THE "GENIUS"

BY THEODORE DREISER

THE
"GENIUS"

BY
THEODORE DREISER

NEW YORK: JOHN LANE COMPANY
LONDON: JOHN LANE, THE BODLEY HEAD
TORONTO: S. B. GUNDY :: MCMXV

Press of
J. J. Little & Ives Company
New York, U. S. A.

"Eugene Witla, wilt thou have this woman to thy wedded wife, to live together after God's ordinance in the holy estate of matrimony? Wilt thou love her, comfort her, honour her, and keep her in sickness and in health; and forsaking all others, keep thee only unto her, so long as ye both shall live?"

"I will."

BOOK I
YOUTH

THE "GENIUS"

CHAPTER I

THIS story has its beginnings in the town of Alexandria, Illinois, between 1884 and 1889, at the time when the place had a population of somewhere near ten thousand. There was about it just enough of the air of a city to relieve it of the sense of rural life. It had one street-car line, a theatre,—or rather, an opera house, so-called (why no one might say, for no opera was ever performed there)—two railroads, with their stations, and a business district, composed of four brisk sides to a public square. In the square were the county court-house and four newspapers. These two morning and two evening papers made the population fairly aware of the fact that life was full of issues, local and national, and that there were many interesting and varied things to do. On the edge of town, several lakes and a pretty stream— perhaps Alexandria's most pleasant feature—gave it an atmosphere not unakin to that of a moderate-priced summer resort. Architecturally the town was not new. It was mostly built of wood, as all American towns were at this time, but laid out prettily in some sections, with houses that sat back in great yards, far from the streets, with flower beds, brick walks, and green trees as concomitants of a comfortable home life. Alexandria was a city of young Americans. Its spirit was young. Life was all before almost everybody. It was really good to be alive.

In one part of this city there lived a family which in its character and composition might well have been considered typically American and middle western. It was not by any means poor— or, at least, did not consider itself so; it was in no sense rich. Thomas Jefferson Witla, the father, was a sewing machine agent with the general agency in that county of one of the best known and best selling machines made. From each twenty, thirty-five or sixty-dollar machine which he sold, he took a profit of thirty-five per cent. The sale of machines was not great, but it was enough to yield him nearly two thousand dollars a year; and on that he had managed to buy a house and lot, to furnish it comfortably, to send his children to school, and to maintain a local store on the public square where the latest styles of machines were displayed. He also took old machines of other makes in

9

exchange, allowing ten to fifteen dollars on the purchase price of a new machine. He also repaired machines,—and with that peculiar energy of the American mind, he tried to do a little insurance business in addition. His first idea was that his son, Eugene Tennyson Witla, might take charge of this latter work, once he became old enough and the insurance trade had developed sufficiently. He did not know what his son might turn out to be, but it was always well to have an anchor to windward.

He was a quick, wiry, active man of no great stature, sandy-haired, with blue eyes with noticeable eye-brows, an eagle nose, and a rather radiant and ingratiating smile. Service as a canvassing salesman, endeavoring to persuade recalcitrant wives and indifferent or conservative husbands to realize that they really needed a new machine in their home, had taught him caution, tact, savoir faire. He knew how to approach people pleasantly. His wife thought too much so.

Certainly he was honest, hard working, and thrifty. They had been waiting a long time for the day when they could say they owned their own home and had a little something laid away for emergencies. That day had come, and life was not half bad. Their house was neat,—white with green shutters, surrounded by a yard with well kept flower beds, a smooth lawn, and some few shapely and broad spreading trees. There was a front porch with rockers, a swing under one tree, a hammock under another, a buggy and several canvassing wagons in a nearby stable. Witla liked dogs, so there were two collies. Mrs. Witla liked live things, so there were a canary bird, a cat, some chickens, and a bird house set aloft on a pole where a few blue-birds made their home. It was a nice little place, and Mr. and Mrs. Witla were rather proud of it.

Miriam Witla was a good wife to her husband. A daughter of a hay and grain dealer in Wooster, a small town near Alexandria in McLean County, she had never been farther out into the world than Springfield and Chicago. She had gone to Springfield as a very young girl, to see Lincoln buried, and once with her husband she had gone to the state fair or exposition which was held annually in those days on the lake front in Chicago. She was well preserved, good looking, poetic under a marked outward reserve. It was she who had insisted upon naming her only son Eugene Tennyson, a tribute at once to a brother Eugene, and to the celebrated romanticist of verse, because she had been so impressed with his "Idylls of the King."

Eugene Tennyson seemed rather strong to Witla père, as the name of a middle-western American boy, but he loved his wife

and gave her her way in most things. He rather liked the
names of Sylvia and Myrtle with which she had christened the
two girls. All three of the children were good looking,—Sylvia,
a girl of twenty-one, with black hair, dark eyes, full blown like
a rose, healthy, active, smiling. Myrtle was of a less vigorous
constitution, small, pale, shy, but intensely sweet—like the flower
she was named after, her mother said. She was inclined to be
studious and reflective, to read verse and dream. The young
bloods of the high school were all crazy to talk to Myrtle and
to walk with her, but they could find no words. And she herself
did not know what to say to them.

Eugene Witla was the apple of his family's eye, younger than
either of his two sisters by two years. He had straight smooth
black hair, dark almond-shaped eyes, a straight nose, a shapely
but not aggressive chin; his teeth were even and white, showing
with a curious delicacy when he smiled, as if he were proud of
them. He was not very strong to begin with, moody, and to a
notable extent artistic. Because of a weak stomach and a semi-
anæmic condition, he did not really appear as strong as he was.
He had emotion, fire, longings, that were concealed behind a
wall of reserve. He was shy, proud, sensitive, and very uncertain
of himself.

When at home he lounged about the house, reading Dickens,
Thackeray, Scott and Poe. He browsed idly through one book
after another, wondering about life. The great cities appealed
to him. He thought of travel as a wonderful thing. In school
he read Taine and Gibbon between recitation hours, wondering
at the luxury and beauty of the great courts of the world. He
cared nothing for grammar, nothing for mathematics, nothing
for botany or physics, except odd bits here and there. Curious
facts would strike him—the composition of clouds, the composition of water, the chemical elements of the earth. He liked to
lie in the hammock at home, spring, summer or fall, and look
at the blue sky showing through the trees. A soaring buzzard
poised in speculative flight held his attention fixedly. The wonder of a snowy cloud, high piled like wool, and drifting as an
island, was like a song to him. He had wit, a keen sense of
humor, a sense of pathos. Sometimes he thought he would
draw; sometimes write. He had a little talent for both, he
thought, but did practically nothing with either. He would
sketch now and then, but only fragments—a small roof-top, with
smoke curling from a chimney and birds flying; a bit of water
with a willow bending over it and perhaps a boat anchored;
a mill pond with ducks afloat, and a boy or woman on the

bank. He really had no great talent for interpretation at this time, only an intense sense of beauty. The beauty of a bird in flight, a rose in bloom, a tree swaying in the wind—these held him. He would walk the streets of his native town at night, admiring the brightness of the store windows, the sense of youth and enthusiasm that went with a crowd; the sense of love and comfort and home that spoke through the glowing windows of houses set back among trees.

He admired girls,—was mad about them,—but only about those who were truly beautiful. There were two or three in his school who reminded him of poetic phrases he had come across— "beauty like a tightened bow," "thy hyacinth hair, thy classic face," "a dancing shape, an image gay"—but he could not talk to them with ease. They were beautiful but so distant. He invested them with more beauty than they had; the beauty was in his own soul. But he did not know that. One girl whose yellow hair lay upon her neck in great yellow braids like ripe corn, was constantly in his thoughts. He worshiped her from afar but she never knew. She never knew what solemn black eyes burned at her when she was not looking. She left Alexandria, her family moving to another town, and in time he recovered, for there is much of beauty. But the color of her hair and the wonder of her neck stayed with him always.

There was some plan on the part of Witla to send these children to college, but none of them showed any great desire for education. They were perhaps wiser than books, for they were living in the realm of imagination and feeling. Sylvia longed to be a mother, and was married at twenty-one to Henry Burgess, the son of Benjamin C. Burgess, editor of the *Morning Appeal*. There was a baby the first year. Myrtle was dreaming through algebra and trigonometry, wondering whether she would teach or get married, for the moderate prosperity of the family demanded that she do something. Eugene mooned through his studies, learning nothing practical. He wrote a little, but his efforts at sixteen were puerile. He drew, but there was no one to tell him whether there was any merit in the things he did or not. Practical matters were generally without significance to him. But he was overawed by the fact that the world demanded practical service—buying and selling like his father, clerking in stores, running big business. It was a confusing maze, and he wondered, even at this age, what was to become of him. He did not object to the kind of work his father was doing, but it did not interest him. For himself he knew it would be a pointless, dreary way of making a living, and as for insurance, that was equally bad. He could hardly bring himself to read through the long rigamarole of specifications which each insurance paper itemized. There were times—evenings and Saturdays—when he clerked in his father's store, but it was painful work. His mind was not in it.

As early as his twelfth year his father had begun to see that Eugene was not cut out for business, and by the time he was sixteen he was convinced of it. From the trend of his reading and his percentage marks at school, he was equally convinced that the boy was not interested in his studies. Myrtle, who was two classes ahead of him but sometimes in the same room, reported that he dreamed too much. He was always looking out of the window.

Eugene's experience with girls had not been very wide. There were those very minor things that occur in early youth—girls whom we furtively kiss, or who furtively kiss us—the latter had been the case with Eugene. He had no particular interest in any one girl. At fourteen he had been picked by a little girl at a party as an affinity, for the evening at least, and in a game of "post-office" had enjoyed the wonder of a girl's arms around him in a dark room and a girl's lips against his; but since then there had been no re-encounter of any kind. He had dreamed of love, with this one experience as a basis, but always in a shy, distant way. He was afraid of girls, and they, to tell the truth, were afraid of him. They could not make him out.

But in the fall of his seventeenth year Eugene came into contact with one girl who made a profound impression on him. Stella Appleton was a notably beautiful creature. She was very fair, Eugene's own age, with very blue eyes and a slender sylph-like body. She was gay and debonair in an enticing way, without really realizing how dangerous she was to the average, susceptible male heart. She liked to flirt with the boys because it amused her, and not because she cared for anyone in particular. There was no petty meanness about it, however, for she thought they were all rather nice, the less clever appealing to her almost more than the sophisticated. She may have liked Eugene originally because of his shyness.

He saw her first at the beginning of his last school year when she came to the city and entered the second high school class. Her father had come from Moline, Illinois, to take a position as manager of a new pulley manufactory which was just starting. She had quickly become friends with his sister Myrtle, being perhaps attracted by her quiet ways, as Myrtle was by Stella's gaiety.

One afternoon, as Myrtle and Stella were on Main Street, walking home from the post office, they met Eugene, who was on his way to visit a boy friend. He was really bashful; and when he saw them approaching he wanted to escape, but there was no way. They saw him, and Stella approached confidently enough. Myrtle was anxious to intercept him, because she had her pretty companion with her.

"You haven't been home, have you?" she asked, stopping. This was her chance to introduce Stella; Eugene couldn't escape. "Miss Appleton, this is my brother Eugene."

Stella gave him a sunny encouraging smile, and her hand, which he took gingerly. He was plainly nervous.

"I'm not very clean," he said apologetically. "I've been helping father fix a buggy."

"Oh, we don't mind," said Myrtle. "Where are you going?"

"Over to Harry Morris's," he explained.

"What for?"

"We're going for hickory nuts."

"Oh, I wish I had some," said Stella.

"I'll bring you some," he volunteered gallantly.

She smiled again. "I wish you would."

She almost proposed that they should be taken along, but inexperience hindered her.

Eugene was struck with all her charm at once. She seemed like one of those unattainable creatures who had swum into his ken a little earlier and disappeared. There was something of the girl with the corn-colored hair about her, only she had been more human, less like a dream. This girl was fine, delicate, pink, like porcelain. She was fragile and yet virile. He caught his breath, but he was more or less afraid of her. He did not know what she might be thinking of him.

"Well, we're going on to the house," said Myrtle.

"I'd go along if I hadn't promised Harry I'd come over."

"Oh, that's all right," replied Myrtle. "We don't mind."

He withdrew, feeling that he had made a very poor impression. Stella's eyes had been on him in a very inquiring way. She looked after him when he had gone.

"Isn't he nice?" she said to Myrtle frankly.

"I think so," replied Myrtle; "kind o'. He's too moody, though."

"What makes him?"

"He isn't very strong."

"I think he has a nice smile."

"I'll tell him!"

"No, please don't! You won't, will you?"

"No."

"But he *has* a nice smile."

"I'll ask you round to the house some evening and you can meet him again."

"I'd like to," said Stella. "It would be a lot of fun."

"Come out Saturday evening and stay all night. He's home then."

"I will," said Stella. "Won't that be fine!"

"I believe you like him!" laughed Myrtle.

"I think he's awfully nice," said Stella, simply.

The second meeting happened on Saturday evening as arranged, when he came home from his odd day at his father's insurance office. Stella had come to supper. Eugene saw her through the open sitting room door, as he bounded upstairs to change his clothes, for he had a fire of youth which no sickness of stomach or weakness of lungs could overcome at this age. A thrill of anticipation ran over his body. He took especial pains with his toilet, adjusting a red tie to a nicety, and parting his hair carefully in the middle. He came down after a while, conscious that he had to say something smart, worthy of himself, or she would not see how attractive he was; and yet he was fearful as to the result. When he entered the sitting room she was sitting with his sister before an open fire-place, the glow of a lamp with a red-flowered shade warmly illuminating the room. It was a commonplace room, with its blue cloth-covered center table, its chairs of stereotyped factory design, and its bookcase of novels and histories, but it was homey, and the sense of hominess was strong.

Mrs. Witla was in and out occasionally, looking for things which appertained to her functions as house-mother. The father was not home yet; he would get there by supper-time, having been to some outlying town of the county trying to sell a machine. Eugene was indifferent to his presence or absence. Mr. Witla had a fund of humor which extended to joking with his son and daughters, when he was feeling good, to noting their budding interest in the opposite sex; to predicting some commonplace climax to their one grand passion when it should come. He was fond of telling Myrtle that she would one day marry a horse-doctor. As for Eugene, he predicted a certain Elsa Brown, who, his wife said, had greasy curls. This did not irritate either Myrtle or Eugene. It even brought a wry smile to Eugene's face for he was fond of a jest; but he saw his father pretty clearly even at this age. He saw the smallness of his business, the ridiculousness of any such profession having any claim on him. He never wanted to say anything, but there was in him a burning opposition to the commonplace, a molten pit in a crater of reserve, which smoked ominously now and then for anyone who could have read. Neither his father nor his mother understood him. To them he was a peculiar boy, dreamy, sickly, unwitting, as yet, of what he really wanted.

"Oh, here you are!" said Myrtle, when he came in. "Come and sit down."

Stella gave him an enticing smile.

He walked to the mantel-piece and stood there, posing. He wanted to impress this girl, and he did not quite know how. He was almost lost for anything to say.

"You can't guess what we've been doing!" his sister chirped helpfully.

"Well—what?" he replied blankly.

"You ought to guess. Can't you be nice and guess?"

"One guess, anyhow," put in Stella.

"Toasting pop-corn," he ventured with a half smile.

"You're warm." It was Myrtle speaking.

Stella looked at him with round blue eyes. "One more guess," she suggested.

"Chestnuts!" he guessed.

She nodded her head gaily. "What hair!" he thought. Then—"Where are they?"

"Here's one," laughed his new acquaintance, holding out a tiny hand.

Under her laughing encouragement he was finding his voice. "Stingy!" he said.

"Now isn't that mean," she exclaimed. "I gave him the only one I had. Don't you give him any of yours, Myrtle."

"I take it back," he pleaded. "I didn't know."

"I won't!" exclaimed Myrtle. "Here, Stella," and she held out the few nuts she had left, "take these, and don't you give him any!" She put them in Stella's eager hands.

He saw her meaning. It was an invitation to a contest. She wanted him to try to make her give him some. He fell in with her plan.

"Here!" He stretched out his palm. "That's not right!" She shook her head.

"One, anyhow," he insisted.

Her head moved negatively from side to side slowly.

"One," he pleaded, drawing near.

Again the golden negative. But her hand was at the side

nearest him, where he could seize it. She started to pass its contents behind her to the other hand but he jumped and caught it.

"Myrtle! Quick!" she called.

Myrtle came. It was a three-handed struggle. In the midst of the contest Stella twisted and rose to her feet. Her hair brushed his face. He held her tiny hand firmly. For a moment he looked into her eyes. What was it? He could not say. Only he half let go and gave her the victory.

"There," she smiled. "Now I'll give you one."

He took it, laughing. What he wanted was to take her in his arms.

A little while before supper his father came in and sat down, but presently took a Chicago paper and went into the dining room to read. Then his mother called them to the table, and he sat by Stella. He was intensely interested in what she did and said. If her lips moved he noted just how. When her teeth showed he thought they were lovely. A little ringlet on her forehead beckoned him like a golden finger. He felt the wonder of the poetic phrase, "the shining strands of her hair."

After dinner he and Myrtle and Stella went back to the sitting room. His father stayed behind to read, his mother to wash dishes. Myrtle left the room after a bit to help her mother, and then these two were left alone. He hadn't much to say, now that they were together—he couldn't talk. Something about her beauty kept him silent.

"Do you like school?" she asked after a time. She felt as if they must talk.

"Only fairly well," he replied. "I'm not much interested. I think I'll quit one of these days and go to work."

"What do you expect to do?"

"I don't know yet—I'd like to be an artist." He confessed his ambition for the first time in his life—why, he could not have said.

Stella took no note of it.

"I was afraid they wouldn't let me enter second year high school, but they did," she remarked. "The superintendent at Moline had to write the superintendent here."

"They're mean about those things," he cogitated.

She got up and went to the bookcase to look at the books. He followed after a little.

"Do you like Dickens?" she asked.

He nodded his head solemnly in approval. "Pretty much," he said.

"I can't like him. He's too long drawn out. I like Scott better."

"I like Scott," he said.

"I'll tell you a lovely book that I like." She paused, her lips parted trying to remember the name. She lifted her hand as though to pick the title out of the air. "The Fair God," she exclaimed at last.

"Yes—it's fine," he approved. "I thought the scene in the old Aztec temple where they were going to sacrifice Ahwahee was so wonderful!"

"Oh, yes, I liked that," she added. She pulled out "Ben Hur" and turned its leaves idly. "And this was so good."

"Wonderful!"

They paused and she went to the window, standing under the cheap lace curtains. It was a moonlight night. The rows of trees that lined the street on either side were leafless; the grass brown and dead. Through the thin, interlaced twigs that were like silver filigree they could see the lamps of other houses shining through half-drawn blinds. A man went by, a black shadow in the half-light.

"Isn't it lovely?" she said.

Eugene came near. "It's fine," he answered.

"I wish it were cold enough to skate. Do you skate?" She turned to him.

"Yes, indeed," he replied.

"My, it's so nice on a moonlit night. I used to skate a lot at Moline."

"We skate a lot here. There're two lakes, you know."

He thought of the clear crystal nights when the ice of Green Lake had split every so often with a great resounding rumble. He thought of the crowds of boys and girls shouting, the distant shadows, the stars. Up to now he had never found any girl to skate with successfully. He had never felt just easy with anyone. He had tried it, but once he had fallen with a girl, and it had almost cured him of skating forever. He felt as though he could skate with Stella. He felt that she might like to skate with him.

"When it gets colder we might go," he ventured. "Myrtle skates."

"Oh, that'll be fine!" she applauded.

Still she looked out into the street.

After a bit she came back to the fire and stood before him, pensively looking down.

"Do you think your father will stay here?" he asked.

"He says so. He likes it very much."

"Do you?"

"Yes—now."

"Why *now*?"

"Oh, I didn't like it at first."

"Why?"

"Oh, I guess it was because I didn't know anybody. I like it though, now." She lifted her eyes.

He drew a little nearer.

"It's a nice place," he said, "but there isn't much for me here. I think I'll leave next year."

"Where do you think you'll go?"

"To Chicago. I don't want to stay here."

She turned her body toward the fire and he moved to a chair behind her, leaning on its back. She felt him there rather close, but did not move. He was surprising himself.

"Aren't you ever coming back?" she asked.

"Maybe. It all depends. I suppose so."

"I shouldn't think you'd want to leave yet."

"Why?"

"You say it's so nice."

He made no answer and she looked over her shoulder. He was leaning very much toward her.

"Will you skate with me this winter?" he asked meaningly.

She nodded her head.

Myrtle came in.

"What are you two talking about?" she asked.

"The fine skating we have here," he said.

"I love to skate," she exclaimed.

"So do I," added Stella. "It's heavenly."

CHAPTER II

SOME of the incidents of this courtship that followed, ephemeral as it was, left a profound impression on Eugene's mind. They met to skate not long after, for the snow came and the ice and there was wonderful skating on Green Lake. The frost was so prolonged that men with horses and ice-saws were cutting blocks a foot thick over at Miller's Point, where the ice houses were. Almost every day after Thanksgiving there were crowds of boys and girls from the schools scooting about like water skippers. Eugene could not always go on week evenings and Saturdays because he had to assist his father at the store. But at regular intervals he could ask Myrtle to get Stella and let them all go together at night. And at other times he would ask her to go alone. Not infrequently she did.

On one particular occasion they were below a group of houses which crept near the lake on high ground. The moon was up, its wooing rays reflected in the polished surfaces of the ice. Through the black masses of trees that lined the shore could be seen the glow of windows, yellow and homey. Eugene and Stella had slowed up to turn about, having left the crowd of skaters some distance back. Stella's golden curls were covered, except for a few ringlets, with a French cap; her body, to below the hips, encased in a white wool Jersey, close-fitting and shapely. The skirt below was a grey mixture of thick wool and the stockings were covered by white woolen leggings. She looked tempting and knew it.

Suddenly, as they turned, one of her skates came loose and she hobbled and exclaimed about it. "Wait," said Eugene, "I'll fix it."

She stood before him and he fell to his knees, undoing the twisted strap. When he had the skate off and ready for her foot he looked up, and she looked down on him, smiling. He dropped the skate and flung his arms around her hips, laying his head against her waist.

"You're a bad boy," she said.

For a few minutes she kept silent, for as the center of this lovely scene she was divine. While he held her she pulled off his wool cap and laid her hand on his hair. It almost brought tears to his eyes, he was so happy. At the same time it awakened a tremendous passion. He clutched her significantly.

"Fix my skate, now," she said wisely.

He got up to hug her but she would not let him.

"No, no," she protested. "You mustn't do like that. I won't come with you if you do."

"Oh, Stella!" he pleaded.

"I mean it," she insisted. "You mustn't do like that."

He subsided, hurt, half angry. But he feared her will. She was really not as ready for caresses as he had thought.

Another time a sleighing party was given by some school girls, and Stella, Eugene and Myrtle were invited. It was a night of snow and stars, not too cold but bracing. A great box-wagon had been dismantled of its body and the latter put on runners and filled with straw and warm robes. Eugene and Myrtle, like the others, had been picked up at their door after the sleigh had gone the rounds of some ten peaceful little homes. Stella was not in yet, but in a little while her house was reached.

"Get in here," called Myrtle, though she was half the length of the box away from Eugene. Her request made him angry. "Sit by me," he called, fearful that she would not. She climbed in by Myrtle but finding the space not to her liking moved farther down. Eugene made a special effort to have room by him, and she came there as though by accident. He drew a buffalo robe around her and thrilled to think that she was really there. The sleigh went jingling around the town for others, and finally struck out into the country. It passed great patches of dark woods silent in the snow, little white frame farmhouses snuggled close to the ground, and with windows that gleamed in a vague romantic way. The stars were countless and keen. The whole scene made a tremendous impression on him, for he was in love, and here beside him, in the shadow, her face palely outlined, was this girl. He could make out the sweetness of her cheek, her eyes, the softness of her hair.

There was a good deal of chatter and singing, and in the midst of these distractions he managed to slip an arm about her waist, to get her hand in his, to look close into her eyes, trying to divine their expression. She was always coy with him, not wholly yielding. Three or four times he kissed her cheek furtively and once her mouth. In a dark place he pulled her vigorously to him, putting a long, sensuous kiss on her lips that frightened her.

"No," she protested, nervously. "You mustn't."

He ceased for a time, feeling that he had pressed his advantage too closely. But the night in all its beauty, and she in hers made a lasting impression.

*   *   *   *   *

"I think we ought to get Eugene into newspaper work or something like that," Witla senior suggested to his wife.

"It looks as though that's all he would be good for, at least now," replied Mrs. Witla, who was satisfied that her boy had not yet found himself. "I think he'll do something better later on. His health isn't very good, you know."

Witla half suspected that his boy was naturally lazy, but he wasn't sure. He suggested that Benjamin C. Burgess, the prospective father-in-law of Sylvia and the editor and proprietor of the *Morning Appeal,* might give him a place as a reporter or type-setter in order that he might learn the business from the ground up. The *Appeal* carried few employees, but Mr. Burgess might have no objections to starting Eugene as a reporter if he could write, or as a student of type-setting, or both. He appealed to Burgess one day on the street.

"Say, Burgess," he said, "you wouldn't have a place over in your shop for that boy of mine, would you? He likes to scribble a little, I notice. I think he pretends to draw a little, too, though I guess it doesn't amount to much. He ought to get into something. He isn't doing anything at school. Maybe he could learn type-setting. It wouldn't hurt him to begin at the bottom if he's going to follow that line. It wouldn't matter what you paid him to begin with."

Burgess thought. He had seen Eugene around town, knew no harm of him except that he was lackadaisical and rather moody.

"Send him in to see me some day," he replied noncommittally. "I might do something for him."

"I'd certainly be much obliged to you if you would," said Witla. "He is not doing much good as it is now," and the two men parted.

He went home and told Eugene. "Burgess says he might give you a position as a type-setter or a reporter on the *Appeal* if you'd come in and see him some day," he explained, looking over to where his son was reading by the lamp.

"Does he?" replied Eugene calmly. "Well, I can't write. I might set type. Did you ask him?"

"Yes," said Witla. "You'd better go to him some day."

Eugene bit his lip. He realized this was a commentary on his loafing propensities. He wasn't doing very well, that was certain. Still type-setting was no bright field for a person of his temperament. "I will," he concluded, "when school's over."

"Better speak before school ends. Some of the other fellows

might ask for it around that time. It wouldn't hurt you to try
your hand at it."

"I will," said Eugene obediently.

He stopped in one sunny April afternoon at Mr. Burgess'
office. It was on the ground floor of the three-story *Appeal*
building in the public square. Mr. Burgess, a fat man, slightly
bald, looked at him quizzically over his steel rimmed spectacles.
What little hair he had was gray.

"So you think you would like to go into the newspaper business, do you?" queried Burgess.

"I'd like to try my hand at it," replied the boy. "I'd like to
see whether I like it."

"I can tell you right now there's very little in it. Your father
says you like to write."

"I'd like to well enough, but I don't think I can. I wouldn't
mind learning type-setting. If I ever could write I'd be perfectly willing to."

"When do you think you'd like to start?"

"At the end of school, if it's all the same to you."

"It doesn't make much difference. I'm not really in need of
anybody, but I could use you. Would you be satisfied with
five a week?"

"Yes, sir."

"Well, come in when you are ready. I'll see what I can do."

He waved the prospective type-setter away with a movement
of his fat hand, and turned to his black walnut desk, dingy,
covered with newspapers, and lit by a green shaded electric
light. Eugene went out, the smell of fresh printing ink in his
nose, and the equally aggressive smell of damp newspapers. It
was going to be an interesting experience, he thought, but perhaps a waste of time. He did not think so much of Alexandria.
Some time he was going to get out of it.

The office of the *Appeal* was not different from that of any
other country newspaper office within the confines of our two
hemispheres. On the ground floor in front was the business
office, and in the rear the one large flat bed press and the job
presses. On the second floor was the composing room with its
rows of type cases on their high racks—for this newspaper was,
like most other country newspapers, still set by hand; and in front
was the one dingy office of the so-called editor, or managing
editor, or city editor—for all three were the same person, a Mr.
Caleb Williams whom Burgess had picked up in times past from
heaven knows where. Williams was a small, lean, wiry man,
with a black pointed beard and a glass eye which fixed you oddly

with its black pupil. He was talkative, skipped about from duty
to duty, wore most of the time a green shade pulled low over
his forehead, and smoked a brown briar pipe. He had a fund
of knowledge, piled up in metropolitan journalistic experience,
but he was anchored here with a wife and three children, after
sailing, no doubt, a chartless sea of troubles, and was glad to
talk life and experiences after office hours with almost anybody.
It took him from eight in the morning until two in the afternoon
to gather what local news there was, and either write it or edit
it. He seemed to have a number of correspondents who sent
him weekly batches of news from surrounding points. The
Associated Press furnished him with a few minor items by telegraph, and there was a "patent insides," two pages of fiction,
household hints, medicine ads. and what not, which saved him
considerable time and stress. Most of the news which came
to him received short shrift in the matter of editing. "In Chicago we used to give a lot of attention to this sort of thing,"
Williams was wont to declare to anyone who was near, "but you
can't do it down here. The readers really don't expect it.
They're looking for local items. I always look after the local
items pretty sharp."

Mr. Burgess took care of the advertising sections. In fact he
solicited advertising personally, saw that it was properly set up
as the advertiser wanted it, and properly placed according to the
convenience of the day and the rights and demands of others.
He was the politician of the concern, the handshaker, the guider
of its policy. He wrote editorials now and then, or, with
Williams, decided just what their sense must be, met the visitors
who came to the office to see the editor, and arbitrated all known
forms of difficulties. He was at the beck and call of certain
Republican party-leaders in the county; but that seemed natural,
for he was a Republican himself by temperament and disposition.
He was appointed postmaster once to pay him for some useful
services, but he declined because he was really making more out
of his paper than his postmastership would have brought. He
received whatever city or county advertising it was in the power
of the Republican leaders to give him, and so he did very well.
The complications of his political relationships Williams knew in
part, but they never troubled that industrious soul. He dispensed with moralizing. "I have to make a living for myself,
my wife and three children. That's enough to keep me going
without bothering my head about other people." So this office
was really run very quietly, efficiently, and in most ways pleasantly. It was a sunny place to work.

Witla, who came here at the end of his eleventh school year and when he had just turned seventeen, was impressed with the personality of Mr. Williams. He liked him. He came to like a Jonas Lyle who worked at what might be called the head desk of the composing room, and a certain John Summers who worked at odd times—whenever there was an extra rush of job printing. He learned very quickly that John Summers, who was fifty-five, grey, and comparatively silent, was troubled with weak lungs and drank. Summers would slip out of the office at various times in the day and be gone from five to fifteen minutes. No one ever said anything, for there was no pressure here. What work was to be done was done. Jonas Lyle was of a more interesting nature. He was younger by ten years, stronger, better built, but still a character. He was semi-phlegmatic, philosophic, feebly literary. He had worked, as Eugene found out in the course of time, in nearly every part of the United States—Denver, Portland, St. Paul, St. Louis, where not, and had a fund of recollections of this proprietor and that. Whenever he saw a name of particular distinction in the newspapers he was apt to bring the paper to Williams—and later, when they became familiar, to Eugene—and say, "I knew that fellow out in——. He was postmaster (or what not) at X——. He's come up considerably since I knew him." In most cases he did not know these celebrities personally at all, but he knew of them, and the echo of their fame sounding in this out-of-the-way corner of the world impressed him. He was a careful reader of proof for Williams in a rush, a quick type-setter, a man who stayed by his tasks faithfully. But he hadn't got anywhere in the world, for, after all, he was little more than a machine. Eugene could see that at a glance.

It was Lyle who taught him the art of type-setting. He demonstrated the first day the theory of the squares or pockets in a case, how some letters were placed more conveniently to the hand than others, why some letters were well represented as to quantity, why capitals were used in certain offices for certain purposes, in others not. "Now on the Chicago *Tribune* we used to italicize the names of churches, boats, books, hotels, and things of that sort. That's the only paper I ever knew to do that," he remarked. What slugs, sticks, galleys, turnovers, meant, came rapidly to the surface. That the fingers would come to recognize weights of leads by the touch, that a letter would almost instinctively find its way back to its proper pocket, even though you were not thinking, once you became expert, were facts which he cheerfully communicated. He wanted his knowledge taken seriously, and this serious attention, Eugene, because of his innate respect for learning of any kind, was only too glad to give him. He did not know what he wanted to do, but he knew quite well that he wanted to see everything. This shop was interesting to him for some little time for this reason, for though he soon found that he did not want to be a type-setter or a reporter, or indeed anything much in connection with a country newspaper, he was learning about life. He worked at his desk cheerfully, smiling out upon the world, which indicated its presence to him through an open window, read the curious bits of news or opinion or local advertisements as he set them up, and dreamed of what the world might have in store for him. He was not vastly ambitious as yet, but hopeful and, withal, a little melancholy. He could see boys and girls whom he knew, idling in the streets or on the corner squares; he could see where Ted Martinwood was driving by in his father's buggy, or George Anderson was going up the street with the air of someone who would never need to work. George's father owned the one and only hotel. There were thoughts in his mind of fishing, boating, lolling somewhere with some pretty girl, but alas, girls did not apparently take to him so very readily. He was too shy. He thought it must be nice to be rich. So he dreamed.

Eugene was at that age when he wished to express himself in ardent phrases. He was also at the age when bashfulness held him in reserve, even though he were in love and intensely emotional. He could only say to Stella what seemed trivial things, and look his intensity, whereas it was the trivial things that were most pleasing to her, not the intensity. She was even then beginning to think he was a little strange, a little too tense for her disposition. Yet she liked him. It became generally understood around town that Stella was *his* girl. School day mating usually goes that way in a small city or village. He was seen to go out with her. His father teased him. Her mother and father deemed this a manifestation of calf love, not so much on her part, for they were aware of her tendency to hold lightly any manifestation of affection on the part of boys, but on his. They thought his sentimentalism would soon be wearisome to Stella. And they were not far wrong about her. On one occasion at a party given by several high school girls, a "country post office" was organized. That was one of those games which mean kissing only. A system of guessing results in a series of forfeits. If you miss you must be postmaster, and call someone for "mail." *Mail* means to be kissed in a dark room (where the postmaster stands) by someone whom you like or who likes you. You, as postmaster, have authority or compulsion—however you feel about it —to call whom you please.

In this particular instance Stella, who was caught before Eugene, was under compulsion to call someone to kiss. Her first thought was of him, but on account of the frankness of the deed, and because there was a lurking fear in her of his eagerness, the name she felt impelled to speak was Harvey Rutter. Harvey was a handsome boy whom Stella had met after her first encounter with Eugene. He was not as yet fascinating to her, but pleasing. She had a coquettish desire to see what he was like. This was her first direct chance.

He stepped gaily in, and Eugene was at once insane with jealousy. He could not understand why she should treat him in that way. When it came to his turn he called for Bertha Shoemaker, whom he admired, and who was sweet in a way, but who was as nothing to Stella in his estimation. The pain of kissing her when he really wanted the other girl was great. When he came out Stella saw moodiness in his eyes, but chose to ignore it. He was obviously half-hearted and downcast in his simulation of joy.

A second chance came to her and this time she called him. He went, but was in a semi-defiant mood. He wanted to punish her. When they met in the dark she expected him to put his arms around her. Her own hands were up to about where his shoulders should be. Instead he only took hold of one of her arms with his hand and planted a chilly kiss on her lips. If he had only asked, "Why did you?" or held her close and pleaded with her not to treat him so badly, the relationship might have lasted longer. Instead he said nothing, and she grew defiant and she went out gaily. There was a strain of reserve running between them until the party broke up and he took her home.

"You must be melancholy tonight," she remarked, after they had walked two blocks in complete silence. The streets were dark, and their feet sounded hollowly on the brick pavement.

"Oh, I'm feeling all right," he replied moodily.

"I think it's awfully nice at the Weimers', we always have so much fun there."

"Yes, lots of fun," he echoed contemptuously.

"Oh, don't be so cross!" she flared. "You haven't any reason for fussing."

"Haven't I?"

"No, you haven't."

"Well if that's the way you feel about it I suppose I haven't. I don't see it that way."

"Well, it doesn't make any difference to me how you see it."

"Oh, doesn't it?"

"No, it doesn't." Her head was up and she was angry.

"Well I'm sure then it doesn't to me."

There was another silence which endured until they were almost home.

"Are you coming to the sociable next Thursday?" he inquired. He was referring to a Methodist evening entertainment which, although he cared very little about it, was a convenience as it enabled him to see her and take her home. He was prompted to ask by the fear that an open rupture was impending.

"No," she said. "I don't think I will."

"Why not?"

"I don't care to."

"I think you're mean," he said reprovingly.

"I don't care," she replied. "I think you're too bossy. I don't think I like you very much anyhow."

His heart contracted ominously.

"You can do as you please," he persisted.

They reached her gate. It was his wont to kiss her in the shadow—to hold her tight for a few minutes in spite of her protests. Tonight, as they approached, he thought of doing it, but she gave him no chance. When they reached the gate she opened it quickly and slipped in. "Good-night," she called.

"Good-night," he said, and then as she reached her door, "Stella!"

It was open, and she slipped in. He stood in the dark, hurt, sore, oppressed. What should he do? He strolled home cudgelling his brain whether never to speak to or look at her again until she came to him, or to hunt her up and fight it all out with her. She was in the wrong, he knew that. When he went to bed he was grieving over it, and when he awoke it was with him all day.

He had been gaining rather rapidly as a student of type-setting, and to a certain extent of the theory of reporting, and he worked diligently and earnestly at his proposed trade. He loved to look out of the window and draw, though of late, after knowing Stella so well and coming to quarrel with her because of her indifference, there was little heart in it. This getting to the office, putting on an apron, and starting in on some local correspondence left over from the day before, or some telegraph copy which had been freshly filed on his hook, had its constructive value. Williams endeavored to use him on some local items of news as a reporter, but he was a slow worker and almost a failure at getting all the facts. He did not appear to know how to interview anybody, and would come back with a story which needed to be filled in from other sources. He really did not understand the theory of news, and Williams could only make it partially clear to him. Mostly he worked at his case, but he did learn some things.

For one thing, the theory of advertising began to dawn on him. These local merchants put in the same ads. day after day, and many of them did not change them noticeably. He saw Lyle and Summers taking the same ads. which had appeared unchangingly from month to month in so far as their main features were concerned, and alter only a few words before returning them to the forms. He wondered at the sameness of them, and when, at last, they were given to him to revise he often wished he could change them a little. The language seemed so dull.

"Why don't they ever put little drawings in these ads?" he asked Lyle one day. "Don't you think they'd look a little better?"

"Oh, I don't know," replied Jonas. "They look pretty good. These people around here wouldn't want anything like that. They'd think it was too fancy." Eugene had seen and in a way studied the ads. in the magazines. They seemed so much more fascinating to him. Why couldn't newspaper ads. be different?

Still it was never given to him to trouble over this problem. Mr. Burgess dealt with the advertisers. He settled how the ads. were to be. He never talked to Eugene or Summers about them, not always to Lyle. He would sometimes have Williams explain just what their character and layout was to be. Eugene was so young that Williams at first did not pay very much attention to him, but after a while he began to realize that there was a personality here, and then he would explain things,—why space had to be short for some items and long for others, why county news, news of small towns around Alexandria, and about people, was much more important financially to the paper than the correct reporting of the death of the sultan of Turkey. The most important thing was to get the local names right. "Don't ever misspell them," he once cautioned him. "Don't ever leave out a part of a name if you can help it. People are awfully sensitive about that. They'll stop their subscription if you don't watch out, and you won't know what's the matter."

Eugene took all these things to heart. He wanted to see how the thing was done, though basically it seemed to be a little small. In fact people seemed a little small, mostly.

One of the things that did interest him was to see the paper put on the press and run off. He liked to help lock up the forms, and to see how they were imposed and registered. He liked to hear the press run, and to help carry the wet papers to the mailing tables and the distributing counter out in front. The paper hadn't a very large circulation but there was a slight hum of life about that time and he liked it. He liked the sense of getting his hands and face streaked and not caring, and of seeing his hair tousled, in the mirror. He tried to be useful and the various people on the paper came to like him, though he was often a little awkward and slow. He was not strong at this period and his stomach troubled him. He thought, too, that the smell of the ink might affect his lungs, though he did not seriously fear it. In the main it was interesting but small; there was a much larger world outside, he knew that. He hoped to go to it some day; he hoped to go to Chicago.

CHAPTER III

EUGENE grew more and more moody and rather restless under Stella's increasing independence. She grew steadily more indifferent because of his moods. The fact that other boys were crazy for her consideration was a great factor; the fact that one particular boy, Harvey Rutter, was persistently genial, not insistent, really better looking than Eugene and much better tempered, helped a great deal. Eugene saw her with him now and then, saw her go skating with him, or at least with a crowd of which he was a member. Eugene hated him heartily; he hated her at times for not yielding to him wholly; but he was none the less wild over her beauty. It stamped his brain with a type or ideal. Thereafter he knew in a really definite way what womanhood ought to be, to be really beautiful.

Another thing it did was to bring home to him a sense of his position in the world. So far he had always been dependent on his parents for food, clothes and spending money, and his parents were not very liberal. He knew other boys who had money to run up to Chicago or down to Springfield—the latter was nearer—to have a Saturday and Sunday lark. No such gaieties were for him. His father would not allow it, or rather would not pay for it. There were other boys who, in consequence of amply provided spending money, were the town dandies. He saw them kicking their heels outside the corner book store, the principal loafing place of the élite, on Wednesdays and Saturdays and sometimes on Sunday evenings preparatory to going somewhere, dressed in a luxury of clothing which was beyond his wildest dreams. Ted Martinwood, the son of the principal drygoods man, had a frock coat in which he sometimes appeared when he came down to the barber shop for a shave before he went to call on his girl. George Anderson was possessed of a dress suit, and wore dancing pumps at all dances. There was Ed Waterbury, who was known to have a horse and runabout of his own. These youths were slightly older, and were interested in girls of a slightly older set, but the point was the same. These things hurt him.

He himself had no avenue of progress which, so far as he could see, was going to bring him to any financial prosperity. His father was never going to be rich, anybody could see that. He himself had made no practical progress in schoolwork—he knew that. He hated insurance—soliciting or writing, despised the sewing machine business, and did not know where he would get with anything which he might like to do in literature or art. His drawing seemed a joke, his writing, or wish for writing, pointless. He was broodingly unhappy.

One day Williams, who had been watching him for a long time, stopped at his desk.

"I say, Witla, why don't you go to Chicago?" he said. "There's a lot more up there for a boy like you than down here. You'll never get anywhere working on a country newspaper."

"I know it," said Eugene.

"Now with me it's different," went on Williams. "I've had my rounds. I've got a wife and three children and when a man's got a family he can't afford to take chances. But you're young yet. Why don't you go to Chicago and get on a paper? You could get something."

"What could I get?" asked Eugene.

"Well, you might get a job as type-setter if you'd join the union. I don't know how good you'd be as a reporter—I hardly think that's your line. But you might study art and learn to draw. Newspaper artists make good money."

Eugene thought of his art. It wasn't much. He didn't do much with it. Still he thought of Chicago; the world appealed to him. If he could only get out of here—if he could only make more than seven or eight dollars a week. He brooded about this.

One Sunday afternoon he and Stella went with Myrtle to Sylvia's home, and after a brief stay Stella announced that she would have to be going; her mother would be expecting her back. Myrtle was for going with her, but altered her mind when Sylvia asked her to stay to tea. "Let Eugene take her home," Sylvia said. Eugene was delighted in his persistent, hopeless way. He was not yet convinced that she could not be won to love. When they walked out in the fresh sweet air—it was nearing spring—he felt that now he should have a chance of saying something which would be winning—which would lure her to him.

They went out on a street next to the one she lived on quite to the confines of the town. She wanted to turn off at her street, but he had urged her not to. "Do you have to go home just yet?" he asked, pleadingly.

"No, I can walk a little way," she replied.

They reached a vacant place—the last house a little distance back—talking idly. It was getting hard to make talk. In his

efforts to be entertaining he picked up three twigs to show her
how a certain trick in balancing was performed. It consisted in
laying two at right angles with each other and with a third,
using the latter as an upright. She could not do it, of course.
She was not really very much interested. He wanted her to
try and when she did, took hold of her right hand to steady her
efforts.

"No, don't," she said, drawing her hand away. "I can do it."

She trifled with the twigs unsuccessfully and was about to let
them fall, when he took hold of both her hands. It was so sudden that she could not free herself, and so she looked him
straight in the eye.

"Let go, Eugene, please let go."

He shook his head, gazing at her.

"Please let go," she went on. "You mustn't do this. I don't
want you to."

"Why?"

"Because."

"Because why?"

"Well, because I don't."

"Don't you like me any more, Stella, really?" he asked.

"I don't think I do, not that way."

"But you did."

"I thought I did."

"Have you changed your mind?"

"Yes, I think I have."

He dropped her hands and looked at her fixedly and dramatically. The attitude did not appeal to her. They strolled back
to the street, and when they neared her door he said, "Well, I
suppose there's no use in my coming to see you any more."

"I think you'd better not," she said simply.

She walked in, never looking back, and instead of going back
to his sister's he went home. He was in a very gloomy mood,
and after sitting around for a while went to his room. The night
fell, and he sat there looking out at the trees and grieving about
what he had lost. Perhaps he was not good enough for her—he
could not make her love him. Was it that he was not handsome
enough—he did not really consider himself good looking—or
what was it, a lack of courage or strength?

After a time he noticed that the moon was hanging over the
trees like a bright shield in the sky. Two layers of thin clouds
were moving in different directions on different levels. He
stopped in his cogitations to think where these clouds came from.
On sunny days when there were great argosies of them he had

seen them disappear before his eyes, and then, marvel of marvels, reappear out of nothingness. The first time he ever saw this it astonished him greatly, for he had never known up to then when what clouds were. Afterward he read about them in his physical geography. Tonight he thought of that, and of the great plains over which these winds swept, and of the grass and trees—great forests of them—miles and miles. What a wonderful world! Poets wrote about these things, Longfellow, and Bryant, and Tennyson. He thought of "Thanatopsis," and of the "Elegy," both of which he admired greatly. What was this thing, life?

Then he came back to Stella with an ache. She was actually gone, and she was so beautiful. She would never really talk to him any more. He would never get to hold her hand or kiss her. He clenched his hands with the hurt. Oh, that night on the ice; that night in the sleigh! How wonderful they were! Finally he undressed and went to bed. He wanted to be alone— to be lonely. On his clean white pillow he lay and dreamed of the things that might have been, kisses, caresses, a thousand joys.

One Sunday afternoon he was lying in his hammock thinking, thinking of what a dreary place Alexandria was, anyhow, when he opened a Chicago Saturday afternoon paper, which was something like a Sunday one because it had no Sunday edition,—and went gloomily through it. It was as he had always found, full of a subtle wonder, the wonder of the city, which drew him like a magnet. Here was the drawing of a big hotel someone was going to build; there was a sketch of a great pianist who was coming to play. An account of a new comedy drama; of a little romantic section of Goose Island in the Chicago river, with its old decayed boats turned into houses and geese waddling about; an item of a man falling through a coal hole on South Halstead street fascinated him. This last was at sixty-two hundred and something and the idea of such a long street seized on his imagination. What a tremendous city Chicago must be. The thought of car lines, crowds, trains, came to him with almost a yearning appeal.

All at once the magnet got him. It gripped his very soul, this wonder, this beauty, this life.

"I'm going to Chicago," he thought, and got up.

There was his nice, quiet little home laid out before him. Inside were his mother, his father, Myrtle. Still he was going. He could come back. "Sure I can come back," he thought. Propelled by this magnetic power he went in and upstairs to his room, and got a little grip or portmanteau he had. He put in it the things he thought he would immediately need. In his pocket were nine dollars, money he had been saving for some time. Finally he came downstairs and stood in the door of the sitting room.

"What's the matter?" asked his mother, looking at his solemn introspective face.

"I'm going to Chicago," he said.

"When?" she asked, astonished, a little uncertain of just what he meant.

"Today," he said.

"No, you're joking." She smiled unbelievingly. This was a boyish prank.

"I'm going today," he said. "I'm going to catch that four o'clock train."

Her face saddened. "You're not?" she said.

"I can come back," he replied, "if I want to. I want to get something else to do."

His father came in at this time. He had a little work room out in the barn where he sometimes cleaned machines and re-paired vehicles. He was fresh from such a task now.

"What's up?" he asked, seeing his wife close to her boy.

"Eugene's going to Chicago."

"Since when?" he inquired amusedly.

"Today. He says he's going right now."

"You don't mean it," said Witla, astonished. He really did not believe it. "Why don't you take a little time and think it over? What are you going to live on?"

"I'll live," said Eugene. "I'm going. I've had enough of this place. I'm going to get out."

"All right," said his father, who, after all, believed in initiative. Evidently after all he hadn't quite understood this boy. "Got your trunk packed?"

"No, but mother can send me that."

"Don't go today," pleaded his mother. "Wait until you get something ready, Eugene. Wait and do a little thinking about it. Wait until tomorrow."

"I want to go today, ma." He slipped his arm around her. "Little ma." He was bigger than she by now, and still growing.

"All right, Eugene," she said softly, "but I wish you wouldn't." Her boy was leaving her—her heart was hurt.

"I can come back, ma. It's only a hundred miles."

"Well, all right," she said finally, trying to brighten. "I'll pack your bag."

"I have already."

She went to look.

"Well, it'll soon be time," said Witla, who was thinking that Eugene might back down. "I'm sorry. Still it may be a good thing for you. You're always welcome here, you know."

"I know," said Eugene.

They went finally to the train together, he and his father and Myrtle. His mother couldn't. She stayed to cry.

On the way to the depot they stopped at Sylvia's.

"Why, Eugene," she exclaimed, "how ridiculous! Don't go."

"He's set," said Witla.

Eugene finally got loose. He seemed to be fighting love, home ties, everything, every step of the way. Finally he reached the depot. The train came. Witla grabbed his hand affectionately. "Be a good boy," he said, swallowing a gulp.

Myrtle kissed him. "You're so funny, Eugene. Write me."

"I will."

He stepped on the train. The bell rang. Out the cars rolled —out and on. He looked out on the familiar scenes and then a real ache came to him—Stella, his mother, his father, Myrtle, the little home. They were all going out of his life.

"Hm," he half groaned, clearing his throat. "Gee!"

And then he sank back and tried, as usual, not to think. He must succeed. That's what the world was made for. That was what he was made for. That was what he would have to do. . . .

CHAPTER IV

THE city of Chicago—who shall portray it! This vast ruck of life that had sprung suddenly into existence upon the dank marshes of a lake shore. Miles and miles of dreary little houses; miles and miles of wooden block-paved streets, with gas lamps placed and water mains laid, and empty wooden walks set for pedestrians; the beat of a hundred thousand hammers; the ring of a hundred thousand trowels! Long, converging lines of telegraph poles; thousands upon thousands of sentinel cottages, factory plants, towering smoke stacks, and here and there a lone, shabby church steeple, sitting out pathetically upon vacant land. The raw prairie stretch was covered with yellow grass; the great broad highways of the tracks of railroads, ten, fifteen, twenty, thirty, laid side by side and strung with thousands upon thousands of shabby cars, like beads upon a string. Engines clanging, trains moving, people waiting at street crossings—pedestrians, wagon drivers, street car drivers, drays of beer, trucks of coal, brick, stone, sand—a spectacle of new, raw, necessary life!

As Eugene began to draw near it he caught for the first time the sense and significance of a great city. What were these newspaper shadows he had been dealing with in his reading compared to this vivid, articulate, eager thing? Here was the substance of a new world, substantial, fascinating, different. The handsome suburban station at South Chicago, the first of its kind he had ever seen, took his eye, as the train rolled cityward. He had never before seen a crowd of foreigners—working men—and here were Lithuanians, Poles, Czechs, waiting for a local train. He had never seen a really large factory plant, and here was one, and another, and another—steel works, potteries, soap-factories, foundries, all gaunt and hard in the Sunday evening air. There seemed to be, for all it was Sunday, something youthful, energetic and alive about the streets. He noted the streetcars waiting; at one place a small river was crossed on a draw,—dirty, gloomy, but crowded with boats and lined with great warehouses, grain elevators, coal pockets—that architecture of necessity and utility. His imagination was fired by this for here was something that could be done brilliantly in black—a spot of red or green for ship and bridge lights. There were some men on the magazines who did things like this, only not so vivid.

The train threaded its way through long lines of cars coming finally into an immense train shed where arc lights were spluttering—a score under a great curved steel and glass roof, where people were hurrying to and fro. Engines were hissing; bells clanging raucously. He had no relatives, no soul to turn to, but somehow he did not feel lonely. This picture of life, this newness, fascinated him. He stepped down and started leisurely to the gate, wondering which way he should go. He came to a corner where a lamp post already lit blazoned the name Madison. He looked out on this street and saw, as far as the eye could reach, two lines of stores, jingling horse cars, people walking. What a sight, he thought, and turned west. For three miles he walked, musing, and then as it was dark, and he had arranged for no bed, he wondered where he should eat and sleep. A fat man sitting outside a livery stable door in a tilted, cane-seated chair offered a possibility of information.

"Do you know where I can get a room around here?" asked Eugene.

The lounger looked him over. He was the proprietor of the place.

"There's an old lady living over there at seven-thirty-two," he said, "who has a room, I think. She might take you in." He liked Eugene's looks.

Eugene crossed over and rang a downstairs bell. The door was opened shortly by a tall, kindly woman, of a rather matriarchal turn. Her hair was gray.

"Yes?" she inquired.

"The gentleman at the livery stable over there said I might get a room here. I'm looking for one."

She smiled pleasantly. This boy looked his strangeness, his wide-eyed interest, his freshness from the country. "Come in," she said. "I have a room. You can look at it."

It was a front room—a little bed-room off the one main living room, clean, simple, convenient. "This looks all right," he said.

She smiled.

"You can have it for two dollars a week," she proffered.

"That's all right," he said, putting down his grip. "I'll take it."

"Have you had supper?" she asked.

"No, but I'm going out soon. I want to see the streets. I'll find some place."

"I'll give you something," she said.

Eugene thanked her, and she smiled. This was what Chicago did to the country. It took the boys.

He opened the closed shutters of his window and knelt before it, leaning on the sill. He looked out idly, for it was all so wonderful. Bright lights were burning in store windows. These people hurrying—how their feet sounded—clap, clap, clap. And away east and away west it was all like this. It was all like this everywhere, a great big, wonderful city. It was nice to be here. He felt that now. It was all worth while. How could he have stayed in Alexandria so long! He would get along here. Certainly he would. He was perfectly sure of that. He knew.

Chicago at this time certainly offered a world of hope and opportunity to the beginner. It was so new, so raw; everything was in the making. The long lines of houses and stores were mostly temporary make-shifts—one and two story frame affairs—with here and there a three and four story brick building which spoke of better days to come. Down in the business heart which lay between the lake and the river, the North Side and the South Side, was a region which spoke of a tremendous future, for here were stores which served the buying public, not only of Chicago, but of the Middle West. There were great banks, great office buildings, great retail stores, great hotels. The section was running with a tide of people which represented the youth, the illusions, the untrained aspirations, of millions of souls. When you walked into this area you could feel what Chicago meant—eagerness, hope, desire. It was a city that put vitality into almost every wavering heart: it made the beginner dream dreams; the aged to feel that misfortune was never so grim that it might not change.

Underneath, of course, was struggle. Youth and hope and energy were setting a terrific pace. You had to work here, to move, to step lively. You had to have ideas. This city demanded of you your very best, or it would have little to do with you. Youth in its search for something—and age—were quickly to feel this. It was no fool's paradise.

Eugene, once he was settled, realized this. He had the notion, somehow, that the printer's trade was all over for him. He wanted no more of that. He wanted to be an artist or something like that, although he hardly knew how to begin. The papers offered one way, but he was not sure that they took on beginners. He had had no training whatever. His sister Myrtle had once said that some of his little thumb-nail sketches were pretty, but what did she know? If he could study somewhere, find someone who would teach him. . . . Meanwhile he would have to work.

He tried the newspapers first of course, for those great institutions seemed the ideal resort for anyone who wanted to get up in the world, but the teeming offices with frowning art directors and critical newspaper workers frightened him. One art director did see something in the three or four little sketches he showed, but he happened to be in a crusty mood, and did not want anybody anyway. He simply said no, there was nothing. Eugene thought that perhaps as an artist also, he was destined to be a failure.

The trouble with this boy was really that he was not half awake yet. The beauty of life, its wonder, had cast a spell over him, but he could not yet interpret it in line and color. He walked about these wonderful streets, gazing in the windows, looking at the boats on the river, looking at the ships on the lake. One day, while he was standing on the lake shore, there came a ship in full sail in the offing—the first he had ever seen. It gripped his sense of beauty. He clasped his hands nervously and thrilled to it. Then he sat down on the lake wall and looked and looked and looked until it gradually sank below the horizon. So this was how the great lakes were; and how the great seas must be—the Atlantic and the Pacific and the Indian Ocean. Ah, the sea! Some day, perhaps he would go to New York. That was where the sea was. But here it was also, in miniature, and it was wonderful.

One cannot moon by lake shores and before store windows and at bridge draws and live, unless one is provided with the means of living, and this Eugene was not. He had determined when he left home that he would be independent. He wanted to get a salary in some way that he could at least live on. He wanted to write back and be able to say that he was getting along nicely. His trunk came, and a loving letter from his mother, and some money, but he sent that back. It was only ten dollars, but he objected to beginning that way. He thought he ought to earn his own way, and he wanted to try, anyhow.

After ten days his funds were very low, a dollar and seventy-five cents, and he decided that any job would have to do. Never mind about art or type-setting now. He could not get the last without a union card, he must take anything, and so he applied from store to store. The cheap little shops in which he asked were so ugly they hurt, but he tried to put his artistic sensibilities aside. He asked for anything, to be made a clerk in a bakery, in a dry goods store, in a candy store. After a time a hardware store loomed up, and he asked there. The man looked at him curiously. "I might give you a place at storing stoves."

Eugene did not understand, but he accepted gladly. It only paid six dollars a week, but he could live on that. He was shown to a loft in charge of two rough men, stove fitters, polishers, and repairers, who gruffly explained to him that his work was to brush the rust off the decayed stoves, to help piece and screw them together, to polish and lift things, for this was a second hand stove business which bought and repaired stoves from junk dealers all over the city. Eugene had a low bench near a window where he was supposed to do his polishing, but he very frequently wasted his time here looking out into the green yards of some houses in a side street. The city was full of wonder to him—its every detail fascinating. When a ragpicker would go by calling "rags, old iron," or a vegetable vender crying "tomatoes, potatoes, green corn, peas," he would stop and listen, the musical pathos of the cries appealing to him. Alexandria had never had anything like this. It was all so strange. He saw himself making pen and ink sketches of things, of the clothes lines in the back yards and of the maids with baskets.

On one of the days when he thought he was working fairly well (he had been there two weeks), one of the two repairers said, "Hey, get a move on you. You're not paid to look out the window." Eugene stopped. He had not realized that he was loafing.

"What have you got to do with it?" he asked, hurt and half defiant. He was under the impression that he was working with these men, not under them.

"I'll show you, you fresh kid," said the older of the two, who was an individual built on the order of "Bill Sykes." "You're under me. You get a move on you, and don't give me any more of your lip."

Eugene was startled. It was a flash of brutality out of a clear sky. The animal, whom he had been scanning as an artist would, as a type, out of the corner of his eye, was revealing himself.

"You go to the devil," said Eugene, only half awake to the grim reality of the situation.

"What's that!" exclaimed the man, making for him. He gave him a shove toward the wall, and attempted to kick him with his big, hob-nailed boot. Eugene picked up a stove leg. His face was wax white.

"Don't you try that again," he said darkly. He fixed the leg in his hand firmly.

"Call it off, Jim," said the other man, who saw the uselessness of so much temper. "Don't hit him. Send him down stairs if you don't like him."

"You get to hell out of here, then," said Eugene's noble superior.

Eugene walked to a nail where his hat and coat were, carrying the stove leg. He edged past his assailant cautiously, fearing a second attack. The man was inclined to kick at him again because of his stubbornness, but forebore.

"You're too fresh, Willie. You want to wake up, you dough face," he said as Eugene went.

Eugene slipped out quietly. His spirit was hurt and torn. What a scene! He, Eugene Witla, kicked at, and almost kicked out, and that in a job that paid six dollars a week. A great lump came up in his throat, but it went down again. He wanted to cry but he could not. He went downstairs, stovepolish on his hands and face and slipped up to the desk.

"I want to quit," he said to the man who had hired him.

"All right, what's the matter?"

"That big brute up there tried to kick me," he explained.

"They're pretty rough men," answered the employer. "I was afraid you wouldn't get along. I guess you're not strong enough. Here you are." He laid out three dollars and a half. Eugene wondered at this queer interpretation of his complaint. He must get along with these men? They musn't get along with him? So the city had that sort of brutality in it.

He went home and washed up, and then struck out again, for it was no time now to be without a job. After a week he found one,—as a house runner for a real estate concern, a young man to bring in the numbers of empty houses and post up the "For Rent" signs in the windows. It paid eight dollars and seemed to offer opportunities of advancement. Eugene might have stayed there indefinitely had it not failed after three months. He had reached the season of fall clothes then, and the need of a winter overcoat, but he made no complaint to his family. He wanted to appear to be getting along well, whether he was or not.

One of the things which tended to harden and sharpen his impressions of life at this time was the show of luxury seen in some directions. On Michigan Avenue and Prairie Avenue, on Ashland Avenue and Washington Boulevard, were sections which were crowded with splendid houses such as Eugene had never seen before. He was astonished at the magnificence of their appointments, the beauty of the lawns, the show of the windows, the distinction of the equipages which accompanied them and served them. For the first time in his life he saw liveried footmen at doors: he saw at a distance girls and women grown who seemed marvels of beauty to him—they were so distinguished in their dress; he saw young men carrying themselves with an air of distinction which he had never seen before. These must be the society people the newspapers were always talking about. His mind made no distinctions as yet. If there were fine clothes, fine trappings, of course social prestige went with them. It made him see for the first time what far reaches lay between the conditions of a beginner from the country and what the world really had to offer—or rather what it showered on some at the top. It subdued and saddened him a little. Life was unfair.

These fall days, too, with their brown leaves, sharp winds, scudding smoke and whirls of dust showed him that the city could be cruel. He met shabby men, sunken eyed, gloomy, haggard, who looked at him, apparently out of a deep despair. These creatures all seemed to be brought where they were by difficult circumstances. If they begged at all,—and they rarely did of him, for he did not look prosperous enough,—it was with the statement that unfortunate circumstances had brought them where they were. You could fail so easily. You could really starve if you didn't look sharp,—the city quickly taught him that.

During these days he got immensely lonely. He was not very sociable, and too introspective. He had no means of making friends, or thought he had none. So he wandered about the streets at night, marveling at the sights he saw, or staying at home in his little room. Mrs. Woodruff, the landlady, was nice and motherly enough, but she was not young and did not fit into his fancies. He was thinking about girls and how sad it was not to have one to say a word to him. Stella was gone—that dream was over. When would he find another like her?

After wandering around for nearly a month, during which time he was compelled to use some money his mother sent him to buy a suit of clothes on an instalment plan, he got a place as driver of a laundry, which, because it paid ten dollars a week, seemed very good. He sketched now and then when he was not tired, but what he did seemed pointless. So he worked here, driving a wagon, when he should have been applying for an art opening, or taking art lessons.

During this winter Myrtle wrote him that Stella Appleton had moved to Kansas, whither her father had gone; and that his mother's health was bad, and that she did so want him to come home and stay awhile. It was about this time that he became acquainted with a little Scotch girl named Margaret Duff, who worked in the laundry, and became quickly involved in a relationship which established a precedent in his experiences with women. Before this he had never physically known a girl. Now, and of a sudden, he was plunged into something which awakened a new, and if not evil, at least disrupting and disorganizing propensity of his character. He loved women, the beauty of the curves of their bodies. He loved beauty of feature and after a while was to love beauty of mind,—he did now, in a vague, unformed way,—but his ideal was as yet not clear to him. Margaret Duff represented some simplicity of attitude, some generosity of spirit, some shapeliness of form, some comeliness of feature,—it was not more. But, growing by what it fed on, his sex appetite became powerful. In a few weeks it had almost mastered him. He burned to be with this girl daily—and she was perfectly willing that he should, so long as the relationship did not become too conspicuous. She was a little afraid of her parents, although those two, being working people, retired early and slept soundly. They did not seem to mind her early philanderings with boys. This latest one was no novelty. It burned fiercely for three months—Eugene was eager, insatiable: the girl not so much so, but complaisant. She liked this evidence of fire in him,—the hard, burning flame she had aroused, and yet after a time she got a little tired. Then little personal differences arose,—differences of taste, differences of judgment, differences of interest. He really could not talk to her of anything serious, could not get a response to his more delicate emotions. For her part she could not find in him any ready appreciation of the little things she liked—theater jests, and the bright remarks of other boys and girls. She had some conception of what was tasteful in dress, but as for anything else, art, literature, public affairs, she knew nothing at all, while Eugene, for all his youth, was intensely alive to what was going on in the great world. The sound of great names and great fames was in his ears,—Carlyle, Emerson, Thoreau, Whitman. He read of great philosophers, painters, musicians, meteors that sped across the intellectual sky of the western world, and he wondered. He felt as though some day he would be called to do something—in his youthful enthusiasm he half-thought it might be soon. He knew that this girl he was trifling with could not hold him. She had lured him, but once lured he was master, judge, critic. He was beginning to feel that he could get along without her,—that he could find someone better.

Naturally such an attitude would make for the death of passion, as the satiation of passion would make for the development of such an attitude. Margaret became indifferent. She resented his superior airs, his top-lofty tone at times. They quarreled over little things. One night he suggested something that she ought to do in the haughty manner customary with him.

"Oh, don't be so smart!" she said. "You always talk as though you owned me."

"I do," he said jestingly.

"Do you?" she flared. "There are others."

"Well, whenever you're ready you can have them. I'm willing."

The tone cut her, though actually it was only an ill-timed bit of teasing, more kindly meant than it sounded.

"Well, I'm ready now. You needn't come to see me unless you want to. I can get along."

She tossed her head.

"Don't be foolish, Margy," he said, seeing the ill wind he had aroused. "You don't mean that."

"Don't I? Well, we'll see." She walked away from him to another corner of the room. He followed her, but her anger re-aroused his opposition. "Oh, all right," he said after a time. "I guess I'd better be going."

She made no response, neither pleas nor suggestions. He went and secured his hat and coat and came back. "Want to kiss me good-bye?" he inquired.

"No," she said simply.

"Good-night," he called.

"Good-night," she replied indifferently.

The relationship was never amicably readjusted after this, although it did endure for some time.

CHAPTER V

FOR the time being this encounter stirred to an almost unbridled degree Eugene's interest in women. Most men are
secretly proud of their triumph with woman—their ability to
triumph—and any evidence of their ability to attract, entertain,
hold, is one of those things which tends to give them an air of
superiority and self-sufficiency which is sometimes lacking in
those who are not so victorious. This was, in its way, his first
victory of the sort, and it pleased him mightily. He felt much
more sure of himself instead of in any way ashamed. What, he
thought, did the silly boys back in Alexandria know of life compared to this? Nothing. He was in Chicago now. The world
was different. He was finding himself to be a man, free, individual, of interest to other personalities. Margaret Duff had
told him many pretty things about himself. She had complimented his looks, his total appearance, his taste in the selection
of particular things. He had felt what it is to own a woman.
He strutted about for a time, the fact that he had been dismissed
rather arbitrarily having little weight with him because he was
so very ready to be dismissed, sudden dissatisfaction with his job
now stirred up in him, for ten dollars a week was no sum wherewith any self-respecting youth could maintain himself,—particularly with a view to sustaining any such relationship as that
which had just ended. He felt that he ought to get a better
place.

Then one day a woman to whom he was delivering a parcel
at her home in Warren Avenue, stopped him long enough to ask:
"What do you drivers get a week for your work?"

"I get ten dollars," said Eugene. "I think some get more."

"You ought to make a good collector," she went on. She
was a large, homely, incisive, straight-talking woman. "Would
you like to change to that kind of work?"

Eugene was sick of the laundry business. The hours were
killing. He had worked as late as one o'clock Sunday morning.

"I think I would," he exclaimed. "I don't know anything
about it, but this work is no fun."

"My husband is the manager of The People's Furniture Company," she went on. "He needs a good collector now and then.
I think he's going to make a change very soon. I'll speak to
him."

Eugene smiled joyously and thanked her. This was surely a windfall. He was anxious to know what collectors were paid but he thought it scarcely tactful to ask.

"If he gives you a job you will probably get fourteen dollars to begin with," she volunteered.

Eugene thrilled. That would be really a rise in the world. Four dollars more! He could get some nice clothes out of that and have spending money besides. He might get a chance to study art. His visions began to multiply. One could get up in the world by trying. The energetic delivery he had done for this laundry had brought him this. Further effort in the other field might bring him more. And he was young yet.

He had been working for the laundry company for six months. Six weeks later, Mr. Henry Mitchly, manager of the People's Furniture, wrote him care of the laundry company to call at his home any evening after eight and he would see him. "My wife has spoken to me of you," he added.

Eugene complied the same day that he received the note, and was looked over by a lean, brisk, unctuous looking man of forty, who asked him various questions as to his work, his home, how much money he took in as a driver, and what not. Finally he said, "I need a bright young man down at my place. It's a good job for one who is steady and honest and hardworking. My wife seems to think you work pretty well, so I'm willing to give you a trial. I can put you to work at fourteen dollars. I want you to come to see me a week from Monday."

Eugene thanked him. He decided, on Mr. Mitchly's advice, to give his laundry manager a full week's notice. He told Margaret that he was leaving and she was apparently glad for his sake. The management was slightly sorry, for Eugene was a good driver. During his last week he helped break in a new man in his place, and on Monday appeared before Mr. Mitchly.

Mr. Mitchly was glad to have him, for he had seen him as a young man of energy and force. He explained the simple nature of the work, which was to take bills for clocks, silverware, rugs, anything which the company sold, and go over the various routes collecting the money due,—which would average from seventy five to a hundred and twenty-five dollars a day. "Most companies in our line require a bond," he explained, "but we haven't come to that yet. I think I know honest young men when I see them. Anyhow we have a system of inspection. If a man's inclined to be dishonest he can't get very far with us."

Eugene had never thought of this question of honesty very much. He had been raised where he did not need to worry about the matter of a little pocket change, and he had made enough at the *Appeal* to supply his immediate wants. Besides, among the people he had always associated with it was considered a very right and necessary thing to be honest. Men were arrested for not being. He remembered one very sad case of a boy he knew being arrested at Alexandria for breaking into a store at night. That seemed a terrible thing to him at the time. Since then he had been speculating a great deal, in a vague way as to what honesty was, but he had not yet decided. He knew that it was expected of him to account for the last penny of anything that was placed in his keeping and he was perfectly willing to do so. The money he earned seemed enough if he had to live on it. There was no need for him to aid in supporting anyone else. So he slipped along rather easily and practically untested.

Eugene took the first day's package of bills as laid out for him, and carefully went from door to door. In some places money was paid him for which he gave a receipt, in others he was put off or refused because of previous difficulties with the company. In a number of places people had moved, leaving no trace of themselves, and packing the unpaid for goods with them. It was his business, as Mr. Mitchly explained, to try to get track of them from the neighbors.

Eugene saw at once that he was going to like the work. The fresh air, the out-door life, the walking, the quickness with which his task was accomplished, all pleased him. His routes took him into strange and new parts of the city, where he had never been before, and introduced him to types he had never met. His laundry work, taking him from door to door, had been a freshening influence, and this was another. He saw scenes that he felt sure he could, when he had learned to draw a little better, make great things of,—dark, towering factory-sites, great stretches of railroad yards laid out like a puzzle in rain, snow, or bright sunlight; great smoke-stacks throwing their black heights athwart morning or evening skies. He liked them best in the late afternoon when they stood out in a glow of red or fading purple. "Wonderful," he used to exclaim to himself, and think how the world would marvel if he could ever come to do great pictures like those of Doré. He admired the man's tremendous imagination. He never thought of himself as doing anything in oils or water colors or chalk—only pen and ink, and that in great, rude splotches of black and white. That was the way. That was the way force was had.

But he could not do them. He could only think them.

One of his chief joys was the Chicago river, its black, mucky water churned by puffing tugs and its banks lined by great red grain elevators and black coal chutes and yellow lumber yards. Here was real color and life—the thing to draw; and then there were the low, drab, rain-soaked cottages standing in lonely, shabby little rows out on flat prairie land, perhaps a scrubby tree somewhere near. He loved these. He would take an envelope and try to get the sense of them—the feel, as he called it—but it wouldn't come. All he did seemed cheap and commonplace, mere pointless lines and stiff wooden masses. How did the great artists get their smoothness and ease? He wondered.

CHAPTER VI

EUGENE collected and reported faithfully every day, and had managed to save a little money. Margaret was now a part of his past. His landlady, Mrs. Woodruff, had gone to live with a daughter in Sedalia, Missouri, and he had moved to a comparatively nice house in East Twenty-first Street on the South Side. It had taken his eye because of a tree in a fifty foot space of ground before it. Like his other room it cost him little, and he was in a private family. He arranged a twenty cent rate per meal for such meals as he took there, and thus he managed to keep his bare living expenses down to five dollars a week. The remaining nine he spent sparingly for clothes, carfare, and amusements—almost nothing of the latter. When he saw he had a little money in reserve he began to think of looking up the Art Institute, which had been looming up in his mind as an avenue of advancement, and find out on what condition he could join a night class in drawing. They were very reasonable, he heard, only fifteen dollars a quarter, and he decided to begin if the conditions were not too severe. He was beginning to be convinced that he was born to be an artist— how soon he could not tell.

The old Art Institute, which preceded the present impressive structure, was located at Michigan Avenue and Monroe Street, and presented an atmosphere of distinction which was not present in most of the structures representing the public taste of the period. It was a large six storey building of brown stone, and contained a number of studios for painters, sculptors, and music teachers, besides the exhibition rooms and the rooms for the classes. There were both day and evening classes, and even at that time a large number of students. The western soul, to a certain extent, was fired by the wonder of art. There was so little of it in the life of the people—the fame of those who could accomplish things in this field and live in a more refined atmosphere was great. To go to Paris! To be a student in any one of the great ateliers of that city! Or of Munich or Rome, to know the character of the artistic treasures of Europe—the life of the Art quarter—that was something. There was what might have been termed a wild desire in the breast of many an untutored boy and girl to get out of the ranks of the commonplace; to assume the character and the habiliments of the artistic temperament as they were then supposed to be; to have a refined, semi-languorous, semi-indifferent manner; to live in a studio, to have a certain freedom in morals and temperament not accorded to the ordinary person—these were the great things to do and be. Of course, art composition was a part of this. You were supposed ultimately to paint great pictures or do noble sculptures, but in the meanwhile you could and should live the life of the artist. And that was beautiful and wonderful and free.

Eugene had long had some sense of this. He was aware that there were studios in Chicago; that certain men were supposed to be doing good work—he saw it in the papers. There were mentions now and then of exhibitions, mostly free, which the public attended but sparingly. Once there was an exhibition of some of the war pictures of Verestchagin, a great Russian painter who had come West for some purpose. Eugene saw them one Sunday afternoon, and was enthralled by the magnificence of their grasp of the elements of battle; the wonder of color; the truth of character; the dramatic quality; the sense of force and danger and horror and suffering which was somehow around and in and through everything that was shown. This man had virility and insight; stupendous imagination and temperament. Eugene stood and stared, wondering how such things could be done. Ever afterward the name of Verestchagin was like a great call to his imagination; that was the kind of an artist to be if you were going to be one.

Another picture came there once, which appealed to another side of his nature, although primarily the basis of its appeal was artistic. It was a great, warm tinted nude by Bouguereau, a French artist who was startling his day with his daring portrayal of the nude. The types he depicted were not namby-pamby little slim-bodied women with spindling qualities of strength and passion, but great, full-blown women whose voluptuous contour of neck and arms and torso and hip and thigh was enough to set the blood of youth at fever heat. The man obviously understood and had passion, love of form, love of desire, love of beauty. He painted with a sense of the bridal bed in the background; of motherhood and of fat, growing babies, joyously nursed. These women stood up big in their sense of beauty and magnetism, the soft lure of desire in their eyes, their full lips parted, their cheeks flushed with the blood of health. As such they were anathema to the conservative and puritanical in mind, the religious in temperament, the cautious in training or taste. The very bringing of this picture to Chicago as a product for sale was enough to create a furore of objection. Such pictures should not be painted, was the cry of the press; or if painted, not exhibited. Bouguereau was conceived of by many as one of those dastards of art who were endeavoring to corrupt by their talent the morals of the world; there was a cry raised that the thing should be suppressed; and as is always the case in all such outbursts of special class opposition, the interest of the general public was aroused.

Eugene was one of those who noted the discussion. He had never seen a picture by Bouguereau or, indeed, an original nude by any other artist. Being usually at liberty after three o'clock, he was free to visit some of these things, and having found it possible to do his work in good clothes he had come to wear his best suit every day. He was a fairly presentable youth with a solemn mien, and his request to be shown anything in any art store would have aroused no surprise. He looked as though he belonged to the intellectual and artistic classes.

Not being sure of what reception would be accorded one so young—he was now nearing twenty—he nevertheless ventured to stop at the gallery where the Bouguereau was being exhibited and ask to see it. The attendant in charge eyed him curiously, but led him back to a room hung in dark red, and turning on a burst of incandescent bulbs set in the ceiling of a red plush hung cabinet, pulled back the curtain revealing the picture. Eugene had never seen such a figure and face. It was a dream of beauty—his ideal come to life. He studied the face and neck, the soft mass of brown, sensuous hair massed at the back of the head, the flowerlike lips and soft cheeks. He marveled at the suggestion of the breasts and the abdomen, that potentiality of motherhood that is so firing to the male. He could have stood there hours dreaming, luxuriating, but the attendant who had left him alone with it for a few minutes returned.

"What is the price of this?" Eugene asked.

"Ten thousand dollars," was the reply.

He smiled solemnly. "It's a wonderful thing," he said, and turned to go. The attendant put out the light.

This picture, like those of Verestchagin, made a sharp impression on him. Curiously he had no longing to paint anything of this kind. He only rejoiced to look at it. It spoke to him of his present ideal of womanhood—physical beauty, and he longed with all his heart to find a creature like that who would look on him with favor.

There were other exhibitions—one containing a genuine Rembrandt—which impressed him, but none like these that had definitely stirred him. His interest in art was becoming eager. He wanted to find out all about it—to do something himself. One day he ventured to call at the Art Institute building and consult the secretary, who explained to him what the charges were. He learned from her, for she was a woman of a practical, clerical turn, that the classes ran from October to May, that he could enter a life or antique class or both, though the antique alone was advisable for the time, and a class in illustration, where costumes of different periods were presented on different models. He found that each class had an instructor of supposed note, whom it was not necessary for him to see. Each class had a monitor and each student was supposed to work faithfully for his own benefit. Eugene did not get to see the class rooms, but he gained a sense of the art of it all, nevertheless, for the halls and offices were decorated in an artistic way, and there were many plaster casts of arms, legs, busts, and thighs and heads. It was as though one stood in an open doorway and looked out upon a new world. The one thing that gratified him was that he could study pen and ink or brush in the illustration class, and that he could also join a sketch class from five to six every afternoon without extra charges if he preferred to devote his evening hours to studying drawing in the life class. He was a little astonished to learn from a printed prospectus given him that the life class meant nude models to work from—both men and women. He was surely approaching a different world now. It seemed necessary and natural enough, and yet there was an aloof atmosphere about it, something that suggested the inner precincts of a shrine, to which only talent was admitted. Was he talented? Wait! He would show the world, even if he was a raw country boy.

The classes which he decided to enter were first a life class which convened Monday, Wednesday and Friday evenings at seven in one of the study rooms and remained in session until ten o'clock, and second a sketch class which met from five to six every afternoon. Eugene felt that he knew little or nothing about figure and anatomy and had better work at that. Costume and illustration would have to wait, and as for the landscapes, or rather city-scapes, of which he was so fond, he could afford to defer those until he learned something of the fundamentals of art.

Heretofore he had rarely attempted the drawing of a face or figure except in miniature and as details of a larger scene. Now he was confronted with the necessity of sketching in char-

coal the head or body of a living person, and it frightened him
a little.   He knew that he would be in a class with fifteen
or twenty other male students.   They would be able to see and
comment on what he was doing.   Twice a week an instructor
would come around and pass upon his work.   There were
honors for those who did the best work during any one month,
he learned from the prospectus, namely: first choice of seats
around the model at the beginning of each new pose.   The
class instructors must be of considerable significance in the
American art world, he thought, for they were N. A.'s, and that
meant National Academicians.   He little knew with what contempt this honor was received in some quarters, or he would
not have attached so much significance to it.

One Monday evening in October, armed with the several
sheets of paper which he had been told to purchase by his all-
informing prospectus, he began his work.   He was a little nervous
at sight of the brightly lighted halls and class rooms, and the
moving crowd of young men and women did not tend to allay
his fears.   He was struck at once with the quality of gaiety,
determination and easy grace which marked the different members
of this company.   The boys struck him as interesting, virile,
in many cases good looking; the girls as graceful, rather dashing and confident.   One or two whom he noted were beautiful
in a dark way.   This was a wonderful world.

The rooms too, were exceptional.   They were old enough
in use to be almost completely covered, as to the walls,
with the accumulation of paint scraped from the palettes.
There were no easels or other paraphernalia, but simply
chairs and little stools—the former, as Eugene learned,
to be turned upside down for easels, the latter for the students
to sit on.   In the center of the room was a platform, the
height of an ordinary table, for the model to pose on, and in
one corner a screen which constituted a dressing room.   There
were no pictures or statuary—just the bare walls—but curiously,
in one corner, a piano.   Out in the halls and in the general
lounging center were pictures of nude figures or parts of
figures posed in all sorts of ways which Eugene, in his raw,
youthful way, thought suggestive.   He secretly rejoiced to
look at them but he felt that he must not say anything about
what he thought.   An art student, he felt sure, must appear to
be indifferent to such suggestion—to be above such desire.
They were here to work, not to dream of women.

When the time came for the classes to assemble there was a
scurrying to and fro, conferring between different students, and

then the men found themselves in one set of rooms and the
women in another. Eugene saw a young girl in his room,
sitting up near the screen, idly gazing about. She was pretty,
of a slightly Irish cast of countenance, with black hair and
black eyes. She wore a cap that was an imitation of the Polish
national head-dress, and a red cape. Eugene assumed her to be
the class model and secretly wondered if he was really to see
her in the nude. In a few minutes all the students were
gathered, and then there was a stir as there strolled in a rather
vigorous and picturesque man of thirty-six or thereabouts, who
sauntered to the front of the room and called the class to order.
He was clad in a shabby suit of grey tweed and crowned with a
little brown hat, shoved rakishly over one ear, which he did not
trouble to take off. He wore a soft blue hickory shirt without
collar or tie, and looked immensely self-sufficient. He was tall
and lean and raw-boned, with a face which was long and narrow; his eyes were large and wide set, his mouth big and firm
in its lines; he had big hands and feet, and an almost rolling
gait. Eugene assumed instinctively that this was Mr. Temple
Boyle, N. A., the class instructor, and he imagined there
would be an opening address of some kind. But the instructor
merely announced that Mr. William Ray had been appointed
monitor and that he hoped that there would be no disorder
or wasting of time. There would be regular criticism days by
him—Wednesdays and Fridays. He hoped that each pupil
would be able to show marked improvement. The class would
now begin work. Then he strolled out.

Eugene soon learned from one of the students that this really
was Mr. Boyle. The young Irish girl had gone behind the
screen. Eugene could see partially, from where he was sitting,
that she was disrobing. It shocked him a little, but he kept
his courage and his countenance because of the presence of so
many others. He turned a chair unside down as he saw the
others do, and sat down on a stool. His charcoal was lying
in a little box beside him. He straightened his paper on its
board and fidgeted, keeping as still as he could. Some of the
students were talking. Suddenly he saw the girl divest herself
of a thin, gauze shirt, and the next moment she came out, naked
and composed, to step upon the platform and stand perfectly
erect, her arms by her side, her head thrown back. Eugene
tingled and blushed and was almost afraid to look directly at
her. Then he took a stick of charcoal and began sketching
feebly, attempting to convey something of this personality and
this pose to paper. It seemed a wonderful thing for him to be

doing—to be in this room, to see this girl posing so; in short, to be an art student. So this was what it was, a world absolutely different from anything he had ever known. And he was self-called to be a member of it.

CHAPTER VII

IT was after he had decided to enter the art class that Eugene paid his first visit to his family. Though they were only a hundred miles away, he had never felt like going back, even at Christmas. Now it seemed to him he had something definite to proclaim. He was going to be an artist; and as to his work, he was getting along well in that. Mr. Mitchly appeared to like him. It was to Mr. Mitchly that he reported daily with his collections and his unsatisfied bills. The collections were checked up by Mr. Mitchly with the cash, and the unpaid bills certified. Sometimes Eugene made a mistake, having too much or too little, but the "too much" was always credited against the "too little," so that in the main he came out even. In money matters there was no tendency on Eugene's part to be dishonest. He thought of lots of things he wanted, but he was fairly well content to wait and come by them legitimately. It was this note in him that appealed to Mitchly. He thought that possibly something could be made of Eugene in a trade way.

He left the Friday night preceding Labor Day, the first Monday in September, which was a holiday throughout the city. He had told Mr. Mitchly that he thought of leaving Saturday after work for over Sunday and Monday, but Mr. Mitchly suggested that he might double up his Saturday's work with Thursday's and Friday's if he wished, and go Friday evening.

"Saturday's a short day, anyhow," he said. "That would give three days at home and still you wouldn't be behind in your work."

Eugene thanked his employer and did as suggested. He packed his bag with the best he had in the way of clothes, and journeyed homeward, wondering how he would find things. How different it all was! Stella was gone. His youthful unsophistication had passed. He could go home as a city man with some prospects. He had no idea of how boyish he looked —how much the idealist he was—how far removed from hard, practical judgment which the world values so highly.

When the train reached Alexandria, his father and Myrtle and Sylvia were at the depot to greet him—the latter with her two year old son. They had all come down in the family carryall, which left one seat for Eugene. He greeted them warmly and received their encomiums on his looks with a befitting sense of humility.

"You're bigger," his father exclaimed. "You're going to be a tall man after all, Eugene. I was afraid you had stopped growing."

"I hadn't noticed that I had grown any," said Eugene.

"Ah, yes," put in Myrtle. "You're much bigger, Gene. It makes you look a little thinner. Are you good and strong?"

"I ought to be," laughed Eugene. "I walk about fifteen or twenty miles a day, and I'm out in the air all the time. If I don't get strong now I never will."

Sylvia asked him about his "stomach trouble." About the same, he told her. Sometimes he thought it was better, sometimes worse. A doctor had told him to drink hot water in the morning but he didn't like to do it. It was so hard to swallow the stuff.

While they were talking, asking questions, they reached the front gate of the house, and Mrs. Witla came out on the front porch. Eugene, at sight of her in the late dusk, jumped over the front wheel and ran to meet her.

"Little ma," he exclaimed. "Didn't expect me back so soon, did you?"

"So soon," she said, her arms around his neck. Then she held him so, quite still for a few moments. "You're getting to be a big man," she said when she released him.

He went into the old sitting room and looked around. It was all quite the same—no change. There were the same books, the same table, the same chairs, the same pulley lamp hanging from the center of the ceiling. In the parlor there was nothing new, nor in the bed rooms or the kitchen. His mother looked a little older—his father not. Sylvia had changed greatly—being slightly "peaked" in the face compared to her former plumpness; it was due to motherhood, he thought. Myrtle seemed a little more calm and happy. She had a real "steady" now, Frank Bangs, the superintendent of the local furniture factory. He was quite young, good-looking, going to be well-off some day, so they thought. "Old Bill," one of the big horses, had been sold. Rover, one of the two collies, was dead. Jake the cat had been killed in a night brawl somewhere.

Somehow, as Eugene stood in the kitchen watching his mother fry a big steak and make biscuits and gravy in honor of his coming, he felt that he did not belong to this world any more. It was smaller, narrower than he had ever thought. The town had seemed smaller as he had come through its streets, the houses too; and yet it was nice. The yards were sweet and simple, but countrified. His father, running a sewing machine business, seemed tremendously limited. He had a country or small town mind. It struck Eugene as curious now, that they had never had a piano. And Myrtle liked music, too. As for himself, he had learned that he was passionately fond of it. There were organ recitals in the Central Music Hall, of Chicago, on Tuesday and Friday afternoons, and he had managed to attend some after his work. There were great preachers like Prof. Swing and the Rev. H. W. Thomas and the Rev F. W. Gunsaulus and Prof. Saltus, liberal thinkers all, whose public services in the city were always accompanied by lovely music. Eugene had found all these men and their services in his search for life and to avoid being lonely. Now they had taught him that his old world was no world at all. It was a small town. He would never come to this any more.

After a sound night's rest in his old room he went down the next day to see Mr. Caleb Williams at the *Appeal* office, and Mr. Burgess, and Jonas Lyle, and John Summers. As he went, on the court house square he met Ed Mitchell and George Taps and Will Groniger, and four or five others whom he had known in school. From them he learned how things were. It appeared that George Anderson had married a local girl and was in Chicago, working out in the stock yards. Ed Waterbury had gone to San Francisco. The pretty Sampson girl, Bessie Sampson, who had once gone with Ted Martinwood so much, had run away with a man from Anderson, Indiana. There had been a lot of talk about it at the time. Eugene listened.

It all seemed less, though, than the new world that he had entered. Of these fellows none knew the visions that were now surging in his brain. Paris—no less—and New York—by what far route he could scarcely tell. And Will Groniger had got to be a baggage clerk at one of the two depots and was proud of it. Good Heavens!

At the office of the *Appeal* things were unchanged. Somehow Eugene had had the feeling that two years would make a lot of difference, whereas the difference was in him only. He was the one who had undergone cataclysmic changes. He had a been a stove polisher, a real estate assistant, a driver and a collector. He had known Margaret Duff, and Mr. Redwood, of the laundry, and Mr. Mitchly. The great city had dawned on him; Verestchagin, and Bouguereau, and the Art Institute. He was going on at one pace, the town was moving at another one—a slower, but quite as fast as it had ever gone.

Caleb Williams was there, skipping about as of yore, cheerful, communicative, interested. "I'm glad to see you back, Eugene," he declared, fixing him with the one good eye which watered. "I'm glad you're getting along—that's fine. Going to be an artist, eh? Well, I think that's what you were cut out for. I wouldn't advise every young fellow to go to Chicago, but that's where you belong. If it wasn't for my wife and three children I never would have left it. When you get a wife and family though—" he paused and shook his head. "I gad! You got to do the best you can." Then he went to look up some missing copy.

Jonas Lyle was as portly, phlegmatic and philosophic as ever. He greeted Eugene with a solemn eye in which there was inquiry. "Well, how is it?" he asked.

Eugene smiled. "Oh, pretty good."

"Not going to be a printer, then?"

"No, I think not."

"Well, it's just as well, there're an awful lot of them."

While they were talking John Summers sidled up.

"How are you, Mr. Witla?" he inquired.

Eugene looked at him. John was certainly marked for the grave in the near future. He was thinner, of a bluish-grey color, bent at the shoulders.

"Why, I'm fine, Mr. Summers," Eugene said.

"I'm not so good," said the old printer. He tapped his chest significantly. "This thing's getting the best of me."

"Don't you believe it," put in Lyle. "John's always gloomy. He's just as good as ever. I tell him he'll live twenty years yet."

"No, no," said Summers, shaking his head, "I know."

He left after a bit to "go across the street," his customary drinking excuse.

"He can't last another year," Lyle observed the moment the door was closed. "Burgess only keeps him because it would be a shame to turn him out. But he's done for."

"Anyone can see that," said Eugene. "He looks terrible." So they talked.

At noon he went home. Myrtle announced that he was to come with her and Mr. Bangs to a party that evening. There were going to be games and refreshments. It never occurred to him that in this town there had never been dancing among the boys and girls he moved with, and scarcely any music. People did not have pianos—or at least only a few of them.

After supper Mr. Bangs called, and the three of them went to a typical small town party. It was not much different from the ones Eugene had attended with Stella, except that the participants were, in the main, just that much older. Two years make a great deal of difference in youth. There were some twenty-two young men and women all crowded into three fair sized rooms and on a porch, the windows and doors leading to which were open. Outside were brown grass and some autumn flowers. Early crickets were chirping, and there were late fire-flies. It was warm and pleasant.

The opening efforts to be sociable were a little stiff. There were introductions all around, much smart badinage among town dandies, for most of them were here. There were a number of new faces—girls who had moved in from other towns or blossomed into maturity since Eugene had left.

"If you'll marry me, Madge, I'll buy you a nice new pair of seal skin earrings," he heard one of the young bloods remark.

Eugene smiled, and the girl laughed back. "He always thinks he's so cute."

It was almost impossible for Eugene to break through the opening sense of reserve which clogged his actions at everything in the way of social diversion. He was a little nervous because he was afraid of criticism. That was his vanity and deep egotism. He stood about, trying to get into the swing of the thing with a bright remark or two. Just as he was beginning to bubble, a girl came in from one of the other rooms. Eugene had not met her. She was with his prospective brother-in-law, Bangs, and was laughing in a sweet, joyous way which arrested his attention. She was dressed in white, he noticed, with a band of golden brown ribbon pulled through the loops above the flounces at the bottom of her dress. Her hair was a wonderful ashen yellow, a great mass of it—and laid in big, thick braids above her forehead and ears. Her nose was straight, her lips were thin and red, her cheek-bones faintly but curiously noticeable. Somehow there was a sense of distinction about her —a faint aroma of personality which Eugene did not understand. It appealed to him.

Bangs brought her over. He was a tight, smiling youth, as sound as oak, as clear as good water.

"Here's Miss Blue, Eugene. She's from up in Wisconsin, and comes down to Chicago occasionally. I told her you ought to know her. You might meet up there sometime."

"Say, but that's good luck, isn't it?" smiled Eugene. "I'm

sure I'm glad to know you. What part of Wisconsin do you come from?"

"Blackwood," she laughed, her greenish-blue eyes dancing.

"Her hair is yellow, her eyes are blue, and she comes from Blackwood," commented Bangs. "How's that?" His big mouth, with its even teeth, was wide with a smile.

"You left out the blue name and the white dress. She ought to wear white all the time."

"Oh, it does harmonize with my name, doesn't it?" she cried. "At home I do wear white mostly. You see I'm just a country girl, and I make most of my things."

"Did you make that?" asked Eugene.

"Of course I did."

Bangs moved away a little, looking at her as if critically. "Well, that's really pretty," he pronounced.

"Mr. Bangs is such a flatterer," she smiled at Eugene. "He doesn't mean any thing he says. He just tells me one thing after another."

"He's right," said Eugene. "I agree as to the dress, and it fits the hair wonderfully."

"You see, he's lost, too," laughed Bangs. "That's the way they all do. Well, I'm going to leave you two. I've got to get back. I left your sister in the hands of a rival of mine."

Eugene turned to this girl and laughed his reserved laugh. "I was just thinking what was going to become of me. I've been away for two years, and I've lost track of some of these people."

"I'm worse yet. I've only been here two weeks and I scarcely know anybody. Mrs. King takes me around everywhere, but it's all so new I can't get hold of it. I think Alexandria is lovely."

"It is nice. I suppose you've been out on the lakes?"

"Oh, yes. We've fished and rowed and camped. I have had a lovely time but I have to go back tomorrow."

"Do you?" said Eugene. "Why I do too. I'm going to take the four-fifteen."

"So am I!" she laughed. "Perhaps we can go together."

"Why, certainly. That's fine. I thought I'd have to go back alone. I only came down for over Sunday. I've been working up in Chicago."

They fell to telling each other their histories. She was from Blackwood, only eighty-five miles from Chicago, and had lived there all her life. There were several brothers and sisters. Her father was evidently a farmer and politician and what not, and Eugene gleaned from stray remarks that they must be well thought of, though poor. One brother-in-law was spoken of as a banker; another as the owner of a grain elevator; she herself was a school teacher at Blackwood—had been for several years.

Eugene did not realize it, but she was fully five years older than himself, with the tact and the superior advantage which so much difference in years brings. She was tired of school-teaching, tired of caring for the babies of married sisters, tired of being left to work and stay at home when the ideal marrying age was rapidly passing. She was interested in able people, and silly village boys did not appeal to her. There was one who was begging her to marry him at this moment, but he was a slow soul up in Blackwood, not actually worthy of her nor able to support her well. She was hopefully, sadly, vaguely, madly longing for something better, and as yet nothing had ever turned up. This meeting with Eugene was not anything which promised a way out to her. She was not seeking so urgently—nor did she give introductions that sort of a twist in her consciousness. But this young man had an appeal for her beyond anyone she had met recently. They were in sympathetic accord, apparently. She liked his clear, big eyes, his dark hair, his rather waxen complexion. He seemed something better than she had known, and she hoped that he would be nice to her.

CHAPTER VIII

THE rest of that evening Eugene spent not exactly with, but near Miss Blue—Miss Angela Blue, as he found her name to be. He was interested in her not so much from the point of view of looks, though she was charming enough, but because of some peculiarity of temperament which lingered with him as a grateful taste might dwell on the palate. He thought her young; and was charmed by what he considered her innocence and unsophistication. As a matter of fact she was not so much young and unsophisticated as an unconscious simulator of simplicity. In the conventional sense she was a thoroughly good girl, loyal, financially honest, truthful in all commonplace things, and thoroughly virtuous, moreover, in that she considered marriage and children the fate and duty of all women. Having had so much trouble with other peoples' children she was not anxious to have any, or at least many, of her own. Of course, she did not believe that she would escape with what seemed to be any such good fortune. She fancied that she would be like her sisters, the wife of a good business or professional man; the mother of three or four or five healthy children; the keeper of an ideal middle class home; the handmaiden of her husband's needs. There was a deep current of passion in her which she had come to feel would never be satisfied. No man would ever understand, no man at least whom she was likely to meet; but she knew she had a great capacity to love. If someone would only come along and arouse that—be worthy of it—what a whirlwind of affection she would return to him! How she would love, how sacrifice! But it seemed now that her dreams were destined never to be fulfilled, because so much time had slipped by and she had not been courted by the right one. So here she was now at twenty-five, dreaming and longing—the object of her ideals thus accidentally brought before her, and no immediate consciousness that that was the case.

It does not take sexual affinity long to manifest itself, once its subjects are brought near to each other. Eugene was older in certain forms of knowledge, broader in a sense, potentially greater than she would ever comprehend; but nevertheless, swayed helplessly by emotion and desire. Her own emotions, though perhaps stronger than his, were differently aroused. The stars, the night, a lovely scene, any exquisite attribute of nature

64

could fascinate him to the point of melancholy. With her, nature in its largest aspects passed practically unnoticed. She responded to music feelingly, as did Eugene. In literature, only realism appealed to him; for her, sentiment, strained though not necessarily unreal, had the greatest charm. Art in its purely æsthetic forms meant nothing at all to her. To Eugene it was the last word in the matter of emotional perception. History, philosophy, logic, psychology, were sealed books to her. To Eugene they were already open doors, or, better yet, flowery paths of joy, down which he was wandering. Yet in spite of these things they were being attracted toward each other.

And there were other differences. With Eugene convention meant nothing at all, and his sense of evil and good was something which the ordinary person would not have comprehended. He was prone to like all sorts and conditions of human beings—the intellectual, the ignorant, the clean, the dirty, the gay, the sorrowful, white, yellow, black. As for Angela, she had a distinct preference for those who conducted themselves according to given standards of propriety. She was brought up to think of those people as best who worked the hardest, denied themselves the most, and conformed to the ordinary notions of right and wrong. There was no questioning of current standards in her mind. As it was written socially and ethically upon the tables of the law, so was it. There might be charming characters outside the pale, but they were not admitted to association or sympathy. To Eugene a human being was a human being. The ruck of misfits or ne'er-do-wells he could laugh joyously with or at. It was all wonderful, beautiful, amusing. Even its grimness and tragedy were worth while, although they hurt him terribly at times. Why, under these circumstances, he should have been so thoroughly attracted to Angela remains a mystery. Perhaps they complemented each other at this time as a satellite complements a larger luminary—for Eugene's egoism required praise, sympathy, feminine coddling; and Angela caught fire from the warmth and geniality of his temperament.

On the train next day Eugene had nearly three hours of what he deemed most delightful talk with her. They had not journeyed far before he had told her how he had traveled this way, on this train, at this hour, two years before; how he had walked about the streets of the big city, looking for a place to sleep, how he had got work and stayed away until he felt that he had found himself. Now he was going to study art and then to New York or Paris, and do magazine illustrating and possibly paint pictures. He was truly your flamboyant youth of talent when he got to talking—when he had a truly sympathetic ear. He loved to boast to someone who really admired him, and he felt that he had admiration here. Angela looked at him with swimming eyes. He was really different from anything she had ever known, young, artistic, imaginative, ambitious. He was going out into a world which she had longed for but never hoped to see—that of art. Here he was telling her of his prospective art studies, and talking of Paris. What a wonderful thing!

As the train neared Chicago she explained that she would have to make an almost immediate connection with one which left over the Chicago Milwaukee and St. Paul, for Blackwood. She was a little lonely, to tell the truth, a little sick at heart, for the summer vacation was over and she was going back to teach school. Alexandria, for the two weeks she had been there visiting Mrs. King (formerly a Blackwood girl and school-day chum of hers), was lovely. Her girlhood friend had tried to make things most pleasant and now it was all over. Even Eugene was over, for he said nothing much of seeing her again, or had not so far. She was wishing she might see more of this world he painted in such glowing colors, when he said:

"Mr. Bangs said that you come down to Chicago every now and then?"

"I do," she replied. "I sometimes come down to go to the theatres and shop." She did not say that there was an element of practical household commercialism in it, for she was considered one of the best buyers in the family and that she was sent to buy by various members of the family in quantities. From a practical household point of view she was a thoroughbred and was valued by her sisters and friends as someone who loved to do things. She might have come to be merely a family pack horse, solely because she loved to work. It was instinct to do everything she did thoroughly, but she worked almost exclusively in minor household matters.

"How soon do you expect to come down again?" he asked.

"Oh, I can't tell. I sometimes come down when Opera is on in the winter. I may be here around Thanksgiving."

"Not before that?"

"I don't think so," she replied archly.

"That's too bad. I thought maybe I'd see you a few times this fall. When you do come I wish you could let me know. I'd like to take you to the theatre."

Eugene spent precious little money on any entertainment, but he thought he could venture this. She would not be down often. Then, too, he had the notion that he might get a rise

one of these days—that would make a difference. When she
came again he would be in art school, opening up another field
for himself. Life looked hopeful.

"That's so nice of you," she replied. "And when I come
I'll let you know. I'm just a country girl," she added, with a
toss of her head, "and I don't get to the city often."

Eugene liked what he considered the guileless naïveté of her
confessions—the frankness with which she owned up to simplicity and poverty. Most girls didn't. She almost made a
virtue out of these things—at least they were charming as a
confession in her.

"I'll hold you to that," he assured her.

"Oh, you needn't. I'll be glad to let you know."

They were nearing the station. He forgot, for the moment
that she was not as remote and delicate in her beauty as Stella,
that she was apparently not as passionate temperamentally as
Margaret. He saw her wonderfully dull hair and her thin lips
and peculiar blue eyes, and admired her honesty and simplicity.
He picked up her grip and helped her to find her train. When
they came to part he pressed her hand warmly, for she had been
very nice to him, so attentive and sympathetic and interested.

"Now remember!" he said gaily, after he had put her in her
seat in the local.

"I won't forget."

"You wouldn't mind if I wrote you now and then?"

"Not at all. I'd like it."

"Then I will," he said, and went out.

He stood outside and looked at her through the train window
as it pulled out. He was glad to have met her. This was
the right sort of girl, clean, honest, simple, attractive. That
was the way the best women were—good and pure—not wild
pieces of fire like Margaret; nor unconscious, indifferent beauties
like Stella, he was going to add, but couldn't. There was a
voice within him that said that artistically Stella was perfect
and even now it hurt him a little to remember. But Stella
was gone forever, there was no doubt about that.

During the days that followed he thought of the girl often.
He wondered what sort of a town Blackwood was; what sort
of people she moved with, what sort of a house she lived in.
They must be nice, simple people like his own in Alexandria.
These types of city bred people whom he saw—girls particularly
—and those born to wealth, had no appeal for him as yet. They
were too distant, too far removed from anything he could
aspire to. A good woman such as Miss Blue obviously was,

must be a treasure anywhere in the world. He kept thinking
he would write to her—he had no other girl acquaintance now;
and just before he entered art school he did this, penning a little
note saying that he remembered so pleasantly their ride; and
when was she coming? Her answer, after a week, was that
she expected to be in the city about the middle or the end of
October and that she would be glad to have him call. She
gave him the number of an aunt who lived out on the North
Side in Ohio Street, and said she would notify him further. She
was hard at work teaching school now, and didn't even have
time to think of the lovely summer she had had.

"Poor little girl," he thought. She deserved a better fate.
"When she comes I'll surely look her up," he thought, and there
was a lot that went with the idea. Such wonderful hair!

CHAPTER IX

THE succeeding days in the art school after his first admission revealed many new things to Eugene. He understood now, or thought he did, why artists were different from the rank and file of mankind. This Art Institute atmosphere was something so refreshing after his days rambling among poor neighborhoods collecting, that he could hardly believe that he, Eugene Witla, belonged there. These were exceptional young people; some of them, anyhow. If they weren't cut out to be good artists they still had imagination—the dream of the artist. They came, as Eugene gradually learned, from all parts of the West and South, from Chicago and St. Louis—from Kansas, Nebraska and Iowa—from Texas and California and Minnesota. One boy was in from Saskatchewan of the Canadian north west, another from the then territory of New Mexico. Because his name was Gill they called him the Gila monster—the difference in the pronunciation of the "G's" not troubling them at all. A boy who came down from Minnesota was a farmer's son, and talked about going back to plow and sow and reap during the next spring and summer. Another boy was the son of a Kansas City millionaire.

The mechanics of drawing interested Eugene from the first. He learned the first night that there was some defect in his understanding of light and shade as it related to the human form. He could not get any roundness or texture in his drawings.

"The darkest shadow is always closest to the high light," observed his instructor laconically on Wednesday evening, looking over his shoulder. "You're making everything a dull, even tone." So that was it.

"You're drawing this figure as a bricklayer who isn't an architect might start to build a house. You're laying bricks without having a plan. Where's your plan?" The voice was that of Mr. Boyle looking over his shoulder.

Eugene looked up. He had begun to draw the head only.

"A plan! A plan!" said his instructor, making a peculiar motion with his hands which described the outline of the pose in a single motion. "Get your general lines first. Then you can put in the details afterward."

Eugene saw at once.

Another time his instructor was watching him draw the female breast. He was doing it woodenly—without much beauty of contour.

"They're round! They're round! I tell you!" exclaimed Boyle. "If you ever see any square ones let me know."

This caught Eugene's sense of humor. It made him laugh, even though he flushed painfully, for he knew he had a lot to learn.

The cruelest thing he heard this man say was to a boy who was rather thick and fat but conscientious. "You can't draw," he said roughly. "Take my advice and go home. You'll make more money driving a wagon."

The class winced, but this man was ugly in his intolerance of futility. The idea of anybody wasting his time was obnoxious to him. He took art as a business man takes business, and he had no time for the misfit, the fool, or the failure. He wanted his class to know that art meant effort.

Aside from this brutal insistence on the significance of art, there was another side to the life which was not so hard and in a way more alluring. Between the twenty-five minute poses which the model took, there were some four or five minute rests during the course of the evening in which the students talked, relighted their pipes and did much as they pleased. Sometimes students from other classes came in for a few moments.

The thing that astonished Eugene though, was the freedom of the model with the students and the freedom of the students with her. After the first few weeks he observed some of those who had been there the year before going up to the platform where the girl sat, and talking with her. She had a little pink gauze veil which she drew around her shoulders or waist that instead of reducing the suggestiveness of her attitudes heightened them.

"Say, ain't that enough to make everything go black in front of your eyes," said one boy sitting next to Eugene.

"Well, I guess," he laughed. "There's some edge to that."

The boys would sit and laugh and jest with this girl, and she would laugh and coquette in return. He saw her strolling about looking at some of the students' drawings of her over their shoulders, standing face to face with others—and so calmly. The strong desire which it invariably aroused in Eugene he quelled and concealed, for these things were not to be shown on the surface. Once, while he was looking at some photographs that a student had brought, she came and looked over his shoulder, this little flower of the streets, her body graced by the thin scarf, her lips and cheeks red with color. She came so close that she leaned against his shoulder and arm with her soft flesh. It pulled him tense, like a great current; but he made no sign, pretending that it was the veriest commonplace. Several times, because the piano was there, and because students would sing and play in the interludes, she came and sat on the piano stool herself, strumming out an accompaniment to which some one or three or four would sing. Somehow this, of all things, seemed most sensuous to him—most oriental. It set him wild. He felt his teeth click without volition on his part. When she resumed her pose, his passion subsided, for then the cold, æsthetic value of her beauty became uppermost. It was only the incidental things that upset him.

In spite of these disturbances, Eugene was gradually showing improvement as a draughtsman and an artist. He liked to draw the figure. He was not as quick at that as he was at the more varied outlines of landscapes and buildings, but he could give lovely sensuous touches to the human form—particularly to the female form—which were beginning to be impressive. He'd got past the place where Boyle had ever to say "They're round." He gave a sweep to his lines that attracted the instructor's attention.

"You're getting the thing as a whole, I see," he said quietly, one day. Eugene thrilled with satisfaction. Another Wednesday he said:—"A little colder, my boy, a little colder. There's sex in that. It isn't in the figure. You ought to make a good mural decorator some day, if you have the inclination," Boyle went on; "you've got the sense of beauty." The roots of Eugene's hair tingled. So art was coming to him. This man saw his capacity. He really had art in him.

One evening a paper sign pasted up on the bulletin board bore the significant legend: "Artists! Attention! We eat! We eat! Nov. 16th. at Sofroni's. All those who want to get in give their names to the monitor."

Eugene had heard nothing of this, but he judged that it originated in one of the other classes. He spoke to the monitor and learned that only seventy-five cents was required of him. Students could bring girls if they wished. Most of them would. He decided that he would go. But where to get a girl? Sofroni's was an Italian restaurant in lower Clark Street, which had originally started out as an eating place for Italian laborers, because it was near an Italian boarding house section. It was located in an old house that was not exactly homely. A yard in the back had been set with plain wooden tables, and benches had been placed for use in the summer time and, later, this had been covered with a mouldy tent-cloth to protect the diners from rain. Still later this became glass and was used in winter. The place was clean and the food good. Some struggling craftsman in journalism and art had found it and by degrees Signor Sofroni had come to realize that he was dealing with a better element. He began to exchange greetings with these people—to set aside a little corner for them. Finally he entertained a small group of them at dinner—charging them hardly more than cost price—and so he was launched. One student told another. Sofroni now had his yard covered in so that he could entertain a hundred at dinner, even in winter. He could serve several kinds of wines and liquors with a dinner for seventy-five cents a piece. So he was popular.

The dinner was the culmination of several other class treats. It was the custom of a class, whenever a stranger, or even a new member appeared, to yell "Treat! Treat!" at which the victim or new member was supposed to produce two dollars as a contribution to a beer fund. If the money was not produced—the stranger was apt to be thrown out or some ridiculous trick played upon him—if it was forthcoming, work for the evening ceased. A collection was immediately taken up. Kegs of beer were sent for, with sandwiches and cheese. Drinking, singing, piano playing, jesting followed. Once, to Eugene's utter astonishment, one of the students—a big, good natured, carousing boy from Omaha—lifted the nude model to his shoulders, set her astride his neck and proceeded around the room, jigging as he went—the girl meantime pulling his black hair, the other students following and shouting uproariously. Some of the girls in an adjoining room, studying in an evening life class, stopped their work to peep through a half dozen small holes which had been punched in the intervening partition. The sight of Showalter carrying the girl so astonished the eavesdroppers that the news of it was soon all over the building. Knowledge of the escapade reached the Secretary and the next day the student was dropped. But the Bacchic dance had been enacted —its impression was left.

There were other treats like this in which Eugene was urged to drink, and he did—a very little. He had no taste for beer. He also tried to smoke, but he did not care for it. He could become nervously intoxicated at times, by the mere sight of such revelry, and then he grew witty, easy in his motions, quick to say bright things. On one of these occasions one of the models said to him: "Why, you're nicer than I thought. I imagined you were very solemn."

"Oh, no," he said, "only at times. You don't know me."

He seized her about the waist, but she pushed him away. He wished now that he danced, for he saw that he might have whirled her about the room then and there. He decided to learn at once.

The question of a girl for the dinner, troubled him. He knew of no one except Margaret, and he did not know that she danced. There was Miss Blue, of Blackwood—whom he had seen when she made her promised visit to the city—but the thought of her in connection with anything like this was to him incongruous. He wondered what she would think if she saw such scenes as he had witnessed.

It chanced that one day when he was in the members' room, he met Miss Kenny, the girl whom he had seen posing the night he had entered the school. Eugene remembered her fascination, for she was the first nude model he had ever seen and she was pretty. She was also the one who had come and stood by him when she was posing. He had not seen her since then. She had liked Eugene, but he had seemed a little distant and, at first, a little commonplace. Lately he had taken to a loose, flowing tie and a soft round hat which became him. He turned his hair back loosely and emulated the independent swing of Mr. Temple Boyle. That man was a sort of god to him—strong and successful. To be like that!

The girl noted a change for what she deemed the better. He was so nice now, she thought, so white-skinned and clear-eyed and keen.

She pretended to be looking at the drawing of a nude when she saw him.

"How are you?" he asked, smiling, venturing to speak to her because he was lonely and because he knew no other girl.

She turned gaily, and returned the question, facing him with smiling lips and genial eyes.

"I haven't seen you for some time," he said. "Are you back here now?"

"For this week," she said. "I'm doing studio work. I don't care for classes when I can get the other."

"I thought you liked them!" he replied, recalling her gaiety of mood.

"Oh, I don't dislike it. Only, studio work is better."

"We've missed you," he said. "The others haven't been nearly as nice."

"Aren't you complimentary," she laughed, her black eyes looking into his with a twinkle.

"No, it's so," he returned, and then asked hopefully, "Are you going to the dinner on the 16th?"

"Maybe," she said. "I haven't made up my mind. It all depends."

"On what?"

"On how I feel and who asks me."

"I shouldn't think there'd be any trouble about that," he observed. "If I had a girl I'd go," he went on, making a terrific effort to reach the point where he could ask her. She saw his intention.

"Well?" she laughed.

"Would you go with me?" he ventured, thus so shamelessly assisted.

"Sure!" she said, for she liked him.

"That's fine!" he exclaimed. "Where do you live? I'll want to know that." He searched for a pencil.

She gave him her number on West Fifty-seventh Street.

Because of his collecting he knew the neighborhood. It was a street of shabby frame houses far out on the South Side. He remembered great mazes of trade near it, and unpaved streets and open stretches of wet prairie land. Somehow it seemed fitting to him that this little flower of the muck and coal yard area should be a model.

"I'll be sure and get you," he laughed. "You won't forget, will you, Miss—"

"Just Ruby," she interrupted. "Ruby Kenny."

"It's a pretty name, isn't it?" he said. "It's euphonious. You wouldn't let me come out some Sunday and see just where it is?"

"Yes, you may," she replied, pleased by his comment on her name. "I'm home most every Sunday. Come out next Sunday afternoon, if you want to."

"I will," said Eugene.

He walked out to the street with her in a very buoyant mood.

CHAPTER X

RUBY KENNY was the adopted child of an old Irish laborer and his wife who had taken her from a quarrelling couple when they had practically deserted her at the age of four years. She was bright, good natured, not at all informed as to the social organization of the world, just a simple little girl with a passion for adventure and no saving insight which would indicate beforehand whither adventure might lead. She began life as a cash girl in a department store and was spoiled of her virtue at fifteen. She was rather fortunate in that her smartness attracted the rather superior, capable, self-protecting type of man; and these were fortunate too, in that she was not utterly promiscuous, appetite with her waiting on strong liking, and in one or two cases real affection, and culminating only after a period of dalliance which made her as much a victim of her moods as were her lovers. Her foster parents provided no guidance of any intelligent character. They liked her, and since she was brighter than they were, submitted to her rule, her explanations of conduct, her taste. She waved aside with a laughing rejoinder any slight objections they might make, and always protested that she did not care what the neighbors thought.

The visits which Eugene paid, and the companionship which ensued, were of a piece with every other relationship of this character which he ever entered into. He worshiped beauty as beauty, and he never wholly missed finding a certain quality of mind and heart for which he longed. He sought in women, besides beauty, good nature and sympathy; he shunned criticism and coldness, and was never apt to select for a sweetheart anyone who could outshine him either in emotion or rapidity or distinction of ideas.

He liked, at this time, simple things, simple homes, simple surroundings, the commonplace atmosphere of simple life, for the more elegant and imposing overawed him. The great mansions which he saw, the great trade structures, the great, significant personalities, seemed artificial and cold. He liked little people—people who were not known, but who were sweet and kindly in their moods. If he could find female beauty with anything like that as a background he was happy and settled down near it, if he could, in comfort. His drawing near to Ruby was governed by this mood.

The Sunday Eugene called, it rained and the neighborhood
in which she lived was exceedingly dreary. Looking around
here and there one could see in the open spaces between the
houses pools of water standing in the brown, dead grass. He
had crossed a great maze of black cindered car tracks, where
engines and cars were in great masses, and speculated on the
drawings such scenes would make—big black engines throwing
up clouds of smoke and steam in a grey, wet air; great mazes of
parti-colored cars dank in the rain but lovely. At night the
switch lights in these great masses of yards bloomed like flowers.
He loved the sheer yellows, reds, greens, blues, that burned
like eyes. Here was the stuff that touched him magnificently,
and somehow he was glad that this raw flowering girl lived
near something like this.

When he reached the door and rang the bell he was greeted
by an old shaky Irish-American who seemed to him rather low
in the scale of intelligence—the kind of a man who would
make a good crossing guard, perhaps. He had on common,
characterful clothes, the kind that from long wear have taken
the natural outlines of the body. In his fingers was a short pipe
which he had been smoking.

"Is Miss Kenny in?" Eugene inquired.

"Yus," said the man. "Come in. I'll git her." He poked
back through a typical workingman's parlor to a rear room.
Someone had seen to it that almost everything in the room was
red—the big silk-shaded lamp, the family album, the carpet
and the red flowered wall paper.

While he was waiting he opened the album and looked at
what he supposed were her relatives—commonplace people, all
—clerks, salesmen, store-keepers. Presently Ruby came, and
then his eye lighted, for there was about her a smartness of youth
—she was not more than nineteen—which captivated his fancy.
She had on a black cashmere dress with touches of red velvet
at the neck and elsewhere, and she wore a loose red tie, much
as a boy might. She looked gay and cheerful and held out her
hand.

"Did you have much trouble in getting here?" she asked.

He shook his head. "I know this country pretty well. I
collect all through here week days. I work for the Peoples'
Furniture Company, you know."

"Oh, then it's all right," she said, enjoying his frankness.
"I thought you'd have a hard time finding it. It's a pretty bad
day, isn't it?"

Eugene admitted that it was, but commented on the car tracks he had seen. "If I could paint at all I'd like to paint those things. They're so big and wonderful."

He went to the window and gazed out at the neighborhood. Ruby watched him with interest. His movements were pleasing to her. She felt at home in his company—as though she were going to like him very much. It was so easy to talk to him. There were the classes, her studio work, his own career, this neighborhood, to give her a feeling of congeniality with him.

"Are there many big studios in Chicago?" he asked when they finally got around to that phase of her work. He was curious to know what the art life of the city was.

"No, not so very many—not, at least, of the good ones. There are a lot of fellows who think they can paint."

"Who are the big ones?" he asked.

"Well, I only know by what I hear artists say. Mr. Rose is pretty good. Byam Jones is pretty fine on *genre* subjects, so they say. Walter Low is a good portrait painter, and so is Manson Steele. And let's see—there's Arthur Biggs—he does landscapes only; I've never been in his studio; and Finley Wood, he's another portrait man; and Wilson Brooks, he does figures —Oh! I don't know, there are quite a number."

Eugene listened entranced. This patter of art matters was more in the way of definite information about personalities than he had heard during all the time he had been in the city. The girl knew these things. She was in the movement. He wondered what her relationship to these various people was?

He got up after a time and looked out of the window again. She came also. "It's not very nice around here," she explained, "but papa and mamma like to live here. It's near papa's work."

"Was that your father I met at the door?"

"They're not my real parents," she explained. "I'm an adopted child. They're just like real parents to me, though, I certainly owe them a lot."

"You can't have been posing in art very long," said Eugene thoughtfully, thinking of her age.

"No; I only began about a year ago."

She told how she had been a clerk in The Fair and how she and another girl had got the idea from seeing articles in the Sunday papers. There was once a picture in the Tribune of a model posing in the nude before the local life class. This had taken her eye and she had consulted with the other girl as to whether they had not better try posing, too. Her friend, like herself, was still posing. She was coming to the dinner.

Eugene listened entranced. It reminded him of how he was

caught by the picture of Goose Island in the Chicago River, of the little tumble-down huts and upturned hulls of boats used for homes. He told her of that and of how he came, and it touched her fancy. She thought he was sentimental but nice— and then he was big, too, and she was so much smaller.

"You play?" he asked, "don't you?"

"Oh, just a little. But we haven't got a piano. I learned what I know by practising at the different studios."

"Do you dance?" asked Eugene.

"Yes, indeed," she replied.

"I wish I did," he commented ruefully.

"Why don't you? It's easy. You could learn in no time. I could teach you in a lesson."

"I wish you would," he said persuasively.

"It isn't hard," she went on, moving away from him. "I can show you the steps. They always begin with the waltz."

She lifted her skirts and exposed her little feet. She explained what to do and how to do it. He tried it alone, but failed; so she got him to put his arm around her and placed her hand in his. "Now, follow me," she said.

It was so delightful to find her in his arms! And she was apparently in no hurry to conclude the lesson, for she worked with him quite patiently, explaining the steps, stopping and correcting him, laughing at her mistakes and his. "You're getting it, though," she said, after they had turned around a few times.

They had looked into each other's eyes a number of times and she gave him frank smiles in return for his. He thought of the time when she stood by him in the studio, looking over his shoulder. Surely, surely this gap of formalities might be bridged over at once if he tried—if he had the courage. He pulled her a little closer and when they stopped he did not let go.

"You're mighty sweet to me," he said with an effort.

"No, I'm just good natured," she laughed, not endeavoring to break away.

He became emotionally tense, as always.

She rather liked what seemed the superiority of his mood. It was different, stronger than was customary in the men she knew.

"Do you like me?" he asked, looking at her.

She studied his face and hair and eyes.

"I don't know," she returned calmly.

"Are you sure you don't?"

There was another pause in which she looked almost mockingly at him and then, sobering, away at the hall door.

"Yes, I think I do," she said.

He picked her up in his arms. "You're as cute as a doll," he said and carried her to the red settee. She spent the rest of the rainy afternoon resting in his arms and enjoying his kisses. He was a new and peculiar kind of boy.

CHAPTER XI

A LITTLE while before, Angela Blue at Eugene's earnest solicitation had paid her first Fall visit to Chicago. She had made a special effort to come, lured by a certain poignancy of expression which he could give to any thought, particularly when it concerned his desires. In addition to the art of drawing he had the gift of writing—very slow in its development from a structural and interpretative point of view, but powerful already on its descriptive side. He could describe anything, people, houses, horses, dogs, landscapes, much as he could draw them and give a sense of tenderness and pathos in the bargain which was moving. He could describe city scenes and the personal atmosphere which surrounded him in the most alluring fashion. He had little time to write, but he took it in this instance to tell this girl what he was doing and how he was doing it. She was captivated by the quality of the world in which he was moving, and the distinction of his own personality, which he indicated rather indirectly than otherwise. By contrast her own little world began to look very shabby indeed.

She came shortly after his art school opened, and at her invitation he went out to the residence of her aunt on the North Side, a nice, pleasant brick house in a quiet side street, which had all the airs of middle class peace and comfort. He was impressed with what seemed to him a sweet, conservative atmosphere—a fitting domicile for a girl so dainty and refined as Angela. He paid his respects early Saturday morning because her neighborhood happened to be in the direction of his work.

She played for him—better than anyone he had ever known. It seemed to him a great accomplishment. Her temperament attracted her to music of a high emotional order and to songs and instrumental compositions of indefinable sweetness. In the half hour he stayed she played several things, and he noted with a new pleasure her small shapely body in a dress of a very simple, close fitting design; her hair hung in two great braids far below her waist. She reminded him the least bit of Marguerite in "Faust."

He went again in the evening, shining and eager, and arrayed in his best. He was full of the sense of his art prospects, and happy to see her again, for he was satisfied that he was going to fall in love with her. She had a strong, sympathetic attitude

80

which allured him. She wanted to be nice to this youth—wanted him to like her—and so the atmosphere was right.

That evening he took her to the Chicago Opera House, where there was playing an extravaganza. This fantasy, so beautiful in its stage-craft, so gorgeous in its show of costumes and pretty girls, so idle in its humor and sweet in its love songs, captivated both Eugene and Angela. Neither had been to a theatre for a long time; both were en rapport with some such fantastic interpretation of existence. After the short acquaintance at Alexandria it was a nice coming together. It gave point to their reunion.

After the performance he guided her through the surging crowds to a North Division Street car—they had laid cables since his arrival—and together they went over the beauties and humor of the thing they had seen. He asked permission to call again next day, and at the end of an afternoon in her company, proposed that they go to hear a famous preacher who was speaking in Central Music Hall evenings.

Angela was pleased at Eugene's resourcefulness. She wanted to be with him; this was a good excuse. They went early and enjoyed it. Eugene liked the sermon as an expression of youth and beauty and power to command. He would have liked to be an orator like that, and he told Angela so. And he confided more and more of himself to her. She was impressed by his vivid interest in life, his selective power, and felt that he was destined to be a notable personality.

There were other meetings. She came again in early November and before Christmas and Eugene was fast becoming lost in the meshes of her hair. Although he met Ruby in November and took up a tentative relation on a less spiritual basis—as he would have said at the time—he nevertheless held this acquaintanceship with Angela in the background as a superior and more significant thing. She was purer than Ruby; there was in her certainly a deeper vein of feeling, as expressed in her thoughts and music. Moreover she represented a country home, something like his own, a nice simple country town, nice people. Why should he part with her, or ever let her know anything of this other world that he touched? He did not think he ought to. He was afraid that he would lose her, and he knew that she would make any man an ideal wife. She came again in December and he almost proposed to her—he must not be free with her or draw too near too rapidly. She made him feel the sacredness of love and marriage. And he did propose in January.

The artist is a blend of subtleties in emotion which can not be

classified. No one woman could have satisfied all sides of
Eugene's character at that time. Beauty was the point with him.
Any girl who was young, emotional or sympathetic to the right
degree and beautiful would have attracted and held him for a
while. He loved beauty—not a plan of life. He was interested in an artistic career, not in the founding of a family.
Girlhood—the beauty of youth—was artistic, hence he craved
it.

Angela's mental and emotional composition was stable. She
had learned to believe from childhood that marriage was a
fixed thing. She believed in one life and one love. When you
found that, every other relationship which did not minister
to it was ended. If children came, very good; if not, very good;
marriage was permanent anyhow. And if you did not marry
happily it was nevertheless your duty to endure and suffer for
whatever good might remain. You might suffer badly in such a
union, but it was dangerous and disgraceful to break it. If
you could not stand it any more, your life was a failure.

Of course, Eugene did not know what he was trifling with.
He had no conception of the nature of the relationship he was
building up. He went on blindly dreaming of this girl as
an ideal, and anticipating eventual marriage with her. When
that would be, he had no idea, for though his salary had been
raised at Christmas he was getting only eighteen dollars a
week; but he deemed it would come within a reasonable time.

Meanwhile, his visits to Ruby had brought the inevitable result. The very nature of the situation seemed to compel it. She
was young, brimming over with a love of adventure, admiring
youth and strength in men. Eugene, with his pale face, which
had just a touch of melancholy about it, his sex magnetism, his
love of beauty, appealed to her. Uncurbed passion was perhaps
uppermost to begin with; very shortly it was confounded with
affection, for this girl could love. She was sweet, good natured,
ignorant of life from many points of view. Eugene represented
the most dramatic imagination she had yet seen. She described
to him the character of her foster parents, told how simple they
were and how she could do about as she pleased. They did not
know that she posed in the nude. She confided to him her particular friendship for certain artists, denying any present intimacies. She admitted them in the past, but asserted that they
were bygones. Eugene really did not believe this. He suspected
her of meeting other approaches in the spirit in which she had
met his own. It aroused his jealousy, and he wished at once that
she were not a model. He said as much and she laughed. She

knew he would act like that, it was the first proof of real, definite
interest in her on his part.

From that time on there were lovely days and evenings spent
in her company. Before the dinner she invited him over to
breakfast one Sunday. Her foster parents were to be away
and she was to have the house to herself. She wanted to cook
Eugene a breakfast—principally to show him she could cook—
and then it was novel. She waited till he arrived at nine to
begin operations and then, arrayed in a neat little lavender,
close fitting house dress, and a ruffled white apron, went about
her work, setting the table, making biscuit, preparing a kidney
ragout with strong wine, and making coffee.

Eugene was delighted. He followed her about, delaying her
work by taking her in his arms and kissing her. She got flour
on her nose and he brushed it off with his lips.

It was on this occasion that she showed him a very pleasing
little dance she could do—a clog dance, which had a running,
side-ways motion, with frequent and rapid clicking of the heels.
She gathered her skirts a little way above her ankles and twinkled
her feet through a maze of motions. Eugene was beside himself with admiration. He told himself he had never met such
a girl—to be so clever at posing, playing and dancing, and so
young. He thought she would make a delightful creature to
live with, and he wished now he had money enough to make it
possible. At this high-flown moment and at some others he
thought he might almost marry her.

On the night of the dinner he took her to Sofroni's, and was
surprised to find her arrayed in a red dress with a row of large
black leather buttons cutting diagonally across the front. She
had on red stockings and shoes and wore a red carnation in her
hair. The bodice was cut low in the neck and the sleeves were
short. Eugene thought she looked stunning and told her so.
She laughed. They went in a cab, for she had warned him beforehand that they would have to. It cost him two dollars each
way but he excused his extravagance on the ground of necessity.
It was little things like this that were beginning to make him
think strongly of the problem of getting on.

The students who had got up this dinner were from all
the art classes, day and night. There were over two hundred of
them, all of them young, and there was a mixed collection of
girl art students, artist's models and girl friends of various grades
of thought and condition, who were brought as companions. The
big dining-room was tempestuous with the rattling of dishes,
the shouting of jests, the singing of songs and the exchange of

greetings. Eugene knew a few of these people outside his own classes, enough to give him the chance to be sociable and not appear lonely or out of it.

From the outset it was apparent that she, Ruby, was generally known and liked. Her costume—a little bold—made her conspicuous. From various directions there were cries of "Hey! Rube!" which was a familiar interpretation of her first name, Ruby.

Eugene was surprised at this—it shocked him a little. All sorts of boys he did not know came and talked to her, exchanging familiar gossip. She was called away from him a dozen times in as many minutes. He saw her laughing and chatting at the other end of the hall, surrounded by half a dozen students. It made him jealous.

As the evening progressed the attitude of each toward the other and all toward anyone became more and more familiar. When the courses were over, a space was cleared at one end and a screen of green cloth rigged up in one corner as a dressing room for *stunts*. Eugene saw one of the students called with much applause to do an Irish monologue, wearing green whiskers, which he adjusted in the presence of the crowd. There was another youth who pretended to have with him an immense roll of verse—an epic, no less—wound in so tight a manner that it looked as though it might take all night to read it. The crowd groaned. With amazing savoir faire he put up one hand for silence, dropped the roll, holding, of course, to the outer end and began reading. It was not bad verse, but the amusing part was that it was really short, not more than twenty lines. The rest of the paper had been covered with scribbling to deceive the crowd. It secured a round of applause. There was one second-year man who sang a song—"Down in the Lehigh Valley"—and another who gave imitations of Temple Boyle and other instructors at their work of criticising and painting for the benefit of the class. These were greatly enjoyed. Finally one of the models, after much calling by the crowd of "Desmond! Desmond!"—her last name—went behind the green cloth screen and in a few moments reappeared in the short skirt of a Spanish dancer, with black and silver spangles, and castanets. Some friendly student had brought a mandolin and "La Paloma" was danced.

Eugene had little of Ruby's company during all these doings. She was too much sought after. As the other girl was concluding her dance he heard the cry of "Hey, Rube! Why don't you do your turn?" Someone else, eager to see her dance, called

"Come on, Ruby!" The rest of the room, almost unthinkingly took it up. Some boys surrounding her had started to push her toward the dancing space. Before Eugene knew it she was up in someone's arms being passed from group to group for a joke. The crowd cheered. Eugene, however, having come so close to her, was irritated by this familiarity. She did not appear to belong to him, but to the whole art-student body. And she was laughing. When she was put down in the clear space she lifted her skirts as she had done for him and danced. A crowd of students got very close. He had to draw near to see her at all. And there she was, unconscious of him, doing her gay clog dance. When she stopped, three or four of the more daring youths urged her, seizing her by the hands and arms, to do something else. Someone cleared a table and someone else picked her up and put her on it. She did still other dances. Someone cried, "Hey, Kenny, do you need the red dress?" So this was his temporary sweetheart.

When she was finally ready to go home at four o'clock in the morning, or when the others were agreed to let her go, she hardly remembered that she had Eugene with her. She saw him waiting as two students were asking for the privilege of taking her home.

"No," she exclaimed, seeing him, "I have my escort. I'm going now. Good-bye," and came toward him. He felt rather frozen and out of it.

"Are you ready?" she asked.

He nodded gloomily, reproachfully.

CHAPTER XII

FROM drawing from the nude, which Eugene came to do very successfully that winter, his interest switched to his work in the illustration class where costume figures were used. Here, for the first time, he tried his hand at wash drawings, the current medium for magazine work, and was praised after a time for his execution. Not always, however; for the instructors, feeling that harsh criticism would make for steadier effort, pooh-poohed some of his best work. But he had faith in what he was destined to do, and after sinking to depths of despair he would rise to great heights of self-confidence.

His labor for the Peoples' Furniture Company was becoming a rather dreary grind when Vincent Beers, the instructor in the illustration class, looking over his shoulder one Wednesday afternoon said:— "You ought to be able to make a little money by your work pretty soon, Witla."

"Do you think so?" questioned Eugene.

"It's pretty good. There ought to be a place on one of the newspapers here for a man like you—an afternoon newspaper possibly. Did you ever try to get on?"

"I did when I first came to the city, but they didn't want anyone. I'm rather glad they didn't now. I guess they wouldn't have kept me very long."

"You draw in pen and ink pretty well, don't you?"

"I thought I liked that best of all at first."

"Well, then, they ought to be able to use you. I wouldn't stay very long at it though. You ought to go to New York to get in the magazine illustration field—there's nothing out here. But a little newspaper work now wouldn't hurt you."

Eugene decided to try the afternoon papers, for he knew that if he got work on one of these he could still continue his night classes. He could give the long evening session to the illustration class and take an occasional night off to work on the life studies. That would make an admirable arrangement. For several days he took an hour after his work to make inquiry, taking with him some examples of his pen and inks. Several of the men he saw liked what he had to show, but he found no immediate opening. There was only one paper, one of the poorest, that offered him any encouragement. The editor-in-chief said he might be in need of a man shortly. If Eugene would come in again in three or four weeks he could tell him. They did not pay very much—twenty-five dollars to beginners.

Eugene thought of this as a great opportunity, and when he went back in three weeks and actually secured the place, he felt that he was now fairly on the road to prosperity. He was given a desk in a small back room on a fourth floor where there was accidentally west and north light. He was in a department which held two other men, both several years older than himself, one of whom posed as "dean" of the staff.

The work here was peculiar in that it included not only pen and ink but the chalk plate process which was a method of drawing with a steel point upon a zinc plate covered with a deposit of chalk, which left a design which was easily reproduced. Eugene had never done this, he had to be shown by the "dean," but he soon picked it up. He found it hard on his lungs, for he had constantly to keep blowing the chalk away as he scratched the surface of the plate, and sometimes the dust went up into his nostrils. He hoped sincerely there would not be much of this work, but there was rather an undue proportion at first owing to the fact that it was shouldered on to him by the other two—he being the beginner. He suspected as much after a little time, but by that time he was beginning to make friends with his companions and things were not so bad.

These two, although they did not figure vastly in his life, introduced him to conditions and personalities in the Chicago newspaper world which broadened him and presented points of view which were helpful. The elder of the two, the "dean," was dressy and art-y; his name was Horace Howe. The other, Jeremiah Mathews, Jerry for short, was short and fat, with a round, cheerful, smiling countenance and a wealth of coarse black hair. He loved chewing tobacco, was a little mussy about his clothes, but studious, generous and good natured. Eugene found that he had several passions, one for good food, another for oriental curios and a third for archæology. He was alive to all that was going on in the world, and was utterly without any prejudices, social, moral or religious. He liked his work, and whistled or talked as he did it. Eugene took a secret like for him from the beginning.

It was while working on this paper that Eugene first learned that he really could write. It came about accidentally for he had abandoned the idea that he could ever do anything in newspaper work, which was the field he had originally contemplated. Here there was great need for cheap Sunday specials of a local character, and in reading some of these, which were given to him for illustration, he came to the conclusion that he could do much better himself.

"Say," he asked Mathews, "who writes the articles in here?" He was looking over the Sunday issue.

"Oh, the reporters on the staff—anyone that wants to. I think they buy some from outsiders. They only pay four dollars a column."

Eugene wondered if they would pay him, but pay or no pay he wanted to do them. Maybe they would let him sign his name. He saw that some were signed. He suggested he believed he could do that sort of thing but Howe, as a writer himself, frowned on this. He wrote and drew. Howe's opposition piqued Eugene who decided to try when the opportunity offered. He wanted to write about the Chicago River, which he thought he could illustrate effectively. Goose Island, because of the description he had read of it several years before, the simple beauties of the city parks where he liked to stroll and watch the lovers on Sundays. There were many things, but these stood as susceptible of delicious, feeling illustration and he wanted to try his hand. He suggested to the Sunday Editor, Mitchell Goldfarb, with whom he had become friendly, that he thought something nice in an illustrative way could be done on the Chicago River.

"Go ahead, try your hand," exclaimed that worthy, who was a vigorous, robust, young American of about thirty-one, with a gaspy laugh that sounded as if someone had thrown cold water down his back. "We need all that stuff. Can you write?"

"I sometimes think I might if I practiced a little."

"Why not," went on the other, who saw visions of a little free copy. "Try your hand. You might make a good thing of it. If your writing is anything like your drawing it will be all right. We don't pay people on the staff, but you can sign your name to it."

This was enough for Eugene. He tried his hand at once. His art work had already begun to impress his companions. It was rough, daring, incisive, with a touch of soul to it. Howe was already secretly envious, Mathews full of admiration. Encouraged thus by Goldfarb Eugene took a Sunday afternoon and followed up the branches of the Chicago River, noting its wonders and peculiarities, and finally made his drawings. Afterward he went to the Chicago library and looked up its history—accidentally coming across the reports of some government engineers who dwelt on the oddities of its traffic. He did not write an article so much as a panegyric on its beauty and littleness, finding the former where few would have believed it to exist. Gold-farb was oddly surprised when he read it. He had not thought Eugene could do it.

The charm of Eugene's writing was that while his mind was full of color and poetry he had logic and a desire for facts which gave what he wrote stability. He liked to know the history of things and to comment on the current phases of life. He wrote of the parks, Goose Island, the Bridewell, whatever took his fancy.

His real passion was for art, however. It was a slightly easier medium for him—quicker. He thrilled to think, sometimes, that he could tell a thing in words and then actually draw it. It seemed a beautiful privilege and he loved the thought of making the commonplace dramatic. It was all dramatic to him—the wagons in the streets, the tall buildings, the street lamps—anything, everything.

His drawing was not neglected meantime, but seemed to get stronger.

"I don't know what there is about your stuff, Witla, that gets me," Mathews said to him one day, "but you do something to it. Now why did you put those birds flying above that smoke-stack?"

"Oh, I don't know," replied Eugene. "It's just the way I feel about it. I've seen pigeons flying like that."

"It's all to the good," replied Mathews. "And then you handle your masses right. I don't see anybody doing this sort of thing over here."

He meant in America, for these two art workers considered themselves connoisseurs of pen and ink and illustration generally. They were subscribers to *Jugend, Simplicissimus, Pick-Me-Up* and the radical European art journals. They were aware of Steinlen and Cheret and Mucha and the whole rising young school of French poster workers. Eugene was surprised to hear of these men and these papers. He began to gain confidence in himself—to think of himself as somebody.

It was while he was gaining this knowledge—finding out who was who and what and why that he followed up his relationship with Angela Blue to its logical conclusion—he became engaged to her. In spite of his connection with Ruby Kenny, which continued unbroken after the dinner, he nevertheless felt that he must have Angela; partly because she offered more resistance than any girl since Stella, and partly because she appeared to be so innocent, simple and good hearted. And she was altogether lovely. She had a beautiful figure, which no

crudity of country dressmaking could conceal. She had her wonderful wealth of hair and her large, luring, water-clear blue eyes.
She had colorful lips and cheeks, a natural grace in walking, could
dance and play the piano. Eugene looked at her and came to
the conclusion after a time that she was as beautiful as any
girl he had ever seen—that she had more soul, more emotion,
more sweetness. He tried to hold her hand, to kiss her, to take
her in his arms, but she eluded him in a careful, wary and yet
half yielding way. She wanted him to propose to her, not because
she was anxious to trap him, but because her conventional conscience told her these things were not right outside a definite engagement and she wanted to be engaged first. She was already
in love with him. When he pleaded, she was anxious to throw
herself in his arms in a mad embrace, but she restrained herself,
waiting. At last he flung his arms about her as she was sitting
at the piano one evening and holding her tight pressed his lips
to her cheek.

She struggled to her feet. "You musn't," she said. "It isn't
right. I can't let you do that."

"But I love you," he exclaimed, pursuing her. "I want to
marry you. Will you have me, Angela? Will you be mine?"

She looked at him yearningly, for she realized that she had
made him do things her way—this wild, unpractical, artistic
soul. She wanted to yield then and there but something told her
to wait.

"I won't tell you now," she said, "I want to talk to papa and
mamma. I haven't told them anything as yet. I want to ask
them about you, and then I'll tell you when I come again."

"Oh, Angela," he pleaded.

"Now, please wait, Mr. Witla," she pleaded. She had never
yet called him Eugene. "I'll come again in two or three weeks.
I want to think it over. It's better."

He curbed his desire and waited, but it made all the more vigorous and binding the illusion that she was the one woman in
the world for him. She aroused more than any woman yet a
sense of the necessity of concealing the eagerness of his senses—
of pretending something higher. He even tried to deceive himself
into the belief that this was a spiritual relationship, but underneath all was a burning sense of her beauty, her physical charm,
her passion. She was sleeping as yet, bound in convention and
a semi-religious interpretation of life. If she were aroused!
He closed his eyes and dreamed.

CHAPTER XIII

IN two weeks Angela came back, ready to plight her faith; and Eugene was waiting, eager to receive it. He had planned to meet her under the smoky train shed of the Chicago, Milwaukee and St. Paul depot, to escort her to Kinsley's for dinner, to bring her some flowers, to give her a ring he had secured in anticipation, a ring which had cost him seventy-five dollars and consumed quite all his savings; but she was too regardful of the drama of the situation to meet him anywhere but in the parlor of her aunt's house, where she could look as she wished. She wrote that she must come down early and when he arrived at eight of a Saturday evening she was dressed in the dress that seemed most romantic to her, the one she had worn when she first met him at Alexandria. She half suspected that he would bring flowers and so wore none, and when he came with pink roses, she added those to her corsage. She was a picture of rosy youth and trimness and not unlike the character by whose name he had christened her—the fair Elaine of Arthur's court. Her yellow hair was done in a great mass that hung sensuously about her neck; her cheeks were rosy with the elation of the hour; her lips moist; her eyes bright. She fairly sparkled her welcome as he entered.

At the sight of her Eugene was beside himself. He was always at the breaking point over any romantic situation. The beauty of the idea—the beauty of love as love; the delight of youth filled his mind as a song might, made him tense, feverish, enthusiastic.

"You're here at last, Angela!" he said, trying to keep hold of her hands. "What word?"

"Oh, you musn't ask so soon," she replied. "I want to talk to you first. I'll play you something."

"No," he said, following her as she backed toward the piano. "I want to know. I must. I can't wait."

"I haven't made up my mind," she pleaded evasively. "I want to think. You had better let me play."

"Oh, no," he urged.

"Yes, let me play."

She ignored him and swept into the composition, but all the while she was conscious of him hovering over her—a force. At the close, when she had been made even more emotionally responsive by the suggestion of the music, he slipped his arms about her as he had once before, but she struggled away again, slipping to a corner and standing at bay. He liked her flushed face, her shaken hair, the roses awry at her waist.

"You must tell me now," he said, standing before her. "Will you have me?"

She dropped her head down as though doubting, and fearing familiarities; he slipped to one knee to see her eyes. Then, looking up, he caught her about the waist. "Will you?" he asked.

She looked at his soft hair, dark and thick, his smooth pale brow, his black eyes and even chin. She wanted to yield dramatically and this was dramatic enough. She put her hands to his head, bent over and looked into his eyes; her hair fell forward about her face. "Will you be good to me?" she asked, yearning into his eyes.

"Yes, yes," he declared. "You know that. Oh, I love you so."

She put his head far back and laid her lips to his. There was fire, agony in it. She held him so and then he stood up heaping kisses upon her cheeks, her lips, her eyes, her neck.

"Good God!" he exclaimed, "how wonderful you are!"

The expression shocked her.

"You mustn't," she said.

"I can't help it. You are so beautiful!"

She forgave him for the compliment.

There were burning moments after this, moments in which they clung to each other desperately, moments in which he took her in his arms, moments in which he whispered his dreams of the future. He took the ring he had bought and put it on her finger. He was going to be a great artist, she was going to be an artist's bride; he was going to paint her lovely face, her hair, her form. If he wanted love scenes he would paint these which they were now living together. They talked until one in the morning and then she begged him to go, but he would not. At two he left, only to come early the next morning to take her to church.

There ensued for Eugene a rather astonishing imaginative and emotional period in which he grew in perception of things literary and artistic and in dreams of what marriage with Angela would mean to him. There was a peculiar awareness about Eugene at this time, which was leading him into an understanding of things. The extraordinary demands of some phases of dogma in the matter of religion; the depths of human perversity in the matter of morality; the fact that there were worlds within worlds of our social organism; that really basically and actually there was no fixed and definite understanding of anything by anybody. From Mathews he learned of philosophies—Kant, Hegel, Schopenhauer—faint inklings of what they believed. From association with Howe he heard of current authors who expressed new moods, Pierre Loti, Thomas Hardy, Maeterlinck, Tolstoi. Eugene was no person to read—he was too eager to live,—but he gained much by conversation and he liked to talk. He began to think he could do almost anything if he tried—write poems, write plays, write stories, paint, illustrate, etc. He used to conceive of himself as a general, an orator, a politician— thinking how wonderful he would be if he could set himself definitely to any one thing. Sometimes he would recite passages from great speeches he had composed in his imagination as he walked. The saving grace in his whole make-up was that he really loved to work and he would work at the things he could do. He would not shirk his assignments or dodge his duties.

After his evening class Eugene would sometimes go out to Ruby's house, getting there by eleven and being admitted by an arrangement with her that the front door be left open so that he could enter quietly. More than once he found her sleeping in her little room off the front room, arrayed in a red silk dressing gown and curled up like a little black-haired child. She knew he liked her art instincts and she strove to gratify them, affecting the peculiar and the exceptional. She would place a candle under a red shade on a small table by her bed and pretend to have been reading, the book being usually tossed to one side on the coverlet where he would see it lying when he came. He would enter silently, gathering her up in his arms as she dozed, kissing her lips to waken her, carrying her in his arms into the front room to caress her and whisper his passion. There was no cessation of this devotion to Ruby the while he was declaring his love for Angela, and he really did not see that the two interfered greatly. He loved Angela, he thought. He liked Ruby, thought she was sweet. He felt sorry for her at times because she was such a little thing, so unthinking. Who was going to marry her eventually? What was going to become of her?

Because of this very attitude he fascinated the girl who was soon ready to do anything for him. She dreamed dreams of how nice it would be if they could live in just a little flat together— all alone. She would give up her art posing and just keep house for him. He talked to her of this—imagining it might possibly come to pass—realizing quite fully that it probably wouldn't. He wanted Angela for his wife, but if he had money he thought

Ruby and he might keep a separate place—somehow. What Angela would think of this did not trouble him—only that she should not know. He never breathed anything to either of the other, but there were times when he wondered what they would think each of the other if they knew. Money, money, that was the great deterrent. For lack of money he could not marry anybody at present—neither Angela nor Ruby nor anyone else. His first duty, he thought, was so to place himself financially that he could talk seriously to any girl. That was what Angela expected of him, he knew. That was what he would have to have if he wanted Ruby.

There came a time when the situation began to grow irksome. He had reached the point where he began to understand how limited his life was. Mathews and Howe, who drew more money, were able to live better than he. They went out to mid-night suppers, theatre parties, and expeditions to the tenderloin section (not yet known by that name). They had time to browse about the sections of the city which had peculiar charms for them as Bohemians after dark—the levee, as a certain section of the Chicago River was called; Gambler's Row in South Clark Street; the Whitechapel Club, as a certain organization of news-paper men was called, and other places frequented by the literati and the more talented of the newspaper makers. Eugene, first because of a temperament which was introspective and reflective, and second because of his æsthetic taste, which was offended by much that he thought was tawdry and cheap about these places, and third by what he considered his lack of means, took practi-cally no part in these diversions. While he worked in his class he heard of these things—usually the next day—and they were amplified and made more showy and interesting by the narrative powers of the participants. Eugene hated coarse, vulgar women and ribald conduct, but he felt that he was not even permitted to see them at close range had he wanted to. It took money to carouse and he did not have it.

Perhaps, because of his youth and a certain air of unsophisti-cation and impracticability which went with him, his employers were not inclined to consider money matters in connection with him. They seemed to think he would work for little and would not mind. He was allowed to drift here six months without a sign of increase, though he really deserved more than any one of those who worked with him during the same period. He was not the one to push his claims personally but he grew restless and slightly embittered under the strain and ached to be free, though his work was as effective as ever.

It was this indifference on their part which fixed his determination to leave Chicago, although Angela, his art career, his natural restlessness and growing judgment of what he might possibly become were deeper incentives. Angela haunted him as a dream of future peace. If he could marry her and settle down he would be happy. He felt now, having fairly satiated himself in the direction of Ruby, that he might leave her. She really would not care so very much. Her sentiments were not deep enough. Still, he knew she would care, and when he began going less regularly to her home, really becoming indifferent to what she did in the artists' world, he began also to feel ashamed of himself, for he knew that it was a cruel thing to do. He saw by her manner when he absented himself that she was hurt and that she knew he was growing cold.

"Are you coming out Sunday night?" she asked him once, wistfully.

"I can't," he apologized; "I have to work."

"Yes, I know how you have to work. But go on. I don't mind, I know."

"Oh, Ruby, how you talk. I can't always be here."

"I know what it is, Eugene," she replied. "You don't care any more. Oh, well, don't mind me."

"Now, sweet, don't talk like that," he would say, but after he was gone she would stand by her window and look out upon the shabby neighborhood and sigh sadly. He was more to her than anyone she had met yet, but she was not the kind that cried.

"He is going to leave me," was her one thought. "He is going to leave me."

Goldfarb had watched Eugene a long time, was interested in him, realized that he had talent. He was leaving shortly to take a better Sunday-Editorship himself on a larger paper, and he thought Eugene was wasting his time and ought to be told so.

"I think you ought to try to get on one of the bigger papers here, Witla," he said to him one Saturday afternoon when things were closing up. "You'll never amount to anything on this paper. It isn't big enough. You ought to get on one of the big ones. Why don't you try the *Tribune*—or else go to New York? I think you ought to do magazine work."

Eugene drank it all in. "I've been thinking of that," he said. "I think I'll go to New York. I'll be better off there."

"I would either do one or the other. If you stay too long in a place like this it's apt to do you harm."

Eugene went back to his desk with the thought of change ringing in his ears. He would go. He would save up his money until he had one hundred and fifty or two hundred dollars and then try his luck in the East. He would leave Ruby and Angela, the latter only temporarily, the former for good very likely, though he only vaguely confessed this to himself. He would make some money and then he would come back and marry his dream from Blackwood. Already his imaginative mind ran forward to a poetic wedding in a little country church, with Angela standing beside him in white. Then he would bring her back with him to New York—he, Eugene Witla, already famous in the East. Already the lure of the big eastern city was in his mind, its palaces, its wealth, its fame. It was the great world he knew; this side of Paris and London. He would go to it now, shortly. What would he be there? How great? How soon?

So he dreamed.

CHAPTER XIV

ONCE this idea of New York was fixed in his mind as a necessary step in his career, it was no trouble for him to carry it out. He had already put aside sixty dollars in a savings bank since he had given Angela the ring and he decided to treble it as quickly as possible and then start. He fancied that all he needed was just enough to live on for a little while until he could get a start. If he could not sell drawings to the magazines he might get a place on a newspaper and anyhow he felt confident that he could live. He communicated to Howe and Mathews his intention of going East pretty soon and aroused in their respective bosoms the emotions which were characteristic of each. Howe, envious from the start, was glad to have him off the paper, but regretful of the stellar career which his determination foreboded. He half suspected now that Eugene would do something exceptional—he was so loose in his moods—so eccentric. Mathews was glad for Eugene and a little sorry for himself. He wished he had Eugene's courage, his fire, his talent.

"You'll make good when you get down there," Mathews said to him one afternoon when Howe was out of the room, for he realized that the latter was jealous. "You've got the stuff. Some of the work you have done here will give you a fine introduction. I wish I were going."

"Why don't you?" suggested Eugene.

"Who? me? What good would it do me? I'm not ready yet. I can't do that sort of stuff. I might go down some time."

"I think you do good work," said Eugene generously. He really did not believe it was good art, but it was fair newspaper sketching.

"Oh, no, you don't mean that, Witla," replied Mathews. "I know what I can do."

Eugene was silent.

"I wish when you get down there," went on Mathews, "you would write us occasionally. I would like to know how you are getting along."

"Sure, I'll write," replied Eugene, flattered by the interest his determination had aroused. "Sure I will." But he never did.

In Ruby and Angela he had two problems to adjust which were not so easy. In the one case it was sympathy, regret, sorrow for her helplessness, her hopelessness. She was so sweet and lovely in her way, but not quite big enough mentally or emotionally for him. Could he really live with her if he wanted to? Could he substitute her for a girl like Angela? Could he? And now he had involved Angela, for since her return to tell him that she accepted him as her affianced lover, there had been some scenes between them in which a new standard of emotion had been set for him. This girl who looked so simple and innocent was burning at times with a wild fire. It snapped in her eyes when Eugene undid her wonderful hair and ran his hands through its heavy strands. "The Rhine Maiden," he would say. "Little Lorelei! You are like the mermaid waiting to catch the young lover in the strands of her hair. You are Marguerite and I Faust. You are a Dutch Gretchen. I love this wonderful hair when it is braided. Oh, sweet, you perfect creature! I will put you in a painting yet. I will make you famous."

Angela thrilled to this. She burned in a flame which was of his fanning. She put her lips to his in long hot kisses, sat on his knee and twined her hair about his neck; rubbed his face with it as one might bathe a face in strands of silk. Finding such a response he went wild, kissed her madly, would have been still more masterful had she not, at the slightest indication of his audacity, leaped from his embrace, not opposition but self protection in her eyes. She pretended to think better of his love, and Eugene, checked by her ideal of him, tried to restrain himself. He did manage to desist because he was sure that he could not do what he wanted to. Daring such as that would end her love. So they wrestled in affection.

It was the fall following his betrothal to Angela that he actually took his departure. He had drifted through the summer, pondering. He had stayed away from Ruby more and more, and finally left without saying good-bye to her, though he thought up to the last that he intended to go out and see her.

As for Angela, when it came to parting from her, he was in a depressed and downcast mood. He thought now that he did not really want to go to New York, but was being drawn by fate. There was no money for him in the West; they could not live on what he could earn there. Hence he must go and in doing so must lose her. It looked very tragic.

Out at her aunt's house, where she came for the Saturday and Sunday preceding his departure, he walked the floor with her gloomily, counted the lapse of the hours after which he would be with her no more, pictured the day when he would return successful to fetch her. Angela had a faint foreboding fear of the events which might intervene. She had read stories of artists who had gone to the city and had never come back. Eugene seemed such a wonderful person, she might not hold him; and yet he had given her his word and he was madly in love with her—no doubt of that. That fixed, passionate, yearning look in his eyes—what did it mean if not enduring, eternal love? Life had brought her a great treasure—a great love and an artist for a lover.

"Go, Eugene!" she cried at last tragically, almost melodramatically. His face was in her hands. "I will wait for you. You need never have one uneasy thought. When you are ready I will be here, only, come soon—you will, won't you?"

"Will I!" he declared, kissing her, "will I? Look at me. Don't you know?"

"Yes! Yes! Yes!" she exclaimed, "of course I know. Oh, yes! yes!"

The rest was a passionate embrace. And then they parted. He went out brooding over the subtlety and the tragedy of life. The sharp October stars saddened him more. It was a wonderful world but bitter to endure at times. Still it could be endured and there was happiness and peace in store for him probably. He and Angela would find it together living in each other's company, living in each other's embrace and by each other's kisses. It must be so. The whole world believed it—even he, after Stella and Margaret and Ruby and Angela. Even he.

The train which bore him to New York bore a very meditative young man. As it pulled out through the great railroad yards of the city, past the shabby back yards of the houses, the street crossings at grade, the great factories and elevators, he thought of that other time when he had first ventured in the city. How different! Then he was so green, so raw. Since then he had become a newspaper artist, he could write, he could find his tongue with women, he knew a little something about the organization of the world. He had not saved any money, true, but he had gone through the art school, had given Angela a diamond ring, had this two hundred dollars with which he was venturing to reconnoitre the great social metropolis of the country. He was passing Fifty-seventh Street; he recognized the neighborhood he traversed so often in visiting Ruby. He had not said good-bye to her and there in the distance were the rows of commonplace, two family frame dwellings, one of which she occupied with her foster parents. Poor little Ruby! and she liked him. It was a shame, but what was he to do about it? He didn't care for her. It really hurt him to think and then he tried not to remember. These tragedies of the world could not be healed by thinking.

The train passed out into the flat fields of northern Indiana and as little country towns flashed past he thought of Alexandria and how he had pulled up his stakes and left it. What was Jonas Lyle doing and John Summers? Myrtle wrote that she was going to be married in the spring. She had delayed solely because she wanted to delay. He thought sometimes that Myrtle was a little like himself, fickle in her moods. He was sure he would never want to go back to Alexandria except for a short visit, and yet the thought of his father and his mother and his old home were sweet to him. His father! How little he knew of the real world!

As they passed out of Pittsburgh he saw for the first time the great mountains, raising their heads in solemn majesty in the dark, and great lines of coke ovens, flaming red tongues of fire. He saw men working, and sleeping towns succeeding one another. What a great country America was! What a great thing to be an artist here! Millions of people and no vast artistic voice to portray these things—these simple dramatic things like the coke ovens in the night. If he could only do it! If he could only stir the whole country, so that his name would be like that of Doré in France or Verestchagin in Russia. If he could but get fire into his work, the fire he felt!

He got into his berth after a time and looked out on the dark night and the stars, longing, and then he dozed. When he awoke again the train had already passed Philadelphia. It was morning and the cars were speeding across the flat meadows toward Trenton. He arose and dressed, watching the array of towns the while, Trenton, New Brunswick, Metuchen, Elizabeth. Somehow this country was like Illinois, flat. After Newark they rushed out upon a great meadow and he caught the sense of the sea. It was beyond this. These were tide-water streams, the Passaic and the Hackensack, with small ships and coal and brick barges tied at the water side. The thrill of something big overtook him as the brakeman began to call "Jersey City," and as he stepped out into the vast train shed his heart misgave him a little. He was all alone in New York. It was wealthy, cold and critical. How should he prosper here? He walked out through the gates to where low arches concealed ferry boats, and in another moment it was before him, sky line, bay, the Hudson, the Statue of Liberty, ferry boats, steamers, liners, all in a grey mist of fierce rain and the tugs and liners blowing mournfully upon great whistles. It was something he could never have imagined without seeing it, and this swish of real salt water, rolling in heavy waves, spoke to him as music might, exalting his soul. What a wonderful thing this was, this sea—where ships were and whales and great mysteries. What a wonderful thing New York was, set down by it, surrounded by it, this metropolis of the country. Here was the sea; yonder were the great docks that held the vessels that sailed to the ports of all the world. He saw them—great grey and black hulls, tied to long piers jutting out into the water. He listened to the whistles, the swish of the water, saw the circling gulls, realized emotionally the mass of people. Here were Jay Gould and Russell Sage and the Vanderbilts and Morgan—all alive and all here. Wall Street, Fifth Avenue, Madison Square, Broadway—he knew of these by reputation. How would he do here—how fare? Would the city ever acclaim him as it did some? He looked wide eyed, with an open heart, with intense and immense appreciation. Well, he was going to enter, going to try. He could do that—perhaps, perhaps. But he felt lonely. He wished he were back with Angela where her soft arms could shut him safe. He wished he might feel her hands on his cheeks, his hair. He would not need to fight alone then. But now he was alone, and the city was roaring about him, a great noise like the sea. He must enter and do battle.

CHAPTER XV

NOT knowing routes or directions in New York, Eugene took a Desbrosses Street ferry, and coming into West Street wandered along that curious thoroughfare staring at the dock entrances. Manhattan Island seemed a little shabby to him from this angle but he thought that although physically, perhaps, it might not be distinguished, there must be other things which made it wonderful. Later when he saw the solidity of it, the massed houses, the persistent streams of people, the crush of traffic, it dawned on him that mere humanity in packed numbers makes a kind of greatness, and this was the island's first characteristic. There were others, like the prevailing lowness of the buildings in its old neighborhoods, the narrowness of the streets in certain areas, the shabbiness of brick and stone when they have seen an hundred years of weather, which struck him as curious or depressing. He was easily touched by exterior conditions.

As he wandered he kept looking for some place where he might like to live, some house that had a yard or a tree. At length he found a row of houses in lower Seventh Avenue with an array of iron balconies in front which appealed to him. He applied here and in one house found a room for four dollars which he thought he had better take for the present. It was cheaper than any hotel. His hostess was a shabby woman in black who made scarcely any impression on him as a personality, merely giving him a thought as to what a dreary thing it was to keep roomers and the room itself was nothing, a commonplace, but he had a new world before him and all his interests were outside. He wanted to see this city. He deposited his grip and sent for his trunk and then took to the streets, having come to see and hear things which would be of advantage to him.

He went about this early relationship to the city in the right spirit. For a little while he did not try to think what he would do, but struck out and walked, here, there and everywhere, this very first day down Broadway to the City Hall and up Broadway from 14th to 42nd street the same night. Soon he knew all Third Avenue and the Bowery, the wonders of Fifth Avenue and Riverside Drive, the beauties of the East River, the Battery, Central Park and the lower East Side. He sought out quickly the wonders of metropolitan life—its crowds at dinner and theatre time in Broadway, its tremendous throngs morning and afternoon in the shopping district, its amazing world of carriages in Fifth Avenue and Central Park. He had marveled at wealth and luxury in Chicago, but here it took his breath away. It was obviously so much more fixed, so definite and comprehensible. Here one felt intuitively the far reaches which separate the ordinary man from the scion of wealth. It curled him up like a frozen leaf, dulled his very soul, and gave him a clear sense of his position in the social scale. He had come here with a pretty high estimate of himself, but daily, as he looked, he felt himself crumbling. What was he? What was art? What did the city care? It was much more interested in other things, in dressing, eating, visiting, riding abroad. The lower part of the island was filled with cold commercialism which frightened him. In the upper half, which concerned only women and show—a voluptuous sybaritism—caused him envy. He had but two hundred dollars with which to fight his way, and this was the world he must conquer.

Men of Eugene's temperament are easily depressed. He first gorged the spectacle of life and then suffered from mental indigestion. He saw too much of it too quickly. He wandered about for weeks, looking in the shop windows, the libraries, the museums, the great streets, growing all the while more despondent. At night he would return to his bare room and indite long epistles to Angela, describing what he had seen and telling her of his undying love for her—largely because he had no other means of ridding himself of his superabundant vitality and moods. They were beautiful letters, full of color and feeling, but to Angela they gave a false impression of emotion and sincerity because they appeared to be provoked by absence from her. In part of course they were, but far more largely they were the result of loneliness and the desire for expression which this vast spectacle of life itself incited. He also sent her some tentative sketches of things he had seen—a large crowd in the dark at 34th Street; a boat off 86th Street in the East River in the driving rain; a barge with cars being towed by a tug. He could not think exactly what to do with these things at that time, but he wanted to try his hand at illustrating for the magazines. He was a little afraid of these great publications, however, for now that he was on the ground with them his art did not appear so significant.

It was during the first few weeks that he received his only letter from Ruby. His parting letter to her, written when he reached New York, had been one of those makeshift affairs which faded passion indites. He was so sorry he had to leave without seeing her. He had intended to come out but the rush of preparation at the last moment, and so forth; he hoped to come back to Chicago one of these days and he would look her up. He still loved her, but it was necessary for him to leave—to come where the greatest possibilities were. "I remember how sweet you were when I first saw you," he added. "I shall never forget my first impressions, little Ruby."

It was cruel to add this touch of remembrance, but the artist in him could not refrain. It cut Ruby as a double edged sword, for she understood that he cared well enough that way—æsthetically. It was not her but beauty that he loved, and her particular beauty had lost its appeal.

She wrote after a time, intending to be defiant, indifferent, but she really could not be. She tried to think of something sharp to say, but finally put down the simple truth.

"Dear Eugene:" she wrote, "I got your note several weeks ago, but I could not bring myself to answer it before this. I know everything is over between us and that is all right, for I suppose it has to be. You couldn't love any woman long, I think. I know what you say about your having to go to New York to broaden your field is true. You ought to, but I'm sorry you didn't come out. You might have. Still I don't blame you, Eugene. It isn't much different from what has been going on for some time. I have cared but I'll get over that, I know, and I won't ever think hard of you. Won't you return me the notes I have sent you from time to time and my pictures? You won't want them now.

"RUBY."

There was a little blank space on the paper and then:—

"I stood by the window last night and looked out on the street. The moon was shining and those dead trees were waving in the wind. I saw the moon on that pool of water over in the field. It looked like silver. Oh, Eugene, I wish I were dead."

He jumped up as he read these words and clenched the letter in his hands. The pathos of it all cut him to the quick, raised his estimate of her, made him feel as if he had made a mistake in leaving her. He really cared for her after all. She was sweet. If she were here now he could live with her. She might as well be a model in New York as in Chicago. He was on the verge of writing this, when one of the long, almost daily epistles Angela was sending arrived and changed his mood. He did not see how, in the face of so great and clean a love as hers, he could go on with Ruby. His affection had obviously been dying. Should he try to revive it now?

This conflict of emotions was so characteristic of Eugene's nature, that had he been soundly introspective, he would have seen that he was an idealist by temperament, in love with the æsthetic, in love with love, and that there was no permanent faith in him for anybody—except the impossible she.

As it was, he wrote Ruby a letter breathing regret and sorrow but not inviting her to come. He could not have supported her long if she had, he thought. Besides he was anxious to secure Angela. So that affair lapsed.

In the meantime he visited the magazine offices. On leaving Chicago he had put in the bottom of his trunk a number of drawings which he had done for the *Globe*—his sketches of the Chicago River, of Blue Island Avenue, of which he had once made a study as a street, of Goose Island and of the Lake front. There were some street scenes, too, all forceful in the peculiar massing of their blacks, the unexpected, almost flashing, use of a streak of white at times. There was emotion in them, a sense of life. He should have been appreciated at once, but, oddly, there was just enough of the radically strange about what he did to make his work seem crude, almost coarse. He drew a man's coat with a single dash of his pen. He indicated a face by a spot. If you looked close there was seldom any detail, frequently none at all. From the praise he had received at the art school and from Mathews and Goldfarb he was slowly coming to the conclusion that he had a way of his own. Being so individual he was inclined to stick to it. He walked with an air of conviction which had nothing but his own belief in himself to back it up, and it was not an air which drew anybody to him. When he showed his pictures at the *Century, Harper's, Scribner's,* they were received with an air of weary consideration. Dozens of magnificent drawings were displayed on their walls signed by men whom Eugene now knew to be leaders in the illustration world. He returned to his room convinced that he had made no impression at all. They must be familiar with artists a hundred times better than himself.

As a matter of fact Eugene was simply overawed by the material face of things. These men whose pictures he saw displayed on the walls of the art and editorial rooms of the magazines were really not, in many instances, any better than himself, if as good. They had the advantage of solid wood frames and artistic acceptance. He was a long way as yet from magazine distinction but the work he did later had no more of the fire than had this early stuff. It was a little broader in treatment, a little less intolerant of detail, but no more vigorous if as much so. The various art directors were weary of smart young artists showing drawings. A little suffering was good for them in the beginning. So Eugene was incontinently turned away with a little faint praise which was worse than opposition. He sank very low in spirits.

There were still the smaller magazines and the newspapers, however, and he hunted about faithfully, trying to get something to do. From one or two of the smaller magazines, he secured commissions, after a time, three or four drawings for thirty-five dollars; and from that had to be extracted models' fees. He had to have a room where he could work as an artist, receiving models to pose, and he finally found one in West 14th Street, a back bedroom, looking out over an open court and with a public stair which let all come who might without question. This cost him twenty-five dollars a month, but he thought he had better risk it. If he could get a few commissions he could live.

CHAPTER XVI

THE art world of New York is peculiar. It was then and for some time after, broken up into cliques with scarcely any unity. There was a world of sculptors, for instance, in which some thirty or forty sculptors had part—but they knew each other slightly, criticised each other severely and retired for the most part into a background of relatives and friends. There was a painting world, as distinguished from an illustrating world, in which perhaps a thousand alleged artists, perhaps more, took part. Most of these were men and women who had some ability—enough to have their pictures hung at the National Academy of Design exhibition—to sell some pictures, get some decorative work to do, paint some portraits. There were studio buildings scattered about various portions of the city; in Washington Square; in Ninth and Tenth Streets; in odd places, such as Macdougal Alley and occasional cross streets from Washington Square to Fifty-ninth Street, which were filled with painters, illustrators, sculptors and craftsmen in art generally. This painting world had more unity than the world of sculptors and, in a way, included the latter. There were several art clubs—the Salmagundi, the Kit-Kat and the Lotus—and there were a number of exhibitions, ink, water color, oil, with their reception nights where artists could meet and exchange the courtesies and friendship of their world. In addition to this there were little communal groups such as those who resided in the Tenth Street studios; the Twenty-third Street Y. M. C. A.; the Van Dyck studios, and so on. It was possible to find little crowds, now and then, that harmonized well enough for a time and to get into a group, if, to use a colloquialism, one *belonged.* If you did not, art life in New York might be a very dreary thing and one might go a long time without finding just the particular crowd with which to associate.

Beside the painting world there was the illustrating world, made up of beginners and those who had established themselves firmly in editorial favor. These were not necessarily a part of the painting or sculpture worlds and yet, in spirit, were allied to them, had their clubs also, and their studios were in the various neighborhoods where the painters and sculptors were. The only difference was that in the case of the embryo illustrators they were to be found living three or four in one studio, partly because of the saving in expense, but also because of the love of companionship and because they could hearten and correct one another in their work. A number of such interesting groups were in existence when Eugene arrived, but of course he did not know of them.

It takes time for the beginner to get a hearing anywhere. We all have to serve an apprenticeship, whatever field we enter. Eugene had talent and determination, but no experience, no savoir faire, no circle of friends and acquaintances. The whole city was strange and cold, and if he had not immediately fallen desperately in love with it as a spectacle he would have been unconscionably lonely and unhappy. As it was the great fresh squares, such as Washington, Union and Madison; the great streets, such as Broadway, Fifth Avenue and Sixth Avenue; the great spectacles, such as the Bowery at night, the East River, the water front, the Battery, all fascinated him with an unchanging glamor.

He was hypnotized by the wonder of this thing—the beauty of it. Such seething masses of people! such whirlpools of life! The great hotels, the opera, the theatres, the restaurants, all gripped him with a sense of beauty. These lovely women in magnificent gowns; these swarms of cabs, with golden eyes, like monstrous insects; this ebb and surge of life at morning and evening, made him forget his loneliness. He had no money to spend, no immediate hope of a successful career, he could walk these streets, look in these windows, admire these beautiful women; thrill at the daily newspaper announcements of almost hourly successes in one field or another. Here and there in the news an author had made a great success with a book; a scientist with a discovery; a philosopher with a new theory; a financier with an investment. There was news of great plays being put on; great actors and actresses coming from abroad; great successes being made by débutantes in society; great movements forwarded generally. Youth and ambition had the call—he saw that. It was only a question of time, if you had talent, when you would get your hearing. He longed ardently for his but he had no feeling that it was coming to him quickly, so he got the blues. It was a long road to travel.

One of his pet diversions these days and nights was to walk the streets in rain or fog or snow. The city appealed to him, wet or white, particularly the public squares. He saw Fifth Avenue once in a driving snowstorm and under sputtering arc lights, and he hurried to his easel next morning to see if he could not put it down in black and white. It was unsuccessful, or at least he felt so, for after an hour of trying he threw it aside in disgust. But these spectacles were drawing him. He was wanting to do them—wanting to see them shown somewhere in color. Possible success was a solace at a time when all he could pay for a meal was fifteen cents and he had no place to go and not a soul with whom to talk.

It was an interesting phase of Eugene's character that he had a passion for financial independence. He might have written home from Chicago at times when he was hard pressed; he might have borrowed some money from his father now, but preferred to earn it—to appear to be further along than he was. If anyone had asked him he would have said he was doing fine. Practically he so wrote to Angela, giving as an excuse for further delay that he wanted to wait until he had ample means. He was trying all this time to make his two hundred dollars go as far as possible and to add to it by any little commissions he could get, however small. He figured his expenses down to ten dollars a week and managed to stay within that sum.

The particular building in which he had settled was really not a studio building but an old, run-down boarding and apartment house turned partially to uses of trade. The top floor contained three fair sized rooms and two hall bedrooms, all occupied by lonely individuals plying some craft or other. Eugene's next door neighbor chanced to be a hack illustrator, who had had his training in Boston and had set up his easel here in the hope of making a living. There were not many exchanges of courtesies between them at first, although, the door being open the second day he arrived, he saw that an artist worked there, for the easel was visible.

No models applying at first he decided to appeal to the Art Students' League. He called on the Secretary and was given the names of four, who replied to postal cards from him. One he selected, a young Swedish American girl who looked somewhat like the character in the story he had in mind. She was neat and attractive, with dark hair, a straight nose and pointed chin, and Eugene immediately conceived a liking for her. He was ashamed of his surroundings, however, and consequently diffident. This particular model was properly distant, and he finished his pictures with as much expedition and as little expense as he possibly could.

Eugene was not given to scraping odd acquaintances, though he made friends fast enough when the balance of intellect was right. In Chicago he had become friendly with several young artists as a result of working with them at the Institute, but here he knew no one, having come without introductions. He did become acquainted with his neighbor, Philip Shotmeyer. He wanted to find out about local art life from him, but Shotmeyer was not brilliant, and could not supply him with more than minor details of what Eugene desired to know. Through him he learnt a little of studio regions, art personalities; the fact that young beginners worked in groups. Shotmeyer had been in such a group the year before, though why he was alone now he did not say. He sold drawings to some of the minor magazines, better magazines than Eugene had yet had dealings with. One thing he did at once for Eugene which was very helpful: he admired his work. He saw, as had others before him, something of his peculiar distinction as an artist, attended every show and one day he gave him a suggestion which was the beginning of Eugene's successful magazine career. Eugene was working on one of his street scenes—a task which he invariably essayed when he had nothing else to do. Shotmeyer had drifted in and was following the strokes of his brush as he attempted to portray a mass of East Side working girls flooding the streets after six o'clock. There were dark walls of buildings, a flaring gas lamp or two, some yellow lighted shop windows, and many shaded, half seen faces—bare suggestions of souls and pulsing life.

"Say," said Shotmeyer at one point, "that kind o' looks like the real thing to me. I've seen a crowd like that."

"Have you?" replied Eugene.

"You ought to be able to get some magazine to use that as a frontispiece. Why don't you try *Truth* with that?"

"Truth" was a weekly which Eugene, along with many others in the West, had admired greatly because it ran a double page color insert every week and occasionally used scenes of this character. Somehow he always needed a shove of this kind to make him act when he was drifting. He put more enthusiasm into his work because of Shotmeyer's remark, and when it was done decided to carry it to the office of *Truth*. The Art Director approved it on sight, though he said nothing, but carried it in to the Editor.

"Here's a thing that I consider a find in its way."

He set it proudly upon the editorial desk.

"Say," said the Editor, laying down a manuscript, "that's the real thing, isn't it? Who did that?"

"A young fellow by the name of Witla, who has just blown in here. He looks like the real thing to me."

"Say," went on the Editor, "look at the suggestion of faces

back there! What? Reminds me just a little of the masses in Doré stuff—It's good, isn't it?"

"It's fine," echoed the Art Director. "I think he's a comer, if nothing happens to him. We ought to get a few centre pages out of him."

"How much does he want for this?"

"Oh, he doesn't know. He'll take almost anything. I'll give him seventy-five dollars."

"That's all right," said the Editor as the Art Director took the drawing down. "There's something new there. You ought to hang on to him."

"I will," replied his associate. "He's young yet. He doesn't want to be encouraged too much."

He went out, pulling a solemn countenance.

"I like this fairly well," he said. "We may be able to find room for it. I'll send you a check shortly if you'll let me have your address."

Eugene gave it. His heart was beating a gay tattoo in his chest. He did not think anything of price, in fact it did not occur to him. All that was in his mind was the picture as a double page spread. So he had really sold one after all and to *Truth!* Now he could honestly say he had made some progress. Now he could write Angela and tell her. He could send her copies when it came out. He could really have something to point to after this and best of all, now he knew he could do street scenes.

He went out into the street treading not the grey stone pavement but air. He threw back his head and breathed deep. He thought of other scenes like this which he could do. His dreams were beginning to be realized—he, Eugene Witla, the painter of a double page spread in *Truth!* Already he was doing a whole series in his imagination, all he had ever dreamed of. He wanted to run and tell Shotmeyer—to buy him a good meal. He almost loved him, commonplace hack that he was—because he had suggested to him the right thing to do.

"Say, Shotmeyer," he said, sticking his head in that worthy's door, "you and I eat tonight. *Truth* took that drawing."

"Isn't that fine," said his floor-mate, without a trace of envy. "Well, I'm glad. I thought they'd like it."

Eugene could have cried. Poor Shotmeyer! He wasn't a good artist, but he had a good heart. He would never forget him.

CHAPTER XVII

THIS one significant sale with its subsequent check of seventy-five dollars and later the appearance of the picture in color, gave Eugene such a lift in spirit that he felt, for the time being, as though his art career had reached a substantial basis, and he began to think of going to Blackwood to visit Angela. But first he must do some more work.

He concentrated his attention on several additional scenes, doing a view of Greeley Square in a sopping drizzle, and a picture of an L train speeding up the Bowery on its high, thin trestle of steel. He had an eye for contrasts, picking out lights and shadows sharply, making wonderful blurs that were like colors in precious stones, confused and suggestive. He took one of these after a month to *Truth,* and again the Art Director was his victim. He tried to be indifferent, but it was hard. The young man had something that he wanted.

"You might show me anything else you do in this line," he said. "I can use a few if they come up to these two."

Eugene went away with his head in the air. He was beginning to get the courage of his ability.

It takes quite a number of drawings at seventy-five and one hundred dollars each to make a living income, and artists were too numerous to make anyone's opportunity for immediate distinction easy. Eugene waited months to see his first drawing come out. He stayed away from the smaller magazines in the hope that he would soon be able to contribute to the larger ones, but they were not eagerly seeking new artists. He met, through Shotmeyer, two artists who were living in one studio in Waverly Place and took a great liking to them. One of them, McHugh, was an importation from Wyoming with delicious stories of mountain farming and mining; the other, Smite, was a fisher lad from Nova Scotia. McHugh, tall and lean, with a face that looked like that of a raw yokel, but with some gleam of humor and insight in the eyes which redeemed it instantly, was Eugene's first choice of a pleasing, genial personality. Joseph Smite had a sense of the sea about him. He was short and stout, and rather solidly put together, like a blacksmith. He had big hands and feet, a big mouth, big, bony eye sockets and coarse brown hair. When he talked, ordinarily, it was with a slow, halting air and when he smiled or laughed it was with his whole face. When he became excited or gay something seemed to happen distinctly to every part of his body. His face became a curious cross-hatch of genial lines. His tongue loosened and he talked fast. He had a habit of emphasizing his language with oaths on these occasions—numerous and picturesque, for he had worked with sea-faring men and had accumulated a vast vocabulary of picturesque expressions. They were vacant of evil intent so far as he was concerned, for there was no subtlety or guile in him. He was kindly and genial all through. Eugene wanted to be friendly and struck a gay relationship with these two. He found that he got along excellently well with them and could swap humorous incidents and character touches by the hour. It was some months before he could actually say that he was intimate with them, but he began to visit them regularly and after a time they called on him.

It was during this year that he came to know several models passingly well, to visit the various art exhibitions, to be taken up by Hudson Dula, the Art Director of *Truth* and invited to two or three small dinners given to artists and girls. He did not find anyone he liked exceptionally well barring one Editor of a rather hopeless magazine called *Craft,* devoted to art subjects, a young blond, of poetic temperament, who saw in him a spirit of beauty and tried to make friends with him. Eugene responded cheerfully and thereafter Richard Wheeler was a visitor at his studio from time to time. He was not making enough to house himself much better these days, but he did manage to buy a few plaster casts and to pick up a few nice things in copper and brass for his studio. His own drawings, his street scenes, were hung here and there. The way in which the exceptionally clever looked at them convinced him by degrees that he had something big to say.

It was while he was settling himself in this atmosphere—the spring of the second year—that he decided to go back and visit Angela and incidentally Alexandria and Chicago. He had been away now sixteen months, had not seen anyone who had won his affections or alienated him from his love of Angela. He wrote in March that he thought he would be coming in May or June. He did get away in July—a season when the city was suffering from a wave of intense heat. He had not done so much—illustrated eight or ten stories and drawn four double page pictures for *Truth,* one of which had appeared; but he was getting along. Just as he was starting for Chicago and Blackwood a second one was put on the news-stand and he proudly carried a copy of it with him on the train. It was the Bowery by night, with the L train rushing overhead and, as reproduced, it had color and life. He felt intensely proud and knew that Angela would also. She had written him such a glowing appreciation of the East Side picture called "Six O'clock."

As he rode he dreamed.

He reached it at last, the long stretch between New York and Chicago traversed; he arrived in the Lake city in the afternoon, and without pausing to revisit the scenes of his earlier efforts took a five o'clock train for Blackwood. It was sultry, and on the way heavy thunder clouds gathered and broke in a short, splendid summer rain. The trees and grass were thoroughly wet and the dust of the roads was laid. There was a refreshing coolness about the air which caressed the weary flesh. Little towns nestling among green trees came into view and passed again, and at last Blackwood appeared. It was smaller than Alexandria, but not so different. Like the other it was marked by a church steeple, a saw mill, a pretty brick business street and many broad branching green trees. Eugene felt drawn to it at sight. It was such a place as Angela should live in.

It was seven o'clock and nearing dusk when he arrived. He had not given Angela the definite hour of his arrival and so decided to stay over night at the little inn or so-called hotel which he saw up the street. He had brought only a large suit case and a traveling bag. He inquired of the proprietor the direction and distance of the Blue house from the town, found that he could get a vehicle any time in the morning which would take him over, as the phrase ran, for a dollar. He ate his supper of fried steak and poor coffee and fried potatoes and then sat out on the front porch facing the street in a rocking chair, to see how the village of Blackwood wagged and to enjoy the cool of the evening. As he sat he thought of Angela's home and how nice it must be. This town was such a little place—so quiet. There would not be another train coming up from the city until after eleven.

After a time he rose and took a short walk, breathing the night air. Later he came back and throwing wide the windows of the stuffy room sat looking out. The summer night with its early rain, its wet trees, its smell of lush, wet, growing things, was impressing itself on Eugene as one might impress wet clay with a notable design. Eugene's mood was soft toward the little houses with their glowing windows, the occasional pedestrians with their "howdy Jakes" and "evenin' Henrys." He was touched by the noise of the crickets, the chirp of the tree toads, the hang of the lucent suns and planets

above the tree tops. The whole night was quick with the richness of fertility, stirring subtly about some work which concerned man very little or not at all, yet of which he was at
least a part, till his eyelids drooped after a time and he went
to bed to sleep deeply and dreamlessly.

Next morning he was up early, eager for the hour to arrive
when he might start. He did not think it advisable to leave
before nine o'clock, and attracted considerable attention by
strolling about, his tall, spare, graceful figure and forceful
profile being an unusual sight to the natives. At nine o'clock
a respectable carryall was placed at his disposal and he was
driven out over a long yellow road, damp with the rain of the
night before and shaded in places by overhanging trees. There
were so many lovely wild flowers growing in the angles of the
rail fences—wild yellow and pink roses, elder flower, Queen
Anne's lace, dozens of beautiful blooms, that Eugene was lost in
admiration. His heart sang over the beauty of yellowing wheat-
fields, the young corn, already three feet high, the vistas of hay
and clover, with patches of woods enclosing them, and over all,
house martens and swallows scudding after insects and high up
in the air his boyhood dream of beauty, a soaring buzzard.

As he rode the moods of his boyhood days came back to him—
his love of winging butterflies and birds; his passion for the
voice of the wood-dove (there was one crying in the still
distance now)—his adoration for the virile strength of the
men of the countryside. He thought as he rode that he would
like to paint a series of country scenes that would be as simple
as those cottage dooryards that they now and then passed; this
little stream that cut the road at right angles and made a drinking
place for the horses; this skeleton of an old abandoned home,
doorless and windowless, where the roof sagged and hollyhocks
and morning glories grew high under the eaves. "We city
dwellers do not know," he sighed, as though he had not taken
the country in his heart and carried it to town as had every
other boy and girl who had gone the way of the metropolis.

The Blue homestead was located in the centre of a rather
wide rolling stretch of country which lay between two gently
rising ridges of hill covered with trees. One corner of the farm,
and that not so very far from the house, was cut by a stream,
a little shallow thing, singing over pebbles and making willows
and hazel bushes to grow in profusion along its banks, and
there was a little lake within a mile of the house. In front
of it was a ten acre field of wheat, to the right of it a grazing
patch of several acres, to the left a field of clover; and near

the house by a barn, a well, a pig pen, a corn crib and some smaller sheds. In front of the house was a long open lawn, down the centre of which ran a gravel path, lined on either side by tall old elm trees. The immediate dooryard was shut from this noble lawn by a low picket fence along the length of which grew lilac bushes and inside which, nearer the house, were simple beds of roses, calycanthus and golden glow. Over an arbor leading from the backdoor to a rather distant summer kitchen flourished a grapevine, and there was a tall remnant of a tree trunk covered completely with a yellow blooming trumpet vine. The dooryard's lawn was smooth enough, and the great lawn was a dream of green grass, graced with the shadows of a few great trees. The house was long and of no great depth, the front a series of six rooms ranged in a row, without an upper storey. The two middle rooms which had originally, perhaps seventy years before, been all there was of the house. Since then all the other rooms had been added, and there was in addition to these a lean-to containing a winter kitchen and dining room, and to the west of the arbor leading to the summer kitchen, an old unpainted frame storehouse. In all its parts the place was shabby and run down but picturesque and quaint.

Eugene was surprised to find the place so charming. It appealed to him, the long, low front, with doors opening from the centre and end rooms direct upon the grass, with windows set in climbing vines and the lilac bushes forming a green wall between the house and the main lawn. The great rows of elm trees throwing a grateful shade seemed like sentinel files. As the carryall turned in at the wagon gate in front he thought "What a place for love! and to think Angela should live here."

The carryall rattled down the pebble road to the left of the lawn and stopped at the garden gate. Marietta came out. Marietta was twenty-two years old, and as gay and joyous as her elder sister Angela was sober and in a way morbid. Light souled as a kitten, looking always on the bright side of things, she made hosts of friends everywhere she went, having a perfect swarm of lovers who wrote her eager notes, but whom she rebuffed with good natured, sympathetic simplicity. Here on this farm there was not supposed to be so much opportunity for social life as in town, but beaux made their way here on one pretext and another. Marietta was the magnet, and in the world of gaiety which she created Angela shared.

Angela was now in the dining room—easy to be called— but Marietta wanted to see for herself what sort of lover her sister had captured. She was surprised at his height, his presence, the keenness of his eyes. She hardly understood so fine a lover for her own sister, but held out her hand smilingly.

"This is Mr. Witla, isn't it?" she asked.

"The same," he replied, a little pompously. "Isn't it a lovely drive over here?"

"We think it nice in nice weather," she laughed. "You wouldn't like it so much in winter. Won't you come in and put your grip here in the hall? David will take it to your room."

Eugene obeyed, but he was thinking of Angela and when she would appear and how she would look. He stepped into the large, low ceiled, dark, cool parlor and was delighted to see a piano and some music piled on a rack. Through an open window he saw several hammocks out on the main lawn, under the trees. It seemed a wonderful place to him, the substance of poetry—and then Angela appeared. She was dressed in plain white linen. Her hair, braided as he liked it in a great rope, lay as a band across her forehead. She had picked a big pink rose and put it in her waist. At sight of her Eugene held out his arms and she flew to them. He kissed her vigorously, for Marietta had discreetly retired and they were left alone.

"So I have you at last," he whispered, and kissed her again.

"Oh, yes, yes, and it has been so long," she sighed.

"You couldn't have suffered any more than I have," he consoled. "Every minute has been torture, waiting, waiting, waiting!"

"Let's not think of that now," she urged. "We have each other. You are here."

"Yes, here I am," he laughed, "all the virtues done up in one brown suit. Isn't it lovely—these great trees, that beautiful lawn?"

He paused from kissing to look out of the window.

"I'm glad you like it," she replied joyously. "We think it's nice, but this place is so old."

"I love it for that," he cried appreciatively. "Those bushes are so nice—those roses. Oh, dear, you don't know how sweet it all seems—and you—you are so nice."

He held her off at arm's length and surveyed her while she blushed becomingly. His eager, direct, vigorous onslaught confused her at times—caused her pulse to beat at a high rate.

They went out into the dooryard after a time and then Marietta appeared again, and with her Mrs. Blue, a comfortable, round bodied mother of sixty, who greeted Eugene cordially. He could feel in her what he felt in his own mother—in every good mother—love of order and peace, love of the well being of her children, love of public respect and private honor and morality. All these things Eugene heartily respected in others. He was glad to see them, believed they had a place in society, but was uncertain whether they bore any fixed or important relationship to him. He was always thinking in his private conscience that life was somehow bigger and subtler and darker than any given theory or order of living. It might well be worth while for a man or woman to be honest and moral within a given condition or quality of society, but it did not matter at all in the ultimate substance and composition of the universe. Any form or order of society which hoped to endure must have individuals like Mrs. Blue, who would conform to the highest standards and theories of that society, and when found they were admirable, but they meant nothing in the shifting, subtle forces of nature. They were just accidental harmonies blossoming out of something which meant everything here to this order, nothing to the universe at large. At twenty-two years of age he was thinking these things, wondering whether it would be possible ever to express them; wondering what people would think of him if they actually knew what he did think; wondering if there was anything, anything, which was really stable—a rock to cling to—and not mere shifting shadow and unreality.

Mrs. Blue looked at her daughter's young lover with a kindly eye. She had heard a great deal about him. Having raised her children to be honest, moral and truthful she trusted them to associate only with those who were equally so. She assumed that Eugene was such a man, and his frank open countenance and smiling eyes and mouth convinced her that he was basically good. Also, what to her were his wonderful drawings, sent to Angela in the form of proofs from time to time, particularly the one of the East Side crowd, had been enough to prejudice her in his favor. No other daughter of the family, and there were three married, had approximated to this type of man in her choice. Eugene was looked upon as a prospective son-in-law who would fulfill all the conventional obligations joyfully and as a matter of course.

"It's very good of you to put me up, Mrs. Blue," Eugene said pleasantly. "I've always wanted to come out here for a visit—I've heard so much of the family from Angela."

"It's just a country home we have, not much to look at, but we like it," replied his hostess. She smiled blandly, asked if he wouldn't make himself comfortable in one of the hammocks, wanted to know how he was getting along with his work in New York and then returned to her cooking, for she was already preparing his first meal. Eugene strolled with Angela to the big lawn under the trees and sat down. He was experiencing the loftiest of human emotions on earth—love in youth, accepted and requited, hope in youth, justified in action by his success in New York; peace in youth, for he had a well earned holiday in his grasp, was resting with the means to do so and with love and beauty and admiration and joyous summer weather to comfort him.

As he rocked to and fro in the hammock gazing at the charming lawn and realizing all these things, his glance rested at last upon Angela, and he thought, "Life can really hold no finer thing than this."

CHAPTER XVIII

TOWARD noon old Jotham Blue came in from a cornfield where he had been turning the earth between the rows. Although sixty-five and with snowy hair and beard he looked to be vigorous, and good to live until ninety or a hundred. His eyes were blue and keen, his color rosy. He had great broad shoulders set upon a spare waist, for he had been a handsome figure of a man in his youth.

"How do you do, Mr. Witla," he inquired with easy grace as he strolled up, the yellow mud of the fields on his boots. He had pulled a big jackknife out of his pocket and begun whittling a fine twig he had picked up. "I'm glad to see you. My daughter, Angela, has been telling me one thing and another about you."

He smiled as he looked at Eugene. Angela, who was sitting beside him, rose and strolled toward the house.

"I'm glad to see you," said Eugene. "I like your country around here. It looks prosperous."

"It is prosperous," said the old patriarch, drawing up a chair which stood at the foot of a tree and seating himself. Eugene sank back into the hammock.

"It's a soil that's rich in lime and carbon and sodium—the things which make plant life grow. We need very little fertilizer here—very little. The principal thing is to keep the ground thoroughly cultivated and to keep out the bugs and weeds."

He cut at his stick meditatively. Eugene noted the chemical and physical knowledge relative to farming. It pleased him to find brain coupled with crop cultivation.

"I noticed some splendid fields of wheat as I came over," he observed.

"Yes, wheat does well here," Blue went on, "when the weather is moderately favorable. Corn does well. We have a splendid apple crop and grapes are generally successful in this state. I have always thought that Wisconsin had a little the best of the other valley states, for we are blessed with a moderate climate, plenty of streams and rivers and a fine, broken landscape. There are good mines up north and lots of lumber. We are a prosperous people, we Wisconsiners, decidedly prosperous. This state has a great future."

Eugene noted the wide space between his clear blue eyes as

he talked. He liked the bigness of his conception of his state and of his country. No petty little ground-harnessed ploughman this, but a farmer in the big sense of the word—a cultivator of the soil, with an understanding of it—an American who loved his state and his country.

"I have always thought of the Mississippi valley as the country of the future," said Eugene. "We have had the Valley of the Nile and the Valley of the Euphrates with big populations, but this is something larger. I rather feel as though a great wave of population were coming here in the future."

"It is the new paradise of the world," said Jotham Blue, pausing in his whittling and holding up his right hand for emphasis. "We haven't come to realize its possibilities. The fruit, the corn, the wheat, to feed the nations of the world can be raised here. I sometimes marvel at the productivity of the soil. It is so generous. It is like a great mother. It only asks to be treated kindly to give all that it has."

Eugene smiled. The bigness of his prospective father-in-law's feelings lured him. He felt as though he could love this man.

They talked on about other things, the character of the surrounding population, the growth of Chicago, the recent threat of a war with Venezuela, the rise of a new leader in the Democratic party, a man whom Jotham admired very much. As he was telling of the latter's exploits—it appeared he had recently met him at Blackwood—Mrs. Blue appeared in the front door.

"Jotham!" she called.

He rose. "My wife must want a bucket of water," he said, and strolled away.

Eugene smiled. This was lovely. This was the way life should be—compounded of health, strength, good nature, understanding, simplicity. He wished he were a man like Jotham, as sound, as hearty, as clean and strong. To think he had raised eight children. No wonder Angela was lovely. They all were, no doubt.

While he was rocking, Marietta came back smiling, her blond hair blowing about her face. Like her father she had blue eyes, like him a sanguine temperament, warm and ruddy. Eugene felt drawn to her. She reminded him a little of Ruby—a little of Margaret. She was bursting with young health.

"You're stronger than Angela," he said, looking at her.

"Oh, yes, I can always outrun Angel-face," she exclaimed. "We fight sometimes but I can get things away from her.

She has to give in. Sometimes I feel older—I always take the lead."

Eugene rejoiced in the sobriquet of Angel-face. It suited Angela, he thought. She looked like pictures of Angels in the old prints and in the stained glass windows he had seen. He wondered in a vague way, however, whether Marietta did not have the sweeter temperament—were not really more lovable and cosy. But he put the thought forcefully out of his mind. He felt he must be loyal to Angela here.

While they were talking the youngest boy, David, came up and sat down on the grass. He was short and stocky for his years—sixteen—with an intelligent face and an inquiring eye. Eugene noted stability and quiet force in his character at once. He began to see that these children had inherited character as well as strength from their parents. This was a home in which successful children were being reared. Benjamin came up after awhile, a tall, overgrown, puritanical youth, with western modifications and then Samuel, the oldest of the living boys and the most impressive. He was big and serene like his father, of brown complexion and hickory strength. Eugene learned in the conversation that he was a railroad man in St. Paul—home for a brief vacation, after three years of absence. He was with a road called the Great Northern, already a Second Assistant Passenger Agent and with great prospects, so the family thought. Eugene could see that all the boys and girls, like Angela, were ruggedly and honestly truthful. They were written all over with Christian precept—not church dogma—but Christian precept, lightly and good naturedly applied. They obeyed the ten commandments in so far as possible and lived within the limits of what people considered sane and decent. Eugene wondered at this. His own moral laxity was a puzzle to him. He wondered whether he were not really all wrong and they all right. Yet the subtlety of the universe was always with him— the mystery of its chemistry. For a given order of society no doubt he was out of place—for life in general, well, he could not say.

At 12.30 dinner was announced from the door by Mrs. Blue and they all rose. It was one of those simple home feasts common to any intelligent farming family. There was a generous supply of fresh vegetables, green peas, new potatoes, new string beans. A steak had been secured from the itinerant butcher who served these parts and Mrs. Blue had made hot light biscuit. Eugene expressed a predilection for fresh buttermilk and they brought him a pitcherful, saying that as a rule it was given to the pigs; the children did not care for it. They talked and jested and he heard odd bits of information concerning people here and there—some farmer who had lost a horse by colic; some other farmer who was preparing to cut his wheat. There were frequent references to the three oldest sisters, who lived in other Wisconsin towns. Their children appeared to be numerous and fairly troublesome. They all came home frequently, it appeared, and were bound up closely with the interests of the family as a whole.

"The more you know about the Blue family," observed Samuel to Eugene, who expressed surprise at the solidarity of interest, "the more you realize that they're a clan not a family. They stick together like glue."

"That's a rather nice trait, I should say," laughed Eugene, who felt no such keen interest in his relatives.

"Well, if you want to find out how the Blue family stick together just do something to one of them," observed Jake Doll, a neighbor who had entered.

"That's sure true, isn't it, Sis," observed Samuel, who was sitting next to Angela, putting his hand affectionately on his sister's arm. Eugene noted the movement. She nodded her head affectionately.

"Yes, we Blues all hang together."

Eugene almost begrudged him his sister's apparent affection. Could such a girl be cut out of such an atmosphere—separated from it completely, brought into a radically different world, he wondered. Would she understand him; would he stick by her. He smiled at Jotham and Mrs. Blue and thought he ought to, but life was strange. You never could tell what might happen.

During the afternoon there were more lovely impressions. He and Angela sat alone in the cool parlor for two hours after dinner while he restated his impressions of her over and over. He told her how charming he thought her home was, how nice her father and mother, what interesting brothers she had. He made a genial sketch of Jotham as he had strolled up to him at noon, which pleased Angela and she kept it to show to her father. He made her pose in the window and sketched her head and her halo of hair. He thought of his double page illustration of the Bowery by night and went to fetch it, looking for the first time at the sweet cool room at the end of the house which he was to occupy. One window, a west one, had hollyhocks looking in, and the door to the north gave out on the cool, shady grass. He moved in beauty, he thought; was treading on showered happiness. It hurt him to think that

such joy might not always be, as though beauty were not everywhere and forever present.

When Angela saw the picture which *Truth* had reproduced,
she was beside herself with joy and pride and happiness. It
was such a testimony to her lover's ability. He had written
almost daily of the New York art world, so she was familiar
with that in exaggerated ideas, but these actual things, like
reproduced pictures, were different. The whole world would
see this picture. He must be famous already, she imagined.

That evening and the next and the next as they sat in the
parlor alone he drew nearer and nearer to that definite understanding which comes between a man and woman when they
love. Eugene could never stop with mere kissing and caressing
in a reserved way, if not persistently restrained. It seemed
natural to him that love should go on. He had not been married.
He did not know what its responsibilities were. He had never
given a thought to what his parents had endured to make him
worth while. There was no instinct in him to tell him. He had
no yearnings for parenthood, that normal desire which gives
visions of a home and the proper social conditions for rearing a
family. All he thought of was the love making period—the
billing and cooing and the transports of delight which come
with it. With Angela he felt that these would be super-
normal precisely because she was so slow in yielding—so on
the defensive against herself. He could look in her eyes at
times and see a swooning veil which foreshadowed a storm of
emotion. He would sit by her stroking her hands, touching her
cheek, smoothing her hair, or at other times holding her in
his arms. It was hard for her to resist those significant pressures
he gave, to hold him at arm's length, for she herself was eager
for the delights of love.

It was on the third night of his stay and in the face of his
growing respect for every member of this family, that he swept
Angela to the danger line—would have carried her across it had
it not been for a fortuitous wave of emotion, which was not
of his creation, but of hers.

They had been to the little lake, Okoonee, a little way from
the house during the afternoon for a swim.

Afterward he and Angela and David and Marietta had
taken a drive. It was one of those lovely afternoons that come
sometimes in summer and speak direct to the heart of love and
beauty. It was so fair and warm, the shadows of the trees
so comforting that they fairly made Eugene's heart ache. He
was young now, life was beautiful, but how would it be when

he was old? A morbid anticipation of disaster seemed to harrow his soul.

The sunset had already died away when they drew near home. Insects hummed, a cow-bell tinkled now and then; breaths of cool air, those harbingers of the approaching eve, swept their cheeks as they passed occasional hollows. Approaching the house they saw the blue smoke curls rising from the kitchen chimney, foretelling the preparation of the evening meal. Eugene clasped Angela's hand in an ecstasy of emotion.

He wanted to dream—sitting in the hammock with Angela as the dusk fell, watching the pretty scene. Life was all around. Jotham and Benjamin came in from the fields and the sound of their voices and of the splashing water came from the kitchen door where they were washing. There was an anticipatory stamping of horses' feet in the barn, the lowing of a distant cow, the hungry grunt of pigs. Eugene shook his head—it was so pastoral, so sweet.

At supper he scarcely touched what was put before him, the group at the dining table holding his attention as a spectacle. Afterwards he sat with the family on the lawn outside the door, breathing the odor of flowers, watching the stars over the trees, listening to Jotham and Mrs. Blue, to Samuel, Benjamin, David, Marietta and occasionally Angela. Because of his mood, sad in the face of exquisite beauty, she also was subdued. She said little, listening to Eugene and her father, but when she did talk her voice was sweet.

Jotham arose, after a time, and went to bed, and one by one the others followed. David and Marietta went into the sitting room and then Samuel and Benjamin left. They gave as an excuse hard work for the morning. Samuel was going to try his hand again at thrashing. Eugene took Angela by the hand and led her out where some hydrangeas were blooming, white as snow by day, but pale and silvery in the dark. He took her face in his hands, telling her again of love.

"It's been such a wonderful day I'm all wrought up," he said. "Life is so beautiful here. This place is so sweet and peaceful. And you! oh, you!" kisses ended his words.

They stood there a little while, then went back into the parlor where she lighted a lamp. It cast a soft yellow glow over the room, just enough to make it warm, he thought. They sat first side by side on two rocking chairs and then later on a settee, he holding her in his arms. Before supper she had changed to a loose cream colored house gown. Now Eugene persuaded her to let her hair hang in the two braids.

Real passion is silent. It was so intense with him that he sat contemplating her as if in a spell. She leaned back against his shoulder stroking his hair, but finally ceased even that, for her own feeling was too intense to make movement possible. She thought of him as a young god, strong, virile, beautiful—a brilliant future before him. All these years she had waited for someone to truly love her and now this splendid youth had apparently cast himself at her feet. He stroked her hands, her neck, cheeks, then slowly gathered her close and buried his head against her bosom.

Angela was strong in convention, in the precepts of her parents, in the sense of her family and its attitude, but this situation was more than she could resist. She accepted first the pressure of his arm, then the slow subtlety with which he caressed her. Resistance seemed almost impossible now for he held her close—tight within the range of his magnetism. When finally she felt the pressure of his hand upon her quivering limbs, she threw herself back in a transport of agony and delight.

"No, no, Eugene," she begged. "No, no! Save me from myself. Save me from myself. Oh, Eugene!"

He paused a moment to look at her face. It was wrought in lines of intense suffering—pale as though she were ill. Her body was quite limp. Only the hot, moist lips told the significant story. He could not stop at once. Slowly he drew his hand away, then let his sensitive artists' fingers rest gently on her neck—her bosom.

She struggled lamely at this point and slipped to her knees, her dress loosened at the neck.

"Don't, Eugene," she begged, "don't. Think of my father, my mother. I, who have boasted so. I of whom they feel so sure. Oh, Eugene, I beg of you!"

He stroked her hair, her cheeks, looking into her face as Abélard might have looked at Héloïse.

"Oh, I know why it is," she exclaimed, convulsively. "I am no better than any other, but I have waited so long, so long! But I mustn't! Oh, Eugene, I mustn't! Help me!"

Vaguely Eugene understood. She had been without lovers. Why? he thought. She was beautiful. He got up, half intending to carry her to his room, but he paused, thinking. She was such a pathetic figure. Was he really as bad as this? Could he not be fair in this one instance? Her father had been so nice to him—her mother—He saw Jotham Blue before him, Mrs. Blue, her admiring brothers and sisters, as they had been a little while before. He looked at her and still the prize lured him—almost swept him on in spite of himself, but he stayed.

"Stand up, Angela," he said at last, pulling himself together, looking at her intensely. She did so. "Leave me now," he went on, "right away! I won't answer for myself if you don't. I am really trying. Please go."

She paused, looking at him fearfully, regretfully.

"Oh, forgive me, Eugene," she pleaded.

"Forgive me," he said. "I'm the one. But you go now, sweet. You don't know how hard this is. Help me by going."

She moved away and he followed her with his eyes, yearningly, burningly, until she reached the door. When she closed it softly he went into his own room and sat down. His body was limp and weary. He ached from head to foot from the intensity of the mood he had passed through. He went over the recent incidents, almost stunned by his experience and then went outside and stood under the stairs, listening. Tree toads were chirping, there were suspicious cracklings in the grass as of bugs stirring. A duck quacked somewhere feebly. The bell of the family cow tinkled somewhere over near the water of the little stream. He saw the great dipper in the sky, Sirius, Canopus, the vast galaxy of the Milky Way.

"What is life anyway?" he asked himself. "What is the human body? What produces passion? Here we are for a few years surging with a fever of longing and then we burn out and die." He thought of some lines he might write, of pictures he might paint. All the while, reproduced before his mind's eye like a cinematograph, were views of Angela as she had been tonight in his arms, on her knees. He had seen her true form. He had held her in his arms. He had voluntarily resigned her charms for tonight; anyhow, no harm had come. It never should.

CHAPTER XIX

IT would be hard to say in what respect, if any, the experiences of this particular night altered Eugene's opinion of Angela. He was inclined to like her better for what he would have called her humanness. Thus frankly to confess her weakness and inability to save herself was splendid. That he was given the chance to do a noble deed was fortunate and uplifting. He knew now that he could take her if he wished, but once calm again he resolved to be fair and not to insist. He could wait.

The state of Angela's mind, on the contrary, once she had come out of her paroxysm and gained the privacy of her own room, or rather the room she shared with Marietta at the other extreme of the house, was pitiable. She had for so long considered herself an estimable and virtuous girl. There was in her just a faint trace of prudery which might readily have led to an unhappy old maid existence for her if Eugene, with his superiority, or non-understanding, or indifference to conventional theories and to old-maidish feelings, had not come along and with his customary blindness to material prosperity and age limitations, seized upon and made love to her. He had filled her brain with a whirlwind of notions hitherto unfamiliar to her world and set himself up in her brain as a law unto himself. He was not like other men—she could see that. He was superior to them. He might not make much money, being an artist, but he could make other things which to her seemed more desirable. Fame, beautiful pictures, notable friends, were not these things far superior to money? She had had little enough money in all conscience, and if Eugene made anything at all it would be enough for her. He seemed to be under the notion that he needed a lot to get married, whereas she would have been glad to risk it on almost anything at all.

This latest revelation of herself, besides tearing her mind from a carefully nurtured belief in her own virtuous impregnability, raised at the same time a spectre of disaster in so far as Eugene's love for her was concerned. Would he, now that she had allowed him those precious endearments which should have been reserved for the marriage bed only, care for her as much as he had before? Would he not think of her as a light minded, easily spoiled creature who was waiting only for a propitious moment to yield herself? She had been lost to all sense of right and wrong in that hour, that she knew. Her father's character and what he stood for, her mother's decency and love of virtue, her cleanly-minded, right-living brothers and sisters,—all had been forgotten and here she was, a tainted maiden, virtuous in technical sense it is true, but tainted. Her convention-trained conscience smote her vigorously and she groaned in her heart. She went outside the door of her own room and sat down on the damp grass in the early morning to think. It was so cool and calm everywhere but in her own soul. She held her face in her hands, feeling her hot cheeks, wondering what Eugene was thinking now. What would her father think, her mother? She wrung her hands more than once and finally went inside to see if she could not rest. She was not unconscious of the beauty and joy of the episode, but she was troubled by what she felt she ought to think, what the consequences to her future might be. To hold Eugene now—that was a subtle question. To hold up her head in front of him as she had, could she? To keep him from going further. It was a difficult situation and she tossed restlessly all night, getting little sleep. In the morning she arose weary and disturbed, but more desperately in love than ever. This wonderful youth had revealed an entirely new and intensely dramatic world to her.

When they met on the lawn again before breakfast, Angela was garbed in white linen. She looked waxen and delicate and her eyes showed dark rings as well as the dark thoughts that were troubling her. Eugene took her hand sympathetically.

"Don't worry," he said, "I know. It isn't as bad as you think." And he smiled tenderly.

"Oh, Eugene, I don't understand myself now," she said sorrowfully. "I thought I was better than that."

"We're none of us better than that," he replied simply. "We just think we are sometimes. You are not any different to me. You just think you are."

"Oh, are you sure?" she asked eagerly.

"Quite sure," he replied. "Love isn't a terrible thing between any two. It's just lovely. Why should I think worse of you?"

"Oh, because good girls don't do what I have done. I have been raised to know better—to do better."

"All a belief, my dear, which you get from what has been taught you. You think it wrong. Why? Because your father and mother told you so. Isn't that it?"

"Oh, not that alone. Everybody thinks it's wrong. The Bible teaches that it is. Everybody turns his back on you when he finds out."

"Wait a minute," pleaded Eugene argumentatively. He was trying to solve this puzzle for himself. "Let's leave the Bible out of it, for I don't believe in the Bible—not as a law of action anyhow. The fact that everybody thinks it's wrong wouldn't necessarily make it so, would it?" He was ignoring completely the significance of *everybody* as a reflection of those principles which govern the universe.

"No-o-o," ventured Angela doubtfully.

"Listen," went on Eugene. "Everybody in Constantinople believes that Mahomet is the Prophet of God. That doesn't make him so, does it?"

"No."

"Well, then, everyone here might believe that what we did last night was wrong without making it so. Isn't that true?"

"Yes," replied Angela confusedly. She really did not know. She could not argue with him. He was too subtle, but her innate principles and instincts were speaking plainly enough, nevertheless.

"Now what you're really thinking about is what people will do. They'll turn their backs on you, you say. That is a practical matter. Your father might turn you out of doors—"

"I think he would," replied Angela, little understanding the bigness of the heart of her father.

"I think he wouldn't," said Eugene, "but that's neither here nor there. Men might refuse to marry you. Those are material considerations. You wouldn't say they had anything to do with real right or wrong, would you?"

Eugene had no convincing end to his argument. He did not know any more than anyone else what was right or wrong in this matter. He was merely talking to convince himself, but he had enough logic to confuse Angela.

"I don't know," she said vaguely.

"Right," he went on loftily, "is something which is supposed to be in accordance with a standard of truth. Now no one in all the world knows what truth is, no one. There is no way of telling. You can only act wisely or unwisely as regards your personal welfare. If that's what you're worrying about, and it is, I can tell you that you're no worse off. There's nothing the matter with your welfare. I think you're better off, for I like you better."

Angela wondered at the subtlety of his brain. She was not

sure but that what he said might be true. Could her fears be baseless? She felt sure she had lost some of the bloom of her youth anyhow.

"How can you?" she asked, referring to his saying that he liked her better.

"Easily enough," he replied. "I know more about you. I admire your frankness. You're lovely—altogether so. You are sweet beyond compare." He started to particularize.

"Don't, Eugene," she pleaded, putting her finger over her lips. The color was leaving her cheeks. "Please don't, I can't stand it."

"All right," he said, "I won't. But you're altogether lovely. Let's go and sit in the hammock."

"No. I'm going to get you your breakfast. It's time you had something."

He took comfort in his privileges, for the others had all gone. Jotham, Samuel, Benjamin and David were in the fields. Mrs. Blue was sewing and Marietta had gone to see a girl friend up the road. Angela, as Ruby before her, bestirred herself about the youth's meal, mixing biscuit, broiling him some bacon, cleaning a basket of fresh dewberries for him.

"I like your man," said her mother, coming out where she was working. "He looks to be good-natured. But don't spoil him. If you begin wrong you'll be sorry."

"You spoiled papa, didn't you?" asked Angela sagely, recalling all the little humorings her father had received.

"Your father has a keen sense of duty," retorted her mother. "It didn't hurt him to be spoiled a little."

"Maybe Eugene has," replied her daughter, turning her slices of bacon.

Her mother smiled. All her daughters had married well. Perhaps Angela was doing the best of all. Certainly her lover was the most distinguished. Yet, "well to be careful," she suggested.

Angela thought. If her mother only knew, or her father. Dear Heaven! And yet Eugene was altogether lovely. She wanted to wait on him, to spoil him. She wished she could be with him every day from now on—that they need not part any more.

"Oh, if he would only marry me," she sighed. It was the one divine event which would complete her life.

Eugene would have liked to linger in this atmosphere indefinitely. Old Jotham, he found, liked to talk to him. He took an interest in national and international affairs, was aware of distinguished and peculiar personalities, seemed to follow world currents everywhere. Eugene began to think of him as a distinguished personality in himself, but old Jotham waved the suggestion blandly aside.

"I'm a farmer," he said. "I've seen my greatest success in raising good children. My boys will do well, I know."

For the first time Eugene caught the sense of fatherhood, of what it means to live again in your children, but only vaguely. He was too young, too eager for a varied life, too lustful. So its true import was lost for the time.

Sunday came and with it the necessity to leave. He had been here nine days, really two days more than he had intended to stay. It was farewell to Angela, who had come so close, so much in his grasp that she was like a child in his hands. It was farewell, moreover, to an ideal scene, a bit of bucolic poetry. When would he see again an old patriarch like Jotham, clean, kindly, intelligent, standing upright amid his rows of corn, proud to be a good father, not ashamed to be poor, not afraid to be old or to die. Eugene had drawn so much from him. It was like sitting at the feet of Isaiah. It was farewell to the lovely fields and the blue hills, the long rows of trees down the lawn walk, the white and red and blue flowers about the dooryard. He had slept so sweetly in his clean room, he had listened so joyously to the voices of birds, the wood dove and the poet thrush; he had heard the water in the Blue's branch rippling over its clean pebbles. The pigs in the barnyard pen, the horses, the cows, all had appealed to him. He thought of Gray's "Elegy"—of Goldsmith's "Deserted Village" and "The Traveller." This was something like the things those men had loved.

He walked down the lawn with Angela, when the time came, repeating how sorry he was to go. David had hitched up a little brown mare and was waiting at the extreme end of the lawn.

"Oh, Sweet," he sighed. "I shall never be happy until I have you."

"I will wait," sighed Angela, although she was wishing to exclaim: "Oh, take me, take me!" When he was gone she went about her duties mechanically, for it was as if all the fire and joy had gone out of her life. Without this brilliant imagination of his to illuminate things, life seemed dull.

And he rode, parting in his mind with each lovely thing as he went—the fields of wheat, the little stream, Lake Okoonee, the pretty Blue farmhouse, all.

He said to himself: "Nothing more lovely will ever come again. Angela in my arms in her simple little parlor. Dear God! and there are only seventy years of life—not more than ten or fifteen of true youth, all told."

CHAPTER XX

EUGENE carried home with him not only a curiously deepened feeling for Angela, due to their altered and more intimate relationship, but moreover a growing respect for her family. Old Jotham was so impressive a figure of a man; his wife so kindly and earnest. Their attitude toward their children and to each other was so sound, and their whole relationship to society so respectable. Another observer might have been repelled by the narrowness and frugality of their lives. But Eugene had not known enough of luxury to be scornful of the material simplicity of such existence. Here he had found character, poetry of location, poetry of ambition, youth and happy prospects. These boys, so sturdy and independent, were sure to make for themselves such places in the world as they desired. Marietta, so charming a girl, could not but make a good marriage. Samuel was doing well in his position with the railroad company; Benjamin was studying to be a lawyer and David was to be sent to West Point. He liked them for their familiar, sterling worth. And they all treated him as the destined husband of Angela. By the end of his stay he had become as much en rapport with the family as if he had known it all his life.

Before going back to New York he had stopped in Chicago, where he had seen Howe and Mathews grinding away at their old tasks, and then for a few days in Alexandria, where he found his father busy about his old affairs. Sewing machines were still being delivered by him in person, and the long roads of the country were as briskly traversed by his light machine-carrying buggy as in his earliest days. Eugene saw him now as just a little futile, and yet he admired him, his patience, his industry. The brisk sewing machine agent was considerably impressed by his son's success, and was actually trying to take an interest in art. One evening coming home from the post office he pointed out a street scene in Alexandria as a subject for a painting. Eugene knew that art had only been called to his father's attention by his own efforts. He had noticed these things all his life, no doubt, but attached no significance to them until he had seen his son's work in the magazines. "If you ever paint country things, you ought to paint Cook's Mill, over here by the falls. That's one of the prettiest things I know anywhere," he said to him one evening, trying to make his son feel the interest he took. Eugene knew the place. It was attractive, a little branch of bright water running at the base of a forty foot wall of red sandstone and finally tumbling down a fifteen foot declivity of grey mossy stones. It was close to a yellow road which carried a good deal of traffic and was surrounded by a company of trees which ornamented it and sheltered it on all sides. Eugene had admired it in his youth as beautiful and peaceful.

"It is nice," he replied to his father. "I'll take a look at it some day."

Witla senior felt set up. His son was doing him honor. Mrs. Witla, like her husband, was showing the first notable traces of the flight of time. The crow's-feet at the sides of her eyes were deeper, the wrinkles in her forehead longer. At the sight of Eugene the first night she fairly thrilled, for he was so well developed now, so self-reliant. He had come through his experiences to a kind of poise which she realized was manhood. Her boy, requiring her careful guidance, was gone. This was someone who could guide her, tease her as a man would a child.

"You've got so big I hardly know you," she said, as he folded her in his arms.

"No, you're just getting little, ma. I used to think I'd never get to the point where you couldn't shake me, but that's all over, isn't it?"

"You never did need much shaking," she said fondly.

Myrtle, who had married Frank Bangs the preceding year, had gone with her husband to live in Ottumwa, Iowa, where he had taken charge of a mill, so Eugene did not see her, but he spent some little time with Sylvia, now the mother of two children. Her husband was the same quiet, conservative plodder Eugene had first noted him to be. Revisiting the office of the *Appeal* he found that John Summers had recently died. Otherwise things were as they had been. Jonas Lyle and Caleb Williams were still in charge—quite the same as before. Eugene was glad when his time was up, and took the train back to Chicago with a light heart.

Again as on his entrance to Chicago from the East, and on his return to it from Blackwood, he was touched keenly by the remembrance of Ruby. She had been so sweet to him. His opening art experiences had in a way been centred about her. But in spite of all, he did not want to go out and see her. Or did he? He asked himself this question with a pang of sorrow,

for in a way he cared. He cared for her as one might care
for a girl in a play or book. She had the quality of a tragedy
about her. She—her life, her surroundings, her misfortune in
loving him, constituted an artistic composition. He thought
he might be able to write a poem about it some time. He
was able to write rather charming verse which he kept to
himself. He had the knack of saying things in a simple way
and with feeling—making you see a picture. The trouble
with his verse was that it lacked as yet any real nobility of
thought—was not as final in understanding as it might have
been.

He did not go to see Ruby. The reason he assigned to himself was that it would not be nice. She might not want him
to now. She might be trying to forget. And he had Angela.
It really wasn't fair to her. But he looked over toward the
region in which she lived, as he travelled out of the city eastward
and wished that some of those lovely moments he had spent with
her might be lived again.

Back in New York, life seemed to promise a repetition of
the preceding year, with some minor modifications. In the fall
Eugene went to live with McHugh and Smite, the studio
they had consisting of one big working room and three bedrooms. They agreed that they could get along together, and
for a while it was good for them all. The criticism they
furnished each other was of real value. And they found it
pleasant to dine together, to walk, to see the exhibitions. They
stimulated each other with argument, each having a special
point of view. It was much as it had been with Howe and
Mathews in Chicago.

During this winter Eugene made his first appearance in one of
the leading publications of the time—*Harper's Magazine*. He
had gone to the Art Director with some proofs of his previous
work, and had been told that it was admirable; if some suitable
story turned up he would be considered. Later a letter came
asking him to call, and a commission involving three pictures
for $125 was given him. He worked them out successfully
with models and was complimented on the result. His associates cheered him on also, for they really admired what he was
doing. He set out definitely to *make Scribner's* and the *Century,* as getting into those publications was called, and after a
time he succeeded in making an impression on their respective Art
Directors, though no notable commissions were given him.
From one he secured a poem, rather out of his mood to decorate,
and from the other a short story; but somehow he could not feel

that either was a real opportunity. He wanted an appropriate subject or to sell them some of his scenes.

Building up a paying reputation was slow work. Although he was being mentioned here and there among artists, his name was anything but a significant factor with the public or with the Art Directors. He was still a promising beginner—growing, but not yet arrived by a long distance.

There was one editor who was inclined to see him at his real worth, but had no money to offer. This was Richard Wheeler, editor of *Craft,* a rather hopeless magazine in a commercial sense, but devoted sincerely enough to art. Wheeler was a blond young man of poetic temperament, whose enthusiasm for Eugene's work made it easy for them to become friends.

It was through Wheeler that he met that winter Miriam Finch and Christina Channing, two women of radically different temperaments and professions, who opened for Eugene two entirely new worlds.

Miriam Finch was a sculptor by profession—a critic by temperament, with no great capacity for emotion in herself but an intense appreciation of its significance in others. To see her was to be immediately impressed with a vital force in womanhood. She was a woman who had never had a real youth or a real love affair, but clung to her ideal of both with a passionate, almost fatuous, faith that they could still be brought to pass. Wheeler had invited him to go round to her studio with him one evening. He was interested to know what Eugene would think of her. Miriam, already thirty-two when Eugene met her—a tiny, brown haired, brown eyed girl, with a slender, rather cat-like figure and a suavity of address and manner which was artistic to the finger tips. She had none of that budding beauty that is the glory of eighteen, but she was altogether artistic and delightful. Her hair encircled her head in a fluffy cloudy mass; her eyes moved quickly, with intense intelligence, feeling, humor, sympathy. Her lips were sweetly modelled after the pattern of a Cupid's bow and her smile was subtly ingratiating. Her sallow complexion matched her brown hair and the drab velvet or corduroy of her dress. There was a striking simplicity about the things she wore which gave her a distinctive air. Her clothes were seldom fashionable but always exceedingly becoming, for she saw herself as a whole and arrayed herself as a decorative composition from head to foot, with a sense of fitness in regard to self and life.

To such a nature as Eugene's, an intelligent, artistic, self-regulating and self-poised human being was always intensely

magnetic and gratifying. He turned to the capable person as
naturally as a flower turns toward the light, finding a joy in
contemplating the completeness and sufficiency of such a being.
To have ideas of your own seemed to him a marvellous thing.
To be able definitely to formulate your thoughts and reach
positive and satisfying conclusions was a great and beautiful
thing. From such personalities Eugene drank admiringly until
his thirst was satiated—then he would turn away. If his
thirst for what they had to give returned, he might come back—
not otherwise.

Hitherto all his relationships with personages of this quality
had been confined to the male sex, for he had not known any
women of distinction. Beginning with Temple Boyle, instructor in the life class in Chicago, and Vincent Beers, instructor
in the illustration class, he had encountered successively Jerry
Mathews, Mitchell Goldfarb, Peter McHugh, David Smite and
Jotham Blue, all men of intense personal feeling and convictions
and men who had impressed him greatly. Now he was to
encounter for the first time some forceful, really exceptional
women of the same calibre. Stella Appleton, Margaret Duff,
Ruby Kenny and Angela Blue were charming girls in their way,
but they did not think for themselves. They were not organized,
self-directed, self-controlled personalities in the way that Miriam
Finch was. She would have recognized herself at once as being
infinitely superior intellectually and artistically to any or all of
them, while entertaining at the same time a sympathetic, appreciative understanding of their beauty, fitness, equality of value
in the social scheme. She was a student of life, a critic of emotions and understanding, with keen appreciative intelligence,
and yet longing intensely for just what Stella and Margaret
and Ruby and even Angela had—youth, beauty, interest for
men, the power or magnetism or charm of face and form to
compel the impetuous passion of a lover. She wanted to be
loved by someone who could love madly and beautifully, and
this had never come to her.

Miss Finch's home, or rather studio, was with her family in
East Twenty-sixth Street, where she occupied a north room on
the third floor, but her presence in the bosom of that family did
not prevent her from attaining an individuality and an exclusive-
ness which was most illuminating to Eugene. Her room was
done in silver, brown and grey, with a great wax-festooned
candlestick fully five feet high standing in one corner and a
magnificent carved chest of early Flemish workmanship standing
in another. There was a brown combination writing desk and

book-shelf which was arrayed with some of the most curious volumes—Pater's "Marius the Epicurean," Daudet's "Wives of Men of Genius," Richard Jefferies' "Story of My Heart," Stevenson's "Aes Triplex," "The Kasidah" of Richard Burton, "The House of Life" by Dante Gabriel Rossetti, "Also sprach Zarathustra" by Friedrich Nietzsche. The fact that they were here, after he had taken one look at the woman and the room, was to Eugene sufficient proof that they were important. He handled them curiously, reading odd paragraphs, nosing about, looking at pictures, and making rapid notes in his mental note-book. This was someone worth knowing, he felt that. He wanted to make a sufficiently favorable impression to be permitted to know her better.

Miriam Finch was at once taken with Eugene. There was such an air of vigor, inquiry, appreciation and understanding about him that she could not help being impressed. He seemed somewhat like a lighted lamp casting a soft, shaded, velvety glow. He went about her room, after his introduction, looking at her pictures, her bronzes and clays, asking after the creator of this, the painter of that, where a third thing came from.

"I never heard of one of these books," he said frankly, when he looked over the small, specially selected collection.

"There are some very interesting things here," she volunteered, coming to his side. His simple confession appealed to her. He was like a breath of fresh air. Richard Wheeler, who had brought him in, made no objection to being neglected. He wanted her to enjoy his find.

"You know," said Eugene, looking up from Burton's "Kasidah" and into her brown eyes, "New York gets me dizzy. It's so wonderful!"

"Just how?" she asked.

"It's so compact of wonderful things. I saw a shop the other day full of old jewelry and ornaments and quaint stones and clothes, and O Heaven! I don't know what all—more things than I had ever seen in my whole life before; and here in this quiet side street and this unpretentious house I find this room. Nothing seems to show on the outside; everything seems crowded to suffocation with luxury or art value on the inside."

"Are you talking about this room?" she ventured.

"Why, yes," he replied.

"Take note, Mr. Wheeler," she called, over her shoulder to her young editor friend. "This is the first time in my life that I have been accused of possessing luxury. When you write me up again I want you to give me credit for luxury. I like it."

"I'll certainly do it," said Wheeler.

"Yes. 'Art values' too."

"Yes. 'Art values.' I have it," said Wheeler.

Eugene smiled. He liked her vivacity. "I know what you mean," she added. "I've felt the same thing about Paris. You go into little unpretentious places there and come across such wonderful things—heaps and heaps of fine clothes, antiques, jewels. Where was it I read such an interesting article about that?"

"Not in *Craft* I hope?" ventured Wheeler.

"No, I don't think so. *Harper's Bazaar*, I believe."

"Oh, pshaw!" exclaimed Wheeler. *Harper's Bazaar!* What rot!"

"But that's just what you ought to have. Why don't you do it—right?"

"I will," he said.

Eugene went to the piano and turned over a pile of music. Again he came across the unfamiliar, the strange, the obviously distinguished—Grieg's "Arabian Dance"; "Es war ein Traum" by Lassen; "Elegie" by Massenet; "Otidi" by Davydoff; "Nymphs and Shepherds" by Purcell—things whose very titles smacked of color and beauty. Gluck, Sgambati, Rossini, Tschaikowsky—the Italian Scarlatti—Eugene marvelled at what he did not know about music.

"Play something," he pleaded, and with a smile Miriam stepped to the piano.

"Do you know 'Es war ein Traum'?" she inquired.

"No," said he.

"That's lovely," put in Wheeler. "Sing it!"

Eugene had thought that possibly she sang, but he was not prepared for the burst of color that came with her voice. It was not a great voice, but sweet and sympathetic, equal to the tasks she set herself. She selected her music as she selected her clothes—to suit her capacity. The poetic, sympathetic reminiscence of the song struck home. Eugene was delighted.

"Oh," he exclaimed, bringing his chair close to the piano and looking into her face, "you sing beautifully."

She gave him a glittering smile.

"Now I'll sing anything you want for you if you go on like that."

"I'm crazy about music," he said; "I don't know anything about it, but I like this sort of thing."

"You like the really good things. I know. So do I."

He felt flattered and grateful. They went through "Otidi," "The Nightingale," "Elegie," "The Last Spring"—music Eugene had never heard before. But he knew at once that he was listening to playing which represented a better intelligence, a keener selective judgment, a finer artistic impulse than anyone he had ever known had possessed. Ruby played and Angela, the latter rather well, but neither had ever heard of these things he was sure. Ruby had only liked popular things; Angela the standard melodies—beautiful but familiar. Here was someone who ignored popular taste—was in advance of it. In all her music he had found nothing he knew. It grew on him as a significant fact. He wanted to be nice to her, to have her like him. So he drew close and smiled and she always smiled back. Like the others she liked his face, his mouth, his eyes, his hair.

"He's charming," she thought, when he eventually left; and his impression of her was of a woman who was notably and significantly distinguished.

CHAPTER XXI

BUT Miriam Finch's family, of which she seemed so independent, had not been without its influence on her. This family was of Middle West origin, and did not understand or sympathize very much with the artistic temperament. Since her sixteenth year, when Miriam had first begun to exhibit a definite striving toward the artistic, her parents had guarded her jealously against what they considered the corrupting atmosphere of the art world. Her mother had accompanied her from Ohio to New York, and lived with her while she studied art in the art school, chaperoning her everywhere. When it became advisable, as she thought, for Miriam to go abroad, she went with her. Miriam's artistic career was to be properly supervised. When she lived in the Latin Quarter in Paris her mother was with her; when she loitered in the atmosphere of the galleries and palaces in Rome it was with her mother at her side. At Pompeii and Herculaneum—in London and in Berlin—her mother, an iron-willed little woman at forty-five at that time, was with her. She was convinced that she knew exactly what was good for her daughter and had more or less made the girl accept her theories. Later, Miriam's personal judgment began to diverge slightly from that of her mother and then trouble began.

It was vague at first, hardly a definite, tangible thing in the daughter's mind, but later it grew to be a definite feeling that her life was being cramped. She had been warned off from association with this person and that; had been shown the pitfalls that surround the free, untrammelled life of the art studio. Marriage with the average artist was not to be considered. Modelling from the nude, particularly the nude of a man, was to her mother at first most distressing. She insisted on being present and for a long time her daughter thought that was all right. Finally the presence, the viewpoint, the intellectual insistence of her mother, became too irksome, and an open break followed. It was one of those family tragedies which almost kill conservative parents. Mrs. Finch's heart was practically broken.

The trouble with this break was that it came a little too late for Miriam's happiness. In the stress of this insistent chaperonage she had lost her youth—the period during which she felt she should have had her natural freedom. She had lost the interest of several men who in her nineteenth, twentieth and twenty-first years had approached her longingly, but who could not stand the criticism of her mother. At twenty-eight when the break came the most delightful love period was over and she felt grieved and resentful.

At that time she had insisted on a complete and radical change for herself. She had managed to get, through one art dealer and another, orders for some of her spirited clay figurines. There was a dancing girl, a visualization of one of the moods of Carmencita, a celebrated dancer of the period, which had caught the public fancy—at least the particular art dealer who was handling her work for her had managed to sell some eighteen replicas of it at $175 each. Miss Finch's share of this was $100, each. There was another little thing, a six-inch bronze called "Sleep," which had sold some twenty replicas at $150 each, and was still selling. "The Wind," a figure crouching and huddling as if from cold, was also selling. It looked as though she might be able to make from three to four thousand dollars a year steadily.

She demanded of her mother at this time the right to a private studio, to go and come when she pleased, to go about alone wherever she wished, to have men and women come to her private apartment, and be entertained by her in her own manner. She objected to supervision in any form, cast aside criticism and declared roundly that she would lead her own life. She realized sadly while she was doing it, however, that the best was gone—that she had not had the wit or the stamina to do as she pleased at the time she most wanted to do so. Now she would be almost automatically conservative. She could not help it.

Eugene when he first met her felt something of this. He felt the subtlety of her temperament, her philosophic conclusions, what might be called her emotional disappointment. She was eager for life, which seemed to him odd, for she appeared to have so much. By degrees he got it out of her, for they came to be quite friendly and then he understood clearly just how things were.

By the end of three months and before Christina Channing appeared, Eugene had come to the sanest, cleanest understanding with Miss Finch that he had yet reached with any woman. He had dropped into the habit of calling there once and sometimes twice a week. He had learned to understand her point of view, which was detachedly æsthetic and rather removed from the world of the sensuous. Her ideal of a lover had been fixed

to a certain extent by statues and poems of Greek youth—
Hylas, Adonis, Perseus, and by those men of the Middle Ages
painted by Millais, Burne-Jones, Dante Gabriel Rossetti and
Ford Madox Brown. She had hoped for a youth with a classic
outline of face, distinction of form, graciousness of demeanor
and an appreciative intellect. He must be manly but artistic.
It was a rather high ideal, not readily capable of attainment
by a woman already turned thirty, but nevertheless worth dreaming about.

Although she had surrounded herself with talented youth as
much as possible—both young men and young women—she had
not come across *the one.* There had been a number of times
when, for a very little while, she had imagined she had found
him, but had been compelled to see her fancies fail. All the
youths she knew had been inclined to fall in love with girls
younger than themselves—some to the interesting maidens she
had introduced them to. It is hard to witness an ideal turning
from yourself, its spiritual counterpart, and fixing itself upon
some mere fleshly vision of beauty which a few years will cause
to fade. Such had been her fate, however, and she was at times
inclined to despair. When Eugene appeared she had almost
concluded that love was not for her, and she did not flatter
herself that he would fall in love with her. Nevertheless she
could not help but be interested in him and look at times with
a longing eye at his interesting face and figure. It was so
obvious that if he loved at all it would be dramatically, in all
probability, beautifully.

As time went on she took pains to be agreeable to him.
He had, as it were, the freedom of her room. She knew of
exhibitions, personalities, movements—in religion, art, science,
government, literature. She was inclined to take an interest in
socialism, and believed in righting the wrongs of the people.
Eugene thought he did, but he was so keenly interested in life
as a spectacle that he hadn't as much time to sympathize as he
thought he ought to have. She took him to see exhibitions, and
to meet people, being rather proud of a boy with so much talent;
and she was pleased to find that he was so generally acceptable.
People, particularly writers, poets, musicians—beginners in every
field, were inclined to remember him. He was an easy talker,
witty, quick to make himself at home and perfectly natural. He
tried to be accurate in his judgments of things, and fair, but he
was young and subject to strong prejudices. He appreciated her
friendship, and did not seek to make their relationship more
intimate. He knew that only a sincere proposal of marriage

could have won her, and he did not care enough for her for that. He felt himself bound to Angela and, curiously, he felt Miriam's age as a bar between them. He admired her tremendously and was learning in part through her what his ideal ought to be, but he was not drawn sufficiently to want to make love to her.

But in Christina Channing, whom he met shortly afterward, he found a woman of a more sensuous and lovable type, though hardly less artistic. Christina Channing was a singer by profession, living also in New York with her mother, but not, as Miss Finch had been, dominated by her so thoroughly, although she was still at the age when her mother could and did have considerable influence with her. She was twenty-seven years of age and so far, had not yet attained the eminence which subsequently was hers, though she was full of that buoyant self-confidence which makes for eventual triumph. So far she had studied ardently under various teachers, had had several love affairs, none serious enough to win her away from her chosen profession, and had gone through the various experiences of those who begin ignorantly to do something in art and eventually reach experience and understanding of how the world is organized and what they will have to do to succeed.

Although Miss Channing's artistic sense did not rise to that definite artistic expression in her material surroundings which characterized Miss Finch's studio atmosphere, it went much farther in its expression of her joy in life. Her voice, a rich contralto, deep, full, colorful, had a note of pathos and poignancy which gave a touch of emotion to her gayest songs. She could play well enough to accompany herself with delicacy and emphasis. She was at present one of the soloists with the New York Symphony Orchestra, with the privilege of accepting occasional outside engagements. The following Fall she was preparing to make a final dash to Germany to see if she could not get an engagement with a notable court opera company and so pave the way for a New York success. She was already quite well known in musical circles as a promising operatic candidate and her eventual arrival would be not so much a question of talent as of luck.

While these two women fascinated Eugene for the time being, his feeling for Angela continued unchanged; for though she suffered in an intellectual or artistic comparison, he felt that she was richer emotionally. There was a poignancy in her love letters, an intensity about her personal feelings when in his presence which moved him in spite of himself—an ache went with her which brought a memory of the tales of Sappho and

Marguerite Gautier. It occurred to him now that if he flung her aside it might go seriously with her. He did not actually think of doing anything of the sort, but he was realizing that there was a difference between her and intellectual women like Miriam Finch. Besides that, there was a whole constellation of society women swimming into his ken—women whom he only knew, as yet, through the newspapers and the smart weeklies like Town Topics and Vogue, who were presenting still a third order of perfection. Vaguely he was beginning to see that the world was immense and subtle, and that there were many things to learn about women that he had never dreamed of.

Christina Channing was a rival of Angela's in one sense, that of bodily beauty. She had a tall perfectly rounded form, a lovely oval face, a nut brown complexion with the rosy glow of health showing in cheeks and lips, and a mass of blue black hair. Her great brown eyes were lustrous and sympathetic.

Eugene met her through the good offices of Shotmeyer, who had been given by some common friend in Boston a letter of introduction to her. He had spoken of Eugene as being a very brilliant young artist and his friend, and remarked that he would like to bring him up some evening to hear her sing. Miss Channing acquiesced, for she had seen some of his drawings and was struck by the poetic note in them. Shotmeyer, vain of his notable acquaintances—who in fact tolerated him for his amusing gossip—described Miss Channing's voice to Eugene and asked him if he did not want to call on her some evening. "Delighted," said Eugene.

The appointment was made and together they went to Miss Channing's suite in a superior Nineteenth Street boarding house. Miss Channing received them, arrayed in a smooth, close fitting dress of black velvet, touched with red. Eugene was reminded of the first costume in which he had seen Ruby. He was dazzled. As for her, as she told him afterward, she was conscious of a peculiar illogical perturbation.

"When I put on my ribbon that night," she told him, "I was going to put on a dark blue silk one I had just bought and then I thought 'No, he'll like me better in a red one.' Isn't that curious? I just felt as though you were going to like me—as though we might know each other better. That young man—what's his name—described you so accurately." It was months afterward when she confessed that.

When Eugene entered it was with the grand air he had acquired since his life had begun to broaden in the East. He took his relationship with talent, particularly female talent, seriously.

He stood up very straight, walked with a noticeable stride, drove an examining glance into the very soul of the person he was looking at. He was quick to get impressions, especially of talent. He could feel ability in another. When he looked at Miss Channing he felt it like a strong wave—the vibrating wave of an intense consciousness.

She greeted him, extending a soft white hand. They spoke of how they had heard of each other. Eugene somehow made her feel his enthusiasm for her art. "Music is the finer thing," he said, when she spoke of his own gift.

Christina's dark brown eyes swept him from head to foot. He was like his pictures, she thought—and as good to look at.

He was introduced to her mother. They sat down, talking, and presently Miss Channing sang—"Che faro senza Euridice." Eugene felt as if she were singing to him. Her cheeks were flushed and her lips red.

Her mother remarked after she had finished, "You're in splendid voice this evening, Christina."

"I feel particularly fit," she replied.

"A wonderful voice—it's like a big red poppy or a great yellow orchid!" cried Eugene.

Christina thrilled. The description caught her fancy. It seemed true. She felt something of that in the sounds to which she gave utterance.

"Please sing 'Who is Sylvia,'" he begged a little later. She complied gladly.

"That was written for you," he said softly as she ceased, for he had come close to the piano. "You image Sylvia for me." Her cheeks colored warmly.

"Thanks," she nodded, and her eyes spoke too. She welcomed his daring and she was glad to let him know it.

CHAPTER XXII

THE chief trouble with his present situation, and with the entrance of these two women into his life, and it had begun to be a serious one to him, was that he was not making money. He had been able to earn about $1200 the first year; the second he made a little over two thousand, and this third year he was possibly doing a little better. But in view of what he saw around him and what he now knew of life, it was nothing. New York presented a spectacle of material display such as he had never known existed. The carriages on Fifth Avenue, the dinners at the great hotels, the constant talk of society functions in the newspapers, made his brain dizzy. He was inclined to idle about the streets, to watch the handsomely dressed crowds, to consider the evidences of show and refinement everywhere, and he came to the conclusion that he was not living at all, but existing. Art as he had first dreamed of it, art had seemed not only a road to distinction but also to affluence. Now, as he studied those about him, he found that it was not so. Artists were never tremendously rich, he learned. He remembered reading in Balzac's story "Cousin Betty," of a certain artist of great distinction who had been allowed condescendingly by one of the rich families of Paris to marry a daughter, but it was considered a great come down for her. He had hardly been able to credit the idea at the time, so exalted was his notion of the artist. But now he was beginning to see that it represented the world's treatment of artists. There were in America a few who were very popular—meretriciously so he thought in certain cases—who were said to be earning from ten to fifteen thousand a year. How high would that place them, he asked himself, in that world of real luxury which was made up of the so-called *four hundred*—the people of immense wealth and social position. He had read in the papers that it took from fifteen to twenty-five thousand dollars a year to clothe a débutante. It was nothing uncommon, he heard, for a man to spend from fifteen to twenty dollars on his dinner at the restaurant. The prices he heard that tailors demanded—that dressmakers commanded, the display of jewels and expensive garments at the opera, made the poor little income of an artist look like nothing at all. Miss Finch was constantly telling him of the show and swagger she met with in her circle of acquaintances, for her tact and adaptability had gained her the friendship of a number of society people. Miss Channing, when he came to know her better, made constant references to things she came in contact with—great singers or violinists paid $1000 a night, or the tremendous salaries commanded by the successful opera stars. He began, as he looked at his own meagre little income, to feel shabby again, and run down, much as he had during those first days in Chicago. Why, art, outside the fame, was nothing. It did not make for real living. It made for a kind of mental blooming, which everybody recognized, but you could be a poor, sick, hungry, shabby genius— you actually could. Look at Verlaine, who had recently died in Paris.

A part of this feeling was due to the opening of a golden age of luxury in New York, and the effect the reiterated sight of it was having on Eugene. Huge fortunes had been amassed in the preceding fifty years and now there were thousands of residents in the great new city who were worth anything from one to fifty and in some instances a hundred million dollars. The metropolitan area, particularly Manhattan Island above Fifty-ninth Street, was growing like a weed. Great hotels were being erected in various parts of the so-called "white light" district. There was beginning, just then, the first organized attempt of capital to supply a new need—the modern sumptuous, eight, ten and twelve story apartment house, which was to house the world of newly rich middle class folk who were pouring into New York from every direction. Money was being made in the West, the South and the North, and as soon as those who were making it had sufficient to permit them to live in luxury for the rest of their days they were moving East, occupying these expensive apartments, crowding the great hotels, patronizing the sumptuous restaurants, giving the city its air of spendthrift luxury. All the things which catered to showy material living were beginning to flourish tremendously, art and curio shops, rug shops, decorative companies dealing with the old and the new in hangings, furniture, objects of art; dealers in paintings, jewelry stores, china and glassware houses—anything and everything which goes to make life comfortable and brilliant. Eugene, as he strolled about the city, saw this, felt the change, realized that the drift was toward greater population, greater luxury, greater beauty. His mind was full of the necessity of living *now*. He was young *now*; he was vigorous *now*; he was keen *now*; in a few years he might not be—seventy years was the allotted span and twenty-five of his had already gone. How would it be if he never came into this luxury, was never allowed to enter society, was never permitted to live as wealth was now living! The thought hurt him. He felt an eager desire to tear wealth and fame from the bosom of the world. Life must give him his share. If it did not he would curse it to his dying day. So he felt when he was approaching twenty-six.

The effect of Christina Channing's friendship for him was particularly to emphasize this. She was not so much older than he, was possessed of very much the same temperament, the same hopes and aspirations, and she discerned almost as clearly as he did the current of events. New York was to witness a golden age of luxury. It was already passing into it. Those who rose to distinction in any field, particularly music or the stage, were likely to share in a most notable spectacle of luxury. Christina hoped to. She was sure she would. After a few conversations with Eugene she was inclined to feel that he would. He was so brilliant, so incisive.

"You have such a way with you," she said the second time he came. "You are so commanding. You make me think you can do almost anything you want to."

"Oh, no," he deprecated. "Not as bad as that. I have just as much trouble as anyone getting what I want."

"Oh, but you will though. You have ideas."

It did not take these two long to reach an understanding. They confided to each other their individual histories, with reservations, of course, at first. Christina told him of her musical history, beginning at Hagerstown, Maryland, and he went back to his earliest days in Alexandria. They discussed the differences in parental control to which they had been subject. He learned of her father's business, which was that of oyster farming, and confessed on his part to being the son of a sewing machine agent. They talked of small town influences, early illusions, the different things they had tried to do. She had sung in the local Methodist church, had once thought she would like to be a milliner, had fallen in the hands of a teacher who tried to get her to marry him and she had been on the verge of consenting. Something happened—she went away for the summer, or something of that sort, and changed her mind.

After an evening at the theatre with her, a late supper one night and a third call, to spend a quiet evening in her room, he took her by the hand. She was standing by the piano and he was looking at her cheeks, her large inquiring eyes, her smooth rounded neck and chin.

"You like me," he said suddenly à propos of nothing save the mutual attraction that was always running strong between them.

Without hesitation she nodded her head, though the bright blood mounted to her neck and cheeks.

"You are so lovely to me," he went on, "that words are of no value. I can paint you. Or you can sing me what you are, but mere words won't show it. I have been in love before, but never with anyone like you."

"Are you in love?" she asked naïvely.

"What is this?" he asked and slipped his arms about her, drawing her close.

She turned her head away, leaving her rosy cheek near his lips. He kissed that, then her mouth and her neck. He held her chin and looked into her eyes.

"Be careful," she said, "mamma may come in."

"Hang mamma!" he laughed.

"She'll hang you if she sees you. Mamma would never suspect me of anything like this."

"That shows how little mamma knows of her Christina," he answered.

"She knows enough at that," she confessed gaily. "Oh, if we were only up in the mountains now," she added.

"What mountains," he inquired curiously.

"The Blue Ridge. We have a bungalow up at Florizel. You must come up when we go there next summer."

"Will mamma be there?" he asked.

"And papa," she laughed.

"And I suppose Cousin Annie."

"No, brother George will be."

"Nix for the bungalow," he replied, using a slang word that had become immensely popular.

"Oh, but I know all the country round there. There are some lovely walks and drives." She said this archly, naïvely, suggestively, her bright face lit with an intelligence that seemed perfection.

"Well—such being the case!" he smiled, "and meanwhile—"

"Oh, meanwhile you just have to wait. You see how things are." She nodded her head towards an inside room where Mrs. Channing was lying down with a slight headache. "Mamma doesn't leave me very often."

Eugene did not know exactly how to take Christina. He had never encountered this attitude before. Her directness, in connection with so much talent, such real ability, rather took him by surprise. He did not expect it—did not think she would confess affection for him; did not know just what she meant by speaking in the way she did of the bungalow and Florizel. He was flattered, raised in his own self-esteem. If such a beautiful, talented creature as this could confess her love for him, what a personage he must be. And she was thinking of freer conditions—just what?

He did not want to press the matter too closely then and she was not anxious to have him do so—she preferred to be enigmatic. But there was a light of affection and admiration in her eye which made him very proud and happy with things just as they were.

As she said, there was little chance for love-making under conditions then existing. Her mother was with her most of the time. Christina invited Eugene to come and hear her sing at the Philharmonic Concerts; so once in a great ball-room at the Waldorf-Astoria and again in the imposing auditorium of Carnegie Hall and a third time in the splendid auditorium of the Arion Society, he had the pleasure of seeing her walk briskly to the footlights, the great orchestra waiting, the audience expectant, herself arch, assured—almost defiant, he thought, and so beautiful. When the great house thundered its applause he was basking in one delicious memory of her.

"Last night she had her arms about my neck. Tonight when I call and we are alone she will kiss me. That beautiful, distinguished creature standing there bowing and smiling loves me and no one else. If I were to ask her she would marry me—if I were in a position and had the means."

"If I were in a position—" that thought cut him, for he knew that he was not. He could not marry her. In reality she would not have him knowing how little he made—or would she? He wondered.

CHAPTER XXIII

TOWARDS the end of spring Eugene concluded he would rather go up in the mountains near Christina's bungalow this summer, than back to see Angela. The memory of that precious creature was, under the stress and excitement of metropolitan life, becoming a little tarnished. His recollections of her were as delightful as ever, as redolent of beauty, but he was beginning to wonder. The smart crowd in New York was composed of a different type. Angela was sweet and lovely, but would she fit in?

Meanwhile Miriam Finch with her subtle eclecticism continued her education of Eugene. She was as good as a school. He would sit and listen to her descriptions of plays, her appreciation of books, her summing up of current philosophies, and he would almost feel himself growing. She knew so many people, could tell him where to go to see just such and such an important thing. All the startling personalities, the worth while preachers, the new actors, somehow she knew all about them.

"Now, Eugene," she would exclaim on seeing him, "you positively must go and see Haydon Boyd in 'The Signet,'" or—"see Elmina Deming in her new dances," or—"look at the pictures of Winslow Homer that are being shown at Knoedler's."

She would explain with exactness why she wanted him to see them, what she thought they would do for him. She frankly confessed to him that she considered him a genius and always insisted on knowing what new thing he was doing. When any work of his appeared and she liked it she was swift to tell him. He almost felt as if he owned her room and herself, as if all that she was—her ideas, her friends, her experiences—belonged to him. He could go and draw on them by sitting at her feet or going with her somewhere. When spring came she liked to walk with him, to listen to his comments on nature and life.

"That's splendid!" she would exclaim. "Now, why don't you write that?" or "why don't you paint that?"

He showed her some of his poems once and she had made copies of them and pasted them in a book of what she called exceptional things. So he was coddled by her.

In another way Christina was equally nice. She was fond of telling Eugene how much she thought of him, how nice she thought he was. "You're so big and smarty," she said to him once, affectionately, pinioning his arms and looking into his eyes. "I like the way you part your hair, too! You're kind o' like an artist ought to be!"

"That's the way to spoil me," he replied. "Let me tell you how nice you are. Want to know how nice you are?"

"Uh-uh," she smiled, shaking her head to mean "no."

"Wait till we get to the mountains. I'll tell you." He sealed her lips with his, holding her until her breath was almost gone.

"Oh," she exclaimed; "you're terrible. You're like steel."

"And you're like a big red rose. Kiss me!"

From Christina he learned all about the musical world and musical personalities. He gained an insight into the different forms of music, operatic, symphonic, instrumental. He learned of the different forms of composition, the terminology, the mystery of the vocal cords, the methods of training. He learned of the jealousies within the profession, and what the best musical authorities thought of such and such composers, or singers. He learned how difficult it was to gain a place in the operatic world, how bitterly singers fought each other, how quick the public was to desert a fading star. Christina took it all so unconcernedly that he almost loved her for her courage. She was so wise and so good natured.

"You have to give up a lot of things to be a good artist," she said to Eugene one day. "You can't have the ordinary life, and art too."

"Just what do you mean, Chrissy?" he asked, petting her hand, for they were alone together.

"Why, you can't get married very well and have children, and you can't do much in a social way. Oh, I know they do get married, but sometimes I think it is a mistake. Most of the singers I know don't do so very well tied down by marriage."

"Don't you intend to get married?" asked Eugene curiously.

"I don't know," she replied, realizing what he was driving at. "I'd want to think about that. A woman artist is in a d— of a position anyway," using the letter d only to indicate the word "devil." "She has so many things to think about."

"For instance?"

"Oh, what people think and her family think, and I don't know what all. They ought to· get a new sex for artists—like they have for worker bees."

Eugene smiled. He knew what she was driving at. But he did not know how long she had been debating the problem of her virginity as conflicting with her love of distinction in art.

She was nearly sure she did not want to complicate her art life with marriage. She was almost positive that success on the operatic stage—particularly the great opportunity for the beginner abroad—was complicated with some liaison. Some escaped, but it was not many. She was wondering in her own mind whether she owed it to current morality to remain absolutely pure. It was assumed generally that girls should remain virtuous and marry, but this did not necessarily apply to her—should it apply to the artistic temperament? Her mother and her family troubled her. She was virtuous, but youth and desire had given her some bitter moments. And here was Eugene to emphasize it.

"It is a difficult problem," he said sympathetically, wondering what she would eventually do. He felt keenly that her attitude in regard to marriage affected his relationship to her. Was she wedded to her art at the expense of love?

"It's a big problem," she said and went to the piano to sing.

He half suspected for a little while after this that she might be contemplating some radical step—what, he did not care to say to himself, but he was intensely interested in her problem. This peculiar freedom of thought astonished him—broadened his horizon. He wondered what his sister Myrtle would think of a girl discussing marriage in this way—the to be or not to be of it—what Sylvia? He wondered if many girls did that. Most of the women he had known seemed to think more logically along these lines than he did. He remembered asking Ruby once whether she didn't think illicit love was wrong and hearing her reply, "No. Some people thought it was wrong, but that didn't make it so to her." Here was another girl with another theory.

They talked more of love, and he wondered why she wanted him to come up to Florizel in the summer. She could not be thinking—no, she was too conservative. He began to suspect, though, that she would not marry him—would not marry anyone at present. She merely wanted to be loved for awhile, no doubt.

May came and with it the end of Christina's concert work and voice study so far as New York was concerned. She had been in and out of the city all the winter—to Pittsburgh, Buffalo, Chicago, St. Paul and now after a winter's hard work retired to Hagerstown with her mother for a few weeks prior to leaving for Florizel.

"You ought to come down here," she wrote to Eugene early in June. "There is a sickle moon that shines in my garden and the roses are in bloom. Oh, the odors are so sweet, and

the dew! Some of our windows open out level with the grass
and I sing! I sing!! I sing!!!"

He had a notion to run down but restrained himself, for she
told him that they were leaving in two weeks for the mountains. He had a set of drawings to complete for a magazine
for which they were in a hurry. So he decided to wait till
that was done.

In late June he went up to the Blue Ridge, in Southern Pennsylvania, where Florizel was situated. He thought at first
he would be invited to stay at the Channing bungalow, but
Christina warned him that it would be safer and better for him
to stay at one of the adjoining hotels. There were several
on the slope of adjacent hills at prices ranging from five to
ten dollars a day. Though this was high for Eugene he
decided to go. He wanted to be with this marvellous creature—
to see just what she did mean by wishing they were in the
mountains together.

He had saved some eight hundred dollars, which was in a
savings bank and he withdrew three hundred for his little
outing. He took Christina a very handsomely bound copy of
Villon, of whom she was fond, and several volumes of new verse.
Most of these, chosen according to his most recent mood, were
sad in their poetic texture; they all preached the nothingness
of life, its sadness, albeit the perfection of its beauty.

At this time Eugene had quite reached the conclusion that
there was no hereafter—there was nothing save blind, dark
force moving aimlessly—where formerly he had believed vaguely
in a heaven and had speculated as to a possible hell. His
reading had led him through some main roads and some odd
by-paths of logic and philosophy. He was an omnivorous reader
now and a fairly logical thinker. He had already tackled
Spencer's "First Principles," which had literally torn him up
by the roots and set him adrift and from that had gone back
to Marcus Aurelius, Epictetus, Spinoza and Schopenhauer—men
who ripped out all his private theories and made him wonder
what life really was. He had walked the streets for a long
time after reading some of these things, speculating on the play
of forces, the decay of matter, the fact that thought-forms had
no more stability than cloud-forms. Philosophies came and
went, governments came and went, races arose and disappeared.
He walked into the great natural history museum of New
York once to discover enormous skeletons of prehistoric animals—
things said to have lived two, three, five millions of years
before his day and he marvelled at the forces which produced

them, the indifference, apparently, with which they had been allowed to die. Nature seemed lavish of its types and utterly indifferent to the persistence of anything. He came to the conclusion that he was nothing, a mere shell, a sound, a leaf which had no general significance, and for the time being it almost broke his heart. It tended to smash his egotism, to tear away his intellectual pride. He wandered about dazed, hurt, moody, like a lost child. But he was thinking persistently.

Then came Darwin, Huxley, Tyndall, Lubbock—a whole string of British thinkers who fortified the original conclusions of the others, but showed him a beauty, a formality, a lavishness of form and idea in nature's methods which fairly transfixed him. He was still reading—poets, naturalists, essayists, but he was still gloomy. Life was nothing save dark forces moving aimlessly.

The manner in which he applied this thinking to his life was characteristic and individual. To think that beauty should blossom for a little while and disappear for ever seemed sad. To think that his life should endure but for seventy years and then be no more was terrible. He and Angela were chance acquaintances—chemical affinities—never to meet again in all time. He and Christina, he and Ruby—he and anyone—a few bright hours were all they could have together, and then would come the great silence, dissolution, and he would never be anymore. It hurt him to think of this, but it made him all the more eager to live, to be loved while he was here. If he could only have a lovely girl's arms to shut him in safely always!

It was while he was in this mood that he reached Florizel after a long night's ride, and Christina who was a good deal of a philosopher and thinker herself at times was quick to notice it. She was waiting at the depot with a dainty little trap of her own to take him for a drive.

The trap rolled out along the soft, yellow, dusty roads. The mountain dew was still in the earth though and the dust was heavy with damp and not flying. Green branches of trees hung low over them, charming vistas came into view at every turn. Eugene kissed her, for there was no one to see, twisting her head to kiss her lips at leisure.

"It's a blessed thing this horse is tame or we'd be in for some accident. What makes you so moody?" she said.

"I'm not moody—or am I? I've been thinking a lot of things of late—of you principally."

"Do I make you sad?"

"From one point of view, yes."

"And what is that, sir?" she asked with an assumption of severity.

"You are so beautiful, so wonderful, and life is so short."

"You have only fifty years to love me in," she laughed, calculating his age. "Oh, Eugene, what a boy you are!—Wait a minute," she added after a pause, drawing the horse to a stop under some trees. "Hold these," she said, offering him the reins. He took them and she put her arms about his neck. "Now, you silly," she exclaimed, "I love you, love you, love you! There was never anyone quite like you. Will that help you?" she smiled into his eyes.

"Yes," he answered, "but it isn't enough. Seventy years isn't enough. Eternity isn't enough of life as it is now."

"As it is now," she echoed and then took the reins, for she felt what he felt, the need of persistent youth and persistent beauty to keep it as it should be, and these things would not stay.

CHAPTER XXIV

THE days spent in the mountains were seventeen exactly, and during that time with Christina, Eugene reached a curious exaltation of spirit different from anything he had experienced before. In the first place he had never known a girl like Christina, so beautiful, so perfect physically, so incisive mentally, so full of a fine artistic perception. She was so quick to perceive exactly what he meant. She was so suggestive to him in her own thoughts and feelings. The mysteries of life employed her mind quite as fully as they did his. She thought much of the subtlety of the human body, of its mysterious emotions, of its conscious and subconscious activities and relationships. The passions, the desires, the necessities of life, were as a fine tapestry for her mind to contemplate. She had no time to sit down and formulate her thoughts; she did not want to write—but she worked out through her emotions and through her singing the beautiful and pathetic things she felt. And she could talk in a fine, poetic melancholy vein on occasion, though there was so much courage and strength in her young blood that she was not afraid of any phase of life or what nature might do with the little substance which she called herself, when it should dissolve. "Time and change happeneth to us all," she would quote to Eugene and he would gravely nod his head.

The hotel where he stopped was more pretentious than any he had been previously acquainted with. He had never had so much money in his life before, nor had he ever felt called upon to spend it lavishly. The room he took was—because of what Christina might think—one of the best. He took Christina's suggestion and invited her, her mother and her brother to dinner on several occasions; the remainder of the family had not arrived yet. In return he was invited to breakfast, to lunch and dinner at the bungalow.

Christina showed on his arrival that she had planned to be with him alone as much as possible, for she suggested that they make expeditions to High Hill, to Bold Face, and The Chimney —three surrounding mountains. She knew of good hotels at seven, ten, fifteen miles distance to which they could go by train, or else they drive and return by moonlight. She had selected two or three secluded spots in thickets and groves where the trees gave way to little open spaces of grass, and in these they would string a hammock, scatter their books of verse about and sit down to enjoy the delights of talk and love-making.

Under the influence of this companionship, under cloudless skies and in the heart of the June weather, Christina finally yielded to an arrangement which brought Eugene into a relationship which he had never dreamed possible with her. They had progressed by degrees through all the subtleties of courtship. They had come to discuss the nature of passion and emotion, and had swept aside as negligible the conviction that there was any inherent evil in the most intimate relationship. At last Christina said frankly:

"I don't want to be married. It isn't for me—not until I've thoroughly succeeded, anyhow. I'd rather wait—If I could just have you and singleness too."

"Why do you want to yield yourself to me?" Eugene asked curiously.

"I don't know that I exactly want to. I could do with just your love—if you were satisfied. It's you that I want to make happy. I want to give you anything you want."

"Curious girl," observed her lover, smoothing her high forehead with his hand. "I don't understand you, Christina. I don't know how your mind works. Why should you? You have everything to lose if worst came to worst."

"Oh, no," she smiled. "I'd marry you then."

"But to do this out of hand, because you love me, because you want me to be happy!" he paused.

"I don't understand it either, honey boy," she offered, "I just do."

"But why, if you are willing to do this, you wouldn't prefer to live with me, is what I don't understand."

She took his face between her hands. "I think I understand you better than you do yourself. I don't think you'd be happy married. You might not always love me. I might not always love you. You might come to regret. If we could be happy now you might reach the point where you wouldn't care any more. Then you see I wouldn't be remorseful thinking that we had never known happiness."

"What logic!" he exclaimed. "Do you mean to say you wouldn't care any more?"

"Oh, I'd care, but not in the same way. Don't you see, Eugene, I would have the satisfaction of knowing that even if we did separate you had had the best of me."

It seemed astounding to Eugene that she should talk in this

way—reason this way. What a curious, sacrificial, fatalistic turn of mind. Could a young, beautiful, talented girl really be like this? Would anybody on earth really believe it if they knew? He looked at her and shook his head sorrowfully.

"To think that the quintessence of life should not stay with us always." He sighed.

"No, honey boy," she replied, "you want too much. You think you want it to stay, but you don't. You want it to go. You wouldn't be satisfied to live with me always, I know it. Take what the gods provide and have no regrets. Refuse to think; you can, you know."

Eugene gathered her up in his arms. He kissed her over and over, forgetting in her embrace all the loves he had ever known. She yielded herself to him gladly, joyously, telling him over and over that it made her happy.

"If you could only see how nice you are to me you wouldn't wonder," she explained.

He concluded she was the most wonderful being he had ever known. No woman had ever revealed herself to him so unselfishly in love. No woman he had ever known appeared to have the courage and the insight to go thus simply and directly to what she desired. To hear an artist of her power, a girl of her beauty, discussing calmly whether she should sacrifice her virtue to love; whether marriage in the customary form was good for her art; whether she should take him now when they were young or bow to the conventions and let youth pass, was enough to shock his still trammelled soul. For after all, and despite his desire for personal freedom, his intellectual doubts and mental exceptions, he still had a profound reverence for a home such as that maintained by Jotham Blue and his wife, and for its results in the form of normal, healthy, dutiful children. Nature had no doubt attained to this standard through a long series of difficulties and experiments, and she would not readily relinquish it. Was it really necessary to abandon it entirely? Did he want to see a world in which a woman would take him for a little while as Christina was doing now, and then leave him? His experience here was making him think, throwing his theories and ideas up in the air, making a mess of all the notions he had ever formed about things. He racked his brain over the intricacies of sex and life, sitting on the great verandas of the hotel and wondering over and over just what the answer was, and why he could not like other men be faithful to one woman and be happy. He wondered whether this was really so, and whether he could not. It seemed to

him then that he might. He knew that he did not understand himself very clearly; that he had no grasp on himself at
all as yet—his tendencies, his possibilities.

These days, under such halcyon conditions, made a profound
impression on him. He was struck with the perfection life could
reach at odd moments. These great quiet hills, so uniform in
their roundness, so green, so peaceful, rested his soul. He
and Christina climbed, one day, two thousand feet to a ledge
which jutted out over a valley and commanded what seemed
to him the kingdoms and the powers of the earth—vast stretches
of green land and subdivided fields, little cottage settlements
and towns, great hills that stood up like friendly brothers to
this one in the distance.

"See that man down in that yard," said Christina, pointing
to a speck of a being chopping wood in a front space serving as
a garden to a country cottage fully a mile distant.

"Where?" asked Eugene.

"See where that red barn is, just this side of that clump of
trees?—don't you see? there, where the cows are in that field."

"I don't see any cows."

"Oh, Eugene, what's the matter with your eyes?"

"Oh, now I see," he replied, squeezing her fingers. "He looks
like a cockroach, doesn't he?"

"Yes," she laughed.

"How wide the earth is and how small we are. Now think
of that speck with all his hopes and ambitions—all the machinery
of his brain and nerves and tell me whether any God can care.
How can He, Christina?"

"He can't care for any one particular speck much, sweet.
He might care for the idea of man or a race of men as a
whole. Still, I'm not sure, honey. All I know is that I'm
happy now."

"And I," he echoed.

Still they dug at this problem, the question of the origin of
life—its why. The tremendous and wearisome age of the
earth; the veritable storms of birth and death that seemed to
have raged at different periods, held them in discussion.

"We can't solve it, Eugenio mio," she laughed. "We might
as well go home. Poor, dear mamma will be wondering where
her Christina is. You know I think she suspects that I'm
falling in love with you. She doesn't care how many men fall
in love with me, but if I show the least sign of a strong preference she begins to worry."

"Have there been many preferences?" he inquired.

"No, but don't ask. What difference does it make? Oh, Eugene, what difference does it make? I love you now."

"I don't know what difference it makes," he replied, "only there is an ache that goes with the thought of previous experience. I can't tell you why it is. It just is."

She looked thoughtfully away.

"Anyhow, no man ever was to me before what you have been. Isn't that enough? Doesn't that speak?"

"Yes, yes, sweet, it does. Oh, yes it does. Forgive me. I won't grieve any more."

"Don't, please," she said, "you hurt me as much as you hurt yourself."

There were evenings when he sat on some one of the great verandas and watched them trim and string the interspaces between the columns with soft, glowing, Chinese lanterns, preparatory to the evening's dancing. He loved to see the girls and men of the summer colony arrive, the former treading the soft grass in filmy white gowns and white slippers, the latter in white ducks and flannels, gaily chatting as they came. Christina would come to these affairs with her mother and brother, beautifully clad in white linen or lawns and laces, and he would be beside himself with chagrin that he had not practised dancing to the perfection of the art. He could dance now, but not like her brother or scores of men he saw upon the waxen floor. It hurt him. At times he would sit all alone after his splendid evenings with his love, dreaming of the beauty of it all. The stars would be as a great wealth of diamond seed flung from the lavish hand of an aimless sower. The hills would loom dark and tall. There was peace and quiet everywhere.

"Why may not life be always like this?" he would ask, and then he would answer himself out of his philosophy that it would become deadly after awhile, as does all unchanging beauty. The call of the soul is for motion, not peace. Peace after activity for a little while, then activity again. So must it be. He understood that.

Just before he left for New York, Christina said to him:

"Now, when you see me again I will be Miss Channing of New York. You will be Mr. Witla. We will almost forget that we were ever here together. We will scarcely believe that we have seen what we have seen and done what we have done."

"But, Christina, you talk as though everything were over. It isn't, is it?"

"We can't do anything like this in New York," she sighed. "I haven't time and you must work."

There was a shade of finality in her tone.

"Oh, Christina, don't talk so. I can't think that way. Please don't."

"I won't," she said. "We'll see. Wait till I get back."

He kissed her a dozen farewells and at the door held her close once more.

"Will you forsake me?" he asked.

"No, you will forsake me. But remember, dear! Don't you see? You've had all. Let me be your wood nymph. The rest is commonplace."

He went back to his hotel with an ache in his heart, for he knew they had gone through all they ever would. She had had her summer with him. She had given him of herself fully. She wanted to be free to work now. He could not understand it, but he knew it to be so.

CHAPTER XXV

IT is a rather dreary thing to come back into the hot city in the summer after a period of beauty in the mountains. The quiet of the hills was in Eugene's mind, the glisten and babble of mountain streams, the soar and poise of hawks and buzzards and eagles sailing the crystal blue. He felt lonely and sick for awhile, out of touch with work and with practical life generally. There were little souvenirs of his recent happiness in the shape of letters and notes from Christina, but he was full of the premonition of the end which had troubled him on leaving.

He must write to Angela. He had not thought of her all the time he had been gone. He had been in the habit of writing to her every third or fourth day at least; while of late his letters had been less passionate they had remained fairly regular. But now this sudden break coming—it was fully three weeks— made her think he must be ill, although she had begun to feel also that he might be changing. His letters had grown steadily less reminiscent of the joys they had experienced together and of the happiness they were anticipating, and more inclined to deal with the color and character of city life and of what he hoped to achieve. Angela was inclined to excuse much of this on the grounds of the special effort he was making to achieve distinction and a living income for themselves. But it was hard to explain three weeks of silence without something quite serious having happened.

Eugene understood this. He tried to explain it on the grounds of illness, stating that he was now up and feeling much better. But when his explanation came, it had the hollow ring of insincerity. Angela wondered what the truth could be. Was he yielding to the temptation of that looser life that all artists were supposed to lead? She wondered and worried, for time was slipping away and he was setting no definite date for their much discussed nuptials.

The trouble with Angela's position was that the delay involved practically everything which was important in her life. She was five years older than Eugene. She had long since lost that atmosphere of youth and buoyancy which is so characteristic of a girl between eighteen and twenty-two. Those few short years following, when the body of maidenhood blooms like a rose and there is about it the freshness and color of all rich, new, lush life, were behind her. Ahead was that persistent decline towards something harder, shrewder and less beautiful. In the case of some persons the decline is slow and the fragrance of youth lingers for years, the artifices of the dressmaker, the chemist, and the jeweller being but little needed. In others it is fast and no contrivance will stay the ravages of a restless, eager, dissatisfied soul. Sometimes art combines with slowness of decay to make a woman of almost perennial charm, loveliness of mind matching loveliness of body, and taste and tact supplementing both. Angela was fortunate in being slow to fade and she had a loveliness of imagination and emotion to sustain her; but she had also a restless, anxious disposition of mind which, if it had not been stayed by the kindly color of her home life and by the fortunate or unfortunate intervention of Eugene at a time when she considered her ideal of love to have fairly passed out of the range of possibility, would already have set on her face the signs of old maidenhood. She was not of the newer order of femininity, eager to get out in the world and follow some individual line of self-development and interest. Rather was she a home woman wanting some one man to look after and love. The wonder and beauty of her dream of happiness with Eugene now made the danger of its loss and the possible compulsory continuance of a humdrum, underpaid, backwoods existence, heart-sickening.

Meanwhile, as the summer passed, Eugene was casually enlarging his acquaintance with women. MacHugh and Smite had gone back home for the summer, and it was a relief from his loneliness to encounter one day in an editorial office, Norma Whitmore, a dark, keen, temperamental and moody but brilliant writer and editor who, like others before her, took a fancy to Eugene. She was introduced to him by Jans Jansen, Art Director of the paper, and after some light banter she offered to show him her office.

She led the way to a little room no larger than six by eight where she had her desk. Eugene noticed that she was lean and sallow, about his own age or older, and brilliant and vivacious. Her hands took his attention for they were thin, shapely and artistic. Her eyes burned with a peculiar lustre and her loose-fitting clothes were draped artistically about her. A conversation sprang up as to his work, which she knew and admired, and he was invited to her apartment. He looked at Norma with an unconsciously speculative eye.

Christina was out of the city, but the memory of her made

it impossible for him to write to Angela in his old vein of devotion. Nevertheless he still thought of her as charming. He thought that he ought to write more regularly. He thought that he ought pretty soon to go back and marry her. He was approaching the point where he could support her in a studio if they lived economically. But he did not want to exactly.

He had known her now for three years. It was fully a year and a half since he had seen her last. In the last year his letters had been less and less about themselves and more and more about everything else. He was finding the conventional love letters difficult. But he did not permit himself to realize just what that meant—to take careful stock of his emotions. That would have compelled him to the painful course of deciding that he could not marry her, and asking her to be released from his promise. He did not want to do that. Instead he parleyed, held by pity for her passing youth and her undeniable affection for him, by his sense of the unfairness of having taken up so much of her time to the exclusion of every other person who might have proposed to her, by sorrow for the cruelty of her position in being left to explain to her family that she had been jilted. He hated to hurt any person's feelings. He did not want to be conscious of the grief of any person who had come to suffering through him and he could not make them suffer very well and not be conscious. He was too tender hearted. He had pledged himself to Angela, giving her a ring, begging her to wait, writing her fulsome letters of protest and desire. Now, after three years, to shame her before her charming family —old Jotham, her mother, her sisters and brothers—it seemed a cruel thing to do, and he did not care to contemplate it.

Angela, with her morbid, passionate, apprehensive nature, did not fail to see disaster looming in the distance. She loved Eugene passionately and the pent-up fires of her nature had been waiting all these years the warrant to express their ardor which marriage alone could confer. Eugene, by the charm of his manner and person, no less than by the sensuous character of some of his moods and the subtleties and refinements of his references to the ties of sex, had stirred her to anticipate a perfect fruition of her dreams, and she was now eager for that fruition almost to the point of being willing to sacrifice virginity itself. The remembrance of the one significant scene between her and Eugene tormented her. She felt that if his love was to terminate in indifference now it would have been better to have yielded then. She wished that she had not tried to save

herself. Perhaps there would have been a child, and he would
have been true to her out of a sense of sympathy and duty. At
least she would have had that crowning glory of womanhood,
ardent union with her lover, and if worst had come to worst she
could have died.

She thought of the quiet little lake near her home, its glassy
bosom a mirror to the sky, and how, in case of failure, she
would have looked lying on its sandy bottom, her pale hair
diffused by some aimless motion of the water, her eyes sealed by
the end of consciousness, her hands folded. Her fancy outran
her daring. She would not have done this, but she could dream
about it, and it made her distress all the more intense.

As time went by and Eugene's ardor did not revive, this
problem of her love became more harrassing and she began to
wonder seriously what she could do to win him back to her.
He had expressed such a violent desire for her on his last
visit, had painted his love in such glowing terms that she
felt convinced he must love her still, though absence and the
excitements of city life had dimmed the memory of her temporarily. She remembered a line in a comic opera which she
and Eugene had seen together: "Absence is the dark room in
which lovers develop negatives" and this seemed a case in
point. If she could get him back, if he could be near her again,
his old fever would develop and she would then find some way
of making him take her, perhaps. It did not occur to her
quite clearly just how this could be done at this time but some
vague notion of self-immolation was already stirring vaguely
and disturbingly in her brain.

The trying and in a way disheartening conditions of her
home went some way to sustain this notion. Her sister Marietta
was surrounded by a score of suitors who were as eager for her
love as a bee is for the honey of a flower, and Angela could see
that they were already looking upon herself as an elderly
chaperon. Her mother and father watched her going about her
work and grieved because so good a girl should be made to
suffer for want of a proper understanding. She could not conceal
her feelings entirely and they could see at times that she was
unhappy. She could see that they saw it. It was hard to
have to explain to her sisters and brothers, who occasionally
asked after Eugene, that he was doing all right, and never
be able to say that he was coming for her some day soon.

At first Marietta had been envious of her. She thought
she would like to win Eugene for herself, and only consideration for Angela's age and the fact that she had not been

so much sought after had deterred her. Now that Eugene was obviously neglecting her, or at least delaying beyond any reasonable period, she was deeply sorry. Once, before she had grown into the age of courtship, she had said to Angela: "I'm going to be nice to the men. You're too cold. You'll never get married." And Angela had realized that it was not a matter of "too cold," but an innate prejudice against most of the types she met. And then the average man did not take to her. She could not spur herself to pleasure in their company. It took a fire like Eugene's to stir her mightily, and once having known that she could brook no other. Marietta realized this too. Now because of these three years she had cut herself off from other men, particularly the one who had been most attentive to her—faithful Victor Dean. The one thing that might save Angela from being completely ignored was a spirit of romance which kept her young in looks as in feelings.

With the fear of desertion in her mind Angela began to hint in her letters to Eugene that he should come back to see her, to express the hope in her letters that their marriage need not— because of any difficulty of establishing himself—be postponed much longer. She said to him over and over that she could be happy with him in a cottage and that she so longed to see him again. Eugene began to ask himself what he wanted to do.

The fact that on the passional side Angela appealed to him more than any woman he had ever known was a saving point in her favor at this juncture. There was a note in her make-up which was stronger, deeper, more suggestive of joy to come than anything he had found elsewhere. He remembered keenly the wonderful days he had spent with her—the one significant night when she begged him to save her against herself. All the beauty of the season with which she was surrounded at that time; the charm of her family, the odor of flowers and the shade of trees served to make a setting for her delightfulness which still endured with him as fresh as yesterday. Now, without having completed that romance—a very perfect flower— could he cast it aside?

At this time he was not entangled with any woman. Miriam Finch was too conservative and intellectual; Norma Whitmore not attractive enough. As for some other charming examples of femininity whom he had met here and there, he had not been drawn to them or they to him. Emotionally he was lonely and this for him was always a very susceptible mood. He could not make up his mind that the end had come with Angela.

It so happened that Marietta, after watching her sister's

love affair some time, reached the conclusion that she ought to try to help her. Angela was obviously concealing a weariness of heart which was telling on her peace of mind and her sweetness of disposition. She was unhappy and it grieved her sister greatly. The latter loved her in a whole-hearted way, in spite of the fact that their affections might possibly have clashed over Eugene, and she thought once of writing in a sweet way and telling him how things were. She thought he was good and kind, that he loved Angela, that perhaps he was delaying as her sister said until he should have sufficient means to marry well, and that if the right word were said now he would cease chasing a phantom fortune long enough to realize that it were better to take Angela while they were still young, than to wait until they were so old that the romance of marriage would for them be over. She revolved this in her mind a long time, picturing to herself how sweet Angela really was, and finally nerved herself to pen the following letter, which she sent.

"Dear Eugene:
    You will be surprised to get a letter from me and I want you to promise me that you will never say anything about it to anyone—above all never to Angela. Eugene, I have been watching her for a long time now and I know she is not happy. She is so desperately in love with you. I notice when a letter does not come promptly she is downcast and I can't help seeing that she is longing to have you here with her. Eugene, why don't you marry Angela? She is lovely and attractive now and she is as good as she is beautiful. She doesn't want to wait for a fine house and luxuries—no girl wants to do that, Eugene, when she loves as I know Angela does you. She would rather have you now when you are both young and can enjoy life than any fine house or nice things you might give her later. Now, I haven't talked to her at all, Eugene—never one word—and I know it would hurt her terribly if she thought I had written to you. She would never forgive me. But I can't help it. I can't bear to see her grieving and longing, and I know that when you know you will come and get her. Don't ever indicate in any way, please, that I wrote to you. Don't write to me unless you want to very much. I would rather you didn't. And tear up this letter. But do come for her soon, Eugene, please do. She wants you. And she will make you a perfectly wonderful wife for she is a wonderful girl. We all love her so—papa and mamma and all. I hope you will forgive me. I can't help it.   "With love I am yours,
                                                "MARIETTA."

When Eugene received this letter he was surprised and astonished, but also distressed for himself and Angela and Marietta and the whole situation. The tragedy of this situation appealed to him perhaps as much from the dramatic as from the personal point of view. Little Angela, with her yellow hair and classic face. What a shame that they could not be together as she wished; as really, in a way, he wished. She was beautiful—no doubt of that. And there was a charm about her which was as alluring as that of any girl barring the intellectually exceptional. Her emotions in a way were deeper than those of Miriam Finch and Christina Channing. She could not reason about them—that was all. She just felt them. He saw all the phases of her anguish—the probable attitude of her parents, her own feelings at being looked at by them, the way her friends wondered. It was a shame, no doubt of that—a cruel situation. Perhaps he had better go back. He could be happy with her. They could live in a studio and no doubt things would work out all right. Had he better be cruel and not go? He hated to think of it.

Anyhow he did not answer Marietta's letter, and he did tear it up into a thousand bits, as she requested. "If Angela knew no doubt she would feel wretched," he thought.

In the meanwhile Angela was thinking, and her brooding led her to the conclusion that it might be advisable, if ever her lover came back, to yield herself in order that he might feel compelled to take her. She was no reasoner about life in any big sense. Her judgment of affairs was more confused at this time than at a later period. She had no clear conception of how foolish any trickery of this sort would be. She loved Eugene, felt that she must have him, felt that she would be willing to die rather than lose him and the thought of trickery came only as a last resource. If he refused her she was determined on one thing—the lake. She would quit this dreary world where love was crossed with despair in its finest moments; she would forget it all. If only there were rest and silence on the other side that would be enough.

The year moved on toward spring and because of some note of this, reiterated in pathetic phrases, he came to feel that he must go back. Marietta's letter preyed on his mind. The intensity of Angela's attitude made him feel that something desperate would happen. He could not, in cold blood, sit down and write her that he would not see her any more. The impressions of Blackwood were too fresh in his mind—the summer incense and green beauty of the world in which she lived. He wrote in April that he would come again in June, and Angela was beside herself with joy.

One of the things which helped Eugene to this conclusion was the fact that Christina Channing was not coming back from

Europe that year. She had written a few times during the winter, but very guardedly. A casual reader could not have drawn from what she said that there had ever been anything between them. He had written much more ardently, of course, but she had chosen to ignore his eager references, making him feel by degrees that he was not to know much of her in the future. They were going to be good friends, but not necessarily lovers nor eventually husband and wife. It irritated him to think she could be so calm about a thing which to him seemed so important. It hurt his pride to think she could so deliberately throw him over. Finally he began to be incensed, and then Angela's fidelity appeared in a much finer light. There was a girl who would not treat him so. She really loved him. She was faithful and true. So his promised trip began to look much more attractive, and by June he was in a fever to see her.

CHAPTER XXVI

THE beautiful June weather arrived and with it Eugene took his departure once more for Blackwood. He was in a peculiar mood, for while he was anxious to see Angela again it was with the thought that perhaps he was making a mistake. A notion of fatality was beginning to run through his mind. Perhaps he was destined to take her! and yet, could anything be more ridiculous? He could decide. He had deliberately decided to go back there—or had he? He admitted to himself that his passion was drawing him—in fact he could not see that there was anything much in love outside of passion. Desire! Wasn't that all that pulled two people together? There was some little charm of personality above that, but desire was the keynote. And if the physical attraction were strong enough, wasn't that sufficient to hold two people together? Did you really need so much more? It was logic based on youth, enthusiasm and inexperience, but it was enough to hold him for the time being—to soothe him. To Angela he was not drawn by any of the things which drew him to Miriam Finch and Norma Whitmore, nor was there the wonderful art of Christina Channing. Still he was going.

His interest in Norma Whitmore had increased greatly as the winter passed. In this woman he had found an intellect as broadening and refining as any he had encountered. Her taste for the exceptional in literature and art was as great as that of anyone he had ever known and it was just as individual. She ran to impressive realistic fiction in literature and to the kind of fresh-from-the-soil art which Eugene represented. Her sense of just how big and fresh was the thing he was trying to do was very encouraging, and she was carrying the word about town to all her friends that he was doing it. She had even gone so far as to speak to two different art dealers asking them why they had not looked into what seemed to her his perfectly wonderful drawings.

"Why, they're astonishing in their newness," she told Eberhard Zang, one of the important picture dealers on Fifth Avenue. She knew him from having gone there to borrow pictures for reproduction.

"Witla! Witla!" he commented in his conservative German way, rubbing his chin, "I doand remember seeing anything by him."

"Of course you don't," replied Norma persistently. "He's new, I tell you. He hasn't been here so very long. You get *Truth* for some week in last month—I forget which one—and see that picture of Greeley Square. It will show you what I mean."

"Witla! Witla!" repeated Zang, much as a parrot might fix a sound in its memory. "Tell him to come in here and see me some day. I should like to see some of his things."

"I will," said Norma, genially. She was anxious to have Eugene go, but he was more anxious to get a lot of things done before he had an exhibition. He did not want to risk an impression with anything short of a rather extensive series. And his collection of views was not complete at that time. Besides he had a much more significant art dealer in mind.

He and Norma had reached the point by this time where they were like brother and sister, or better yet, two good men friends. He would slip his arm about her waist when entering her rooms and was free to hold her hands or pat her on the arm or shoulder. There was nothing more than strong good feeling on his part, while on hers a burning affection might have been inspired, but his genial, brotherly attitude convinced her that it was useless. He had never told her of any of his other women friends and he was wondering as he rode west how she and Miriam Finch would take his marriage with Angela, supposing that he ever did marry her. As for Christina Channing, he did not want to think—really did not dare to think of her very much. Some sense of lost beauty came to him out of that experience—a touch of memory that had a pang in it.

Chicago in June was just a little dreary to him with its hurry of life, its breath of past experience, the Art Institute, the *Daily Globe* building, the street and house in which Ruby had lived. He wondered about her (as he had before) the moment he neared the city, and had a strong desire to go and look her up. Then he visited the *Globe* offices, but Mathews had gone. Genial, cheerful Jerry had moved to Philadelphia recently, taking a position on the Philadelphia *North American,* leaving Howe alone, more finicky and picayune than ever. Goldfarb, of course, was gone and Eugene felt out of it. He was glad to take the train for Blackwood, for he felt lonesome. He left the city with quite an ache for old times in his heart and the feeling that life was a jumble of meaningless, strange and pathetic things.

"To think that we should grow old," he pondered, "that things that were as real as these things were to me, should become mere memories."

The time just before he reached Blackwood was one of great emotional, stress for Angela. Now she was to learn whether he really loved her as much as he had. She was to feel the joy of his presence, the subtle influence of his attitude. She was to find whether she could hold him or not. Marietta, who on hearing that he was coming, had rather plumed herself that her letter had had something to do with it, was afraid that her sister would not make good use of this opportune occasion. She was anxious that Angela should look her best, and made suggestions as to things she might wear, games she might play (they had installed tennis and croquet as part of the home pleasures since he had been there last) and places they might go to. Marietta was convinced that Angela was not artful enough—not sufficiently subtle in her presentation of her charms. He could be made to feel very keen about her if she dressed right and showed herself to the best advantage. Marietta herself intended to keep out of the way as much as possible when Eugene arrived, and to appear at great disadvantage in the matter of dress and appearance when seen; for she had become a perfect beauty and was a breaker of hearts without conscious effort.

"You know that string of coral beads I have, Angel Face," she asked Angela one morning some ten days before Eugene arrived. "Wear them with that tan linen dress of mine and your tan shoes some day for Eugene. You'll look stunning in those things and he'll like you. Why don't you take the new buggy and drive over to Blackwood to meet him? That's it. You must meet him."

"Oh, I don't think I want to, Babyette," she replied. She was afraid of this first impression. She did not want to appear to run after him. Babyette was a nickname which had been applied to Marietta in childhood and had never been dropped.

"Oh, pshaw, Angel Face, don't be so backward! You're the shyest thing I know. Why that's nothing. He'll like you all the better for treating him just a little smartly. You do that now, will you?"

"I can't," replied Angela. "I can't do it that way. Let him come over here first; then I'll drive him over some afternoon."

"Oh, Angel Face! Well, anyhow, when he comes you must wear that little rose flowered house dress and put a wreath of green leaves in your hair."

"Oh, I won't do anything of the sort, Babyette," exclaimed Angela.

"Yes, you will," replied her sister. "Now you just have to do what I tell you for once. That dress looks beautiful on you and the wreath will make it perfect."

"It isn't the dress. I know that's nice. It's the wreath."

Marietta was incensed by this bit of pointless reserve.

"Oh, Angela," she exclaimed, "don't be so silly. You're older than I am, but I know more about men in a minute than you'll ever know. Don't you want him to like you? You'll have to be more daring—goodness! Lots of girls would go a lot farther than that."

She caught her sister about the waist and looked into her eyes. "Now you've got to wear it," she added finally, and Angela understood that Marietta wanted her to entice Eugene by any means in her power to make him declare himself finally and set a definite date or take her back to New York with him.

There were other conversations in which a trip to the lake was suggested, games of tennis, with Angela wearing her white tennis suit and shoes, a country dance which might be got up—there were rumors of one to be given in the new barn of a farmer some seven miles away. Marietta was determined that Angela should appear youthful, gay, active, just the things which she knew instinctively would fascinate Eugene.

Finally Eugene came. He arrived at Blackwood at noon. Despite her objections Angela met him, dressed smartly and, as urged by Marietta, carrying herself with an air. She hoped to impress Eugene with a sense of independence, but when she saw him stepping down from the train in belted corduroy travelling suit with a grey English travelling cap, carrying a green leather bag of the latest design, her heart misgave her. He was so worldly now, so experienced. You could see by his manner that this country place meant little or nothing to him. He had tasted of the world at large.

Angela had stayed in her buggy at the end of the depot platform and she soon caught Eugene's eye and waved to him. He came briskly forward.

"Why, sweet," he exclaimed, "here you are. How nice you look!" He jumped up beside her, surveying her critically and she could feel his examining glance. After the first pleasant impression he sensed the difference between his new world and hers and was a little depressed by it. She was a little older, no doubt of that. You cannot hope and yearn and worry for three years and not show it. And yet she was fine and tender and sympathetic and emotional. He felt all this. It hurt him a little for her sake and his too.

"Well, how have you been?" he asked. They were in the confines of the village and no demonstration could be made. Until the quiet of a country road could be reached all had to be formal.

"Oh, just the same, Eugene, longing to see you."

She looked into his eyes and he felt the impact of that emotional force which governed her when she was near him. There was something in the chemistry of her being which roused to blazing the ordinarily dormant forces of his sympathies. She tried to conceal her real feeling—to pretend gaiety and enthusiasm, but her eyes betrayed her. Something roused in him now at her look—a combined sense of emotion and desire.

"It's so fine to be out in the country again," he said, pressing her hand, for he was letting her drive. "After the city, to see you and the green fields!" He looked about at the little one-storey cottages, each with a small plot of grass, a few trees, a neat confining fence. After New York and Chicago, a village like this was quaint.

"Do you love me just as much as ever?"

She nodded her head. They reached a strip of yellow road, he asking after her father, her mother, her brothers and sisters, and when he saw that they were unobserved he slipped his arm about her and drew her head to him.

"Now we can," he said.

She felt the force of his desire but she missed that note of adoration which had seemed to characterize his first lovemaking. How true it was he had changed! He must have. The city had made her seem less significant. It hurt her to think that life should treat her so. But perhaps she could win him back—could hold him anyhow.

They drove over toward Okoonee, a little crossroads settlement, near a small lake of the same name, a place which was close to the Blue house, and which the Blue's were wont to speak of as "home." On the way Eugene learned that her youngest brother David was a cadet at West Point now and doing splendidly. Samuel had become western freight agent of the Great Northern and was on the way to desirable promotion. Benjamin had completed his law studies and was practising

in Racine. He was interested in politics and was going to
run for the state legislature. Marietta was still the gay carefree girl she had always been, not at all inclined to choose yet
among her many anxious suitors. Eugene thought of her letter
to him—wondered if she would look her thoughts into his eyes
when he saw her.

"Oh, Marietta," Angela replied when Eugene asked after
her, "she's just as dangerous as ever. She makes all the men
make love to her."

Eugene smiled. Marietta was always a pleasing thought to
him. He wished for the moment that it was Marietta instead of Angela that he was coming to see.

She was as shrewd as she was kind in this instance. Her
appearance on meeting Eugene was purposely indifferent and her
attitude anything but coaxing and gay. At the same time
she suffered a genuine pang of feeling, for Eugene appealed
to her. If it were anybody but Angela, she thought, how she
would dress and how quickly she would be coquetting with
him. Then his love would be won by her and she felt that she
could hold it. She had great confidence in her ability to keep
any man, and Eugene was a man she would have delighted
to hold. As it was she kept out of his way, took sly glances
at him here and there, wondered if Angela would truly win
him. She was so anxious for Angela's sake. Never, never,
she told herself, would she cross her sister's path.

At the Blue homestead he was received as cordially as before.
After an hour it quite brought back the feeling of three years
before. These open fields, this old house and its lovely lawn, all
served to awaken the most poignant sensations. One of Marietta's beaux, over from Waukesha, appeared after Eugene had
greeted Mrs. Blue and Marietta, and the latter persuaded him to
play a game of tennis with Angela. She invited Eugene to
make it a four with her, but not knowing how he refused.

Angela changed to her tennis suit and Eugene opened his
eyes to her charms. She was very attractive on the court, quick,
flushed, laughing. And when she laughed she had a charming
way of showing her even, small, white teeth. She quite awakened
a feeling of interest—she looked so dainty and frail. When
he saw her afterward in the dark, quiet parlor, he gathered her
to his heart with much of the old ardour. She felt the quick
change of feeling. Marietta was right. Eugene loved gaiety
and color. Although on the way home she had despaired this
was much more promising.

Eugene rarely entered on anything half heartedly. If interested at all he was greatly interested. He could so yield himself to the glamour of a situation as to come finally to believe that he was something which he was not. Thus, now he was beginning to accept this situation as Angela and Marietta wished he should, and to see her in somewhat the old light. He overlooked things which in his New York studio, surrounded by the influences which there modified his judgment, he would have seen. Angela was not young enough for him. She was not liberal in her views. She was charming, no doubt of that, but he could not bring her to an understanding of his casual acceptance of life. She knew nothing of his real disposition and he did not tell her. He played the part of a seemingly single-minded Romeo, and as such he was from a woman's point of view beautiful to contemplate. In his own mind he was coming to see that he was fickle but he still did not want to admit it to himself.

There was a night of stars after an evening of June perfection. At five old Jotham came in from the fields, as dignified and patriarchal as ever. He greeted Eugene with a hearty handshake, for he admired him. "I see some of your work now and then," he said, "in these monthly magazines. It's fine. There's a young minister down here near the lake that's very anxious to meet you. He likes to get hold of anything you do, and I always send the books down as soon as Angela gets through with them."

He used the words books and magazines interchangeably, and spoke as though they were not much more important to him than the leaves of the trees, as indeed, they were not. To a mind used to contemplating the succession of crops and seasons, all life with its multitudinous interplay of shapes and forms seemed passing shadows. Even men were like leaves that fall.

Eugene was drawn to old Jotham as a filing to a magnet. His was just the type of mind that appealed to him, and Angela gained by the radiated glory of her father. If he was so wonderful she must be something above the average of womanhood. Such a man could not help but produce exceptional children.

Left alone together it was hardly possible for Angela and Eugene not to renew the old relationship on the old basis. Having gone as far as he had the first time it was natural that he should wish to go as far again and further. After dinner, when she turned to him from her room, arrayed in a soft evening dress of clinging texture—somewhat low in the neck by request of Marietta, who had helped her to dress—Eugene was con-

scious of her emotional perturbation. He himself was distraught,
for he did not know what he would do—how far he would dare
to trust himself. He was always troubled when dealing with his
physical passion, for it was a raging lion at times. It seemed
to overcome him quite as a drug might or a soporific fume. He
would mentally resolve to control himself, but unless he instantly
fled there was no hope, and he did not seem able to run away.
He would linger and parley, and in a few moments it was master
and he was following its behest blindly, desperately, to the point
almost of exposure and destruction.

Tonight when Angela came back he was cogitating, wondering
what it might mean. Should he? Would he marry her? Could
he escape? They sat down to talk, but presently he drew her to
him. It was the old story—moment after moment of increasing
feeling. Presently she, from the excess of longing and waiting
was lost to all sense of consideration. And he—

"I shall have to go away, Eugene," she pleaded, when he
carried her recklessly into his room, "if anything happens. I
cannot stay here."

"Don't talk," he said. "You can come to me."

"You mean it, Eugene, surely?" she begged.

"As sure as I'm holding you here," he replied.

At midnight Angela lifted frightened, wondering, doubting
eyes, feeling herself the most depraved creature. Two pictures
were in her mind alternately and with pendulum-like reiteration.
One was a composite of a marriage altar and a charming New
York studio with friends coming in to see them much as he had
often described to her. The other was of the still blue waters
of Okoonee with herself lying there pale and still. Yes, she
would die if he did not marry her now. Life would not be
worth while. She would not force him. She would slip out
some night when it was too late and all hope had been abandoned
—when exposure was near—and the next day they would find
her.

Little Marietta—how she would cry. And old Jotham—she
could see him, but he would never be really sure of the truth.
And her mother. "Oh God in heaven," she thought, "how
hard life is! How terrible it can be."

CHAPTER XXVII

THE atmosphere of the house after this night seemed charged with reproach to Eugene, although it took on no semblance of reality in either look or word. When he awoke in the morning and looked through the half closed shutters to the green world outside he felt a sense of freshness and of shame. It was cruel to come into such a home as this and do a thing as mean as he had done. After all, philosophy or no philosophy, didn't a fine old citizen like Jotham, honest, upright, genuine in his moral point of view and his observance of the golden rule, didn't he deserve better from a man whom he so sincerely admired? Jotham had been so nice to him. Their conversations together were so kindly and sympathetic. Eugene felt that Jotham believed him to be an honest man. He knew he had that appearance. He was frank, genial, considerate, not willing to condemn anyone—but this sex question—that was where he was weak. And was not the whole world keyed to that? Did not the decencies and the sanities of life depend on right moral conduct? Was not the world dependent on how the homes were run? How could anyone be good if his mother and father had not been good before him? How could the children of the world expect to be anything if people rushed here and there holding illicit relations? Take his sister Myrtle, now—would he have wanted her rifled in this manner? In the face of this question he was not ready to say exactly what he wanted or was willing to countenance. Myrtle was a free agent, as was every other girl. She could do as she pleased. It might not please him exactly but—he went round and round from one problem to another, trying to untie this Gordian knot. One thing, this home had appeared sweet and clean when he came into it; now it was just a little tarnished, and by him! Or was it? His mind was always asking this question. There was nothing that he was actually accepting as true any more. He was going round in a ring asking questions of this proposition and that. Are you true? And are you true? And are you true? And all the while he was apparently not getting anywhere. It puzzled him, this life. Sometimes it shamed him. This deed shamed him. And he asked himself whether he was wrong to be ashamed or not. Perhaps he was just foolish. Was not life made for living, not worrying? He had not created his passions and desires.

He threw open the shutters and there was the bright day. Everything was so green outside, the flowers in bloom, the trees casting a cool, lovely shade, the birds twittering. Bees were humming. He could smell the lilacs. "Dear God," he exclaimed, throwing his arms above his head, "How lovely life is! How beautiful! Oh!" He drew in a deep breath of the flower and privet laden air. If only he could live always like this—for ever and ever.

When he had sponged himself with cold water and dressed, putting on a soft negligée shirt with turn-down collar and dark flowing tie, he issued forth clean and fresh. Angela was there to greet him. Her face was pale but she looked intensely sweet because of her sadness.

"There, there," he said, touching her chin, "less of that now!"

"I told them that I had a headache," she said. "So I have. Do you understand?"

"I understand your headache," he laughed. "But everything is all right—very much all right. Isn't this a lovely day!"

"Beautiful," replied Angela sadly.

"Cheer up," he insisted. "Don't worry. Everything is coming out fine." He walked to the window and stared out.

"I'll have your breakfast ready in a minute," she said, and, pressing his hand, left him.

Eugene went out to the hammock. He was so deliciously contented and joyous now that he saw the green world about him, that he felt that everything was all right again. The vigorous blooming forces of nature everywhere present belied the sense of evil and decay to which mortality is so readily subject. He felt that everything was justified in youth and love, particularly where mutual affection reigned. Why should he not take Angela? Why should they not be together? He went in to breakfast at her call, eating comfortably of the things she provided. He felt the easy familiarity and graciousness of the conqueror. Angela on her part felt the fear and uncertainty of one who has embarked upon a dangerous voyage. She had set sail—whither? At what port would she land? Was it the lake or his studio? Would she live and be happy or would she die to face a black uncertainty? Was there a hell as some preachers insisted? Was there a gloomy place of lost souls such as the poets described? She looked into the face of this same world which Eugene found so beautiful and its very beauty trembled with forebodings of danger.

And there were days and days yet to be lived of this. For

all her fear, once having tasted of the forbidden fruit, it was sweet and inviting. She could not go near Eugene, nor he near her but this flush of emotion would return.

In the daylight she was too fearful, but when the night came with its stars, its fresh winds, its urge to desire, her fears could not stand in their way. Eugene was insatiable and she was yearning. The slightest touch was as fire to tow. She yielded saying she would not yield.

The Blue family were of course blissfully ignorant of what was happening. It seemed so astonishing to Angela at first that the very air did not register her actions in some visible way. That they should be able thus to be alone was not so remarkable, seeing that Eugene's courtship was being aided and abetted, for her sake, but that her lapse should not be exposed by some sinister influence seemed strange—accidental and subtly ominous. Something would happen—that was her fear. She had not the courage of her desire or need.

By the end of the week, though Eugene was less ardent and more or less oppressed by the seeming completeness with which he had conquered, he was not ready to leave. He was sorry to go, for it ended a honeymoon of sweetness and beauty—all the more wonderful and enchanting because so clandestine— yet he was beginning to be aware that he had bound himself in chains of duty and responsibility. Angela had thrown herself on his mercy and his sense of honor to begin with. She had exacted a promise of marriage—not urgently, and as one who sought to entrap him, but with the explanation that otherwise life must end in disaster for her. Eugene could look in her face and see that it would. And now that he had had his way and plumbed the depths of her emotions and desires he had a higher estimate of her personality. Despite the fact that she was older than he, there was a breath of youth and beauty here that held him. Her body was exquisite. Her feeling about life and love was tender and beautiful. He wished he could make true her dreams of bliss without injury to himself.

It so turned out that as his visit was drawing to a close Angela decided that she ought to go to Chicago, for there were purchases which must be made. Her mother wanted her to go and she decided that she would go with Eugene. This made the separation easier, gave them more time to talk. Her usual plan was to stay with her aunt and she was going there now.

On the way she asked over and over what he would think of her in the future; whether what had passed would not lower

her in his eyes. He did not feel that it would. Once she said
to him sadly—"only death or marriage can help me now."

"What do you mean?" he asked, her yellow head pillowed
on his shoulder, her dark blue eyes looking sadly into his.

"That if you don't marry me I'll have to kill myself. I can't
stay at home."

He thought of her with her beautiful body, her mass of soft
hair all tarnished in death.

"You wouldn't do that?" he asked unbelievingly.

"Yes, I would," she said sadly. "I must, I will."

"Hush, Angel Face," he pleaded. "You won't do anything
like that. You won't have to. I'll marry you—How would
you do it?"

"Oh, I've thought it all out," she continued gloomily. "You
know that little lake. I'd drown myself."

"Don't, sweetheart," he pleaded. "Don't talk that way. It's
terrible. You won't have to do anything like that."

To think of her under the waters of little Okoonee, with
its green banks, and yellow sandy shores. All her love come
to this! All her passion! Her death would be upon his head
and he could not stand the thought of that. It frightened him.
Such tragedies occasionally appeared in the papers with all the
pathetic details convincingly set forth, but this should not enter
his life. He would marry her. She was lovely after all. He
would have to. He might as well make up his mind to that
now. He began to speculate how soon it might be. For the
sake of her family she wanted no secret marriage but one which,
if they could not be present at it, they could at least know was
taking place. She was willing to come East—that could be
arranged. But they must be married. Eugene realized the
depth of her conventional feeling so keenly that it never occurred to him to suggest an alternative. She would not consent, would scorn him for it. The only alternative, she appeared to believe, was death.

One evening—the last—when it was necessary for her to return to Blackwood, and he had seen her off on the train, her
face a study in sadness, he rode out gloomily to Jackson Park
where he had once seen a beautiful lake in the moonlight. When
he reached there the waters of the lake were still suffused and
tinged with lovely suggestions of lavender, pink and silver, for
this was near the twenty-first of June. The trees to the east
and west were dark. The sky showed a last blush of orange.
Odours were about—warm June fragrance. He thought now,
as he walked about the quiet paths where the sand and pebbles

crunched lightly beneath his feet, of all the glory of this wonderful week. How dramatic was life; how full of romance. This love of Angela's, how beautiful. Youth was with him— love. Would he go on to greater days of beauty or would he stumble, idling his time, wasting his substance in riotous living? Was this riotous living? Would there be evil fruition of his deeds? Would he really love Angela after he married her? Would they be happy?

Thus he stood by the bank of this still lake, studying the water, marvelling at the subtleties of reflected radiance, feeling the artist's joy in perfect natural beauty, twining and intertwining it all with love, death, failure, fame. It was romantic to think that in such a lake, if he were unkind, would Angela be found. By such a dark as was now descending would all her bright dreams be submerged. It would be beautiful as romance. He could imagine a great artist like Daudet or Balzac making a great story out of it. It was even a subject for some form of romantic expression in art. Poor Angela! If he were a great portrait painter he would paint her. He thought of some treatment of her in the nude with that mass of hair of hers falling about her neck and breasts. It would be beautiful. Should he marry her? Yes, though he was not sure of the outcome, he must. It might be a mistake but—

He stared at the fading surface of the lake, silver, lavender, leaden gray. Overhead a vivid star was already shining. How would it be with her if she were really below those still waters? How would it be with him? It would be too desperate, too regretful. No, he must marry her. It was in this mood that he returned to the city, the ache of life in his heart. It was in this mood that he secured his grip from the hotel and sought the midnight train for New York. For once Ruby, Miriam, Christina, were forgotten. He was involved in a love drama which meant life or death to Angela, peace or reproach of conscience to himself in the future. He could not guess what the outcome would be, but he felt that he must marry her—how soon he could not say. Circumstances would dictate that. From present appearances it must be immediately. He must see about a studio, announce the news of his departure to Smite and MacHugh; make a special effort to further his art ambitions so that he and Angela would have enough to live on. He had talked so glowingly of his art life that now, when the necessity for demonstrating it was at hand, he was troubled as to what the showing might be. The studio had to be attractive. He would need to introduce his friends. All the way back to New York he turned this over in his mind—Smite, MacHugh, Miriam, Norma, Wheeler, Christina—what would Christina think if she ever returned to New York and found him married? There was no question but that there was a difference between Angela and these. It was something—a matter of courage—more soul, more daring, more awareness, perhaps—something. When they saw her would they think he had made a mistake, would they put him down as a fool? MacHugh was going with a girl, but she was a different type—intellectual, smart. He thought and thought, but he came back to the same conclusion always. He would have to marry her. There was no way out. He would have to.

CHAPTER XXVIII

THE studio of Messrs. Smite, MacHugh and Witla in
Waverley Place was concerned the following October with
a rather picturesque event. Even in the city the time when the
leaves begin to yellow and fall brings a sense of melancholy,
augmented by those preliminaries of winter, gray, lowery days,
with scraps of paper, straws, bits of wood blown about by gusty
currents of air through the streets, making it almost disagreeable to be abroad. The fear of cold and storm and suffering
among those who have little was already apparent. Apparent
too was the air of renewed vitality common to those who have
spent an idle summer and are anxious to work again. Shopping
and marketing and barter and sale were at high key. The
art world, the social world, the manufacturing world, the professional worlds of law, medicine, finance, literature, were bub-
bling with a feeling of the necessity to do and achieve. The
whole city, stung by the apprehension of winter, had an atmosphere of emprise and energy.

In this atmosphere, with a fairly clear comprehension of the
elements which were at work making the colour of the life about
him, was Eugene, digging away at the task he had set himself.
Since leaving Angela he had come to the conclusion that he
must complete the jointings for the exhibition which had been
running in his mind during the last two years. There was no other
way for him to make a notable impression—he saw that. Since
he had returned he had gone through various experiences: the
experience of having Angela tell him that she was sure there
was something wrong with her; an impression sincere enough,
but based on an excited and overwrought imagination of evil to
follow, and having no foundation in fact. Eugene was as yet,
despite his several experiences, not sufficiently informed in such
affairs to know. His lack of courage would have delayed him
from asking if he had known. In the next place, facing this
crisis, he had declared that he would marry her, and because of
her distressed condition he thought he might as well do it now.
He had wanted time to do some of the pictures he was working
on, to take in a little money for drawing, to find a suitable place
to live in. He had looked at various studios in various sections
of the city and had found nothing, as yet, which answered to
his taste or his purse. Anything with a proper light, a bath,

a suitable sleeping room, and an inconspicuous chamber which might be turned into a kitchen, was difficult to find. Prices were high, ranging from fifty to one hundred and twenty-five and one hundred and fifty a month. There were some new studios being erected for the rich loungers and idlers which commanded, so he understood, three or four thousand dollars a year. He wondered if he should ever attain to any such magnificence through his art.

Again, in taking a studio for Angela and himself there was the matter of furniture. The studio he had with Smite and MacHugh was more or less of a camp. The work room was bare of carpets or rugs. The two folding beds and the cot which graced their individual chambers were heirlooms from ancient predecessors—substantial but shabby. Beyond various drawings, three easels, and a chest of drawers for each, there was no suitable household equipment. A woman came twice a week to clean, send out the linen, and make up the beds.

To live with Angela required, in his judgment, many and much more significant things. His idea of a studio was some such one as that now occupied by Miriam Finch or Norma Whitmore. There ought to be furniture of a period—old Flemish or Colonial, Heppelwhite or Chippendale or Sheraton, such as he saw occasionally knocking about in curio shops and second hand stores. It could be picked up if he had time. He was satisfied that Angela knew nothing of these things. There ought to be rugs, hangings of tapestry, bits of brass, pewter, copper, old silver, if he could afford it. He had an idea of some day obtaining a figure of the Christ in brass or plaster, hung upon a rough cross of walnut or teak, which he could hang or stand in some corner as one might a shrine and place before it two great candlesticks with immense candles smoked and dripping with wax. These lighted in a dark studio, with the outlines of the Christ flickering in the shadows behind would give the desired atmosphere to his studio. Such an equipment as he dreamed of would have cost in the neighborhood of two thousand dollars.

Of course this was not to be thought of at this period. He had no more than that in ready cash. He was writing to Angela about his difficulties in finding a suitable place, when he heard of a studio in Washington Square South, which its literary possessor was going to quit for the winter. It was, so he understood, handsomely furnished, and was to be let for the rent of the studio. The owner wanted someone who would take care of it by occupying it for him until he should return the following fall. Eugene hurried round to look at it and, taken with the location, the appearance of the square from the windows, the beauty of the furnishings, felt that he would like to live here. This would be the way to introduce Angela to New York. This would be the first and proper impression to give her. Here, as in every well arranged studio he had yet seen were books, pictures, bits of statuary, implements of copper and some few of silver. There was a great fish net dyed green and spangled with small bits of mirror to look like scales which hung as a veil between the studio proper and an alcove. There was a piano done in black walnut, and odd pieces of furniture, Mission, Flemish, Venetian of the sixteenth century and English of the seventeenth, which, despite that diversity offered a unity of appearance and a harmony of usefulness. There was one bed room, a bath, and a small partitioned section which could be used as a kitchen. With a few of his pictures judiciously substituted he could see a perfect abode here for himself and his wife. The rent was fifty dollars. He decided that he would risk it.

Having gone so far as to indicate that he would take it—he was made to feel partially resigned to marriage by the very appearance of this place—he decided that he would marry in October. Angela could come to New York or Buffalo—she had never seen Niagara Falls—and they could be married there. She had spoken recently of visiting her brother at West Point. Then they could come here and settle down. He decided that this must be so, wrote to her to that effect, and vaguely hinted to Smite and MacHugh that he might get married shortly.

This was a great blow to his partners in art, for Eugene was very popular with them. He had the habit, with those he liked, of jesting constantly. "Look at the look of noble determination on Smite's brow this morning," he would comment cheerfully on getting up; or "MacHugh, you lazy lout, crawl out and earn your living."

MacHugh's nose, eyes and ears would be comfortably buried in the folds of a blanket.

"These hack artists," Eugene would sigh disconsolately. "There's not much to be made out of them. A pile of straw and a couple of boiled potatoes a day is all they need."

"Aw, cut it out," MacHugh would grunt.

"To hell, to hell, I yell, I yell," would come from somewhere in the voice of Smite.

"If it weren't for me," Eugene would go on, "God knows

what would become of this place. A lot of farmers and fishermen trying to be artists."

"And laundry wagon drivers, don't forget that," MacHugh would add, sitting up and rubbing his tousled head, for Eugene had related some of his experiences. "Don't forget the contribution made by the American Steam Laundry Company to the world of true art."

"Collars and cuffs I would have you know is artistic," Eugene at once declared with mock dignity, "whereas plows and fish is trash."

Sometimes this "kidding" would continue for a quarter of an hour at a stretch, when some one remark really brighter than any other would dissolve the whole in laughter. Work began after breakfast, to which they usually sallied forth together, and would continue unbroken save for necessary engagements or periods of entertainment, lunch and so on, until five in the afternoon.

They had worked together now for a couple of years. They had, by experience, learned of each other's reliability, courtesy, kindness and liberality. Criticism was free, generous, and sincerely intended to be helpful. Pleasure trips, such as walks on grey, lowery days, or in rain or brilliant sunshine, or trips to Coney Island, Far Rockaway, the theatres, the art exhibitions, the odd and peculiar restaurants of different nationalities, were always undertaken in a spirit of joyous camaraderie. Jesting as to morality, their respective abilities, their tendencies and characteristics were all taken and given in good part. At one time it would be Joseph Smite who would come in for a united drubbing and excoriation on the part of Eugene and MacHugh. At another time Eugene or MacHugh would be the victim, the other two joining forces vigorously. Art, literature, personalities, phases of life, philosophy, were discussed by turn. As with Jerry Mathews, Eugene had learned of new things from these men—the life of fisher-folk, and the characteristics of the ocean from Joseph Smite; the nature and spirit of the great West from MacHugh. Each appeared to have an inexhaustible fund of experiences and reminiscences which refreshed and entertained the trio day by day year in and year out. They were at their best strolling through some exhibit or preliminary view of an art collection offered for sale, when all their inmost convictions of what was valuable and enduring in art would come to the surface. All three were intolerant of reputations as such, but were strong for individual merit whether it carried a great name or not. They were constantly becoming acquainted with the work of some genius little known here, and celebrating his talents, each to the others. Thus Monet, Degas, Manet, Ribera, Monticelli, by turns came up for examination and praise.

When Eugene then, toward the end of September, announced that he might be leaving them shortly, there was a united wail of opposition. Joseph Smite was working on a sea scene at the time, doing his best to get the proper colour harmony between the worm-eaten deck of a Gold Coast trading ship, a half naked West Coast negro handling a broken wheel, and a mass of blue black undulations in the distance which represented the boundless sea.

"G'wan!" said Smite, incredulously, for he assumed that Eugene was jesting. There had been a steady stream of letters issuing from somewhere in the West and delivered here week after week, as there had been for MacHugh, but this by now was a commonplace, and apparently meant nothing. "You marry? What the hell do you want to get married for? A fine specimen you will make! I'll come around and tell your wife."

"Sure," returned Eugene. "It's true, I may get married." He was amused at Smite's natural assumption that it was a jest.

"Stow that," called MacHugh, from his easel. He was working on a country corner picture, a group of farmers before a country post office. "You don't want to break up this shack, do you?" Both of these men were fond of Eugene. They found him inspiring, helpful, always intensely vigorous and apparently optimistic.

"I don't want to break up any shack. But haven't I a right to get married?"

"I vote no, by God!" said Smite emphatically. "You'll never go out of here with my consent. Peter, are we going to stand for anything like that?"

"We are not," replied MacHugh. "We'll call out the reserves if he tries any game like that on us. I'll prefer charges against him. Who's the lady, Eugene?"

"I bet I know," suggested Smite. "He's been running up to Twenty-sixth Street pretty regularly." Joseph was thinking of Miriam Finch, to whom Eugene had introduced both him and MacHugh.

"Nothing like that, surely," inquired MacHugh, looking over at Eugene to see if it possibly could be so.

"It's all true, fellers," replied Eugene, "—as God is my judge. I'm going to leave you soon."

"You're not really talking seriously, are you, Witla?" inquired Joseph soberly.

"I am, Joe," said Eugene quietly. He was studying the perspective of his sixteenth New York view,—three engines coming abreast into a great yard of cars. The smoke, the haze, the dingy reds and blues and yellows and greens of kicked about box cars were showing with beauty—the vigor and beauty of raw reality.

"Soon?" asked MacHugh, equally quietly. He was feeling that touch of pensiveness which comes with a sense of vanishing pleasures.

"I think some time in October, very likely," replied Eugene.

"Jesus Christ, I'm sorry to hear that," put in Smite.

He laid down his brush and strolled over to the window. MacHugh, less expressive in extremes, worked on medatively.

"When'd you reach that conclusion, Witla?" he asked after a time.

"Oh, I've been thinking it over for a long time, Peter," he returned. "I should really have married before if I could have afforded it. I know how things are here or I wouldn't have sprung this so suddenly. I'll hold up my end on the rent here until you get someone else."

"To hell with the rent," said Smite. "We don't want anyone else, do we, Peter? We didn't have anyone else before."

Smite was rubbing his square chin and contemplating his partner as if they were facing a catastrophe.

"There's no use talking about that," said Peter. "You know we don't care about the rent. Do you mind telling us who you're going to marry? Do we know her?"

"You don't," returned Eugene. "She's out in Wisconsin. It's the one who writes the letters. Angela Blue is her name."

"Well, here's to Angela Blue, by God, say I," said Smite, recovering his spirits and picking up his paint brush from his board to hold aloft. "Here's to Mrs. Eugene Witla, and may she never reef a sail to a storm or foul an anchor, as they say up Nova Scotia way."

"Right oh," added MacHugh, catching the spirit of Smite's generous attitude. "Them's my sentiments. When d'you expect to get married really, Eugene?"

"Oh I haven't fixed the time exactly. About November first, I should say. I hope you won't say anything about it though, either of you. I don't want to go through any explanations."

"We won't, but it's tough, you old walrus. Why the hell

didn't you give us time to think it over? You're a fine jelly-fish, you are."

He poked him reprimandingly in the ribs.

"There isn't anyone any more sorry than I am," said Eugene. "I hate to leave here, I do. But we won't lose track of each other. I'll still be around here."

"Where do you expect to live? Here in the city?" asked MacHugh, still a little gloomy.

"Sure. Right here in Washington Square. Remember that Dexter studio Weaver was telling about? The one in the third floor at sixty-one? That's it."

"You don't say!" exclaimed Smite. "You're in right. How'd you get that?"

Eugene explained.

"Well, you sure are a lucky man," observed MacHugh. "Your wife ought to like that. I suppose there'll be a cozy corner for an occasional strolling artist?"

"No farmers, no sea-faring men, no artistic hacks—nothing!" declared Eugene dramatically.

"You to Hell," said Smite. "When Mrs. Witla sees us—"

"She'll wish she'd never come to New York," put in Eugene.

"She'll wish she'd seen us first," said MacHugh.

BOOK II

THE STRUGGLE

CHAPTER I

THE marriage ceremony between Eugene and Angela was solemnized at Buffalo on November second. As planned, Marietta was with them. They would go, the three of them, to the Falls, and to West Point, where the girls would see their brother David, and then Marietta would return to tell the family about it. Naturally, under the circumstances, it was a very simple affair, for there were no congratulations to go through with and no gifts—at least immediately—to consider and acknowledge. Angela had explained to her parents and friends that it was quite impossible for Eugene to come West at this time. She knew that he objected to a public ceremony where he would have to run the gauntlet of all her relatives, and so she was quite willing to meet him in the East and be married there. Eugene had not troubled to take his family into his confidence as yet. He had indicated on his last visit home that he might get married, and that Angela was the girl in question, but since Myrtle was the only one of his family who had seen her and she was now in Ottumwa, Iowa, they could not recall anything about her. Eugene's father was a little disappointed, for he expected to hear some day that Eugene had made a brilliant match. His boy, whose pictures were in the magazines so frequently and whose appearance was so generally distinguished, ought in New York, where opportunities abounded, to marry an heiress at least. It was all right of course if Eugene wanted to marry a girl from the country, but it robbed the family of a possible glory.

The spirit of this marriage celebration, so far as Eugene was concerned, was hardly right. There was the consciousness, always with him, of his possibly making a mistake; the feeling that he was being compelled by circumstances and his own weakness to fulfil an agreement which might better remain unfulfilled. His only urge was his desire, in the gratification of which he might find compensation, for saving Angela from an unhappy spinsterhood. It was a thin reed to lean on; there could be no honest satisfaction in it. Angela was sweet, devoted, painstaking in her attitude toward life, toward him, toward everything with which she came in contact, but she was not what he had always fancied his true mate would be—the be all and the end all of his existence. Where was the divine fire which on this occasion should have animated him; the lofty thoughts of future companionship; that intense feeling he had first felt about her when he had called on her at her aunt's house in Chicago? Something had happened. Was it that he had cheapened his ideal by too close contact with it? Had he taken a beautiful flower and trailed it in the dust? Was passion all there was to marriage? Or was it that true marriage was something higher—a union of fine thoughts and feelings? Did Angela share his with him? Angela did have exalted feelings and moods at times. They were not sensibly intellectual—but she seemed to respond to the better things in music and to some extent in literature. She knew nothing about art, but she was emotionally responsive to many fine things. Why was not this enough to make life durable and comfortable between them? Was it not really enough? After he had gone over all these points, there was still the thought that there was something wrong in this union. Despite his supposedly laudable conduct in fulfilling an obligation which, in a way, he had helped create or created, he was not happy. He went to his marriage as a man goes to fulfil an uncomfortable social obligation. It might turn out that he would have an enjoyable and happy life and it might turn out very much otherwise. He could not face the weight and significance of the social theory that this was for life—that if he married her today he would have to live with her all the rest of his days. He knew that was the generally accepted interpretation of marriage, but it did not appeal to him. Union ought in his estimation to be based on a keen desire to live together and on nothing else. He did not feel the obligation which attaches to children, for he had never had any and did not feel the desire for any. A child was a kind of a nuisance. Marriage was a trick of Nature's by which you were compelled to carry out her scheme of race continuance. Love was a lure; desire a scheme of propagation devised by the way. Nature, the race spirit, used you as you would use a work-horse to pull a load. The load in this case was race progress and man was the victim. He did not think he owed anything to nature, or to this race spirit. He had not asked to come here. He had not been treated as generously as he might have been since he arrived. Why should he do what nature bid?

When he met Angela he kissed her fondly, for of course the sight of her aroused the feeling of desire which had been running in his mind so keenly for some time. Since last seeing Angela he had touched no woman, principally because the right one had not presented herself and because the memories and the

anticipations in connection with Angela were so close. Now
that he was with her again the old fire came over him and he
was eager for the completion of the ceremony. He had seen to
the marriage license in the morning,—and from the train on
which Angela and Marietta arrived they proceeded in a carriage direct to the Methodist preacher. The ceremony which
meant so much to Angela meant practically nothing to him. It
seemed a silly formula—this piece of paper from the marriage
clerk's office and this instructed phraseology concerning "love,
honor and cherish." Certainly he would love, honor and
cherish if it were possible—if not, then not. Angela, with the
marriage ring on her finger and the words "with this ring I thee
wed" echoing in her ears, felt that all her dreams had come true.
Now she was, really, truly, Mrs. Eugene Witla. She did not
need to worry about drowning herself, or being disgraced, or
enduring a lonely, commiserated old age. She was the wife of
an artist—a rising one, and she was going to live in New York.
What a future stretched before her! Eugene loved her after
all. She imagined she could see that. His slowness in marrying
her was due to the difficulty of establishing himself properly.
Otherwise he would have done it before. They drove to the
Iroquois hotel and registered as man and wife, securing a separate room for Marietta. The latter pretending an urgent desire
to bathe after her railroad journey, left them, promising to be
ready in time for dinner. Eugene and Angela were finally
alone.

He now saw how, in spite of his fine theories, his previous
experiences with Angela had deadened to an extent his joy in
this occasion. He had her again it was true. His desire that he
had thought of so keenly was to be gratified, but there was no
mystery connected with it. His real nuptials had been celebrated at Blackwood months before. This was the commonplace
of any marriage relation. It was intense and gratifying, but
the original, wonderful mystery of unexplored character was
absent. He eagerly took her in his arms, but there was more
of crude desire than of awed delight in the whole proceeding.

Nevertheless Angela was sweet to him. Hers was a loving
disposition and Eugene was the be all and end all of her love.
His figure was of heroic proportions to her. His talent was divine fire. No one could know as much as Eugene, of course!
No one could be as artistic. True, he was not as practical as
some men—her brothers and brothers-in-law, for instance—but
he was a man of genius. Why should he be practical? She was
beginning to think already of how thoroughly she would help

him shape his life toward success—what a good wife she would
be to him. Her training as a teacher, her experience as a buyer,
her practical judgment, would help him so much. They spent
the two hours before dinner in renewed transports and then
dressed and made their public appearance. Angela had had
designed a number of dresses for this occasion, representing the
saving of years, and tonight at dinner she looked exceptionally
pretty in a dress of black silk with neck piece and half sleeves
of mother-of-pearl silk, set off with a decoration of seed pearls
and black beads in set designs. Marietta, in a pale pink silk of
peachblow softness of hue with short sleeves and a low cut
bodice was, with all her youth and natural plumpness and gaiety
of soul, ravishing. Now that she had Angela safely married,
she was under no obligations to keep out of Eugene's way nor
to modify her charms in order that her sister's might shine. She
was particularly ebullient in her mood and Eugene could not
help contrasting, even in this hour, the qualities of the two sisters. Marietta's smile, her humor, her unconscious courage,
contrasted so markedly with Angela's quietness.

The luxuries of the modern hotel have become the commonplaces of ordinary existence, but to the girls they were still
strange enough to be impressive. To Angela they were a fore-
taste of what was to be an enduring higher life. These carpets, hangings, elevators, waiters, seemed in their shabby ma-
terialism to speak of superior things.

One day in Buffalo, with a view of the magnificent falls at
Niagara, and then came West Point with a dress parade accidentally provided for a visiting general and a ball for the ca-
dets. Marietta, because of her charm and her brother's popularity, found herself so much in demand at West Point that
she extended her stay to a week, leaving Eugene and Angela free
to come to New York together and have a little time to themselves. They only stayed long enough to see Marietta safely
housed and then came to the city and the apartment in Washington Square.

It was dark when they arrived and Angela was impressed
with the glittering galaxy of lights the city presented across the
North River from Forty-second Street. She had no idea of the
nature of the city, but as the cab at Eugene's request turned into
Broadway at Forty-second Street and clattered with interrupted
progress south to Fifth Avenue she had her first glimpse of that
tawdry world which subsequently became known as the "Great
White Way." Already its make-believe and inherent cheapness
had come to seem to Eugene largely characteristic of the city

and of life, but it still retained enough of the lure of the flesh and of clothes and of rush-light reputations to hold his attention. Here were dramatic critics and noted actors and actresses and chorus girls, the gods and toys of avid, inexperienced, unsatisfied wealth. He showed Angela the different theatres, called her attention to distinguished names; made much of restaurants and hotels and shops and stores that sell trifles and trash, and finally turned into lower Fifth Avenue, where the dignity of great houses and great conservative wealth still lingered. At Fourteenth Street Angela could already see Washington Arch glowing cream white in the glare of electric lights.

"What is that?" she asked interestedly.

"It's Washington Arch," he replied. "We live in sight of that on the south side of the Square."

"Oh! but it is beautiful!" she exclaimed.

It seemed very wonderful to her, and as they passed under it, and the whole Square spread out before her, it seemed a perfect world in which to live.

"Is this where it is?" she asked, as they stopped in front of the studio building.

"Yes, this is it. How do you like it?"

"I think it's beautiful," she said.

They went up the white stone steps of the old Bride house in which was Eugene's leased studio, up two flights of red-carpeted stairs and finally into the dark studio where he struck a match and lit, for the art of it, candles. A soft waxen glow irradiated the place as he proceeded and then Angela saw old Chippendale chairs, a Heppelwhite writing-table, a Flemish strong box containing used and unused drawings, the green stained fish-net studded with bits of looking glass in imitation of scales, a square, gold-framed mirror over the mantel, and one of Eugene's drawings—the three engines in the gray, lowering weather, standing large and impressive upon an easel. It seemed to Angela the perfection of beauty. She saw the difference now between the tawdry gorgeousness of a commonplace hotel and this selection and arrangement of individual taste. The glowing candelabrum of seven candles on either side of the square mirror surprised her deeply. The black walnut piano in the alcove behind the half draped net drew forth an exclamation of delight. "Oh, how lovely it all is!" she exclaimed and ran to Eugene to be kissed. He fondled her for a few minutes and then she left again to examine in detail pictures, pieces of furniture, ornaments of brass and copper.

"When did you get all this?" she asked, for Eugene had not

told her of his luck in finding the departing Dexter and leasing it for the rent of the studio and its care. He was lighting the fire in the grate which had been prepared by the house attendant.

"Oh, it isn't mine," he replied easily. "I leased this from Russell Dexter. He's going to be in Europe until next winter. I thought that would be easier than waiting around to fix up a place after you came. We can get our things together next fall."

He was thinking he would be able to have his exhibition in the spring, and perhaps that would bring some notable sales. Anyhow it might bring a few, increase his repute and give him a greater earning power.

Angela's heart sank just a little but she recovered in a moment, for after all it was very exceptional even to be able to lease a place of this character. She went to the window and looked out. There was the great square with its four walls of houses, the spread of trees, still decorated with a few dusty leaves, and the dozens of arc lights sputtering their white radiance in between, the graceful arch, cream white over at the entrance of Fifth Avenue.

"It's so beautiful," she exclaimed again, coming back to Eugene and putting her arms about him. "I didn't think it would be anything as fine as this. You're so good to me." She put up her lips and he kissed her, pinching her cheeks. Together they walked to the kitchen, the bedroom, the bathroom. Then after a time they blew out the candles and retired for the night.

CHAPTER II

AFTER the quiet of a small town, the monotony and simplicity of country life, the dreary, reiterated weariness of teaching a country school, this new world into which Angela was plunged seemed to her astonished eyes to be compounded of little save beauties, curiosities and delights. The human senses, which weary so quickly of reiterated sensory impressions, exaggerate with equal readiness the beauty and charm of the unaccustomed. If it is new, therefore it must be better than that which we have had of old. The material details with which we are able to surround ourselves seem at times to remake our point of view. If we have been poor, wealth will seem temporarily to make us happy; when we have been amid elements and personages discordant to our thoughts, to be put among harmonious conditions seems, for the time being, to solve all our woes. So little do we have that interior peace which no material conditions can truly affect or disturb.

When Angela awoke the next morning, this studio in which she was now to live seemed the most perfect habitation which could be devised by man. The artistry of the arrangement of the rooms, the charm of the conveniences—a bathroom with hot and cold water next to the bedroom; a kitchen with an array of necessary utensils. In the rear portion of the studio used as a dining-room a glimpse of the main studio gave her the sense of art which dealt with nature, the beauty of the human form, colors, tones—how different from teaching school. To her the difference between the long, low rambling house at Blackwood with its vine ornamented windows, its somewhat haphazard arrangement of flowers and its great lawn, and this peculiarly compact and ornate studio apartment looking out upon Washington Square, was all in favor of the latter. In Angela's judgment there was no comparison. She could not have understood if she could have seen into Eugene's mind at this time how her home town, her father's single farm, the blue waters of the little lake near her door, the shadows of the tall trees on her lawn were somehow, compounded for him not only with classic beauty itself, but with her own charm. When she was among these things she partook of their beauty and was made more beautiful thereby. She did not know how much she had lost in leaving them behind. To her all these older elements of her life were shabby and unimportant, pointless and to be neglected.

This new world was in its way for her an Aladdin's cave of delight. When she looked out on the great square for the first time the next morning, seeing it bathed in sunlight, a dignified line of red brick dwellings to the north, a towering office building to the east, trucks, carts, cars and vehicles clattering over the pavement below, it all seemed gay with youth and energy.

"We'll have to dress and go out to breakfast," said Eugene. "I didn't think to lay anything in. As a matter of fact I wouldn't have known what to buy if I had wanted to. I never tried house-keeping for myself."

"Oh, that's all right," said Angela, fondling his hands, "only let's not go out to breakfast unless we have to. Let's see what's here," and she went back to the very small room devoted to cooking purposes to see what cooking utensils had been provided. She had been dreaming of housekeeping and cooking for Eugene, of petting and spoiling him, and now the opportunity had arrived. She found that Mr. Dexter, their generous lessor, had provided himself with many conveniences—breakfast and dinner sets of brown and blue porcelain, a coffee percolator, a charming dull blue teapot with cups to match, a chafing dish, a set of waffle irons, griddles, spiders, skillets, stew and roasting pans and knives and forks of steel and silver in abundance. Obviously he had entertained from time to time, for there were bread, cake, sugar, flour and salt boxes and a little chest containing, in small drawers, various spices.

"Oh, it will be easy to get something here," said Angela, lighting the burners of the gas stove to see whether it was in good working order. "We can just go out to market if you'll come and show me once and get what we want. It won't take a minute. I'll know after that." Eugene consented gladly.

She had always fancied she would be an ideal housekeeper and now that she had her Eugene she was anxious to begin. It would be such a pleasure to show him what a manager she was, how everything would go smoothly in her hands, how careful she would be of his earnings—their joint possessions.

She was sorry, now that she saw that art was no great producer of wealth, that she had no money to bring him, but she knew that Eugene in the depth of his heart thought nothing of that. He was too impractical. He was a great artist, but when it came to practical affairs she felt instinctively that she was much the wiser. She had bought so long, calculated so well for her sisters and brothers.

Out of her bag (for her trunks had not yet arrived) she extracted a neat house dress of pale green linen which she put on after she had done up her hair in a cosy coil, and together with Eugene for a temporary guide, they set forth to find the stores. He had told her, looking out the windows, that there were lines of Italian grocers, butchers and vegetable men in the side streets, leading south from the square, and into one of these they now ventured. The swarming, impressive life of the street almost took her breath away, it was so crowded. Potatoes, tomatoes, eggs, flour, butter, lamb chops, salt—a dozen little accessories were all purchased in small quantities, and then they eagerly returned to the studio. Angela was a little disgusted with the appearance of some of the stores, but some of them were clean enough. It seemed so strange to her to be buying in an Italian street, with Italian women and children about, their swarthy leathern faces set with bright, almost feverish eyes. Eugene in his brown corduroy suit and soft green hat, watching and commenting at her side, presented such a contrast. He was so tall, so exceptional, so laconic.

"I like them when they wear rings in their ears," he said at one time.

"Get the coal man who looks like a bandit," he observed at another.

"This old woman here might do for the witch of Endor."

Angela attended strictly to her marketing. She was gay and smiling, but practical. She was busy wondering in what quantities she should buy things, how she would keep fresh vegetables, whether the ice box was really clean; how much delicate dusting the various objects in the studio would require. The raw brick walls of the street, the dirt and slops in the gutter, the stray cats and dogs hungry and lean, the swarming stream of people, did not appeal to her as picturesque at all. Only when she heard Eugene expatiating gravely did she begin to realize that all this must have artistic significance. If Eugene said so it did. But it was a fascinating world whatever it was, and it was obvious that she was going to be very, very happy.

There was a breakfast in the studio then of hot biscuit with fresh butter, an omelette with tomatoes, potatoes stewed in cream, and coffee. After the long period of commonplace restaurant dining which Eugene had endured, this seemed ideal. To sit in your own private apartment with a charming wife opposite you ready to render you any service, and with an array of food before you which revived the finest memories in your gustatory experience, seemed perfect. Nothing could be better. He saw visions of a happy future if he could finance this sort of thing. It would require a lot of money, more than he had been making, but he thought he could make out. After breakfast Angela played on the piano, and then, Eugene wanting to work, she started housekeeping in earnest. The trunks arriving gave her the task of unpacking and with that and lunch and dinner to say nothing of love she had sufficient to do.

It was a charming existence for a little while. Eugene suggested that they should have Smite and MacHugh to dinner first of all, these being his closest friends. Angela agreed heartily for she was only too anxious to meet the people he knew. She wanted to show him she knew how to receive and entertain as well as anyone. She made great preparations for the Wednesday evening following—the night fixed for the dinner—and when it came was on the qui vive to see what his friends were like and what they would think of her.

The occasion passed off smoothly enough and was the occasion of considerable jollity. These two cheerful worthies were greatly impressed with the studio. They were quick to praise it before Angela, and to congratulate him on his good fortune in having married her. Angela, in the same dress in which she had appeared at dinner in Buffalo, was impressive. Her mass of yellow hair fascinated the gaze of both Smite and MacHugh.

"Gee, what hair!" Smite observed secretly to MacHugh when neither Angela nor Eugene were within hearing distance.

"You're right," returned MacHugh. "She's not at all bad looking, is she?"

"I should say not," returned Smite who admired Angela's simple, good-natured western manners. A little later, more subtly, they expressed their admiration to her, and she was greatly pleased.

Marietta, who had arrived late that afternoon, had not made her appearance yet. She was in the one available studio bedroom making her toilet. Angela, in spite of her fine raiment, was busy superintending the cooking, for although through the janitor she had managed to negotiate the loan of a girl to serve, she could not get anyone to cook. A soup, a fish, a chicken and a salad, were the order of procedure. Marietta finally appeared, ravishing in pink silk. Both Smite and MacHugh sat up and Marietta proceeded to bewitch them. Marietta knew no order or distinctions in men. They were all slaves to her—victims to be stuck on the spit of her beauty and broiled in their amorous uncertainties at her leisure. In after years Eugene learned to speak of Marietta's smile as "the dagger." The moment she appeared smiling he would say, "Ah, we have it out again, have we? Who gets the blade this evening? Poor victim!"

Being her brother-in-law now, he was free to slip his arm about her waist and she took this family connection as license to kiss him. There was something about Eugene which held her always. During these very first days she gratified her desire to be in his arms, but always with a sense of reserve which kept him in check. She wondered secretly how much he liked her.

Smite and MacHugh, when she appeared, both rose to do her service. MacHugh offered her his chair by the fire. Smite bestirred himself in an aimless fashion.

"I've just had such a dandy week up at West Point," began Marietta cheerfully, "dancing, seeing dress parades, walking with the soldier boys."

"I warn you two, here and now," began Eugene, who had already learned to tease Marietta, "that you're not safe. This woman here is dangerous. As artists in good standing you had better look out for yourselves."

"Oh, Eugene, how you talk," laughed Marietta, her teeth showing effectively. "Mr. Smite, I leave it to you. Isn't that a mean way to introduce a sister-in-law? I'm here for just a few days too, and have so little time. I think it cruel!"

"It's a shame!" said Smite, who was plainly a willing victim. "You ought to have another kind of brother-in-law. If you had some people I know now——"

"It's an outrage," commented MacHugh. "There's one thing though. You may not require so very much time."

"Now I think that's ungallant," Marietta laughed. "I see I'm all alone here except for Mr. Smite. Never mind. You all will be sorry when I'm gone."

"I believe that," replied MacHugh, feelingly.

Smite simply stared. He was lost in admiration of her cream and peach complexion, her fluffy, silky brown hair, her bright blue eyes and plump rounded arms. Such radiant good nature would be heavenly to live with. He wondered what sort of a family this was that Eugene had become connected with. Angela, Marietta, a brother at West Point. They must be nice, conservative, well-to-do western people. Marietta went to help her sister, and Smite, in the absence of Eugene, said: "Say, he's in right, isn't he? She's a peach. She's got it a little on her sister."

MacHugh merely stared at the room. He was taken with the complexion and arrangement of things generally. The old furniture, the rugs, the hangings, the pictures, Eugene's borrowed maid servant in a white apron and cap, Angela, Marietta, the bright table set with colored china and an arrangement of

silver candlesticks—Eugene had certainly changed the tenor
of his life radically within the last ten days. Why he was mar-
vellously fortunate. This studio was a wonderful piece of
luck. Some people—and he shook his head meditatively.

"Well," said Eugene, coming back after some final touches to
his appearance, "what do you think of it, Peter?"

"You're certainly moving along, Eugene. I never expected
to see it. You ought to praise God. You're plain lucky."

Eugene smiled enigmatically. He was wondering whether he
was. Neither Smite nor MacHugh nor anyone could dream of
the conditions under which this came about. What a sham
the world was anyhow. It's surface appearances so ridiculously
deceptive! If anyone had known of the apparent necessity
when he first started to look for an apartment, of his own mood
toward it!

Marietta came back, and Angela. The latter had taken
kindly to both these men, or boys as she already considered them.
Eugene had a talent for reducing everybody to "simply folks,"
as he called them. So these two capable and talented men were
mere country boys like himself—and Angela caught his attitude.

"I'd like to have you let me make a sketch of you some day,
Mrs. Witla," MacHugh said to Angela when she came back
to the fire. He was essaying portraiture as a side line and he
was anxious for good opportunities to practice.

Angela thrilled at the invitation, and the use of her new name,
Mrs. Witla, by Eugene's old friends.

"I'd be delighted," she replied, flushing.

"My word, you look nice, Angel-Face," exclaimed Marietta,
catching her about the waist. "You paint her with her hair down
in braids, Mr. MacHugh. She makes a stunning Gretchen."

Angela flushed anew.

"I've been reserving that for myself, Peter," said Eugene,
"but you try your hand at it. I'm not much in portraiture anyhow."

Smite smiled at Marietta. He wished he could paint her, but
he was poor at figure work except as incidental characters in
sea scenes. He could do men better than he could women.

"If you were an old sea captain now, Miss Blue," he said
to Marietta gallantly, "I could make a striking thing out of
you."

"I'll try to be, if you want to paint me," she replied gaily.
"I'd look fine in a big pair of boots and a raincoat, wouldn't I,
Eugene?"

"You certainly would, if I'm any judge," replied Smite. "Come over to the studio and I'll rig you out. I have all those things on hand."

"I will," she replied, laughing. "You just say the word."

MacHugh felt as if Smite were stealing a march on him. He wanted to be nice to Marietta, to have her take an interest in him.

"Now, looky, Joseph," he protested. "I was going to suggest making a study of Miss Blue myself."

"Well, you're too late," replied Smite. "You didn't speak quick enough."

Marietta was greatly impressed with this atmosphere in which Angela and Eugene were living. She expected to see something artistic, but nothing so nice as this particular studio. Angela explained to her that Eugene did not own it, but that made small difference in Marietta's estimate of its significance. Eugene had it. His art and social connections brought it about. They were beginning excellently well. If she could have as nice a home when she started on her married career she would be satisfied.

They sat down about the round teak table which was one of Dexter's prized possessions, and were served by Angela's borrowed maid. The conversation was light and for the most part pointless, serving only to familiarize these people with each other. Both Angela and Marietta were taken with the two artists because they felt in them a note of homely conservatism. These men spoke easily and naturally of the trials and triumphs of art life, and the difficulty of making a good living, and seemed to be at home with personages of repute in one world and another, its greatest reward.

During the dinner Smite narrated experiences in his sea-faring life, and MacHugh of his mountain camping experiences in the West. Marietta described experiences with her beaux in Wisconsin and characteristics of her yokel neighbors at Blackwood, Angela joining in. Finally MacHugh drew a pencil sketch of Marietta followed by a long train of admiring yokels, her eyes turned up in a very shy, deceptive manner.

"Now I think that's cruel," she declared, when Eugene laughed heartily. "I never look like that."

"That's just the way you look and do," he declared. "You're the broad and flowery path that leadeth to destruction."

"Never mind, Babyette," put in Angela, "I'll take your part if no one else will. You're a nice, demure, shrinking girl and you wouldn't look at anyone, would you?"

Angela got up and was holding Marietta's head mock sympathetically in her arms.

"Say, that's a dandy pet name," called Smite, moved by Marietta's beauty.

"Poor Marietta," observed Eugene. "Come over here to me and I'll sympathize with you."

"You don't take my drawing in the right spirit, Miss Blue," put in MacHugh cheerfully. "It's simply to show how popular you are."

Angela stood beside Eugene as her guests departed, her slender arm about his waist. Marietta was coquetting finally with MacHugh. These two friends of his, thought Eugene, had the privilege of singleness to be gay and alluring to her. With him that was over now. He could not be that way to any girl any more. He had to behave—be calm and circumspect. It cut him, this thought. He saw at once it was not in accord with his nature. He wanted to do just as he had always done—make love to Marietta if she would let him, but he could not. He walked to the fire when the studio door was closed.

"They're such nice boys," exclaimed Marietta. "I think Mr. MacHugh is as funny as he can be. He has such droll wit."

"Smite is nice too," replied Eugene defensively.

"They're both lovely—just lovely," returned Marietta.

"I like Mr. MacHugh a little the best—he's quainter," said Angela, "but I think Mr. Smite is just as nice as he can be. He's so old fashioned. There's not anyone as nice as my Eugene, though," she said affectionately, putting her arm about him.

"Oh, dear, you two!" exclaimed Marietta. "Well, I'm going to bed."

Eugene sighed.

They had arranged a couch for her which could be put behind the silver-spangled fish net in the alcove when company was gone.

Eugene thought what a pity that already this affection of Angela's was old to him. It was not as it would be if he had taken Marietta or Christina. They went to their bed room to retire and then he saw that all he had was passion. Must he be satisfied with that? Could he be? It started a chain of thought which, while persistently interrupted or befogged, was really never broken. Momentary sympathy, desire, admiration, might obscure it, but always fundamentally it was there. He had made a mistake. He had put his head in a noose. He had subjected himself to conditions which he did not sincerely approve of. How was he going to remedy this—or could it ever be remedied?

CHAPTER III

WHATEVER were Eugene's secret thoughts, he began his married life with the outward air of one who takes it seriously enough. Now that he was married, was actually bound by legal ties, he felt that he might as well make the best of it. He had once had the notion that it might be possible to say nothing of his marriage, and keep Angela in the background, but this notion had been dispelled by the attitude of MacHugh and Smite, to say nothing of Angela. So he began to consider the necessity of notifying his friends—Miriam Finch and Norma Whitmore and possibly Christina Channing, when she should return. These three women offered the largest difficulty to his mind. He felt the commentary which their personalities represented. What would they think of him? What of Angela? Now that she was right here in the city he could see that she represented a different order of thought. He had opened the campaign by suggesting that they invite Smite and MacHugh. The thing to do now was to go further in this matter.

The one thing that troubled him was the thought of breaking the news to Miriam Finch, for Christina Channing was away, and Norma Whitmore was not of sufficient importance. He argued now that he should have done this beforehand, but having neglected that it behoved him to act at once. He did so, finally, writing to Norma Whitmore and saying, for he had no long explanation to make—"Yours truly is married. May I bring my wife up to see you?" Miss Whitmore was truly taken by surprise. She was sorry at first—very—because Eugene interested her greatly and she was afraid he would make a mistake in his marriage; but she hastened to make the best of a bad turn on the part of fate and wrote a note which ran as follows:

"Dear Eugene and Eugene's Wife:
        "This is news as is news. Congratulations. And I am coming right down as soon as I get my breath. And then you two must come to see me.
                                "Norma Whitmore."

Eugene was pleased and grateful that she took it so nicely, but Angela was the least big chagrined secretly that he had not told her before. Why hadn't he? Was this someone that he

was interested in? Those three years in which she had doubt-
ingly waited for Eugene had whetted her suspicions and nurtured
her fears. Still she tried to make little of it and to put on an air
of joyousness. She would be so glad to meet Miss Whitmore.
Eugene told her how kind she had been to him, how much she
admired his art, how helpful she was in bringing together young
literary and artistic people and how influential with those who
counted. She could do him many a good turn. Angela listened
patiently, but she was just the least bit resentful that he should
think so much of any one woman outside of herself. Why should
he, Eugene Witla, be dependent on the favor of any woman?
Of course she must be very nice and they would be good friends,
but—

Norma came one afternoon two days later with the atmosphere
of enthusiasm trailing, as it seemed to Eugene, like a cloud of
glory about her. She was both fire and strength to him in her
regard and sympathy, even though she resented, ever so slightly,
his affectional desertion.

"You piggy-wiggy Eugene Witla," she exclaimed. "What do
you mean by running off and getting married and never saying
a word. I never even had a chance to get you a present and now
I have to bring it. Isn't this a charming place—why it's perfectly delightful," and as she laid her present down unopened she
looked about to see where Mrs. Eugene Witla might be.

Angela was in the bedroom finishing her toilet. She was
expecting this descent and so was prepared, being suitably dressed
in the light green house gown. When she heard Miss Whitmore's familiar mode of address she winced, for this spoke volumes for a boon companionship of long endurance. Eugene
hadn't said so much of Miss Whitmore in the past as he had recently, but she could see that they were very intimate. She
looked out and saw her—this tall, not very shapely, but graceful woman, whose whole being represented dynamic energy,
awareness, subtlety of perception. Eugene was shaking her hand
and looking genially into her face.

"Why should Eugene like her so much?" she asked herself instantly. "Why did his face shine with that light of intense enthusiasm?" The "piggy-wiggy Eugene Witla" expression irritated her. It sounded as though she might be in love with him.
She came out after a moment with a glad smile on her face and
approached with every show of good feeling, but Miss Whitmore could sense opposition.

"So this is Mrs. Witla," she exclaimed, kissing her. "I'm delighted to know you. I have always wondered what sort of a

girl Mr. Witla would marry. You'll just have to pardon my calling him Eugene. I'll get over it after a bit, I suppose, now that he's married. But we've been such good friends and I admire his work so much. How do you like studio life—or are you used to it?"

Angela, who was taking in every detail of Eugene's old friend, replied in what seemed an affected tone that no, she wasn't used to studio life: she was just from the country, you know—a regular farmer girl—Blackwood, Wisconsin, no less! She stopped to let Norma express friendly surprise, and then went on to say that she supposed Eugene had not said very much about her, but he wrote her often enough. She was rejoicing in the fact that whatever slight Eugene's previous silence seemed to put upon her, she had the satisfaction that she had won him after all and Miss Whitmore had not. She fancied from Miss Whitmore's enthusiastic attitude that she must like Eugene very much, and she could see now what sort of women might have made him wish to delay. Who were the others, she wondered?

They talked of metropolitan experiences generally. Marietta came in from a shopping expedition with a Mrs. Link, wife of an army captain acting as an instructor at West Point, and tea was served immediately afterward. Miss Whitmore was insistent that they should come and take dinner with her some evening. Eugene confided that he was sending a painting to the Academy.

"They'll hang it, of course," assured Norma, "but you ought to have an exhibition of your own."

Marietta gushed about the wonder of the big stores and so it finally came time for Miss Whitmore to go.

"Now you will come up, won't you?" she said to Angela, for in spite of a certain feeling of incompatibility and difference she was determined to like her. She thought Angela a little inexperienced and presumptuous in marrying Eugene. She was afraid she was not up to his standard. Still she was quaint, piquant. Perhaps she would do very well. Angela was thinking all the while that Miss Whitmore was presuming on her old acquaintance with Eugene—that she was too affected and enthusiastic.

There was another day on which Miriam Finch called. Richard Wheeler, having learned at Smite's and MacHugh's studio of Eugene's marriage and present whereabouts, had hurried over, and then immediately afterwards off to Miriam Finch's studio. Surprised himself, he knew that she would be more so.

"Witla's married!" he exclaimed, bursting into her room, and for the moment Miriam lost her self-possession sufficiently to reply almost dramatically: "Richard Wheeler, what are you talking about! You don't mean that, do you?"

"He's married," insisted Wheeler, "and he's living down in Washington Square, 61 is the number. He has the cutest yellow-haired wife you ever saw."

Angela had been nice to Wheeler and he liked her. He liked the air of this domicile and thought it was going to be a good thing for Eugene. He needed to settle down and work hard.

Miriam winced mentally at the picture. She was hurt by this deception of Eugene's, chagrined because he had not thought enough of her even to indicate that he was going to get married.

"He's been married ten days," communicated Wheeler, and this added force to her temporary chagrin. The fact that Angela was yellow-haired and cute was also disturbing.

"Well," she finally exclaimed cheerfully, "he might have said something to us, mightn't he?" and she covered her own original confusion by a gay nonchalance which showed nothing of what she was really thinking. This was certainly indifference on Eugene's part, and yet, why shouldn't he? He had never proposed to her. Still they had been so intimate mentally.

She was interested to see Angela. She wondered what sort of a woman she really was. "Yellow-haired! Cute!" Of course, like all men, Eugene had sacrificed intellect and mental charm for a dainty form and a pretty face. It seemed queer, but she had fancied that he would not do that—that his wife, if he ever took one, would be tall perhaps, and gracious, and of a beautiful mind—someone distinguished. Why would men, intellectual men, artistic men, any kind of men, invariably make fools of themselves! Well, she would go and see her.

Because Wheeler informed him that he had told Miriam, Eugene wrote, saying as briefly as possible that he was married and that he wanted to bring Angela to her studio. For reply she came herself, gay, smiling, immaculately dressed, anxious to hurt Angela because she had proved the victor. She also wanted to show Eugene how little difference it all made to her.

"You certainly are a secretive young man, Mr. Eugene Witla," she exclaimed, when she saw him. "Why didn't you make him tell us, Mrs. Witla?" she demanded archly of Angela, but with a secret dagger thrust in her eyes. "You'd think he didn't want us to know."

Angela cowered beneath the sting of this whip cord. Miriam made her feel as though Eugene had attempted to conceal his relationship to her—as though he was ashamed of her. How many more women were there like Miriam and Norma Whitmore?

Eugene was gaily unconscious of the real animus in Miriam's conversation, and now that the first cruel moment was over, was talking glibly of things in general, anxious to make everything seem as simple and natural as possible. He was working at one of his pictures when Miriam came in and was eager to obtain her critical opinion, since it was nearly done. She squinted at it narrowly but said nothing when he asked. Ordinarily she would have applauded it vigorously. She did think it exceptional, but was determined to say nothing. She walked indifferently about, examining this and that object in a superior way, asking how he came to obtain the studio, congratulating him upon his good luck. Angela, she decided, was interesting, but not in Eugene's class mentally, and should be ignored. He had made a mistake, that was plain.

"Now you must bring Mrs. Witla up to see me," she said on leaving. "I'll play and sing all my latest songs for you. I have made some of the daintest discoveries in old Italian and Spanish pieces."

Angela, who had posed to Eugene as knowing something about music, resented this superior invitation, without inquiry as to her own possible ability or taste, as she did Miriam's entire attitude. Why was she so haughty—so superior? What was it to her whether Eugene had said anything about her or not?

She said nothing to show that she herself played, but she wondered that Eugene said nothing. It seemed neglectful and inconsiderate of him. He was busy wondering what Miriam thought of his picture. Miriam took his hand warmly at parting, looked cheerfully into his eyes, and said, "I know you two are going to be irrationally happy," and went out.

Eugene felt the irritation at last. He knew Angela felt something. Miriam was resentful, that was it. She was angry at him for his seeming indifference. She had commented to herself on Angela's appearance and to her disadvantage. In her manner had been the statement that his wife was not very important after all, not of the artistic and superior world to which she and he belonged.

"How do you like her?" he asked tentatively after she had gone, feeling a strong current of opposition, but not knowing on what it might be based exactly.

"I don't like her," returned Angela petulantly. "She thinks she's sweet. She treats you as though she thought you were her

personal property. She openly insulted me about your not telling her. Miss Whitmore did the same thing—they all do! They
all will! Oh!!"

She suddenly burst into tears and ran crying toward their
bedroom.

Eugene followed, astonished, ashamed, rebuked, guilty minded,
almost terror-stricken—he hardly knew what.

"Why, Angela," he urged pleadingly, leaning over her and
attempting to raise her. "You know that isn't true."

"It is! It is!!" she insisted. "Don't touch me! Don't come
near me! You know it is true! You don't love me. You
haven't treated me right at all since I've been here. You haven't
done anything that you should have done. She insulted me
openly to my face."

She was speaking with sobs, and Eugene was at once pained
and terrorized by the persistent and unexpected display of
emotion. He had never seen Angela like this before. He had
never seen any woman so.

"Why, Angelface," he urged, "how can you go on like this?
You know what you say isn't true. What have I done?"

"You haven't told your friends—that's what you haven't
done," she exclaimed between gasps. "They still think you're
single. You keep me here hidden in the background as though
I were a—were a—I don't know what! Your friends come
and insult me openly to my face. They do! They do! Oh!"
and she sobbed anew.

She knew very well what she was doing in her anger and
rage. She felt that she was acting in the right way. Eugene
needed a severe reproof; he had acted very badly, and this
was the way to administer it to him now in the beginning.
His conduct was indefensible, and only the fact that he was
an artist, immersed in cloudy artistic thoughts and not really
subject to the ordinary conventions of life, saved him in her
estimation. It didn't matter that she had urged him to marry
her. It didn't absolve him that he had done so. She thought
he owed her that. Anyhow they were married now, and he
should do the proper thing.

Eugene stood there cut as with a knife by this terrific charge.
He had not meant anything by concealing her presence, he
thought. He had only endeavored to protect himself very
slightly, temporarily.

"You oughtn't to say that, Angela," he pleaded. "There
aren't any more that don't know—at least any more that I
care anything about. I didn't think. I didn't mean to conceal

anything. I'll write to everybody that might be interested."

He still felt hurt that she should brutally attack him this way even in her sorrow. He was wrong, no doubt, but she? Was this a way to act, this the nature of true love? He mentally writhed and twisted.

Taking her up in his arms, smoothing her hair, he asked her to forgive him. Finally, when she thought she had punished him enough, and that he was truly sorry and would make amends in the future, she pretended to listen and then of a sudden threw her arms about his neck and began to hug and kiss him. Passion, of course, was the end of this, but the whole thing left a disagreeable taste in Eugene's mouth. He did not like scenes. He preferred the lofty indifference of Miriam, the gay subterfuge of Norma, the supreme stoicism of Christina Channing. This noisy, tempestuous, angry emotion was not quite the thing to have introduced into his life. He did not see how that would make for love between them.

Still Angela was sweet, he thought. She was a little girl— not as wise as Norma Whitmore, not as self-protective as Miriam Finch or Christina Channing. Perhaps after all she needed his care and affection. Maybe it was best for her and for him that he had married her.

So thinking he rocked her in his arms, and Angela, lying there, was satisfied. She had won a most important victory. She was starting right. She was starting Eugene right. She would get the moral, mental and emotional upper hand of him and keep it. Then these women, who thought themselves so superior, could go their way. She would have Eugene and he would be a great man and she would be his wife. That was all she wanted.

CHAPTER IV

THE result of Angela's outburst was that Eugene hastened to notify those whom he had not already informed—Shotmeyer, his father and mother, Sylvia, Myrtle, Hudson Dula—and received in return cards and letters of congratulation expressing surprise and interest, which he presented to Angela in a conciliatory spirit. She realized, after it was all over, that she had given him an unpleasant shock, and was anxious to make up to him in personal affection what she had apparently compelled him to suffer for policy's sake. Eugene did not know that in Angela, despite her smallness of body and what seemed to him her babyishness of spirit, he had to deal with a thinking woman who was quite wise as to ways and means of handling her personal affairs. She was, of course, whirled in the maelstrom of her affection for Eugene and this was confusing, and she did not understand the emotional and philosophic reaches of his mind; but she did understand instinctively what made for a stable relationship between husband and wife and between any married couple and the world. To her the utterance of the marriage vow meant just what it said, that they would cleave each to the other; there should be henceforth no thoughts, feelings, or emotions, and decidedly no actions which would not conform with the letter and the spirit of the marriage vow.

Eugene had sensed something of this, but not accurately or completely. He did not correctly estimate either the courage or the rigidity of her beliefs and convictions. He thought that her character might possibly partake of some of his own easy tolerance and good nature. She must know that people—men particularly—were more or less unstable in their make-up. Life could not be governed by hard and fast rules. Why, everybody knew that. You might try, and should hold yourself in check as much as possible for the sake of self-preservation and social appearances, but if you erred—and you might easily—it was no crime. Certainly it was no crime to look at another woman longingly. If you went astray, overbalanced by your desires, wasn't it after all in the scheme of things? Did we make our desires? Certainly we did not, and if we did not succeed completely in controlling them—well—

The drift of life into which they now settled was interesting enough, though for Eugene it was complicated with the thought of possible failure, for he was, as might well be expected of such a temperament, of a worrying nature, and inclined, in his hours of ordinary effort, to look on the dark side of things. The fact that he had married Angela against his will, the fact that he had no definite art connections which produced him as yet anything more than two thousand dollars a year, the fact that he had assumed financial obligations which doubled the cost of food, clothing, entertainment, and rent—for their studio was costing him thirty dollars more than had his share of the Smite-MacHugh chambers—weighed on him. The dinner which he had given to Smite and MacHugh had cost about eight dollars over and above the ordinary expenses of the week. Others of a similar character would cost as much and more. He would have to take Angela to the theatre occasionally. There would be the need of furnishing a new studio the following fall, unless another such windfall as this manifested itself. Although Angela had equipped herself with a varied and serviceable trousseau, her clothes would not last forever. Odd necessities began to crop up not long after they were married, and he began to see that if they lived with anything like the freedom and care with which he had before he was married, his income would have to be larger and surer.

The energy which these thoughts provoked was not without result. For one thing he sent the original of the East Side picture, "Six O'clock" to the American Academy of Design exhibition—a thing which he might have done long before but failed to do.

Angela had heard from Eugene that the National Academy of Design was a forum for the display of art to which the public was invited or admitted for a charge. To have a picture accepted by this society and hung on the line was in its way a mark of merit and approval, though Eugene did not think very highly of it. All the pictures were judged by a jury of artists which decided whether they should be admitted or rejected, and if admitted whether they should be given a place of honor or hung in some inconspicuous position. To be hung "on the line" was to have your picture placed in the lower tier where the light was excellent and the public could get a good view of it. Eugene had thought the first two years he was in New York that he was really not sufficiently experienced or meritorious, and the previous year he had thought that he would hoard all that he was doing for his first appearance in some exhibition of his own, thinking the National Academy commonplace and retrogressive. The exhibitions he had seen thus far had been full of commonplace, dead-and-alive stuff, he thought. It was no great honor to be admitted to such a collection. Now, because MacHugh was trying, and because he had accumulated nearly enough pictures for exhibition at a private gallery which he hoped to interest, he was anxious to see what the standard body of American artists thought of his work. They might reject him. If so that would merely prove that they did not recognize a radical departure from accepted methods and subject matter as art. The impressionists, he understood, were being so ignored. Later they would accept him. If he were admitted it would simply mean that they knew better than he believed they did.

"I believe I will do it," he said; "I'd like to know what they think of my stuff anyhow."

The picture was sent as he had planned, and to his immense satisfaction it was accepted and hung. It did not, for some reason, attract as much attention as it might, but it was not without its modicum of praise. Owen Overman, the poet, met him in the general reception entrance of the Academy on the opening night, and congratulated him sincerely. "I remember seeing that in *Truth*," he said, "but it's much better in the original. It's fine. You ought to do a lot of those things."

"I am," replied Eugene. "I expect to have a show of my own one of these days."

He called Angela, who had wandered away to look at a piece of statuary, and introduced her.

"I was just telling your husband how much I like his picture," Overman informed her.

Angela was flattered that her husband was so much of a personage that he could have his picture hung in a great exhibition such as this, with its walls crowded with what seemed to her magnificent canvases, and its rooms filled with important and distinguished people. As they strolled about Eugene pointed out to her this well known artist and that writer, saying almost always that they were very able. He knew three or four of the celebrated collectors, prize givers, and art patrons by sight, and told Angela who they were. There were a number of striking looking models present whom Eugene knew either by reputation, whispered comment of friends, or personally— Zelma Desmond, who had posed for Eugene, Hedda Anderson, Anna Magruder and Laura Matthewson among others. Angela was struck and in a way taken by the dash and beauty of these girls. They carried themselves with an air of personal freedom and courage which surprised her. Hedda Anderson was bold in her appearance but immensely smart. Her manner seemed to comment on the ordinary woman as being indifferent and not worth while. She looked at Angela walking with Eugene and wondered who she was.

"Isn't she striking," observed Angela, not knowing she was anyone whom Eugene knew.

"I know her well," he replied; "she's a model."

Just then Miss Anderson in return for his nod gave him a fetching smile. Angela chilled.

Elizabeth Stein passed by and he nodded to her.

"Who is she?" asked Angela.

"She's a socialist agitator and radical. She sometimes speaks from a soap-box on the East Side."

Angela studied her carefully. Her waxen complexion, smooth black hair laid in even plaits over her forehead, her straight, thin, chiseled nose, even red lips and low forehead indicated a daring and subtle soul. Angela did not understand her. She could not understand a girl as good looking as that doing any such thing as Eugene said, and yet she had a bold, rather free and easy air. She thought Eugene certainly knew strange people. He introduced to her William McConnell, Hudson Dula, who had not yet been to see them, Jan Jansen, Louis Deesa, Leonard Baker and Paynter Stone.

In regard to Eugene's picture the papers, with one exception, had nothing to say, but this one in both Eugene's and Angela's minds made up for all the others. It was the *Evening Sun,* a most excellent medium for art opinion, and it was very definite in its conclusions in regard to this particular work. The statement was:

"A new painter, Eugene Witla, has an oil entitled 'Six O'clock' which for directness, virility, sympathy, faithfulness to detail and what for want of a better term we may call totality of spirit, is quite the best thing in the exhibition. It looks rather out of place surrounded by the weak and spindling interpretations of scenery and water which so readily find a place in the exhibition of the Academy, but it is none the weaker for that. The artist has a new, crude, raw and almost rough method, but his picture seems to say quite clearly what he sees and feels. He may have to wait—if this is not a single burst of ability—but he will have a hearing. There is no question of that. Eugene Witla is an artist."

Eugene thrilled when he read this commentary. It was quite what he would have said himself if he had dared. Angela was beside herself with joy. Who was the critic who had said this, they wondered? What was he like? He must be truly an intellectual personage. Eugene wanted to go and look him up. If one saw his talent now, others would see it later. It was for this reason—though the picture subsequently came back to him unsold, and unmentioned so far as merit or prizes were concerned—that he decided to try for an exhibition of his own.

CHAPTER V

THE hope of fame—what hours of speculation, what pulses of enthusiasm, what fevers of effort, are based on that peculiarly subtle illusion! It is yet the lure, the ignis fatuus of almost every breathing heart. In the young particularly it burns with the sweetness and perfume of spring fires. Then most of all does there seem substantial reality in the shadow of fame—those deep, beautiful illusions which tremendous figures throw over the world. Attainable, it seems, must be the peace and plenty and sweet content of fame—that glamour of achievement that never was on sea or land. Fame partakes of the beauty and freshness of the morning. It has in it the odour of the rose, the feel of rich satin, the color of the cheeks of youth. If we could but be famous when we dream of fame, and not when locks are tinged with grey, faces seamed with the lines that speak of past struggles, and eyes wearied with the tensity, the longings and the despairs of years! To bestride the world in the morning of life, to walk amid the plaudits and the huzzahs when love and faith are young; to feel youth and the world's affection when youth and health are sweet—what dream is that, of pure sunlight and moonlight compounded. A sun-kissed breath of mist in the sky; the reflection of moonlight upon water; the remembrance of dreams to the waking mind—of such is fame in our youth, and never afterward.

By such an illusion was Eugene's mind possessed. He had no conception of what life would bring him for his efforts. He thought if he could have his pictures hung in a Fifth Avenue gallery much as he had seen Bouguereau's "Venus" in Chicago, with people coming as he had come on that occasion—it would be of great comfort and satisfaction to him. If he could paint something which would be purchased by the Metropolitan Museum in New York he would then be somewhat of a classic figure, ranking with Corot and Daubigny and Rousseau of the French or with Turner and Watts and Millais of the English, the leading artistic figures of his pantheon. These men seemed to have something which he did not have, he thought, a greater breadth of technique, a finer comprehension of color and character, a feeling for the subtleties at the back of life which somehow showed through what they did. Larger experience, larger vision, larger feeling—these things seemed to be imminent in the great pictures exhibited here, and it made him a little uncertain of himself. Only the criticism in the *Evening Sun* fortified him against all thought of failure. *He was an artist.*

He gathered up the various oils he had done—there were some twenty-six all told now, scenes of the rivers, the streets, the night life, and so forth—and went over them carefully, touching up details which in the beginning he had merely sketched or indicated, adding to the force of a spot of color here, modifying a tone or shade there, and finally, after much brooding over the possible result, set forth to find a gallery which would give them place and commercial approval.

Eugene's feeling was that they were a little raw and sketchy—that they might not have sufficient human appeal, seeing that they dealt with factory architecture at times, scows, tugs, engines, the elevated roads in raw reds, yellows and blacks; but MacHugh, Dula, Smite, Miss Finch, Christina, the *Evening Sun,* Norma Whitmore, all had praised them, or some of them. Was not the world much more interested in the form and spirit of classic beauty such as that represented by Sir John Millais? Would it not prefer Rossetti's "Blessed Damozel" to any street scene ever painted? He could never be sure. In the very hour of his triumph when the *Sun* had just praised his picture, there lurked the spectre of possible intrinsic weakness. Did the world wish this sort of thing? Would it ever buy of him? Was he of any real value?

"No, artist heart!" one might have answered, "of no more value than any other worker of existence and no less. The sunlight on the corn, the color of dawn in the maid's cheek, the moonlight on the water—these are of value and of no value according to the soul to whom is the appeal. Fear not. Of dreams and the beauty of dreams is the world compounded."

Kellner and Son, purveyors of artistic treasures by both past and present masters, with offices in Fifth Avenue near Twenty-eighth Street, was the one truly significant firm of art-dealers in the city. The pictures in the windows of Kellner and Son, the exhibitions in their very exclusive show rooms, the general approval which their discriminating taste evoked, had attracted the attention of artists and the lay public for fully thirty years. Eugene had followed their shows with interest ever since he had been in New York. He had seen, every now and then, a most astonishing picture of one school or another displayed in their imposing shop window, and had heard artists comment from time to time on other things there with considerable enthusiasm. The first important picture of the impressionistic school—a heavy spring rain in a grove of silver poplars by Winthrop—had been shown in the window of this firm, fascinating Eugene with its technique. He had encountered here collections of Aubrey Beardsley's decadent drawings, of Helleu's silverpoints, of Rodin's astonishing sculptures and Thaulow's solid Scandinavian eclecticism. This house appeared to have capable artistic connections all over the world, for the latest art force in Italy, Spain, Switzerland, or Sweden, was quite as likely to find its timely expression here as the more accredited work of England, Germany or France. Kellner and Son were art connoisseurs in the best sense of the word, and although the German founder of the house had died many years before, its management and taste had never deteriorated.

Eugene did not know at this time how very difficult it was to obtain an exhibition under Kellner's auspices, they being over-crowded with offers of art material and appeals for display from celebrated artists who were quite willing and able to pay for the space and time they occupied. A fixed charge was made, never deviated from except in rare instances where the talent of the artist, his poverty, and the advisability of the exhibition were extreme. Two hundred dollars was considered little enough for the use of one of their show rooms for ten days.

Eugene had no such sum to spare, but one day in January, without any real knowledge as to what the conditions were, he carried four of the reproductions which had been made from time to time in *Truth* to the office of Mr. Kellner, certain that he had something to show. Miss Whitmore had indicated to him that Eberhard Zang wanted him to come and see him, but he thought if he was going anywhere he would prefer to go to Kellner and Son. He wanted to explain to Mr. Kellner, if there were such a person, that he had many more paintings which he considered even better—more expressive of his growing understanding of American life and of himself and his technique. He went in timidly, albeit with quite an air, for this adventure disturbed him much.

The American manager of Kellner and Son, M. Anatole Charles, was a Frenchman by birth and training, familiar with the spirit and history of French art, and with the drift and tendency of art in various other sections of the world. He had been sent here by the home office in Berlin not only because of his very thorough training in English art ways, and because of his ability to select that type of picture which would attract attention and bring credit and prosperity to the house here and abroad; but also because of his ability to make friends among the rich and powerful wherever he was, and to sell one type of important picture after another—having some knack or magnetic capacity for attracting to him those who cared for good art and were willing to pay for it. His specialties, of course, were the canvases of the eminently successful artists in various parts of the world—the living successful. He knew by experience what sold—here, in France, in England, in Germany. He was convinced that there was practically nothing of value in American art as yet—certainly not from the commercial point of view, and very little from the artistic. Beyond a few canvases by Inness, Homer, Sargent, Abbey, Whistler, men who were more foreign, or rather universal, than American in their attitude, he considered that the American art spirit was as yet young and raw and crude. "They do not seem to be grown up as yet over here," he said to his intimate friends. "They paint little things in a forceful way, but they do not seem as yet to see things as a whole. I miss that sense of the universe in miniature which we find in the canvases of so many of the great Europeans. They are better illustrators than artists over here—why I don't know."

M. Anatole Charles spoke English almost more than perfectly. He was an example of your true man of the world—polished, dignified, immaculately dressed, conservative in thought and of few words in expression. Critics and art enthusiasts were constantly running to him with this and that suggestion in regard to this and that artist, but he only lifted his sophisticated eyebrows, curled his superior mustachios, pulled at his highly artistic goatee, and exclaimed: "Ah!" or "So?" He asserted always that he was most anxious to find talent—profitable talent— though on occasion (and he would demonstrate that by an outward wave of his hands and a shrug of his shoulders), the house of Kellner and Son was not averse to doing what it could for art—and that for art's sake without any thought of profit whatsoever. "Where are your artists?" he would ask. "I look and look. Whistler, Abbey, Inness, Sargent—ah— they are old, where are the new ones?"

"Well, this one"—the critic would probably persist.

"Well, well, I go. I shall look. But I have little hope— very, very little hope."

He was constantly appearing under such pressure, at this studio and that—examining, criticising. Alas, he selected the work of but few artists for purposes of public exhibition and usually charged them well for it.

It was this man, polished, artistically superb in his way, whom

Eugene was destined to meet this morning. When he entered the sumptuously furnished office of M. Charles the latter arose. He was seated at a little rosewood desk lighted by a lamp with green silk shade. One glance told him that Eugene was an artist—very likely of ability, more than likely of a sensitive, high-strung nature. He had long since learned that politeness and savoir faire cost nothing. It was the first essential so far as the good will of an artist was concerned. Eugene's card and message brought by a uniformed attendant had indicated the nature of his business. As he approached, M. Charles' raised eyebrows indicated that he would be very pleased to know what he could do for Mr. Witla.

"I should like to show you several reproductions of pictures of mine," began Eugene in his most courageous manner. "I have been working on a number with a view to making a show and I thought that possibly you might be interested in looking at them with a view to displaying them for me. I have twenty-six all told and—"

"Ah! that is a difficult thing to suggest," replied M. Charles cautiously. "We have a great many exhibitions scheduled now—enough to carry us through two years if we considered nothing more. Obligations to artists with whom we have dealt in the past take up a great deal of our time. Contracts, which our Berlin and Paris branches enter into, sometimes crowd out our local shows entirely. Of course, we are always anxious to make interesting exhibitions if opportunity should permit. You know our charges?"

"No," said Eugene, surprised that there should be any.

"Two hundred dollars for two weeks. We do not take exhibitions for less than that time."

Eugene's countenance fell. He had expected quite a different reception. Nevertheless, since he had brought them, he untied the tape of the portfolio in which the prints were laid.

M. Charles looked at them curiously. He was much impressed with the picture of the East Side Crowd at first, but looking at one of Fifth Avenue in a snow storm, the battered, shabby bus pulled by a team of lean, unkempt, bony horses, he paused, struck by its force. He liked the delineation of swirling, wind-driven snow. The emptiness of this thoroughfare, usually so crowded, the buttoned, huddled, hunched, withdrawn look of those who traveled it, the exceptional details of piles of snow sifted on to window sills and ledges and into doorways and on to the windows of the bus itself, attracted his attention.

"An effective detail," he said to Eugene, as one critic might

say to another, pointing to a line of white snow on the window
of one side of the bus. Another dash of snow on a man's hat
rim took his eye also. "I can feel the wind," he added.

Eugene smiled.

M. Charles passed on in silence to the steaming tug coming up
the East River in the dark hauling two great freight barges.
He was saying to himself that after all Eugene's art was that
of merely seizing upon the obviously dramatic. It wasn't so much
the art of color composition and life analysis as it was stage
craft. The man before him had the ability to see the dramatic
side of life. Still—

He turned to the last reproduction which was that of
Greeley Square in a drizzling rain. Eugene by some mystery
of his art had caught the exact texture of seeping water on gray
stones in the glare of various electric lights. He had caught the
values of various kinds of lights, those in cabs, those in cable
cars, those in shop windows, those in the street lamp—re-
lieving by them the black shadows of the crowds and of the sky.
The color work here was unmistakably good.

"How large are the originals of these?" he asked thoughtfully.

"Nearly all of them thirty by forty."

Eugene could not tell by his manner whether he were merely
curious or interested.

"All of them done in oil, I fancy."

"Yes, all."

"They are not bad, I must say," he observed cautiously. "A
little persistently dramatic but—"

"These reproductions—" began Eugene, hoping by criticising
the press work to interest him in the superior quality of the
originals.

"Yes, I see," M. Charles interrupted, knowing full well what
was coming. "They are very bad. Still they show well enough
what the originals are like. Where is your studio?"

"61 Washington Square."

"As I say," went on M. Charles, noting the address on
Eugene's card, "the opportunity for exhibition purposes is very
limited and our charge is rather high. We have so many
things we would like to exhibit—so many things we must exhibit. It is hard to say when the situation would permit—If
you are interested I might come and see them sometime."

Eugene looked perturbed. Two hundred dollars! Two hundred dollars! Could he afford it? It would mean so much to
him. And yet the man was not at all anxious to rent him the
show room even at this price.

"I will come," said M. Charles, seeing his mood, "if you wish. That is what you want me to do. We have to be careful of what we exhibit here. It isn't as if it were an ordinary show room. I will drop you a card some day when occasion offers, if you wish, and you can let me know whether the time I suggest is all right. I am rather anxious to see these scenes of yours. They are very good of their kind. It may be—one never can tell—an opportunity might offer—a week or ten days, somewhere in between other things."

Eugene sighed inwardly. So this was how these things were done. It wasn't very flattering. Still, he must have an exhibition. He could afford two hundred if he had to. An exhibition elsewhere would not be so valuable. He had expected to make a better impression than this.

"I wish you would come," he said at last meditatively. "I think I should like the space if I can get it. I would like to know what you think."

M. Charles raised his eyebrows.

"Very well," he said, "I will communicate with you."

Eugene went out.

What a poor thing this exhibiting business was, he thought. Here he had been dreaming of an exhibition at Kellners which should be brought about without charge to him because they were tremendously impressed with his work. Now they did not even want his pictures—would charge him two hundred dollars to show them. It was a great come down—very discouraging.

Still he went home thinking it would do him some good. The critics would discuss his work just as they did that of other artists. They would have to see what he could do should it be that at last this thing which he had dreamed of and so deliberately planned had come true. He had thought of an exhibition at Kellner's as the last joyous thing to be attained in the world of rising art and now it looked as though he was near it. It might actually be coming to pass. This man wanted to see the rest of his work. He was not opposed to looking at them. What a triumph even that was!

CHAPTER VI

IT was some little time before M. Charles condescended to write saying that if it was agreeable he would call Wednesday morning, January 16th, at 10 A. M., but the letter finally did come and this dispelled all his intermediary doubts and fears. At last he was to have a hearing! This man might see something in his work, possibly take a fancy to it. Who could tell? He showed the letter to Angela with an easy air as though it were quite a matter of course, but he felt intensely hopeful.

Angela put the studio in perfect order for she knew what this visit meant to Eugene, and in her eager, faithful way was anxious to help him as much as possible. She bought flowers from the Italian florist at the corner and put them in vases here and there. She swept and dusted, dressed herself immaculately in her most becoming house dress and waited with nerves at high tension for the fateful ring of the door bell. Eugene pretended to work at one of his pictures which he had done long before—the raw jangling wall of an East Side street with its swarms of children, its shabby push-carts, its mass of eager, shuffling, pushing mortals, the sense of rugged ground life running all through it, but he had no heart for the work. He was asking himself over and over what M. Charles would think. Thank heaven this studio looked so charming! Thank heaven Angela was so dainty in her pale green gown with a single red coral pin at her throat. He walked to the window and stared out at Washington Square, with its bare, wind-shaken branches of trees, its snow, its ant-like pedestrians hurrying here and there. If he were only rich— how peacefully he would paint! M. Charles could go to the devil.

The door bell rang.

Angela clicked a button and up came M. Charles quietly. They could hear his steps in the hall. He knocked and Eugene answered, decidedly nervous in his mind, but outwardly calm and dignified. M. Charles entered, clad in a fur-lined over-coat, fur cap and yellow chamois gloves.

"Ah, good morning!" said M. Charles in greeting. "A fine bracing day, isn't it? What a charming view you have here. Mrs. Witla! I'm delighted to meet you. I am a little late but I was unavoidably detained. One of our German associates is in the city."

He divested himself of his great coat and rubbed his hands before the fire. He tried, now that he had unbent so far, to be genial and considerate. If he and Eugene were to do any business in the future it must be so. Besides the picture on the easel before him, near the window, which for the time being he pretended not to see, was an astonishingly virile thing. Of whose work did it remind him—anybody's? He confessed to himself as he stirred around among his numerous art memories that he recalled nothing exactly like it. Raw reds, raw greens, dirty grey paving stones—such faces! Why this thing fairly shouted its facts. It seemed to say: "I'm dirty, I am commonplace, I am grim, I am shabby, but I am life." And there was no apologizing for anything in it, no glossing anything over. Bang! Smash! Crack! came the facts one after another, with a bitter, brutal insistence on their so-ness. Why, on moody days when he had felt sour and depressed he had seen somewhere a street that looked like this, and there it was—dirty, sad, slovenly, immoral, drunken—anything, everything, but here it was. "Thank God for a realist," he said to himself as he looked, for he knew life, this cold connoisseur; but he made no sign. He looked at the tall, slim frame of Eugene, his cheeks slightly sunken, his eyes bright—an artist every inch of him, and then at Angela, small, eager, a sweet, loving, little woman, and he was glad that he was going to be able to say that he would exhibit these things.

"Well," he said, pretending to look at the picture on the easel for the first time, "we might as well begin to look at these things. I see you have one here. Very good, I think, quite forceful. What others have you?"

Eugene was afraid this one hadn't appealed to him as much as he hoped it would, and set it aside quickly, picking up the second in the stock which stood against the wall, covered by a green curtain. It was the three engines entering the great freight yard abreast, the smoke of the engines towering straight up like tall whitish-grey plumes, in the damp, cold air, the sky lowering with blackish-grey clouds, the red and yellow and blue cars standing out in the sodden darkness because of the water. You could feel the cold, wet drizzle, the soppy tracks, the weariness of "throwing switches." There was a lone brakeman in the foreground, "throwing" a red brake signal. He was quite black and evidently wet.

"A symphony in grey," said M. Charles succinctly.

They came swiftly after this, without much comment from either, Eugene putting one canvas after another before him, leaving it for a few moments and replacing it with another. His estimate of his own work did not rise very rapidly, for M. Charles was persistently distant, but the latter could not help voicing approval of "After The Theatre," a painting full of the wonder and bustle of a night crowd under sputtering electric lamps. He saw that Eugene had covered almost every phase of what might be called the dramatic spectacle in the public life of the city and much that did not appear dramatic until he touched it—the empty canyon of Broadway at three o'clock in the morning; a long line of giant milk wagons, swinging curious lanterns, coming up from the docks at four o'clock in the morning; a plunging parade of fire vehicles, the engines steaming smoke, the people running or staring open-mouthed; a crowd of polite society figures emerging from the opera; the bread line; an Italian boy throwing pigeons in the air from a basket on his arm in a crowded lower West-side street. Everything he touched seemed to have romance and beauty, and yet it was real and mostly grim and shabby.

"I congratulate you, Mr. Witla," finally exclaimed M. Charles, moved by the ability of the man and feeling that caution was no longer necessary. "To me this is wonderful material, much more effective than the reproductions show, dramatic and true. I question whether you will make any money out of it. There is very little sale for American art in this country. It might almost do better in Europe. It *ought* to sell, but that is another matter. The best things do not always sell readily. It takes time. Still I will do what I can. I will give these pictures a two weeks' display early in April without any charge to you whatever." (Eugene started.) "I will call them to the attention of those who know. I will speak to those who buy. It is an honor, I assure you, to do this. I consider you an artist in every sense of the word—I might say a great artist. You ought, if you preserve yourself sanely and with caution, to go far, very far. I shall be glad to send for these when the time comes."

Eugene did not know how to reply to this. He did not quite understand the European seriousness of method, its appreciation of genius, which was thus so easily and sincerely expressed in a formal way. M. Charles meant every word he said. This was one of those rare and gratifying moments of his life when he was permitted to extend to waiting and unrecognized genius the assurance of the consideration and approval of the world.

He stood there waiting to hear what Eugene would say, but the latter only flushed under his pale skin.

"I'm very glad," he said at last, in his rather commonplace, off-hand, American way. "I thought they were pretty good but I wasn't sure. I'm very grateful to you."

"You need not feel gratitude toward me," returned M. Charles, now modifying his formal manner. "You can congratulate yourself—your art. I am honored, as I tell you. We will make a fine display of them. You have no frames for these? Well, never mind, I will lend you frames."

He smiled and shook Eugene's hand and congratulated Angela. She had listened to this address with astonishment and swelling pride. She had perceived, despite Eugene's manner, the anxiety he was feeling, the intense hopes he was building on the outcome of this meeting. M. Charles' opening manner had deceived her. She had felt that he did not care so much after all, and that Eugene was going to be disappointed. Now, when this burst of approval came, she hardly knew what to make of it. She looked at Eugene and saw that he was intensely moved by not only a sense of relief, but pride and joy. His pale, dark face showed it. To see this load of care taken off him whom she loved so deeply was enough to unsettle Angela. She found herself stirred in a pathetic way and now, when M. Charles turned to her, tears welled to her eyes.

"Don't cry, Mrs. Witla," he said grandly on seeing this. "You have a right to be proud of your husband. He is a great artist. You should take care of him."

"Oh, I'm so happy," half-laughed and half-sobbed Angela, "I can't help it."

She went over to where Eugene was and put her face against his coat. Eugene slipped his arm about her and smiled sympathetically. M. Charles smiled also, proud of the effect of his words. "You both have a right to feel very happy," he said.

"Little Angela!" thought Eugene. This was your true wife for you, your good woman. Her husband's success meant all to her. She had no life of her own—nothing outside of him and his good fortune.

M. Charles smiled. "Well, I will be going now," he said finally. "I will send for the pictures when the time comes. And meanwhile you two must come with me to dinner. I will let you know."

He bowed himself out with many assurances of good will, and then Angela and Eugene looked at each other.

"Oh, isn't it lovely, Honeybun," she cried, half giggling,

half crying. (She had begun to call him Honeybun the first day they were married.) "My Eugene a great artist. He said it was a great honor! Isn't that lovely? And all the world is going to know it soon, now. Isn't that fine! Oh dear, I'm so proud." And she threw her arms ecstatically about his neck.

Eugene kissed her affectionately. He was not thinking so much of her though as he was of Kellner and Son—their great exhibit room, the appearance of these twenty-seven or thirty great pictures in gold frames; the spectators who might come to see; the newspaper criticisms; the voices of approval. Now all his artist friends would know that he was considered a great artist; he was to have a chance to associate on equal terms with men like Sargent and Whistler if he ever met them. The world would hear of him widely. His fame might go to the uttermost parts of the earth.

He went to the window after a time and looked out. There came back to his mind Alexandria, the printing shop, the Peoples' Furniture Company in Chicago, the Art Students League, the *Daily Globe*. Surely he had come by devious paths.

"Gee!" he exclaimed at last simply. "Smite and MacHugh'll be glad to hear this. I'll have to go over and tell them."

CHAPTER VII

THE exhibition which followed in April was one of those things which happen to fortunate souls—a complete flowering out before the eyes of the world of its feelings, emotions, perceptions, and understanding. We all have our feelings and emotions, but lack the power of self-expression. It is true, the work and actions of any man are to some degree expressions of character, but this is a different thing. The details of most lives are not held up for public examination at any given time. We do not see succinctly in any given place just what an individual thinks and feels. Even the artist is not always or often given the opportunity of collected public expression under conspicuous artistic auspices. Some are so fortunate—many are not. Eugene realized that fortune was showering its favors upon him.

When the time came, M. Charles was so kind as to send for the pictures and to arrange all the details. He had decided with Eugene that because of the vigor of treatment and the prevailing color scheme black frames would be the best. The principal exhibition room on the ground floor in which these paintings were to be hung was heavily draped in red velvet and against this background the different pictures stood out effectively. Eugene visited the show room at the time the pictures were being hung, with Angela, with Smite and MacHugh, Shotmeyer and others. He had long since notified Norma Whitmore and Miriam Finch, but not the latter until after Wheeler had had time to tell her. This also chagrined her, for she felt in this as she had about his marriage, that he was purposely neglecting her.

The dream finally materialized—a room eighteen by forty, hung with dark red velvet, irradiated with a soft, illuminating glow from hidden lamps in which Eugene's pictures stood forth in all their rawness and reality—almost as vigorous as life itself. To some people, those who do not see life clearly and directly, but only through other people's eyes, they seemed more so.

For this reason Eugene's exhibition of pictures was an astonishing thing to most of those who saw it. It concerned phases of life which in the main they had but casually glanced at, things which because they were commonplace and customary were supposedly beyond the pale of artistic significance. One picture in particular, a great hulking, ungainly negro, a positively animal man, his ears thick and projecting, his lips fat, his nose flat, his cheek bones prominent, his whole body expressing brute strength and animal indifference to dirt and cold, illustrated this point particularly. He was standing in a cheap, commonplace East Side street. The time evidently was a January or February morning. His business was driving an ash cart, and his occupation at the moment illustrated by the picture was that of lifting a great can of mixed ashes, paper and garbage to the edge of the ungainly iron wagon. His hands were immense and were covered with great red patched woolen and leather gloves—dirty, bulbous, inconvenient, one would have said. His head and ears were swaddled about by a red flannel shawl or strip of cloth which was knotted under his pugnacious chin, and his forehead, shawl and all, surmounted by a brown canvas cap with his badge and number as a garbage driver on it. About his waist was tied a great piece of rough coffee sacking and his arms and legs looked as though he might have on two or three pairs of trousers and as many vests. He was looking purblindly down the shabby street, its hard crisp snow littered with tin cans, paper, bits of slop and offal. Dust—gray ash dust, was flying from his upturned can. In the distance behind him was a milk wagon, a few pedestrians, a little thinly clad girl coming out of a delicatessen store. Over head were dull small-paned windows, some shutters with a few of their slats broken out, a frowsy headed man looking out evidently to see whether the day was cold.

Eugene was so cruel in his indictment of life. He seemed to lay on his details with bitter lack of consideration. Like a slavedriver lashing a slave he spared no least shade of his cutting brush. "Thus, and thus and thus" (he seemed to say) "is it." "What do you think of this? and this? and this?"

People came and stared. Young society matrons, art dealers, art critics, the literary element who were interested in art, some musicians, and, because the newspapers made especial mention of it, quite a number of those who run wherever they imagine there is something interesting to see. It was quite a notable two weeks' display. Miriam Finch (though she never admitted to Eugene that she had seen it—she would not give him that satisfaction) Norma Whitmore, William McConnell, Louis Deesa, Owen Overman, Paynter Stone, the whole ruck and rabble of literary and artistic life, came. There were artists of great ability there whom Eugene had never seen before. It would have pleased him immensely if he had chanced to see several of the city's most distinguished social leaders looking, at one time and another, at his pictures. All his observers were astonished at his virility, curious as to his personality, curious as to what motive, or significance, or point of view it might have. The more eclectically cultured turned to the newspapers to see what the art critics would say of this—how they would label it. Because of the force of the work, the dignity and critical judgment of Kellner and Son, the fact that the public of its own instinct and volition was interested, most of the criticisms were favorable. One art publication, connected with and representative of the conservative tendencies of a great publishing house, denied the merit of the collection as a whole, ridiculed the artist's insistence on shabby details as having artistic merit, denied that he could draw accurately, denied that he was a lover of pure beauty, and accused him of having no higher ideal than that of desire to shock the current mass by painting brutal things brutally.

"Mr. Witla," wrote this critic, "would no doubt be flattered if he were referred to as an American Millet. The brutal exaggeration of that painter's art would probably testify to him of his own merit. He is mistaken. The great Frenchman was a lover of humanity, a reformer in spirit, a master of drawing and composition. There was nothing of this cheap desire to startle and offend by what he did. If we are to have ash cans and engines and broken-down bus-horses thrust down our throats as art, Heaven preserve us. We had better turn to commonplace photography at once and be done with it. Broken window shutters, dirty pavements, half frozen ash cart drivers, over-drawn, heavily exaggerated figures of policemen, tenement harridans, beggars, panhandlers, sandwich men—of such is *Art* according to Eugene Witla."

Eugene winced when he read this. For the time being it seemed true enough. His art was shabby. Yet there were others like Luke Severas who went to the other extreme.

"A true sense of the pathetic, a true sense of the dramatic, the ability to endow color—not with its photographic value, though to the current thought it may seem so—but with its higher spiritual significance; the ability to indict life with its own grossness, to charge it prophetically with its own meanness and cruelty in order that mayhap it may heal itself; the ability to see wherein is beauty—even in shame and pathos and degradation; of such is this man's work. He comes from the soil apparently, fresh to a great task. There is no fear here, no bowing to traditions, no recognition of any of the accepted methods. It is probable that he may not know what the accepted methods are. So much the better. We have a new method. The world is the richer for that. As we have said before, Mr. Witla may have to wait for his recognition. It is certain that these pictures will not be quickly purchased and hung in parlors. The average art lover does not take to a new thing so readily. But if he persevere, if his art does not fail him, his turn will come. It cannot fail. He is a great artist. May he live to realize it consciously and in his own soul."

Tears leaped to Eugene's eyes whan he read this. The thought that he was a medium for some noble and super-human purpose thickened the cords in his throat until they felt like a lump. He wanted to be a great artist, he wanted to be worthy of the appreciation that was thus extended to him. He thought of all the writers and artists and musicians and connoisseurs of pictures who would read this and remember him. It was just possible that from now onwards some of his pictures would sell. He would be so glad to devote himself to this sort of thing—to quit magazine illustration entirely. How ridiculous the latter was, how confined and unimportant. Henceforth, unless driven by sheer necessity, he would do it no more. They should beg in vain. He was an artist in the true sense of the word—a great painter, ranking with Whistler, Sargent, Velasquez and Turner. Let the magazines with their little ephemeral circulation go their way. He was for the whole world.

He stood at the window of his studio one day while the exhibition was still in progress, Angela by his side, thinking of all the fine things that had been said. No picture had been sold, but M. Charles had told him that some might be taken before it was all over.

"I think if I make any money out of this," he said to Angela, "we will go to Paris this summer. I have always wanted to see Paris. In the fall we'll come back and take a studio up town. They are building some dandy ones up in Sixty-fifth Street." He was thinking of the artists who could pay three and four thousand dollars a year for a studio. He was thinking of men who made four, five, six and even eight hundred dollars out of every picture they painted. If he could do that! Or if he could get a contract for a mural decoration for next winter. He had very little money laid by. He had spent most of his time this winter working with these pictures.

"Oh, Eugene," exclaimed Angela, "it seems so wonderful. I can hardly believe it. You a really, truly, great artist! And us

going to Paris! Oh, isn't that beautiful. It seems like a dream.
I think and think, but it's hard to believe that I am here sometimes, and that your pictures are up at Kellner's and oh!—"
she clung to him in an ecstasy of delight.

Out in the park the leaves were just budding. It looked as
though the whole square were hung with a transparent green
net, spangled, as was the net in his room, with tiny green
leaves. Songsters were idling in the sun. Sparrows were flying
noisily about in small clouds. Pigeons were picking lazily
between the car tracks of the street below.

"I might get a group of pictures illustrative of Paris. You
can't tell what we'll find. Charles says he will have another
exhibition for me next spring, if I'll get the material ready."
He pushed his arms above his head and yawned deliciously.

He wondered what Miss Finch thought now. He wondered
where Christina Channing was. There was never a word in the
papers yet as to what had become of her. He knew what
Norma Whitmore thought. She was apparently as happy
as though the exhibition had been her own.

"Well, I must go and get your lunch, Honeybun!" exclaimed
Angela. "I have to go to Mr. Gioletti, the grocer, and to Mr.
Ruggiere, the vegetable man." She laughed, for the Italian
names amused her.

Eugene went back to his easel. He was thinking of Christina
—where was she? At that moment, if he had known, she was
looking at his pictures, only newly returned from Europe. She
had seen a notice in the *Evening Post*.

"Such work!" Christina thought, "such force! Oh, what a
delightful artist. And he was with me."

Her mind went back to Florizel and the amphitheatre among
the trees. "He called me 'Diana of the Mountains,'" she
thought, "his 'hamadryad,' his 'huntress of the morn.'" She
knew he was married. An acquaintance of hers had written in
December. The past was past with her—she wanted no more
of it. But it was beautiful to think upon—a delicious memory.

"What a queer girl I am," she thought.

Still she wished she could see him again—not face to face,
but somewhere where he could not see her. She wondered if he
was changing—if he would ever change. He was so beautiful
then—to her.

CHAPTER VIII

PARIS now loomed bright in Eugene's imagination, the prospect mingling with a thousand other delightful thoughts. Now that he had attained to the dignity of a public exhibition, which had been notably commented upon by the newspapers and art journals and had been so generally attended by the elect, artists, critics, writers generally, seemed to know of him. There were many who were anxious to meet and greet him, to speak approvingly of his work. It was generally understood, apparently, that he was a great artist, not exactly arrived to the fullness of his stature as yet, being so new, but on his way. Among those who knew him he was, by this one exhibition, lifted almost in a day to a lonely height, far above the puny efforts of such men as Smite and MacHugh, McConnell and Deesa, the whole world of small artists whose canvases packed the semi-annual exhibition of the National Academy of Design and the Water color society, and with whom in a way, he had been associated. He was a great artist now—recognized as such by the eminent critics who knew; and as such, from now on, would be expected to do the work of a great artist. One phrase in the criticisms of Luke Severas in the *Evening Sun* as it appeared during the run of his exhibition remained in his memory clearly—"If he perseveres, if his art does not fail him." Why should his art fail him?—he asked himself. He was immensely pleased to hear from M. Charles at the close of the exhibition that three of his pictures had been sold—one for three hundred dollars to Henry McKenna, a banker; another, the East Side street scene which M. Charles so greatly admired, to Isaac Wertheim, for five hundred dollars; a third, the one of the three engines and the railroad yard, to Robert C. Winchon, a railroad man, first vice-president of one of the great railroads entering New York, also for five hundred dollars. Eugene had never heard of either Mr. McKenna or Mr. Winchon, but he was assured that they were men of wealth and refinement. At Angela's suggestion he asked M. Charles if he would not accept one of his pictures as a slight testimony of his appreciation for all he had done for him. Eugene would not have thought to do this, he was so careless and unpractical. But Angela thought of it, and saw that he did it. M. Charles was greatly pleased, and took the picture of Greeley Square, which he considered a masterpiece of color interpretation. This somehow sealed the friendship be-tween these two, and M. Charles was anxious to see Eugene's interests properly forwarded. He asked him to leave three of his scenes on sale for a time and he would see what he could do. Meanwhile, Eugene, with thirteen hundred added to the thou-sand and some odd dollars he had left in his bank from previous earnings, was convinced that his career was made, and decided, as he had planned to go to Paris, for the summer at least.

This trip, so exceptional to him, so epoch-making, was easily arranged. All the time he had been in New York he had heard more in his circle of Paris than of any other city. Its streets, its quarters, its museums, its theatres and opera were already almost a commonplace to him. The cost of living, the ideal methods of living, the way to travel, what to see—how often he had sat and listened to descriptions of these things. Now he was going. Angela took the initiative in arranging all the practical details—such as looking up the steamship routes, decid-ing on the size of trunks required, what to take, buying the tickets, looking up the rates of the different hotels and pensions at which they might possibly stay. She was so dazed by the glory that had burst upon her husband's life that she scarcely knew what to do or what to make of it.

"That Mr. Bierdat," she said to Eugene, referring to one of the assistant steam-ship agents with whom she had taken coun-sel, "tells me that if we are just going for the summer it's foolish to take anything but absolute necessaries. He says we can buy so many nice little things to wear over there if we need them, and then I can bring them back duty free in the fall."

Eugene approved of this. He thought Angela would like to see the shops. They finally decided to go via London, re-turning direct from Havre, and on the tenth of May they de-parted, arriving in London a week later and in Paris on the first of June. Eugene was greatly impressed with London. He had arrived in time to miss the British damp and cold and to see London through a golden haze which was entrancing. Angela objected to the shops, which she described as "punk," and to the condition of the lower classes, who were so poor and wretchedly dressed. She and Eugene discussed the interesting fact that all Englishmen looked exactly alike, dressed, walked, and wore their hats and carried their canes exactly alike. Eu-gene was impressed with the apparent "go" of the men—their smartness and dapperness. The women he objected to in the main as being dowdy and homely and awkward.

But when he reached Paris, what a difference! In London,

because of the lack of sufficient means (he did not feel that as yet he had sufficient to permit him to indulge in the more expensive comforts and pleasures of the city) and for the want of someone to provide him with proper social introductions, he was compelled to content himself with that superficial, exterior aspect of things which only the casual traveler sees—the winding streets, the crush of traffic, London Tower, Windsor Castle, the Inns of court, the Strand, Piccadilly, St. Paul's and, of course, the National Gallery and the British Museum. South Kensington and all those various endowed palaces where objects of art are displayed pleased him greatly. In the main he was struck with the conservatism of London, its atmosphere of Empire, its soldiery and the like, though he considered it drab, dull, less strident than New York, and really less picturesque. When he came to Paris, however, all this was changed. Paris is of itself a holiday city—one whose dress is always gay, inviting, fresh, like one who sets forth to spend a day in the country. As Eugene stepped onto the dock at Calais and later as he journeyed across and into the city, he could feel the vast difference between France and England. The one country seemed young, hopeful, American, even foolishly gay, the other serious, speculative, dour.

Eugene had taken a number of letters from M. Charles, Hudson Dula, Louis Deesa, Leonard Baker and others, who, on hearing that he was going, had volunteered to send him to friends in Paris who might help him. The principal thing, if he did not wish to maintain a studio of his own, and did wish to learn, was to live with some pleasant French family where he could hear French and pick it up quickly. If he did not wish to do this, the next best thing was to settle in the Montmartre district in some section or court where he could obtain a nice studio, and where there were a number of American or English students. Some of the Americans to whom he had letters were already domiciled here. With a small calling list of friends who spoke English he would do very well.

"You will be surprised, Witla," said Deesa to him one day, "how much English you can get understood by making intelligent signs."

Eugene had laughed at Deesa's descriptions of his own difficulties and successes, but he found that Deesa was right. Signs went very far and they were, as a rule, thoroughly intelligible.

The studio which he and Angela eventually took after a few days spent at an hotel, was a comfortable one on the third floor of a house which Eugene found ready to his hand, recommended by M. Arkquin, of the Paris branch of Kellner and Son. Another artist, Finley Wood, whom afterwards Eugene recalled as having been mentioned to him by Ruby Kenny, in Chicago, was leaving Paris for the summer. Because of M. Charles' impressive letter, M. Arkquin was most anxious that Eugene should be comfortably installed and suggested that he take this, the charge being anything he cared to pay—forty francs the month. Eugene looked at it and was delighted. It was in the back of the house, looking out on a little garden, and because of a westward slope of the ground from this direction and an accidental breach in the building line, commanded a wide sweep of the city of Paris, the twin towers of Notre Dame, the sheer rise of the Eiffel tower. It was fascinating to see the lights of the city blinking of an evening. Eugene would invariably draw his chair close to his favorite window when he came in, while Angela made lemonade or iced tea or practised her culinary art on a chafing dish. In presenting to him an almost standard American menu she exhibited the executive ability and natural industry which was her chief characteristic. She would go to the neighboring groceries, rotisseries, patisseries, green vegetable stands, and get the few things she needed in the smallest quantities, always selecting the best and preparing them with the greatest care. She was an excellent cook and loved to set a dainty and shining table. She saw no need of company, for she was perfectly happy alone with Eugene and felt that he must be with her. She had no desire to go anywhere by herself—only with him; and she would hang on every thought and motion waiting for him to say what his pleasure would be.

The wonder of Paris to Eugene was its freshness and the richness of its art spirit as expressed on every hand. He was never weary of looking at the undersized French soldiery with their wide red trousers, blue coats and red caps, or the police with their capes and swords and the cab drivers with their air of leisurely superiority. The Seine, brisk with boats at this season of the year, the garden of the Tuileries, with its white marble nudes and formal paths and stone benches, the Bois, the Champ de Mars, the Trocadero Museum, the Louvre—all the wonder streets and museums held him as in a dream.

"Gee," he exclaimed to Angela one afternoon as he followed the banks of the Seine toward Issy, "this is certainly the home of the blessed for all good artists. Smell that perfume. (It was from a perfume factory in the distance.) See that barge!"

He leaned on the river wall. "Ah," he sighed, "this is perfect."

They went back in the dusk on the roof of an open car. "When I die," he sighed, "I hope I come to Paris. It is all the heaven I want."

Yet like all perfect delights, it lost some of its savour after a time, though not much. Eugene felt that he could live in Paris if his art would permit him—though he must go back, he knew, for the present anyhow.

Angela, he noticed after a time, was growing in confidence, if not in mentality. From a certain dazed uncertainty which had characterized her the preceding fall when she had first come to New York, heightened and increased for the time being by the rush of art life and strange personalities she had encountered there and here she was blossoming into a kind of assurance born of experience. Finding that Eugene's ideas, feelings and interests were of the upper world of thought entirely— concerned with types, crowds, the aspect of buildings, streets, skylines, the humors and pathetic aspects of living, she concerned herself solely with the managerial details. It did not take her long to discover that if anyone would relieve Eugene of all care for himself he would let him do it. It was no satisfaction to him to buy himself anything. He objected to executive and commercial details. If tickets had to be bought, time tables consulted, inquiries made, any labor of argument or dispute engaged in, he was loath to enter on it. "You get these, will you, Angela?" he would plead, or "you see him about that. I can't now. Will you?"

Angela would hurry to the task, whatever it was, anxious to show that she was of real use and necessity. On the busses of London or Paris, as in New York, he was sketching, sketching, sketching—cabs, little passenger boats of the Seine, characters in the cafés, parks, gardens, music halls, anywhere, anything, for he was practically tireless. All that he wanted was not to be bothered very much, to be left to his own devices. Sometimes Angela would pay all the bills for him for a day. She carried his purse, took charge of all the express orders into which their cash had been transferred, kept a list of all their expenditures, did the shopping, buying, paying. Eugene was left to see the thing that he wanted to see, to think the things that he wanted to think. During all those early days Angela made a god of him and he was very willing to cross his legs, Buddha fashion, and act as one.

Only at night when there were no alien sights or sounds to engage his attention, when not even his art could come between them, and she could draw him into her arms and submerge his restless spirit in the tides of her love did she feel his equal—really worthy of him. These transports which came with the darkness, or with the mellow light of the little oil lamp that hung in chains from the ceiling near their wide bed, or in the faint freshness of dawn with the birds cheeping in the one tree of the little garden below—were to her at once utterly generous and profoundly selfish. She had eagerly absorbed Eugene's philosophy of self-indulgent joy where it concerned themselves—all the more readily as it coincided with her own vague ideas and her own hot impulses.

Angela had come to marriage through years of self-denial, years of bitter longing for the marriage that perhaps would never be, and out of those years she had come to the marriage bed with a cumulative and intense passion. Without any knowledge either of the ethics or physiology of sex, except as pertained to her state as a virgin, she was vastly ignorant of marriage itself; the hearsay of girls, the equivocal confessions of newly married women, and the advice of her elder sister (conveyed by Heaven only knows what process of conversation) had left her almost as ignorant as before, and now she explored its mysteries with abandon, convinced that the unrestrained gratification of passion was normal and excellent—in addition to being, as she came to find, a universal solvent for all differences of opinion or temperament that threatened their peace of mind. Beginning with their life in the studio on Washington Square, and continuing with even greater fervor now in Paris, there was what might be described as a prolonged riot of indulgence between them, bearing no relation to any necessity in their natures, and certainly none to the demands which Eugene's intellectual and artistic tasks laid upon him. She was to Eugene astonishing and delightful; and yet perhaps not so much delightful as astonishing. Angela was in a sense elemental, but Eugene was not: he was the artist, in this as in other things, rousing himself to a pitch of appreciation which no strength so undermined by intellectual subtleties could continuously sustain. The excitement of adventure, of intrigue in a sense, of discovering the secrets of feminine personality—these were really what had constituted the charm, if not the compelling urge, of his romances. To conquer was beautiful: but it was in essence an intellectual enterprise. To see his rash dreams come true in the yielding of the last sweetness possessed by the desired woman, had been to him imaginatively as well as physically an irresistible thing. But these enterprises were like thin silver strands spun out across

an abyss, whose beauty but not whose dangers were known to
him. Still, he rejoiced in this magnificent creature-joy which
Angela supplied; it was, so far as it was concerned, what he
thought he wanted. And Angela interpreted her power to respond to what seemed his inexhaustible desire as not only a
kindness but a duty.

Eugene set up his easel here, painted from nine to noon some
days, and on others from two to five in the afternoon. If it were
dark, he would walk or ride with Angela or visit the museums,
the galleries and the public buildings or stroll in the factory
or railroad quarters of the city. Eugene sympathized most with
sombre types and was constantly drawing something which represented grim care. Aside from the dancers in the music halls,
the toughs, in what later became known as the Apache district,
the summer picnicking parties at Versailles and St. Cloud, the
boat crowds on the Seine, he drew factory throngs, watchmen
and railroad crossings, market people, market in the dark, street
sweepers, newspaper vendors, flower merchants, always with
a memorable street scene in the background. Some of the
most interesting bits of Paris, its towers, bridges, river views,
façades, appeared in backgrounds to the grim or picturesque or
pathetic character studies. It was his hope that he could interest America in these things—that his next exhibition would not
only illustrate his versatility and persistence of talent, but show
an improvement in his art, a surer sense of color values, a greater
analytical power in the matter of character, a surer selective
taste in the matter of composition and arrangement. He did
not realize that all this might be useless—that he was, aside
from his art, living a life which might rob talent of its finest
flavor, discolor the aspect of the world for himself, take scope
from imagination and hamper effort with nervous irritation,
and make accomplishment impossible. He had no knowledge of
the effect of one's sexual life upon one's work, nor what such a
life when badly arranged can do to a perfect art—how it can
distort the sense of color, weaken that balanced judgment of
character which is so essential to a normal interpretation of life,
make all striving hopeless, take from art its most joyous conception, make life itself seem unimportant and death a relief.

CHAPTER IX

THE summer passed, and with it the freshness and novelty of Paris, though Eugene never really wearied of it. The peculiarities of a different national life, the variations between this and his own country in national ideals, an obviously much more complaisant and human attitude toward morals, a matter-of-fact acceptance of the ills, weaknesses and class differences, to say nothing of the general physical appearance, the dress, habitations and amusements of the people, astonished as much as they entertained him. He was never weary of studying the differences between American and European architecture, noting the pacific manner in which the Frenchman appeared to take life, listening to Angela's unwearied comments on the cleanliness, economy, thoroughness with which the French women kept house, rejoicing in the absence of the American leaning to incessant activity. Angela was struck by the very moderate prices for laundry, the skill with which their concierge—who governed this quarter and who knew sufficient English to talk to her—did her marketing, cooking, sewing and entertaining. The richness of supply and aimless waste of Americans was alike unknown. Because she was naturally of a domestic turn Angela became very intimate with Madame Bourgoche and learned of her a hundred and one little tricks of domestic economy and arrangement.

"You're a peculiar girl, Angela," Eugene once said to her. "I believe you would rather sit down stairs and talk to that Frenchwoman than meet the most interesting literary or artistic personage that ever was. What do you find that's so interesting to talk about?"

"Oh, nothing much," replied Angela, who was not unconscious of the implied hint of her artistic deficiencies. "She's such a smart woman. She's so practical. She knows more in a minute about saving and buying and making a little go a long way than any American woman I ever saw. I'm not interested in her any more than I am in anyone else. All the artistic people do, that I can see, is to run around and pretend that they're a whole lot when they're not."

Eugene saw that he had made an irritating reference, not wholly intended in the way it was being taken.

"I'm not saying she isn't able," he went on. "One talent is

247

as good as another, I suppose. She certainly looks clever enough
to me. Where is her husband?"

"He was killed in the army," returned Angela dolefully.

"Well I suppose you'll learn enough from her to run a hotel
when you get back to New York. You don't know enough about
housekeeping now, do you?"

Eugene smiled with his implied compliment. He was anxious
to get Angela's mind off the art question. He hoped she would
feel or see that he meant nothing, but she was not so easily
pacified.

"You don't think I'm so bad, Eugene, do you?" she asked
after a moment. "You don't think it makes so much difference
whether I talk to Madame Bourgoche? She isn't so dull. She's
awfully smart. You just haven't talked to her. She says she
can tell by looking at you that you're a great artist. You're
different. You remind her of a Mr. Degas that once lived
here. Was he a great artist?"

"Was he!" said Eugene. "Well I guess yes. Did he have
this studio?"

"Oh, a long time ago—fifteen years ago."

Eugene smiled beatifically. This was a great compliment.
He could not help liking Madame Bourgoche for it. She was
bright, no doubt of that, or she would not be able to make such
a comparison. Angela drew from him, as before, that her do-
mesticity and housekeeping skill was as important as anything
else in the world, and having done this was satisfied and cheerful once more. Eugéne thought how little art or conditions or
climate or country altered the fundamental characteristics of
human nature. Here he was in Paris, comparatively well supplied with money, famous, or in process of becoming so, and
quarreling with Angela over little domestic idiosyncrasies, just
as in Washington Square.

By late September Eugene had most of his Paris sketches so
well laid in that he could finish them anywhere. Some
fifteen were as complete as they could be made. A number of
others were nearly so. He decided that he had had a profitable
summer. He had worked hard and here was the work to show
for it—twenty-six canvases which were as good, in his judgment, as those he had painted in New York. They had not
taken so long, but he was surer of himself—surer of his method.
He parted reluctantly with all the lovely things he had seen,
believing that this collection of Parisian views would be as impressive to Americans as had been his New York views. M.
Arquin for one, and many others, including the friends of Deesa

and Dula were delighted with them. The former expressed the belief that some of them might be sold in France.

Eugene returned to America with Angela, and learning that he might stay in the old studio until December first, settled down to finish the work for his exhibition there.

The first suggestion that Eugene had that anything was wrong with him, aside from a growing apprehensiveness as to what the American people would think of his French work, was in the fall, when he began to imagine—or perhaps it was really true—that coffee did not agree with him. He had for several years now been free of his old-time complaint,—stomach trouble; but gradually it was beginning to reappear and he began to complain to Angela that he was feeling an irritation after his meals, that coffee came up in his throat. "I think I'll have to try tea or something else if this doesn't stop," he observed. She suggested chocolate and he changed to that, but this merely resulted in shifting the ill to another quarter. He now began to quarrel with his work—not being able to get a certain effect, and having sometimes altered and re-altered and re-re-altered a canvas until it bore little resemblance to the original arrangement, he would grow terribly discouraged; or believe that he had attained perfection at last, only to change his mind the following morning.

"Now," he would say, "I think I have that thing right at last, thank heaven!"

Angela would heave a sigh of relief, for she could feel instantly any distress or inability that he felt, but her joy was of short duration. In a few hours she would find him working at the same canvas changing something. He grew thinner and paler at this time and his apprehensions as to his future rapidly became morbid.

"By George! Angela," he said to her one day, "it would be a bad thing for me if I were to become sick now. It's just the time that I don't want to. I want to finish this exhibition up right and then go to London. If I could do London and Chicago as I did New York I would be just about made, but if I'm going to get sick—"

"Oh, you're not going to get sick, Eugene," replied Angela, "you just think you are. You want to remember that you've worked very hard this summer. And think how hard you worked last winter! You need a good rest, that's what you need. Why don't you stop after you get this exhibition ready and rest awhile? You have enough to live on for a little bit. M. Charles will probably sell a few more of those pictures, or some of those will sell and then you can wait. Don't try to go to London in the spring. Go on a walking tour or go down South or just rest awhile, anywhere,—that's what you need."

Eugene realized vaguely that it wasn't rest that he needed so much as peace of mind. He was not tired. He was merely nervously excited and apprehensive. He began to sleep badly, to have terrifying dreams, to feel that his heart was failing him. At two o'clock in the morning, the hour when for some reason human vitality appears to undergo a peculiar disturbance, he would wake with a sense of sinking physically. His pulse would appear to be very low, and he would feel his wrists nervously. Not infrequently he would break out in a cold perspiration and would get up and walk about to restore himself. Angela would rise and walk with him. One day at his easel he was seized with a peculiar nervous disturbance—a sudden glittering light before his eyes, a rumbling in his ears, and a sensation which was as if his body were being pricked with ten million needles. It was as though his whole nervous system had given way at every minute point and division. For the time being he was intensely frightened, believing that he was going crazy, but he said nothing. It came to him as a staggering truth that the trouble with him was over-indulgence physically; that the remedy was abstinence, complete or at least partial; that he was probably so far weakened mentally and physically that it would be very difficult for him to recover; that his ability to paint might be seriously affected—his life blighted.

He stood before his canvas holding his brush, wondering. When the shock had completely gone he laid the brush down with a trembling hand. He walked to the window, wiped his cold, damp forehead with his hand and then turned to get his coat from the closet.

"Where are you going?" asked Angela.

"For a little walk. I'll be back soon. I don't feel just as fresh as I might."

She kissed him good-bye at the door and let him go, but her heart troubled her.

"I'm afraid Eugene is going to get sick," she thought. "He ought to stop work."

CHAPTER X

IT was the beginning of a period destined to last five or six years, in which, to say the least, Eugene was not himself. He was not in any sense out of his mind, if power to reason clearly, jest sagely, argue and read intelligently are any evidences of sanity; but privately his mind was a maelstrom of contradictory doubts, feelings and emotions. Always of a philosophic and introspective turn, this peculiar faculty of reasoning deeply and feeling emotionally were now turned upon himself and his own condition and, as in all such cases where we peer too closely into the subtleties of creation, confusion was the result. Previously he had been well satisfied that the world knew nothing. Neither in religion, philosophy nor science was there any answer to the riddle of existence. Above and below the little scintillating plane of man's thought was—what? Beyond the opic strength of the greatest telescope,—far out upon the dim horizon of space—were clouds of stars. What were they doing out there? Who governed them? When were their sidereal motions calculated? He figured life as a grim dark mystery, a sad semi-conscious activity turning aimlessly in the dark. No one knew anything. God knew nothing—himself least of all. Malevolence, life living on death, plain violence—these were the chief characteristics of existence. If one failed of strength in any way, if life were not kind in its bestowal of gifts, if one were not born to fortune's pampering care—the rest was misery. In the days of his strength and prosperity the spectacle of existence had been sad enough: in the hours of threatened delay and defeat it seemed terrible. Why, if his art failed him now, what had he? Nothing. A little puny reputation which he could not sustain, no money, a wife to take care of, years of possible suffering and death. The abyss of death! When he looked into that after all of life and hope, how it shocked him, how it hurt! Here was life and happiness and love in health—there was death and nothingness—æons and æons of nothingness.

He did not immediately give up hope—immediately succumb to the evidences of a crumbling reality. For months and months he fancied each day that this was a temporary condition; that drugs and doctors could heal him. There were various remedies that were advertised in the papers, blood purifiers, nerve restorers, brain foods, which were announced at once as specifics and cures, and while he did not think that the ordinary patent medicine had anything of value in it, he did imagine that some good could be had from tonics, or *the* tonic. A physician whom he consulted recommended rest and an excellent tonic which he knew of. He asked whether he was subject to any wasting disease. Eugene told him no. He confessed to an over-indulgence in the sex-relationship, but the doctor did not believe that ordinarily this should bring about a nervous de-cline. Hard work must have something to do with it, over-anxiety. Some temperaments such as his were predisposed at birth to nervous breakdowns; they had to guard themselves. Eugene would have to be very careful. He should eat regularly, sleep as long as possible, observe regular hours. A system of ex-ercise might not be a bad thing for him. He could get him a pair of Indian clubs or dumb-bells or an exerciser and bring himself back to health that way.

Eugene told Angela that he believed he would try exercising and joined a gymnasium. He took a tonic, walked with her a great deal, sought to ignore the fact that he was nervously depressed. These things were of practically no value, for the body had apparently been drawn a great distance below normal and all the hell of a subnormal state had to be endured before it could gradually come into its own again.

In the meantime he was continuing his passional relations with Angela, in spite of a growing judgment that they were in some way harmful to him. But it was not easy to refrain, and each failure to do so made it harder. It was a customary re-mark of his that "he must quit this," but it was like the self-apologetic assurance of the drunkard that he must reform.

Now that he had stepped out into the limelight of public observation—now that artists and critics and writers some-what knew of him, and in their occasional way were wondering what he was doing, it was necessary that he should bestir him-self to especial effort in order to satisfy the public as to the enduring quality of his art. He was glad, once he realized that he was in for a siege of bad weather, that his Paris drawings had been so nearly completed before the break came. By the day he suffered the peculiar nervousness which seemed to mark the opening of his real decline, he had completed twenty-two paintings, which Angela begged him not to touch; and by sheer strength of will, though he misdoubted gravely, he managed to complete five more. All of these M. Charles came to see on occasion, and he approved of them highly. He was not so sure that they would have the appeal of the American pictures, for after all the city of Paris had been pretty well done over and over in illustration and genré work. It was not so new as New York; the things Eugene chose were not as unconventional. Still, he could say truly they were exceptional. They might try an exhibition of them later in Paris if they did not take here. He was very sorry to see that Eugene was in poor health and urged him to take care of himself.

It seemed as if some malign planetary influence were affecting him. Eugene knew of astrology and palmistry and one day, in a spirit of curiosity and vague apprehensiveness, consulted a practitioner of the former, receiving for his dollar the statement that he was destined to great fame in either art or literature but that he was entering a period of stress which would endure for a number of years. Eugene's spirits sank perceptibly. The musty old gentleman who essayed his books of astrological lore shook his head. He had a rather noble growth of white hair and a white beard, but his coffee-stained vest was covered with tobacco ash and his collar and cuffs were dirty.

"It looks pretty bad between your twenty-eighth and your thirty-second years, but after that there is a notable period of prosperity. Somewhere around your thirty-eighth or thirty-ninth year there is some more trouble—a little—but you will come out of that—that is, it looks as though you would. Your stars show you to be of a nervous, imaginative character, inclined to worry; and I see that your kidneys are weak. You ought never to take much medicine. Your sign is inclined to that but it is without benefit to you. You will be married twice, but I don't see any children."

He rambled on dolefully and Eugene left in great gloom. So it was written in the stars that he was to suffer a period of decline and there was to be more trouble for him in the future. But he did see a period of great success for him between his thirty-second and his thirty-eighth years. That was some comfort. Who was the second woman he was to marry? Was Angela going to die? He walked the streets this early December afternoon, thinking, thinking.

The Blue family had heard a great deal of Eugene's success since Angela had come to New York. There had never been a week but at least one letter, and sometimes two, had gone the rounds of the various members of the family. It was written to Marietta primarily, but Mrs. Blue, Jotham, the boys and the several sisters all received it by turns. Thus the whole regiment of Blue connections knew exactly how it was with Angela and even better than it was; for although things had looked prosperous enough, Angela had not stayed within the limits of bare fact in describing her husband's success. She added atmosphere, not fictitious, but the seeming glory which dwelt in her mind, until the various connections of the Blue family, Marietta in particular, were convinced that there was nothing but dignity and bliss in store for the wife of so talented a man. The studio life which Angela had seen, here and in Paris, the picturesque descriptions which came home from London and Paris, the personalities of M. Charles, M. Arkquin, Isaac Wertheim, Henry L. Tomlins, Luke Severas—all the celebrities whom they met, both in New York and abroad, had been described at length. There was not a dinner, a luncheon, a reception, a tea party, which was not pictured in all its native colors and more. Eugene had become somewhat of a demi-god to his Western connections. The quality of his art was never questioned. It was only a little time now before he would be rich or at least well-to-do.

All the relatives hoped that he would bring Angela home some day on a visit. To think that she should have married such a distinguished man!

In the Witla family it was quite the same. Eugene had not been home to see his parents since his last visit to Blackwood, but they had not been without news. For one thing, Eugene had been neglectful, and somewhat because of this Angela had taken it upon herself to open up a correspondence with his mother. She wrote that of course she didn't know her but that she was terribly fond of Eugene, that she hoped to make him a good wife and that she hoped to make her a satisfactory daughter-in-law. Eugene was so dilatory about writing. She would write for him now and his mother should hear every week. She asked if she and her husband couldn't manage to come and see them sometime. She would be so glad and it would do Eugene so much good. She asked if she couldn't have Myrtle's address— they had moved from Ottumwa—and if Sylvia wouldn't write occasionally. She sent a picture of herself and Eugene, a sketch of the studio which Eugene had made one day, a sketch of herself looking pensively out of the window into Washington Square. Pictures from his first show published in the newspapers, accounts of his work, criticisms,—all reached the members of both families impartially and they were kept well aware of how things were going.

During the time that Eugene was feeling so badly and because, if he were going to lose his health, it might be necessary to economize greatly, it occurred to Angela that it might be advisable for them to go home for a visit. While her family were not rich, they had sufficient means to live on. Eugene's mother also was constantly writing, wanting to know why they didn't come out there for a while. She could not see why Eugene could not paint his pictures as well in Alexandria as in New York or Paris. Eugene listened to this willingly, for it occurred to him that instead of going to London he might do Chicago next, and he and Angela could stay awhile at Blackwood and another while at his own home. They would be welcome guests.

The condition of his finances at this time was not exactly bad, but it was not very good. Of the thirteen hundred dollars he had received for the first three pictures sold, eleven hundred had been used on the foreign trip. He had since used three hundred dollars of his remaining capital of twelve hundred, but M. Charles' sale of two pictures at four hundred each had swelled his bank balance to seventeen hundred dollars; however, on this he had to live now until additional pictures were disposed of. He daily hoped to hear of additional sales, but none occurred.

Moreover, his exhibition in January did not produce quite the impression he thought it would. It was fascinating to look at; the critics and the public imagined that by now he must have created a following for himself, else why should M. Charles make a feature of his work. But Charles pointed out that these foreign studies could not hope to appeal to Americans as did the American things. He indicated that they might take better in France. Eugene was depressed by the general tone of the opinions, but this was due more to his unhealthy state of mind than to any inherent reason for feeling so. There was still Paris to try and there might be some sales of his work here. The latter were slow in materializing, however, and because by February he had not been able to work and because it was necessary that he should husband his resources as carefully as possible, he decided to accept Angela's family's invitation as well as that of his own parents and spend some time in Illinois and Wisconsin. Perhaps his health would become better. He decided also that, if his health permitted, he would work in Chicago.

CHAPTER XI

IT was in packing the trunks and leaving the studio in Washington Square (owing to the continued absence of Mr. Dexter they had never been compelled to vacate it) that Angela came across the first evidence of Eugene's duplicity. Because of his peculiar indifference to everything except matters which related to his art, he had put the letters which he had received in times past from Christina Channing, as well as the one and only one from Ruby Kenny, in a box which had formerly contained writing paper and which he threw carelessly in a corner of his trunk. He had by this time forgotten all about them, though his impression was that he had placed them somewhere where they would not be found. When Angela started to lay out the various things which occupied it she came across this box and opening it took out the letters.

Curiosity as to things relative to Eugene was at this time the dominant characteristic of her life. She could neither think nor reason outside of this relationship which bound her to him. He and his affairs were truly the sum and substance of her existence. She looked at the letters oddly and then opened one—the first from Christina. It was dated Florizel, the summer of three years before when she was waiting so patiently for him at Blackwood. It began conservatively enough—"Dear E—," but it concerned itself immediately with references to an apparently affectionate relationship. "I went this morning to see if by chance there were any tell-tale evidences of either Diana or Adonis in Arcady. There were none of importance. A hairpin or two, a broken mother-of-pearl button from a summer waist, the stub of a lead-pencil wherewith a certain genius sketched. The trees seemed just as unconscious of any nymphs or hamadryads as they could be. The smooth grass was quite unruffled of any feet. It is strange how much the trees and forest know and keep their counsel.

"And how is the hot city by now? Do you miss a certain evenly-swung hammock? Oh, the odor of leaves and the dew! Don't work too hard. You have an easy future and almost too much vitality. More repose for you, sir, and considerably more optimism of thought. I send you good wishes.—Diana."

Angela wondered at once who Diana was, for before she had begun the letter she had looked for the signature on the suc-

ceeding page. Then after reading this she hurried feverishly
from letter to letter, seeking a name. There was none. "Diana
of the Mountains," "The Hamadryad," "The Wood-Nymph,"
"C," "C C"—so they ran, confusing, badgering, enraging
her until all at once it came to light—her first name at least. It
was on the letter from Baltimore suggesting that he come to
Florizel—"Christina."

"Ah," she thought, "Christina! That is her name." Then
she hurried back to read the remaining epistles, hoping to find
some clue to her surname. They were all of the same character, in the manner of writing she despised,—top-lofty, make-
believe, the nasty, hypocritical, cant and make-believe superiority
of the studios. How Angela hated her from that moment. How
she could have taken her by the throat and beaten her head
against the trees she described. Oh, the horrid creature! How
dare she! And Eugene—how could he! What a way to reward
her love! What an answer to make to all her devotion! At
the very time when she was waiting so patiently, he was in the
mountains with this Diana. And here she was packing his trunk
for him like the little slave that she was when he cared so little,
had apparently cared so little all this time. How could he ever
have cared for her and done anything like this! He didn't!
He never had! Dear Heaven!

She began clenching and unclenching her hands dramatically,
working herself into that frenzy of emotion and regret which
was her most notable characteristic. All at once she stopped.
There was another letter in another handwriting on cheaper
paper. "Ruby" was the signature.

"Dear Eugene:"—she read— "I got your note several weeks
ago, but I couldn't bring myself to answer it before this. I
know everything is over between us and that is all right I suppose. It has to be. You couldn't love any woman long, I
think. I know what you say about having to go to New York
to broaden your field is true. You ought to, but I'm sorry you
didn't come out. You might have. Still I don't blame you,
Eugene. It isn't much different from what has been going on
for some time. I have cared, but I'll get over that, I know, and
I won't ever think hard of you. Won't you return me the notes
I have sent you from time to time, and my picture? You won't
want them now.—Ruby."

"I stood by the window last night and looked out on the street.
The moon was shining and those dead trees were waving in the
wind. I saw the moon on that pool of water over in the field.
It looked like silver. Oh, Eugene, I wish that I were dead."

Angela got up (as Eugene had) when she read this.   The
pathos struck home, for somehow it matched her own.   Ruby!
Who was she?   Where had she been concealed while she, Angela,
was coming to Chicago?   Was this the fall and winter of their
engagement?   It certainly was.   Look at the date.   He had
given her the diamond ring on her finger that fall!   He had
sworn eternal affection!   He had sworn there was never another
girl like her in all the world and yet, at that very time, he was
apparently paying *court* to this woman if nothing worse. Heaven!
Could anything like this really be?   He was telling her that
he loved her and making love to this Ruby at the same time.
He was kissing and fondling her and Ruby too! !   Was there
ever such a situation?   He, Eugene Witla, to deceive her this
way.   No wonder he wanted to get rid of her when he came to
New York.   He would have treated her as he had this Ruby.
And Christina!   This Christina! !   Where was she?   Who
was she?   What was she doing now?   She jumped up prepared
to go to Eugene and charge him with his iniquities, but remembered that he was out of the studio—that he had gone
for a walk.   He was sick now, very sick.   Would she dare to
reproach him with these reprehensible episodes?
She came back to the trunk where she was working and sat
down.   Her eyes were hard and cold for the time, but at the
same time there was a touch of terror and of agonized affection.
A face that, in the ordinary lines of its repose, was very much
like that of a madonna, was now drawn and peaked and gray.
Apparently Christina had forsaken him, or it might be that
they still corresponded secretly.   She got up again at that
thought.   Still the letters were old.   It looked as though all
communication had ceased two years ago.   What had he written
to her?—love notes.   Letters full of wooing phrases such as he
had written to her.   Oh, the instability of men, the insincerity,
the lack of responsibility and sense of duty.   Her father,—
what a different man he was; her brothers,—their word was
their bond.   And here was she married to a man who, even in
the days of his most ardent wooing, had been deceiving her.
She had let him lead her astray, too,—disgrace her own home.
Tears came after a while, hot, scalding tears that seared her
cheeks.   And now she was married to him and he was sick
and she would have to make the best of it.   She wanted to make
the best of it, for after all she loved him.
But oh, the cruelty, the insincerity, the unkindness, the brutality of it all.
The fact that Eugene was out for several hours following

her discovery gave her ample time to reflect as to a suitable course of action. Being so impressed by the genius of the man, as imposed upon her by the opinion of others and her own affection, she could not readily think of anything save some method of ridding her soul of this misery and him of his evil tendencies, of making him ashamed of his wretched career, of making him see how badly he had treated her and how sorry he ought to be. She wanted him to feel sorry, very sorry, so that he would be a long time repenting in suffering, but she feared at the same time that she could not make him do that. He was so ethereal, so indifferent, so lost in the contemplation of life that he could not be made to think of her. That was her one complaint. He had other gods before her—the god of his art, the god of nature, the god of people as a spectacle. Frequently she had complained to him in this last year—"you don't love me! you don't love me!" but he would answer, "oh, yes I do. I can't be talking to you all the time, Angel-face. I have work to do. My art has to be cultivated. I can't be making love all the time."

"Oh, it isn't that, it isn't that!" she would exclaim passionately. "You just don't love me, like you ought to. You just don't care. If you did I'd feel it."

"Oh, Angela," he answered, "why do you talk so? Why do you carry on so? You're the funniest girl I ever knew. Now be reasonable. Why don't you bring a little philosophy to bear? We can't be billing and cooing all the time!"

"Billing and cooing! That's the way you think of it. That's the way you talk of it! As though it were something you had to do. Oh, I hate love! I hate life! I hate philosophy! I wish I could die."

"Now, Angela, for Heaven's sake, why will you take on so? I can't stand this. I can't stand these tantrums of yours. They're not reasonable. You know I love you. Why, haven't I shown it? Why should I have married you if I didn't? I wasn't obliged to marry you!"

"Oh, dear! oh, dear!" Angela would sob on, wringing her hands. "Oh, you really don't love me! You don't care! And it will go on this way, getting worse and worse, with less and less of love and feeling until after awhile you won't even want to see me any more—you'll hate me! Oh, dear! oh, dear!"

Eugene felt keenly the pathos involved in this picture of decaying love. In fact, her fear of the disaster which might overtake her little bark of happiness was sufficiently well founded. It might be that his affection would cease—it wasn't even affection now in the true sense of the word,—a passionate intellectual

desire for her companionship. He never had really loved her
for her mind, the beauty of her thoughts. As he meditated he
realized that he had never reached an understanding with her
by an intellectual process at all. It was emotional, subconscious,
a natural drawing together which was not based on reason and
spirituality of contemplation apparently, but on grosser emotions and desires. Physical desire had been involved—strong,
raging, uncontrollable. And for some reason he had always felt
sorry for her—he always had. She was so little, so conscious of
disaster, so afraid of life and what it might do to her. It was
a shame to wreck her hopes and desires. At the same time he
was sorry now for this bondage he had let himself into—this
yoke which he had put about his neck. He could have done so
much better. He might have married a woman of wealth or
a woman with artistic perceptions and philosophic insight like
Christina Channing, who would be peaceful and happy with
him. Angela couldn't be. He really didn't admire her enough,
couldn't fuss over her enough. Even while he was soothing her
in these moments, trying to make her believe that there was no
basis for her fears, sympathizing with her subconscious intuitions that all was not well, he was thinking of how different his
life might have been.

"It won't end that way," he would soothe. "Don't cry. Come
now, don't cry. We're going to be very happy. I'm going to
love you always, just as I'm loving you now, and you're going
to love me. Won't that be all right? Come on, now. Cheer
up. Don't be so pessimistic. Come on, Angela. Please do.
Please!"

Angela would brighten after a time, but there were spells of
apprehension and gloom; they were common, apt to burst forth
like a summer storm when neither of them was really expecting it.

The discovery of these letters now checked the feeling, with
which she tried to delude herself at times, that there might be
anything more than kindness here. They confirmed her suspicions that there was not and brought on that sense of defeat and
despair which so often and so tragically overcame her. It did
it at a time, too, when Eugene needed her undivided consideration and feeling, for he was in a wretched state of mind. To
have her quarrel with him now, lose her temper, fly into rages
and compel him to console her, was very trying. He was in
no mood for it; could not very well endure it without injury
to himself. He was seeking for an atmosphere of joyousness,
wishing to find a cheerful optimism somewhere which would pull

him out of himself and make him whole. Not infrequently he dropped in to see Norma Whitmore, Isadora Crane, who was getting along very well on the stage, Hedda Andersen, who had a natural charm of intellect with much vivacity, even though she was a model, and now and then Miriam Finch. The latter was glad to see him alone, almost as a testimony against Angela, though she would not go out of her way to conceal from Angela the fact that he had been there. The others, though he said nothing, assumed that since Angela did not come with him he wanted nothing said and observed his wish. They were inclined to think that he had made a matrimonial mistake and was possibly artistically or intellectually lonely. All of them noted his decline in health with considerate apprehension and sorrow. It was too bad, they thought, if his health was going to fail him just at this time. Eugene lived in fear lest Angela should become aware of any of these visits. He thought he could not tell her because in the first place she would resent his not having taken her with him; and in the next, if he had proposed it first, she would have objected, or set another date, or asked pointless questions. He liked the liberty of going where he pleased, saying nothing, not feeling it necessary to say anything. He longed for the freedom of his old pre-matrimonial days. Just at this time, because he could not work artistically and because he was in need of diversion and of joyous artistic palaver, he was especially miserable. Life seemed very dark and ugly.

Eugene, returning and feeling, as usual, depressed about his state, sought to find consolation in her company. He came in at one o'clock, their usual lunch hour, and finding Angela still working, said, "George! but you like to keep at things when you get started, don't you? You're a regular little work-horse. Having much trouble?"

"No-o," replied Angela, dubiously.

Eugene noted the tone of her voice. He thought she was not very strong and this packing was getting on her nerves. Fortunately there were only some trunks to look after, for the vast mass of their housekeeping materials belonged to the studio. Still no doubt she was weary.

"Are you very tired?" he asked.

"No-o," she replied.

"You look it," he said, slipping his arm about her. Her face, which he turned up with his hand, was pale and drawn.

"It isn't anything physical," she replied, looking away from him in a tragic way. "It's just my heart. It's here!" and she laid her hand over her heart.

"What's the matter now?" he asked, suspecting something emotional, though for the life of him he could not imagine what. "Does your heart hurt you?"

"It isn't my real heart," she returned, "it's just my mind, my feelings; though I don't suppose they ought to matter."

"What's the matter now, Angel-face," he persisted, for he was sorry for her. This emotional ability of hers had the power to move him. It might have been acting, or it might not have been. It might be either a real or a fancied woe;—in either case it was real to her. "What's come up?" he continued. "Aren't you just tired? Suppose we quit this and go out somewhere and get something to eat. You'll feel better."

"No, I couldn't eat," she replied. "I'll stop now and get your lunch, but I don't want anything."

"Oh, what's the matter, Angela?" he begged. "I know there's something. Now what is it? You're tired, or you're sick, or something has happened. Is it anything that I have done? Look at me! Is it?"

Angela held away from him, looking down. She did not know how to begin this but she wanted to make him terribly sorry if she could, as sorry as she was for herself. She thought he ought to be; that if he had any true feeling of shame and sympathy in him he would be. Her own condition in the face of his shameless past was terrible. She had no one to love her. She had no one to turn to. Her own family did not understand her life any more—it had changed so. She was a different woman now, greater, more important, more distinguished. Her experiences with Eugene here in New York, in Paris, in London and even before her marriage, in Chicago and Blackwood, had changed her point of view. She was no longer the same in her ideas, she thought, and to find herself deserted in this way emotionally—not really loved, not ever having been really loved but just toyed with, made a doll and a plaything, was terrible.

"Oh, dear!" she exclaimed in a shrill staccato, "I don't know what to do! I don't know what to say! I don't know what to think! If I only knew how to think or what to do!"

"What's the matter?" begged Eugene, releasing his hold and turning his thoughts partially to himself and his own condition as well as to hers. His nerves were put on edge by these emotional tantrums—his brain fairly ached. It made his hands tremble. In his days of physical and nervous soundness it did not matter, but now, when he was sick, when his own heart was weak, as he fancied, and his nerves set to jangling by the least discord, it was almost more than he could bear. "Why don't you speak?" he insisted. "You know I can't stand this. I'm in no condition. What's the trouble? What's the use of carrying on this way? Are you going to tell me?"

"There!" Angela said, pointing her finger at the box of letters she had laid aside on the window-sill. She knew he would see them, would remember instantly what they were about.

Eugene looked. The box came to his memory instantly. He picked it up nervously, sheepishly, for this was like a blow in the face which he had no power to resist. The whole peculiar nature of his transactions with Ruby and with Christina came back to him, not as they had looked to him at the time, but as they were appearing to Angela now. What must she think of him? Here he was protesting right along that he loved her, that he was happy and satisfied to live with her, that he was not interested in any of these other women whom she knew to be interested in him and of whom she was inordinately jealous, that he had always loved her and her only, and yet here were these letters suddenly come to light, giving the lie to all these protestations and asseverations—making him look like the coward, the blackguard, the moral thief that he knew himself to be. To be dragged out of the friendly darkness of lack of knowledge and understanding on her part and set forth under the clear white light of positive proof—he stared helplessly, his nerves trembling, his brain aching, for truly he was in no condition for an emotional argument.

And yet Angela was crying now. She had walked away from him and was leaning against the mantel-piece sobbing as if her heart would break. There was a real convincing ache in the sound—the vibration expressing the sense of loss and defeat and despair which she felt. He was staring at the box wondering why he had been such an idiot as to leave them in his trunk, to have saved them at all.

"Well, I don't know that there is anything to say to that," he observed finally, strolling over to where she was. There wasn't anything that he could say—that he knew. He was terribly sorry—sorry for her, sorry for himself. "Did you read them all?" he asked, curiously.

She nodded her head in the affirmative.

"Well, I didn't care so much for Christina Channing," he observed, deprecatingly. He wanted to say something, anything which would relieve her depressed mood. He knew it couldn't be much. If he could only make her believe that there wasn't anything vital in either of these affairs, that his interests and protestations had been of a light, philandering character. Still the Ruby Kenny letter showed that she cared for him desperately. He could not say anything against Ruby.

Angela caught the name of Christina Channing clearly. It seared itself in her brain. She recalled now that it was she of whom she had heard him speak in a complimentary way from time to time. He had told in studios of what a lovely voice she had, what a charming platform presence she had, how she could sing so feelingly, how intelligently she looked upon life, how good looking she was, how she was coming back to grand opera some day. And he had been in the mountains with her—had made love to her while she, Angela, was out in Blackwood waiting for him patiently. It aroused on the instant all the fighting jealousy that was in her breast; it was the same jealousy that had determined her once before to hold him in spite of the plotting and scheming that appeared to her to be going on about her. They should not have him—these nasty studio superiorities—not any one of them, nor all of them combined, if they were to unite and try to get him. They had treated her shamefully since she had been in the East. They had almost uniformly ignored her. They would come to see Eugene, of course, and now that he was famous they could not be too nice to him, but as for her—well, they had no particular use for her. Hadn't she seen it! Hadn't she watched the critical, hypocritical, examining expressions in their eyes! She wasn't smart enough! She wasn't literary enough or artistic enough. She knew as much about life as they did and more—ten times as much; and yet because she couldn't strut and pose and stare and talk in an affected voice they thought themselves superior. And so did Eugene, the wretched creature! Superior! The cheap, mean, nasty, selfish upstarts! Why, the majority of them had nothing. Their clothes were mere rags and tags, when you came to examine them closely—badly sewed, of poor material, merely slung together, and yet they wore them with such a grand air! She would show them. She would dress herself too, one of these days, when Eugene had the means. She was doing it now—a great deal more than when she first came, and she would do it a great deal more before long. The nasty, mean, cheap, selfish, make-belief things. She would show them! O-oh! how she hated them.

Now as she cried she also thought of the fact that Eugene could write love letters to this horrible Christina Channing—one of the same kind, no doubt; her letters showed it. O-oh! how she hated her! If she could only get at her to poison her. And her sobs sounded much more of the sorrow she felt than of the rage. She was helpless in a way and she knew it. She did not dare to show him exactly what she felt. She was afraid of him. He might possibly leave her. He really did not care for her enough to stand everything from her—or did he? This doubt was the one terrible, discouraging, annihilating feature of the whole thing—if he only cared.

"I wish you wouldn't cry, Angela," said Eugene appealingly, after a time. "It isn't as bad as you think. It looks pretty bad, but I wasn't married then, and I didn't care so very much for these people—not as much as you think; really I didn't. It may look that way to you, but I didn't."

"Didn't care!" sneered Angela, all at once, flaring up. "Didn't care! It looks as though you didn't care, with one of them calling you Honey Boy and Adonis, and the other saying she wishes she were dead. A fine time you'd have convincing anyone that you didn't care. And I out in Blackwood at that very time, longing and waiting for you to come, and you up in the mountains making love to another woman. Oh, I know how much you cared. You showed how much you cared when you could leave me out there to wait for you eating my heart out while you were off in the mountains having a good time with another woman. 'Dear E—,' and 'Precious Honey Boy,' and 'Adonis'! That shows how much you cared, doesn't it!"

Eugene stared before him helplessly. Her bitterness and wrath surprised and irritated him. He did not know that she was capable of such an awful rage as showed itself in her face and words at this moment, and yet he did not know but that she was well justified. Why so bitter though—so almost brutal? He was sick. Had she no consideration for him?

"I tell you it wasn't as bad as you think," he said stolidly, showing for the first time a trace of temper and opposition. "I wasn't married then. I did like Christina Channing; I did like Ruby Kenny. What of it? I can't help it now. What am I going to say about it? What do you want me to say? What do you want me to do?"

"Oh," whimpered Angela, changing her tone at once from helpless accusing rage to pleading, self-commiserating misery. "And you can stand there and say to me 'what of it'? What of it! What of it! What shall you say? What do you think you ought to say? And me believing that you were so honorable and faithful! Oh, if I had only known! If I had only known! I had better have drowned myself a hundred times over than have waked and found that I wasn't loved. Oh, dear, oh, dear! I don't know what I ought to do! I don't know what I can do!"

"But I do love you," protested Eugene soothingly, anxious to say or do anything which would quiet this terrific storm. He could not imagine how he could have been so foolish as to leave these letters lying around. Dear Heaven! What a mess he had made of this! If only he had put them safely outside the home or destroyed them. Still he had wanted to keep Christina's letters; they were so charming.

"Yes, you love me!" flared Angela. "I see how you love me. Those letters show it! Oh, dear! oh, dear! I wish I were dead."

"Listen to me, Angela," replied Eugene desperately, "I know this correspondence looks bad. I did make love to Miss Kenny and to Christina Channing, but you see I didn't care enough to marry either of them. If I had I would have. I cared for you. Believe it or not. I married you. Why did I marry you? Answer me that? I needn't have married you. Why did I? Because I loved you, of course. What other reason could I have?"

"Because you couldn't get Christina Channing," snapped Angela, angrily, with the intuitive sense of one who reasons from one material fact to another, "that's why. If you could have, you would have. I know it. Her letters show it."

"Her letters don't show anything of the sort," returned Eugene angrily. "I couldn't get her? I could have had her, easily enough. I didn't want her. If I had wanted her, I would have married her—you can bet on that."

He hated himself for lying in this way, but he felt for the time being that he had to do it. He did not care to stand in the rôle of a jilted lover. He half-fancied that he could have married Christina if he had really tried.

"Anyhow," he said, "I'm not going to argue that point with you. I didn't marry her, so there you are; and I didn't marry Ruby Kenny either. Well you can think all you want; but I know. I cared for them, but I didn't marry them. I married you instead. I ought to get credit for something on that score. I married you because I loved you, I suppose. That's perfectly plain, isn't it?" He was half convincing himself that he had loved her—in some degree.

"Yes, I see how you love me," persisted Angela, cogitating this very peculiar fact which he was insisting on and which it was very hard intellectually to overcome. "You married me because you couldn't very well get out of it, that's why. Oh, I know. You didn't want to marry me. That's very plain. You wanted to marry someone else. Oh, dear! oh, dear!"

"Oh, how you talk!" replied Eugene defiantly. "Marry someone else! Who did I want to marry? I could have married
often enough if I had wanted to. I didn't want to marry,
that's all. Believe it or not. I wanted to marry you and I
did. I don't think you have any right to stand there and argue
so. What you say isn't so, and you know it."

Angela cogitated this argument further. He had married her!
Why had he? He might have cared for Christina and Ruby,
but he must have cared for her too. Why hadn't she thought
of that? There was something in it—something besides a mere
desire to deceive her. Perhaps he did care for her a little. Anyway it was plain that she could not get very far by arguing
with him—he was getting stubborn, argumentative, contentious.
She had not seen him that way before.

"Oh!" she sobbed, taking refuge from this very difficult
realm of logic in the safer and more comfortable one of illogical
tears. "I don't know what to do! I don't know what to think!"

She was badly treated, no doubt of that. Her life was a
failure, but even so there was some charm about him. As he
stood there, looking aimlessly around, defiant at one moment,
appealing at another, she could not help seeing that he was not
wholly bad. He was just weak on this one point. He loved
pretty women. They were always trying to win him to them.
He was probably not wholly to blame. If he would only be repentant enough, this thing might be allowed to blow over.
It couldn't be forgiven. She never could forgive him for the
way he had deceived her. Her ideal of him had been pretty
hopelessly shattered—but she might live with him on probation.

"Angela!" he said, while she was still sobbing, and feeling
that he ought to apologize to her. "Won't you believe me?
Won't you forgive me? I don't like to hear you cry this way.
There's no use saying that I didn't do anything. There's no
use my saying anything at all, really. You won't believe me. I
don't want you to; but I'm sorry. Won't you believe that?
Won't you forgive me?"

Angela listened to this curiously, her thoughts going around
in a ring for she was at once despairing, regretful, revengeful,
critical, sympathetic toward him, desirous of retaining her state,
desirous of obtaining and retaining his love, desirous of punish-
ing him, desirous of doing any one of a hundred things. Oh,
if he had only never done this! And he was sickly, too. He
needed her sympathy.

"Won't you forgive me, Angela?" he pleaded softly, laying
his hand on her arm. "I'm not going to do anything like

that any more. Won't you believe me? Come on now. Quit crying, won't you?"

Angela hesitated for a while, lingering dolefully. She did not know what to do, what to say. It might be that he would not sin against her any more. He had not thus far, in so far as she knew. Still this was a terrible revelation. All at once, because he manœuvred himself into a suitable position and because she herself was weary of fighting and crying, and because she was longing for sympathy, she allowed herself to be pulled into his arms, her head to his shoulder, and there she cried more copiously than ever. Eugene for the moment felt terribly grieved. He was really sorry for her. It wasn't right. He ought to be ashamed of himself. He should never have done anything like that.

"I'm sorry," he whispered, "really I am. Won't you forgive me?"

"Oh, I don't know what to do! what to think!" moaned Angela after a time.

"Please do, Angela," he urged, holding her questioningly.

There was more of this pleading and emotional badgering until finally out of sheer exhaustion Angela said yes. Eugene's nerves were worn to a thread by the encounter. He was pale, exhausted, distraught. Many scenes like this, he thought, would set him crazy; and still he had to go through a world of petting and love-making even now. It was not easy to bring her back to her normal self. It was bad business, this philandering, he thought. It seemed to lead to all sorts of misery for him, and Angela was jealous. Dear Heaven! what a wrathful, vicious, contentious nature she had when she was aroused. He had never suspected that. How could he truly love her when she acted like that? How could he sympathize with her? He recalled how she sneered at him—how she taunted him with Christina's having discarded him. He was weary, excited, desirous of rest and sleep, but now he must make more love. He fondled her, and by degrees she came out of her blackest mood; but he was not really forgiven even then. He was just understood better. And she was not truly happy again but only hopeful—and watchful.

CHAPTER XII

SPRING, summer and fall came and went with Eugene and Angela first in Alexandria and then in Blackwood. In suffering this nervous breakdown and being compelled to leave New York, Eugene missed some of the finest fruits of his artistic efforts, for M. Charles, as well as a number of other people, were interested in him and were prepared to entertain him in an interesting and conspicuous way. He could have gone out a great deal, but his mental state was such that he was poor company for anyone. He was exceedingly morbid, inclined to discuss gloomy subjects, to look on life as exceedingly sad and to believe that people generally were evil. Lust, dishonesty, selfishness, envy, hypocrisy, slander, hate, theft, adultery, murder, dementia, insanity, inanity—these and death and decay occupied his thoughts. There was no light anywhere. Only a storm of evil and death. These ideas coupled with his troubles with Angela, the fact that he could not work, the fact that he felt he had made a matrimonial mistake, the fact that he feared he might die or go crazy, made a terrible and agonizing winter for him.

Angela's attitude, while sympathetic enough, once the first storm of feeling was over, was nevertheless involved with a substratum of criticism. While she said nothing, agreed that she would forget, Eugene had the consciousness all the while that she wasn't forgetting, that she was secretly reproaching him and that she was looking for new manifestations of weakness in this direction, expecting them and on the alert to prevent them.

The spring-time in Alexandria, opening as it did shortly after they reached there, was in a way a source of relief to Eugene. He had decided for the time being to give up trying to work, to give up his idea of going either to London or Chicago, and merely rest. Perhaps it was true that he was tired. He didn't feel that way. He couldn't sleep and he couldn't work, but he felt brisk enough. It was only because he couldn't work that he was miserable. Still he decided to try sheer idleness. Perhaps that would revive his wonderful art for him. Meantime he speculated ceaselessly on the time he was losing, the celebrities he was missing, the places he was not seeing. Oh, London, London! If he could only do that.

Mr. and Mrs. Witla were immensely pleased to have their boy back with them again. Being in their way simple, unsophisticated people, they could not understand how their son's health could have undergone such a sudden reverse.

"I never saw Gene looking so bad in all his life," observed Witla pére to his wife the day Eugene arrived. "His eyes are so sunken. What in the world do you suppose is ailing him?"

"How should I know?" replied his wife, who was greatly distressed over her boy. "I suppose he's just tired out, that's all. He'll probably be all right after he rests awhile. Don't let on that you think he's looking out of sorts. Just pretend that he's all right. What do you think of his wife?"

"She appears to be a very nice little woman," replied Witla. "She's certainly devoted to him. I never thought Eugene would marry just that type, but he's the judge. I suppose people thought that I would never marry anybody like you, either," he added jokingly.

"Yes, you did make a terrible mistake," jested his wife in return. "You worked awfully hard to make it."

"I was young! I was young! You want to remember that," retorted Witla. "I didn't know much in those days."

"You don't appear to know much better yet," she replied, "do you?"

He smiled and patted her on the back. "Well, anyhow I'll have to make the best of it, won't I? It's too late now."

"It certainly is," replied his wife.

Eugene and Angela were given his old room on the second floor, commanding a nice view of the yard and the street corner, and they settled down to spend what the Witla parents hoped would be months of peaceful days. It was a curious sensation to Eugene to find himself back here in Alexandria looking out upon the peaceful neighborhood in which he had been raised, the trees, the lawn, the hammock replaced several times since he had left, but still in its accustomed place. The thought of the little lakes and the small creek winding about the town were a comfort to him. He could go fishing now and boating, and there were some interesting walks here and there. He began to amuse himself by going fishing the first week, but it was still a little cold, and he decided, for the time being, to confine himself to walking.

Days of this kind grow as a rule quickly monotonous. To a man of Eugene's turn of mind there was so little in Alexandria to entertain him. After London and Paris, Chicago and New York, the quiet streets of his old home town were a joke. He visited the office of the *Appeal* but both Jonas Lyle and Caleb Williams had gone, the former to St. Louis, the latter to Bloomington. Old Benjamin Burgess, his sister's husband's father, was unchanged except in the matter of years. He told Eugene that he was thinking of running for Congress in the next campaign—the Republican organization owed it to him. His son Henry, Sylvia's husband, had become a treasurer of the local bank. He was working as patiently and quietly as ever, going to church Sundays, going to Chicago occasionally on business, consulting with farmers and business men about small loans. He was a close student of the several banking journals of the country, and seemed to be doing very well financially. Sylvia had little to say of how he was getting along. Having lived with him for eleven years, she had become somewhat close-mouthed like himself. Eugene could not help smiling at the lean, slippered subtlety of the man, young as he was. He was so quiet, so conservative, so intent on all the little things which make a conventionally successful life. Like a cabinet maker, he was busy inlaying the little pieces which would eventually make the perfect whole.

Angela took up the household work, which Mrs. Witla grudgingly consented to share with her, with a will. She liked to work and would put the house in order while Mrs. Witla was washing the dishes after breakfast. She would make special pies and cakes for Eugene when she could without giving offense, and she tried to conduct herself so that Mrs. Witla would like her. She did not think so much of the Witla household. It wasn't so much better than her own—hardly as good. Still it was Eugene's birthplace and for that reason important. There was a slight divergence of view-point though, between his mother and herself, over the nature of life and how to live it. Mrs. Witla was of an easier, more friendly outlook on life than Angela. She liked to take things as they came without much worry, while Angela was of a naturally worrying disposition. The two had one very human failing in common—they could not work with anyone else at anything. Each preferred to do all that was to be done rather than share it at all. Both being so anxious to be conciliatory for Eugene's sake and for permanent peace in the family, there was small chance for any disagreement, for neither was without tact. But there was just a vague hint of something in the air— that Angela was a little hard and selfish, on Mrs. Witla's part; that Mrs. Witla was just the least bit secretive, or shy or distant—from Angela's point of view. All was serene and

lovely on the surface, however, with many won't-you-let-me's
and please-do-now's on both sides. Mrs. Witla, being so much
older, was, of course, calmer and in the family seat of dignity
and peace.

To be able to sit about in a chair, lie in a hammock, stroll in
the woods and country fields and be perfectly happy in idle
contemplation and loneliness, requires an exceptional talent for
just that sort of thing. Eugene once fancied he had it, as did his
parents, but since he had heard the call of fame he could never
be still any more. And just at this time he was not in need
of solitude and idle contemplation but of diversion and entertainment. He needed companionship of the right sort, gayety,
sympathy, enthusiasm. Angela had some of this, when she was
not troubled about anything, his parents, his sister, his old acquaintances had a little more to offer. They could not, however,
be forever talking to him or paying him attention, and beyond
them there was nothing. The town had no resources. Eugene
would walk the long country roads with Angela or go boating
or fishing sometimes, but still he was lonely. He would sit on
the porch or in the hammock and think of what he had seen
in London and Paris—how he might be at work. St. Paul's
in a mist, the Thames Embankment, Piccadilly, Blackfriars
Bridge, the muck of Whitechapel and the East End—how he
wished he was out of all this and painting them. If he could
only paint. He rigged up a studio in his father's barn, using a
north loft door for light and essayed certain things from memory, but there was no making anything come out right. He
had this fixed belief, which was a notion purely, that there was
always something wrong. Angela, his mother, his father, whom
he occasionally asked for an opinion, might protest that it was
beautiful or wonderful, but he did not believe it. After a few
altering ideas of this kind, under the influences of which he
would change and change and change things, he would find
himself becoming wild in his feelings, enraged at his condition,
intensely despondent and sorry for himself.

"Well," he would say, throwing down his brush, "I shall
simply have to wait until I come out of this. I can't do anything this way." Then he would walk or read or row on the
lakes or play solitaire, or listen to Angela playing on the piano
that his father had installed for Myrtle long since. All the time
though he was thinking of his condition, what he was missing,
how the gay world was surging on rapidly elsewhere, how long
it would be before he got well, if ever. He talked of going to
Chicago and trying his hand at scenes there, but Angela per-

suaded him to rest for a while longer. In June she promised him they would go to Blackwood for the summer, coming back here in the fall if he wished, or going on to New York or staying in Chicago, just as he felt about it. Now he needed rest.

"Eugene will probably be all right by then," Angela volunteered to his mother, "and he can make up his mind whether he wants to go to Chicago or London."

She was very proud of her ability to talk of where they would go and what they would do.

CHAPTER XIII

IF it had not been for the lurking hope of some fresh exciting experience with a woman, he would have been unconscionably lonely. As it was, this thought with him—quite as the confirmed drunkard's thought of whiskey—buoyed him up, kept him from despairing utterly, gave his mind the only diversion it had from the ever present thought of failure. If by chance he should meet some truly beautiful girl, gay, enticing, who would fall in love with him! that would be happiness. Only, Angela was constantly watching him these days and, besides, more girls would simply mean that his condition would be aggravated. Yet so powerful was the illusion of desire, the sheer animal magnetism of beauty, that when it came near him in the form of a lovely girl of his own temperamental inclinations he could not resist it. One look into an inviting eye, one glance at a face whose outlines were soft and delicate—full of that subtle suggestion of youth and health which is so characteristic of girlhood—and the spell was cast. It was as though the very form of the face, without will or intention on the part of the possessor, acted hypnotically upon its beholder. The Arabians believed in the magic power of the word Abracadabra to cast a spell. For Eugene the form of a woman's face and body was quite as powerful.

While he and Angela were in Alexandria from February to May, he met one night at his sister's house a girl who, from the point of view of the beauty which he admired and to which he was so susceptible, was extremely hypnotic, and who for the ease and convenience of a flirtation was very favorably situated. She was the daughter of a traveling man, George Roth by name, whose wife, the child's mother, was dead, but who lived with his sister in an old tree-shaded house on the edge of Green Lake not far from the spot where Eugene had once attempted to caress his first love, Stella Appleton. Frieda was the girl's name. She was extremely attractive, not more than eighteen years of age, with large, clear, blue eyes, a wealth of yellowish-brown hair and a plump but shapely figure. She was a graduate of the local high school, well developed for her years, bright, rosy-cheeked, vivacious and with a great deal of natural intelligence which attracted the attention of Eugene at once. Normally he was extremely fond of a natural, cheerful, laughing disposition. In his present state he was abnormally so. This girl and her foster mother had heard of him a long time since through his parents and his sister, whom they knew well and whom they visited frequently. George Roth had moved here since Eugene had first left for Chicago, and because he was so much on the road he had not seen him since. Frieda, on all his previous visits, had been too young to take an interest in men, but now at this age, when she was just blossoming into womanhood, her mind was fixed on them. She did not expect to be interested in Eugene because she knew he was married, but because of his reputation as an artist she was curious about him. Everybody knew who he was. The local papers had written up his success and published his portrait. Frieda expected to see a man of about forty, stern and sober. Instead she met a smiling youth of twenty-nine, rather gaunt and hollow-eyed, but none the less attractive for that. Eugene, with Angela's approval, still affected a loose, flowing tie, a soft turn-down collar, brown corduroy suits as a rule, the coat cut with a belt, shooting jacket fashion, a black iron ring of very curious design upon one of his fingers, and a soft hat. His hands were very thin and white, his skin pale. Frieda, rosy, as thoughtless as a butterfly, charmingly clothed in a dress of blue linen, laughing, afraid of him because of his reputation, attracted his attention at once. She was like all the young, healthy, laughing girls he had ever known, delightful. He wished he were single again that he might fall into a jesting conversation with her. She seemed inclined to be friendly from the first.

Angela being present, however, and Frieda's foster mother, it was necessary for him to be circumspect and distant. The latter, Sylvia and Angela, talked of art and listened to Angela's descriptions of Eugene's eccentricities, idiosyncrasies and experiences, which were a never-failing source of interest to the common run of mortals whom they met. Eugene would sit by in a comfortable chair with a weary, genial or indifferent look on his face as his mood happened to be. To-night he was bored and a little indifferent in his manner. No one here interested him save this girl, the beauty of whose face nourished his secret dreams. He longed to have some such spirit of youth near him always. Why could not women remain young?

While they were laughing and talking, Eugene picked up a copy of Howard Pyle's "Knights of the Round Table" with its warm heavy illustrations of the Arthurian heroes and heroines, and began to study the stately and exaggerated characteristics of the various characters. Sylvia had purchased it for her seven-year old boy Jack, asleep upstairs, but Frieda had read it in her girlhood a few years before. She had been moving restlessly about, conscious of an interest in Eugene but not knowing how to find an opportunity for conversation. His smile, which he sometimes directed toward her, was to her entrancing.

"Oh, I read that," she said, when she saw him looking at it. She had drifted to a position not far behind his chair and near one of the windows. She pretended to be looking out at first, but now began to talk to him. "I used to be crazy about every one of the Knights and Ladies—Sir Launcelot, Sir Galahad, Sir Tristram, Sir Gawaine, Queen Guinevere."

"Did you ever hear of Sir Bluff?" he asked teasingly, "or Sir Stuff? or Sir Dub?" He looked at her with a mocking light of humor in his eyes.

"Oh, there aren't such people," laughed Frieda, surprised at the titles but tickled at the thought of them.

"Don't you let him mock you, Frieda," put in Angela, who was pleased at the girl's gayety and glad that Eugene had found someone in whom he could take an interest. She did not fear the simple Western type of girl like Frieda and her own sister Marietta. They were franker, more kindly, better intentioned than the Eastern studio type, and besides they did not consider themselves superior. She was playing the rôle of the condescending leader here.

"Certainly there are," replied Eugene solemnly, addressing Frieda. "They are the new Knights of the Round Table. Haven't you ever heard of that book?"

"No, I haven't," answered Frieda gaily, "and there isn't any such. You're just teasing me."

"Teasing you? Why I wouldn't think of such a thing. And there is such a book. It's published by Harper and Brothers and is called 'The New Knights of the Round Table.' You simply haven't heard of it, that's all."

Frieda was impressed. She didn't know whether to believe him or not. She opened her eyes in a curiously inquiring girlish way which appealed to Eugene strongly. He wished he were free to kiss her pretty, red, thoughtlessly-parted lips. Angela herself was faintly doubtful as to whether he was speaking of a real book or not.

"Sir Stuff is a very famous Knight," he went on, "and so is Sir Bluff. They're inseparable companions in the book. As for Sir Dub and Sir Hack, and the Lady Dope—"

"Oh, hush, Eugene," called Angela gaily. "Just listen to what he's telling Frieda," she remarked to Miss Roth. "You mustn't mind him though. He's always teasing someone. Why didn't you raise him better, Sylvia?" she asked of Eugene's sister.

"Oh, don't ask me. We never could do anything with Gene. I never knew he had much jesting in him until he came back this time."

"They're very wonderful," they heard him telling Frieda, "all fine rosy gentlemen and ladies."

Frieda was impressed by this charming, good-natured man. His spirit was evidently as youthful and gay as her own. She sat before him looking into his smiling eyes while he teased her about this, that and the other foible of youth. Who were her sweethearts? How did she make love? How many boys lined up to see her come out of church on Sunday? He knew. "I'll bet they look like a line of soldiers on dress parade," he volunteered, "all with nice new ties and clean pocket handkerchiefs and their shoes polished and—"

"Oh, ha! ha!" laughed Frieda. The idea appealed to her immensely. She started giggling and bantering with him and their friendship was definitely sealed. She thought he was delightful.

CHAPTER XIV

THE opportunity for further meetings seemed to come about quite naturally. The Witla boathouse, where the family kept one small boat, was at the foot of the Roth lawn, reached by a slightly used lane which came down that side of the house; and also by a grape-arbor which concealed the lake from the lower end of the house and made a sheltered walk to the waterside, at the end of which was a weather-beaten wooden bench. Eugene came here sometimes to get the boat to row or to fish. On several occasions Angela had accompanied him, but she did not care much for rowing or fishing and was perfectly willing that he should go alone if he wanted to. There was also the friendship of Miss Roth for Mr. and Mrs. Witla, which occasionally brought her and Frieda to the house. And Frieda came from time to time to his studio in the barn, to see him paint. Because of her youth and innocence Angela thought very little of her presence there, which struck Eugene as extremely fortunate. He was interested in her charms, anxious to make love to her in a philandering sort of way, without intending to do her any harm. It struck him as a little curious that he should find her living so near the spot where once upon a winter's night he had made love to Stella. There was something not unlike Stella about her, though she was softer, more whole souledly genial and pliable to his moods.

He saw her one day, when he went for his boat, standing out in the yard, and she came down to the waterside to greet him.

"Well," he said, smiling at her fresh morning appearance, and addressing her with that easy familiarity with which he knew how to take youth and life generally, "we're looking as bright as a butterfly. I don't suppose we butterflies have to work very hard, do we?"

"Oh, don't we," replied Frieda. "That's all you know."

"Well, I don't know, that's true, but perhaps one of these butterflies will tell me. Now you, for instance."

Frieda smiled. She scarcely knew how to take him, but she thought he was delightful. She hadn't the faintest conception either of the depth and subtlety of his nature or of the genial, kindly inconstancy of it. She only saw him as a handsome, smiling man, not at all too old, witty, good-natured, here by the bright green waters of this lake, pulling out his boat. He

278

looked so cheerful to her, so care free. She had him indissolubly mixed in her impressions with the freshness of the ground, the newness of the grass, the brightness of the sky, the chirping of the birds and even the little scintillating ripples on the water.

"Butterflies never work, that I know," he said, refusing to take her seriously. "They just dance around in the sunlight and have a good time. Did you ever talk to a butterfly about that?"

Frieda merely smiled at him.

He pushed his boat into the water, holding it lightly by a rope, got down a pair of oars from a rack and stepped into it. Then he stood there looking at her.

"Have you lived in Alexandria long?" he asked.

"About eight years now."

"Do you like it?"

"Sometimes, not always. I wish we lived in Chicago. O-oh!" she sniffed, turning up her pretty nose, "isn't that lovely!" She was smelling some odor of flowers blown from a garden.

"Yes, I get it too. Geraniums, isn't it? They're blooming here, I see. A day like this sets me crazy." He sat down in his boat and put his oars in place.

"Well, I have to go and try my luck for whales. Wouldn't you like to go fishing?"

"I would, all right," said Frieda, "only aunt wouldn't let me, I think. I'd just love to go. It's lots of fun, catching fish."

"Yes, *catching* fish," laughed Eugene. "Well, I'll bring you a nice little shark—one that bites. Would you like that? Down in the Atlantic Ocean they have sharks that bite and bark. They come up out of the water at night and bark like a dog."

"O-o-oh, dear! how funny!" giggled Frieda, and Eugene began slowly rowing his boat lakeward.

"Be sure you bring me a nice fish," she called.

"Be sure you're here to get it when I come back," he answered.

He saw her with the lattice of spring leaves behind her, the old house showing pleasantly on its rise of ground, some house-martens turning in the morning sky.

"What a lovely girl," he thought. "She's beautiful—as fresh as a flower. That is the one great thing in the world—the beauty of girlhood."

He came back after a time expecting to find her, but her foster-mother had sent her on an errand. He felt a keen sense of disappointment.

There were other meetings after this, once on a day when he

came back practically fishless and she laughed at him; once
when he saw her sunning her hair on the back porch after she
had washed it and she came down to stand under the trees near
the water, looking like a naiad. He wished then he could take
her in his arms, but he was a little uncertain of her and of
himself. Once she came to his studio in the barn to bring him
a piece of left-over dough which his mother had "turned" on
the top of the stove.

"Eugene used to be crazy about that when he was a boy," his
mother had remarked.

"Oh, let me take it to him," said Frieda gaily, gleeful over
the idea of the adventure.

"That's a good idea," said Angela innocently. "Wait, I'll put
it on this saucer."

Frieda took it and ran. She found Eugene staring oddly at his
canvas, his face curiously dark. When her head came above
the loft floor his expression changed immediately. His guileless,
kindly smile returned.

"Guess what," she said, pulling a little white apron she
had on over the dish.

"Strawberries." They were in season.

"Oh, no."

"Peaches and cream."

"Where would we get peaches now?"

"At the grocery store."

"I'll give you one more guess."

"Angel cake!" He was fond of that, and Angela occasionally made it.

"Your guesses are all gone. You can't have any."

He reached out his hand, but she drew back. He followed
and she laughed. "No, no, you can't have any now."

He caught her soft arm and drew her close to him. "Sure
I can't?"

Their faces were close together.

She looked into his eyes for a moment, then dropped her
lashes. Eugene's brain swirled with the sense of her beauty.
It was the old talisman. He covered her sweet lips with his
own and she yielded feverishly.

"There now, eat your dough," she exclaimed when he let
her go, pushing it shamefacedly toward him. She was flustered
—so much so that she failed to jest about it. "What would
Mrs. Witla think," she added, "if she could see us?"

Eugene paused solemnly and listened. He was afraid of
Angela.

"I've always liked this stuff, ever since I was a boy," he said in an offhand way.

"So your mother said," replied Frieda, somewhat recovered. "Let me see what you're painting." She came round to his side and he took her hand. "I'll have to go now," she said wisely. "They'll be expecting me back."

Eugene speculated on the intelligence of girls—at least on that of those he liked. Somehow they were all wise under these circumstances—cautious. He could see that instinctively Frieda was prepared to protect him and herself. She did not appear to be suffering from any shock from this revelation. Rather she was inclined to make the best of it.

He folded her in his arms again.

"You're the angel cake and the strawberries and the peaches and cream," he said.

"Don't!" she pleaded. "Don't! I have to go now."

And when he released her she ran quickly down the stairs, giving him a swift, parting smile.

So Frieda was added to the list of his conquests and he pondered over it gravely. If Angela could have seen this scene, what a storm there would have been! If she ever became conscious of what was going on, what a period of wrath there would be! It would be terrible. After her recent discovery of his letters he hated to think of that. Still this bliss of caressing youth—was it not worth any price? To have a bright, joyous girl of eighteen put her arms about you—could you risk too much for it? The world said one life, one love. Could he accede to that? Could any one woman satisfy him? Could Frieda if he had her? He did not know. He did not care to think about it. Only this walking in a garden of flowers— how delicious it was. This having a rose to your lips!

Angela saw nothing of this attraction for some time. She was not prepared yet to believe, poor little depender on the conventions as she understood them, that the world was full of plots and counter-plots, snares, pitfalls and gins. The way of the faithful and well-meaning woman in marriage should be simple and easy. She should not be harassed by uncertainty of affection, infelicities of temper, indifference or infidelity. If she worked hard, as Angela was trying to do, trying to be a good wife, saving, serving, making a sacrifice of her time and services and moods and wishes for her husband's sake, why shouldn't he do the same for her? She knew of no double standard of virtue. If she had she would not have believed in it. Her parents had raised her to see marriage in a different

light. Her father was faithful to her mother. Eugene's father
was faithful to his wife—that was perfectly plain. Her brothers-
in-law were faithful to her sisters, Eugene's brothers-in-law
were faithful to his sisters. Why should not Eugene be faithful
to her?

So far, of course, she had no evidence to the contrary. He
probably was faithful and would remain so. He had said so,
but this pre-matrimonial philandering of his looked very curious.
It was an astonishing thing that he could have deceived her
so. She would never forget it. He was a genius to be sure.
The world was waiting to hear what he had to say. He was
a great man and should associate with great men, or, failing
that, should not want to associate with anyone at all. It was
ridiculous for him to be running around after silly women. She
thought of this and decided to do her best to prevent it. The
seat of the mighty was in her estimation the place for Eugene,
with her in the foreground as a faithful and conspicuous acolyte,
swinging the censer of praise and delight.

The days went on and various little meetings—some accidental, some premeditated—took place between Eugene and
Frieda. There was one afternoon when he was at his sister's
and she came there to get a pattern for her foster-mother from
Sylvia. She lingered for over an hour, during which time
Eugene had opportunities to kiss her a dozen times. The beauty
of her eyes and her smile haunted him after she was gone. There
was another time when he saw her at dusk near his boathouse,
and kissed her in the shadow of the sheltering grape-arbor. In
his own home there were clandestine moments and in his studio,
the barn loft, for Frieda made occasion a few times to come
to him—a promise to make a sketch of her being the excuse.
Angela resented this, but she could not prevent it. In the main
Frieda exhibited that curious patience in love which women so
customarily exhibit and which a man can never understand.
She could wait for her own to come to her—for him to find
her; while he, with that curious avidness of the male in love,
burned as a fed fire to see her. He was jealous of the little
innocent walks she took with boys she knew. The fact that
it was necessary for her to be away from him was a great
deprivation. The fact that he was married to Angela was a
horrible disaster. He would look at Angela, when she was with
him, preventing him from his freedom in love, with almost
calculated hate in his eyes. Why had he married her? As for
Frieda, when she was near, and he could not draw near her,

his eyes followed her movements with a yearning, devouring glance. He was fairly beside himself with anguish under the spell of her beauty. Frieda had no notion of the consuming flame she had engendered.

It was a simple thing to walk home with her from the post-office—quite accidentally on several occasions. It was a fortuitous thing that Anna Roth should invite Angela and himself, as well as his father and mother, to her house to dinner. On one occasion when Frieda was visiting at the Witla homestead, Angela thought Frieda stepped away from Eugene in a curiously disturbed manner when she came into the parlor. She was not sure. Frieda hung round him in a good-natured way most of the time when various members of the family were present. She wondered if by any chance he was making love to her, but she could not prove it. She tried to watch them from then on, but Eugene was so subtle, Frieda so circumspect, that she never did obtain any direct testimony. Nevertheless, before they left Alexandria there was a weeping scene over this, hysterical, tempestuous, in which she accused him of making love to Frieda, he denying it stoutly.

"If it wasn't for your relatives' sake," she declared, "I would accuse her to her face, here before your eyes. She couldn't dare deny it."

"Oh, you're crazy," said Eugene. "You're the most suspicious woman I ever knew. Good Lord! Can't I look at a woman any more? This little girl! Can't I even be nice to her?"

"Nice to her? Nice to her? I know how you're nice to her. I can see! I can feel! Oh, God! Why can't you give me a faithful husband!"

"Oh, cut it out!" demanded Eugene defiantly. "You're always watching. I can't turn around but you have your eye on me. I can tell. Well, you go ahead and watch. That's all the good it will do you. I'll give you some real reason for watching one of these days. You make me tired!"

"Oh, hear how he talks to me," moaned Angela, "and we're only married one year! Oh, Eugene, how can you? Have you no pity, no shame? Here in your own home, too! Oh! oh! oh!"

To Eugene such hysterics were maddening. He could not understand how anyone should want or find it possible to carry on in this fashion. He was lying "out of the whole cloth" about Frieda, but Angela didn't know and he knew she didn't know. All these tantrums were based on suspicion. If she would do this on a mere suspicion, what would she not do when she had a proved cause?

Still by her tears she as yet had the power of rousing his sympathies and awakening his sense of shame. Her sorrow made him slightly ashamed of his conduct or rather sorry, for the tougher nature was constantly presenting itself. Her suspicions made the further pursuit of this love quest practically impossible. Secretly he already cursed the day he had married her, for Frieda's face was ever before him, a haunting lure to love and desire. In this hour life looked terribly sad to him. He couldn't help feeling that all the perfect things one might seek or find were doomed to the searing breath of an inimical fate. Ashes of roses—that was all life had to offer. Dead sea fruit, turning to ashes upon the lips. Oh, Frieda! Frieda! Oh, youth, youth! That there should dance before him for evermore an unattainable desire—the holy grail of beauty. Oh life, oh death! Which was really better, waking or sleeping? If he could only have Frieda now it would be worth living, but without her—

CHAPTER XV

THE weakness of Eugene was that he was prone in each of these new conquests to see for the time being the sum and substance of bliss, to rise rapidly in the scale of uncontrollable, exaggerated affection, until he felt that here and nowhere else, now and in this particular form was ideal happiness. He had been in love with Stella, with Margaret, with Ruby, with Angela, with Christina, and now with Frieda, quite in this way, and it had taught him nothing as yet concerning love except that it was utterly delightful. He wondered at times how it was that the formation of a particular face could work this spell. There was plain magic in the curl of a lock of hair, the whiteness or roundness of a forehead, the shapeliness of a nose or ear, the arched redness of full-blown petal lips. The cheek, the chin, the eye—in combination with these things —how did they work this witchery? The tragedies to which he laid himself open by yielding to these spells—he never stopped to think of them.

It is a question whether the human will, of itself alone, ever has cured or ever can cure any human weakness. Tendencies are subtle things. They are involved in the chemistry of one's being, and those who delve in the mysteries of biology frequently find that curious anomaly, a form of minute animal life born to be the prey of another form of animal life—chemically and physically attracted to its own disaster. Thus, to quote Calkins, "some protozoa are apparently limited to special kinds of food. The 'slipper-animal' (Paramecium) and the 'bell-animal' (Vorticella) live on certain kinds of bacteria, and many others, which live upon smaller protozoa, seem to have a marked affinity for certain kinds. I have watched one of these creatures (Actinobolus) lie perfectly quiet while hundreds of bacteria and smaller kinds of protozoa bumped against it, until a certain variety (Halteria grandinella) came near, when a minute dart, or 'trochocyst,' attached to a relatively long thread, was launched. The victim was invariably hit, and after a short struggle was drawn in and devoured. The results of many experiments indicate that the apparently *willful* selection in these cases is the inevitable action of definite chemical and physical laws which the individual organism can no more change than it can change the course of gravitation. The killing dart mentioned above is called out by the particular kind of prey with the irresistible attraction of an iron filing for a magnet."

Eugene did not know of these curious biologic experiments at this time, but he suspected that these attractions were deeper than human will. He thought at times that he ought to resist his impulses. At other times he asked himself why. If his treasure was in this and he lost it by resistance, what had he? A sense of personal purity? It did not appeal to him. The respect of his fellow-citizens? He believed that most of his fellow-citizens were whited sepulchres. What good did their hypocritical respect do him? Justice to others? Others were not concerned, or should not be in the natural affinity which might manifest itself between two people. That was for them to settle. Besides, there was very little justice in the world. As for his wife—well, he had given her his word, but he had not done so willingly. Might one swear eternal fealty and abide by it when the very essence of nature was lack of fealty, inconsiderateness, destruction, change? A gloomy Hamlet to be sure, asking "can honor set a leg?"—a subtle Machiavelli believing that might made right, sure that it was a matter of careful planning, not ethics which brought success in this world, and yet one of the poorest planners in it. An anarchistic manifestation of selfishness surely; but his additional plea was that he did not make his own mind, nor his emotions, nor anything else. And worst of all, he counselled himself that he was not seizing anything ruthlessly. He was merely accepting that which was thrust temptingly before him by fate.

Hypnotic spells of this character like contagion and fever have their period of duration, their beginning, climax and end. It is written that love is deathless, but this was not written of the body nor does it concern the fevers of desire. The marriage of true minds to which Shakespeare would admit no impediment is of a different texture and has little sex in it. The friendship of Damon and Pythias was a marriage in the best sense, though it concerned two men. The possibilities of intellectual union between a man and a woman are quite the same. This is deathless in so far as it reflects the spiritual ideals of the universe—not more so. All else is illusion of short duration and vanishes in thin air.

When the time came for Eugene to leave Alexandria as he had originally wanted to do, he was not at all anxious to depart; rather it was an occasion of great suffering for him. He could not see any solution to the problem which confronted him in connection with Frieda's love for him. As a matter of fact, when he thought about it at all he was quite sure that she did not understand or appreciate the nature of her affection for him or his for her. It had no basis in responsibility. It was one of those things born of thin air—sunlight, bright waters, the reflection of a bright room—things which are intangible and insubstantial. Eugene was not one who, if he thought anything at all about it, would persuade a girl to immorality for the mere sake of indulgence. His feelings were invariably compounded of finer things, love of companionship, love of beauty, a variable sense of the consequences which must ensue, not so much to him as to her, though he took himself into consideration. If she were not already experienced and he had no method of protecting her, if he could not take her as his wife or give her the advantages of his presence and financial support, secretly or openly, if he could not keep all their transactions a secret from the world, he was inclined to hesitate. He did not want to do anything rash—as much for her sake as for his. In this case, the fact that he could not marry her, that he could not reasonably run away with her, seeing that he was mentally sick and of uncertain financial condition, the fact that he was surrounded by home conditions which made it of the greatest importance that he should conduct himself circumspectly, weighed greatly with him. Nevertheless a tragedy could easily have resulted here. If Frieda had been of a headstrong, unthinking nature; if Angela had been less watchful, morbid, appealing in her mood; if the family and town conditions had been less weighty; if Eugene had had health and ample means, he would probably have deserted Angela, taken Frieda to some European city—he dreamed of Paris in this connection—and found himself confronted later by an angry father or a growing realization that Frieda's personal charms were not the sum and substance of his existence, or both. George Roth, for all he was a traveling salesman, was a man of considerable determination. He might readily have ended the life of his daughter's betrayer—art reputation or no. He worshiped Frieda as the living image of his dead wife, and at best he would have been heartbroken.

As it was, there was not much chance of this, for Eugene was not rash. He was too philosophic. Conditions might have arisen in which he would have shown the most foolhardy bravado, but not in his present state. There was not sufficient anguish in his own existence to drive him to action. He saw no clear way. So, in June, with Angela he took his departure for Blackwood, pretending, to her, outward indifference as to his departure, but inwardly feeling as though his whole life were coming to nothing.

When he reached Blackwood he was now, naturally, disgusted with the whole atmosphere of it. Frieda was not there. Alexandria, from having been the most wearisome sidepool of aimless inactivity, had suddenly taken on all the characteristics of paradise. The little lakes, the quiet streets, the court house square, his sister's home, Frieda's home, his own home, had been once more invested for him with the radiance of romance —that intangible glory of feeling which can have no existence outside the illusion of love. Frieda's face was everywhere in it, her form, the look of her eyes. He could see nothing there now save the glory of Frieda. It was as though the hard, weary face of a barren landscape were suddenly bathed in the soft effulgence of a midnight moon.

As for Blackwood, it was as lovely as ever but he could not see it. The fact that his attitude had changed toward Angela for the time being made all the difference. He did not really hate her—he told himself that. She was not any different from that she had been, that was perfectly plain. The difference was in him. He really could not be madly in love with two people at once. He had entertained joint affections for Angela and Ruby, and Angela and Christina, but those were not the dominating fevers which this seemed to be. He could not for the time get the face of this girl out of his mind. He was sorry for Angela at moments. Then, because of her insistence on his presence with her—on her being in his company, "following him around" as he put it, he hated her. Dear Heaven! if he could only be free without injuring her. If he could only get loose. Think, at this moment he might be with Frieda walking in the sun somewhere, rowing on the lake at Alexandria, holding her in his arms. He would never forget how she looked the first morning she came into his barn studio at home—how enticing she was the first night he saw her at Sylvia's. What a rotten mess living was, anyhow. And so he sat about in the hammock at the Blue homestead, or swung in a swing that old Jotham had since put up for Marietta's beaux, or dreamed in a chair in the shade of the house, reading. He was dreary and lonely with just one ambition in the world —Frieda.

Meanwhile, as might be expected, his health was not getting any better. Instead of curing himself of those purely carnal expressions of passion which characterized his life with Angela, the latter went on unbroken. One would have thought that his passion for Frieda would have interrupted this, but the presence of Angela, the comparatively enforced contact, her insistence on his attentions, broke down again and again the protecting barrier of distaste. Had he been alone, he would have led a chaste life until some new and available infatuation seized him. As it was there was no refuge either from himself or Angela, and the at times almost nauseating relationship went on and on.

Those of the Blue family, who were in the home or near it, were delighted to see him. The fact that he had achieved such a great success, as the papers had reported, with his first exhibition and had not lost ground with the second—a very interesting letter had come from M. Charles saying that the Paris pictures would be shown in Paris in July—gave them a great estimate of him. Angela was a veritable queen in this home atmosphere; and as for Eugene, he was given the privilege of all geniuses to do as he pleased. On this occasion Eugene was the centre of interest, though he appeared not to be, for his four solid Western brothers-in-law gave no indication that they thought he was unusual. He was not their type— banker, lawyer, grain merchant and real estate dealer—but they felt proud of him just the same. He was different, and at the same time natural, genial, modest, inclined to appear far more interested in their affairs than he really was. He would listen by the hour to the details of their affairs, political, financial, agricultural, social. The world was a curious compost to Eugene and he was always anxious to find out how other people lived. He loved a good story, and while he rarely told one he made a splendid audience for those who did. His eyes would sparkle and his whole face light with the joy of the humor he felt.

Through all this—the attention he was receiving, the welcome he was made to feel, the fact that his art interests were not yet dead (the Paris exhibition being the expiring breath of his original burst of force),—he was nevertheless feeling the downward trend of his affairs most keenly. His mind was not right. That was surely true. His money affairs were getting worse, not better, for while he could hope for a few sales yet (the Paris pictures did not sell in New York) he was not certain that this would be the case. This homeward trip had cost him two hundred of his seventeen hundred dollars and there would be additional expenses if he went to Chicago, as he planned in the fall. He could not live a single year on fifteen hundred dollars—scarcely more than six months, and he could not paint or illustrate anything new in his present state. Additional sales of the pictures of the two original exhibitions must be effected in a reasonable length of time or he would find himself in hard straits.

Meanwhile, Angela, who had obtained such a high estimate of his future by her experience in New York and Paris, was beginning to enjoy herself again, for after all, in her judgment, she seemed to be able to manage Eugene very well. He might have had some slight understanding with Frieda Roth—it couldn't have been much or she would have seen it, she thought—but she had managed to break it up. Eugene was cross, naturally, but that was due more to her quarreling than anything else. These storms of feeling on her part—not always premeditated—seemed very essential. Eugene must be made to understand that he was married now; that he could not look upon or run after girls as he had in the old days. She was well aware that he was considerably younger than she was in temperament, inclined to be exceedingly boyish, and this was apt to cause trouble anywhere. But if she watched over him, kept his attention fixed on her, everything would come out all right. And then there were all these other delightful qualities—his looks, his genial manner, his reputation, his talent. What a delightful thing it had become to announce herself as Mrs. Eugene Witla and how those who knew about him sat up. Big people were his friends, artists admired him, common, homely, everyday people thought he was nice and considerate and able and very worth while. He was generally liked everywhere. What more could one want?

Angela knew nothing of his real thoughts, for because of sympathy, a secret sense of injustice toward her on his part, a vigorous, morbid impression of the injustice of life as a whole, a desire to do things in a kindly or at least a secret and not brutal way, he was led to pretend at all times that he really cared for her; to pose as being comfortable and happy; to lay all his moods to his inability to work. Angela, who could not read him clearly, saw nothing of this. He was too subtle for her understanding at times. She was living in a fool's paradise; playing over a sleeping volcano.

He grew no better and by fall began to get the notion that he could do better by living in Chicago. His health would come back to him there perhaps. He was terribly tired of Blackwood. The long tree-shaded lawn was nothing to him now. The little lake, the stream, the fields that he had rejoiced in at first were to a great extent a commonplace. Old Jotham was a perpetual source of delight to him with his kindly, stable, enduring attitude toward things and his interesting comment on life, and Marietta entertained him with her wit, her good nature, her intuitive understanding; but he could not be happy just talking to everyday, normal, stable people, interesting and worthwhile as they might be. The doing of simple things, living a simple life, was just now becoming irritating. He must go to London, Paris—do things. He couldn't loaf this way. It mattered little that he could not work. He must try. This isolation was terrible.

There followed six months spent in Chicago in which he painted not one picture that was satisfactory to him, that was not messed into nothingness by changes and changes and changes. There were then three months in the mountains of Tennessee because someone told him of a wonderfully curative spring in a delightful valley where the spring came as a dream of color and the expense of living was next to nothing. There were four months of summer in southern Kentucky on a ridge where the air was cool, and after that five months on the Gulf of Mexico, at Biloxi, in Mississippi, because some comfortable people in Kentucky and Tennessee told Angela of this delightful winter resort farther South. All this time Eugene's money, the fifteen hundred dollars he had when he left Blackwood, several sums of two hundred, one hundred and fifty and two hundred and fifty, realized from pictures sold in New York and Paris during the fall and winter following his Paris exhibition, and two hundred which had come some months afterward from a fortuitous sale by M. Charles of one of his old New York views, had been largely dissipated. He still had five hundred dollars, but with no pictures being sold and none painted he was in a bad way financially in so far as the future was concerned. He could possibly return to Alexandria with Angela and live cheaply there for another six months, but because of the Frieda incident both he and she objected to it. Angela was afraid of Frieda and was resolved that she would not go there so long as Frieda was in the town, and Eugene was ashamed because of the light a return would throw on his fading art prospects. Blackwood was out of the question to him. They had lived on her parents long enough. If he did not get better he must soon give up this art idea entirely, for he could not live on trying to paint.

He began to think that he was possessed—obsessed of a devil— and that some people were pursued by evil spirits, fated by stars, doomed from their birth to failure or accident. How did the astrologer in New York know that he was to have four years of bad luck? He had seen three of them already. Why did a man who read his palm in Chicago once say that his hand showed two periods of disaster, just as the New York astrologer had and that he was likely to alter the course of his life radically in the middle portion of it? Were there any fixed laws of being? Did any of the so-called naturalistic school of philosophers and scientists whom he had read know anything at all? They were always talking about the fixed laws of the universe—the unalterable laws of chemistry and physics. Why didn't chemistry or physics throw some light on his peculiar physical condition, on the truthful prediction of the astrologer, on the signs and portents which he had come to observe for himself as foretelling trouble or good fortune for himself. If his left eye twitched he had observed of late he was going to have a quarrel with someone—invariably Angela. If he found a penny or any money, he was going to get money; for every notification of a sale of a picture with the accompanying check had been preceded by the discovery of a coin somewhere: once a penny in State Street, Chicago, on a rainy day—M. Charles wrote that a picture had been sold in Paris for two hundred; once a three-cent piece of the old American issue in the dust of a road in Tennessee—M. Charles wrote that one of his old American views had brought one hundred and fifty; once a penny in sands by the Gulf in Biloxi—another notification of a sale. So it went. He found that when doors squeaked, people were apt to get sick in the houses where they were; and a black dog howling in front of a house was a sure sign of death. He had seen this with his own eyes, this sign which his mother had once told him of as having been verified in her experience, in connection with the case of a man who was sick in Biloxi. He was sick, and a dog came running along the street and stopped in front of this place—a black dog—and the man died. Eugene saw this with his own eyes,—that is, the dog and the sick man's death notice. The dog howled at four o'clock in the afternoon and the next morning the man was dead. He saw the crape on the door. Angela mocked at his superstition, but he was convinced. "There are more things in heaven and earth, Horatio, than are dreamt of in your philosophy."

CHAPTER XVI

EUGENE was reaching the point where he had no more money and was compelled to think by what process he would continue to make a living in the future. Worry and a hypochondriacal despair had reduced his body to a comparatively gaunt condition. His eyes had a nervous, apprehensive look. He would walk about speculating upon the mysteries of nature, wondering how he was to get out of this, what was to become of him, how soon, if ever, another picture would be sold, when? Angela, from having fancied that his illness was a mere temporary indisposition, had come to feel that he might be seriously affected for some time. He was not sick physically: he could walk and eat and talk vigorously enough, but he could not work and he was worrying, worrying, worrying.

Angela was quite as well aware as Eugene that their finances were in a bad way or threatening to become so, though he said nothing at all about them. He was ashamed to confess at this day, after their very conspicuous beginning in New York, that he was in fear of not doing well. How silly—he with all his ability! Surely he would get over this, and soon.

Angela's economical upbringing and naturally saving instinct stood her in good stead now, for she could market with the greatest care, purchase to the best advantage, make every scrap and penny count. She knew how to make her own clothes, as Eugene had found out when he first visited Blackwood, and was good at designing hats. Although she had thought in New York, when Eugene first began to make money, that now she would indulge in tailor-made garments and the art of an excellent dressmaker, she had never done so. With true frugality she had decided to wait a little while, and then Eugene's health having failed she had not the chance any more. Fearing the possible long duration of this storm she had begun to mend and clean and press and make over whatever seemed to require it. Even when Eugene suggested that she get something new she would not do it. Her consideration for their future—the difficulty he might have in making a living, deterred her.

Eugene noted this, though he said nothing. He was not unaware of the fear that she felt, the patience she exhibited, the sacrifice she made of her own whims and desires to his, and he was not entirely unappreciative. It was becoming very apparent to him that she had no life outside his own—no interests. She was his shadow, his alter ego, his servant, his anything he wanted her to be. "Little Pigtail" was one of his jesting pet names for her because in the West as a boy they had always called anyone who ran errands for others a pigtailer. In playing "one old cat," if one wanted another to chase the struck balls he would say: "You pig-tail for me, Willie, will you?" And Angela was his "little pigtail."

There were no further grounds for jealousy during the time, almost two years, in which they were wandering around together, for the reason that she was always with him, almost his sole companion, and that they did not stay long enough in any one place and under sufficiently free social conditions to permit him to form those intimacies which might have resulted disastrously. Some girls did take his eye—the exceptional in youth and physical perfection were always doing that, but he had no chance or very little of meeting them socially. They were not living with people they knew, were not introduced in the local social worlds, which they visited. Eugene could only look at these maidens whom he chanced to spy from time to time, and wish that he might know them better. It was hard to be tied down to a conventional acceptance of matrimony—to pretend that he was interested in beauty only in a sociological way. He had to do it before Angela though (and all conventional people for that matter), for she objected strenuously to the least interest he might manifest in any particular woman. All his remarks had to be general and guarded in their character. At the least show of feeling or admiration Angela would begin to criticize his choice and to show him wherein his admiration was ill-founded. If he were especially interested she would attempt to tear his latest ideal to pieces. She had no mercy, and he could see plainly enough on what her criticism was based. It made him smile but he said nothing. He even admired her for her heroic efforts to hold her own, though every victory she seemed to win served only to strengthen the bars of his own cage.

It was during this time that he could not help learning and appreciating just how eager, patient and genuine was her regard for his material welfare. To her he was obviously the greatest man in the world, a great painter, a great thinker, a great lover, a great personality every way. It didn't make so much difference to her at this time that he wasn't making any money. He would sometime, surely, and wasn't she getting it all in fame anyhow, now? Why, to be Mrs. Eugene Witla, after what she had seen of him in New York and Paris, what more could she want? Wasn't it all right for her to rake and scrape now, to make her own clothes and hats, save, mend, press and patch? He would come out of all this silly feeling about other women once he became a little older, and then he would be all right. Anyhow he appeared to love her now; and that was something. Because he was lonely, fearsome, uncertain of himself, uncertain of the future, he welcomed these unsparing attentions on her part, and this deceived her. Who else would give them to him, he thought; who else would be so faithful in times like these? He almost came to believe that he could love her again, be faithful to her, if he could keep out of the range of these other enticing personalities. If only he could stamp out this eager desire for other women, their praise and their beauty!

But this was more because he was sick and lonely than anything else. If he had been restored to health then and there, if prosperity had descended on him as he so eagerly dreamed, it would have been the same as ever. He was as subtle as nature itself; as changeable as a chameleon. But two things were significant and real—two things to which he was as true and unvarying as the needle to the pole—his love of the beauty of life which was coupled with his desire to express it in color, and his love of beauty in the form of the face of a woman, or rather that of a girl of eighteen. That blossoming of life in womanhood at eighteen!—there was no other thing under the sun like it to him. It was like the budding of the trees in spring; the blossoming of flowers in the early morning; the odor of roses and dew, the color of bright waters and clear jewels. He could not be faithless to that. He could not get away from it. It haunted him like a joyous vision, and the fact that the charms of Stella and Ruby and Angela and Christina and Frieda in whom it had been partially or wholly shadowed forth at one time or another had come and gone, made little difference. It remained clear and demanding. He could not escape it—the thought; he could not deny it. He was haunted by this, day after day, and hour after hour; and when he said to himself that he was a fool, and that it would lure him as a will-o'-the-wisp to his destruction and that he could find no profit in it ultimately, still it would not down. The beauty of youth; the beauty of eighteen! To him life without it was a joke, a shabby scramble, a work-horse job, with only silly material details like furniture and houses and steel cars and stores all involved in a struggle for what? To make a habitation for more shabby humanity? Never! To make a habitation for beauty? Certainly! What beauty? The beauty of old age?—How silly! The beauty of middle age? Nonsense! The beauty of maturity? No! The beauty of youth? Yes. The beauty of eighteen. No more and no less. That was the standard, and the history of the world proved it. Art, literature, romance, history, poetry—if they did not turn on this and the lure of this and the wars and sins because of this, what did they turn on? He was for beauty. The history of the world justified him. Who could deny it?

CHAPTER XVII

FROM Biloxi, because of the approach of summer when it would be unbearably warm there, and because his funds were so low that it was necessary to make a decisive move of some kind whether it led to complete disaster or not, he decided to return to New York. In storage with Kellners (M. Charles had kindly volunteered to take care of them for him) were a number of the pictures left over from the original show, and nearly all the paintings of the Paris exhibition. The latter had not sold well. Eugene's idea was that he could slip into New York quietly, take a room in some side street or in Jersey City or Brooklyn where he would not be seen, have the pictures in the possession of M. Charles returned to him, and see if he could not get some of the minor art dealers or speculators of whom he had heard to come and look at them and buy them outright. Failing that, he might take them himself, one by one, to different dealers here and there and dispose of them. He remembered now that Eberhard Zang had, through Norma Whitmore, asked him to come and see him. He fancied that, as Kellners had been so interested, and the newspaper critics had spoken of him so kindly the smaller dealers would be eager to take up with him. Surely they would buy this material. It was exceptional—very. Why not?

Eugene forgot or did not know the metaphysical side of prosperity and failure. He did not realize that "as a man thinketh so is he," and so also is the estimate of the whole world at the time he is thinking of himself thus—not as he is but as he thinks he is. The sense of it is abroad—by what processes we know not, but so it is.

Eugene's mental state, so depressed, so helpless, so fearsome—a rudderless boat in the dark, transmitted itself as an impression, a wireless message to all those who knew him or knew of him. His breakdown, which had first astonished M. Charles, depressed and then weakened the latter's interest in him. Like all other capable, successful men in the commercial world M. Charles was for strong men—men in the heyday of their success, the zenith of their ability. The least variation from this standard of force and interest was noticeable to him. If a man was going to fail—going to get sick and lose his interest in life or have

297

his viewpoint affected, it might be very sad, but there was just one thing to do under such circumstances—get away from him. Failures of any kind were dangerous things to countenance. One must not have anything to do with them. They were very unprofitable. Such people as Temple Boyle and Vincent Beers, who had been his instructors in the past and who had heard of him in Chicago at the time of his success, Luke Severas, William McConnell, Oren Benedict, Hudson Dula, and others wondered what had become of him. Why did he not paint any more? He was never seen in the New York haunts of art! It was rumored at the time of the Paris exhibition that he was going to London to do a similar group of views, but the London exhibition never came off. He had told Smite and MacHugh the spring he left that he might do Chicago next, but that came to nothing. There was no evidence of it. There were rumors that he was very rich, that his art had failed him, that he had lost his mind even, and so the art world that knew him and was so interested in him no longer cared very much. It was too bad but—so thought the rival artists—there was one less difficult star to contend with. As for his friends, they were sorry, but such was life. He might recover. If not,—well—.

As time went on, one year, another year, another year, the strangeness of his suddenly brilliant burst and disappearance became to the talented in this field a form of classic memory. He was a man of such promise! Why did he not go on painting? There was an occasional mention in conversation or in print, but Eugene to all intents and purposes was dead.

When he came to New York it was after his capital had been reduced to three hundred dollars and he had given Angela one hundred and twenty-five of this to take her back to Blackwood and keep her there until he could make such arrangements as would permit her to join him. After a long discussion they had finally agreed that this would be best, for, seeing that he could neither paint nor illustrate, there was no certainty as to what he would do. To come here on so little money with her was not advisable. She had her home where she was welcome to stay for a while anyhow. Meanwhile he figured he could weather any storm alone.

The appearance of the metropolis, after somewhat over two years of absence during which he had wandered everywhere, was most impressive to Eugene. It was a relief after the mountains of Kentucky and Tennessee and the loneliness of the Biloxi coast, to get back to this swarming city where millions were hurrying to and fro, and where one's misery as well as one's prosperity was apparently swallowed up in an inconceivable mass of life. A subway was being built. The automobile, which only a few years before was having a vague, uncertain beginning, was now attaining a tremendous vogue. Magnificent cars of new design were everywhere. From the ferry-house in Jersey City he could see notable changes in the skyline, and a single walk across Twenty-third Street and up Seventh Avenue showed him a changing world—great hotels, great apartment houses, a tremendous crush of vainglorious life which was moulding the city to its desires. It depressed him greatly, for he had always hoped to be an integral part of this magnificence and display and now he was not—might never be again.

It was still raw and cold, for the spring was just beginning to break, and Eugene was compelled to buy a light overcoat, his own imperishable great coat having been left behind, and he had no other fit to wear. Appearances, he thought, demanded this. He had spent forty of his closely-guarded one hundred and seventy-five dollars coming from Biloxi to New York, and now an additional fifteen was required for this coat, leaving him one hundred and twenty-five dollars with which to begin his career anew. He was greatly worried as to the outcome, but curiously also he had an abiding subconscious feeling that it could not be utterly destructive to him.

He rented a cheap room in a semi-respectable neighborhood in West Twenty-fourth Street near Eleventh Avenue solely because he wanted to keep out of the run of intellectual life and hide until he could get on his feet. It was an old and shabby residence in an old and shabby red brick neighborhood such as he had drawn in one of his views, but it was not utterly bad. The people were poor but fairly intellectual. He chose this particular neighborhood with all its poverty because it was near the North River where the great river traffic could be seen, and where, because of some open lots in which were stored wagons, his one single west window gave him a view of all this life. About the corner in Twenty-third Street, in another somewhat decayed residence, was a moderate priced restaurant and boarding house. Here he could get a meal for twenty-five cents. He cared nothing for the life that was about him. It was cheap, poor, from a money point of view, dingy, but he would not be here forever he hoped. These people did not know him. Besides the number 552 West 24th Street did not sound bad. It might be one of the old neighborhoods with which New York was dotted, and which artists were inclined to find and occupy.

After he had secured this room from a semi-respectable Irish landlady, a dock weigher's wife, he decided to call upon M. Charles. He knew that he looked quite respectable as yet, despite his poverty and decline. His clothes were good, his overcoat new, his manner brisk and determined. But what he could not see was that his face in its thin sallowness, and his eyes with their semi-feverish lustre bespoke a mind that was harassed by trouble of some kind. He stood outside the office of Kellner and Son in Fifth Avenue—a half block from the door, wondering whether he should go in, and just what he should say. He had written to M. Charles from time to time that his health was bad and that he couldn't work—always that he hoped to be better soon. He had always hoped that a reply would come that another of his pictures had been sold. One year had gone and then two, and now a third was under way and still he was not any better. M. Charles would look at him searchingly. He would have to bear his gaze unflinchingly. In his present nervous state this was difficult and yet he was not without a kind of defiance even now. He would force himself back into favor with life sometime.

He finally mustered up his courage and entered and M. Charles greeted him warmly.

"This certainly is good,—to see you again. I had almost given up hope that you would ever come back to New York. How is your health now? And how is Mrs. Witla? It doesn't seem as though it had been three years. You're looking excellent. And how is painting going now? Getting to the point where you can do something again?"

Eugene felt for the moment as though M. Charles believed him to be in excellent condition, whereas that shrewd observer of men was wondering what could have worked so great a change. Eugene appeared to be eight years older. There were marked wrinkles between his eyes and an air of lassitude and weariness. He thought to himself, "Why, this man may possibly be done for artistically. Something has gone from him which I noted the first time I met him: that fire and intense enthusiasm which radiated force after the fashion of an arclight. Now he seems to be seeking to draw something in,—to save himself from drowning as it were. He is making a voiceless appeal for consideration. What a pity!"

The worst of it all was that in his estimation nothing could be done in such a case. You couldn't do anything for an artist who could do nothing for himself. His art was gone. The sanest thing for him to do would be to quit trying, go at some other form of labor and forget all about it. It might be that he would recover, but it was a question. Nervous breakdowns were not infrequently permanent.

Eugene noticed something of this in his manner. He couldn't tell exactly what it was, but M. Charles seemed more than ordinarily preoccupied, careful and distant. He wasn't exactly chilly in his manner, but reserved, as though he were afraid he might be asked to do something which he could not very well do.

"I noticed that the Paris scenes did not do very well either here or in Paris," observed Eugene with an air of nonchalance, as though it were a matter of small importance, at the same time hoping that he would have some favorable word. "I had the idea that they would take better than they did. Still I don't suppose I ought to expect everything to sell. The New York ones did all right."

"They did very well indeed, much better than I expected. I didn't think as many would be sold as were. They were very new and considerably outside the lines of current interest. The Paris pictures, on the other hand, were foreign to Americans in the wrong sense. By that I mean they weren't to be included in that genre art which comes from abroad, but is not based on any locality and is universal in its appeal—thematically speaking. Your Paris pictures were, of course, pictures in the best sense to those who see art as color and composition and idea, but to the ordinary lay mind they were, I take it, merely Paris scenes. You get what I mean. In that sense they were foreign, and Paris has been done illustratively anyhow. You might have done better with London or Chicago. Still you have every reason to congratulate yourself. Your work made a distinct impression both here and in France. When you feel able to return to it I have no doubt you will find that time has done you no harm."

He tried to be polite and entertaining, but he was glad when Eugene went away again.

The latter turned out into the street disconsolate. He could see how things were. He was down and out for the present and would have to wait.

CHAPTER XVIII

THE next thing was to see what could be done with the other art dealers and the paintings that were left. There were quite a number of them. If he could get any reasonable price at all he ought to be able to live quite awhile—long enough anyhow to get on his feet again. When they came to his quiet room and were unpacked by him in a rather shamefaced and disturbed manner and distributed about, they seemed wonderful things. Why, if the critics had raved over them and M. Charles had thought they were so fine, could they not be sold? Art dealers would surely buy them! Still, now that he was on the ground again and could see the distinctive art shops from the sidewalks his courage failed him. They were not running after pictures. Exceptional as he might be, there were artists in plenty—good ones. He could not run to other well known art dealers very well for his work had become identified with the house of Kellner and Son. Some of the small dealers might buy them but they would not buy them all—probably one or two at the most, and that at a sacrifice. What a pass to come to!—he, Eugene Witla, who three years before had been in the heyday of his approaching prosperity, wondering as he stood in the room of a gloomy side-street house how he was going to raise money to live through the summer, and how he was going to sell the paintings which had seemed the substance of his fortune but two years before. He decided that he would ask several of the middle class dealers whether they would not come and look at what he had to show. To a number of the smaller dealers in Fourth, Sixth, Eighth Avenues and elsewhere he would offer to sell several outright when necessity pinched. Still he had to raise money soon. Angela could not be left at Blackwood indefinitely.

He went to Jacob Bergman, Henry LaRue, Pottle Frères and asked if they would be interested to see what he had. Henry Bergman, who was his own manager, recalled his name at once. He had seen the exhibition but was not eager. He asked curiously how the pictures of the first and second exhibitions had sold, how many there were of them, what prices they brought. Eugene told him.

"You might bring one or two here and leave them on sale. You know how that is. Someone might take a fancy to them. You never can tell."

He explained that his commission was twenty-five per cent. and that he would report when a sale was made. He was not interested to come and see them. Eugene could select any two pictures he pleased. It was the same with Henry LaRue and Pottle Frères, though the latter had never heard of him. They asked him to show them one of his pictures. Eugene's pride was touched the least bit by this lack of knowledge on their part, though seeing how things were going with him he felt as though he might expect as much and more.

Other art dealers he did not care to trust with his paintings on sale, and he was now ashamed to start carrying them about to the magazines, where at least one hundred and twenty-five to one hundred and fifty per picture might be expected for them, if they were sold at all. He did not want the magazine art world to think that he had come to this. His best friend was Hudson Dula, and he might no longer be Art Director of *Truth*. As a matter of fact Dula was no longer there. Then there were Jan Jansen and several others, but they were no doubt thinking of him now as a successful painter. It seemed as though his natural pride were building insurmountable barriers for him. How was he to live if he could not do this and could not paint? He decided on trying the small art dealers with a single picture, offering to sell it outright. They might not recognize him and so might buy it direct. He could accept, in such cases, without much shock to his pride, anything which they might offer, if it were not too little.

He tried this one bright morning in May, and though it was not without result it spoiled the beautiful day for him. He took one picture, a New York scene, and carried it to a third rate art dealer whose place he had seen in upper Sixth Avenue, and without saying anything about himself asked if he would like to buy it. The proprietor, a small, dark individual of Semitic extraction, looked at him curiously and at his picture. He could tell from a single look that Eugene was in trouble, that he needed money and that he was anxious to sell his picture. He thought of course that he would take anything for it and he was not sure that he wanted the picture at that. It was not very popular in theme, a view of a famous Sixth Avenue restaurant showing behind the track of the L road, with a driving rain pouring in between the interstices of light. Years after this picture was picked up by a collector from Kansas City at an old furniture sale and hung among his gems, but this morning its merits were not very much in evidence.

"I see that you occasionally exhibit a painting in your window for sale. Do you buy originals?"

"Now and again," said the man indifferently—"not often. What have you?"

"I have an oil here that I painted not so long ago. I occasionally do these things. I thought maybe you would like to buy it."

The proprietor stood by indifferently while Eugene untied the string, took off the paper and stood the picture up for inspection. It was striking enough in its way but it did not appeal to him as being popular. "I don't think it's anything that I could sell here," he remarked, shrugging his shoulders. "It's good, but we don't have much call for pictures of any kind. If it were a straight landscape or a marine or a figure of some kind—. Figures sell best. But this—I doubt if I could get rid of it. You might leave it on sale if you want to. Somebody might like it. I don't think I'd care to buy it."

"I don't care to leave it on sale," replied Eugene irritably. Leave one of his pictures in a cheap side-street art store—and that on sale! He would not. He wanted to say something cutting in reply but he curbed his welling wrath to ask,

"How much do you think it would be worth if you did want it?"

"Oh," replied the proprietor, pursing his lips reflectively, "not more than ten dollars. We can't ask much for anything we have on view here. The Fifth Avenue stores take all the good trade."

Eugene winced. Ten dollars! Why, what a ridiculous sum! What was the use of coming to a place like this anyhow? He could do better dealing with the art directors or the better stores. But where were they? Whom could he deal with? Where were there any stores much better than this outside the large ones which he had already canvassed. He had better keep his pictures and go to work now at something else. He only had thirty-five of them all told and at this rate he would have just three hundred and fifty dollars when they were all gone. What good would that do him? His mood and this preliminary experience convinced him that they could not be sold for any much greater sum. Fifteen dollars or less would probably be offered and he would be no better off at the end. His pictures would be gone and he would have nothing. He ought to get something to do and save his pictures. But what?

To a man in Eugene's position—he was now thirty-one years of age, with no training outside what he had acquired in developing his artistic judgment and ability—this proposition of finding something else which he could do was very difficult. His mental sickness was, of course, the first great bar. It made him appear nervous and discouraged and so more or less objectionable to anyone who was looking for vigorous healthy manhood in the shape of an employee. In the next place, his look and manner had become decidedly that of the artist—refined, retiring, subtle. He also had an air at times of finicky standoffishness, particularly in the presence of those who appeared to him commonplace or who by their look or manner appeared to be attempting to set themselves over him. In the last place, he could think of nothing that he really wanted to do—the idea that his art ability would come back to him or that it ought to serve him in this crisis, haunting him all the time. Once he had thought he might like to be an art director; he was convinced that he would be a good one. And another time he had thought he would like to write, but that was long ago. He had never written anything since the Chicago newspaper specials, and several efforts at concentrating his mind for this quickly proved to him that writing was not for him now. It was hard for him to formulate an intelligent consecutive-idea'd letter to Angela. He harked back to his old Chicago days and remembering that he had been a collector and a driver of a laundry wagon, he decided that he might do something of that sort. Getting a position as a street-car conductor or a drygoods clerk appealed to him as possibilities. The necessity of doing something within regular hours and in a routine way appealed to him as having curative properties. How should he get such a thing?

If it had not been for the bedeviled state of his mind this would not have been such a difficult matter, for he was physically active enough to hold any ordinary position. He might have appealed frankly and simply to M. Charles or Isaac Wertheim and through influence obtained something which would have tided him over, but he was too sensitive to begin with and his present weakness made him all the more fearful and retiring. He had but one desire when he thought of doing anything outside his creative gift, and that was to slink away from the gaze of men. How could he, with his appearance, his reputation, his tastes and refinement, hobnob with conductors, drygoods clerks, railroad hands or drivers? It wasn't possible—he hadn't the strength. Besides all that was a thing of the past, or he thought it was. He had put it behind him in his art student days. Now

to have to get out and look for a job! How could he? He
walked the streets for days and days, coming back to his room to
see if by any chance he could paint yet, writing long, rambling,
emotional letters to Angela. It was pitiful. In fits of gloom
he would take out an occasional picture and sell it, parting with
it for ten or fifteen dollars after he had carried it sometimes for
miles. His one refuge was in walking, for somehow he could not
walk and feel very, very bad. The beauty of nature, the activity
of people entertained and diverted his mind. He would come
back to his room some evenings feeling as though a great change
had come over him, as though he were going to do better now;
but this did not last long. A little while and he would be back
in his old mood again. He spent three months this way, drifting,
before he realized that he must do something—that fall and winter would be coming on again in a little while and he would have
nothing at all.

In his desperation he first attempted to get an art directorship,
but two or three interviews with publishers of magazines proved
to him pretty quickly that positions of this character were not
handed out to the inexperienced. It required an apprenticeship,
just as anything else did, and those who had positions in this field
elsewhere had the first call. His name or appearance did not
appear to strike any of these gentlemen as either familiar or important in any way. They had heard of him as an illustrator and
a painter, but his present appearance indicated that this was a
refuge in ill health which he was seeking, not a vigorous, constructive position, and so they would have none of him. He
next tried at three of the principal publishing houses, but they
did not require anyone in that capacity. Truth to tell he knew
very little of the details and responsibilities of the position, though
he thought he did. After that there was nothing save drygoods
stores, street-car registration offices, the employment offices of
the great railroads and factories. He looked at sugar refineries,
tobacco factories, express offices, railroad freight offices, wondering whether in any of these it would be possible for him to obtain a position which would give him a salary of ten dollars a
week. If he could get that, and any of the pictures now on
show with Jacob Bergman, Henry LaRue and Pottle Frères
should be sold, he could get along. He might even live on this
with Angela if he could sell an occasional picture for ten or fifteen dollars. But he was paying seven dollars a week for nothing save food and room, and scarcely managing to cling to the
one hundred dollars which had remained of his original traveling
fund after he had paid all his opening expenses here in New

York. He was afraid to part with all his pictures in this way for fear he would be sorry for it after a while.

Work is hard to get under the most favorable conditions of health and youth and ambition, and the difficulties of obtaining it under unfavorable ones need not be insisted on. Imagine if you can the crowds of men, forty, fifty, one hundred strong, that wait at the door of every drygoods employment office, every street-car registration bureau, on the special days set aside for considering applications, at every factory, shop or office where an advertisement calling for a certain type of man or woman was inserted in the newspapers. On a few occasions that Eugene tried or attempted to try, he found himself preceded by peculiar groups of individuals who eyed him curiously as he approached, wondering, as he thought, whether a man of his type could be coming to apply for a job. They seemed radically different from himself to his mind, men with little education and a grim consciousness of the difficulties of life; young men, vapid looking men, shabby, stale, discouraged types—men who, like himself, looked as though they had seen something very much better, and men who looked as though they had seen things a great deal worse. The evidence which frightened him was the presence of a group of bright, healthy, eager looking boys of nineteen, twenty, twenty-one and twenty-two who, like himself when he first went to Chicago years before, were everywhere he went. When he drew near he invariably found it impossible to indicate in any way that he was looking for anything. He couldn't. His courage failed him; he felt that he looked too superior; self-consciousness and shame overcame him.

He learned now that men rose as early as four o'clock in the morning to buy a newspaper and ran quickly to the address mentioned in order to get the place at the head of the line, thus getting the first consideration as an applicant. He learned that some other men, such as waiters, cooks, hotel employees and so on, frequently stayed up all night in order to buy a paper at two in the morning, winter or summer, rain or snow, heat or cold, and hurry to the promising addresses they might find. He learned that the crowds of applicants were apt to become surly or sarcastic or contentious as their individual chances were jeopardized by ever-increasing numbers. And all this was going on all the time, in winter or summer, heat or cold, rain or snow. Pretending interest as a spectator, he would sometimes stand and watch, hearing the ribald jests, the slurs cast upon life, fortune, individuals in particular and in general by those who were wearily or hopelessly waiting. It was a horrible picture to him in his present condition. It was like the grinding of the millstones, upper and nether. These were the chaff. He was a part of the chaff at present, or in danger of becoming so. Life was winnowing him out. He might go down, down, and there might never be an opportunity for him to rise any more.

Few, if any of us, understand thoroughly the nature of the unconscious stratification which takes place in life, the layers and types and classes into which it assorts itself and the barriers which these offer to a free migration of individuals from one class to another. We take on so naturally the material habiliments of our temperaments, necessities and opportunities. Priests, doctors, lawyers, merchants, appear to be born with their particular mental attitude and likewise the clerk, the ditch-digger, the janitor. They have their codes, their guilds and their class feelings. And while they may be spiritually closely related, they are physically far apart. Eugene, after hunting for a place for a month, knew a great deal more about this stratification than he had ever dreamed of knowing. He found that he was naturally barred by temperament from some things, from others by strength and weight, or rather the lack of them; from others, by inexperience; from others, by age; and so on. And those who were different from him in any or all of these respects were inclined to look at him askance. "You are not as we are," their eyes seemed to say; "why do you come here?"

One day he approached a gang of men who were waiting outside a car barn and sought to find out where the registration office was. He did not lay off his natural manner of superiority —could not, but asked a man near him if he knew. It had taken all his courage to do this.

"He wouldn't be after lookin' fer a place as a conductor now, would he?" he heard someone say within his hearing. For some reason this remark took all his courage away. He went up the wooden stairs to the little office where the application blanks were handed out, but did not even have the courage to apply for one. He pretended to be looking for someone and went out again. Later, before a drygoods superintendent's office, he heard a youth remark, "Look what wants to be a clerk." It froze him.

It is a question how long this aimless, nervous wandering would have continued if it had not been for the accidental recollection of an experience which a fellow artist once related to him of a writer who had found himself nervously depressed and who, by application to the president of a railroad, had secured as a courtesy to the profession which he represented so ably a position as an apprentice in a surveying corps, being given transportation to a distant section of the country and employed at a laborer's wages until he was well. Eugene now thought of this as quite an idea for himself. Why it had not occurred to him before he did not know. He could apply as an artist—his appearance would bear him out, and being able to speak from the vantage point of personal ability temporarily embarrassed by ill health, his chances of getting something would be so much better. It would not be the same as a position which he had secured for himself without fear or favor, but it would be a position, different from farming with Angela's father because it would command a salary.

CHAPTER XIX

THIS idea of appealing to the president of one of the great railroads that entered New York was not so difficult to execute. Eugene dressed himself very carefully the next morning, and going to the office of the company in Forty-second Street, consulted the list of officers posted in one of the halls, and finding the president to be on the third floor, ascended. He discovered, after compelling himself by sheer will power to enter, that this so-called office was a mere anteroom to a force of assistants serving the president, and that no one could see him except by appointment.

"You might see his secretary if he isn't busy," suggested the clerk who handled his card gingerly.

Eugene was for the moment undetermined what to do but decided that maybe the secretary could help him. He asked that his card might be taken to him and that no explanation be demanded of him except by the secretary in person. The latter came out after a while, an under secretary of perhaps twenty-eight years of age, short and stout. He was bland and apparently good natured.

"What is it I can do for you?" he asked.

Eugene had been formulating his request in his mind—some method of putting it briefly and simply.

"I came up to see Mr. Wilson," he said, "to see if he would not send me out as a day-laborer of some kind in connection with some department of the road. I am an artist by profession and I am suffering from neurasthenia. All the doctors I have consulted have recommended that I get a simple, manual position of some kind and work at it until I am well. I know of an instance in which Mr. Wilson, assisted, in this way, Mr. Savin the author, and I thought he might be willing to interest himself in my case."

At the sound of Henry Savin's name the under-secretary pricked up his ears. He had, fortunately, read one of his books, and this together with Eugene's knowledge of the case, his personal appearance, a certain ring of sincerity in what he was saying, caused him to be momentarily interested.

"There is no position in connection with any clerical work which the president could give you, I am sure," he replied. "All of these things are subject to a system of promotion. It might be that he could place you with one of the construction gangs in one of the departments under a foreman. I don't know. It's very hard work, though. He might consider your case." He smiled commiseratingly. "I question whether you're strong enough to do anything of that sort. It takes a pretty good man to wield a pick or a shovel."

"I don't think I had better worry about that now," replied Eugene in return, smiling wearily. "I'll take the work and see if it won't help me. I think I need it badly enough."

He was afraid the under-secretary would repent of his suggestion and refuse him entirely.

"Can you wait a little while?" asked the latter curiously. He had the idea that Eugene was someone of importance, for he had suggested as a parting argument that he could give a number of exceptional references.

"Certainly," said Eugene, and the secretary went his way, coming back in half an hour to hand him an enveloped letter.

"We have the idea," he said quite frankly waiving any suggestion of the president's influence in the matter and speaking for himself and the secretary-in-chief, with whom he had agreed that Eugene ought to be assisted, "that you had best apply to the engineering department. Mr. Hobsen, the chief-engineer, can arrange for you. This letter I think will get you what you want."

Eugene's heart bounded. He looked at the superscription and saw it addressed to Mr. Woodruff Hobsen, Chief Engineer, and putting it in his pocket without stopping to read it, but thanking the under-secretary profusely, went out. In the hall at a safe distance he stopped and opened it, finding that it spoke of him familiarly as "Mr. Eugene Witla, an artist, temporarily incapacitated by neurasthenia," and went on to say that he was "desirous of being appointed to some manual toil in some construction corps. The president's office recommends this request to your favor."

When he read this he knew it meant a position. It roused curious feelings as to the nature and value of stratification. As a laborer he was nothing: as an artist he could get a position as a laborer. After all, his ability as an artist was worth something. It obtained him this refuge. He hugged it joyously, and a few moments later handed it to an under-secretary in the Chief-Engineer's office. Without being seen by anyone in authority he was in return given a letter to Mr. William Haverford, "Engineer of Maintenance of Way," a pale, anæmic gentleman of perhaps forty years of age, who, as Eugene learned from him when he was eventually ushered into his presence a half hour later, was a captain of thirteen thousand men. The latter read the letter from the Engineer's office curiously. He was struck by Eugene's odd mission and his appearance as a man. Artists were queer. This was like one. Eugene reminded him of himself a little in his appearance.

"An artist," he said interestedly. "So you want to work as a day laborer?" He fixed Eugene with clear, coal-black eyes looking out of a long, pear-shaped face. Eugene noticed that his hands were long and thin and white and that his high, pale forehead was crowned by a mop of black hair.

"Neurasthenia. I've heard a great deal about that of late, but have never been troubled that way myself. I find that I derive considerable benefit when I am nervous from the use of a rubber exerciser. You have seen them perhaps?"

"Yes," Eugene replied, "I have. My case is much too grave for that, I think. I have traveled a great deal. But it doesn't seem to do me any good. I want work at something manual, I fancy—something at which I have to work. Exercise in a room would not help me. I think I need a complete change of environment. I will be much obliged if you will place me in some capacity."

"Well, this will very likely be it," suggested Mr. Haverford blandly. "Working as a day-laborer will certainly not strike you as play. To tell you the truth, I don't think you can stand it." He reached for a glass-framed map showing the various divisions of the railroad stretching from New England to Chicago and St. Louis, and observed quietly. "I could send you to a great many places, Pennsylvania, New York, Ohio, Michigan, Canada." His finger roved idly about. "I have thirteen thousand men in my department and they are scattered far and wide."

Eugene marveled. Such a position! Such authority! This pale, dark man sitting as an engineer at a switch board directing so large a machine.

"You have a large force," he said simply. Mr. Haverford smiled wanly.

"I think, if you will take my advice, you will not go in a construction corps right away. You can hardly do manual labor. There is a little carpenter shop which we have at Speonk, not very far outside the city, which I should think would answer your needs admirably. A little creek joins the Hudson there and it's out on a point of land, the shop is. It's summer now, and to put you in a broiling sun with a gang of Italians would be a little rough. Take my advice and go here. It will be hard enough. After you are broken in and you think you want a change I can easily arrange if for you. The money may not make so much difference to you but you may as well have it. It will be fifteen cents an hour. I will give you a letter to Mr. Litlebrown, our division engineer, and he will see that you are properly provided for."

Eugene bowed. Inwardly he smiled at the thought that the money would not be acceptable to him. Anything would be acceptable. Perhaps this would be best. It was near the city. The description of the little carpenter shop out on the neck of land appealed to him. It was, as he found when he looked at the map of the immediate division to which this belonged, almost within the city limits. He could live in New York—the upper portion of it anyhow.

Again there was a letter, this time to Mr. Henry C. Litlebrown, a tall, meditative, philosophic man whom Eugene found two days later in the division offices at Yonkers, who in turn wrote a letter to Mr. Joseph Brooks, Superintendent of Buildings, at Mott Haven, whose secretary finally gave Eugene a letter to Mr. Jack Stix, foreman carpenter at Speonk. This letter, when presented on a bright Friday afternoon, brought him the advice to come Monday at seven A. M., and so Eugene saw a career as a day laborer stretching very conspicuously before him.

The "little shop" in question was located in the most charming manner possible. If it had been set as a stage scene for his especial artistic benefit it could not have been better. On a point of land between the river and the main line of the railroad and a little creek, which was east of the railroad and which the latter crossed on a trestle to get back to the mainland again, it stood, a long, low two-storey structure, green as to its roof, red as to its body, full of windows which commanded picturesque views of passing yachts and steamers and little launches and row-boats anchored safely in the waters of the cove which the creek formed. There was a veritable song of labor which arose from this shop, for it was filled with planes, lathes and wood-turning instruments of various kinds, to say nothing of a great group of carpenters who could make desks, chairs, tables, in short, office furniture of various kinds, and who kept the company's needs of these fittings for its depots and offices well supplied. Each carpenter had a bench before a window on the second floor, and in the centre were the few necessary machines they were always using, small jig, cross cut, band and rip saws, a plane, and four or five lathes. On the ground floor was the engine room, the blacksmith's shop, the giant plane, the great jig and cross cut saws, and the store room and supply closets. Out in the yard were piles of lumber, with tracks in between, and twice every day a local freight called "The Dinky" stopped to switch in or take out loaded cars of lumber or finished furniture and supplies. Eugene, as he approached on the day he presented his letter, stopped to admire the neatness of the low board fence which surrounded it all, the beauty of the water, the droning sweetness of the saws.

"Why, the work here couldn't be very hard," he thought. He saw carpenters looking out of the upper windows, and a couple of men in brown overalls and jumpers unloading a car. They were carrying great three-by-six joists on their shoulders. Would he be asked to do anything like that. He scarcely thought so. Mr. Haverford had distinctly indicated in his letter to Mr. Litlebrown that he was to be built up by degrees. Carrying great joists did not appeal to him as the right way, but he presented his letter. He had previously looked about on the high ground which lay to the back of the river and which commanded this point of land, to see if he could find a place to board and lodge, but had seen nothing. The section was very exclusive, occupied by suburban New Yorkers of wealth, and they were not interested in the proposition which he had formulated in his own mind, namely his temporary reception somewhere as a paying guest. He had visions of a comfortable home somewhere now with nice people, for strangely enough the securing of this very minor position had impressed him as the beginning of the end of his bad luck. He was probably going to get well now, in the course of time. If he could only live with some nice family for the summer. In the fall if he were improving, and he thought he might be, Angela could come on. It might be that one of the dealers, Pottle Frères or Jacob Bergman or Henry LaRue would have sold a picture. One hundred and fifty or two hundred dollars joined to his salary would go a long way towards making their living moderately comfortable. Besides Angela's taste and economy, coupled with his own art judgment, could make any little place look respectable and attractive.

The problem of finding a room was not so easy. He followed the track south to a settlement which was visible from the shop windows a quarter of a mile away, and finding nothing which suited his taste as to location, returned to Speonk proper and followed the little creek inland half a mile. This adventure delighted him for it revealed a semi-circle of charming cottages ranged upon a hill slope which had for its footstool the little silvery-bosomed stream. Between the stream and the hill slope ran a semi-circular road and above that another road. Eugene could see at a glance that here was middle class prosperity, smooth lawns, bright awnings, flower pots of blue and yellow and green upon the porches, doorsteps and verandas. An auto standing in front of one house indicated a certain familiarity with the ways of the rich, and a summer road house, situated at the intersection of a road leading out from New York and the little stream where it was crossed by a bridge, indicated that the charms of this village were not unknown to those who came touring and seeking for pleasure. The road house itself was hung with awnings and one dining balcony out over the water. Eugene's desire was fixed on this village at once. He wanted to live here—anywhere in it. He walked about under the cool shade of the trees looking at first one door yard and then another wishing that he might introduce himself by letter and be received. They ought to welcome an artist of his ability and refinement and would, he thought, if they knew. His working in a furniture factory or for the railroad as a day laborer for his health simply added to his picturesque character. In his wanderings he finally came upon a Methodist church quaintly built of red brick and grey stone trimmings, and the sight of its tall, stained glass windows and square fortress-like bell-tower gave him an idea. Why not appeal to the minister? He could explain to him what he wanted, show him his credentials—for he had with him old letters from editors, publishers and art houses—and give him a clear understanding as to why he wanted to come here at all. His ill health and distinction ought to appeal to this man, and he would probably direct him to some one who would gladly have him. At five in the afternoon he knocked at the door and was received in the pastor's study—a large still room in which a few flies were buzzing in the shaded light. In a few moments the minister himself came in—a tall, grey-headed man, severely simple in his attire and with the easy air of one who is used to public address. He was about to ask what he could do for him when Eugene began with his explanation.

"You don't know me at all. I am a stranger in this section. I am an artist by profession and I am coming to Speonk on Monday to work in the railroad shop there for my health. I have been suffering from a nervous breakdown and am going to try day labor for awhile. I want to find a convenient, pleasant place to live, and I thought you might know of someone here, or near here, who might be willing to take me in for a little while. I can give excellent references. There doesn't appear to be anything in the immediate neighborhood of the shop."

"It is rather isolated there," replied the old minister, studying Eugene carefully. "I have often wondered how all those men like it, traveling so far. None of them live about here." He looked at Eugene solemnly, taking in his various characteristics. He was not badly impressed. He seemed to be a reserved, thoughtful, dignified young man and decidedly artistic. It struck him as very interesting that he should be trying so radical a thing as day labor for his nerves.

"Let me see," he said thoughtfully. He sat down in his chair near his table and put his hand over his eyes. "I don't think of anyone just at the moment. There are plenty of families who have room to take you if they would, but I question very much whether they would. In fact I'm rather sure they wouldn't. Let me see now."

He thought again.

Eugene studied his big aquiline nose, his shaggy grey eyebrows, his thick, crisp, grey hair. Already his mind was sketching him, the desk, the dim walls, the whole atmosphere of the room.

"No, no," he said slowly. "I don't think of anyone. There is one family—Mrs. Hibberdell. She lives in the—let me see—first, second, third, tenth house above here. She has one nephew with her at present, a young man of about your age, and I don't think anyone else. I don't know that she would consider taking you in, but she might. Her house is quite large. She did have her daughter with her at one time, but I'm not sure that she's there now. I think not."

He talked as though he were reporting his own thoughts to himself audibly.

Eugene pricked up his ears at the mention of a daughter. During all the time he had been out of New York he had not, with the exception of Frieda, had a single opportunity to talk intimately with any girl. Angela had been with him all the time. Here in New York since he had been back he had been living under such distressing conditions that he had not thought of either youth or love. He had no business to be thinking of it now, but this summer air, this tree-shaded village, the fact that he had a position, small as it was, on which he could depend and which would no doubt benefit him mentally, and that he was somehow feeling better about himself because he was going to work, made him feel that he might look more interestedly on life again. He was not going to die; he was going to get well.

Finding this position proved it. And he might go to the house now and find some charming girl who would like him very much. Angela was away. He was alone. He had again the freedom of his youth. If he were only well and working!

He thanked the old minister very politely and went his way, recognizing the house by certain details given him by the minister, a double balconied veranda, some red rockers, two yellow jardinières at the doorstep, a greyish white picket fence and gate. He walked up smartly and rang the bell. A very intelligent woman of perhaps fifty-five or sixty with bright grey hair and clear light blue eyes was coming out with a book in her hand. Eugene stated his case. She listened with keen interest, looking him over the while. His appearance took her fancy, for she was of a strong intellectual and literary turn of mind.

"I wouldn't ordinarily consider anything of the kind, but I am alone here with my nephew and the house could easily accommodate a dozen. I don't want to do anything which will irritate him, but if you will come back in the morning I will let you know. It would not disturb me to have you about. Do you happen to know of an artist by the name of Deesa?"

"I know him well," replied Eugene. "He's an old friend of mine."

"He is a friend of my daughter's, I think. Have you enquired anywhere else here in the village?"

"No," said Eugene.

"That is just as well," she replied.

He took the hint.

So there was no daughter here. Well, what matter? The view was beautiful. Of an evening he could sit out here in one of the rocking chairs and look at the water. The evening sun, already low in the west was burnishing it a bright gold. The outline of the hill on the other side was dignified and peaceful. He could sleep and work as a day laborer and take life easy for a while. He could get well now and this was the way to do it. Day laborer! How fine, how original, how interesting. He felt somewhat like a knight-errant reconnoitring a new and very strange world.

CHAPTER XX

THE matter of securing admission to this house was quickly settled. The nephew, a genial, intelligent man of thirty-four, as Eugene discovered later, had no objection. It appeared to Eugene that in some way he contributed to the support of this house, though Mrs. Hibberdell obviously had some money of her own. A charmingly furnished room on the second floor adjoining one of the several baths was assigned him, and he was at once admitted to the freedom of the house. There were books, a piano (but no one to play it), a hammock, a maid-of-all-work, and an atmosphere of content and peace. Mrs. Hibberdell, a widow, presumably of some years of widowhood, was of that experience and judgment in life which gave her intellectual poise. She was not particularly inquisitive about anything in connection with him, and so far as he could see from surface indications was refined, silent, conservative. She could jest, and did, in a subtle understanding way. He told her quite frankly at the time he applied that he was married, that his wife was in the West and that he expected her to return after his health was somewhat improved. She talked with him about art and books and life in general. Music appeared to be to her a thing apart. She did not care much for it. The nephew, Davis Simpson, was neither literary nor artistic, and apparently cared little for music. He was a buyer for one of the larger department stores, a slight, dapper, rather dandified type of man, with a lean, not thin but tight-muscled face, and a short black mustache, and he appeared to be interested only in the humors of character, trade, baseball and methods of entertaining himself. The things that pleased Eugene about him were that he was clean, simple, direct, good-natured and courteous. He had apparently no desire to infringe on anybody's privacy, but was fond of stirring up light discussions and interpolating witty remarks. He liked also to grow flowers and to fish. The care of a border of flowers which glorified a short gravel path in the back yard received his especial attention evenings and mornings.

It was a great pleasure for Eugene to come into this atmosphere after the storm which had been assailing him for the past three years, and particularly for the past ninety days. He was only asked to pay eight dollars a week by Mrs. Hibberdell, though he realized that what he was obtaining in home atmosphere here was not ordinarily purchasable at any price in the public market. The maid saw to it that a little bouquet of flowers was put on his dressing table daily. He was given fresh towels and linen in ample quantities. The bath was his own. He could sit out on the porch of an evening and look at the water uninterrupted or he could stay in the library and read. Breakfast and dinner were invariably delightful occasions, for though he rose at five-forty-five in order to have his bath, breakfast, and be able to walk to the factory and reach it by seven, Mrs. Hibberdell was invariably up, as it was her habit to rise thus early, had been so for years. She liked it. Eugene in his weary mood could scarcely understand this. Davis came to the table some few moments before he would be leaving. He invariably had some cheery remark to offer, for he was never sullen or gloomy. His affairs, whatever they were, did not appear to oppress him. Mrs. Hibberdell would talk to Eugene genially about his work, this small, social centre of which they were a part and which was called Riverwood, the current movements in politics, religion, science and so forth. There were references sometimes to her one daughter, who was married and living in New York. It appeared that she occasionally visited her mother here. Eugene was delighted to think he had been so fortunate as to find this place. He hoped to make himself so agreeable that there would be no question as to his welcome, and he was not disappointed.

Between themselves Mrs. Hibberdell and Davis discussed him, agreeing that he was entirely charming, a good fellow, and well worth having about. At the factory where Eugene worked and where the conditions were radically different, he made for himself an atmosphere which was almost entirely agreeable to him, though he quarreled at times with specific details. On the first morning, for instance, he was put to work with two men, heavy clods of souls he thought at first, familiarly known about the yard as John and Bill. These two, to his artistic eye, appeared machines, more mechanical than humanly self-directive. They were of medium height, not more than five feet, nine inches tall and weighed about one hundred and eighty pounds each. One had a round, poorly modeled face very much the shape of an egg, to which was attached a heavy yellowish mustache. He had a glass eye, complicated in addition by a pair of spectacles which were fastened over his large, protruding red ears with steel hooks. He wore a battered brown hat, now a limp shapeless mass. His name was Bill Jeffords and he responded sometimes to the sobriquet of "One Eye."

The other man was John alias "Jack" Duncan, an individual of the same height and build with but slightly more modeling to his face and with little if any greater intelligence. He looked somewhat the shrewder—Eugene fancied there might be lurking in him somewhere a spark of humor, but he was mistaken. Unquestionably in Jeffords there was none. Jack Stix, the foreman-carpenter, a tall, angular, ambling man with red hair, a red mustache, shifty, uncertain blue eyes and noticeably big hands and feet, had suggested to Eugene that he work with these men for a little while. It was his idea to "try him out," as he told one of the associate foremen who was in charge of a gang of Italians working in the yard for the morning, and he was quite equal to doing it. He thought Eugene had no business here and might possibly be scared off by a little rough work.

"He's up here for his health," he told him. "I don't know where he comes from. Mr. Brooks sent him up here with orders to put him on. I want to see how he takes to real work for awhile."

"Look out you don't hurt him," suggested the other. "He don't look very strong to me."

"He's strong enough to carry a few spiles, I guess. If Jimmy can carry 'em, he can. I don't intend to keep him at it long."

Eugene knew nothing of this, but when he was told to "come along, new man" and shown a pile of round, rough ash trunk cutting six inches in diameter and eight feet long, his courage failed him. He was suffered to carry some of these to the second floor, how many he did not know.

"Take 'em to Thompson up there in the corner," said Jeffords dully.

Eugene grasped one uncertainly in the middle with his thin, artistic hands. He did not know that there were ways of handling lumber just as there were ways of handling a brush. He tried to lift it but could not. The rough bark scratched his fingers cruelly.

"Yah gotta learn somepin about that before yuh begin, I guess," said Jack Duncan, who had been standing by eyeing him narrowly.

Jeffords had gone about some other work.

"I suppose I don't know very much about it," replied Eugene shamefacedly stopping and waiting for further instructions.

"Lemme show you a trick," said his associate. "There's tricks in all these here trades. Take it by the end this-a-way, and push it along until you can stand it up. Stoop down now and put your shoulder right next the middle. Gotta pad under your shirt? You oughtta have one. Now put your right arm out ahead o'yuh, on the spile. Now you're all right."

Eugene straightened up and the rough post balanced itself evenly but crushingly on his shoulder. It appeared to grind his muscles and his back and legs ached instantly. He started bravely forward straining to appear at ease but within fifty feet he was suffering agony. He walked the length of the shop, however, up the stairs and back again to the window where Thompson was, his forehead bursting with perspiration and his ears red with blood. He fairly staggered as he neared the machine and dropped the post heavily.

"Look what you're doin'," said a voice behind him. It was Thompson, the lathe worker. "Can't you put that down easy?"

"No, I can't," replied Eugene angrily, his face tinged with a faint blush from his extreme exertion. He was astonished and enraged to think they should put him to doing work like this, especially since Mr. Haverford had told him it would be easy. He suspected at once a plot to drive him away. He would have added "these are too damn heavy for me," but he restrained himself. He went down stairs wondering how he was to get up the others. He fingered about the pole gingerly hoping that the time taken this way would ease his pain and give him strength for the next one. Finally he picked up another and staggered painfully to the loft again. The foreman had his eye on him but said nothing. It amused him a little to think Eugene was having such a hard time. It wouldn't hurt him for a change, would do him good. "When he gets four carried up let him go," he said to Thompson, however, feeling that he had best lighten the situation a little. The latter watched Eugene out of the tail of his eye noting the grimaces he made and the strain he was under-going, but he merely smiled. When four had been dropped on the floor he said: "That'll do for the present," and Eugene, heaving a groan of relief, went angrily away. In his nervous, fantastic, imaginative and apprehensive frame of mind, he imagined he had been injured for life. He feared he had strained a muscle or broken a blood vessel somewhere.

"Good heavens, I can't stand anything like this," he thought. "If the work is going to be this hard I'll have to quit. I wonder what they mean by treating me this way. I didn't come here to do this."

Visions of days and weeks of back-breaking toil stretched before him. It would never do. He couldn't stand it. He saw his old search for work coming back, and this frightened him in another direction. "I mustn't give up so easily," he counseled

himself in spite of his distress. "I have to stick this out a little
while anyhow." It seemed in this first trying hour as though he
were between the devil and the deep sea. He went slowly
down into the yard to find Jeffords and Duncan. They were
working at a car, one inside receiving lumber to be piled, the
other bringing it to him.

"Get down, Bill," said John, who was on the ground looking
up at his partner indifferently. "You get up there, new man.
What's your name?"

"Witla," said Eugene.

"Well, my name's Duncan. We'll bring this stuff to you and
you pile it."

It was more heavy lumber, as Eugene apprehensively observed,
quarter cut joists for some building—"four by fours" they called
them—but after he was shown the art of handling them they
were not unmanageable. There were methods of sliding and
balancing them which relieved him of a great quantity of labor.
Eugene had not thought to provide himself with gloves though,
and his hands were being cruelly torn. He stopped once to
pick a splinter out of his thumb and Jeffords, who was coming
up, asked, "Ain't cha got no gloves?"

"No," said Eugene, "I didn't think to get any."

"Your hands'll get pretty well bunged up, I'm afraid. Maybe
Joseph'll let you have his for to-day, you might go in and ask
him."

"Where's Joseph?" asked Eugene.

"He's inside there. He's taking from the plane."

Eugene did not understand this quite. He knew what a plane
was, had been listening to it sing mightily all the morning, the
shavings flying as it smoothed the boards, but *taking?*

"Where's Joseph?" he asked of the plane driver.

He nodded his head to a tall hump-shouldered boy of perhaps
twenty-two. He was a big, simple, innocent looking fellow.
His face was long and narrow, his mouth wide, his eyes a watery
blue, his hair a shock of brown, loose and wavy, with a good
sprinkling of sawdust in it. About his waist was a big piece
of hemp bagging tied by a grass rope. He wore an old faded
wool cap with a long visor in order to shield his eyes from the
flying chips and dust, and when Eugene came in one hand was
lifted protectingly to shield his eyes. Eugene approached him
deprecatingly.

"One of the men out in the yard said that you might have a
pair of gloves you would lend me for to-day. I'm piling lumber
and it's tearing my hands. I forgot to get a pair."

"Sure," said Joseph genially waving his hand to the driver to stop. "They're over here in my locker. I know what that is. I been there. When I come here they rubbed it into me jist as they're doin' to you. Doncher mind. You'll come out all right. Up here for your health, are you? It ain't always like that. Somedays there ain't most nothin' to do here. Then somedays ag'in there's a whole lot. Well, it's good healthy work, I can say that. I ain't most never sick. Nice fresh air we git here and all that."

He rambled on, fumbling under his bagging apron for his keys, unlocking his locker and producing a great pair of old yellow lumber gloves. He gave them to Eugene cheerfully and the latter thanked him. He liked Eugene at once and Eugene liked him. "A nice fellow that," he said, as he went back to his car. "Think of how genially he gave me these. Lovely! If only all men were as genial and kindly disposed as this boy, how nice the world would be." He put on the gloves and found his work instantly easier for he could grasp the joists firmly and without pain. He worked on until noon when the whistle blew and he ate a dreary lunch sitting by himself on one side, pondering. After one he was called to carry shavings, one basket after another back through the blacksmith shop to the engine room in the rear where was a big shaving bin. By four o'clock he had seen almost all the characters he was going to associate with for the time that he stayed there. Harry Fornes, the blacksmith or "the village smith," as Eugene came to call him later on, Jimmy Sudds, the blacksmith's helper or "maid-of-all-work" as he promptly named him; John Peters, the engineer, Malachi Dempsey, the driver of the great plane, Joseph Mews and, in addition, carpenters, tin-smiths, plumbers, painters, and those few exceptional cabinet makers who passed through the lower floor now and then, men who were about the place from time to time and away from it at others—all of whom took note of Eugene at first as a curiosity.

Eugene was himself intensely interested in the men. Harry Fornes and Jimmy Sudds attracted him especially. The former was an undersized American of distant Irish extraction who was so broad chested, swollen armed, square-jawed and generally self-reliant and forceful as to seem a minor Titan. He was remarkably industrious, turning out a great deal of work and beating a piece of iron with a resounding lick which could be heard all about the hills and hollows outside. Jimmy Sudds, his assistant, was like his master equally undersized, dirty, gnarled, twisted, his teeth showing like a row of yellow snags, his ears

standing out like small fans, his eye askew, but nevertheless with
so genial a look in his face as to disarm criticism at once. Every
body liked Jimmy Sudds because he was honest, single-minded
and free of malicious intent. His coat was three and his trousers
two times too large for him, and his shoes were obviously bought
at a second-hand store, but he had the vast merit of being a
picture. Eugene was fascinated with him. He learned shortly
that Jimmy Sudds truly believed that buffaloes were to be shot
around Buffalo, New York.

John Peters, the engineer, was another character who fixed his
attention. John was almost helplessly fat and was known for
this reason as "Big John." He was a veritable whale of a man.
Six feet tall, weighing over three hundred pounds and standing
these summer days in his hot engine room, his shirt off, his sus-
penders down, his great welts of fat showing through his thin
cotton undershirt, he looked as though he might be suffering,
but he was not. John, as Eugene soon found out, did not take
life emotionally. He stood mostly in his engine room door when
the shade was there staring out on the glistening water of the
river, occasionally wishing that he didn't need to work but could
lie and sleep indefinitely instead.

"Wouldja think them fellers would feel purty good sittin' out
there on the poop deck of them there yachts smokin' their per-
fectos?" he once asked Eugene, apropos of the magnificent private
vessels that passed up and down the river.

"I certainly would," laughed Eugene.

"Aw! Haw! That's the life fer yer uncle Dudley. I could
do that there with any of 'em. Aw! Haw!"

Eugene laughed joyously.

"Yes, that's the life," he said. "We all could stand our share."

Malachi Dempsey, the driver of the great plane, was dull,
tight-mouthed, silent, more from lack of ideas than anything
else, though oyster-wise he had learned to recede from all manner
of harm by closing his shell tightly. He knew no way to avoid
earthly harm save by being preternaturally silent, and Eugene saw
this quickly. He used to stare at him for long periods at a time,
marvelling at the curiosity his attitude presented. Eugene himself, though, was a curiosity to the others, even more so than
they to him. He did not look like a workingman and could not
be made to do so. His spirit was too high, his eye too flashing and
incisive. He smiled at himself carrying basketful after basketful
of shavings from the planing room, where it rained shavings
and from which, because of the lack of a shaving blower, they
had to be removed back to the hot engine room where Big John

presided. The latter took a great fancy to Eugene, but something after the fashion of a dog for a master. He did not have a single idea above his engine, his garden at home, his wife, his children and his pipe. These and sleep—lots of it—were his joys, his recreations, the totality of his world.

CHAPTER XXI

THERE were many days now, three months all told, in which Eugene obtained insight into the workaday world such as he had not previously had. It is true he had worked before in somewhat this fashion, but his Chicago experience was without the broad philosophic insight which had come to him since. Formerly the hierarchies of power in the universe and on earth were inexplicable to him—all out of order; but here, where he saw by degrees ignorant, almost animal intelligence, being directed by greater, shrewder, and at times it seemed to him possibly malicious intelligences—he was not quite sure about that—who were so strong that the weaker ones must obey them, he began to imagine that in a rough way life might possibly be ordered to the best advantage even under this system. It was true that men quarreled here with each other as to who should be allowed to lead. There was here as elsewhere great seeking for the privileges and honors of direction and leadership in such petty things as the proper piling of lumber, the planing of boards, the making of desks and chairs, and men were grimly jealous of their talents and abilities in these respects, but in the main it was the jealousy that makes for ordered, intelligent control. All were striving to do the work of intelligence, not of unintelligence. Their pride, however ignorant it might be, was in the superior, not the inferior. They might complain of their work, snarl at each other, snarl at their bosses, but after all it was because they were not able or permitted to do the higher work and carry out the orders of the higher mind. All were striving to do something in a better way, a superior way, and to obtain the honors and emoluments that come from doing anything in a superior way. If they were not rewarded according to their estimate of their work there was wrath and opposition and complaint and self-pity, but the work of the superior intelligence was the thing which each in his blind, self-seeking way was apparently trying to do.

Because he was not so far out of his troubles that he could be forgetful of them, and because he was not at all certain that his talent to paint was ever coming back to him, he was not as cheerful at times as he might have been; but he managed to conceal it pretty well. This one thought with its attendant ills of probable poverty and obscurity were terrible to him. Time was slipping away and youth. But when he was not thinking of this he was cheerful enough. Besides he had the ability to simulate cheerfulness even when he did not feel it. Because he did not permanently belong to this world of day labor and because his position which had been given him as a favor was moderately secure, he felt superior to everything about him. He did not wish to show this feeling in any way—was very anxious as a matter of fact to conceal it, but his sense of superiority and ultimate indifference to all these petty details was an abiding thought with him. He went to and fro carrying a basket of shavings, jesting with "the village smith," making friends with "Big John," the engineer, with Joseph, Malachi Dempsey, little Jimmy Sudds, in fact anyone and everyone who came near him who would be friends. He took a pencil one day at the noon hour and made a sketch of Harry Fornes, the blacksmith, his arm upraised at the anvil, his helper, Jimmy Sudds, standing behind him, the fire glowing in the forge. Fornes, who was standing beside him, looking over his shoulder, could scarcely believe his eyes.

"Wotcha doin'?" he asked Eugene curiously, looking over his shoulder, for it was at the blacksmith's table, in the sun of his window that he was sitting, looking out at the water. Eugene had bought a lunch box and was carrying with him daily a delectable lunch put up under Mrs. Hibberdell's direction. He had eaten his noonday meal and was idling, thinking over the beauty of the scene, his peculiar position, the curiosities of this shop—anything and everything that came into his head.

"Wait a minute," he said genially, for he and the smith were already as thick as thieves.

The latter gazed interestedly and finally exclaimed:

"W'y that's me, ain't it?"

"Yep!" said Eugene.

"Wat are you goin' to do with that wen you get through with it?" asked the latter avariciously.

"I'm going to give it to you, of course."

"Say, I'm much obliged fer that," replied the smith delightedly. "Gee, the wife'll be tickled to see that. You're a artist, ain't cher? I hearda them fellers. I never saw one. Gee, that's good, that looks just like me, don't it?"

"Something," said Eugene quietly, still working.

The helper came in.

"Watcha' doin'?" he asked.

"He's drawin' a pitcher, ya rube, watchye suppose he's doin'," informed the blacksmith authoritatively. "Don't git too close. He's gotta have room."

"Aw, whose crowdin'?" asked the helper irritably. He realized at once that his superior was trying to shove him in the background, this being a momentous occasion. He did not propose that any such thing should happen. The blacksmith glared at him irritably but the progress of the art work was too exciting to permit of any immediate opportunities for hostilities, so Jimmy was allowed to crowd close and see.

"Ho, ho! that's you, ain't it," he asked the smith curiously, indicating with a grimy thumb the exact position of that dignitary on the drawing.

"Don't," said the latter, loftily—"sure! He's gotta have room."

"An' there's me. Ho! Ho! Gee, I look swell, don't I? Ho! ho!"

The little helper's tushes were showing joyously—a smile that extended far about either side of his face. He was entirely unconscious of the rebuke administered by the smith.

"If you're perfectly good, Jimmy," observed Eugene cheerfully still working, "I may make a sketch of you, sometime!"

"Na! Will you? Go on! Say, hully chee. Dat'll be fine, won't it? Say, ho! ho! De folks at home won't know me. I'd like to have a ting like dat, say!"

Eugene smiled. The smith was regretful. This dividing of honors was not quite all that it might be. Still his own picture was delightful. It looked exactly like the shop. Eugene worked until the whistle blew and the belts began to slap and the wheels to whirr. Then he got up.

"There you are, Fornes," he said. "Like it?"

"Gee, it's swell," said the latter and carried it to the locker. He took it out after a bit though and hung it up over his bench on the wall opposite his forge, for he wanted everyone to see. It was one of the most significant events in his life. This sketch was the subject immediately of a perfect storm of discussion. Eugene was an artist—could draw pictures—that was a revelation in itself. Then this picture was so life-like. It looked like Fornes and Sudds and the shop. Everyone was interested. Everyone jealous. They could not understand how God had favored the smith in this manner. Why hadn't Eugene sketched them before he did him? Why didn't he immediately offer to sketch them now? Big John came first, tipped off and piloted by Jimmy Sudds.

"Say!" he said his big round eyes popping with surprise.

"There's some class to that, what? That looks like you, Fornes. Jinged if it don't! An' Suddsy! Bless me if there ain't Suddsy. Say, there you are, kid, natural as life, damned if you ain't. That's fine. You oughta keep that, smith."

"I intend to," said the latter proudly.

Big John went back to his engine room regretfully. Next came Joseph Mews, his shoulders humped, his head bobbing like a duck, for he had this habit of nodding when he walked.

"Say, wot d'ye thinka that?" he asked. "Ain't that fine. He kin drawr jist as good as they do in them there magazines. I see them there things in them, now an' then. Ain't that swell? Lookit Suddsy back in there. Eh, Suddsy, you're in right, all right. I wisht he'd make a picture o' us out there. We're just as good as you people. Wats the matter with us, eh?"

"Oh, he ain't goin' to be bothered makin' pitchers of you mokes," replied the smith jestingly. "He only draws real ones. You want to remember that, Mews. He's gotta have good people to make sketches of. None o' your half-class plane-drivers and jig-saw operators."

"Is that so? Is that so?" replied Joseph contemptuously, his love of humor spurred by the slight cast upon his ability. "Well if he was lookin' for real ones he made a mistake wen he come here. They're all up front. You don't want to forget that, smith. They don't live in no blacksmith's shop as I ever seen it."

"Cut it out! Cut it out!" called little Sudds from a position of vantage near the door. "Here comes the boss," and Joseph immediately pretended to be going to the engine room for a drink. The smith blew up his fire as though it were necessary to heat the iron he had laid in the coals. Jack Stix came ambling by.

"Who did that?" he asked, stopping after a single general, glance and looking at the sketch on the wall.

"Mr. Witla, the new man," replied the smith, reverently.

"Say, that's pretty good, ain't it?" the foreman replied pleasantly. "He did that well. He must be an artist."

"I think he is," replied the smith, cautiously. He was always eager to curry favor with the boss. He came near to his side and looked over his arm. "He done it here today at noon in about a half an hour."

"Say, that's pretty good now," and the foreman went on his way, thinking.

If Eugene could do that, why was he here? It must be his run down condition, sure enough. And he must be the friend of someone high in authority. He had better be civil. Hitherto he had stood in suspicious awe of Eugene, not knowing what to make of him. He could not figure out just why he was here— a spy possibly. Now he thought that he might be mistaken. "Don't let him work too hard," he told Bill and John. "He ain't any too strong yet. He came up here for his health."

He was obeyed in this respect, for there was no gain-saying the wishes of a foreman, but this open plea for consideration was the one thing if any which could have weakened Eugene's popularity. The men did not like the foreman. He would have been stronger at any time in the affections of the men if the foreman had been less markedly considerate or against him entirely.

The days which followed were restful enough though hard, for Eugene found that the constant whirl of work which went on here, and of which he had naturally to do his share, was beneficial to him. For the first time in several years he slept soundly. He would don his suit of blue overalls and jumper in the morning a few minutes before the whistle blew at seven and from then on until noon, and from one o'clock until six he would carry shavings, pile lumber for one or several of the men in the yard, load or unload cars, help Big John stoke his boilers, or carry chips and shavings from the second floor. He wore an old hat which he had found in a closet at Mrs. Hibberdell's, a faded, crumpled memory of a soft tan-colored sombrero which he punched jauntily to a peak and wore over one ear. He had big new yellow gloves which he kept on his hands all day, which were creased and frayed, but plenty good enough for this shop and yard. He learned to handle lumber nicely, to pile with skill, to "take" for Malachi Dempsey from the plane, to drive the jig-saw, and other curious bits. He was tireless in his energy because he was weary of thinking and hoped by sheer activity to beat down and over-come his notion of artistic inability—to forget that he believed that he couldn't paint and so be able to paint again. He had surprised himself in these sketches he had made, for his first feeling under the old régime would have been that he could not make them. Here, because the men were so eager and he was so much applauded, he found it rather easy and, strange to say, he thought they were good.

At the home of Mrs. Hibberdell at night he would lay off all his working clothes before dinner, take a cold bath and don a new brown suit, which because of the assurance of this position he had bought for eighteen dollars, ready made. He found it hard to get off to buy anything, for his pay ceased (fifteen cents an hour) the moment he left the shop. He had put his pictures in storage in New York and could not get off (or at least did not want to take the time off) to go and sell any. He found that he could leave without question if he wanted no pay, but if he wanted pay and had a good reason he could sometimes be excused. His appearance about the house and yard after six-thirty in the evening and on Sundays was attractive enough. He looked delicate, refined, conservative, and, when not talking to someone, rather wistful. He was lonely and restless, for he felt terribly out of it. This house was lonely. As at Alexandria, before he met Frieda, he was wishing there were some girls about. He wondered where Frieda was, what she was doing, whether she had married. He hoped not. If life had only given him a girl like Frieda—so young, so beautiful! He would sit and gaze at the water after dark in the moonlight, for this was his one consolation —the beauty of nature—thinking. How lovely it all was! How lovely life was,—this village, the summer trees, the shop where he worked, the water, Joseph, little Jimmy, Big John, the stars. If he could paint again, if he could be in love again. In love! In love! Was there any other sensation in the world like that of being in love?

A spring evening, say, some soft sweet odours blowing as they were tonight, the dark trees bending down, or the twilight angelically silver, hyacinth, orange, some soothing murmurs of the wind; some faint chirping of the tree-toads or frogs and then your girl. Dear God! Could anything be finer than that? Was anything else in life worth while? Your girl, her soft young arms about your neck, her lips to yours in pure love, her eyes speaking like twin pools of color here in the night.

So had it been only a little while ago with Frieda. So had it been once with Angela. So long ago with Stella! Dear, sweet Stella, how nice she was. And now here he was sick and lonely and married and Angela would be coming back soon—and— He would get up frequently to shut out these thoughts, and either read or walk or go to bed. But he was lonely, almost irritably so. There was only one true place of comfort for Eugene anywhere and that was in the spring time in love.

CHAPTER XXII

IT was while he was mooning along in this mood, working, dreaming, wishing, that there came, one day to her mother's house at Riverwood, Carlotta Wilson,—Mrs. Norman Wilson, in the world in which she moved—a tall brunette of thirty-two, handsome after the English fashion, shapely, graceful, with a knowledge of the world which was not only compounded of natural intelligence and a sense of humor, but experiences fortunate and unfortunate which had shown her both the showy and the seamy sides of life. To begin with she was the wife of a gambler—a professional gambler—of that peculiar order which essays the rôle of a gentleman, looks the part, and fleeces unmercifully the unwary partakers of their companionship. Carlotta Hibberdell, living with her mother at that time in Springfield, Massachusetts, had met him at a local series of races, which she was attending with her father and mother, where Wilson happened to be accidentally upon another mission. Her father, a real estate dealer, and fairly successful at one time, was very much interested in racing horses, and owned several of worthy records though of no great fame. Norman Wilson had posed as a real estate speculator himself, and had handled several fairly successful deals in land, but his principal skill and reliance was in gambling. He was familiar with all the gambling opportunities of the city, knew a large circle of those who liked to gamble, men and women in New York and elsewhere, and his luck or skill at times was phenomenal. At other times it was very bad. There were periods when he could afford to live in the most expensive apartment houses, dine at the best restaurants, visit the most expensive country pleasure resorts and otherwise disport himself in the companionship of friends. At other times, because of bad luck, he could not afford any of these things and though he held to his estate grimly had to borrow money to do it. He was somewhat of a fatalist in his interpretation of affairs and would hang on with the faith that his luck would turn. It did turn invariably, of course, for when difficulties began to swarm thick and fast he would think vigorously and would usually evolve some idea which served to help him out. His plan was always to spin a web like a spider and await the blundering flight of some unwary fly.

332

At the time she married him Carlotta Hibberdell did not know of the peculiar tendencies and subtle obsession of her ardent lover. Like all men of his type he was suave, persuasive, passionate, eager. There was a certain cat-like magnetism about him also which fascinated her. She could not understand him at that time and she never did afterwards. The license which he subsequently manifested not only with her but with others astonished and disgusted her. She found him selfish, domineering, outside his own particular field shallow, not at all artistic, emotional, or poetic. He was inclined to insist on the last touch of material refinement in surroundings (so far as he understood them) when he had money, but she found to her regret that he did not understand them. In his manner with her and everyone else he was top-lofty, superior, condescending. His stilted language at times enraged and at other times amused her, and when her original passion passed and she began to see through his pretence to his motives and actions she became indifferent and then weary. She was too big a woman mentally to quarrel with him much. She was too indifferent to life in its totality to really care. Her one passion was for an ideal lover of some type, and having been thoroughly mistaken in him she looked abroad wondering whether there were any ideal men.

Various individuals came to their apartments. There were gamblers, blasé society men, mining experts, speculators, sometimes with, sometimes without a wife. From these and from her husband and her own observation she learned of all sorts of scoundrels, mes-alliances, queer manifestations of incompatibility of temper, queer freaks of sex desire. Because she was good looking, graceful, easy in her manners, there were no end of proposals, overtures, hints and luring innuendos cast in her direction. She had long been accustomed to them. Because her husband deserted her openly for other women and confessed it in a blasé way she saw no valid reason for keeping herself from other men. She chose her lovers guardedly and with subtle taste, beginning after mature deliberation with one who pleased her greatly. She was seeking refinement, emotion, understanding coupled with some ability and they were not so easy to find. The long record of her liaisons is not for this story, but their impress on her character was important.

She was indifferent in her manner at most times and to most people. A good jest or story drew from her a hearty laugh. She was not interested in books except those of a very exceptional character—the realistic school—and these she thought ought not to be permitted except to private subscribers, nevertheless she cared for no others. Art was fascinating—really great art. She loved the pictures of Rembrandt, Frans Hals, Correggio, Titian. And with less discrimination, and more from a sensual point of view the nudes of Cabanel, Bouguereau and Gerome. To her there was reality in the works of these men, lightened by great imagination. Mostly people interested her, the vagaries of their minds, the idiosyncrasies of their characters, their lies, their subterfuges, their pretences, their fears. She knew that she was a dangerous woman and went softly, like a cat, wearing a half-smile not unlike that seen on the lips of Monna Lisa, but she did not worry about herself. She had too much courage. At the same time she was tolerant, generous to a fault, charitable. When someone suggested that she overdid the tolerance, she replied, "Why shouldn't I? I live in such a magnificent glass house."

The reason for her visit home on this occasion was that her husband had practically deserted her for the time being. He was in Chicago for some reason—principally because the atmosphere in New York was getting too hot for him, as she suspected. Because she hated Chicago and was weary of his company she refused to go with him. He was furious for he suspected her of liaisons, but he could not help himself. She was indifferent. Besides she had other resources than those he represented, or could get them.

A certain wealthy Jew had been importuning her for years to get a divorce in order that he might marry her. His car and his resources were at her command but she condescended only the vaguest courtesies. It was within the ordinary possibilities of the day for him to call her up and ask if he could not come with his car. He had three. She waved most of this aside indifferently. "What's the use?" was her pet inquiry. Her husband was not without his car at times. She had means to drive when she pleased, dress as she liked, and was invited to many interesting outings. Her mother knew well of her peculiar attitude, her marital troubles, her quarrels and her tendency to flirt. She did her best to keep her in check, for she wanted to retain for her the privilege of obtaining a divorce and marrying again, the next time successfully. Norman Wilson, however, would not readily give her a legal separation even though the preponderance of evidence was against him and, if she compromised herself, there would be no hope. She half suspected that her daughter might already have compromised herself, but she could not be sure. Carlotta was too subtle. Norman made open charges in their family quarrels, but they were based largely on jealousy. He did not know for sure.

Carlotta Wilson had heard of Eugene. She did not know of him by reputation, but her mother's guarded remarks in regard to him and his presence, the fact that he was an artist, that he was sick and working as a laborer for his health aroused her interest. She had intended to spend the period of her husband's absence at Narragansett with some friends, but before doing so she decided to come home for a few days just to see for herself. Instinctively her mother suspected curiosity on her part in regard to Eugene. She threw out the remark that he might not stay long, in the hope that her daughter might lose interest. His wife was coming back. Carlotta discerned this opposition—this desire to keep her away. She decided that she would come.

"I don't know that I want to go to Narragansett just now," she told her mother. "I'm tired. Norman has just worn my nerves to a frazzle. I think I'll come up home for a week or so."

"All right," said her mother, "but do be careful how you act now. This Mr. Witla appears to be a very nice man and he's happily married. Don't you go casting any looks in his direction. If you do I won't let him stay here at all."

"Oh, how you talk," replied Carlotta irritably. "Do give me a little credit for something. I'm not going up there to see him. I'm tired, I tell you. If you don't want me to come I won't."

"It isn't that, I do want you. But you know how you are. How do you ever expect to get free if you don't conduct yourself circumspectly? You know that you—"

"Oh, for heaven's sake, I hope you're not going to start that old argument again," exclaimed Carlotta defensively. "What's the use beginning on that? We've been all over it a thousand times. I can't go anywhere or do anything but what you want to fuss. Now I'm not coming up there to do anything but rest. Why will you always start in to spoil everything?"

"Well now, you know well enough, Carlotta—" reiterated her mother.

"Oh, chuck it. I'll not come. To hell with the house. I'll go to Narragansett. You make me tired!"

Her mother looked at her tall daughter, graceful, handsome, her black hair parted in rich folds, irritated and yet pleased with her force and ability. If she would only be prudent and careful, what a figure she might yet become! Her complexion was like old rose-tinted ivory, her lips the color of dark raspberries, her eyes bluish grey, wide set, large, sympathetic, kindly. What a pity she had not married some big, worthy man to begin with. To be tied up to this gambler, even though they did live in Central Park West and had a comparatively sumptuous apartment, was a wretched thing. Still it was better than poverty or scandal, though if she did not take care of herself both might ensue. She wanted her to come to Riverwood for she liked her company, but she wanted her to behave herself. Perhaps Eugene would save the day. He was certainly restrained enough in his manner and remarks. She went back to Riverwood, and Carlotta, the quarrel smoothed over, followed her.

Eugene did not see her during the day she arrived, for he was at work; and she did not see him as he came in at night. He had on his old peaked hat and carried his handsome leather lunch box jauntily in one hand. He went to his room, bathed, dressed and then out on the porch to await the call of the dinner gong. Mrs. Hibberdell was in her room on the second floor and "Cousin Dave," as Carlotta called Simpson, was in the back yard. It was a lovely twilight. He was in the midst of deep thoughts about the beauty of the scene, his own loneliness, the characters at the shop-work, Angela and what not, when the screen door opened and she stepped out. She had on a short-sleeved house dress of spotted blue silk with yellow lace set about the neck and the ends of the sleeves. Her shapely figure, beautifully proportioned to her height, was set in a smooth, close fitting corset. Her hair, laid in great braids at the back, was caught in a brown spangled net. She carried herself with thoughtfulness and simplicity, seeming naturally indifferent.

Eugene rose. "I'm in your way, I think. Won't you have this chair?"

"No, thanks. The one in the corner will do. But I might as well introduce myself, since there isn't anyone here to do it. I'm Mrs. Wilson, Mrs. Hibberdell's daughter. You're Mr. Witla?"

"Yes, I answer to that," said Eugene, smiling. He was not very much impressed at first. She seemed nice and he fancied intelligent—a little older than he would have preferred any woman to be who was to interest him. She sat down and looked at the water. He took his chair and held his peace. He was not even interested to talk to her. She was nice to look at, however. Her presence lightened the scene for him.

"I always like to come up here," she volunteered finally. "It's so warm in the city these days. I don't think many people know of this place. It's out of the beaten track."

"I enjoy it," said Eugene. "It's such a rest for me. I don't know what I would have done if your mother hadn't taken me in. It's rather hard to find any place, doing what I am."

"You've taken a pretty strenuous way to get health, I should say," she observed. "Day labor sounds rough to me. Do you mind it?"

"Not at all. I like it. The work is interesting and not so very hard. It's all so new to me, that's what makes it easy. I like the idea of being a day laborer and associating with laborers. It's only because I'm run down in health that I worry. I don't like to be sick."

"It is bad," she replied, "but this will probably put you on your feet. I think we're always inclined to look on our present troubles as the worst. I know I am."

"Thanks for the consolation," he said.

She did not look at him and he rocked to and fro silently. Finally the dinner gong struck. Mrs. Hibberdell came down stairs and they went in.

The conversation at dinner turned on his work for a few moments and he described accurately the personalities of John and Bill and Big John the engineer, and little Suddsy and Harry Fornes, the blacksmith. Carlotta listened attentively without appearing to, for everything about Eugene seemed singular and exceptional to her. She liked his tall, spare body, his lean hands, his dark hair and eyes. She liked the idea of his dressing as a laboring man in the morning, working all day in the shop, and yet appearing so neat and trim at dinner. He was easy in his manner, apparently lethargic in his movements and yet she could feel a certain swift force that filled the room. It was richer for his presence. She understood at a glance that he was an artist, in all probability a good one. He said nothing of that, avoided carefully all reference to his art, and listened attentively. She felt though as if he were studying her and everyone else, and it made her gayer. At the same time she had a strong leaning toward him. "What an ideal man to be associated with," was one of her repeated thoughts.

Although she was about the house for ten days and he met her after the third morning not only at dinner, which was natural enough, but at breakfast (which surprised him a little), he paid not so very much attention to her. She was nice, very, but Eugene was thinking of another type. He thought she was uncommonly pleasant and considerate and he admired her style of dressing and her beauty, studying her with interest, wondering what sort of a life she led, for from various bits of conversation

he overheard not only at table but at other times he judged she
was fairly well to do. There was an apartment in Central Park
West, card parties, automobile parties, theatre parties and a
general sense of people—acquaintances anyhow, who were making
money. He heard her tell of a mining engineer, Dr. Rowland;
of a successful coal-mining speculator, Gerald Woods; of a
Mrs. Hale who was heavily interested in copper mines and apparently very wealthy. "It's a pity Norman couldn't connect
with something like that and make some real money," he heard
her say to her mother one evening. He understood that Norman
was her husband and that he probably would be back soon. So
he kept his distance—interested and curious but hardly more.

Mrs. Wilson was not so easily baffled, however. A car appeared one evening at the door immediately after dinner, a great
red touring car, and Mrs. Wilson announced easily, "We're
going for a little spin after dinner, Mr. Witla. Don't you want
to come along?"

Eugene had never ridden in an automobile at that time. "I'd
be very pleased," he said, for the thought of a lonely evening
in an empty house had sprung up when he saw it appear.

There was a chauffeur in charge—a gallant figure in a brown
straw cap and tan duster, but Mrs. Wilson manœuvred for
place.

"You sit with the driver, coz," she said to Simpson, and when
her mother stepped in she followed after, leaving Eugene the
place to the right of her.

"There must be a coat and cap in the locker," she said to the
chauffeur; "let Mr. Witla have it."

The latter extracted a spare linen coat and straw cap which
Eugene put on.

"I like automobiling, don't you?" she said to Eugene good-
naturedly. "It's so refreshing. If there is any rest from care
on this earth it's in traveling fast."

"I've never ridden before," replied Eugene simply. Something about the way he said it touched her. She felt sorry for
him because he appeared lonely and gloomy. His indifference to
her piqued her curiosity and irritated her pride. Why shouldn't
he take an interest in her? As they sped under leafy lanes, up
hill and down dale, she made out his face in the starlight. It was
pale, reflective, indifferent. "These deep thinkers!" she chided
him. "It's terrible to be a philosopher." Eugene smiled.

When they reached home he went to his room as did all the
others to theirs. He stepped out into the hall a few minutes later
to go to the library for a book, and found that her door which

he had to pass was wide open. She was sitting back in a Morris chair, her feet upon another chair, her skirts slightly drawn up revealing a trim foot and ankle. She did not stir but looked up and smiled winningly.

"Aren't you tired enough to sleep?" he asked.

"Not quite yet," she smiled.

He went down stairs and turning on a light in the library stood looking at a row of books reading the titles. He heard a step and there she was looking at the books also.

"Don't you want a bottle of beer?" she asked. "I think there is some in the ice box. I forgot that you might be thirsty."

"I really don't care," he said. "I'm not much for drinks of any kind."

"That's not very sociable," she laughed.

"Let's have the beer then," he said.

She threw herself back languidly in one of the big dining room chairs when she had brought the drinks and some Swiss cheese and crackers, and said: "I think you'll find some cigarettes on the table in the corner if you like."

He struck her a match and she puffed her cigarette comfortably. "I suppose you find it lonely up here away from all your friends and companions," she volunteered.

"Oh, I've been sick so long I scarcely know whether I have any."

He described some of his imaginary ailments and experiences and she listened to him attentively. When the beer was gone she asked him if he would have more but he said no. After a time because he stirred wearily, she got up.

"Your mother will think we're running some sort of a midnight game down here," he volunteered.

"Mother can't hear," she said. "Her room is on the third floor and besides she doesn't hear very well. Dave don't mind. He knows me well enough by now to know that I do as I please."

She stood closer to Eugene but still he did not see. When he moved away she put out the lights and followed him to the stairs.

"He's either the most bashful or the most indifferent of men," she thought, but she said softly, "Good-night. Pleasant dreams to you," and went her way.

Eugene thought of her now as a good fellow, a little gay for a married woman, but probably circumspect withal. She was simply being nice to him. All this was simply because, as yet, he was not very much interested.

There were other incidents. One morning he passed her door. Her mother had already gone down to breakfast and there was the spectacle of a smooth, shapely arm and shoulder quite bare to his gaze as she lay on her pillow apparently unconscious that her door was open. It thrilled him as something sensuously beautiful for it was a perfect arm. Another time he saw her of an evening just before dinner buttoning her shoes. Her dress was pulled three-quarters of the way to her knees and her shoulders and arms were bare, for she was still in her corset and short skirts. She seemed not to know that he was near. One night after dinner he started to whistle something and she went to the piano to keep him company. Another time he hummed on the porch and she started the same song, singing with him. He drew his chair near the window where there was a couch after her mother had retired for the night, and she came and threw herself on it. "You don't mind if I lie here?" she said, "I'm tired tonight."

"Not at all. I'm glad of your company. I'm lonely."

She lay and stared at him, smiling. He hummed and she sang. "Let me see your palm," she said, "I want to learn something." He held it out. She fingered it temptingly. Even this did not wake him.

She left for five days because of some necessity in connection with her engagements and when she returned he was glad to see her. He had been lonesome, and he knew now that she made the house gayer. He greeted her genially.

"I'm glad to see you back," he said.

"Are you really?" she replied. "I don't believe it."

"Why not?" he asked.

"Oh, signs, omens and portents. You don't like women very well I fancy."

"Don't I!"

"No, I think not," she replied.

She was charming in a soft grayish green satin. He noticed that her neck was beautiful and that her hair looped itself gracefully upon the back of it. Her nose was straight and fine, sensitive because of its thin partitioning walls. He followed her into the library and they went out on the porch. Presently he returned—it was ten o'clock—and she came also. Davis had gone to his room, Mrs. Hibberdell to hers.

"I think I'll read," he said, aimlessly.

"Why anything like that?" she jested. "Never read when you can do anything else."

"What else can I do?"

"Oh, lots of things. Play cards, tell fortunes, read palms, drink beer—" She looked at him wilfully.

He went to his favorite chair near the window, side by side with the window-seat couch. She came and threw herself on it.

"Be gallant and fix my pillows for me, will you?" she asked.

"Of course I will," he said.

He took a pillow and raised her head, for she did not deign to move.

"Is that enough?" he inquired.

"One more."

He put his hand under the first pillow and lifted it up. She took hold of his free hand to raise herself. When she had it she held it and laughed a curious excited laugh. It came over him all at once, the full meaning of all the things she had been doing. He dropped the pillow he was holding and looked at her steadfastly. She relaxed her hold and leaned back, languorous, smiling. He took her left hand, then her right and sat down beside her. In a moment he slipped one arm under her waist and bending over put his lips to hers. She twined her arms about his neck tightly and hugged him close; then looking in his eyes she heaved a great sigh.

"You love me, don't you?" he asked.

"I thought you never would," she sighed, and clasped him to her again.

CHAPTER XXIII

THE form of Carlotta Wilson was perfect, her passion eager, her subtlety a match for almost any situation. She had deliberately set out to win Eugene because he was attractive to her and because, by his early indifference, he had piqued her vanity and self-love. She liked him though, liked every one of his characteristics, and was as proud of her triumph as a child with a new toy. When he had finally slipped his arm under her waist she had thrilled with a burning, vibrating thrill throughout her frame and when she came to him it was with the eagerness of one wild for his caresses. She threw herself on him, kissed him sensuously scores of times, whispered her desire and her affection. Eugene thought, now that he saw her through the medium of an awakened passion, that he had never seen anything more lovely. For the time being he forgot Frieda, Angela, his loneliness, the fact that he was working in supposed prudent self-restraint to effect his recovery, and gave himself up to the full enjoyment of this situation.

Carlotta was tireless in her attentions. Once she saw that he really cared, or imagined he did, she dwelt in the atmosphere of her passion and affection. There was not a moment that she was not with or thinking of Eugene when either was possible. She lay in wait for him at every turn, gave him every opportunity which her skill could command. She knew the movements of her mother and cousin to the least fraction—could tell exactly where they were, how long they were likely to remain, how long it would take them to reach a certain door or spot from where they were standing. Her step was noiseless, her motions and glances significant and interpretative. For a month or thereabouts she guided Eugene through the most perilous situations, keeping her arms about him to the last possible moment, kissing him silently and swiftly at the most unexpected times and in the most unexpected surroundings. Her weary languor, her seeming indifference, disappeared, and she was very much alive—except in the presence of others. There her old manner remained, intensified even, for she was determined to throw a veil of darkness over her mother and her cousin's eyes. She succeeded admirably for the time being, for she lied to her mother out of the whole cloth, pretending that Eugene was nice but a little

342

slow so far as the ways of the world were concerned. "He may be a good artist," she volunteered, "but he isn't very much of a ladies' man. He hasn't the first trace of gallantry."

Mrs. Hibberdell was glad. At least there would be no disturbance here. She feared Carlotta, feared Eugene, but she saw no reason for complaint. In her presence all was seemingly formal and at times almost distant. She did not like to say to her daughter that she should not come to her own home now that Eugene was here, and she did not like to tell him to leave. Carlotta said she liked him fairly well, but that was nothing. Any married woman might do that. Yet under her very eyes was going forward the most disconcerting license. She would have been astounded if she had known the manner in which the bath, Carlotta's chamber and Eugene's room were being used. The hour never struck when they were beyond surveillance but what they were together.

Eugene grew very indifferent in the matter of his work. From getting to the point where he was enjoying it because he looked upon it as a form of exercise which was benefiting him, and feeling that he might not have to work indefinitely if he kept up physical rehabilitation at this pace, he grew languid about it and moody over the time he had to give to it. Carlotta had the privilege of a certain automobile and besides she could afford to hire one of her own. She began by suggesting that he meet her at certain places and times for a little spin and this took him away from his work a good portion of the time.

"You don't have to work every day, do you?" she asked him one Sunday afternoon when they were alone. Simpson and Mrs. Hibberdell had gone out for a walk and they were in her room on the second floor. Her mother's was on the third.

"I don't have to," he said, "if I don't mind losing the money they pay. It's fifteen cents an hour and I need that. I'm not working at my regular profession, you must remember."

"Oh, chuck that," she said. "What's fifteen cents an hour? I'll give you ten times that to come and be with me."

"No, you won't," he said. "You won't give me anything. We won't go anywhere on that basis."

"Oh, Eugene, how you talk. Why won't you?" she asked. "I have lots of it—at least lots more than you have just now. And it might as well be spent this way as some other. It won't be spent right anyhow—that is not for any exceptional purpose. Why shouldn't you have some of it? You can pay it back to me."

"I won't do it," said Eugene. "We won't go anywhere on that basis. I'd rather go and work. It's all right, though. I

can sell a picture maybe. I expect to hear any day of something being sold. What is it you want to do?"

"I want you to come automobiling with me tomorrow. Ma is
going over to her sister Ella's in Brooklyn. Has that shop of
yours a phone?"

"Sure it has. I don't think you'd better call me up there
though."

"Once wouldn't hurt."

"Well, perhaps not. But we'd better not begin that, or at
least not make a practice of it. These people are very strict.
They have to be."

"I know," said Carlotta. "I won't. I was just thinking.
I'll let you know. You know that river road that runs on the
top of the hill over there?"

"Yes."

"You be walking along there tomorrow at one o'clock and I'll
pick you up. You can come this once, can't you?"

"Sure," said Eugene. "I can come. I was just joking. I
can get some money." He had still his hundred dollars which
he had not used when he first started looking for work. He had
been clinging to it grimly, but now in this lightened atmosphere
he thought he might spend some of it. He was going to get well.
Everything was pointing that way. His luck was with him.

"Well, I'll get the car. You don't mind riding in that, do
you?"

"No," he said. "I'll wear a good suit to the shop and change
over there."

She laughed gaily, for his scruples and simplicity amused her.

"You're a prince—my Prince Charming," she said and she
flung herself in his lap. "Oh, you angel man, heaven-born!
I've been waiting for you I don't know how long. Wise man!
Prince Charming! I love you! I love you! I think you're the
nicest thing that ever was."

Eugene caressed her gently.

"And you're my wise girl. But we are no good, neither you
nor I. You're a wastrel and a stray. And I—I hesitate to think
what I am."

"What is a wastrel?" she asked. "That's a new one on me.
I don't remember."

"Something or someone that can be thrown away as useless.
A stray is a pigeon that won't stay with the flock."

"That's me," said Carlotta, holding out her firm, smooth arms
before her and grinning mischievously. "I won't stay with any
flock. Nix for the flocks. I'd rather be off with my wise man.

He is nice enough for me. He's better nor nine or ten flocks."
She was using corrupt English for the joy of it. "Just me and
you, Prince Charming. Am I your lovely wastrel? Do you
like strays? Say you do. Listen! Do you like strays?"

Eugene had been turning his head away, saying "scandalous!
terrible, you're the worst ever," but she stopped his mouth with
her lips.

"Do you?"

"This wastrel, yes. This stray," he replied, smoothing her
cheek. "Ah, you're lovely, Carlotta, you're beautiful. What a
wonderful woman you are."

She gave herself to him completely.

"Whatever I am, I'm yours, wise man," she went on. "You
can have anything you want of me, do anything you please with
me. You're like an opiate to me, Eugene, sweet! You stop my
mouth and close my eyes and seal my ears. You make me forget
everything I suppose I might think now and then but I don't
want to. I don't want to! And I don't care. I wish you were
single. I wish I were free. I wish we had an island somewhere
together. Oh, hell! Life is a wearisome tangle, isn't it? 'Take
the cash and let the credit go.' "

By this time Carlotta had heard enough of Eugene's life to
understand what his present condition was. She knew he was
sick though not exactly why. She thought it was due to overwork. She knew he was out of funds except for certain pictures
he had on sale, but that he would regain his art ability and re-
establish himself she did not doubt. She knew something of
Angela and thought it was all right that she should be away from
him, but now she wished the separation might be permanent.
She went into the city and asking about at various art stores
learned something of Eugene's art history and his great promise.
It made him all the more fascinating in her eyes. One of his
pictures on exhibition at Pottle Frères was bought by her after
a little while and the money sent to Eugene, for she had learned
from him how these pictures, any pictures, were exhibited on
sale and the painter paid, minus the commission, when the sale
was made. She took good care to make it clear to the manager at
Pottle Frères that she was doing this so that Eugene could have
the money and saw to it that the check reached him promptly.
If Eugene had been alone this check of three hundred dollars
would have served to bring Angela to him. As it was it gave
him funds to disport himself with in her company. He did not
know that she had been the means of his getting it, or to whom
the picture had been sold. A fictitious name was given. This

sale somewhat restored Eugene's faith in his future, for if one of his pictures would sell so late in the day for this price, others would.

There were days thereafter of the most curious composition. In the morning he would leave dressed in his old working suit and carrying his lunch box, Carlotta waving him a farewell from her window, or, if he had an engagement outside with carlotta, wearing a good suit, and trusting to his overalls and jumper to protect it, working all day with John and Bill, or Malachi Dempsey and Joseph—for there was rivalry between these two groups as to which should have his company—or leaving the shop early and riding with her a part of the time, coming home at night to be greeted by Carlotta as though she had not seen him at all. She watched for his coming as patiently as a wife and was as eager to see if there was anything she could do for him. In the shop Malachi and Joseph or John and Bill and sometimes some of the carpenters up stairs would complain of a rush of work in order that they might have his assistance or presence. Malachi and Joseph could always enter the complaint that they were in danger of being hampered by shavings, for the latter were constantly piling up in great heaps, beautiful shavings of ash and yellow pine and walnut which smelled like resin and frankincense and had the shape of girl's curls or dry breakfast food, or rich damp sawdust. Or John and Bill would complain that they were being overworked and needed someone in the car to receive. Even Big John, the engineer, tried to figure out some scheme by which he could utilize Eugene as a fireman, but that was impossible; there was no call for any such person. The foreman understood well enough what the point was but said nothing, placing Eugene with the particular group which seemed to need him most. Eugene was genial enough about the matter. Wherever he was was right. He liked to be in the cars or on a lumber pile or in the plane room. He also liked to stand and talk to Big John or Harry Fornes, his basket under his arm— "kidding," as he called it. His progress to and fro was marked by endless quips and jests and he was never weary.

When his work was done at night he would hurry home, following the right bank of the little stream until he reached a path which led up to the street whereon was the Hibberdell house. On his way he would sometimes stop and study the water, its peaceful current bearing an occasional stick or straw upon its bosom, and contrasting the seeming peace of its movement with his own troubled life. The subtlety of nature as expressed in water appealed to him. The difference between this idyllic

stream bank and his shop and all who were of it, struck him forcefully. Malachi Dempsey had only the vaguest conception of the
beauty of nature. Jack Stix was scarcely more artistic than the
raw piles of lumber with which he dealt. Big John had no
knowledge of the rich emotions of love or of beauty which troubled Eugene's brain. They lived on another plane, apparently.

And at the other end of the stream awaiting him was Carlotta, graceful, sophisticated, eager in her regard for him, luke-
warm in her interest in morals, sybaritic in her moods, representing in a way a world which lived upon the fruits of this ex-
ploited toil and caring nothing about it. If he said anything to
Carlotta about the condition of Joseph Mews, who carried
bundles of wood home to his sister of an evening to help save
the expense of fuel, she merely smiled. If he talked of the poverty of the masses she said, "Don't be doleful, Eugene." She
wanted to talk of art and luxury and love, or think of them at
least. Her love of the beauty of nature was keen. There were
certain inns they could reach by automobile where they could sit
and dine and drink a bottle of wine or a pitcher of claret cup,
and here she would muse on what they would do if they were
only free. Angela was frequently in Carlotta's thoughts, persistently in Eugene's, for he could not help feeling that he was
doing her a rank injustice.

She had been so patient and affectionate all this long time past,
had tended him as a mother, waited on him as a servant. Only
recently he had been writing in most affectionate terms, wishing
she were with him. Now all that was dead again. It was hard
work to write. Everything he said seemed a lie and he did not
want to say it. He hated to pretend. Still, if he did not write
Angela would be in a state of mortal agony, he thought, and
would shortly come to look him up. It was only by writing,
protesting his affection, explaining why in his judgment it was
unadvisable for her to come at present, that she could be made
to stay where she was. And now that he was so infatuated with
Carlotta this seemed very desirable. He did not delude himself
that he would ever be able to marry her. He knew that he could
not get a divorce, there being no grounds, and the injustice to
Angela being such a bar to his conscience; and as for Carlotta,
her future was very uncertain. Norman Wilson, for all that he
disregarded her at times, did not want to give her up. He was
writing, threatening to come back to New York if she did not
come to him, though the fact that she was in her mother's home,
where he considered her safe, was some consolation to him. Angela was begging Eugene to let her come. They would get along,

she argued, on whatever he got and he would be better off with her than alone. She pictured him living in some uncomfortable boarding house where he was not half attended to and intensely lonely. Her return meant the leaving of this lovely home—for Mrs. Hibberdell had indicated that she would not like to keep him and his wife—and so the end of this perfect romance with Carlotta. An end to lovely country inns and summer balconies where they were dining together! An end to swift tours in her automobile, which she guided skilfully herself, avoiding the presence of a chauffeur. An end to lovely trysts under trees and by pretty streams where he kissed and fondled her and where she lingered joyously in his arms!

"If ma could only see us now," she would jest; or,

"Do you suppose Bill and John would recognize you here if they saw you?"

Once she said: "This is better than the engine room, isn't it?"

"You're a bad lot, Carlotta," he would declare, and then would come to her lips the enigmatic smile of Monna Lisa.

"You like bad lots, don't you? Strays make fine hunting."

In her own philosophy she was taking the cash and letting the credit go.

CHAPTER XXIV

DAYS like this could not go on forever. The seed of their destruction was in their beginning. Eugene was sad. He used to show his mood at times and if she asked him what was the matter, would say: "We can't keep this thing up much longer. It must come to an end soon."

"You're certainly a gloomy philosopher, Genie," she would say, reproachfully, for she had hopes that it could be made to last a long while under any circumstances. Eugene had the feeling that no pretence would escape Angela's psychology. She was too sensitive to his unspoken moods and feelings. She would come soon, willynilly, and then all this would be ended. As a matter of fact several things combined to bring about change and conclusion.

For one thing Mrs. Hibberdell had been more and more impressed with the fact that Carlotta was not merely content to stay but that once having come she was fairly determined to remain. She had her own apartment in the city, ostensibly closed for the summer, for she had protested that it was too hot to live in town when she first proposed going to Narragansett. After seeing Eugene she figured out a possible use for it, though that use was dangerous, for Norman Wilson might return at any time. Nevertheless, they had been there on occasions—this with the double effect of deceiving her mother and entertaining Eugene. If she could remain away from Riverwood a percentage of the time, she argued with Eugene, it would make her stay less suspicious and would not jeopardize their joy in companionship. So she did this. At the same time she could not stay away from Riverwood entirely, for Eugene was there necessarily morning and evening.

Nevertheless, toward the end of August Mrs. Hibberdell was growing suspicious. She had seen an automobile entering Central Park once when Carlotta had phoned her that she had a sick headache and could not come up. It looked to Mrs. Hibberdell, who had gone down town shopping on the strength of this ailment and who had phoned Carlotta that she was going to call at her apartment in the evening, as though Eugene and Carlotta were in it. Eugene had gone to work that morning, which made it seem doubtful, but it certainly looked very much like him. Still she did not feel sure it was he or Carlotta either. When she came to the latter's apartment Carlotta was there, feeling better, but stating that she had not been out. Mrs. Hibberdell concluded thoughtfully that she must have been mistaken.

Her own room was on the third floor, and several times after all had retired and she had come down to the kitchen or dining room or library for something, she had heard a peculiar noise as of someone walking lightly. She thought it was fancy on her part, for invariably when she reached the second floor all was dark and still. Nevertheless she wondered whether Eugene and Carlotta could be visiting. Twice, between breakfast and the time Eugene departed, she thought she heard Eugene and Carlotta whispering on the second floor, but there was no proof. Carlotta's readiness to rise for breakfast at six-thirty in order to be at the same table with Eugene was peculiar, and her giving up Narragansett for Riverwood was most significant. It remained for one real discovery to resolve all her suspicions into the substance of fact and convict Carlotta of being the most conscienceless of deceivers.

It came about in this fashion. One Sunday morning Davis and Mrs. Hibberdell had decided to go automobiling. Eugene and Carlotta were invited but had refused, for Carlotta on hearing the discussion several days before had warned Eugene and planned to have the day for herself and her lover. She cautioned him to pretend the need of making visits down town. As for herself she had said she would go, but on the day in question did not feel well enough. Davis and Mrs. Hibberdell departed, their destination being Long Island. It was an all day tour. After an hour their machine broke, however, and after sitting in it two hours waiting for repairs—long enough to spoil their plans—they came back by trolley. Eugene had not gone down town. He was not even dressed when the door opened on the ground floor and Mrs. Hibberdell came in.

"Oh, Carlotta," she called, standing at the foot of the stairs and expecting Carlotta to appear from her own room or a sort of lounging and sewing room which occupied the front of the house on the second floor and where she frequently stayed. Carlotta unfortunately was with Eugene and the door to this room was commanded from where Mrs. Hibberdell was standing. She did not dare to answer.

"Oh, Carlotta," called her mother again.

The latter's first thought was to go back in the kitchen and look there, but on second thoughts she ascended the steps and started for the sewing room. Carlotta thought she had entered. In an instant she had seized the opportunity to step into the bath which was next to Eugene's room but she was scarcely quick enough. Her mother had not gone into the room—only opened the door and looked in. She did not see Carlotta step out of Eugene's room, but she did see her entering the bath, in negligee, and she could scarcely have come from anywhere else. Her own door which was between Eugene's room and the sewing room was ten feet away. It did not seem possible that she could have come from there: she had not had time enough, and anyhow why had she not answered?

The first impulse of Mrs. Hibberdell was to call to her. Her second thought was to let the ruse seem successful. She was convinced that Eugene was in his room, and a few moments later a monitory cough on his part—coughed for a purpose—convinced her.

"Are you in the bath, Carlotta?" she called quietly, after looking into Carlotta's room.

"Yes," came the reply, easily enough now. "Did your machine break down?"

A few remarks were exchanged through the door and then Mrs. Hibberdell went to her room. She thought over the situation steadily for it greatly irritated her. It was not the same as the discovered irregularity of a trusted and virtuous daughter. Carlotta had not been led astray. She was a grown woman, married, experienced. In every way she knew as much about life as her mother—in some respects more. The difference between them was in ethical standards and the policy that aligns itself with common sense, decency, self preservation, as against its opposite. Carlotta had so much to look out for. Her future was in her own hands. Besides, Eugene's future, his wife's rights and interests, her mother's home, her mother's standards, were things which she ought to respect—ought to want to respect. To find her lying as she had been this long time, pretending indifference, pretending absence, and no doubt associating with Eugene all the while, was disgusting. She was very angry, not so much at Eugene, though her respect for him was greatly lowered, artist though he was, as at Carlotta. She ought to do better. She ought to be ashamed not to guard herself against a man like Eugene, instead of luring him on. It was Carlotta's fault, and she determined to reproach her bitterly and to break up this wretched alliance at once.

There was an intense and bitter quarrel the next morning, for Mrs. Hibberdell decided to hold her peace until Eugene and Davis should be out of the house. She wanted to have this out with Carlotta alone, and the clash came shortly after breakfast when both the others had left. Carlotta had already warned Eugene that something might happen on account of this, but under no circumstances was he to admit anything unless she told him to. The maid was in the kitchen out of ear shot, and Mrs. Hibberdell and Carlotta were in the library when the opening gun was fired. In a way Carlotta was prepared, for she fancied her mother might have seen other things—what or how much she could not guess. She was not without the dignity of a Circe, for she had been through scenes like this before. Her own husband had charged her with infidelity more than once, and she had been threatened with physical violence by him. Her face was pale but calm.

"Now, Carlotta," observed her mother vigorously, "I saw what was going on yesterday morning when I came home. You were in Mr. Witla's room with your clothes off. I saw you come out. Please don't deny it. I saw you come out. Aren't you ashamed of yourself? How can you treat me that way after your promise not to do anything out of the way here?"

"You didn't see me come out of his room and I wasn't in there," said Carlotta brazenly. Her face was pale, but she was giving a fair imitation of righteous surprise. "Why do you make any such statement as that?"

"Why, Carlotta Hibberdell, how dare you contradict me; how dare you lie! You came out of that room. You know you did. You know that you were in there. You know that I saw you. I should think you would be ashamed of yourself, slipping about this house like a street girl and your own mother in it. Aren't you ashamed of yourself? Have you no sense of decency left? Oh, Carlotta, I know you are bad, but why will you come here to be so? Why couldn't you let this man alone? He was doing well enough. It's a shame, the thing you have done. It's an outrage. Mrs. Witla ought to come here and whip you within an inch of your life."

"Oh, how you talk," said Carlotta, irritably. "You make me tired. You didn't see me. It's the old story—suspicion. You're always full of suspicion. You didn't see me and I wasn't in there. Why do you start a fuss for nothing!"

"A fuss! A fuss for nothing—the idea, you evil woman. A fuss for nothing. How can you talk that way! I can hardly believe my senses. I can hardly believe you would dare to brazenly face me in this way. I saw you and now you deny it."

Mrs. Hibberdell had not seen her, but she was convinced that what she said was true.

Carlotta brazened it out. "You didn't," she insisted.

Mrs. Hibberdell stared. The effrontery of it took her breath away.

"Carlotta," she exclaimed, "I honestly think you are the worst woman in the world. I can't think of you as my daughter—you are too brazen. You're the worst because you're calculating. You know what you're doing, and you are deliberate in your method of doing it. You're evil-minded. You know exactly what you want and you set out deliberately to get it. You have done it in this case. You started out to get this man and you have succeeded in doing it. You have no sense of shame, no pride, no honesty, no honor, no respect for me or anyone else. You do not love this man. You know you don't. If you did you would never degrade him and yourself and me as you have done. You've simply indulged in another vile relationship because you wanted to, and now when you're caught you brazen it out. You're evil, Carlotta. You're as low as a woman can be, even if you are my daughter."

"It isn't true," said Carlotta. "You're just talking to hear yourself talk."

"It is true and you know it," reproved her mother. "You talk about Norman. He never did a thing worse in his life than you have done. He may be a gambler and immoral and inconsiderate and selfish. What are you? Can you stand there and tell me you're any better? Pah! If you only had a sense of shame something could be done for you, but you haven't any. You're just vile, that's all."

"How you talk, ma," she observed, calmly; "how you carry on, and that on a mere suspicion. You didn't see me. I might have been in there but you didn't see me and I wasn't. You're making a storm just because you want to. I like Mr. Witla. I think he's very nice, but I'm not interested in him and I haven't done anything to harm him. You can turn him out if you want to. That's none of my affairs. You're simply raging about as usual without any facts to go upon."

Carlotta stared at her mother, thinking. She was not greatly disturbed. It was pretty bad, no doubt of that, but she was not thinking so much of that as of the folly of being found out. Her mother knew for certain, though she would not admit to her that she knew. Now all this fine summer romance would end—the pleasant convenience of it, anyhow. Eugene would be put to the trouble of moving. Her mother might say something disagreeable to him. Besides, she knew she was better than Norman because she did not associate with the same evil type of people. She was not coarse, she was not thick-witted, she was not cruel, she was not a user of vile language or an expresser of vile ideas, and Norman was at times. She might lie and she might be calculating, but not to anyone's disadvantage—she was simply passion driven—boldly so and only toward love or romance. "Am I evil?" she often asked herself. Her mother said she was evil. Well, she was in one way; but her mother was angry, that was all. She did not mean all she said. She would come round. Still Carlotta did not propose to admit the truth of her mother's charges or to go through this situation without some argument. There were charges which her mother was making which were untenable—points which were inexcusable.

"Carlotta Hibberdell, you're the most brazen creature I ever knew! You're a terrible liar. How can you stand there and look me in the eye and say that, when you know that I know? Why lie in addition to everything else? Oh! Carlotta, the shame of it. If you only had some sense of honor! How can you lie like that? How can you?"

"I'm not lying," declared Carlotta, "and I wish you would quit fussing. You didn't see me. You know you didn't. I came out of my room and you were in the front room. Why do you say you weren't. You didn't see me. Supposing I am a liar. I'm your daughter. I may be vile. I didn't make myself so. Certainly I'm not in this instance. Whatever I am I come by it honestly. My life hasn't been a bed of roses. Why do you start a silly fight? You haven't a thing to go on except suspicion and now you want to raise a row. I don't care what you think of me. I'm not guilty in this case and you can think what you please. You ought to be ashamed to charge me with something of which you are not sure."

She walked to the window and stared out. Her mother shook her head. Such effrontery was beyond her. It was like her daughter, though. She took after her father and herself. Both were self-willed and determined when aroused. At the same time she was sorry for her girl, for Carlotto was a capable woman in her way and very much dissatisfied with life.

"I should think you would be ashamed of yourself, Carlotta, whether you admit it to me or not," she went on. "The truth is the truth and it must hurt you a little. You were in that room. We won't argue that, though. You set out deliberately to do this and you have done it. Now what I have to say is this: You are going back to your apartment today, and Mr. Witla is going to leave here as quick as he can get a room somewhere else. You're not going to continue this wretched relationship any longer if I can help it. I'm going to write to his wife and to

Norman too, if I can't do anything else to break this up. You're going to let this man alone. You have no right to come between him and Mrs. Witla. It's an outrage, and no one but a vile, conscienceless woman would do it. I'm not going to say anything to him now, but he's going to leave here and so are you. When it's all over you can come back if you want to. I'm ashamed for you. I'm ashamed for myself. If it hadn't been for my own feelings and those of Davis, I would have ordered you both out of the house yesterday and you know it. It's consideration for myself that's made me smooth it over as much as I have. He, the vile thing, after all the courtesy I have shown him. Still I don't blame him as much as I do you, for he would never have looked at you if you hadn't made him. My own daughter! My own house! Tch! Tch! Tch!"

There was more conversation—that fulgurous, coruscating reiteration of charges. Eugene was no good. Carlotta was vile. Mrs. Hibberdell wouldn't have believed it possible if she hadn't seen it with her own eyes. She was going to tell Norman if Carlotta didn't reform—over and over, one threat after another.

"Well," she said, finally, "you're going to get your things ready and go into the city this afternoon. I'm not going to have you here another day."

"No I'm not," said Carlotta boldly, pondering over all that had been said. It was a terrible ordeal, but she would not go today. "I'm going in the morning. I'm not going to pack that fast. It's too late. I'm not going to be ordered out of here like a servant."

Her mother groaned, but she gave in. Carlotta could not be made to do anything she did not want to do. She went to her room, and presently Mrs. Hibberdell heard her singing. She shook her head. Such a personality. No wonder Eugene succumbed to her blandishments. What man wouldn't?

CHAPTER XXV

THE sequel of this scene was not to be waited for. At dinner time Mrs. Hibberdell announced in the presence of Carlotta and Davis that the house was going to be closed up for the present, and very quickly. She and Carlotta were going to Narragansett for the month of September and a part of October. Eugene, having been forewarned by Carlotta, took it with a show of polite surprise. He was sorry. He had spent such a pleasant time here. Mrs. Hibberdell could not be sure whether Carlotta had told him or not, he seemed so innocent, but she assumed that she had and that he like Carlotta was "putting on." She had informed Davis that for reasons of her own she wanted to do this. He suspected what they were, for he had seen signs and slight demonstrations which convinced him that Carlotta and Eugene had reached an understanding. He did not consider it anything very much amiss, for Carlotta was a woman of the world, her own boss and a "good fellow." She had always been nice to him. He did not want to put any obstacles in her way. In addition, he liked Eugene. Once he had said to Carlotta jestingly, "Well, his arms are almost as long as Norman's—not quite maybe."

"You go to the devil," was her polite reply.

Tonight a storm came up, a brilliant, flashing summer storm. Eugene went out on the porch to watch it. Carlotta came also. "Well, wise man," she said, as the thunder rolled. "It's all over up here. Don't let on. I'll see you wherever you go, but this was so nice. It was fine to have you near me. Don't get blue, will you? She says she may write your wife, but I don't think she will. If she thinks I'm behaving, she won't. I'll try and fool her. It's too bad, though. I'm crazy about you, Genie."

Now that he was in danger of losing Carlotta, her beauty took on a special significance for Eugene. He had come into such close contact with her, had seen her under such varied conditions, that he had come to feel a profound admiration for not only her beauty but her intellect and ability as well. One of his weaknesses was that he was inclined to see much more in those he admired than was really there. He endowed them with the romance of his own moods—saw in them the ability to do things which he only could do. In doing this of course he flattered their vanity, aroused their self-confidence, made them feel themselves the possessors of latent powers and forces which before him they had only dreamed of. Margaret, Ruby, Angela, Christina and Carlotta had all gained this feeling from him. They had a better opinion of themselves for having known him. Now as he looked at Carlotta he was intensely sorry, for she was so calm, so affable, so seemingly efficient and self reliant, and such a comfort to him in these days.

"Circe!" he said, "this is too bad. I'm sorry. I'm going to hate to lose you."

"You won't lose me," she replied. "You can't. I won't let you. I've found you now and I'm going to keep you. This don't mean anything. We can find places to meet. Get a place where they have a phone if you can. When do you think you'll go?"

"Right away," said Eugene. "I'll take tomorrow morning off and look."

"Poor Eugene," she said sympathetically. "It's too bad. Never mind though. Everything will come out right."

She was still not counting on Angela. She thought that even if Angela came back, as Eugene told her she would soon, a joint arrangement might possibly be made. Angela could be here, but she, Carlotta, could share Eugene in some way. She thought she would rather live with him than any other man on earth.

It was only about noon the next morning when Eugene had found another room, for, in living here so long, he had thought of several methods by which he might have obtained a room in the first place. There was another church, a library, the postmaster and the ticket agent at Speonk who lived in the village. He went first to the postmaster and learned of two families, one the home of a civil engineer, where he might be welcome, and it was here that he eventually settled. The view was not quite so attractive, but it was charming, and he had a good room and good meals. He told them that he might not stay long, for his wife was coming back soon. The letters from Angela were becoming most importunate.

He gathered up his belongings at Mrs. Hibberdell's and took a polite departure. After he was gone Mrs. Hibberdell of course changed her mind, and Carlotta returned to her apartment in New York. She communicated with Eugene not only by phone but by special delivery, and had him meet her at a convenient inn the second evening of his departure. She was planning some sort of a separate apartment for them, when Eugene informed her that Angela was already on her way to New York and that nothing could be done at present.

Since Eugene had left her at Biloxi, Angela had spent a most miserable period of seven months. She had been grieving her heart out, for she imagined him to be most lonely, and at the same time she was regretful that she had ever left him. She might as well have been with him. She figured afterward that she might have borrowed several hundred dollars from one of her brothers, and carried out the fight for his mental recovery by his side. Once he had gone she fancied she might have made a mistake matrimonially, for he was so impressionable—but his condition was such that she did not deem him to be interested in anything save his recovery. Besides, his attitude toward her of late had been so affectionate and in a way dependent. All her letters since he had left had been most tender, speaking of his sorrow at this necessary absence and hoping that the time would soon come when they could be together. The fact that he was lonely finally decided her and she wrote that she was coming whether he wanted her to or not.

Her arrival would have made little difference except that by now he was thoroughly weaned away from her again, had obtained a new ideal and was interested only to see and be with Carlotta. The latter's easy financial state, her nice clothes, her familiarity with comfortable and luxurious things—better things than Eugene had ever dreamed of enjoying—her use of the automobile, her freedom in the matter of expenditures—taking the purchase of champagne and expensive meals as a matter of course—dazzled and fascinated him. It was rather an astonishing thing, he thought, to have so fine a woman fall in love with him. Besides, her tolerance, her indifference to petty conventions, her knowledge of life and literature and art—set her in marked contrast to Angela, and in all ways she seemed rare and forceful to him. He wished from his heart that he could be free and could have her.

Into this peculiar situation Angela precipitated herself one bright Saturday afternoon in September. She was dying to see Eugene again. Full of grave thoughts for his future, she had come to share it whatever it might be. Her one idea was that he was sick and depressed and lonely. None of his letters had been cheerful or optimistic, for of course he did not dare to confess the pleasure he was having in Carlotta's company. In order to keep her away he had to pretend that lack of funds made it inadmissible for her to be here. The fact that he was spending, and by the time she arrived had spent, nearly the whole of the three hundred dollars his picture sold to Carlotta had brought him, had troubled him—not unduly, of course, or he would not have done it. He had qualms of conscience, severe ones, but they passed with the presence of Carlotta or the reading of his letters from Angela.

"I don't know what's the matter with me," he said to himself from time to time. "I guess I'm no good." He thought it was a blessing that the world could not see him as he was.

One of the particular weaknesses of Eugene's which should be set forth here and which will help to illuminate the bases of his conduct was that he was troubled with a dual point of view —a condition based upon a peculiar power of analysis—self-analysis in particular, which was constantly permitting him to tear himself up by the roots in order to see how he was getting along. He would daily and hourly when not otherwise employed lift the veil from his inner mental processes as he might lift the covering from a well, and peer into its depths. What he saw was not very inviting and vastly disconcerting, a piece of machinery that was not going as a true man should, clock fashion, and corresponding in none of its moral characteristics to the recognized standard of a man. He had concluded by now, from watching various specimens, that sane men were honest, some inherently moral, some regulated by a keen sense of duty, and occasionally all of these virtues and others were bound up in one man. Angela's father was such an one. M. Charles appeared to be another. He had concluded from his association with Jerry Mathews, Philip Shotmeyer, Peter MacHugh and Joseph Smite that they were all rather decent in respect to morals. He had never seen them under temptation but he imagined they were. Such a man as William Haverford, the Engineer of Maintenance of Way, and Henry C. Litlebrown, the Division Engineer of this immense road, struck him as men who must have stuck close to a sense of duty and the conventions of the life they represented, working hard all the time, to have attained the positions they had. All this whole railroad system which he was watching closely from day to day from his little vantage point of connection with it, seemed a clear illustration of the need of a sense of duty and reliability. All of these men who worked for this company had to be in good health, all had to appear at their posts on the tick of the clock, all had to perform faithfully the duties assigned them, or there would be disasters. Most of them had climbed by long, arduous years of work to very modest positions of prominence, as conductors, engineers, foremen, division superintendents. Others more gifted or more blessed by fortune became division engineers, superintendents, vice-presidents and presidents. They were all slow climbers, rigid in their sense of duty, tireless in their energy, exact, thoughtful. What was he?

He looked into the well of his being and there he saw nothing but shifty and uncertain currents. It was very dark down there. He was not honest, he said to himself, except in money matters—he often wondered why. He was not truthful. He was not moral. This love of beauty which haunted him seemed much more important than anything else in the world, and his pursuit of that seemed to fly in the face of everything else which was established and important. He found that men everywhere did not think much of a man who was crazy after women. They might joke about an occasional lapse as an amiable vice or one which could be condoned, but they wanted little to do with a man who was overpowered by it. There was a case over in the railroad yard at Speonk recently which he had noted, of a foreman who had left his wife and gone after some hoyden in White Plains, and because of this offense he was promptly discharged. It appeared, though, that before this he had occasionally had such lapses and that each time he had been discharged, but had been subsequently forgiven. This one weakness, and no other, had given him a bad reputation among his fellow railroad men—much as that a drunkard might have. Big John Peters, the engineer, had expressed it aptly to Eugene one day when he told him in confidence that "Ed Bowers would go to hell for his hide," the latter being the local expression for women. Everybody seemed to pity him, and the man seemed in a way to pity himself. He had a hang-dog look when he was re-instated, and yet everybody knew that apart from this he was a fairly competent foreman. Still it was generally understood that he would never get anywhere.

From that Eugene argued to himself that a man who was cursed with this peculiar vice could not get anywhere; that he, if he kept it up, would not. It was like drinking and stealing, and the face of the world was against it. Very frequently it went hand in hand with those things—"birds of a feather" he thought. Still he was cursed with it, and he no more than Ed Bowers appeared to be able to conquer it. At least he was yielding to it now as he had before. It mattered not that the women he chose were exceptionally beautiful and fascinating. They were women, and ought he to want them? He had one. He had taken a solemn vow to love and cherish her, or at least had gone through the formality of such a vow, and here he was running about with Carlotta, as he had with Christina and Ruby before her. Was he not always looking for some such woman as this? Certainly he was. Had he not far better be seeking for wealth, distinction, a reputation for probity, chastity, impeccable moral honor? Certainly he had. It was the way to distinction apparently, assuming the talent, and here he was doing anything but take that way. Conscience was his barrier, a conscience unmodified by cold self-interest. Shame upon himself! Shame upon his weak-kneed disposition, not to be able to recover from this illusion of beauty. Such were some of the thoughts which his moments of introspection brought him.

On the other hand, there came over him that other phase of his duality—the ability to turn his terrible searchlight of intelligence which swept the heavens and the deep as with a great white ray—upon the other side of the question. It revealed constantly the inexplicable subtleties and seeming injustices of nature. He could not help seeing how the big fish fed upon the little ones, the strong were constantly using the weak as pawns; the thieves, the grafters, the murderers were sometimes allowed to prey on society without let or hindrance. Good was not always rewarded—frequently terribly ill-rewarded. Evil was seen to flourish beautifully at times. It was all right to say that it would be punished, but would it? Carlotta did not think so. She did not think the thing she was doing with him was very evil. She had said to him over and over that it was an open question, that he was troubled with an ingrowing conscience. "I don't think it's so bad," she once told him. "It depends somewhat on how you were raised." There was a system apparently in society, but also apparently it did not work very well. Only fools were held by religion, which in the main was an imposition, a graft and a lie. The honest man might be very fine but he wasn't very successful. There was a great to-do about morals, but most people were immoral or unmoral. Why worry? Look to your health! Don't let a morbid conscience get the better of you. Thus she counselled, and he agreed with her. For the rest the survival of the fittest was the best. Why should he worry? He had talent.

It was thus that Eugene floundered to and fro, and it was in this state, brooding and melancholy, that Angela found him on her arrival. He was as gay as ever at times, when he was not thinking, but he was very thin and hollow-eyed, and Angela fancied that it was overwork and worry which kept him in this state. Why had she left him? Poor Eugene! She had clung desperately to the money he had given her, and had most of it with her ready to be expended now for his care. She was so anxious for his recovery and his peace of mind that she was ready to go to work herself at anything she could find, in order to make his path more easy. She was thinking that fate was terribly unjust to him, and when he had gone to sleep beside her the first night she lay awake and cried. Poor Eugene! To think he should be tried so by fate. Nevertheless, he should not be tortured by anything which she could prevent. She was going to make him as comfortable and happy as she could. She set about to find some nice little apartment or rooms where they could live in peace and where she could cook Eugene's meals for him. She fancied that maybe his food had not been exactly right, and when she got him where she could manifest a pretence of self-confidence and courage that he would take courage from her and grow better. So she set briskly about her task, honeying Eugene the while, for she was confident that this above all things was the thing he needed. She little suspected what a farce it all appeared to him, how mean and contemptible he appeared to himself. He did not care to be mean—to rapidly disillusion her and go his way; and yet this dual existence sickened him. He could not help but feel that from a great many points of view Angela was better than Carlotta. Yet the other woman was wider in her outlook, more gracious in her appearance, more commanding, more subtle. She was a princess of the world, subtle, deadly Machiavellian, but a princess nevertheless. Angela was better described by the current and acceptable phrase of the time—a "thoroughly good woman," honest, energetic, resourceful, in all things obedient to the race spirit and the conventional feelings of the time. He knew that society would support her thoroughly and condemn Carlotta, and yet Carlotta interested him more. He wished that he might have both and no fussing. Then all would be beautiful. So he thought.

CHAPTER XXVI

THE situation which here presented itself was subject to no such gracious and generous development. Angela was the soul of watchfulness, insistence on duty, consideration for right conduct and for the privileges, opportunities and emoluments which belonged to her as the wife of a talented artist, temporarily disabled, it is true, but certain to be distinguished in the future. She was deluding herself that this recent experience of reverses had probably hardened and sharpened Eugene's practical instincts, made him less indifferent to the necessity of looking out for himself, given him keener instincts of self-protection and economy. He had done very well to live on so little she thought, but they were going to do better—they were going to save. She was going to give up those silly dreams she had entertained of a magnificent studio and hosts of friends, and she was going to start now saving a fraction of whatever they made, however small it might be, if it were only ten cents a week. If Eugene could only make nine dollars a week by working every day, they were going to live on that. He still had ninety-seven of the hundred dollars he had brought with him, he told her, and this was going in the bank. He did not tell her of the sale of one of his pictures and of the subsequent dissipation of the proceeds. In the bank, too, they were going to put any money from subsequent sales until he was on his feet again. One of these days if they ever made any money, they were going to buy a house somewhere in which they could live without paying rent. Some of the money in the bank, a very little of it, might go for clothes if worst came to worst, but it would not be touched unless it was absolutely necessary. She needed clothes now, but that did not matter. To Eugene's ninety-seven was added Angela's two hundred and twenty-eight which she brought with her, and this total sum of three hundred and twenty-five dollars was promptly deposited in the Bank of Riverwood.

Angela by personal energy and explanation found four rooms in the house of a furniture manufacturer; it had been vacated by a daughter who had married, and they were glad to let it to an artist and his wife for practically nothing so far as real worth was concerned, for this was a private house in a lovely lawn. Twelve dollars per month was the charge. Mrs. Witla seemed very charming to Mrs. Desenas, who was the wife of the manufacturer, and for her especial benefit a little bedroom on the second floor adjoining a bath was turned into a kitchen, with a small gas stove, and Angela at once began housekeeping operations on the tiny basis necessitated by their income. Some furniture had to be secured, for the room was not completely furnished, but Angela by haunting the second-hand stores in New York, looking through all the department stores, and visiting certain private sales, managed to find a few things which she could buy cheaply and which would fit in with the dressing table, library table, dining table and one bed which were already provided. The necessary curtains for the bath and kitchen windows she cut, decorated and hung for herself. She went down to the storage company where the unsold and undisplayed portion of Eugene's pictures were and brought back seven, which she placed in the general living-room and dining-room. All Eugene's clothes, his underwear and socks particularly, received her immediate attention, and she soon had his rather attenuated wardrobe in good condition. From the local market she bought good vegetables and a little meat and made delightful stews, ragouts, combinations of eggs and tasty meat juices after the French fashion. All her housekeeping art was employed to the utmost to make everything look clean and neat, to maintain a bountiful supply of varied food on the table and yet to keep the cost down, so that they could not only live on nine dollars a week, but set aside a dollar or more of that for what Angela called their private bank account. She had a little hollow brown jug, calculated to hold fifteen dollars in change, which could be opened when full, which she conscientiously endeavored to fill and refill. Her one desire was to rehabilitate her husband in the eyes of the world—this time to stay—and she was determined to do it.

For another thing, reflection and conversation with one person and another had taught her that it was not well for herself or for Eugene for her to encourage him in his animal passions. Some woman in Blackwood had pointed out a local case of locomotor-ataxia which had resulted from lack of self-control, and she had learned that it was believed that many other nervous troubles sprang from the same source. Perhaps Eugene's had. She had resolved to protect him from himself. She did not believe she could be injured, but Eugene was so sensitive, so emotional.

The trouble with the situation was that it was such a sharp change from his recent free and to him delightful mode of existence that it was almost painful. He could see that everything appeared to be satisfactory to her, that she thought all his days had been moral and full of hard work. Carlotta's presence in the background was not suspected. Her idea was that they would work hard together now along simple, idealistic lines to the one end—success for him, and of course, by reflection, for her.

Eugene saw the charm of it well enough, but it was only as something quite suitable for others. He was an artist. The common laws of existence could not reasonably apply to an artist. The latter should have intellectual freedom, the privilege of going where he pleased, associating with whom he chose. This marriage business was a galling yoke, cutting off all rational opportunity for enjoyment, and he was now after a brief period of freedom having that yoke heavily adjusted to his neck again. Gone were all the fine dreams of pleasure and happiness which so recently had been so real—the hope of living with Carlotta—the hope of associating with her on easy and natural terms in that superior world which she represented. Angela's insistence on the thought that he should work every day and bring home nine dollars a week, or rather its monthly equivalent, made it necessary for him to take sharp care of the little money he had kept out of the remainder of the three hundred in order to supply any deficiency which might occur from his taking time off. For there was no opportunity now of seeing Carlotta of an evening, and it was necessary to take a regular number of afternoons or mornings off each week, in order to meet her. He would leave the little apartment as usual at a quarter to seven in the morning, dressed suitably for possible out-door expeditions, for in anticipation of difficulty he had told Angela that it was his custom to do this, and sometimes he would go to the factory and sometimes he would not. There was a car line which carried him rapidly cityward to a rendezvous, and he would either ride or walk with her as the case might be. There was constant thought on his and her part of the risk involved, but still they persisted. By some stroke of ill or good fortune Norman Wilson returned from Chicago, so that Carlotta's movements had to be calculated to a nicety, but she did not care. She trusted most to the automobiles which she could hire at convenient garages and which would carry them rapidly away from the vicinity where they might be seen and recognized.

It was a tangled life, difficult and dangerous. There was no peace in it, for there is neither peace nor happiness in deception. A burning joy at one time was invariably followed by a disturbing remorse afterward. There was Carlotta's mother, Nor-

man Wilson, and Angela, to guard against, to say nothing of the
constant pricking of his own conscience.

It is almost a foregone conclusion in any situation of this
kind that it cannot endure. The seed of its undoing is in itself.
We think that our actions when unseen of mortal eyes resolve
themselves into nothingness, but this is not true. They are
woven indefinably into our being, and shine forth ultimately as
the real self, in spite of all our pretences. One could almost
accept the Brahmanistic dogma of a psychic body which sees
and is seen where we dream all to be darkness. There is no
other supposition on which to explain the facts of intuition. So
many individuals have it. They know so well without knowing
why they know.

Angela had this intuitive power in connection with Eugene.
Because of her great affection for him she divined or appre-
hended many things in connection with him long before they
occurred. Throughout her absence from him she had been
haunted by the idea that she ought to be with him, and now that
she was here and the first excitement of contact and adjustment
was over, she was beginning to be aware of something. Eugene
was not the same as he had been a little while before he had left
her. His attitude, in spite of a kindly show of affection, was
distant and preoccupied. He had no real power of concealing
anything. He appeared at times—at most times when he was
with her—to be lost in a mist of speculation. He was lonely
and a little love-sick, because under the pressure of home affairs
Carlotta was not able to see him quite so much. At the same
time, now that the fall was coming on, he was growing weary
of the shop at Speonk, for the gray days and slight chill which
settled upon the earth at times caused the shop windows to be
closed and robbed the yard of that air of romance which had
characterized it when he first came there. He could not take
his way of an evening along the banks of the stream to the arms
of Carlotta. The novelty of Big John and Joseph Mews and
Malachi Dempsey and Little Suddsy had worn off. He was
beginning now to see also that they were nothing but plain work-
ingmen after all, worrying over the fact that they were not
getting more than fifteen or seventeen and a half cents an hour;
jealous of each other and their superiors, full of all the frailties
and weaknesses to which the flesh is heir.

His coming had created a slight diversion for them, for he
was very strange, but his strangeness was no longer a novelty.
They were beginning to see him also as a relatively commonplace
human being. He was an artist, to be sure, but his actions and

intentions were not so vastly different from those of other men.

A shop of this kind, like any other institution where people are compelled by force of circumstances to work together whether the weather be fair or foul, or the mood grave or gay, can readily become and frequently does become a veritable hell. Human nature is a subtle, irritable, irrational thing. It is not so much governed by rules of ethics and conditions of understanding as a thing of moods and temperament. Eugene could easily see, philosopher that he was, that these people would come here enveloped in some mist of home trouble or secret illness or grief and would conceive that somehow it was not their state of mind but the things around them which were the cause of all their woe. Sour looks would breed sour looks in return; a gruff question would beget a gruff answer; there were long-standing grudges between one man and another, based on nothing more than a grouchy observation at one time in the past. He thought by introducing gaiety and persistent, if make-believe, geniality that he was tending to obviate and overcome the general condition, but this was only relatively true. His own gaiety was capable of becoming as much of a weariness to those who were out of the spirit of it, as was the sour brutality with which at times he was compelled to contend. So he wished that he might arrange to get well and get out of here, or at least change his form of work, for it was plain to be seen that this condition would not readily improve. His presence was a commonplace. His power to entertain and charm was practically gone.

This situation, coupled with Angela's spirit of honest conservatism was bad, but it was destined to be much worse. From watching him and endeavoring to decipher his moods, Angela came to suspect something—she could not say what. He did not love her as much as he had. There was a coolness in his caresses which was not there when he left her. What could have happened, she asked herself. Was it just absence, or what? One day when he had returned from an afternoon's outing with Carlotta and was holding her in his arms in greeting, she asked him solemnly:

"Do you love me, Honeybun?"

"You know I do," he asseverated, but without any energy, for he could not regain his old original feeling for her. There was no trace of it, only sympathy, pity, and a kind of sorrow that she was being so badly treated after all her efforts.

"No, you don't," she replied, detecting the hollow ring in what he said. Her voice was sad, and her eyes showed traces of that wistful despair into which she could so readily sink at times.

"Why, yes I do, Angelface," he insisted. "What makes you ask? What's come over you?" He was wondering whether she had heard anything or seen anything and was concealing her knowledge behind this preliminary inquiry.

"Nothing," she replied. "Only you don't love me. I don't know what it is. I don't know why. But I can feel it right here," and she laid her hand on her heart.

The action was sincere, unstudied. It hurt him, for it was like that of a little child.

"Oh, hush! Don't say that," he pleaded. "You know I do. Don't look so gloomy. I love you—don't you know I do?" and he kissed her.

"No, no!" said Angela. "I know! You don't. Oh, dear; oh, dear; I feel so bad!"

Eugene was dreading another display of the hysteria with which he was familiar, but it did not come. She conquered her mood, inasmuch as she had no real basis for suspicion, and went about the work of getting him his dinner. She was depressed, though, and he was fearful. What if she should ever find out!

More days passed. Carlotta called him up at the shop occasionally, for there was no phone where he lived, and she would not have risked it if there had been. She sent him registered notes to be signed for, addressed to Henry Kingsland and directed to the post office at Speonk. Eugene was not known there as Witla and easily secured these missives, which were usually very guarded in their expressions and concerned appointments—the vaguest, most mysterious directions, which he understood. They made arrangements largely from meeting to meeting, saying, "If I can't keep it Thursday at two it will be Friday at the same time; and if not then, Saturday. If anything happens I'll send you a registered special." So it went on.

One noontime Eugene walked down to the little post office at Speonk to look for a letter, for Carlotta had not been able to meet him the previous day and had phoned instead that she would write the following day. He found it safely enough, and after glancing at it—it contained but few words—decided to tear it up as usual and throw the pieces away. A mere expression, "Ashes of Roses," which she sometimes used to designate herself, and the superscription, "Oh, Genie!" made it, however, inexpressibly dear to him. He thought he would hold it in his possession just a little while—a few hours longer. It was enigmatic enough to anyone but himself, he thought, even if found. "The bridge, two, Wednesday." The bridge referred to was one over the Harlem at Morris Heights. He kept the appointment that day as requested, but by some necromancy of fate he forgot the letter until he was within his own door. Then he took it out, tore it up into four or five pieces quickly, put it in his vest pocket, and went upstairs intending at the first opportunity to dispose of it.

Meanwhile, Angela, for the first time since they had been living at Riverwood, had decided to walk over toward the factory about six o'clock and meet Eugene on his way home. She heard him discourse on the loveliness of this stream and what a pleasure it was to stroll along its banks morning and evening. He was so fond of the smooth water and the overhanging leaves! She had walked with him there already on several Sundays. When she went this evening she thought what a pleasant surprise it would be for him, for she had prepared everything on leaving so that his supper would not be delayed when they reached home. She heard the whistle blow as she neared the shop, and, standing behind a clump of bushes on the thither side of the stream, she waited, expecting to pounce out on Eugene with a loving "Boo!" He did not come.

The forty or fifty men who worked here trickled out like a little stream of black ants, and then, Eugene not appearing, Angela went over to the gate which Joseph Mews in the official capacity of gateman, after the whistle blew, was closing.

"Is Mr. Witla here?" asked Angela, peering through the bars at him. Eugene had described Joseph so accurately to her that she recognized him at sight.

"No, ma'am," replied Joseph, quite taken back by this attractive arrival, for good-looking women were not common at the shop gate of the factory. "He left four or five hours ago. I think he left at one o'clock, if I remember right. He wasn't working with us today. He was working out in the yard."

"You don't know where he went, do you?" asked Angela, who was surprised at this novel information. Eugene had not said anything about going anywhere. Where could he have gone?

"No'm, I don't," replied Joseph volubly. "He sometimes goes off this way—quite frequent, ma'am. His wife calls him up—er—now, maybe you're his wife."

"I am," said Angela; but she was no longer thinking of what she was saying, her words on the instant were becoming mechanical. Eugene going away frequently? He had never said anything to her! His wife calling him up! Could there be another woman! Instantly all her old suspicions, jealousies, fears, awoke, and she was wondering why she had not fixed on this fact before. That explained Eugene's indifference, of course. That explained his air of abstraction. He wasn't thinking of her, the miserable creature! He was thinking of someone else. Still she could not be sure, for she had no proof. Two adroit questions elicited the fact that no one in the shop had ever seen his wife. He had just gone out. A woman had called up.

Angela took her way home amid a whirling fire of conjecture. When she reached it Eugene was not there yet, for he sometimes delayed his coming, lingering, as he said, to look at the water. It was natural enough in an artist. She went upstairs and hung the broad-brimmed straw she had worn in the closet, and went into the kitchen to await his coming. Experience with him and the nature of her own temperament determined her to enact a rôle of subtlety. She would wait until he spoke, pretending that she had not been out. She would ask whether he had had a hard day, and see whether he disclosed the fact that he had been away from the factory. That would show her positively what he was doing and whether he was deliberately deceiving her.

Eugene came up the stairs, gay enough but anxious to deposit the scraps of paper where they would not be seen. No opportunity came for Angela was there to greet him.

"Did you have a hard job today?" she asked, noting that he made no preliminary announcement of any absence.

"Not very," he replied; "no. I don't look tired?"

"No," she said bitterly, but concealing her feelings; she wanted to see how thoroughly and deliberately he would lie. "But I thought maybe you might have. Did you stop to look at the water tonight?"

"Yes," he replied smoothly. "It's very lovely over there. I never get tired of it. The sun on the leaves these days now that they are turning yellow is so beautiful. They look a little like stained glass at certain angles."

Her first impulse after hearing this was to exclaim, "Why do you lie to me, Eugene?" for her temper was fiery, almost uncontrollable at times; but she restrained herself. She wanted to find out more—how she did not know, but time, if she could only wait a little, would help her. Eugene went to the bath, congratulating himself on the ease of his escape—the comfortable fact that he was not catechised very much; but in this temporary feeling of satisfaction he forgot the scraps of paper in his

vest pocket—though not for long. He hung his coat and vest
on a hook and started into the bedroom to get himself a fresh
collar and tie. While he was in there Angela passed the bathroom door. She was always interested in Eugene's clothes,
how they were wearing, but tonight there were other thoughts
in her mind. Hastily and by intuition she went through his
pockets, finding the torn scraps, then for excuse took his coat
and vest down to clean certain spots. At the same moment
Eugene thought of his letter. He came hurrying out to get it,
or the pieces, rather, but Angela already had them and was looking at them curiously.

"What was that?" she asked, all her suspicious nature on
the *qui vive* for additional proof. Why should he keep the torn
fragments of a letter in his pocket? For days she had had a
psychic sense of something impending. Everything about him
seemed strangely to call for investigation. Now it was all coming out.

"Nothing," he said nervously. "A memorandum. Throw it
in the paper box."

Angela noted the peculiarity of his voice and manner. She
was taken by the guilty expression of his eyes. Something was
wrong. It concerned these scraps of paper. Maybe it was in
these she would be able to read the riddle of his conduct. The
woman's name might be in here. Like a flash it came to her
that she might piece these scraps together, but there was another
thought equally swift which urged her to pretend indifference.
That might help her. Pretend now and she would know more
later. She threw them in the paper box, thinking to piece them
together at her leisure. Eugene noted her hesitation, her suspicion. He was afraid she would do something, what he could
not guess. He breathed more easily when the papers fluttered
into the practically empty box, but he was nervous. If they
were only burned! He did not think she would attempt to put
them together, but he was afraid. He would have given anything if his sense of romance had not led him into this trap.

CHAPTER XXVII

ANGELA was quick to act upon her thought. No sooner had Eugene entered the bath than she gathered up the pieces, threw other bits of paper like them in their place and tried quickly to piece them together on the ironing board where she was. It was not difficult; the scraps were not small. On one triangular bit were the words, "Oh, Genie!" with a colon after it; on another the words, "The bridge," and on another "Roses." There was no doubt in her mind from this preliminary survey that this was a love note, and every nerve in her body tingled to the terrible import of it. Could it really be true? Could Eugene have found someone else? Was this the cause of his coolness and his hypocritical pretence of affection? and of his not wanting her to come to him? Oh, God! Would her sufferings never cease! She hurried into the front room, her face white, her hand clenching the tell-tale bits, and there set to work to complete her task. It did not take her long. In four minutes it was all together, and then she saw it all. A love note! From some demon of a woman. No doubt of it! Some mysterious woman in the background. "Ashes of Roses!" Now God curse her for a siren, a love thief, a hypnotizing snake, fascinating men with her evil eyes. And Eugene! The dog! The scoundrel! The vile coward! The traitor! Was there no decency, no morality, no kindness, no gratitude in his soul? After all her patience, all her suffering, all her loneliness, her poverty. To treat her like this! Writing that he was sick and lonely and unable to have her with him, and at the same time running around with a strange woman. "Ashes of Roses!" Oh, curses, curses, curses on her harlot's heart and brain! Might God strike her dead for her cynical, brutal seizing upon that sacred possession which belonged to another. She wrung her hands desperately.

Angela was fairly beside herself. Through her dainty little head ran a foaming torrent of rage, hate, envy, sorrow, self-commiseration, brutal desire for revenge. If she could only get at this woman! If she could only denounce Eugene now to his face! If she could only find them together and kill them! How she would like to strike her on the mouth! How tear her hair and her eyes out! Something of the forest cat's cruel rage shone in her gleaming eyes as she thought of her, for if she could

have had Carlotta there alone she would have tortured her with
hot irons, torn her tongue and teeth from their roots, beaten her
into insensibility and an unrecognizable mass. She was a real
tigress now, her eyes gleaming, her red lips wet. She would
kill her! kill her!! kill her!!! As God was judge, she would
kill her if she could find her, and Eugene and herself. Yes, yes,
she would. Better death than this agony of suffering. Better
a thousand times to be dead with this beast of a woman dead
beside her and Eugene than to suffer this way. She didn't deserve it. Why did God torture her so? Why was she made
to bleed at every step by this her sacrificial love? Had she
not been a good wife? Had she not laid every tribute of tenderness, patience, self-abnegation, self-sacrifice and virtue on the
altar of love? What more could God ask? What more could
man want? Had she not waited on Eugene in sickness and
health? She had gone without clothes, gone without friends,
hidden herself away in Blackwood the seven months while he
was here frittering away his health and time in love and immorality, and what was her reward? In Chicago, in Tennessee,
in Mississippi, had she not waited on him, sat up with him of
nights, walked the floor with him when he was nervous, consoled
him in his fear of poverty and failure, and here she was now,
after seven long months of patient waiting and watching—eating her lonely heart out—forsaken. Oh, the inconceivable in-
humanity of the human heart! To think anybody could be so
vile, so low, so unkind, so cruel! To think that Eugene with
his black eyes, his soft hair, his smiling face, could be so treacherous, so subtle, so dastardly! Could he really be as mean as
this note proved him to be? Could he be as brutal, as selfish?
Was she awake or asleep? Was this a dream? Ah, God! no,
no it was not a dream. It was a cold, bitter, agonizing reality.
And the cause of all her suffering was there in the bathroom
now shaving himself.

For one moment she thought she would go in and strike him
where he stood. She thought she could tear his heart out, cut
him up, but then suddenly the picture of him bleeding and dead
came to her and she recoiled. No, no, she could not do that!
Oh, no, not Eugene—and yet and yet——

"Oh, God, let me get my hands on that woman!" she said
to herself. "Let me get my hands on her. I'll kill her, I'll
kill her! I'll kill her!"

This torrent of fury and self-pity was still raging in her
heart when the bathroom knob clicked and Eugene came out.
He was in his undershirt, trousers and shoes, looking for a clean

white shirt. He was very nervous over the note which had been thrown in scraps into the box, but looking in the kitchen and seeing the pieces still there he was slightly reassured. Angela was not there; he could come back and get them when he found out where she was. He went on into the bedroom, looking into the front room as he did so. She appeared to be at the window waiting for him. After all, she was probably not as suspicious as he thought. It was his own imagination. He was too nervous and sensitive. Well, he would get those pieces now if he could and throw them out of the window. Angela should not have a chance to examine them if she wanted to. He slipped out into the kitchen, made a quick grab for the little heap, and sent the pieces flying. Then he felt much better. He would never bring another letter home from anybody, that was a certainty. Fate was too much against him.

Angela came out after a bit, for the click of the bathroom knob had sobered her a little. Her rage was high, her pulse abnormal, her whole being shaken to its roots, but still she realized that she must have time to think. She must see who this woman was first. She must have time to find her. Eugene mustn't know. Where was she now? Where was this bridge? Where did they meet? Where did she live? She wondered for the moment why she couldn't think it all out, why it didn't come to her in a flash, a revelation. If she could only know!

In a few minutes Eugene came in, clean-shaven, smiling, his equanimity and peace of mind fairly well restored. The letter was gone. Angela could never know. She might suspect, but this possible burst of jealousy had been nipped in the bud. He came over toward her to put his arm round her, but she slipped away from him, pretending to need the sugar. He let this effort at love making go—the will for the deed, and sat down at the snow-white little table, set with tempting dishes and waited to be served. The day had been very pleasant, being early in October, and he was pleased to see a last lingering ray of light falling on some red and yellow leaves. This yard was very beautiful. This little flat, for all their poverty, very charming. Angela was neat and trim in a dainty house dress of mingled brown and green. A dark blue studio apron shielded her bosom and skirt. She was very pale and distraught-looking, but Eugene for the time was almost unconscious of it—he was so relieved.

"Are you very tired, Angela?" he finally asked sympathetically.

"Yes, I'm not feeling so well today," she replied.

"What have you been doing, ironing?"

"Oh, yes, and cleaning. I worked on the cupboard."

"You oughtn't to try to do so much," he said cheerfully. "You're not strong enough. You think you're a little horse, but you are only a colt. Better go slow, hadn't you?"

"I will after I get everything straightened out to suit me," she replied.

She was having the struggle of her life to conceal her real feelings. Never at any time had she undergone such an ordeal as this. Once in the studio, when she discovered those two letters, she thought she was suffering—but that, what was that to this? What were her suspicions concerning Frieda? What were the lonely longings at home, her grieving and worrying over his illness? Nothing, nothing! Now he was actually faithless to her. Now she had the evidence. This woman was here. She was somewhere in the immediate background. After these years of marriage and close companionship he was deceiving her. It was possible that he had been with this woman today, yesterday, the day before. The letter was not dated. Could it be that she was related to Mrs. Hibberdell? Eugene had said that there was a married daughter, but never that she was there. If she was there, why should he have moved? He wouldn't have. Was it the wife of the man he was last living with? No; she was too homely. Angela had seen her. Eugene would never associate with her. If she could only know! "Ashes of Roses!" The world went red before her eyes. There was no use bursting into a storm now, though. If she could only be calm it would be better. If she only had someone to talk to—if there were a minister or a bosom friend! She might go to a detective agency. They might help her. A detective could trace this woman and Eugene. Did she want to do this? It cost money. They were very poor now. Paugh! Why should she worry about their poverty, mending her dresses, going without hats, going without decent shoes, and he wasting his time and being upon some shameless strumpet! If he had money, he would spend it on her. Still, he had handed her almost all the money he had brought East with him intact. How was that?

All the time Eugene was sitting opposite her eating with fair heartiness. If the trouble about the letter had not come out so favorably he would have been without appetite, but now he felt at ease. Angela said she was not hungry and could not eat. She passed him the bread, the butter, the hashed brown potatoes, the tea, and he ate cheerfully.

"I think I am going to try and get out of that shop over there," he volunteered affably.

"Why?" asked Angela mechanically.

"I'm tired of it. The men are not so interesting to me now. I'm tired of them. I think Mr. Haverford will transfer me if I write to him. He said he would. I'd rather be outside with some section gang if I could. It's going to be very dreary in the shop when they close it up."

"Well, if you're tired you'd better," replied Angela. "Your mind needs diversion, I know that. Why don't you write to Mr. Haverford?"

"I will," he said, but he did not immediately. He went into the front room and lit the gas eventually, reading a paper, then a book, then yawning wearily. Angela came in after a time and sat down pale and tired. She went and secured a little work-basket in which were socks undarned and other odds and ends and began on those, but she revolted at the thought of doing anything for him and put them up. She got out a skirt of hers which she was making. Eugene watched her a little while lazily, his artistic eye measuring the various dimensions of her features. She had a well-balanced face, he finally concluded. He noted the effect of the light on her hair—the peculiar hue it gave it— and wondered if he could get that in oil. Night scenes were harder than those of full daylight. Shadows were so very treacherous. He got up finally.

"Well, I'm going to turn in," he said. "I'm tired. I have to get up at six. Oh, dear, this darn day labor business gives me a pain. I wish it were over."

Angela did not trust herself to speak. She was so full of pain and despair that she thought if she spoke she would cry. He went out, saying: "Coming soon?" She nodded her head. When he was gone the storm burst and she broke into a blinding flood of tears. They were not only tears of sorrow, but of rage and helplessness. She went out on a little balcony which was there and cried alone, the night lights shining wistfully about. After the first storm she began to harden and dry up again, for helpless tears were foreign to her in a rage. She dried her eyes and became white-faced and desperate as before.

The dog, the scoundrel, the brute, the hound! she thought. How could she ever have loved him? How could she love him now? Oh, the horror of life, its injustice, its cruelty, its shame! That she should be dragged through the mire with a man like this. The pity of it! The shame! If this was art, death take it! And yet hate him as she might—hate this hellish man-trap who signed herself "Ashes of Roses"—she loved him, too. She could not help it. She knew she loved him. Oh, to be crossed by two fevers like this! Why might she not die? Why not die, right now?

CHAPTER XXVIII

THE hells of love are bitter and complete. There were days after that when she watched him, followed him down the pleasant lane from the house to the water's edge, slipping out unceremoniously after he had gone not more than eight hundred feet. She watched the bridge at Riverwood at one and six, expecting that Eugene and his paramour might meet there. It just happened that Carlotta was compelled to leave town for ten days with her husband, and so Eugene was safe. On two occasions he went downtown—into the heart of the great city, anxious to get a breath of the old life that so fascinated him, and Angela followed him only to lose track of him quickly. He did nothing evil, however, merely walked, wondering what Miriam Finch and Christina Channing and Norma Whitmore were doing these days and what they were thinking of him in his long absence. Of all the people he had known, he had only seen Norma Whitmore once and that was not long after he returned to New York. He had given her a garbled explanation of his illness, stated that he was going to work now and proposed to come and see her. He did his best to avoid observation, however, for he dreaded explaining the reason of his non-productive condition. Miriam Finch was almost glad that he had failed, since he had treated her so badly. Christina Channing was in opera, as he quickly discovered, for he saw her name blazoned one day the following November in the newspapers. She was a star of whose talent great hopes were entertained, and was interested almost exclusively in her career. She was to sing in "Bohème" and "Rigoletto."

Another thing, fortunate for Eugene at this time, was that he changed his work. There came to the shop one day an Irish foreman, Timothy Deegan, master of a score of "guineas," as he called the Italian day laborers who worked for him, who took Eugene's fancy greatly. He was of medium height, thick of body and neck, with a cheerful, healthy red face, a keen, twinkling gray eye, and stiff, closely cropped gray hair and mustache. He had come to lay the foundation for a small dynamo in the engine room at Speonk, which was to supply the plant with light in case of night work, and a car of his had been backed in, a tool car, full of boards, barrows, mortar boards, picks and shovels. Eugene was amused and astonished at his insistent, defiant attitude and the brisk manner in which he was handing out orders to his men.

"Come, Matt! Come, Jimmie! Get the shovels now! Get the picks!" he heard him shout. "Bring some sand here! Bring some stone! Where's the cement now? Where's the cement? Jasus Christ! I must have some cement. What arre ye all doing? Hurry now, hurry! Bring the cement."

"Well, he knows how to give orders," commented Eugene to Big John, who was standing near. "He certainly does," replied the latter.

To himself Eugene observed, hearing only the calls at first, "the Irish brute." Later he discovered a subtle twinkle in Deegan's eyes as he stood brazenly in the door, looking defiantly about. There was no brutality in it, only self-confidence and a hearty Irish insistence on the necessity of the hour.

"Well, you're a dandy!" commented Eugene boldly after a time, and laughed.

"Ha! ha! ha!" mocked Deegan in return. "If you had to work as harred as these men you wouldn't laugh."

"I'm not laughing at them. I'm laughing at you," explained Eugene.

"Laugh," said Deegan. "Shure you're as funny to me as I am to you."

Eugene laughed again. The Irishman agreed with himself that there was humor in it. He laughed too. Eugene patted his big rough shoulder with his hands and they were friends immediately. It did not take Deegan long to find out from Big John why he was there and what he was doing.

"An arrtist!" he commented. "Shewer he'd better be outside than in. The loikes of him packin' shavin's and him laughin' at me."

Big John smiled.

"I believe he wants to get outside," he said.

"Why don't he come with me, then? He'd have a foine time workin' with the guineas. Shewer 'twould make a man av him—a few months of that"—and he pointed to Angelo Esposito shoveling clay.

Big John thought this worth reporting to Eugene. He did not think that he wanted to work with the guineas, but he might like to be with Deegan. Eugene saw his opportunity. He liked Deegan.

"Would you like to have an artist who's looking for health come and work for you, Deegan?" Eugene asked genially. He thought Deegan might refuse, but it didn't matter. It was worth the trial.

"Shewer!" replied the latter.

"Will I have to work with the Italians?"

"There'll be plenty av work for ye to do without ever layin' yer hand to pick or shovel unless ye want to. Shewer that's no work fer a white man to do."

"And what do you call them, Deegan? Aren't they white?"

"Shewer they're naat."

"What are they, then? They're not black."

"Nagurs, of coorse."

"But they're not negroes."

"Will, begad, they're naat white. Any man kin tell that be lookin' at thim."

Eugene smiled. He understood at once the solid Irish temperament which could draw this hearty conclusion. There was no malice in it. Deegan did not underestimate these Italians. He liked his men, but they weren't white. He didn't know what they were exactly, but they weren't white. He was standing over them a moment later shouting, "Up with it! Up with it! Down with it! Down with it!" as though his whole soul were intent on driving the last scrap of strength out of these poor underlings, when as a matter of fact they were not working very hard at all. His glance was roving about in a general way as he yelled and they paid little attention to him. Once in a while he would interpolate a "Come, Matt!" in a softer key—a key so soft that it was entirely out of keeping with his other voice. Eugene saw it all clearly. He understood Deegan.

"I think I'll get Mr. Haverford to transfer me to you, if you'll let me come," he said at the close of the day when Deegan was taking off his overalls and the "Eyetalians," as he called them, were putting the things back in the car.

"Shewer!" said Deegan, impressed by the great name of Haverford. If Eugene could accomplish that through such a far-off, wondrous personality, he must be a remarkable man himself. "Come along. I'll be glad to have ye. Ye can just make out the O. K. blanks and the repoarts and watch over the min sich times as I'll naat be there and—well—all told, ye'll have enough to keep ye busy."

Eugene smiled. This was a pleasant prospect. Big John had told him during the morning that Deegan went up and down the road from Peekskill on the main line, Chatham on the Midland Division, and Mt. Kisco on a third branch to New York City. He built wells, culverts, coal bins, building piers—small brick buildings—anything and everything, in short, which a capable foreman-mason ought to be able to build, and in addition he was fairly content and happy in his task. Eugene could see it. The atmosphere of the man was wholesome. He was like a tonic—a revivifying dynamo to this sickly overwrought sentimentalist.

That night he went home to Angela full of the humor and romance of his new situation. He liked the idea of it. He wanted to tell her about Deegan—to make her laugh. He was destined unfortunately to another kind of reception.

For Angela, by this time, had endured the agony of her discovery to the breaking point. She had listened to his pretences, knowing them to be lies, until she could endure it no longer. In following him she had discovered nothing, and the change in his work would make the chase more difficult. It was scarcely possible for anyone to follow him, for he himself did not know where he would be from day to day. He would be here, there, and everywhere. His sense of security as well as of his unfairness made him sensitive about being nice in the unimportant things. When he thought at all he was ashamed of what he was doing—thoroughly ashamed. Like the drunkard he appeared to be mastered by his weakness, and the psychology of his attitude is so best interpreted. He caressed her sympathetically, for he thought from her drawn, weary look that she was verging on some illness. She appeared to him to be suffering from worry for him, overwork, or approaching malady.

But Eugene in spite of his unfaithfulness did sympathize with Angela greatly. He appreciated her good qualities—her truthfulness, economy, devotion and self-sacrifice in all things which related to him. He was sorry that his own yearning for freedom crossed with her desire for simple-minded devotion on his part. He could not love her as she wanted him to, that he knew, and yet he was at times sorry for it, very. He would look at her when she was not looking at him, admiring her industry, her patience, her pretty figure, her geniality in the face of many difficulties, and wish that she could have had a better fate than to have met and married him.

Because of these feelings on his part for her he could not bear to see her suffer. When she appeared to be ill he could not help drawing near to her, wanting to know how she was, endeavoring to make her feel better by those sympathetic, emotional demonstrations which he knew meant so much to her. On this particular evening, noting the still drawn agony of her face, he was moved to insist. "What's the matter with you, Angelface, these days? You look so tired. You're not right. What's troubling you?"

"Oh, nothing," replied Angela wearily.

"But I know there is," he replied. "You can't be feeling well. What's ailing you? You're not like yourself at all. Won't you tell me, sweet? What's the trouble?"

He was thinking because Angela said nothing that it must be a real physical illness. Any emotional complaint vented itself quickly.

"Why should you care?" she asked cautiously, breaking her self-imposed vow of silence. She was thinking that Eugene and this woman, whoever she was, were conspiring to defeat her and that they were succeeding. Her voice had changed from one of weary resignation to subtle semi-concealed complaint and offense, and Eugene noted it. Before she could add any more, he had observed, "Why shouldn't I? Why, how you talk! What's the matter now?"

Angela really did not intend to go on. Her query was dragged out of her by his obvious sympathy. He was sorry for her in some general way. It made her pain and wrath all the greater. And his additional inquiry irritated her the more.

"Why should you?" she asked weepingly. "You don't want me. You don't like me. You pretend sympathy when I look a little bad, but that's all. But you don't care for me. If you could get rid of me, you would. That is so plain."

"Why, what are you talking about?" he asked, astonished. Had she found out anything? Was the incident of the scraps of paper really closed? Had anybody been telling her anything about Carlotta? Instantly he was all at sea. Still he had to pretend.

"You know I care," he said. "How can you say that?"

"You don't. You know you don't!" she flared up suddenly. "Why do you lie? You don't care. Don't touch me. Don't come near me. I'm sick of your hypocritical pretences! Oh!" And she straightened up with her finger nails cutting into her palms.

Eugene at the first expression of disbelief on her part had laid his hand soothingly on her arm. That was why she had jumped away from him. Now he drew back, nonplussed, nervous, a little defiant. It was easier to combat rage than sorrow; but he did not want to do either.

"What's the matter with you?" he asked, assuming a look of bewildered innocence. "What have I done now?"

"What haven't you done, you'd better ask. You dog! You

coward!" flared Angela. "Leaving me to stay out in Wisconsin while you go running around with a shameless woman. Don't deny it! Don't dare to deny it!"—this apropos of a protesting movement on the part of Eugene's head—"I know all! I know more than I want to know. I know how you've been acting. I know what you've been doing. I know how you've been lying to me. You've been running around with a low, vile wretch of a woman while I have been staying out in Blackwood eating my heart out, that's what you've been doing. Dear Angela! Dear Angelface! Dear Madonna Doloroso! Ha! What have you been calling her, you lying, hypocritical coward! What names have you for her, Hypocrite! Brute! Liar! I know what you've been doing. Oh, how well I know! Why was I ever born?—oh, why, why?"

Her voice trailed off in a wail of agony. Eugene stood there astonished to the point of inefficiency. He could not think of a single thing to do or say. He had no idea upon what evidence she based her complaint. He fancied that it must be much more than had been contained in that little note which he had torn up. She had not seen that—of that he was reasonably sure —or was he? Could she have taken it out of the box while he was in the bath and then put it back again? This sounded like it. She had looked very bad that night. How much did she know? Where had she secured this information? Mrs. Hibberdell? Carlotta? No! Had she seen her? Where? When?

"You're talking through your hat," he said aimlessly and largely in order to get time. "You're crazy! What's got into you, anyhow? I haven't been doing anything of the sort."

"Oh, haven't you!" she sneered. "You haven't been meeting her at bridges and road houses and street cars, have you? You liar! You haven't been calling her 'Ashes of Roses' and 'River Nymph' and 'Angel Girl.'" Angela was making up names and places out of her own mind. "I suppose you used some of the pet names on her that you gave to Christina Channing, didn't you? She'd like those, the vile strumpet! And you, you dog, pretending to me—pretending sympathy, pretending loneliness, pretending sorrow that I couldn't be here! A lot you cared what I was doing or thinking or suffering. Oh, I hate you, you horrible coward! I hate her! I hope something terrible happens to you. If I could get at her now I would kill her and you both—and myself. I would! I wish I could die! I wish I could die!"

Eugene was beginning to get the measure of his iniquity as Angela interpreted it. He could see now how cruelly he had

hurt her. He could see now how vile what he was doing looked
in her eyes. It was bad business—running with other women—
no doubt of it. It always ended in something like this—a terrible storm in which he had to sit by and hear himself called
brutal names to which there was no legitimate answer. He had
heard of this in connection with other people, but he had never
thought it would come to him. And the worst of it was that
he was guilty and deserving of it. No doubt of that. It lowered him in his own estimation. It lowered her in his and her
own because she had to fight this way. Why did he do it?
Why did he drag her into such a situation? It was breaking
down that sense of pride in himself which was the only sustaining power a man had before the gaze of the world. Why did he
let himself into these situations? Did he really love Carlotta?
Did he want pleasure enough to endure such abuse as this?
This was a terrible scene. And where would it end? His
nerves were tingling, his brain fairly aching. If he could only
conquer this desire for another type and be faithful, and yet
how dreadful that seemed! To confine himself in all his
thoughts to just Angela! It was not possible. He thought of
these things, standing there enduring the brunt of this storm.
It was a terrible ordeal, but it was not wholly reformatory even
at that.

"What's the use of your carrying on like that, Angela?" he
said grimly, after he had listened to all this. "It isn't as bad
as you think. I'm not a liar, and I'm not a dog! You must
have pieced that note I threw in the paper box together and read
it. When did you do it?"

He was curious about that and about how much she knew.
What were her intentions in regard to him? What in regard
to Carlotta? What would she do next?

"When did I do it?" she replied. "When did I do it? What
has that to do with it? What right have you to ask? Where
is this woman, that's what I want to know? I want to find
her. I want to face her. I want to tell her what a wretched
beast she is. I'll show her how to come and steal another
woman's husband. I'll kill her. I'll kill her and I'll kill you,
too. Do you hear? I'll kill you!" And she advanced on him
defiantly, blazingly.

Eugene was astounded. He had never seen such rage in any
woman. It was wonderful, fascinating, something like a great
lightning-riven storm. Angela was capable of hurling thunder-
bolts of wrath. He had not known that. It raised her in his
estimation—made her really more attractive than she would

otherwise have been, for power, however displayed, is fascinating. She was so little, so grim, so determined! It was in its way a test of great capability. And he liked her for it even though he resented her abuse.

"No, no, Angela," he said sympathetically and with a keen wish to alleviate her sorrow. "You would not do anything like that. You couldn't!"

"I will! I will!" she declared. "I'll kill her and you, too!"

And then having reached this tremendous height she suddenly broke. Eugene's big, sympathetic understanding was after all too much for her. His brooding patience in the midst of her wrath, his innate sorrow for what he could not or would not help (it was written all over his face), his very obvious presentation of the fact by his attitude that he knew that she loved him in spite of this, was too much for her. It was like beating her hands against a stone. She might kill him and this woman, whoever she was, but she would not have changed his attitude toward her, and that was what she wanted. A great torrent of heart-breaking sobs broke from her, shaking her frame like a reed. She threw her arms and head upon the kitchen table, falling to her knees, and cried and cried. Eugene stood there contemplating the wreck he had made of her dreams. Certainly it was hell, he said to himself; certainly it was. He was a liar, as she said, a dog, a scoundrel. Poor little Angela! Well, the damage had been done. What could he do now? Anything? Certainly not. Not a thing. She was broken— heart-broken. There was no earthly remedy for that. Priests might shrive for broken laws, but for a broken heart what remedy was there?

"Angela!" he called gently. "Angela! I'm sorry! Don't cry! Angela!! Don't cry!"

But she did not hear him. She did not hear anything. Lost in the agony of her situation, she could only sob convulsively until it seemed that her pretty little frame would break to pieces.

CHAPTER XXIX

EUGENE'S feelings on this occasion were of reasonable duration. It is always possible under such circumstances to take the victim of our brutalities in our arms and utter a few sympathetic or repentant words. The real kindness and repentance which consists in reformation is quite another matter. One must see with eyes too pure to behold evil to do that. Eugene was not to be reformed by an hour or many hours of agony on anyone's part. Angela was well within the range of his sympathetic interests. He suffered with her keenly, but not enough to outrun or offset his own keen desire for what he considered his spiritual right to enjoy beauty. What harm did it do, he would have asked himself, if he secretly exchanged affectionate looks and feelings with Carlotta or any other woman who fascinated him and in turn was fascinated by him? Could an affinity of this character really be called evil? He was not giving her any money which Angela ought to have, or very little. He did not want to marry her—and she really did not want to marry him, he thought—there was no chance of that, anyhow. He wanted to associate with her. And what harm did that do Angela? None, if she did not know. Of course, if she knew, it was very sad for her and for him. But, if the shoe were on the other foot, and Angela was the one who was acting as he was acting now he would not care, he thought. He forgot to add that if he did not care it would be because he was not in love, and Angela was in love. Such reasoning runs in circles. Only it is not reasoning. It is sentimental and emotional anarchy. There is no will toward progress in it.

When Angela recovered from her first burst of rage and grief it was only to continue it further, though not in quite the same vein. There can only be one superlative in any field of endeavor. Beyond that may be mutterings and thunderings or a shining after-glow, but no second superlative. Angela charged him with every weakness and evil tendency, only to have him look at her in a solemn way, occasionally saying: "Oh, no! You know I'm not as bad as that," or "Why do you abuse me in that way? That isn't true," or "Why do you say that?"

"Because it is so, and you know it's so," Angela would declare.

"Listen, Angela," he replied once, with a certain amount of

386

logic, "there is no use in brow-beating me in this way. It doesn't do any good to call me names. You want me to love you, don't you? That's all that you want. You don't want anything else. Will calling me names make me do it? If I can't I can't, and if I can I can. How will fighting help that?"

She listened to him pitifully, for she knew that her rage was useless, or practically so. He was in the position of power. She loved him. That was the sad part of it. To think that tears and pleadings and wrath might not really avail, after all! He could only love her out of a desire that was not self-generated. That was something she was beginning to see in a dim way as a grim truth.

Once she folded her hands and sat white and drawn, staring at the floor. "Well, I don't know what to do," she declared. "I suppose I ought to leave you. If it just weren't for my family! They all think so highly of the marriage state. They are so naturally faithful and decent. I suppose these qualities have to be born in people. They can't be acquired. You would have to be made over."

Eugene knew she would not leave him. He smiled at the superior condescension of the last remark, though it was not intended as such by her. To think of his being made over after the model Angela and her relatives would lay down!

"I don't know where I'd go or what I'd do," she observed. "I can't go back to my family. I don't want to go there. I haven't been trained in anything except school teaching, and I hate to think of that again. If I could only study stenography or book-keeping!" She was talking as much to clear her own mind as his. She really did not know what to do.

Eugene listened to this self-demonstrated situation with a shamed face. It was hard for him to think of Angela being thrown out on the world as a book-keeper or a stenographer. He did not want to see her doing anything like that. In a way, he wanted to live with her, if it could be done in his way— much as the Mormons might, perhaps. What a lonely life hers would be if she were away from him! And she was not suited to it. She was not suited to the commercial world—she was too homey, too housewifely. He wished he could assure her now that she would not have further cause for grief and mean it, but he was like a sick man wishing he could do the things a hale man might. There was no self-conviction in his thoughts, only the idea that if he tried to do right in this matter he might succeed, but he would be unhappy. So he drifted.

In the meanwhile Eugene had taken up his work with Deegan

and was going through a very curious experience. At the time Deegan had stated that he would take him he had written to Haverford, making a polite request for transfer, and was immediately informed that his wishes would be granted. Haverford remembered Eugene kindly. He hoped he was improving. He understood from inquiry of the Superintendent of Buildings that Deegan was in need of a capable assistant, anyhow, and that Eugene could well serve in that capacity. The foreman was always in trouble about his reports. An order was issued to Deegan commanding him to receive Eugene, and another to Eugene from the office of the Superintendent of Buildings ordering him to report to Deegan. Eugene went, finding him working on the problem of constructing a coal bin under the depot at Fords Centre, and raising as much storm as ever. He was received with a grin of satisfaction.

"So here ye arre. Will, ye're just in time. I want ye to go down to the ahffice."

Eugene laughed. "Sure," he said. Deegan was down in a freshly excavated hole and his clothes were redolent of the freshly turned earth which surrounded him. He had a plumb bob in his hand and a spirit level, but he laid them down. Under the neat train shed to which he crawled when Eugene appeared and where they stood, he fished from a pocket of his old gray coat a soiled and crumpled letter which he carefully unfolded with his thick and clumsy fingers. Then he held it up and looked at it defiantly.

"I want ye to go to Woodlawn," he continued, "and look after some bolts that arre theyer—there's a keg av thim—an' sign the bill fer thim, an' ship thim down to me. They're not miny. An' thin I waant ye to go down to the ahffice an' take thim this O. K." And here he fished around and produced another crumpled slip. "It's nonsinse!" he exclaimed, when he saw it. "It's onraisonable! They're aalways yillen fer thim O. K. blanks. Ye'd think, begad, I was goin' to steal thim from thim. Ye'd think I lived on thim things. O. K. blanks, O. K. blanks. From mornin' 'til night O. K. blanks. It's nonsinse! It's onraisonable!" And his face flushed a defiant red.

Eugene could see that some infraction of the railroad's rules had occurred and that Deegan had been "called down," or "jacked up" about it, as the railroad men expressed it. He was in a high state of dudgeon—as defiant and pugnacious as his royal Irish temper would allow.

"I'll fix it," said Eugene. "That's all right. Leave it to me."

Deegan showed some signs of approaching relief. At last he had a man of "intilligence," as he would have expressed it. He flung a parting shot though at his superior as Eugene departed.

"Tell thim I'll sign fer thim when I git thim and naat before!" he rumbled.

Eugene laughed. He knew no such message would be accepted, but he was glad to give Deegan an opportunity to blow off steam. He entered upon his new tasks with vim, pleased with the out-of-doors, the sunshine, the opportunity for brief trips up and down the road like this. It was delightful. He would soon be all right now, that he knew.

He went to Woodlawn and signed for the bolts; went to the office and met the chief clerk (delivering the desired O. K. blanks in person) who informed him of the chief difficulty in Deegan's life. It appeared that there were some twenty-five of these reports to be made out monthly, to say nothing of endless O. K. blanks to be filled in with acknowledgments of material received. Everything had to be signed for in this way, it mattered not whether it was a section of a bridge or a single bolt or a pound of putty. If a man could sit down and reel off a graphic report of what he was doing, he was the pride of the chief clerk's heart. His doing the work properly was taken as a matter of course. Deegan was not efficient at this, though he was assisted at times by his wife and all three of his children, a boy and two girls. He was constantly in hot water.

"My God!" exclaimed the chief clerk, when Eugene explained that Deegan had thought that he might leave the bolts at the station where they would be safe until he needed them and then sign for them when he took them out. He ran his hands distractedly through his hair. "What do you think of that?" he exclaimed. "He'll leave them there until he needs them, will he? What becomes of my reports? I've got to have those O. K.'s. You tell Deegan he ought to know better than that; he's been long enough on the road. You tell him that I said that I want a signed form for everything consigned to him the moment he learns that it's waiting for him. And I want it without fail. Let him go and get it. The gall! He's got to come to time about this, or something's going to drop. I'm not going to stand it any longer. You'd better help him in this. I've got to make out my reports on time."

Eugene agreed that he would. This was his field. He could help Deegan. He could be really useful.

Time passed. The weather grew colder, and while the work

was interesting at first, like all other things it began after a time to grow monotonous. It was nice enough when the weather was fine to stand out under the trees, where some culvert was being built to bridge a small rivulet or some well to supply the freight engines with water, and survey the surrounding landscape; but when the weather grew colder it was not so nice. Deegan was always interesting. He was forever raising a ruction. He lived a life of hard, narrow activity laid among boards, wheelbarrows, cement, stone, a life which concerned construction and had no particular joy in fruition. The moment a thing was nicely finished they had to leave it and go where everything would be torn up again. Eugene used to look at the wounded ground, the piles of yellow mud, the dirty Italians, clean enough in their spirit, but soiled and gnarled by their labor, and wonder how much longer he could stand it. To think that he, of all men, should be here working with Deegan and the *guineas!* He became lonesome at times—terribly, and sad. He longed for Carlotta, longed for a beautiful studio, longed for a luxurious, artistic life. It seemed that life had wronged him terribly, and yet he could do nothing about it. He had no money-making capacity.

About this time the construction of a rather pretentious machine shop, two hundred by two hundred feet and four storeys high was assigned to Deegan, largely because of the efficiency which Eugene contributed to Deegan's work. Eugene handled his reports and accounts with rapidity and precision, and this so soothed the division management that they had an opportunity to see Deegan's real worth. The latter was beside himself with excitement, anticipating great credit and distinction for the work he was now to be permitted to do.

" 'Tis the foine time we'll have, Eugene, me bye," he exclaimed, "puttin' up that buildin'. 'Tis no culvert we'll be afther buildin' now. Nor no coal bin. Wait till the masons come. Then ye'll see somethin'."

Eugene was pleased that their work was progressing so successfully, but of course there was no future in it for him. He was lonely and disheartened.

Besides, Angela was complaining, and rightfully enough, that they were leading a difficult life—and to what end, so far as she was concerned? He might recover his health and his art (by reason of his dramatic shake-up and changes he appeared to be doing so), but what would that avail her? He did not love her. If he became prosperous again it might be to forsake her, and at best he could only give her money and position if he ever attained these, and how would that help? It was love that she wanted—his love. And she did not have that, or only a mere shadow of it. He had made up his mind after this last fatal argument that he would not pretend to anything he did not feel in regard to her, and this made it even harder. She did believe that he sympathized with her in his way, but it was an intellectual sympathy and had very little to do with the heart. He was sorry for her. Sorry! Sorry! How she hated the thought of that! If he could not do any better than that, what was there in all the years to come but misery?

A curious fact to be noted about this period was that suspicion had so keyed up Angela's perceptions that she could almost tell, and that without knowing, when Eugene was with Carlotta—or had been. There was something about his manner when he came in of an evening, to say nothing of those subtler thought waves which passed from him to her when he was with Carlotta, which told her instantly where he had been and what he had been doing. She would ask him where he had been and he would say: "Oh, up to White Plains" or "out to Scarborough," but nearly always when he had been with Carlotta she would flare up with, "Yes, I know where you've been. You've been out again with that miserable beast of a woman. Oh, God will punish her yet! You will be punished! Wait and see."

Tears would flood her eyes and she would berate him roundly.

Eugene stood in profound awe before these subtle outbreaks. He could not understand how it was that Angela came to know or suspect so accurately. To a certain extent he was a believer in spiritualism and the mysteries of a subconscious mind or self. He fancied that there must be some way of this subconscious self seeing or apprehending what was going on and of communicating its knowledge in the form of fear and suspicion to Angela's mind. If the very subtleties of nature were in league against him, how was he to continue or profit in this career? Obviously it could not be done. He would probably be severely punished for it. He was half terrified by the vague suspicion that there might be some laws which tended to correct in this way all the abuses in nature. There might be much vice and crime going seemingly unpunished, but there might also be much correction going on, as the suicides and deaths and cases of insanity seemed to attest. Was this true? Was there no escape from the results of evil except by abandoning it entirely? He pondered over this gravely.

Getting on his feet again financially was not such an easy thing. He had been out of touch now so long with things artistic—the magazine world and the art agencies—that he felt as if he might not readily be able to get in touch again. Besides he was not at all sure of himself. He had made sketches of men and things at Speonk, and of Deegan and his gang on the road, and of Carlotta and Angela, but he felt that they were weak in their import—lacking in the force and feeling which had once characterized his work. He thought of trying his hand at newspaper work if he could make any sort of a connection—working in some obscure newspaper art department until he should feel himself able to do better; but he did not feel at all confident that he could get that. His severe breakdown had made him afraid of life—made him yearn for the sympathy of a woman like Carlotta, or of a larger more hopeful, more tender attitude, and he dreaded looking for anything anywhere. Besides he hated to spare the time unless he were going to get somewhere. His work was so pressing. But he knew he must quit it. He thought about it wearily, wishing he were better placed in this world; and finally screwed up his courage to leave this work, though it was not until something else was quite safely in his hands.

CHAPTER XXX

IT was only after a considerable lapse of time, when trying to live on nine dollars a week and seeing Angela struggle almost hopelessly in her determination to live on what he earned and put a little aside, that he came to his senses and made a sincere effort to find something better. During all this time he had been watching her narrowly, seeing how systematically she did all her own house work, even under these adverse and trying circumstances, cooking, cleaning, marketing. She made over her old clothes, reshaping them so that they would last longer and still look stylish. She made her own hats, doing everything in short that she could to make the money in the bank hold out until Eugene should be on his feet. She was willing that he should take money and buy himself clothes when she was not willing to spend it on herself. She was living in the hope that somehow he would reform. Consciousness of what she was worth to him might some day strike him. Still she did not feel that things could ever be quite the same again. She could never forget, and neither could he.

The affair between Eugene and Carlotta, because of the various forces that were militating against it, was now slowly drawing to a close. It had not been able to endure all the storm and stress which followed its discovery. For one thing, Carlotta's mother, without telling her husband, made him feel that he had good cause to stay about, which made it difficult for Carlotta to act. Besides she charged her daughter constantly, much as Angela was charging Eugene, with the utmost dissoluteness of character and was as constantly putting her on the defensive. She was too hedged about to risk a separate apartment, and Eugene would not accept money from her to pay for expensive indoor entertainment. She wanted to see him but she kept hoping he would get to the point where he would have a studio again and she could see him as a star in his own field. That would be so much nicer.

By degrees their once exciting engagements began to lapse, and despite his grief Eugene was not altogether sorry. To tell the truth, great physical discomfort recently had painted his romantic tendencies in a very sorry light for him. He thought he saw in a way where they were leading him. That there was no money in them was obvious. That the affairs of the

393

world were put in the hands of those who were content to get their life's happiness out of their management, seemed quite plain. Idlers had nothing as a rule, not even the respect of their fellow men. The licentious were worn threadbare and disgraced by their ridiculous and psychologically diseased propensities. Women and men who indulged in these unbridled relations were sickly sentimentalists, as a rule, and were thrown out or ignored by all forceful society. One had to be strong, eager, determined and abstemious if wealth was to come, and then it had to be held by the same qualities. One could not relax. Otherwise one became much what he was now, a brooding sentimentalist—diseased in mind and body.

So out of love-excitement and poverty and ill health and abuse he was coming to see or thought he was this one fact clearly,—namely that he must behave himself if he truly wished to succeed. Did he want to? He could not say that. But he had to—that was the sad part of it—and since apparently he had to, he would do the best he could. It was grim but it was essential.

At this time Eugene still retained that rather ultra artistic appearance which had characterized his earlier years, but he began to suspect that on this score he was a little bizarre and out of keeping with the spirit of the times. Certain artists whom he met in times past and recently, were quite commercial in their appearance—the very successful ones—and he decided that it was because they put the emphasis upon the hard facts of life and not upon the romance connected with their work. It impressed him and he decided to do likewise, abandoning the flowing tie and the rather indiscriminate manner he had of combing his hair, and thereafter affected severe simplicity. He still wore a soft hat because he thought it became him best, but otherwise he toned himself down greatly. His work with Deegan had given him a sharp impression of what hard, earnest labor meant. Deegan was nothing but a worker. There was no romance in him. He knew nothing about romance. Picks and shovels and mortar boards and concrete forms—such was his life, and he never complained. Eugene remembered commiserating him once on having to get up at four A. M. in order to take a train which would get to work by seven. Darkness and cold made no difference to him, however.

"Shewer, I have to be theyre," he had replied with his quizzical Irish grin. "They're not payin' me me wages fer lyin' in bed. If ye were to get up that way every day fer a year it would make a man of ye!"

"Oh, no," said Eugene teasingly.

"Oh, yes," said Deegan, "it would. An' yere the wan that's needin' it. I can tell that by the cut av ye."

Eugene resented this but it stayed by him. Deegan had the habit of driving home salutary lessons in regard to work and abstemiousness without really meaning to. The two were wholly representative of him—just those two things and nothing more.

One day he went down into Printing House Square to see if he could not make up his mind to apply at one of the newspaper art departments, when he ran into Hudson Dula whom he had not seen for a long while. The latter was delighted to see him.

"Why, hello, Witla!" he exclaimed, shocked to see that he was exceptionally thin and pale. "Where have you been all these years? I'm delighted to see you. What have you been doing? Let's go over here to Hahn's and you tell me all about yourself."

"I've been sick, Dula," said Eugene frankly. "I had a severe case of nervous breakdown and I've been working on the railroad for a change. I tried all sorts of specialists, but they couldn't help me. So I decided to go to work by the day and see what that would do. I got all out of sorts with myself and I've been pretty near four years getting back. I think I am getting better, though. I'm going to knock off on the road one of these days and try my hand at painting again. I think I can do it."

"Isn't that curious," replied Dula reminiscently, "I was just thinking of you the other day and wondering where you were. You know I've quit the art director game. *Truth* failed and I went into the lithographic business. I have a small interest in a plant that I'm managing down in Bond Street. I wish you'd come in and see me some day."

"I certainly will," said Eugene.

"Now this nervousness of yours," said Dula, as they strolled into the restaurant where they were dining. "I have a brother-in-law that was hit that way. He's still doctoring around. I'm going to tell him about your case. You don't look so bad."

"I'm feeling much better," said Eugene. "I really am but I've had a bad spell of it. I'm going to come back in the game, though, I feel sure of it. When I do I'll know better how to take care of myself. I over-worked on that first burst of pictures."

"I must say that was the best stuff of that kind I ever saw done in this country," said Dula. "I saw both your shows, as you remember. They were splendid. What became of all those pictures?"

"Oh, some were sold and the rest are in storage," replied Eugene.

"Curious, isn't it," said Dula. "I should have thought all those things would have been purchased. They were so new and forceful in treatment. You want to pull yourself together and stay pulled. You're going to have a great future in that field."

"Oh, I don't know," replied Eugene pessimistically. "It's all right to obtain a big reputation, but you can't live on that, you know. Pictures don't sell very well over here. I have most of mine left. A grocer with one delivery wagon has the best artist that ever lived backed right off the board for financial results."

"Not quite as bad as that," said Dula smilingly. "An artist has something which a tradesman can never have—you want to remember that. His point of view is worth something. He lives in a different world spiritually. And then financially you can do well enough—you can live, and what more do you want? You're received everywhere. You have what the tradesman cannot possibly attain—distinction; and you give the world a standard of merit—you will, at least. If I had your ability I would never sit about envying any butcher or baker. Why, all the artists know you now—the good ones, anyhow. It only remains for you to do more, to obtain more. There are lots of things you can do."

"What, for instance?" asked Eugene.

"Why, ceilings, mural decorations. I was saying to someone the other day what a mistake it was the Boston Library did not assign some of their panels to you. You would make splendid things of them."

"You certainly have a world of faith in me," replied Eugene, tingling warmly. It was like a glowing fire to hear this after all the dreary days. Then the world still remembered him. He was worth while.

"Do you remember Oren Benedict—you used to know him out in Chicago, didn't you?"

"I certainly did," replied Eugene. "I worked with him."

"He's down on the *World* now, in charge of the art department there. He's just gone there." Then as Eugene exclaimed over the curious shifts of time, he suddenly added, "Why wouldn't that be a good idea for you? You say you're just about to knock off. Why don't you go down and do some

pen work to get your hand in? It would be a good experience
for you. Benedict would be glad to put you on, I'm sure."

Dula suspected that Eugene might be out of funds, and this
would be an easy way for him to slip into something which
would lead back to studio work. He liked Eugene. He was
anxious to see him get along. It flattered him to think he
had been the first to publish his work in color.

"That isn't a bad idea," said Eugene. "I was really thinking of doing something like that if I could. I'll go up and see
him maybe today. It would be just the thing I need now,—a
little preliminary practise. I feel rather rusty and uncertain."

"I'll call him up, if you want," said Dula generously. "I
know him well. He was asking me the other day if I knew one
or two exceptional men. You wait here a minute."

Eugene leaned back in his chair as Dula left. Could it be
that he was going to be restored thus easily to something better?
He had thought it would be so hard. Now this chance was
coming to lift him out of his sufferings at the right time.

Dula came back. "He says 'Sure,'" he exclaimed. "'Come
right down!' You'd better go down there this afternoon.
That'll be just the thing for you. And when you are placed
again, come around and see me. Where are you living?"

Eugene gave him his address.

"That's right, you're married," he added, when Eugene spoke
of himself and Angela having a small place. "How is Mrs.
Witla? I remember her as a very charming woman. Mrs.
Dula and I have an apartment in Gramercy Place. You didn't
know I had tied up, did you? Well, I have. Bring your wife
and come to see us. We'll be delighted. I'll make a dinner
date for you two."

Eugene was greatly pleased and elated. He knew Angela
would be. They had seen nothing of artistic life lately. He
hurried down to see Benedict and was greeted as an old acquaintance. They had never been very chummy but always
friendly. Benedict had heard of Eugene's nervous breakdown.

"Well, I'll tell you," he said, after greeting and reminiscences
were over, "I can't pay very much—fifty dollars is high here
just at present, and I have just one vacancy now at twenty-five
which you can have if you want to try your hand. There's
a good deal of hurry up about at times, but you don't mind
that. When I get things straightened out here I may have
something better."

"Oh, that's all right," replied Eugene cheerfully. "I'm glad

to get that." (He was very glad indeed.) "And I don't mind
the hurry. It will be good for a change."

Benedict gave him a friendly handshake in farewell. He
was glad to have him, for he knew what he could do.

"I don't think I can come before Monday. I have to give
a few days' notice. Is that all right?"

"I could use you earlier, but Monday will do," said Benedict, and they parted genially.

Eugene hurried back home. He was delighted to tell Angela,
for this would rob their condition of part of its gloom. It was
no great comfort to him to be starting in as a newspaper
artist again at twenty-five dollars a week, but it couldn't be
helped, and it was better than nothing. At least it was putting
him back on the track again. He was sure to do still better
after this. He could hold this newspaper job, he felt, and outside that he didn't care very much for the time being; his
pride had received some severe jolts. It was vastly better than
day labor, anyway. He hurried up the four flights of stairs to
the cheap little quarters they occupied, saying when he saw
Angela at the gas range: "Well, I guess our railroad days are
over."

"What's the trouble?" asked Angela apprehensively.

"No trouble," he replied. "I have a better job."

"What is it?"

"I'm going to be a newspaper artist for a while on the
World."

"When did you find that out?" she asked, brightening, for
she had been terribly depressed over their state.

"This afternoon. I'm going to work Monday. Twenty-five
dollars will be some better than nine, won't it?"

Angela smiled. "It certainly will," she said, and tears of
thanksgiving filled her eyes.

Eugene knew what those tears stood for. He was anxious
to avoid painful reminiscences.

"Don't cry," he said. "Things are going to be much better
from now on."

"Oh, I hope so, I hope so," she murmured, and he patted
her head affectionately as it rested on his shoulder.

"There now. Cheer up, girlie, will you! We're going to
be all right from now on."

Angela smiled through her tears. She set the table, exceedingly cheerful.

"That certainly is good news," she laughed afterward. "But
we're not going to spend any more money for a long while,

anyhow. We're going to save something. We don't want to get in this hole again."

"No more for mine," replied Eugene gaily, "not if I know my business," and he went into the one little combination parlor, sitting room, reception room and general room of all work, to open his evening newspaper and whistle. In his excitement he almost forgot his woes over Carlotta and the love question in general. He was going to climb again in the world and be happy with Angela. He was going to be an artist or a business man or something. Look at Hudson Dula. Owning a lithographic business and living in Gramercy Place. Could any artist he knew do that? Scarcely. He would see about this. He would think this art business over. Maybe he could be an art director or a lithographer or something. He had often thought while he was with the road that he could be a good superintendent of buildings if he could only give it time enough.

Angela, for her part, was wondering what this change really spelled for her. Would he behave now? Would he set himself to the task of climbing slowly and surely? He was getting along in life. He ought to begin to place himself securely in the world if he ever was going to. Her love was not the same as it had formerly been. It was crossed with dislike and opposition at times, but still she felt that he needed her to help him. Poor Eugene—if he only were not cursed with this weakness. Perhaps he would overcome it? So she mused.

CHAPTER XXXI

THE work which Eugene undertook in connection with the art department of the *World* was not different from that which he had done ten years before in Chicago. It seemed no less difficult for all his experience—more so if anything, for he felt above it these days and consequently out of place. He wished at once that he could get something which would pay him commensurately with his ability. To sit down among mere boys—there were men there as old as himself and older, though, of course, he did not pay so much attention to them —was galling. He thought Benedict should have had more respect for his talent than to have offered him so little, though at the same time he was grateful for what he had received. He undertook energetically to carry out all the suggestions given him, and surprised his superior with the speed and imagination with which he developed everything. He surprised Benedict the second day with a splendid imaginative interpretation of "the Black Death," which was to accompany a Sunday newspaper article upon the modern possibilities of plagues. The latter saw at once that Eugene could probably only be retained a very little while at the figure he had given him. He had made the mistake of starting him low, thinking that Eugene's talent after so severe an illness might be at a very low ebb. He did not know, being new to the art directorship of a newspaper, how very difficult it was to get increases for those under him. An advance of ten dollars to anyone meant earnest representation and an argument with the business manager, and to double and treble the salary, which should have been done in this case, was out of the question. Six months was a reasonable length of time for anyone to wait for an increase— such was the dictate of the business management—and in Eugene's case it was ridiculous and unfair. However, being still sick and apprehensive, he was content to abide by the situation, hoping with returning strength and the saving of a little money to put himself right eventually.

Angela, of course, was pleased with the turn of affairs. Having suffered so long with only prospects of something worse in store, it was a great relief to go to the bank every Tuesday— Eugene was paid on Monday—and deposit ten dollars against a rainy day. It was agreed between them that they might use six for clothing, which Angela and Eugene very much needed, and some slight entertainment. It was not long before Eugene began to bring an occasional newspaper artist friend up to dinner, and they were invited out. They had gone without much clothing, with scarcely a single visit to the theatre, without friends—everything. Now the tide began slowly to change; in a little while, because they were more free to go to places, they began to encounter people whom they knew.

There was six months of the drifting journalistic work, in which as in his railroad work he grew more and more restless, and then there came a time when he felt as if he could not stand that for another minute. He had been raised to thirty-five dollars and then fifty, but it was a terrific grind of exaggerated and to him thoroughly meretricious art. The only valuable results in connection with it were that for the first time in his life he was drawing a moderately secure living salary, and that his mind was fully occupied with details which gave him no time to think about himself. He was in a large room surrounded by other men who were as sharp as knives in their thrusts of wit, and restless and greedy in their attitude toward the world. They wanted to live brilliantly, just as he did, only they had more self-confidence and in many cases that extreme poise which comes of rare good health. They were inclined to think he was somewhat of a poseur at first, but later they came to like him—all of them. He had a winning smile and his love of a joke, so keen, so body-shaking, drew to him all those who had a good story to tell.

"Tell that to Witla," was a common phrase about the office and Eugene was always listening to someone. He came to lunching with first one and then another, then three or four at a time; and by degrees Angela was compelled to entertain Eugene and two or three of his friends twice and sometimes three times a week. She objected greatly, and there was some feeling over that, for she had no maid and she did not think that Eugene ought to begin so soon to put the burden of entertainment upon their slender income. She wanted him to make these things very formal and by appointment, but Eugene would stroll in genially, explaining that he had Irving Nelson with him, or Henry Hare, or George Beers, and asking nervously at the last minute whether it was all right. Angela would say, "Certainly, to be sure," in front of the guests, but when they were alone there would be tears and reproaches and firm declarations that she would not stand it.

"Well, I won't do it any more," Eugene would apologize. "I forgot, you know."

Still he wanted Angela to get a maid and let him bring all who would come. It was a great relief to get back into the swing of things and see life broadening out once more.

It was not so long after he had grown exceedingly weary of his underpaid relationship to the *World* that he heard of some-thing which promised a much better avenue of advancement. Eugene had been hearing for some time from one source and another of the development of art in advertising. He had read one or two articles on the subject in the smaller magazines, had seen from time to time curious and sometimes beautiful series of ads run by first one corporation and then another, advertising some product. He had always fancied in looking at these things that he could get up a notable series on almost any sub-ject, and he wondered who handled these things. He asked Benedict one night, going up on the car with him, what he knew about it.

"Why so far as I know," said Benedict, "that is coming to be quite a business. There is a man out in Chicago, Saljerian, an American Syrian—his father was a Syrian, but he was born over here—who has built up a tremendous business out of de-signing series of ads like that for big corporations. He got up that Molly Maguire series for the new cleaning fluid. I don't think he does any of the work himself. He hires artists to do it. Some of the best men, I understand, have done work for him. He gets splendid prices. Then some of the big advertis-ing agencies are taking up that work. One of them I know. The Summerville Company has a big art department in con-nection with it. They employ fifteen to eighteen men all the time, sometimes more. They turn out some fine ads, too, to my way of thinking. Do you remember that Korno series?"— Benedict was referring to a breakfast food which had been ad-vertised by a succession of ten very beautiful and very clever pictures.

"Yes," replied Eugene.

"Well, they did that."

Eugene thought of this as a most interesting development. Since the days in which he worked on the Alexandria *Appeal* he had been interested in ads. The thought of ad creation took his fancy. It was newer than anything else he had en-countered recently. He wondered if there would not be some chance in that field for him. His paintings were not selling. He had not the courage to start a new series. If he could make some money first, say ten thousand dollars, so that he could get an interest income of say six or seven hundred dollars a year, he might be willing to risk art for art's sake. He had suffered too much—poverty had scared him so that he was very anxious to lean on a salary or a business income for the time being.

It was while he was speculating over this almost daily that there came to him one day a young artist who had formerly worked on the *World*—a youth by the name of Morgenbau——Adolph Morgenbau—who admired Eugene and his work greatly and who had since gone to another paper. He was very anxious to tell Eugene something, for he had heard of a change coming in the art directorship of the Summerville Company and he fancied for one reason and another that Eugene might be glad to know of it. Eugene had never looked to Morgenbau like a man who ought to be working in a newspaper art department. He was too self-poised, too superior, too wise. Morgenbau had conceived the idea that Eugene was destined to make a great hit of some kind and with that kindling intuition that sometimes saves us whole he was anxious to help Eugene in some way and so gain his favor.

"I have something I'd like to tell you, Mr. Witla," he observed.

"Well, what is it?" smiled Eugene.

"Are you going out to lunch?"

"Certainly, come along."

They went out together and Morgenbau communicated to Eugene what he had heard—that the Summerfield Company had just dismissed, or parted company with, or lost, a very capable director by the name of Freeman, and that they were looking for a new man.

"Why don't you apply for that?" asked Morgenbau. "You could hold it. You're doing just the sort of work that would make great ads. You know how to handle men, too. They like you. All the young fellows around here do. Why don't you go and see Mr. Summerfield? He's up in Thirty-fourth Street. You might be just the man he's looking for, and then you'd have a department of your own."

Eugene looked at this boy, wondering what had put this idea in his head. He decided to call up Dula and did so at once, asking him what he thought would be the best move to make. The latter did not know Summerville, but he knew someone who did.

"I'll tell you what you do, Eugene," he said. "You go and see Baker Bates of the Satina Company. That's at the corner of Broadway and Fourth Street. We do a big business with the Satina Company, and they do a big business with Summerfield. I'll send a letter over to you by a boy and you take that. Then I'll call Bates up on the phone, and if he's favorable he can speak to Summerfield. He'll want to see you, though."

Eugene was very grateful and eagerly awaited the arrival of the letter. He asked Benedict for a little time off and went to Mr. Baker Bates. The latter had heard enough from Dula to be friendly. He had been told by the latter that Eugene was potentially a great artist, slightly down on his luck, but that he was doing exceedingly well where he was and would do better in the new place. He was impressed by Eugene's appearance, for the latter had changed his style from the semi-artistic to the practical. He thought Eugene looked capable. He was certainly pleasant.

"I'll talk to Mr. Summerfield for you," he said, "though I wouldn't put much hope in what will come of it if I were you. He's a difficult man and it's best not to appear too eager in this matter. If he can be induced to send for you it will be much better. You let this rest until tomorrow. I'll call him up on another matter and take him out to lunch, and then I'll see how he stands and who he has in mind, if he has anyone. He may have, you know. If there is a real opening I'll speak of you. We'll see."

Eugene went away once more, very grateful. He was thinking that Dula had always meant good luck to him. He had taken his first important drawing. The pictures he had published for him had brought him the favor of M. Charles. Dula had secured him the position that he now had. Would he be the cause of his getting this one?

On the way down town on the car he encountered a cross-eyed boy. He had understood from someone recently that cross-eyed boys were good luck—cross-eyed women bad luck. A thrill of hopeful prognostication passed over him. In all likelihood he was going to get this place. If this sign came true this time, he would believe in signs. They had come true before, but this would be a real test. He stared cheerfully at the boy and the latter looked him full in the eyes and grinned.

"That settles it!" said Eugene. "I'm going to get it."

Still he was far from being absolutely sure.

CHAPTER XXXII

THE Summerfield Advertising Agency, of which Mr. Daniel C. Summerfield was president, was one of those curious exfoliations or efflorescences of the personality of a single individual which is so often met with in the business world, and which always means a remarkable individual behind them. The ideas, the enthusiasm, the strength of Mr. Daniel C. Summerfield was all there was to the Summerfield Advertising Agency. It was true there was a large force of men working for him, advertising canvassers, advertising writers, financial accountants, artists, stenographers, book-keepers and the like, but they were all as it were an emanation or irradiation of the personality of Mr. Daniel C. Summerfield. He was small, wiry, black-haired, black-eyed, black-mustached, with an olive complexion and even, pleasing, albeit at times wolfish, white teeth which indicated a disposition as avid and hungry as a disposition well might be.

Mr. Summerfield had come up into his present state of affluence or comparative affluence from the direst poverty and by the directest route—his personal efforts. In the State in which he had originated, Alabama, his family had been known, in the small circle to which they were known at all, as poor white trash. His father had been a rather lackadaisical, half-starved cotton planter who had been satisfied with a single bale or less of cotton to the acre on the ground which he leased, and who drove a lean mule very much the worse for age and wear, up and down the furrows of his leaner fields the while he complained of "the misery" in his breast. He was afflicted with slow consumption or thought he was, which was just as effective, and in addition had hook-worm, though that parasitic producer of hopeless tiredness was not yet discovered and named.

Daniel Christopher, his eldest son, had been raised with scarcely any education, having been put in a cotton mill at the age of seven, but nevertheless he soon manifested himself as the brain of the family. For four years he worked in the cotton mill, and then, because of his unusual brightness, he had been given a place in the printing shop of the Wickham Union, where he was so attractive to the slow-going proprietor that he soon became foreman of the printing department and then manager. He knew nothing of printing or newspapers at the time, but the little contact he obtained here soon cleared his vision. He saw instantly what the newspaper business was, and decided to enter it. Later, as he grew older, he suspected that no one knew very much about advertising as yet, or very little, and that he was called by God to revise it. With this vision of a still wider field of usefulness in his mind, he began at once to prepare himself for it, reading all manner of advertising literature and practicing the art of display and effective statement. He had been through such bitter things as personal fights with those who worked under him, knocking one man down with a heavy iron form key; personal altercation with his own father and mother in which he frankly told them that they were failures, and that they had better let him show them something about regulating their hopeless lives. He had quarreled with his younger brothers, trying to dominate them, and had succeeded in controlling the youngest, principally for the very good reason that he had become foolishly fond of him; this younger brother he later introduced into his advertising business. He had religiously saved the little he had earned thus far, invested a part of it in the further development of the Wickham *Union,* bought his father an eight acre farm, which he showed him how to work, and finally decided to come to New York to see if he could not connect himself with some important advertising concern where he could learn something more about the one thing that interested him. He was already married, and he brought his young wife with him from the South.

He soon connected himself as a canvasser with one of the great agencies and advanced rapidly. He was so smiling, so bland, so insistent, so magnetic, that business came to him rapidly. He became the star man in this New York concern and Alfred Cookman, who was its owner and manager, was soon pondering what he could do to retain him. No individual or concern could long retain Daniel C. Summerfield, however, once he understood his personal capabilities. In two years he had learned all that Alfred Cookman had to teach him and more than he could teach him. He knew his customers and what their needs were, and where the lack was in the service which Mr. Cookman rendered them. He foresaw the drift toward artistic representation of saleable products, and decided to go into that side of it. He would start an agency which would render a service so complete and dramatic that anyone who could afford to use his service would make money.

When Eugene first heard of this agency, the Summerfield concern was six years old and rapidly growing. It was already very large and profitable and as hard and forceful as its owner. Daniel C. Summerfield, sitting in his private office, was absolutely ruthless in his calculations as to men. He had studied the life of Napoleon and had come to the conclusion that no individual life was important. Mercy was a joke to be eliminated from business. Sentiment was silly twaddle. The thing to do was to hire men as cheaply as possible, to drive them as vigorously as possible, and to dispose of them quickly when they showed signs of weakening under the strain. He had already had five art directors in as many years, had "hired and fired," as he termed it, innumerable canvassers, ad writers, book-keepers, stenographers, artists—getting rid of anyone and everyone who showed the least sign of incapacity or inefficiency. The great office floor which he maintained was a model of cleanliness, order—one might almost say beauty of a commercial sort, but it was the cleanliness, order and beauty of a hard, polished and well-oiled machine. Daniel C. Summerfield was not much more than that, but he had long ago decided that was what he must be in order not to be a failure, a fool, and as he called it, "a mark," and he admired himself for being so.

When Mr. Baker Bates at Hudson Dula's request went to Mr. Summerfield in regard to the rumored vacancy which really existed, the latter was in a most receptive frame of mind. He had just come into two very important advertising contracts which required a lot of imagination and artistic skill to execute, and he had lost his art director because of a row over a former contract. It was true that in very many cases—in most cases, in fact—his customers had very definite ideas as to what they wanted to say and how they wanted to say it, but not always. They were almost always open to suggestions as to modifications and improvements, and in a number of very important cases they were willing to leave the entire theory of procedure to the Summerfield Advertising Company. This called for rare good judgment not only in the preparation, but in the placing of these ads, and it was in the matter of their preparation—the many striking ideas which they should embody—that the judgment and assistance of a capable art director of real imagination was most valuable.

As has already been said, Mr. Summerfield had had five art directors in almost as many years. In each case he had used the Napoleonic method of throwing a fresh, unwearied mind into the breach of difficulty, and when it wearied or broke under the strain, tossing it briskly out. There was no compunction or pity connected with any detail of this method. "I hire good men and I pay them good wages," was his favorite comment. "Why shouldn't I expect good results?" If he was wearied or angered by failure he was prone to exclaim—"These God-damned cattle of artists! What can you expect of them? They don't know anything outside their little theory of how things ought to look. They don't know anything about life. Why, God damn it, they're like a lot of children. Why should any-body pay any attention to what they think? Who cares what they think? They give me a pain in the neck." Mr. Daniel C. Summerfield was very much given to swearing, more as a matter of habit than of foul intention, and no picture of him would be complete without the interpolation of his favorite expressions.

When Eugene appeared on the horizon as a possible appli-cant for this delightful position, Mr. Daniel C. Summerfield was debating with himself just what he should do in con-nection with the two new contracts in question. The adver-tisers were awaiting his suggestions eagerly. One was for the nation-wide advertising of a new brand of sugar, the second for the international display of ideas in connection with a series of French perfumes, the sale of which depended largely upon the beauty with which they could be interpreted to the lay mind. The latter were not only to be advertised in the United States and Canada, but in Mexico also, and the fulfilment of the contracts in either case was dependent upon the approval given by the advertisers to the designs for newspaper, car and bill-board advertising which he should submit. It was a ticklish business, worth two hundred thousand dollars in ultimate profits, and naturally he was anxious that the man who should sit in the seat of authority in his art department should be one of real force and talent—a genius if possible, who should, through his ideas, help him win his golden harvest.

The right man naturally was hard to find. The last man had been only fairly capable. He was dignified, meditative, thought-ful, with considerable taste and apprehension as to what the material situation required in driving home simple ideas, but he had no great imaginative grasp of life. In fact no man who had ever sat in the director's chair had ever really suited Mr. Summerfield. According to him they had all been weaklings. "Dubs; fakes; hot air artists," were some of his descriptions of them. Their problem, however, was a hard one, for they had to think very vigorously in connection with any product which he might be trying to market, and to offer him endless sugges-

tions as to what would be the next best thing for a manufacturer to say or do to attract attention to what he had to sell. It might be a catch phrase such as "Have You Seen This New Soap?" or "Do You Know Soresda?—It's Red." It might be that a novelty in the way of hand or finger, eye or mouth was all that was required, carrying some appropriate explanation in type. Sometimes, as in the case of very practical products, their very practical display in some clear, interesting, attractive way was all that was needed. In most cases, though, something radically new was required, for it was the theory of Mr. Summerfield that his ads must not only arrest the eye, but fix themselves in the memory, and convey a fact which was or at least could be made to seem important to the reader. It was a struggling with one of the deepest and most interesting phases of human psychology.

The last man, Older Freeman, had been of considerable use to him in his way. He had collected about him a number of fairly capable artists—men temporarily down on their luck—who like Eugene were willing to take a working position of this character, and from them he had extracted by dint of pleading, cajoling, demonstrating and the like a number of interesting ideas. Their working hours were from nine to five-thirty, their pay meagre—eighteen to thirty-five, with experts drawing in several instances fifty and sixty dollars, and their tasks innumerable and really never-ending. Their output was regulated by a tabulated record system which kept account of just how much they succeeded in accomplishing in a week, and how much it was worth to the concern. The ideas on which they worked were more or less products of the brains of the art director and his superior, though they occasionally themselves made important suggestions, but for their proper execution, the amount of time spent on them, the failures sustained, the art director was more or less responsible. He could not carry to his employer a poor drawing of a good idea, or a poor idea for something which required a superior thought, and long hope to retain his position. Mr. Daniel C. Summerfield was too shrewd and too exacting. He was really tireless in his energy. It was his art director's business, he thought, to get him good ideas for good drawings and then to see that they were properly and speedily executed.

Anything less than this was sickening failure in the eyes of Mr. Summerfield, and he was not at all bashful in expressing himself. As a matter of fact, he was at times terribly brutal. "Why the hell do you show me a thing like that?" he once

exclaimed to Freeman. "Jesus Christ; I could hire an ashman
and get better results. Why, God damn it, look at the drawing of the arm of that woman. Look at her ear. Whose going
to take a thing like that? It's tame! It's punk! It's a joke!
What sort of cattle have you got out there working for you,
anyhow? Why, if the Summerfield Advertising Company can't
do better than that I might as well shut up the place and go
fishing. We'll be a joke in six weeks. Don't try to hand me
any such God damned tripe as that, Freeman. You know better. You ought to know our advertisers wouldn't stand for
anything like that. Wake up! I'm paying you five thousand
a year. How do you expect I'm going to get my money back
out of any such arrangement as that? You're simply wasting
my money and your time letting a man draw a thing like that.
Hell!!"

The art director, whoever he was, having been by degrees
initiated into the brutalities of the situation, and having—by reason of the time he had been employed and the privileges he had
permitted himself on account of his comfortable and probably
never before experienced salary—sold himself into bondage to
his now fancied necessities, was usually humble and tractable
under the most galling fire. Where could he go and get five
thousand dollars a year for his services? How could he live at
the rate he was living if he lost this place? Art directorships
were not numerous. Men who could fill them fairly acceptably
were not impossible to find. If he thought at all and was not
a heaven-born genius serene in the knowledge of his God-
given powers, he was very apt to hesitate, to worry, to be humble
and to endure a good deal. Most men under similar circumstances do the same thing. They think before they fling back
into the teeth of their oppressors some of the slurs and brutal
characterizations which so frequently issue therefrom. Most
men do. Besides there is almost always a high percentage of
truth in the charges made. Usually the storm is for the better-
ment of mankind. Mr. Summerfield knew this. He knew also
the yoke of poverty and the bondage of fear which most if not
all his men were under. He had no compunctions about using
these weapons, much as a strong man might use a club. He had
had a hard life himself. No one had sympathized with him
very much. Besides you couldn't sympathize and succeed. Better look the facts in the face, deal only with infinite capacity,
roughly weed out the incompetents and proceed along the line
of least resistance, in so far as your powerful enemies were
concerned. Men might theorize and theorize until the crack

of doom, but this was the way the thing had to be done and this
was the way he preferred to do it.

Eugene had never heard of any of these facts in connection
with the Summerfield Company. The idea had been flung at
him so quickly he had no time to think, and besides if he had
had time it would have made no difference. A little experience
of life had taught him as it teaches everyone else to mistrust
rumor. He had applied for the place on hearing and he was
hoping to get it. At noon the day following his visit to Mr.
Baker Bates, the latter was speaking for him to Mr. Summerfield, but only very casually.

"Say," he asked, quite apropos of nothing apparently, for
they were discussing the chances of his introducing his product
into South America, "do you ever have need of an art director
over in your place?"

"Occasionally," replied Summerfield guardedly, for his impression was that Mr. Baker Bates knew very little of art directors or anything else in connection with the art side of advertising life. He might have heard of his present need and be
trying to palm off some friend of his, an incompetent, of course,
on him. "What makes you ask?"

"Why, Hudson Dula, the manager of the Triple Lithographic Company, was telling me of a man who is connected
with the *World* who might make a good one for you. I know
something of him. He painted some rather remarkable views
of New York and Paris here a few years ago. Dula tells me
they were very good."

"Is he young?" interrupted Summerfield, calculating.

"Yes, comparatively. Thirty-one or two, I should say."

"And he wants to be an art director, does he. Where is he?"

"He's down on the *World,* and I understand he wants to get
out of there. I heard you say last year that you were looking
for a man, and I thought this might interest you."

"What's he doing down on the *World?*"

"He's been sick, I understand, and is just getting on his
feet again."

The explanation sounded sincere enough to Summerfield.

"What's his name?" he asked.

"Witla, Eugene Witla. He had an exhibition at one of
the galleries here a few years ago."

"I'm afraid of these regular high-brow artists," observed Summerfield suspiciously. "They're usually so set up about their
art that there's no living with them. I have to have someone
with hard, practical sense in my work. Someone that isn't a

plain damn fool. He has to be a good manager—a good administrator, mere talent for drawing won't do—though he has to have that, or know it when he sees it. You might send this fellow around sometime if you know him. I wouldn't mind looking at him. I may need a man pretty soon. I'm thinking of making certain changes."

"If I see him I will," said Baker indifferently and dropped the matter. Summerfield, however, for some psychological reason was impressed with the name. Where had he heard it? Somewhere apparently. Perhaps he had better find out something about him.

"If you send him you'd better give him a letter of introduction," he added thoughtfully, before Bates should have forgotten the matter. "So many people try to get in to see me, and I may forget."

Baker knew at once that Summerfield wished to look at Witla. He dictated a letter of introduction that afternoon to his stenographer and mailed it to Eugene.

"I find Mr. Summerfield apparently disposed to see you," he wrote. "You had better go and see him if you are interested. Present this letter. Very truly yours."

Eugene looked at it with astonishment and a sense of foregoneness so far as what was to follow. Fate was fixing this for him. He was going to get it. How strange life was! Here he was down on the *World* working for fifty dollars a week, and suddenly an art directorship, a thing he had thought of for years, was coming to him out of nowhere! Then he decided to telephone Mr. Daniel Summerfield, saying that he had a letter from Mr. Baker Bates and asking when he could see him. Later he decided to waste no time, but to present the letter direct without phoning. At three in the afternoon he received permission from Benedict to be away from the office between three and five, and at three-thirty he was in the anteroom of the general offices of the Summerfield Advertising Company, waiting for a much desired permission to enter.

CHAPTER XXXIII

WHEN Eugene called, Mr. Daniel C. Summerfield was in no great rush about any particular matter, but he had decided in this case as he had in many others that it was very important that anyone who wanted anything from him should be made to wait. Eugene was made to wait a solid hour before he was informed by an underling that he was very sorry but that other matters had so detained Mr. Summerfield that it was now impossible for him to see him at all this day, but that tomorrow at twelve he would be glad to see him. Eugene was finally admitted on the morrow, however, and then, at the first glance, Mr. Summerfield liked him. "A man of intelligence," he thought, as he leaned back in his chair and stared at him. "A man of force. Young still, wide-eyed, quick, clean looking. Perhaps I have found someone in this man who will make a good art director." He smiled, for Summerfield was always good-natured in his opening relationships—usually so in all of them, and took most people (his employees and prospective employees particularly) with an air of superior but genial condescension.

"Sit down! Sit down!" he exclaimed cheerfully and Eugene did so, looking about at the handsomely decorated walls, the floor which was laid with a wide, soft, light brown rug, and the mahogany desk, flat-topped, glass covered, on which lay handsome ornaments of silver, ivory and bronze. This man looked so keen, so dynamic, like a polished Japanese carving, hard and smooth.

"Now tell me all about yourself," began Summerfield. "Where do you come from? Who are you? What have you done?"

"Hold! Hold!" said Eugene easily and tolerantly. "Not so fast. My history isn't so much. The short and simple annals of the poor. I'll tell you in two or three sentences."

Summerfield was a little taken back at this abruptness which was generated by his own attitude; still he liked it. This was something new to him. His applicant wasn't frightened or apparently even nervous so far as he could judge. "He is droll," he thought, "sufficiently so—a man who has seen a number of things evidently. He is easy in manner, too, and kindly."

"Well," he said smilingly, for Eugene's slowness appealed to him. His humor was something new in art directors. So far

413

as he could recall, his predecessors had never had any to speak of.

"Well, I'm an artist," said Eugene, "working on the *World*. Let's hope that don't militate against me very much."

"It don't," said Summerfield.

"And I want to become an art director because I think I'd make a good one."

"Why?" asked Summerfield, his even teeth showing amiably.

"Well, because I like to manage men, or I think I do. And they take to me."

"You know that?"

"I do. In the next place I know too much about art to want to do the little things that I'm doing. I can do bigger things."

"I like that also," applauded Summerfield. He was thinking that Eugene was nice and good looking, a little pale and thin to be wholly forceful, perhaps, he wasn't sure. His hair a little too long. His manner, perhaps, a bit too deliberate. Still he was nice. Why did he wear a soft hat? Why did artists always insist on wearing soft hats, most of them? It was so ridiculous, so unbusinesslike.

"How much do you get?" he added, "if it's a fair question."

"Less than I'm worth," said Eugene. "Only fifty dollars. But I took it as a sort of health cure. I had a nervous breakdown several years ago—better now, as Mulvaney used to say—and I don't want to stay at that. I'm an art director by temperament, or I think I am. Anyhow, here I am."

"You mean," said Summerfield, "you never ran an art department before?"

"Never."

"Know anything about advertising?"

"I used to think so."

"How long ago was that?"

"When I worked on the Alexandria, Illinois, *Daily Appeal*." Summerfield smiled. He couldn't help it.

"That's almost as important as the Wickham *Union,* I fancy. It sounds as if it might have the same wide influence."

"Oh, much more, much more," returned Eugene quietly. "The Alexandria *Appeal* had the largest exclusively country circulation of any county south of the Sangamon."

"I see! I see!" replied Summerfield good-humoredly. "It's all day with the Wickham *Union*. Well, how was it you came to change your mind?"

"Well, I got a few years older for one thing," said Eugene. "And then I decided that I was cut out to be the greatest living artist, and then I came to New York, and in the excitement I almost lost the idea."

"I see."

"But I have it again, thank heaven, tied up back of the house, and here I am."

"Well, Witla, to tell you the truth you don't look like a real live, every day, sure-enough art director, but you might make good. You're not quite art-y enough according to the standards that prevail around this office. Still I might be willing to take one gosh-awful chance. I suppose if I do I'll get stung as usual, but I've been stung so often that I ought to be used to it by now. I feel sort of spotted at times from the hornets I've hired in the past. But, be that as it may, what do you think you could do with a real live art directorship if you had it?"

Eugene mused. This persiflage entertained him. He thought Summerfield would hire him now that they were together.

"Oh, I'd draw my salary first and then I'd see that I had the proper system of approach so that any one who came to see me would think I was the King of England, and then I'd——"

"I was really busy yesterday," interpolated Summerfield apologetically.

"I'm satisfied of that," replied Eugene gaily. "And finally I might condescend, if I were coaxed enough, to do a little work."

This speech at once irritated and amused Mr. Summerfield. He liked a man of spirit. You could do something with someone who wasn't afraid, even if he didn't know so much to begin with. And Eugene knew a good deal, he fancied. Besides, his talk was precisely in his own sarcastic, semi-humorous vein. Coming from Eugene it did not sound so hard as it would have coming from himself, but it had his own gay, bantering attitude of mind in it. He believed Eugene could make good. He wanted to try him, instanter, anyhow.

"Well, I'll tell you what, Witla," he finally observed. "I don't know whether you can run this thing or not—the probabilities are all against you as I have said, but you seem to have some ideas or what might be made some under my direction, and I think I'll give you a chance. Mind you, I haven't much confidence. My personal likes usually prove very fatal to me. Still, you're here, and I like your looks and I haven't seen anyone else, and so——"

"Thanks," said Eugene.

"Don't thank me. You have a hard job ahead of you if I

take you. It's no child's play. You'd better come with me
first and look over the place," and he led the way out into the
great central room where, because it was still noon time, there
were few people working, but where one could see just how
imposing this business really was.

"Seventy-two stenographers, book-keepers, canvassers and
writers and trade-aid people at their desks," he observed with
an easy wave of his hand, and moved on into the art department, which was in another wing of the building where a north
and east light could be secured. "Here's where you come in,"
he observed, throwing open the door where thirty-two artists'
desks and easels were ranged. Eugene was astonished.

"You don't employ that many, do you?" he asked interestedly.
Most of the men were out to lunch.

"From twenty to twenty-five all the time, sometimes more,"
he said. "Some on the outside. It depends on the condition
of business."

"And how much do you pay them, as a rule?"

"Well, that depends. I think I'll give you seventy-five
dollars a week to begin with, if we come to an understanding.
If you make good I'll make it a hundred dollars a week inside
of three months. It all depends. The others we don't pay so
much. The business manager can tell you."

Eugene noticed the evasion. His eyes narrowed. Still there
was a good chance here. Seventy-five dollars was considerably
better than fifty and it might lead to more. He would be his
own boss—a man of some consequence. He could not help
stiffening with pride a little as he looked at the room which
Summerfield pointed out to him as his own if he came—a room
where a large, highly polished oak desk was placed and where
some of the Summerfield Advertising Company's art products
were hung on the walls. There was a nice rug on the floor
and some leather-backed chairs.

"Here's where you will be if you come here," said Summerfield.

Eugene gazed round. Certainly life was looking up. How
was he to get this place? On what did it depend? His mind
was running forward to various improvements in his affairs, a
better apartment for Angela, better clothes for her, more entertainment for both of them, freedom from worry over the future;
for a little bank account would soon result from a place like
this.

"Do you do much business a year?" Eugene asked curiously.

"Oh, about two million dollars' worth."

And you have to make drawings for every ad?"

"Exactly, not one but six or eight sometimes. It depends upon the ability of the art director. If he does his work right I save money."

Eugene saw the point.

"What became of the other man?" he asked, noting the name of Older Freeman on the door.

"Oh, he quit," said Summerville, "or rather he saw what was coming and got out of the way. He was no good. He was too weak. He was turning out work here which was a joke—some things had to be done over eight and nine times."

Eugene discovered the wrath and difficulties and opposition which went with this. Summerfield was a hard man, plainly. He might smile and joke now, but anyone who took that chair would hear from him constantly. For a moment Eugene felt as though he could not do it, as though he had better not try it, and then he thought, "Why shouldn't I? It can't hurt me. If worst comes to worst, I have my art to fall back on."

"Well, so it goes," he said. "If I don't make good, the door for mine, I suppose?"

"No, no, nothing so easy," chuckled Summerfield; "the coal chute."

Eugene noticed that he champed his teeth like a nervous horse, and that he seemed fairly to radiate waves of energy. For himself he winced the least bit. This was a grim, fighting atmosphere he was coming into. He would have to fight for his life here—no doubt of that.

"Now," said Summerfield, when they were strolling back to his own office. "I'll tell you what you might do. I have two propositions, one from the Sand Perfume Company and another from the American Crystal Sugar Refining Company which may mean big contracts for me if I can present them the right line of ideas for advertising. They want to advertise. The Sand Company wants suggestions for bottles, labels, car ads, newspaper ads, posters, and so on. The American Crystal Company wants to sell its sugar in small packages, powdered, grained, cubed, hexagoned. We want package forms, labels, posters ads, and so on for that. It's a question of how much novelty, simplicity and force we can put in the smallest possible space. Now I depend upon my art director to tell me something about these things. I don't expect him to do everything. I'm here and I'll help him. I have men in the trade aid department out there who are wonders at making suggestions along this line, but the art director is supposed to help.

He's the man who is supposed to have the taste and can execute the proposition in its last form. Now suppose you take these two ideas and see what you can do with them. Bring me some suggestions. If they suit me and I think you have the right note, I'll hire you. If not, well then I won't, and no harm done. Is that all right?"

"That's all right," said Eugene.

Mr. Summerfield handed him a bundle of papers, catalogues, prospectuses, communications. "You can look these over if you want to. Take them along and then bring them back."

Eugene rose.

"I'd like to have two or three days for this," he said. "It's a new proposition to me. I think I can give you some ideas —I'm not sure. Anyhow, I'd like to try."

"Go ahead! Go ahead!" said Summerfield, "the more the merrier. And I'll see you any time you're ready. I have a man out there—Freeman's assistant—who's running things for me temporarily. Here's luck," and he waved his hand indifferently.

Eugene went out. Was there ever such a man, so hard, so cold, so practical! It was a new note to him. He was simply astonished, largely because he was inexperienced. He had not yet gone up against the business world as those who try to do anything in a big way commercially must. This man was getting on his nerves already, making him feel that he had a tremendous problem before him, making him think that the quiet realms of art were merely the backwaters of oblivion. Those who did anything, who were out in the front row of effort, were fighters such as this man was, raw products of the soil, ruthless, superior, indifferent. If only he could be that way, he thought. If he could be strong, defiant, commanding, what a thing it would be. Not to wince, not to quail, but to stand up firm, square to the world and make people obey. Oh, what a splendid vision of empire was here before him.

CHAPTER XXXIV

THE designs or suggestions which Eugene offered his prospective employer for the advertising of the products of M. Sand et Cie and the American Crystal Sugar Refining Company, were peculiar. As has been indicated, Eugene had one of those large, effervescent intelligences which when he was in good physical condition fairly bubbled ideas. His imaginings, without any effort on his part, naturally took all forms and shapes. The call of Mr. Summerfield was for street car cards, posters and newspaper ads of various sizes, and what he wanted Eugene specifically to supply was not so much the lettering or rather wording of the ads as it was their artistic form and illustrative point: what one particular suggestion in the form of a drawing or design could be made in each case which would arrest public attention. Eugene went home and took the sugar proposition under consideration first. He did not say anything of what he was really doing to Angela, because he did not want to disappoint her. He pretended that he was making sketches which he might offer to some company for a little money and because it amused him. By the light of his green shaded working lamp at home he sketched designs of hands holding squares of sugar, either in the fingers or by silver and gold sugar tongs, urns piled high with crystalline concoctions, a blue and gold after-dinner cup with one lump of the new form on the side against a section of snow white table cloth, and things of that character. He worked rapidly and with ease until he had some thirty-five suggestions on this one proposition alone, and then he turned his attention to the matter of the perfumery.

His first thought was that he did not know all the designs of the company's bottles, but he originated peculiar and delightful shapes of his own, some of which were afterwards adopted by the company. He designed boxes and labels to amuse himself and then made various still-life compositions such as a box, a bottle, a dainty handkerchief and a small white hand all showing in a row. His mind slipped to the manufacture of perfume, the growing of flowers, the gathering of blossoms, the type of girls and men that might possibly be employed, and then he hurried to the great public library the next day to see if he could find a book or magazine article which would tell him something about it. He found this and several articles on sugar growing and refining which gave him new ideas in that direction. He decided that in each case he would put a beautifully designed bottle of perfume or a handsome package of sugar, say, in the upper right or lower left-hand corner of the design, and then for the rest show some scene in the process of its manufacture. He began to think of men who could carry out his ideas brilliantly if they were not already on his staff, letterers, character artists, men with a keen sense of color combination whom he might possibly hire cheaply. He thought of Jerry Mathews of the old Chicago *Globe* days—where was he now? —and Philip Shotmeyer, who would be almost ideal to work under his direction, for he was a splendid letterer, and Henry Hare, still of the *World,* with whom he had frequently talked on the subject of ads and posters. Then there was young Morgenbau, who was a most excellent character man, looking to him for some opportunity, and eight or ten men whose work he had admired in the magazines—the best known ones. He decided first to see what could be done with the staff that he had, and then to eliminate and fill in as rapidly as possible until he had a capable working group. He had already caught by contact with Summerfield some of that eager personage's ruthlessness and began to manifest it in his own attitude. He was most impressionable to things advantageous to himself, and this chance to rise to a higher level out of the slough of poverty in which he had so greatly suffered nerved him to the utmost effort. In two days he had a most impressive mass of material to show his prospective employer, and he returned to his presence with considerable confidence. The latter looked over his ideas carefully and then began to warm to his attitude of mind.

"I should say!" he said generously, "there's some life to this stuff. I can see you getting the five thousand a year all right if you keep on. You're a little new, but you've caught the drift." And he sat down to show him where some improvements from a practical point of view could be made.

"Now, professor," he said finally when he was satisfied that Eugene was the man he wanted, "you and I might as well call this a deal. It's pretty plain to me that you've got something that I want. Some of these things are fine. I don't know how you're going to make out as a master of men, but you might as well take that desk out there and we'll begin right now. I wish you luck. I really do. You're a live wire, I think."

Eugene thrilled with satisfaction. This was the result he wanted. No half-hearted commendation, but enthusiastic praise.

He must have it. He always felt that he could command it. People naturally ran after him. He was getting used to it by now—taking it as a matter of course. If he hadn't broken down, curse the luck, think where he could have been today. He had lost five years and he was not quite well yet, but thank God he was getting steadily better, and he would try and hold himself in check from now on. The world demanded it.

He went out with Summerfield into the art room and was there introduced by him to the various men employed. "Mr. Davis, Mr. Witla; Mr. Hart, Mr. Witla; Mr. Clemens, Mr. Witla," so it went, and the staff was soon aware of who he was. Summerfield then took him into the next room and introduced him to the various heads of departments, the business manager who fixed his and his artists' salaries, the cashier who paid him, the manager of the ad writing department, the manager of the trade aid department, and the head of the stenographic department, a woman. Eugene was a little disgusted with what he considered the crassness of these people. After the quality of the art atmosphere in which he had moved these people seemed to him somewhat raw and voracious, like fish. They had no refinement. Their looks and manners were unduly aggressive. He resented particularly the fact that one canvasser with whom he shook hands wore a bright red tie and had on yellow shoes. The insistence on department store models for suits and floor-walker manners pained him.

"To hell with such cattle," he thought, but on the surface he smiled and shook hands and said how glad he would be to work with them. Finally when all the introductions were over he went back to his own department, to take up the work which rushed through here like a living stream, pellmell. His own staff was, of course, much more agreeable to him. These artists who worked for him interested him, for they were as he suspected men very much like himself, in poor health probably, or down on their luck and compelled to do this. He called for his assistant, Mr. Davis, whom Summerfield had introduced to him as such, and asked him to let him see how the work stood.

"Have you a schedule of the work in hand?" he asked easily.

"Yes, sir," said his new attendant.

"Let me see it."

The latter brought what he called his order book and showed him just how things worked. Each particular piece of work, or order as it was called, was given a number when it came in, the time of its entry marked on the slip, the name of the artist to whom it was assigned, the time taken to execute it, and so forth. If one artist only put two hours on it and another took it and put four, this was noted. If the first drawing was a failure and a second begun, the records would show all, the slips and errors of the office as well as its speed and capacity. Eugene perceived that he must see to it that his men did not make many mistakes.

After this order book had been carefully inspected by him, he rose and strolled about among the men to see how they were getting on. He wanted to familiarize himself at once with the styles and methods of his men. Some were working on clothing ads, some on designs illustrative of the beef industry, some on a railroad travel series for the street cars, and so forth. Eugene bent over each one graciously, for he wanted to make friends with these people and win their confidence. He knew from experience how sensitive artists were—how they could be bound by feelings of good fellowship. He had a soft, easy, smiling manner which he hoped would smooth his way for him. He leaned over this man's shoulder and that asking what the point was, how long a piece of work of that character ought to take, suggesting where a man appeared to be in doubt what he thought would be advisable. He was not at all certain of himself—this line of work being so new—but he was hopeful and eager. It was a fine sensation, this being a boss, if one could only triumph at it. He hoped to help these men to help themselves; to make them make good in ways which would bring them and him more money. He wanted more money—that five thousand, no less.

"I think you have the right idea there," he said to one pale, anæmic worker who looked as though he might have a lot of talent.

The man, whose name was Dillon, responded to the soothing, caressing tone of his voice. He liked Eugene's appearance, though he was not at all disposed to pass favorable judgment as yet. It was already rumored that he had had an exceptional career as an artist. Summerfield had attended to that. He looked up and smiled and said, "Do you think so?"

"I certainly do," said Eugene cheerfully. "Try a touch of yellow next to that blue. See if you don't like that."

The artist did as requested and squinted at it narrowly. "It helps it a lot, don't it," he observed, as though it were his own.

"It certainly does," said Eugene, "that's a good idea," and somehow Dillon felt as though he had thought of it. Inside of twenty minutes the whole staff was agreeing with itself that he was a nice man to all outward appearances and that he might make good. He appeared to be so sure. They little knew how perturbed he was inwardly, how anxious he was to get all the threads of this in his hand and to see that everything came to an ideal fruition. He dreaded the hour when he might have something to contend with which was not quite right.

Days passed at this new work and then weeks, and by degrees he grew moderately sure of himself and comparatively easy in his seat, though he realized that he had not stepped into a bed of roses. He found this a most tempestuous office to work in, for Summerfield was, as he expressed it, "on the job" early and late, and tireless in his insistence and enthusiasm. He came down from his residence in the upper portion of the city at eight-fifty in the morning and remained almost invariably until six-thirty and seven and not infrequently until eight and nine in the evening. He had the inconsiderate habit of keeping such of his staff as happened to be working upon the thing in which he was interested until all hours of the night; sometimes transferring his deliberations to his own home and that without dinner or the proffer of it to those whom he made to work. He would talk advertising with one big merchant or another until it was time to go home, and would then call in the weary members of his staff before they had time to escape and begin a long and important discussion of something he wanted done. At times, when anything went wrong, he would fly into an insane fury, rave and curse and finally, perhaps, discharge the one who was really not to blame. There were no end of labored and irritating conferences in which hard words and sarcastic references would fly about, for he had no respect for the ability or personality of anyone who worked for him. They were all more or less machines in his estimation and rather poorly constructed ones at that. Their ideas were not good enough unless for the time being they happened to be new, or as in Eugene's case displaying pronounced talent.

He could not fathom Eugene so readily, for he had never met anyone of his kind. He was looking closely in his case, as he was in that of all the others, to see if he could not find some weakness in his ideas. He had a gleaming, insistent, almost demoniac eye, a habit of chewing incessantly and even violently the stub end of a cigar, the habit of twitching, getting up and walking about, stirring things on his desk, doing anything and everything to give his restless, generative energy a chance to escape.

"Now, professor," he would say when Eugene came in and

seated himself quietly and unobtrusively in some corner, "we have a very difficult thing here to solve today. I want to know what you think could be done in such and such a case," describing a particular condition.

Eugene would brace himself up and begin to consider, but rumination was not what Summerfield wanted from anyone.

"Well, professor! well! well!" he would exclaim.

Eugene would stir irritably. This was so embarrassing—in a way so degrading to him.

"Come to life, professor," Summerfield would go on. He seemed to have concluded long before that the gad was the most effective commercial weapon.

Eugene would then make some polite suggestion, wishing instead that he could tell him to go to the devil, but that was not the end of it. Before all the old writers, canvassers, trade aid men—sometimes one or two of his own artists who might be working upon the particular task in question, he would exclaim: "Lord! what a poor suggestion!" or "can't you do any better than that, professor?" or "good heavens, I have three or four ideas better than that myself." The best he would ever say in conference was, "Well, there may be something in that," though privately, afterwards, he might possibly express great pleasure. Past achievements counted for nothing; that was so plain. One might bring in gold and silver all day long; the next day there must be more gold and silver and in larger quantities. There was no end to the man's appetite. There was no limit to the speed at which he wished to drive his men. There was no limit to the venomous commercial idea as an idea. Summerfield set an example of nagging and irritating insistence, and he urged all his employees to the same policy. The result was a bear-garden, a den of prize-fighters, liars, cut-throats and thieves in which every man was for himself openly and avowedly and the devil take the hindmost.

CHAPTER XXXV

STILL time went by, and although things did not improve very much in his office over the standards which he saw prevailing when he came there, he was obviously getting things much better arranged in his private life. In the first place Angela's attitude was getting much better. The old agony which had possessed her in the days when he was acting so badly had modified as day by day she saw him working and conducting himself with reasonable circumspection. She did not trust him as yet. She was not sure that he had utterly broken with Carlotta Wilson (she had never found out who his paramour was), but all the evidence seemed to attest it. There was a telephone down stairs in a drug store by which, during his days on the *World,* Angela would call him up at any time, and whenever she had called him up he was always in the office. He seemed to have plenty of time to take her to the theatre if she wished to go, and to have no especial desire to avoid her company. He had once told her frankly that he did not propose to pretend to love her any more, though he did care for her, and this frightened her. In spite of her wrath and suffering she cared for him, and she believed that he still sympathized with her and might come to care for her again—that he ought to.

She decided to play the rôle of the affectionate wife whether it was true or not, and to hug and kiss him and fuss over him if he would let her, just as though nothing had happened. Eugene did not understand this. He did not see how Angela could still love him. He thought she must hate him, having such just grounds, for having by dint of hard work and absence come out of his vast excitement about Carlotta he was beginning to feel that he had done her a terrific injustice and to wish to make amends. He did not want to love her, he did not feel that he could, but he was perfectly willing to behave himself, to try to earn a good living, to take her to theatre and opera as opportunity permitted, and to build up and renew a social relationship with others which should act as a substitute for love. He was beginning to think that there was no honest or happy solution to any affair of the heart in the world. Most people so far as he could see were unhappily married. It seemed to be the lot of mankind to make mistakes in its matrimonial selections. He was probably no more unhappy than many others. Let the world wag as it would for a time. He would try to make some money now, and restore himself in the eyes of the world. Later, life might bring him something—who could tell?

In the next place their financial condition, even before he left the *World,* was so much better than it had been. By dint of saving and scraping, refusing to increase their expenses more than was absolutely necessary, Angela had succeeded by the time he left the *World* in laying by over one thousand dollars, and since then it had gone up to three thousand. They had relaxed sufficiently so that now they were wearing reasonably good clothes, were going out and receiving company regularly. It was not possible in their little apartment which they still occupied to entertain more than three or four at the outside, and two was all that Angela ever cared to consider as either pleasurable or comfortable; but they entertained this number frequently. There were some slight recoveries of friendship and of the old life—Hudson Dula, Jerry Mathews, who had moved to Newark; William McConnell, Philip Shotmeyer. MacHugh and Smite were away, one painting in Nova Scotia, the other working in Chicago. As for the old art crowd, socialists and radicals included, Eugene attempted to avoid them as much as possible. He knew nothing of the present whereabouts of Miriam Finch and Norma Whitmore. Of Christina Channing he heard much, for she was singing in Grand Opera, her pictures displayed in the paper and upon the billboards. There were many new friends, principally young newspaper artists like Adolph Morgenbau, who took to Eugene and were in a sense his disciples.

Angela's relations showed up from time to time, among them David Blue, now a sub-lieutenant in the army, with all the army officer's pride of place and station. There were women friends of Angela's for whom Eugene cared little—Mrs. Desmas, the wife of the furniture manufacturer at Riverwood, from whom they had rented their four rooms there; Mrs. Wertheim, the wife of the multimillionaire, to whom M. Charles had introduced them; Mrs. Link, the wife of the West Point army captain who had come to the old Washington Square studio with Marietta and who was now stationed at Fort Hamilton in Brooklyn; and a Mrs. Juergens, living in a neighboring apartment. As long as they were very poor, Angela was very careful how she revived acquaintances; but when they began to have a little money she decided that she might indulge her predilection and so make life less lonesome for herself. She had always been anxious to build up solid social connections for Eugene, but as yet she did not see how it was to be done.

When Eugene's new connection with the Summerfield company was consummated, Angela was greatly astonished and rather delighted to think that if he had to work in this practical field for long it was to be under such comforting auspices—that is, as a superior and not as an underling. Long ago she had come to feel that Eugene would never make any money in a commercial way. To see him mounting in this manner was curious, but not wholly reassuring. They must save money; that was her one cry. They had to move soon, that was very plain, but they mustn't spend any more than they had to. She delayed until the attitude of Summerfield, upon an accidental visit to their flat, made it commercially advisable.

Summerfield was a great admirer of Eugene's artistic ability. He had never seen any of his pictures, but he was rather keen to, and once when Eugene told him that they were still on display, one or two of them at Pottle Frères, Jacob Bergman's and Henry LaRue's, he decided to visit these places, but put it off. One night when he was riding uptown on the L road with Eugene he decided because he was in a vagrom mood to accompany him home and see his pictures there. Eugene did not want this. He was chagrined to be compelled to take him into their very little apartment, but there was apparently no way of escaping it. He tried to persuade him to visit Pottle Frères instead, where one picture was still on view, but Summerfield would none of that.

"I don't like you to see this place," finally he said apologetically, as they were going up the steps of the five-story apartment house. "We are going to get out of here pretty soon. I came here when I worked on the road."

Summerfield looked about at the poor neighborhood, the inlet of a canal some two blocks east where a series of black coal pockets were and to the north where there was flat open country and a railroad yard.

"Why, that's all right," he said, in his direct, practical way. "It doesn't make any difference to me. It does to you, though, Witla. You know, I believe in spending money, everybody spending money. Nobody gets anywhere by saving anything. Pay out! Pay out—that's the idea. I found that out for myself long ago. You'd better move when you get a chance soon and surround yourself with clever people."

Eugene considered this the easy talk of a man who was successful and lucky, but he still thought there was much in it. Summerfield came in and viewed the pictures. He liked them, and he liked Angela, though he wondered how Eugene ever came to marry her. She was such a quiet little home body. Eugene looked more like a Bohemian or a club man now that he had been worked upon by Summerfield. The soft hat had long since been discarded for a stiff derby, and Eugene's clothes were of the most practical business type he could find. He looked more like a young merchant than an artist. Summerfield invited them over to dinner at his house, refusing to stay to dinner here, and went his way.

Before long, because of his advice they moved. They had practically four thousand by now, and because of his salary Angela figured that they could increase their living expenses to say two thousand five hundred or even three thousand dollars. She wanted Eugene to save two thousand each year against the day when he should decide to return to art. They sought about together Saturday afternoons and Sundays and finally found a charming apartment in Central Park West overlooking the park, where they thought they could live and entertain beautifully. It had a large dining-room and living-room which when the table was cleared away formed one great room. There was a handsomely equipped bathroom, a nice kitchen with ample pantry, three bedrooms, one of which Angela turned into a sewing room, and a square hall or entry which answered as a temporary reception room. There were plenty of closets, gas and electricity, elevator service with nicely uniformed elevator men, and a house telephone. It was very different from their last place, where they only had a long dark hall, stairways to climb, gas only, and no phone. The neighborhood, too, was so much better. Here were automobiles and people walking in the park or promenading on a Sunday afternoon, and obsequious consideration or polite indifference to your affairs from everyone who had anything to do with you.

"Well, the tide is certainly turning," said Eugene, as they entered it the first day.

He had the apartment redecorated in white and delft-blue and dark blue, getting a set of library and dining-room furniture in imitation rosewood. He bought a few choice pictures which he had seen at various exhibitions to mix with his own, and set a cut-glass bowl in the ceiling where formerly the commonplace chandelier had been. There were books enough, accumulated during a period of years, to fill the attractive white bookcase with its lead-paned doors. Attractive sets of bedroom furniture in bird's-eye maple and white enamel were secured, and the whole apartment given a very cosy and tasteful appearance. A piano was purchased outright and dinner and breakfast sets of Haviland china. There were many other dainty accessories, such as rugs, curtains, portières, and so forth, the hanging of which Angela supervised. Here they settled down to a comparatively new and attractive life.

Angela had never really forgiven him his indiscretions of the past, his radical brutality in the last instance, but she was not holding them up insistently against him. There were occasional scenes even yet, the echoes of a far-off storm; but as long as they were making money and friends were beginning to come back she did not propose to quarrel. Eugene was very considerate. He was very, very hard-working. Why should she nag him? He would sit by a window overlooking the park at night and toil over his sketches and ideas until midnight. He was up and dressed by seven, down to his office by eight-thirty, out to lunch at one or later, and only back home at eight or nine o'clock at night. Sometimes Angela would be cross with him for this, sometimes rail at Mr. Summerfield for an inhuman brute, but seeing that the apartment was so lovely and that Eugene was getting along so well, how could she quarrel? It was for her benefit as much as for his that he appeared to be working. He did not think about spending money. He did not seem to care. He would work, work, work, until she actually felt sorry for him.

"Certainly Mr. Summerfield ought to like you," she said to him one day, half in compliment, half in a rage at a man who would exact so much from him. "You're valuable enough to him. I never saw a man who could work like you can. Don't you ever want to stop?"

"Don't bother about me, Angelface," he said. "I have to do it. I don't mind. It's better than walking the streets and wondering how I'm going to get along"—and he fell to his ideas again.

Angela shook her head. Poor Eugene! If ever a man deserved success for working, he certainly did. And he was really getting nice again—getting conventional. Perhaps it was because he was getting a little older. It might turn out that he would become a splendid man, after all.

CHAPTER XXXVI

THERE came a time, however, when all this excitement and wrath and quarreling began to unnerve Eugene and to make him feel that he could not indefinitely stand the strain. After all, his was the artistic temperament, not that of a commercial or financial genius. He was too nervous and restless. For one thing he was first astonished, then amused, then embittered by the continual travesty on justice, truth, beauty, sympathy, which he saw enacted before his eyes. Life stripped of its illusion and its seeming becomes a rather deadly thing to contemplate. Because of the ruthless, insistent, inconsiderate attitude of this employer, all the employees of this place followed his example, and there was neither kindness nor courtesy—nor even raw justice anywhere. Eugene was compelled to see himself looked upon from the beginning, not so much by his own staff as by the other employees of the company, as a man who could not last long. He was disliked forsooth because Summerfield displayed some liking for him, and because his manners did not coincide exactly with the prevailing standard of the office. Summerfield did not intend to allow his interest in Eugene to infringe in any way upon his commercial exactions, but this was not enough to save or aid Eugene in any way. The others disliked him, some because he was a true artist to begin with, because of his rather distant air, and because in spite of himself he could not take them all as seriously as he should.

Most of them seemed little mannikins to him—little second, third, and fourth editions or copies of Summerfield. They all copied that worthy's insistent air. They all attempted to imitate his briskness. Like children, they were inclined to try to imitate his bitter persiflage and be smart; and they demanded, as he said they should, the last ounce of consideration and duty from their neighbors. Eugene was too much of a philosopher not to take much of this with a grain of salt, but after all his position depended on his activity and his ability to get results, and it was a pity, he thought, that he could expect neither courtesy nor favor from anyone. Departmental chiefs stormed his room daily, demanding this, that, and the other work immediately. Artists complained that they were not getting enough pay, the business manager railed because expenses were not kept low, saying that Eugene might be an improvement in the matter of the quality of the results obtained and the speed of execution, but that he was lavish in his expenditure. Others cursed openly in his presence at times, and about him to his employer, alleging that the execution of certain ideas was rotten, or that certain work was delayed, or that he was slow or discourteous. There was little in these things, as Summerfield well knew from watching Eugene, but he was too much a lover of quarrels and excitement as being productive of the best results in the long run to wish to interfere. Eugene was soon accused of delaying work generally, of having incompetent men (which was true), of being slow, of being an artistic snob. He stood it all calmly because of his recent experience with poverty, but he was determined to fight ultimately. He was no longer, or at least not going to be, he thought, the ambling, cowardly, dreaming Witla he had been. He was going to stand up, and he did begin to.

"Remember, you are the last word here, Witla," Summerfield had told him on one occasion. "If anything goes wrong here, you're to blame. Don't make any mistakes. Don't let anyone accuse you falsely. Don't run to me. I won't help you."

It was such a ruthless attitude that it shocked Eugene into an attitude of defiance. In time he thought he had become a hardened and a changed man—aggressive, contentious, bitter.

"They can all go to hell!" he said one day to Summerfield, after a terrific row about some delayed pictures, in which one man who was animated by personal animosity more than anything else had said hard things about him. "The thing that's been stated here isn't so. My work is up to and beyond the mark. This individual here"—pointing to the man in question—"simply doesn't like me. The next time he comes into my room nosing about I'll throw him out. He's a damned fakir, and you know it. He lied here today, and you know that."

"Good for you, Witla!" exclaimed Summerfield joyously. The idea of a fighting attitude on Eugene's part pleased him. "You're coming to life. You'll get somewhere now. You've got the ideas, but if you let these wolves run over you they'll do it, and they'll eat you. I can't help it. They're all no good. I wouldn't trust a single God-damned man in the place!"

So it went. Eugene smiled. Could he ever get used to such a life? Could he ever learn to live with such cheap, inconsiderate, indecent little pups? Summerfield might like them, but he didn't. This might be a marvellous business policy, but he couldn't see it. Somehow it seemed to reflect the mental attitude and temperament of Mr. Daniel C. Summerfield and nothing more. Human nature ought to be better than that.

It is curious how fortune sometimes binds up the wounds of the past, covers over the broken places as with clinging vines, gives to the miseries and mental wearinesses of life a look of sweetness and comfort. An illusion of perfect joy is sometimes created where still, underneath, are cracks and scars. Here were Angela and Eugene living together now, beginning to be visited by first one and then the other of those they had known in the past, seemingly as happy as though no storm had ever beset the calm of their present sailing. Eugene, despite all his woes, was interested in this work. He liked to think of himself as the captain of a score of men, having a handsome office desk, being hailed as chief by obsequious subordinates and invited here and there by Summerfield, who still liked him. The work was hard, but it was so much more profitable than anything he had ever had before. Angela was happier, too, he thought, than she had been in a long time, for she did not need to worry about money and his prospects were broadening. Friends were coming back to them in a steady stream, and they were creating new ones. It was possible to go to a seaside resort occasionally, winter or summer, or to entertain three or four friends at dinner. Angela had a maid. The meals were served with considerable distinction under her supervision. She was flattered to hear nice things said about her husband in her presence, for it was whispered abroad in art circles with which they were now slightly in touch again that half the effectiveness of the Summerfield ads was due to Eugene's talent. It was no shame for him to come out now and say where he was, for he was getting a good salary and was a department chief. He, or rather the house through him, had made several great hits, issuing series of ads which attracted the attention of the public generally to the products which they advertised. Experts in the advertising world first, and then later the public generally, were beginning to wonder who it was that was primarily responsible for the hits.

The Summerfield company had not had them during the previous six years of its history. There were too many of them coming close together not to make a new era in the history of the house. Summerfield, it was understood about the office, was becoming a little jealous of Eugene, for he could not brook the presence of a man with a reputation; and Eugene, with his five thousand dollars in cash in two savings banks, with practically two thousand five hundred dollars' worth of tasteful furniture in his apartment and with a ten-thousand life-insurance policy in favor of Angela, was carrying himself with quite an air. He was not feeling so anxious about his future.

Angela noted it. Summerfield also. The latter felt that Eugene was beginning to show his artistic superiority in a way which was not entirely pleasant. He was coming to have a direct, insistent, sometimes dictatorial manner. All the driving Summerfield had done had not succeeded in breaking his spirit. Instead, it had developed him. From a lean, pale, artistic soul, wearing a soft hat, he had straightened up and filled out until now he looked more like a business man than an artist, with a derby hat, clothes of the latest cut, a ring of oriental design on his middle finger, and pins and ties which reflected the prevailing modes.

Eugene's attitude had not as yet changed completely, but it was changing. He was not nearly so fearsome as he had been. He was beginning to see that he had talents in more directions than one, and to have the confidence of this fact. Five thousand dollars in cash, with two or three hundred dollars being added monthly, and interest at four per cent. being paid upon it, gave him a reserve of self-confidence. He began to joke Summerfield himself, for he began to realize that other advertising concerns might be glad to have him. Word had been brought to him once that the Alfred Cookman Company, of which Summerfield was a graduate, was considering making him an offer, and the Twine-Campbell Company, the largest in the field, was also interested in what he was doing. His own artists, mostly faithful because he had sought to pay them well and to help them succeed, had spread his fame greatly. According to them, he was the sole cause of all the recent successes which had come to the house, which was not true at all.

A number, perhaps the majority, of things recently had started with him; but they had been amplified by Summerfield, worked over by the ad-writing department, revised by the advertisers themselves, and so on and so forth, until notable changes had been effected and success achieved. There was no doubt that Eugene was directly responsible for a share of this. His presence was inspiring, constructive. He keyed up the whole tone of the Summerfield Company merely by being there; but he was not all there was to it by many a long step. He realized this himself.

He was not at all offensively egotistic—simply surer, calmer, more genial, less easily ruffled; but even this was too much. Summerfield wanted a frightened man, and seeing that Eugene might be getting strong enough to slip away from him, he began to think how he should either circumvent his possible sudden flight, or discredit his fame, so that if he did leave he would gain nothing by it. Neither of them was directly manifesting any ill-will or indicating his true feelings, but such was the situation just the same. The things which Summerfield thought he might do were not easy to do under any circumstances. It was particularly hard in Eugene's case. The man was beginning to have an air. People liked him. Advertisers who met him, the big manufacturers, took note of him. They did not understand him as a trade figure, but thought he must have real force. One man—a great real estate plunger in New York, who saw him once in Summerfield's office—spoke to the latter about him.

"That's a most interesting man you have there, that man Witla," he said, when they were out to lunch together. "Where does he come from?"

"Oh, the West somewhere!" replied Summerfield evasively. "I don't know. I've had so many art directors I don't pay much attention to them."

Winfield (ex-Senator Kenyon C. Winfield, of Brooklyn) perceived a slight undercurrent of opposition and belittling. "He looks like a bright fellow," he said, intending to drop the subject.

"He is, he is," returned Summerfield; "but like all artists, he's flighty. They're the most unstable people in the world. You can't depend upon them. Good for one idea today—worth nothing tomorrow—I have to handle them like a lot of children. The weather sometimes makes all the difference in the world."

Winfield fancied this was true. Artists generally were worth nothing in business. Still, he remembered Eugene pleasantly.

As Summerfield talked here, so was it in the office and elsewhere. He began to say in the office and out that Eugene was really not doing as well as he might, and that in all likelihood he would have to drop him. It was sad; but all directors, even the best of them, had their little day of ability and usefulness, and then ran to seed. He did not see why it was that all these directors failed so, but they did. They never really made good in the company. By this method, his own undiminished ability was made to stand out free and clear, and Eugene was not able to appear as important. No one who knew anything about Eugene, however, at this time believed this; but they did believe— in the office—that he might lose his position. He was too bright —too much of a leader. They felt that this condition could not continue in a one-man concern; and this made the work harder, for it bred disloyalty in certain quarters. Some of his men were disposed to counsel with the enemy.

But as time passed and in spite of the change of attitude which was coming over Summerfield, Eugene became even stronger in his own self-esteem. He was not getting vainglorious as yet— merely sure. Because of his art work his art connections had revived considerably, and he had heard again from such men as Louis Deesa, M. Charles, Luke Severas, and others who now knew where he was and wondered why he did not come back to painting proper. M. Charles was disgusted. "A great error," he said. He always spoke of him to others as a great loss to art. Strange to relate, one of his pictures was sold the spring following his entry into the Summerfield Company, and another the following winter. Each netted him two hundred and fifty dollars, Pottle Frères being the agents in one case, Jacob Bergman in the other. These sales with their consequent calls for additional canvases to show, cheered him greatly. He felt satisfied now that if anything happened to him he could go back to his art and that he could make a living, anyhow.

There came a time when he was sent for by Mr. Alfred Cookman, the advertising agent for whom Summerfield had worked; but nothing came of that, for the latter did not care to pay more than six thousand a year and Summerfield had once told Eugene that he would eventually pay him ten thousand if he stayed with him. He did not think it was fair to leave him just then, and, besides, Cookman's firm had not the force and go and prestige which Summerfield had at this time. His real chance came some six months later, when one of the publishing houses of Philadelphia having an important weekly to market, began looking for an advertising manager.

It was the policy of this house to select young men and to select from among all the available candidates just the one particular one to suit the fancy of the owner and who had a record of successful effort behind him. Now Eugene was not any more an advertising manager by experience than he was an art director, but having worked for Summerfield for nearly two years he had come to know a great deal about advertising, and the public thought he knew a great deal more. He knew by now just how Summerfield had his business organized. He knew how he specialized his forces, giving this line to one and that line to another. He had been able to learn by sitting in conferences and consultations what it was that advertisers wanted, how they wanted their goods displayed, what they wanted said. He had learned that novelty, force and beauty were the keynotes and he had to work these elements out under the most galling fire so often that he knew how it ought to be done. He knew also about commissions, rebates, long-time contracts, and so forth.

He had fancied more than once that he might run a little advertising business of his own to great profit if he only could find an honest and capable business manager or partner. Since this person was not forthcoming, he was content to bide his time.

But the Kalvin Publishing Company of Philadelphia had heard of him. In his search for a man, Obadiah Kalvin, the founder of the company, had examined many individuals through agents in Chicago, in St. Louis, in Baltimore, Boston, and New York, but he had not yet made up his mind. He was slow in his decisions, and always flattered himself that once he made a selection he was sure of a good result. He had not heard of Eugene until toward the end of his search, but one day in the Union Club in Philadelphia, when he was talking to a big advertising agent with whom he did considerable business, the latter said:

"I hear you are looking for an advertising manager for your weekly."

"I am," he said.

"I heard of a man the other day who might suit you. He's with the Summerfield Company in New York. They've been getting up some very striking ads of late, as you may have noticed."

"I think I have seen some of them," replied Kalvin.

"I'm not sure of the man's name—Witla, or Gitla, or some such thing as that; but, anyhow, he's over there, and they say he's pretty good. Just what he is in the house I don't know. You might look him up."

"Thanks; I will," replied Kalvin. He was really quite grateful, for he was not quite satisfied with any of those he had seen or heard of. He was an old man, extremely sensitive to ability, wanting to combine force with refinement if he could; he was a good Christian, and was running Christian, or rather their happy correlatives, decidedly conservative publications. When he went back to his office he consulted with his business partner, a man named Fredericks, who held but a minor share in the company, and asked him if he couldn't find out something about this promising individual. Fredericks did so. He called up Cookman, in New York, who was delighted to injure his old employee, Summerfield, to the extent of taking away his best man if he could. He told Fredericks that he thought Eugene was very capable, probably the most capable young man in the field, and in all likelihood the man he was looking for—a hustler.

"I thought once of hiring him myself here not long ago," he told Fredericks. "He has ideas, you can see that."

The next thing was a private letter from Mr. Fredericks to Mr. Witla asking if by any chance he could come over to Philadelphia the following Saturday afternoon, indicating that there was a business proposition of considerable importance which he wished to lay before him.

From the paper on which it was written Eugene could see that there was something important in the wind, and laid the matter before Angela. The latter's eyes glistened.

"I'd certainly go if I were you," she advised. "He might want to make you business manager or art director or something. You can be sure they don't intend to offer you less than you're getting now, and Mr. Summerfield certainly has not treated you very well, anyhow. You've worked like a slave for him, and he's never kept his agreement to raise your salary as much as he said he would. It may mean our having to leave New York; but that doesn't make any difference for a while. You don't intend to stay in this field, anyhow. You only want to stay long enough to get a good sound income of your own."

Angela's longing for Eugene's art career was nevertheless being slightly stilled these days by the presence and dangled lure of money. It was a great thing to be able to go downtown and buy dresses and hats to suit the seasons. It was a fine thing to be taken by Eugene Saturday afternoons and Sundays in season to Atlantic City, to Spring Lake, and Shelter Island.

"I think I will go over," he said; and he wrote Mr. Fredericks a favorable reply.

The latter met him at the central station in Philadelphia with his auto and took him out to his country place in the Haverford district. On the way he talked of everything but business—the state of the weather, the condition of the territory through which they were traveling, the day's news, the nature and interest of Eugene's present work. When they were in the Fredericks house, where they arrived in time for dinner, and while they were getting ready for it, Mr. Obadiah Kalvin dropped in—ostensibly to see his partner, but really to look at Eugene without committing himself. He was introduced to Eugene, and shook hands with him cordially. During the meal he talked with Eugene a little, though not on business, and Eugene wondered why he had been called. He suspected, knowing as he did that Kalvin was the president of the company, that the latter was there to look at him. After dinner Mr. Kalvin left, and Eugene noted that Mr. Fredericks was then quite ready to talk with him.

"The thing that I wanted you to come over and see me about

is in regard to our weekly and the advertising department. We
have a great paper over here, as you know," he said. "We are
intending to do much more with it in the future than we have
in the past even. Mr. Kalvin is anxious to get just the man to
take charge of the advertising department. We have been looking for someone for quite a little while. Several people have
suggested your name, and I'm rather inclined to think that Mr.
Kalvin would be pleased to see you take it. His visit here today
was purely accidental, but it was fortunate. He had a chance
to look at you, so that if I should propose your name he will
know just who you are. I think you would find this company
a fine background for your efforts. We have no penny-wise-
and-pound-foolish policy over here. We know that any successful thing is made by the men behind it, and we are willing to
pay good money for good men. I don't know what you are
getting where you are, and I don't care very much. If you are
interested I should like to talk to Mr. Kalvin about you, and
if he is interested I should like to bring you two together for a
final conference. The salary will be made right, you needn't
worry about that. Mr. Kalvin isn't a small man. If he likes
a man—and I think he might like you—he'll offer you what he
thinks you're worth and you can take it or leave it. I never
heard anyone complain about the salary he offered."

Eugene listened with extreme self-gratulation. He was thrill-
ing from head to toe. This was the message he had been expecting to hear for so long. He was getting five thousand now,
he had been offered six thousand. Mr. Kalvin could do no less
than offer him seven or eight—possibly ten. He could easily ask
seven thousand five hundred.

"I must say," he said innocently, "the proposition sounds attractive to me. It's a different kind of thing—somewhat—from
what I have been doing, but I think I could handle it successfully. Of course, the salary will determine the whole thing
I'm not at all badly placed where I am. I've just got comfortably settled in New York, and I'm not anxious to move. But I
would not be opposed to coming. I have no contract with Mr.
Summerfield. He has never been willing to give me one."

"Well, we are not keen upon contracts ourselves," said Mr.
Fredericks. "It's not a very strong reed to lean upon, anyhow,
as you know. Still a contract might be arranged if you wish it.
Supposing we talk a little further to Mr. Kalvin today. He
doesn't live so far from here," and with Eugene's consent he
went to the phone.

The latter had supposed that the conversation with Mr. Kalvin was something which would necessarily have to take place at some future date; but from the conversation then and there held over the phone it appeared not. Mr. Fredericks explained elaborately over the phone—as though it was necessary—that he had been about the work of finding an advertising manager for some time, as Mr. Kalvin knew, and that he had some difficulty in finding the right man.

"I have been talking to Mr. Witla, whom you met here today, and he is interested in what I have been telling him about the *Weekly*. He strikes me from my talk with him here as being possibly the man you are looking for. I thought that you might like to talk with him further."

Mr. Kalvin evidently signified his assent, for the machine was called out and they traveled to his house, perhaps a mile away. On the way Eugene's mind was busy with the possibilities of the future. It was all so nebulous, this talk of a connection with the famous Kalvin Publishing Company; but at the same time it was so significant, so potential. Could it be possible that he was going to leave Summerfield, after all, and under such advantageous circumstances? It seemed like a dream.

Mr. Kalvin met them in the library of his house, which stood in a spacious lawn and which save for the lights in the library was quite dark and apparently lonely. And here their conversation was continued. He was a quiet man—small, gray-haired, searching in his gaze. He had, as Eugene noted, little hands and feet, and appeared as still and composed as a pool in dull weather. He said slowly and quietly that he was glad that Eugene and Mr. Fredericks had had a talk. He had heard a little something of Eugene in the past; not much. He wanted to know what Eugene thought of current advertising policies, what he thought of certain new developments in advertising method, and so on, at some length.

"So you think you might like to come with us," he observed drily toward the end, as though Eugene had proposed coming.

"I don't think I would object to coming under certain conditions," he replied.

"And what are those conditions?"

"Well, I would rather hear what you have to suggest, Mr. Kalvin. I really am not sure that I want to leave where I am. I'm doing pretty well as it is."

"Well, you seem a rather likely young man to me," said Mr. Kalvin. "You have certain qualities which I think I need. I'll say eight thousand for this year, and if everything is satisfac-

tory one year from this time I'll make it ten. After that we'll
let the future take care of itself."

"Eight thousand! Ten next year!" thought Eugene. The
title of advertising manager of a great publication! This was
certainly a step forward!

"Well, that isn't so bad," he said, after a moment's apparent
reflection. "I'd be willing to take that, I think."

"I thought you would," said Mr. Kalvin, with a dry smile.
"Well, you and Mr. Fredericks can arrange the rest of the details. Let me wish you good luck," and he extended his hand
cordially.

Eugene took it.

It did not seem as he rode back in the machine with Mr. Fredericks to the latter's house—for he was invited to stay for the
night—that it could really be true. Eight thousand a year!
Was he eventually going to become a great business man instead
of an artist? He could scarcely flatter himself that this was
true, but the drift was strange. Eight thousand this year! Ten
the next if he made good; twelve, fifteen, eighteen—— He had
heard of such salaries in the advertising field alone, and how
much more would his investments bring him. He foresaw an
apartment on Riverside Drive in New York, a house in the
country perhaps, for he fancied he would not always want to
live in the city. An automobile of his own, perhaps; a grand
piano for Angela; Sheraton or Chippendale furniture; friends,
fame—what artist's career could compare to this? Did any
artist he knew enjoy what he was enjoying now, even? Why
should he worry about being an artist? Did they ever get
anywhere? Would the approval of posterity let him ride in an
automobile now? He smiled as he recalled Dula's talk about
class superiority—the distinction of being an artist, even though
poor. Poverty be hanged! Posterity could go to the devil! He
wanted to live now—not in the approval of posterity.

CHAPTER XXXVII

THE best positions are not always free from the most disturbing difficulties, for great responsibility goes with great opportunity; but Eugene went gaily to this new task, for he knew that it could not possibly be much more difficult than the one he was leaving. Truly, Summerfield had been a terrible man to work for. He had done his best by petty nagging, insisting on endless variations, the most frank and brutal criticism, to break down Eugene's imperturbable good nature and make him feel that he could not reasonably hope to handle the situation without Summerfield's co-operation and assistance. But he had only been able, by so doing, to bring out Eugene's better resources. His self-reliance, coolness under fire, ability to work long and ardently even when his heart was scarcely in it, were all strengthened and developed.

"Well, luck to you, Witla," he said, when Eugene informed him one morning that he was going to leave and wished to give him notice.

"You needn't take me into consideration. I don't want you to stay if you're going to go. The quicker the better. These long drawn-out agonies over leaving don't interest me. There's nothing in that. Clinch the job today if you want it. I'll find someone."

Eugene resented his indifference, but he only smiled a cordial smile in reply. "I'll stay a little while if you want me to—one or two weeks—I don't want to tie up your work in any way."

"Oh, no, no! You won't tie up my work. On your way, and good luck!"

"The little devil!" thought Eugene; but he shook hands and said he was sorry. Summerfield grinned imperturbably. He wound up his affairs quickly and got out. "Thank God," he said the day he left, "I'm out of that hell hole!" But he came to realize afterward that Summerfield had rendered him a great service. He had forced him to do his best and utmost, which no one had ever done before. It had told in his character, his spiritual make-up, his very appearance. He was no longer timid and nervous, but rather bold and determined-looking. He had lost that fear of very little things, for he had been sailing through stormy seas. Little storms did not—could never again—really frighten him. He had learned to fight. That was the one great thing Summerfield had done for him.

In the offices of the Kalvin Company it was radically different. Here was comparative peace and quiet. Kalvin had not fought his way up by clubbing little people through little difficulties, but had devoted himself to thinking out a few big things, and letting them because of their very bigness and newness make their own way and his. He believed in big men, honest men— the biggest and most honest he could find. He saw something in Eugene, a tendency toward perfection perhaps which attracted him.

The formalities of this new arrangement were soon concluded, and Eugene came into his new and beautiful offices, heralded by the word recently passed about that he was a most charming man. He was greeted by the editor, Townsend Miller, in the most cordial manner. He was met by his assembled staff in the most friendly spirit. It quite took Eugene's breath away to realize that he was the responsible head of some fifteen capable advertising men here in Philadelphia alone, to say nothing of eight more in a branch office in Chicago and traveling canvassers in the different parts of the country—the far West, the South, the Southwest, the Canadian Northwest. His material surroundings were much more imposing than they had been with the Summerfield Company. The idea of all these men was to follow up business, to lay interesting propositions before successful merchants and manufacturers who had not yet tried the columns of the *North American Weekly,* to make contracts which should be mutually advantageous to the advertiser and the *Weekly,* and to gain and retain good-will according to the results rendered. It was no very difficult task in connection with the *North American Weekly* to do this, because owing to a novel and appealing editorial policy it was already in possession of a circulation of five hundred thousand a week, and was rapidly gaining more. It was not difficult, as Eugene soon found, to show advertisers in most cases that this was a proposition in which worth-while results could be obtained. What with Eugene's fertility in suggesting new methods of advertising, his suaveness of approach and geniality in laying before the most recalcitrant his very desirable schemes, his ability to get ideas and suggestions out of his men in conference, he was really in no danger of not being able to hold his own, and indeed was destined to make a rather remarkable showing.

Eugene and Angela settled into what might have been deemed a fixed attitude of comfort and refinement. Without much inconvenience to himself and with little friction among those about, he had succeeded in reorganizing his staff along lines which were eminently satisfactory to himself. Some men who were formerly with the Summerfield Company were now with him. He had brought them because he found he could inculcate in them the spirit of sympathetic relationship and good understanding such as Kalvin desired. He was not making the progress which Summerfield was making with really less means at his command, but then, on the other hand, this was a rich company which did not ask or expect any such struggle as that which Summerfield had been and was still compelled to make for himself. The business ethics of this company were high. It believed in clean methods, good salaries, honest service. Kalvin liked him, and he had one memorable conversation with Eugene some time after he came there—almost a year—which stuck in his memory and did him much good. Kalvin saw clearly wherein both his strength and his weakness lay, and once said to Fredericks, his business manager: "The one thing I like about that man is his readiness with ideas. He always has one, and he's the most willing man to try I ever knew. He has imagination. He needs to be steadied in the direction of sober thought, so that he doesn't promise more than he can fulfil. Outside this I see nothing the matter with him."

Fredericks agreed. He liked Eugene also. He did as much as he could to make things smooth, but of course Eugene's task was personal and to be worked out by him solely. Kalvin said to him when it became necessary to raise his salary:

"I've watched your work for a year now and I'm going to keep my word and raise your salary. You're a good man. You have many excellent qualities which I want and need in the man who sits at that desk; but you have also some failings. I don't want you to get offended. A man in my position is always like a father who sits at the head of a family, and my lieutenants are like my sons. I have to take an interest in them because they take an interest in me. Now you've done your work well— very well, but you are subject to one fault which may sometime lead into trouble. You're a little too enthusiastic. I don't think you stop to think enough. You have a lot of ideas. They swarm in your head like bees, and sometimes you let them all out at once and they buzz around you and confuse you and everyone else connected with you. You would really be a better man if you had, not less ideas—I wouldn't say that—but better control of them. You want to do too many things at once. Go slow. Take your time. You have lots of time. You're young yet. Think! If you're in doubt, come down and consult with me. I'm older in this business than you are, and I'll help you all I can."

Eugene smiled and said: "I think that's true."

"It is true," said Kalvin; "and now I want to speak of another thing which is a little more of a personal matter, and I don't want you to take offence, for I'm saying it for your benefit. If I'm any judge of men, and I flatter myself sometimes that I am, you're a man whose greatest weakness lies—and, mind you, I have no actual evidence to go upon, not one scrap—your greatest weakness lies perhaps not so much in the direction of women as in a love of luxury generally, of which women might become, and usually are, a very conspicuous part."

Eugene flushed the least bit nervously and resentfully, for he thought he had conducted himself in the most circumspect manner here—in fact, everywhere since the days he had begun to put the Riverwood incident behind him.

"Now I suppose you wonder why I say that. Well, I raised two boys, both dead now, and one was just a little like you. You have so much imagination that it runs not only to ideas in business, but ideas in dress and comfort and friends and entertainment. Be careful of the kind of people you get in with. Stick to the conservative element. It may be hard for you, but it's best for you, materially speaking. You're the kind of man, if my observations and intuitions are correct, who is apt to be carried away by his ideals of anything—beauty, women, show. Now I have no ascetic objections to women, but to you they are dangerous, as yet. At bottom, I don't think you have the making of a real cold business man in you, but you're a splendid lieutenant. I'll tell you frankly I don't think a better man than you has ever sat, or could sit, in that chair. You are very exceptional, but your very ability makes you an uncertain quantity. You're just on the threshold of your career. This additional two thousand dollars is going to open up new opportunities to you. Keep cool. Keep out of the hands of clever people. Don't let subtle women come near. You're married, and for your sake I hope you love your wife. If you don't, pretend to, and stay within the bounds of convention. Don't let any scandal ever attach to you. If you do it will be absolutely fatal so far as I am concerned. I have had to part with a number of excellent men in my time because a little money turned their heads and they went wild over some one woman, or many women. Don't you be that way. I like you. I'd like to see you get along. Be cold if you can. Be careful. Think. That's the best advice I can give you, and I wish you luck."

He waved him a dismissal, and Eugene rose. He wondered how this man had seen so clearly into his character. It was the truth, and he knew it was. His inmost thoughts and feelings were evidently written where this man could see them. Fittingly was he president of a great company. He could read men.

He went back into his office and decided to take this lesson to heart. He must keep cool and sane always. "I guess I've had enough experience to know that, though, by now," he said and dismissed the idea from his mind.

For this year and the year following, when his salary was raised to twelve thousand, Eugene flourished prodigiously. He and Miller became better friends than ever. Miller had advertising ideas which were of value to Eugene. Eugene had art and editorial ideas which were of value to Miller. They were together a great deal at social functions, and were sometimes hailed by their companions as the "Kalvin Kids," and the "Limelight Twins." Eugene learned to play golf with Miller, though he was a slow student and never good, and also tennis. He and Mrs. Miller, Angela and Townsend, frequently made a set on their own court or over at Miller's. They automobiled and rode a great deal. Eugene met some charming women, particularly young ones, at dances, of which he had become very fond, and at dinners and receptions. They and the Millers were invited to a great many affairs, but by degrees it became apparent to him, as it did to Miller and Mrs. Miller, that his presence was much more desired by a certain type of smart woman than was that of his wife.

"Oh, he is so clever!" was an observation which might have been heard in various quarters. Frequently the compliment stopped there and nothing was said of Angela, or later on it would come up that she was not quite so nice. Not that she was not charming and worthy and all that, "But you know, my dear, she isn't quite so available. You can't use her as you can some women."

It was at this time that Angela first conceived the notion seriously that a child might have a sobering effect on Eugene. She had, in spite of the fact that for some time now they had been well able to support one or more, and in spite also of the fact that Eugene's various emotional lapses indicated that he needed a sobering weight of some kind, steadily objected in her mind to the idea of subjecting herself to this ordeal. To tell the truth, aside from the care and worry which always, owing to her early experience with her sister's children, had been associated in her mind with the presence of them, she was decidedly afraid of the result. She had heard her mother say that most girls in their infancy showed very clearly whether they were to be good healthy mothers or not—whether they were to have children—and her recollection was that her mother had once said that she would not have any children. She half believed it to be impossible in her case, though she had never told this to Eugene, and she had guarded herself jealously against the chance of having any.

Now, however, after watching Eugene all these years, seeing the drift of his present mood, feeling the influence of prosperity on him, she wished sincerely that she might have one, without great danger or discomfort to herself, in order that she might influence and control him. He might learn to love it. The sense of responsibility involved would have its effect. People would look to him to conduct himself soberly under these circumstances, and he probably would—he was so subject to public opinion now. She thought of this a long time, wondering, for fear and annoyance were quite strong influences with her, and she did nothing immediately. She listened to various women who talked with her from time to time about the child question, and decided that perhaps it was very wrong not to have children—at least one or two; that it was very likely possible that she could have one, if she wanted to. A Mrs. Sanifore who called on her quite frequently in Philadelphia—she met her at the Millers'—told her that she was sure she could have one even if she was past the usual age for first babies; for she had known so many women who had.

"If I were you, Mrs. Witla, I would see a doctor," she suggested one day. "He can tell you. I'm sure you can if you want to. They have so many ways of dieting and exercising you which make all the difference in the world. I'd like to have you come some day and see my doctor, if you will."

Angela decided that she would, for curiosity's sake, and in case she wished to act in the matter some time; and was informed by the wiseacre who examined her that in his opinion there was no doubt that she could. She would have to subject herself to a strict regimen. Her muscles would have to be softened by some form of manipulation. Otherwise, she was apparently in a healthy, normal condition and would suffer no intolerable hardship. This pleased and soothed Angela greatly. It gave her a club wherewith to strike her lord—a chain wherewith to bind him. She did not want to act at once. It was too serious a matter. She wanted time to think. But it was pleasant to know that she could do this. Unless Eugene sobered down now——

During the time in which he had been working for the Sum-

merfield Company and since then for the Kalvin Company here
in Philadelphia, Eugene, in spite of the large salary he was
receiving—more each year—really had not saved so much money.
Angela had seen to it that some of his earnings were invested
in Pennsylvania Railroad stock, which seemed to her safe
enough, and in a plot of ground two hundred by two hundred
feet at Upper Montclair, New Jersey, near New York, where
she and Eugene might some day want to live. His business engagements had necessitated considerable personal expenditures,
his opportunity to enter the Baltusrol Golf Club, the Yere
Tennis Club, the Philadelphia Country Club, and similar organizations had taken annual sums not previously contemplated,
and the need of having a modest automobile, not a touring car,
was obvious. His short experience with that served as a lesson,
however, for it was found to be a terrific expense, entirely disproportionate to his income. After paying for endless repairs,
salarying a chauffeur wearisomely, and meeting with an accident which permanently damaged the looks of his machine, he
decided to give it up. They could rent autos for all the uses
they would have. And so that luxury ended there.

It was curious, too, how during this time their Western home
relations fell rather shadowily into the background. Eugene
had not been home now for nearly two years, and Angela had
seen only David of all her family since she had been in Philadelphia. In the fall of their third year there Angela's mother
died and she returned to Blackwood for a short time. The following spring Eugene's father died. Myrtle moved to New
York; her husband, Frank Bangs, was connected with a western
furniture company which was maintaining important show rooms
in New York. Myrtle had broken down nervously and taken
up Christian Science, Eugene heard. Henry Burgess, Sylvia's
husband, had become president of the bank with which he had
been so long connected, and had sold his father's paper, the
Alexandria *Appeal,* when the latter suddenly died. Marietta
was promising to come to Philadelphia next year, in order, as
she said, that Eugene might get her a rich husband; but Angela
informed him privately that Marietta was now irrevocably engaged and would, the next year, marry a wealthy Wisconsin
lumber man. Everyone was delighted to hear that Eugene was
doing so well, though all regretted the lapse of his career as an
artist. His fame as an advertising man was growing, and he
was thought to have considerable weight in the editorial direction of the *North American Weekly.* So he flourished.

CHAPTER XXXVIII

IT was in the fall of the third year that the most flattering offer of any was made him, and that without any seeking on his part, for he was convinced that he had found a fairly permanent berth and was happy among his associates. Publishing and other trade conditions were at this time in a peculiar condition, in which lieutenants of any importance in any field might well be called to positions of apparently extraordinary prominence and trust. Most of the great organizations of Eugene's day were already reaching a point where they were no longer controlled by the individuals who had founded and constructed them, but had passed into the hands of sons or holding companies, or groups of stockholders, few of whom knew much, if anything, of the businesses which they were called to engineer and protect.

Hiram C. Colfax was not a publisher at all at heart. He had come into control of the Swinton-Scudder-Davis Company by one of those curious manipulations of finance which sometimes give the care of sheep into the hands of anything but competent or interested shepherds. Colfax was sufficiently alert to handle anything in such a way that it would eventually make money for him, even if that result were finally attained by parting with it. In other words, he was a financier. His father had been a New England soap manufacturer, and having accumulated more or less radical ideas along with his wealth, had decided to propagandize in favor of various causes, the Single Tax theory of Henry George for one, Socialism for another, the promotion of reform ideas in politics generally. He had tried in various ways to get his ideas before the public, but had not succeeded very well. He was not a good speaker, not a good writer, simply a good money maker and fairly capable thinker, and this irritated him. He thought once of buying or starting a newspaper in Boston, but investigation soon showed him that this was a rather hazardous undertaking. He next began subsidizing small weeklies which should advocate his reforms, but this resulted in little. His interest in pamphleteering did bring his name to the attention of Martin W. Davis of the Swinton-Scudder-Davis Company, whose imprint on books, magazines and weeklies was as common throughout the length and breadth of the land as that of Oxford is upon the English bible.

The Swinton-Scudder-Davis Company was in sad financial

straits. Intellectually, for various reasons, it had run to seed. John Jacob Swinton and Owen V. Scudder, the men with book, magazine and true literary instincts, were long since dead. Mr. Davis had tried for the various heirs and assigns involved to run it intelligently and honestly, but intelligence and honesty were of little value in this instance without great critical judgment. This he had not. The house had become filled with editors, readers, critics, foremen of manufacturing and printing departments, business managers, art directors, traveling salesmen and so on without end, each of whom might be reasonably efficient if left alone, but none of whom worked well together and all of whom used up a great deal of money.

The principal literary publication, a magazine of great prestige, was in the hands of an old man who had been editor for nearly forty years. A weekly was being run by a boy, comparatively, a youth of twenty-nine. A second magazine, devoted to adventure fiction, was in the hands of another young man of twenty-six, a national critical monthly was in the hands of salaried critics of great repute and uncompromising attitude. The book department was divided into the hands of a juvenile editor, a fiction editor, a scientific and educational editor and so on. It was Mr. Davis' task to see that competent overseers were in charge of all departments so that they might flourish and work harmoniously under him, but he was neither sufficiently wise or forceful to fill the rôle. He was old and was veered about first by one theory and then by another, and within the house were rings and cliques. One of the most influential of these—the most influential, in fact—was one which was captained and led by Florence J. White, an Irish-American, who as business manager (and really more than that, general manager under Davis) was in charge of the manufacturing and printing departments, and who because of his immense budgets for paper, ink, printing, mailing and distribution generally, was in practical control of the business.

He it was who with Davis' approval said how much was to be paid for paper, ink, composition, press work, and salaries generally. He it was who through his henchman, the head of the printing department, arranged the working schedules by which the magazines and books were to reach the presses, with the practical power to say whether they were to be on time or not. He it was who through another superintendent supervised the mailing and the stock room, and by reason of his great executive ability was coming to have a threatening control over the advertising and circulation departments.

The one trouble with White, and this was something which would affect any man who should come in through Davis' auspices, was that he knew nothing of art, literature, or science, and cared less, his only interest being in manufacture. He had risen so rapidly on the executive side that his power had outrun his financial means. Davis, the present head above him, had no means beyond his own depreciated share. Because of poor editorial judgment, the books and magazines were tottering through a serious loss of prestige to eventual failure. Something had to be done, for at that time the expenditure for three years past had been much greater than the receipts.

So Marshall P. Colfax, the father of Hiram Colfax, had been appealed to, because of his interest in reform ideas which might be to a certain extent looked upon as related to literature, and because he was reported to be a man of great wealth. Rumor reported his fortune as being anywhere between six and eight millions. The proposition which Davis had to put before him was this: that he buy from the various heirs and assigns the whole of the stock outside his (Davis') own, which amounted to somewhere about sixty-five per cent, and then come in as managing director and reorganize the company to suit himself. Davis was old. He did not want to trouble himself about the future of this company or risk his own independent property. He realized as well as anyone that what the company needed was new blood. A receivership at this juncture would injure the value of the house imprint very much indeed. White had no money, and besides he was so new and different that Davis scarcely understood what his ambitions or his true importance might be. There was no real intellectual sympathy between them. In the main, he did not like White's temperament, and so in considering what might be done for the company he passed him by.

Various consultations were held. Colfax was greatly flattered to think that this proposition should be brought to his attention at all. He had three sons, only one of whom was interested in the soap business. Edward and Hiram, the two youngest, wanted nothing to do with it. He thought this might be an outlet for the energies of one or both of them, preferably Hiram, who was more of an intellectual and scientific turn than the others, though his chief interests were financial; and besides these books and publications would give him the opportunity which he had long been seeking. His personal prestige might be immensely heightened thereby. He examined carefully into the financial phases of the situation, using his son Hiram, whose financial judgment he had faith in, as an accountant and mouth-piece, and finally, after seeing that he could secure the stock on a long-time consideration for a very moderate valuation—$1,500,000, while it was worth $3,000,000—he had his son Hiram elected director and president and proceeded to see what could be done with the company.

In this approaching transaction Florence J. White had seen his opportunity and seized it. He had realized on sight that Hiram would need and possibly appreciate all the information and assistance he could get, and being in a position to know he had laid all the facts in connection with the house plainly before him. He saw clearly where the trouble lay, the warring factions, the lack of editorial judgment, the poor financial manipulations. He knew exactly where the stock was and by what representations it could be best frightened and made to release itself cheaply. He worked vigorously for Hiram because he liked him and the latter reciprocated his regard.

"You've been a prince in this transaction, White," he said to that individual one day. "You've put things practically in my hands. I'm not going to forget it."

"Don't mention it," said White. "It's to my interest to see a real live man come in here."

"When I become president, you become vice-president, and that means twenty-five thousand a year." White was then getting twelve.

"When I become vice-president nothing will ever happen to your interests," returned the other man grimly. White was six feet tall, lean, savage, only semi-articulate. Colfax was small, wiry, excitable, with enough energy to explode a cartridge by yelling at it. He was eager, vainglorious, in many respects brilliant. He wanted to shine in the world, and he did not know how to do it as yet exactly.

The two shook hands firmly.

Some three months later Colfax was duly elected director and president, and the same meeting that elected him president elected Florence J. White vice-president. The latter was for clearing out all the old elements and letting in new blood. Colfax was for going slow, until he could see for himself what he wanted to do. One or two men were eliminated at once, an old circulation man and an old advertising man. In six months, while they were still contemplating additional changes and looking for new men, Colfax senior died, and the Swinton-Scudder-Davis Company, or at least Mr. Colfax's control of it, was willed to Hiram. So he sat there, accidentally president, and in full charge, wondering how he should make it a great success, and Florence J. White was his henchman and sworn ally.

At the time that Colfax first heard of Eugene he had been in charge of the Swinton-Scudder-Davis Company (which he was planning to reincorporate as "The United Magazines Corporation") for three years. He had made a number of changes, some radical, some conservative. He had put in an advertising man whom he was now finding unsatisfactory, and had made changes in the art and editorial departments which were more the result of the suggestions of others, principally of White, than the thoughts of his own brain. Martin W. Davis had retired. He was old and sick, and unwilling to ruminate in a back-room position. Such men as the editor of the *National Review, Swinton's Magazine,* and *Scudder's Weekly* were the only figures of importance about the place, and they were now of course immensely subsidiary to Hiram Colfax and Florence White.

The latter had introduced a rather hard, bitter atmosphere into the place. He had been raised under difficult conditions himself in a back street in Brooklyn, and had no sympathy with the airs and intellectual insipidities which characterized the editorial and literary element which filled the place. He had an Irishman's love of organization and politics, but far and away above that he had an Irishman's love of power. Because of the trick he had scored in winning the favor of Hiram Colfax at the time when the tremendous affairs of the concern were in a state of transition, he had become immensely ambitious. He wanted to be not nominally but actually director of the affairs of this house under Colfax, and he saw his way clear to do it by getting editors, art directors, department heads and assistants generally who were agreeable to him. But unfortunately he could not do this directly, for while Colfax cared little about the details of the business his hobby was just this one thing— men. Like Obadiah Kalvin, of the Kalvin Publishing Company, who, by the way, was now his one great rival, Colfax prided himself on his ability to select men. His general idea was that if he could find one more man as good as Florence White to take charge of the art, editorial and book end of the business, not from the manufacturing and commercial, but from the intellectual and spiritual ends—a man with ideas who would draw to him authors, editors, scientific writers and capable assistants generally—the fortune of the house would be made. He thought, sanely enough from some points of view, that this publishing world could be divided in this way. White bringing the inside manufacturing, purchasing and selling interests to a state of perfection; the new man, whoever he might be, bringing the ideas of the house and their literary and artistic representation up to such a state of efficiency that the whole country would know that it was once more powerful and successful. He wanted to be called the foremost publisher of his day, and then he could retire gracefully or devote himself to other financial matters as he pleased.

He really did not understand Florence J. White as well as he did himself. White was a past master at dissembling. He had no desire to see any such thing as Colfax was now planning come to pass. He could not do the things intellectually and spiritually which Colfax wanted done, nevertheless he wanted to be king under this emperor, the real power behind the throne, and he did not propose to brook any interference if he could help it. It was in his power, having the printing and composing room in his hands, to cause any man whom he greatly disliked to suffer severely. Forms could be delayed, material lost, complaints lodged as to dilatoriness in the matter of meeting schedules, and so on, ad infinitum. He had the Irishman's love of chicanery in the matter of morals. If he could get at an enemy's record and there was a flaw in it, the facts were apt to become mysteriously known at the most inconvenient times. He demanded the utmost loyalty of those who worked under him. If a man did not know enough instinctively to work intelligently for his interests, while at the same time appearing to serve the interests of the house at large only, he was soon dismissed on one pretext or another. Intelligent department heads, not sure of their own strength and seeing which way the wind was blowing, soon lined up in his course. Those whom he liked and who did his will prospered. Those whom he disliked suffered greatly in their duties, and were forever explaining or complaining to Colfax, who was not aware of White's subtlety and who therefore thought them incompetent.

Colfax, when he first heard of Eugene, was still cherishing his dream of a literary and artistic primate who should rank in power with White. He had not found him as yet, for all the men he sincerely admired and thought fitted for the position were in business for themselves. He had sounded one man after another, but to no satisfactory end. Then it became necessary to fill the position of advertising manager with someone who would make a conspicuous success of it, and he began to sound various authorities. Naturally he looked at the different advertising men working for various publications, and quickly came to the name of Eugene Witla. The latter was rumored to be making a shining success of his work. He was well liked where he was. Two different business men told Colfax that they had met him and that he was exceptionally clever. A third told him of his record with Summerfield, and through a fourth man who knew Eugene, and who was having him to lunch at the Hardware Club a few weeks later, Colfax had a chance to meet him without appearing to be interested in him in any way.

Not knowing who Colfax was, or rather very little, other than that he was president of this great rival publishing concern, Eugene was perfectly free and easy in his manner. He was never affected at any time, decidedly eager to learn things from anybody and supremely good natured.

"So you're Swinton, Scudder and Davis, are you?" he said to Colfax on introduction. "That trinity must have shrunk some to get condensed into you, but I suppose the power is all there."

"I don't know about that! I don't know about that!" exclaimed Colfax electrically. He was always ready like a greyhound to run another a race. "They tell me Swinton and Scudder were exceptionally big men. If you have as much force as you have length there's nothing the matter with you, though."

"Oh, I'm all right," said Eugene, "when I'm by myself. These little men worry me, though. They are so darned smart."

Colfax cackled ecstatically. He liked Eugene's looks. The latter's manner, easy and not in any way nervous or irritable but coupled with a heavenly alertness of eye, took his fancy. It was a fit companion for his own terrific energy, and it was not unduly soft or yielding.

"So you're the advertising manager of the *North American*. How'd they ever come to tie you down to that?"

"They didn't tie me," said Eugene. "I just lay down. But they put a nice fat salary on top of me to keep me there. I wouldn't lie down for anything except a salary."

He grinned smartly.

Colfax cackled.

"Well, my boy, it doesn't seem to be hurting your ribs, does it? They've not caved in yet. Ha! Ha!—Ha! Ha! They've not, have they? Ha! Ha!"

Eugene studied this little man with great interest. He was taken by his sharp, fierce, examining eye. He was so different from Kalvin, who was about his size, but so much more quiet, peaceful, dignified. Colfax was electric, noisy, insistent, like a pert jack-in-the-box; he seemed to be nothing but energy. Eugene thought of him as having an electric body coated over with some thin veneer of skin. He seemed as direct as a flash of lightning.

"Doing pretty good over there, are you?" he asked. "I've heard a little something about you from time to time. Not much. Not much. Just a little. Not unfavorable, though. Not unfavorable."

"I hope not," said Eugene easily. He wondered why Colfax was so interested in him. The latter kept looking him over much as one might examine a prize animal. Their eyes would meet and Colfax's would gleam with a savage but friendly fire.

"Well?" said Eugene to him finally.

"I'm just thinking, my boy! I'm just thinking!" he returned, and that was all Eugene could get out of him.

It was not long after this very peculiar meeting which stuck in Eugene's memory that Colfax invited him over to his house in New York to dinner. "I wish," he wrote one day not long after this meeting, "that the next time you are in New York you would let me know. I would like to have you come to my house to dine. You and I ought to be pretty good friends. There are a number of things I would like to talk to you about."

This was written on the paper of the United Magazines Corporation, which had just been organized to take over the old company of Swinton, Scudder and Davis, and was labeled "The Office of the President."

Eugene thought this was significant. Could Colfax be going to make him an offer of some kind? Well, the more the merrier! He was doing very well indeed, and liked Mr. Kalvin very much, in fact, all his surroundings, but, as an offer was a testimonial to merit and could be shown as such, he would not be opposed to receiving it. It might strengthen him with Kalvin if it did nothing else. He made an occasion to go over, first talking the letter over with Angela, who was simply curious about the whole thing. He told her how much interested Colfax appeared to be the first time they met and that he fancied it might mean an offer from the United Magazines Corporation at some time or other.

"I'm not particularly anxious about it," said Eugene, "but I'd like to see what is there."

Angela was not sure that it was wise to bother with it. "It's a big firm," she said, "but it isn't bigger than Mr. Kalvin's, and he's been mighty nice to you. You'd better not do anything to injure yourself with him."

Eugene thought of this. It was sound advice. Still he wanted to hear.

"I won't do anything," he said. "I would like to hear what he has to say, though."

A little later he wrote that he was coming on the twentieth and that he would be glad to take dinner with Colfax.

The first meeting between Eugene and Colfax had been conclusive so far as future friendship was concerned. These two, like Eugene and Summerfield, were temperamentally in accord, though Colfax was very much superior to Summerfield in his ability to command men.

This night when they met at dinner at Colfax's house the latter was most cordial. Colfax had invited him to come to his office, and together they went uptown in his automobile. His residence was in upper Fifth Avenue, a new, white marble fronted building with great iron gates at the door and a splendid entry set with small palms and dwarf cedars. Eugene saw at once that this man was living in that intense atmosphere of commercial and financial rivalry which makes living in New York so keen. You could feel the air of hard, cold order about the place, the insistence on perfection of appointment, the compulsion toward material display which was held in check only by that sense of fitness, which knowledge of current taste and the mode in everything demanded. His automobile was very large and very new, the latest model, a great dark blue affair which ran as silently as a sewing machine. The footman who opened the door was six feet tall, dressed in knee breeches and a swallow-tailed coat. The valet was a Japanese, silent, polite, attentive. Eugene was introduced to Mrs. Colfax, a most graceful but somewhat self-conscious woman. A French maid later presented two children, a boy and a girl.

Eugene by now had become used to luxury in various forms, and this house was not superior to many he had seen; but it ranked with the best. Colfax was most free in it. He threw his overcoat to the valet carelessly and tossed his babies in the air by turn, when they were presented to him by the French maid. His wife, slightly taller than himself, received a resounding smack.

"There, Ceta," he exclaimed (a diminutive for Cecile, as Eugene subsequently learned), "how do you like that, eh? Meet Mr. Witla. He's an artist and an art director and an advertising manager and——"

"A most humble person," put in Eugene smilingly. "Not half as bad as you may think. His report is greatly exaggerated."

Mrs. Colfax smiled sweetly. "I discount much that he says at once," she returned. "More later. Won't you come up into the library?"

They ascended together, jesting. Eugene was pleased with what he saw. Mrs. Colfax liked him. She excused herself after a little while and Colfax talked life in general. "I'm going to show you my house now, and after dinner I'm going to talk a little business to you. You interest me. I may as well tell you that."

"Well, you interest me, Colfax," said Eugene genially, "I like you."

"You don't like me any more than I like you, that's a sure thing," replied the other.

CHAPTER XXXIX

THE results of this evening were most pleasant, but in some ways disconcerting. It became perfectly plain that Colfax was anxious to have Eugene desert the Kalvin Company and come over to him.

"You people over there," he said to him at one stage of the conversation, "have an excellent company, but it doesn't compare with this organization which we are revising. Why, what are your two publications to our seven? You have one eminently successful one—the one you're on—and no book business whatsoever! We have seven publications all doing excellently well, and a book business that is second to none in the country. You know that. If it hadn't been that the business had been horribly mismanaged it would never have come into my hands at all. Why, Witla, I want to tell you one little fact in connection with that organization which will illustrate everything else which might be said in connection with it before I came here! They were wasting twenty thousand dollars a year on ink alone. We were publishing a hundred absolutely useless books that did not sell enough to pay for the cost of printing, let alone the paper, plates, typework and cost of distribution. I think it's safe to say we lost over a hundred thousand dollars a year that way. The magazines were running down. They haven't waked up sufficiently yet to suit me. But I'm looking for men. I'm really looking for one man eventually who will take charge of all that editorial and art work and make it into something exceptional. He wants to be a man who can handle men. If I can get the right man I will even include the advertising department, for that really belongs with the literary and art sections. It depends on the man."

He looked significantly at Eugene, who sat there stroking his upper lip with his hand.

"Well," he said thoughtfully, "that ought to make a very nice place for someone. Who have you in mind?"

"No one as yet that I'm absolutely sure of. I have one man in mind who I think might come to fill the position after he had had a look about the organization and a chance to study its needs a little. It's a hard position to hold. It requires a man with imagination, tact, judgment. He would have to be a sort of vice-Colfax, for I can't give my attention permanently to that business. I don't want to. I have bigger fish to fry. But I want someone who will eventually be my other self in these departments, who can get along with Florence White and the men under him and hold his own in his own world. I want a sort of bi-partisan commission down there—each man supreme in his own realm."

"It sounds interesting," said Eugene thoughtfully. "Who's your man?"

"As I say, he isn't quite ready yet, in my judgment, but he is near it, and he's the right man! He's in this room now. You're the man I'm thinking about, Witla."

"No," said Eugene quietly.

"Yes; you," replied Colfax.

"You flatter me," he said, with a deprecatory wave of his hand. "I'm not so sure that he is."

"Oh, yes, he is, if he thinks he is!" replied Colfax emphatically. "Opportunity doesn't knock in vain at a real man's door. At least, I don't believe it will knock here and not be admitted. Why the advertising department of this business alone is worth eighteen thousand dollars a year to begin with."

Eugene sat up. He was getting twelve. Could he afford to ignore that offer? Could the Kalvin Company afford to pay him that much? They were paying him pretty well as it was. Could the Kalvin Company offer him the prospects which this company was offering him?

"What is more, I might say," went on Colfax, "the general publishing control of this organization—the position of managing publisher, which I am going to create and which when you are fitted for it you can have, will be worth twenty-five thousand dollars a year, and that oughtn't to be so very far away, either."

Eugene turned that over in his mind without saying anything. This offer coming so emphatically and definitely at this time actually made him nervous and fearsome. It was such a tremendous thing to talk about—the literary, art and advertising control of the United Magazines Corporation. Who was this man White? What was he like? Would he be able to agree with him? This man beside him was so hard, so brilliant, so dynamic! He would expect so much.

And then his work with Townsend Miller and under Mr. Kalvin. How much he had learned of the editorial game by merely talking and planning with those two men! He had got the whole idea of timely topics, of big progressive, national forecasts and features, of odd departments and interesting pieces of fiction and personality studies, from talking with Miller alone. Kalvin had made clear to him what constituted great craftsmen. Of course, long before, he had suspected just how it was, but in Philadelphia he had sat in conference with Miller and Kalvin, and knew. He had practically managed the former's little art department for him without paying much attention to it either. Couldn't he really handle this greater thing if he tried? If he didn't, someone else would. Would the man who would, be so much greater than himself?

"I'm not anxious that you should act hastily," said Colfax soothingly, after a little bit, for he saw that Eugene was debating the question solemnly and that it was a severe problem for him. "I know how you feel. You have gone into the Kalvin Company and you've made good. They've been nice to you. It's only natural that they should be. You hate to leave. Well, think it over. I won't tempt you beyond your best judgment. Think it over. There's a splendid chance here. Just the same, I like you, and I think you are the man to get away with it. Come down to my place tomorrow and let me show you what we have. I want to show our resources. I don't think you know how big this thing really is."

"Yes, I do," replied Eugene, smiling. "It certainly is a fascinating proposition. But I can't make up my mind about it now. It's something I want to think about. I'd like to take my time, and I'll let you know."

"Take all the time you want, my boy! Take all the time you want!" exclaimed Colfax. "I'll wait for you a little while. I'm in no life-or-death hurry. This position can't be filled satisfactorily in a minute. When you're ready, let me know what you decide. And now let's go to the theatre—what do you say?"

The automobile was called, Mrs. Colfax and her guest, Miss Genier, appeared. There was an interesting evening in a box, with Eugene talking gaily and entertainingly to all, and then an after-theatre bite at Sherry's. The next morning, for he stayed all night at Colfax's, they visited the United Magazines Corporation building together, and at noon Eugene returned to Philadelphia.

His head was fairly seething and ringing with all he had seen and heard. Colfax was a great man, he thought, greater in some respects than Kalvin. He was more forceful, more enthusiastic, younger—more like himself, than Kalvin. He could never fail, he was too rich. He would make a success of this great corporation—a tremendous success—and if he went he might help make it with him. What a thing that would be! Very different from working for a corporation with whose success he had never had anything to do. Should he ignore this offer? New York, a true art and literary standing; a great executive and social standing; fame; money—all these were calling. Why, on eighteen or twenty-five thousand he could have a splendid studio apartment of his own, say on Riverside Drive; he could entertain magnificently; he could keep an automobile without worrying about it. Angela would cease feeling that they had to be careful. It would be the apex of lieutenantship for him. Beyond that he would take stock in the company, or a business of his own. What a long distance he had come from the days when, here as a boy, he had walked the streets, wondering where he would find a $3 room, and when as an art failure he carried his paintings about and sold them for ten and fifteen dollars. Dear Heaven, what peculiar tricks fortune could play!

The discussion with Angela of this proposition led to some additional uncertainty, for although she was greatly impressed with what Colfax offered, she was afraid Eugene might be making a mistake in leaving Kalvin. The latter had been so nice to Eugene. He had never associated with him in any intimate way, but he and Angela had been invited to his home on several formal occasions, and Eugene had reported that Kalvin was constantly giving him good advice. His attitude in the office was not critical but analytic and considerate.

"He's been mighty nice to me," Eugene said to her one morning at breakfast; "they all have. It's a shame to leave him. And yet, now that I look at it, I can see very plainly that there is never going to be the field here that there will be with the United Company. They have the publications and the book business, and the Kalvin Company hasn't and won't have. Kalvin is too old. They're in New York, too; that's one thing I like about it. I'd like to live in New York again. Wouldn't you?"

"It would be fine," said Angela, who had never really cared for Philadelphia and who saw visions of tremendous superiority in this situation. Philadelphia had always seemed a little out of the way of things after New York and Paris. Only Eugene's good salary and the comforts they had experienced here had made it tolerable. "Why don't you speak to Mr. Kalvin and tell him just what Mr. Colfax says," she asked. "It may be that he'll offer to raise your salary so much that you'll want to stay when he hears of this."

"No danger," replied Eugene. "He may raise it a bit, but he never can pay me twenty-five thousand dollars a year. There isn't any reason for paying it. It takes a corporation like the United to do it. There isn't a man in our place gets that, unless it is Fredericks. Besides, I could never be anything more here, or much more, than advertising manager. Miller has that editorial job sewed up. He ought to have it, too, he's a good man. This thing that Colfax offers lets me out into a new field. I don't want to be an advertising manager all my days if I can help it!"

"I don't want you to be, either, Eugene," sighed Angela. "It's a shame you can't quit entirely and take up your art work. I've always thought that if you were to stop now and go to painting you would make a success of it. There's nothing the matter with your nerves now. It's just a question of whether we want to live more simply for a while and let you work at that. I'm sure you'd make a big success of it."

"Art doesn't appeal to me so much as it did once," replied Eugene. "I've lived too well and I know a lot more about living than I once did. Where could I make twelve thousand a year painting? If I had a hundred thousand or a couple of hundred thousand laid aside, it would be a different thing, but I haven't. All we have is that Pennsylvania Railroad stock and those lots in Montclair eating their merry little heads off in taxes, and that Steel common stock. If we go back to New York we ought to build on that Montclair property, and rent it if we don't want to live in it. If I quit now we wouldn't have more than two thousand dollars a year outside of what I could earn, and what sort of a life can you live on that?"

Angela saw, disappearing under those circumstances, the rather pleasant world of entertainment in which they were disporting themselves. Art distinction might be delightful, but would it furnish such a table as they were sitting at this morning? Would they have as nice a home and as many friends? Art was glorious, but would they have as many rides and auto trips as they had now? Would she be able to dress as nicely? It took money to produce a variety of clothing—house, street, evening, morning and other wear. Hats at thirty-five and forty dollars were not in the range of artists' wives, as a rule. Did she want to go back to a simpler life for his art's sake? Wouldn't it be better to have him go with Mr. Colfax and make $25,000 a year for a while and then have him retire?

"You'd better talk to Mr. Kalvin," she counseled. "You'll

have to do that, anyhow. See what he says. After that you can decide what you must do."

Eugene hesitated, but after thinking it all over he decided that he would.

One morning not long after, when he met Mr. Kalvin in the main hall on the editorial floor, he said, "I'd like to talk to you for a few moments some time today alone, Mr. Kalvin, if you can spare me the time."

"Certainly. I'm not busy now," returned the president. "Come right down. What is it you want to see me about?"

"Well, I'll tell you," said Eugene, when they had reached the former's office and he had closed the door. "I've had an offer that I feel that I ought to talk to you about. It's a pretty fascinating proposition and it's troubling me. I owe it to you as well as to myself to speak about it."

"Yes; what is it?" said Kalvin considerately.

"Mr. Colfax of the United Magazines Corporation came to me not long ago and wanted to know if I would not come with him. He offers me eighteen thousand dollars a year as advertising manager to begin with, and a chance to take charge of all the art and editorial ends as well a little later at twenty-five thousand dollars. He calls it the managing-publishing end of the business. I've been thinking of it seriously, for I've handled the art and advertising ends here and at the Summerfield Company, and I have always imagined that I knew something of the book and magazine business. I know it's a rather large proposition, but I'm not at all sure that I couldn't handle it."

Mr. Kalvin listened quietly. He saw what Colfax's scheme was and liked it as a proposition. It was a good idea, but needed an exceptional man for the position. Was Eugene the man? He wasn't sure of that, and yet perchance he might be. Colfax, he thought, was a man of excellent financial if not publishing judgment. He might, if he could get the proper person, make an excellent success of his business. Eugene interested him, perhaps more at first flash than he would later. This man before him had a most promising appearance. He was clean, quick, with an alert mind and eye. He could see how, because of Eugene's success here, Colfax was thinking of him being even more exceptional than he was. He was a good man, a fine man, under direction. Would Colfax have the patience, the interest, the sympathy, to work with and understand him?

"Now, let's think about that a little, Witla," he said quietly. "It's a flattering offer. You'd be foolish if you didn't give it careful consideration. Do you know anything about the organization of that place over there?"

"No," replied Eugene, "nothing except what I learned by casually going over it with Mr. Colfax."

"Do you know much about Colfax as a man?"

"Very little. I've only met him twice. He's forceful, dramatic, a man with lots of ideas. I understand he's very rich, three or four millions, someone told me."

Kalvin's hand moved indifferently. "Do you like him?"

"Well, I can't say yet absolutely whether I do or don't. He interests me a lot. He's wonderfully dynamic. I'm sure I'm favorably impressed with him."

"And he wants to give you charge eventually of all the magazines and books, the publishing end?"

"So he says," said Eugene.

"I'd go a little slow if I were saddling myself with that responsibility. I'd want to be sure that I knew all about it. You want to remember, Witla, that running one department under the direction and with the sympathetic assistance and consideration of someone over you is very different from running four or five departments on your own responsibility and with no one over you except someone who wants intelligent guidance from you. Colfax, as I understand him, isn't a publisher, either by tendency or training or education. He's a financier. He'll want you, if you take that position, to tell him how it shall be done. Now, unless you know a great deal about the publishing business, you have a difficult task in that. I don't want to appear to be throwing cold water on your natural ambition to get up in the world. You're entitled to go higher if you can. No one in your circle of acquaintances would wish you more luck than I will if you decide to go. I want you to think carefully of what you are doing. Where you are here you are perfectly safe, or as nearly safe as any man is who behaves himself and maintains his natural force and energy can be. It's only natural that you should expect more money in the face of this offer, and I shall be perfectly willing to give it to you. I intended, as you possibly expected, to do somewhat better for you by January. I'll say now that if you want to stay here you can have fourteen thousand now and possibly sixteen thousand in a year or a year and a half from now. I don't want to overload this department with what I consider an undue salary. I think sixteen thousand dollars, when it is paid, will be high for the work that is done here, but you're a good man and I'm perfectly willing to pay it to you.

"The thing for you to do is to make up your mind whether this proposition which I now make you is safer and more in accord with your desires than the one Mr. Colfax makes you. With him your eighteen thousand begins at once. With me sixteen thousand is a year away, anyhow. With him you have promise of an outlook which is much more glittering than any you can reasonably hope for here, but you want to remember that the difficulties will be, of course, proportionately greater. You know something about me by now. You still—and don't think I want to do him any injustice; I don't—have to learn about Mr. Colfax. Now, I'd advise you to think carefully before you act. Study the situation over there before you accept it. The United Magazines Corporation is a great concern. I have no doubt that under Mr. Colfax's management it has a brilliant future in store for it. He is an able man. If you finally decide to go, come and tell me and there will be no hard feelings one way or the other. If you decide to stay, the new salary arrangement goes into effect at once. As a matter of fact, I might as well have Mr. Fredericks credit that up to you so that you can say that you have drawn that sum here. It won't do you any harm. Then we can run along as before. I know it isn't good business as a rule to try and keep a man who has been poisoned by a bigger offer, and because I know that is the reason why I am only offering you fourteen thousand dollars this year. I want to be sure that you are sure that you want to stay. See?"

He smiled.

Eugene arose. "I see," he said. "You are one of the best men I have ever known, Mr. Kalvin. You have constantly treated me with more consideration than I ever expected to receive anywhere. It has been a pleasure and a privilege to work for you. If I stay, it will be because I want to—because I value your friendship."

"Well," said Kalvin quietly, "that's very nice, I'm sure, and I appreciate it. But don't let your friendship for me or your sense of gratitude stop you from doing something you think you ought to do. Go ahead if you feel like it. I won't feel the least bit angry with you. I'll feel sorry, but that's neither here nor there. Life is a constant condition of readjustment, and every good business man knows it."

He took Eugene's extended hand.

"Good luck," he said, "whatever you do"—his favorite expression.

CHAPTER XL

THE upshot of Eugene's final speculation was that he accepted the offer of the United Magazines Corporation and left Mr. Kalvin. Colfax had written one day to his house asking him what he thought he would do about it. The more he had turned it over in his mind, the more it had grown in attraction. The Colfax company was erecting a tremendous building, eighteen stories high, in the heart of the middle business district in New York near Union Square, to house all their departments. Colfax had said at the time Eugene took dinner with him that the sixteenth, seventeenth and eighteenth floors would be devoted to the editorial, publication, circulation, art, and advertising departments. He had asked Eugene what he had thought would be a good floor arrangement, and the latter, with his usual facility for scheming such things, had scratched on a piece of paper a tentative layout for the various departments. He had put the editorial and art departments on the topmost floor, giving the publisher, whoever he might eventually prove to be, a commanding position in a central room on the western side of the building which overlooked all the city between the Square and Hudson River, and showed that magnificent body of water as a panorama for the eye to feast upon. He had put the advertising and some overflow editorial rooms on the seventeenth floor, and the circulation with its attendant mailing and cabinet record rooms on the sixteenth. The publisher's and editor's rooms he laid out after an old Flemish scheme he had long had in mind, in which green, dark blue, blood-red and black walnut shades contrasted richly with the flood of light which would be available.

"You might as well do this thing right if you do it at all," he had said to Colfax. "Nearly all the editorial offices I have ever seen have been the flimsiest makeshifts. A rich-looking editorial, art and advertising department would help your company a great deal. It has advertising value."

He recalled as he spoke Summerfield's theory that a look of prosperity was about the most valuable asset a house could have.

Colfax agreed with him, and said when the time came that he wished Eugene would do him the favor to come and look the thing over. "I have two good architects on the job," he explained, "but I would rather trust your ideas as to how those rooms should be laid out."

When he was considering this final call for a decision he was thinking how this floor would look—how rich it would be. Eventually, if he succeeded, his office would be the most sumptuous thing in it. He would be the most conspicuous figure in the great, new building, apart from Colfax himself.

Thoughts of this kind, which ought to have had but very little share in any commercial speculation, were nevertheless uppermost in Eugene's mind; for he was not a business man—he was primarily an artist, and for all his floundering round in the commercial world he remained an artist still. His sense of his coming dignity and standing before the world was almost greater than his sense of the terrifying responsibility which it involved. Colfax was a hard man, he knew, harder even than Summerfield, for he talked less and acted more; but this did not sink into Eugene's consciousness sufficiently to worry him. He fancied he was a strong man, able to hold his own anywhere.

Angela was really not very much opposed to the change, though her natural conservatism made her worry and hesitate to approve. It was a great step forward if Eugene succeeded, but if he failed it would be such a loss.

"Colfax has so much faith in me," he told her. "He's convinced that I can do it, and faith like that is a great help. I'd like to try it, anyhow. It can't do me any harm. If I think I can't handle the publishing proposition I'll stick to the advertising end."

"All right," said Angela, "but I scarcely know what to advise. They've been so nice to you over here."

"I'll try it," said Eugene determinedly. "Nothing venture, nothing have," and he informed Kalvin the same day.

The latter looked at him solemnly, his keen gray eyes contemplating the situation from all points of view. "Well, Eugene," he said, "you're shouldering a great responsibility. It's difficult. Think carefully of everything that you do. I'm sorry to see you go. Good-bye."

He had the feeling that Eugene was making a mistake—that he would do better to rest a while where he was; but persuasion was useless. It would only give Eugene the notion that he was more important than he was—make matters more difficult in the future.

Kalvin had heard a number of things concerning Colfax recently, and he fancied that Eugene might find it hard to deal with him later. The general impression was that he was sub-

ject to sudden likes and dislikes which did not bear the test of
time. He was said to be scarcely human enough to be the effective head of a great working corporation.

The truth was that this general opinion was quite correct.
Colfax was as hard as steel but of a smiling and delightful presence to those he fancied. Vanity was really his other name, and
ambition with him knew no bounds. He hoped to make a tremendous success of his life, to be looked up to as an imposing
financier, and he wanted *men*—only strong men about him. Eugene seemed to Colfax to be a strong man, and the day he
finally communicated with him saying that he thought that he
would accept his offer but that he wished to talk to him further,
Colfax threw his hat up in the air, slapped his side partner White
on the back, and exclaimed: "Whee! Florrie! There's a trick
I've scored for this corporation. There's a man, unless I am
greatly mistaken, will do something here. He's young but he's
all right. He's got the looks on you and me, Florrie, but we
can stand that, can't we?"

White eyed him, with a show of joy and satisfaction which
was purely simulated. He had seen many editors and many
advertising men in his time. To his judgment they were nearly
all lightweights, men who were easily satisfied with the little
toy wherewith he or anyone might decide to gratify their vanity.
This was probably another case in point, but if a real publisher
were coming in here it would not be so well with him. He
might attempt to crowd in on his authority or at least divide it
with him. That did not appeal to his personal vanity. It
really put a stumbling block in his path, for he hoped to rule
here some day alone. Why was it that Colfax was so eager to
have the authority in this house divided? Was it because he
was somewhat afraid of him? He thought so, and he was exceedingly close to the truth when he thought so.

"Florrie's a good lieutenant," Colfax said to himself, "but he
needs to be counterbalanced here by someone who will represent
the refinements and that intellectual superiority which the world
respects."

He wanted this refinement and intellectual superiority to be
popular with the public, and to produce results in the shape of
increased circulation for his magazines and books. These two
would then act as checks each to the other, thus preventing the
house from becoming overweighted in either direction. Then he
could drive this team as a grand master—the man who had selected both, whose ideas they represented, and whose judgment

they respected. The world of finance and trade would know they were nothing without him.

What Eugene thought and what White thought of this prospective situation was that the other would naturally be the minor figure, and that he under Colfax would be the shining light. Eugene was convinced that the house without proper artistic and intellectual dominance was nothing. White was convinced that without sane commercial management it was a failure and that this was the thing to look to. Money could buy brains.

Colfax introduced Eugene to White on the morning he arrived to take charge, for on the previous occasions when he had been there White was absent. The two looked at each other and immediately suspended judgment, for both were able men. Eugene saw White as an interesting type—tall, leathery, swaggering, a back-street bully evolved into the semblance of a gentleman. White saw in Eugene a nervous, refined, semi-emotional literary and artistic type who had, however, a curious versatility and virility not common among those whom he had previously encountered. He was exceedingly forceful but not poised. That he could eventually undermine him if he could not dominate him he did not doubt. Still he was coming in with the backing of Colfax and a great reputation, and it might not be easy. Eugene made him feel nervous. He wondered as he looked at him whether Colfax would really make him general literary, artistic and advertising administrator, or whether he would remain simply advertising manager as he now entered. Colfax had not accepted Eugene for more than that.

"Here he is, Florrie," Colfax had said of Eugene, in introducing him to White. "This is the man I've been talking about. Witla—Mr. White. White—Mr. Witla. You two want to get together for the good of this house in the future. What do you think of each other?"

Eugene had previously noted the peculiarity of this rowdy, rah! rah! attitude on the part of Colfax. He seemed to have no sense of the conventions of social address and conference at any time.

"Now, by God," Colfax exclaimed, striking his right fist against his left palm, "unless I am greatly mistaken, this house is going to begin to move! I'm not positive that I have the man I want, but I think I have. White, let's stroll around and introduce him."

White swaggered to the office door.

"Sure," he said quietly. "An exceptional man," he said to himself.

Colfax was almost beside himself with satisfaction, for he was subject to emotional flushes which, however, related to self-aggrandizement only. He walked with a great stride (little as he was), which was his wont when he was feeling particularly satisfied. He talked in a loud voice, for he wanted everyone to know that he, Hiram Colfax, was about and as forceful as the lord of so great an institution should be. He could yell and scream something like a woman in a paroxysm of rage when he was thwarted or irritated. Eugene did not know that as yet.

"Here's one of the printing floors," he said to Eugene, throwing open a door which revealed a room full of thundering presses of giant size. "Where's Dodson, boy? Where's Dodson? Tell him to come here. He's foreman of our printing department," he added, turning to Eugene, as the printer's devil, who had been working at a press, scurried away to find his master. "I told you, I guess, that we have thirty of these presses. There are four more floors just like this."

"So you did," replied Eugene. "It certainly is a great concern. I can see that the possibilities of a thing like this are almost limitless."

"Limitless—I should say! It depends on what you can do with this," and he tapped Eugene's forehead. "If you do your part right, and he does his"—turning to White—"there won't be any limit to what this house can do. That remains to be seen."

Just then Dodson came bustling up, a shrewd, keen henchman of White's, and looked at Eugene curiously.

"Dodson, Mr. Witla, the new advertising manager. He's going to try to help pay for all this wasteful presswork you're doing. Witla, Mr. Dodson, manager of the printing department."

The two men shook hands. Eugene felt in a way as though he were talking to an underling, and did not pay very definite attention to him. Dodson resented his attitude somewhat, but gave no sign. His loyalty was to White, and he felt himself perfectly safe under that man's supervision.

The next visit was to the composing room where a vast army of men were working away at type racks and linotype machines. A short, fat, ink-streaked foreman in a green striped apron that looked as though it might have been made of bed ticking came forward to greet them ingratiatingly. He was plainly nervous at their presence, and withdrew his hand when Eugene offered to take it.

"It's too dirty," he said. "I'll take the will for the deed, Mr. Witla."

More explanations and laudations of the extent of the business followed.

Then came the circulation department with its head, a tall dark man who looked solemnly at Eugene, uncertain as to what place he was to have in the organization and uncertain as to what attitude he should ultimately have to take. White was "butting into his affairs," as he told his wife, and he did not know where it would end. He had heard rumors to the effect that there was to be a new man soon who was to have great authority over various departments. Was this he?

There came next the editors of the various magazines, who viewed this triumphal procession with more or less contempt, for to them both Colfax and White were raw, uncouth upstarts blazoning their material superiority in loud-mouthed phrases. Colfax talked too loud and was too vainglorious. White was too hard, bitter and unreasoning. They hated them both with a secret hate but there was no escaping their domination. The need of living salaries held all in obsequious subjection.

"Here's Mr. Marchwood," Colfax said inconsiderately of the editor of the *International Review*. "He thinks he's making a wonderful publication of that, but we don't know whether he is yet or not."

Eugene winced for Marchwood. He was so calm, so refined, so professional.

"I suppose we can only go by the circulation department," he replied simply, attracted by Eugene's sympathetic smile.

"That's all! That's all!" exclaimed Colfax.

"That is probably true," said Eugene, "but a good thing ought to be as easily circulated as a poor one. At least it's worth trying."

Mr. Marchwood smiled. It was a bit of intellectual kindness in a world of cruel comment.

"It's a great institution," said Eugene finally, on reaching the president's office again. "I'll begin now and see what I can do."

"Good luck, my boy. Good luck!" said Colfax loudly. "I'm laying great stress on what you're going to do, you know."

"Don't lean too hard," returned Eugene. "Remember, I'm just one in a great organization."

"I know, I know, but *the one* is all I need up there—*the one,* see?"

"Yes, yes," laughed Eugene, "cheer up. We'll be able to do a little something, I'm sure."

"A great man, that," Colfax declared to White as he went away. "The real stuff in that fellow, no flinching there you notice. He knows how to think. Now, Florrie, unless I miss my guess you and I are going to get somewhere with this thing."

White smiled gloomily, almost cynically. He was not so sure. Eugene was pretty good, but he was obviously too independent, too artistic, to be really stable and dependable. He would never run to him for advice, but he would probably make mistakes. He might lose his head. What must he do to offset this new invasion of authority? Discredit him? Certainly. But he needn't worry about that. Eugene would do something. He would make mistakes of some kind. He felt sure of it. He was almost positive of it.

CHAPTER XLI

THE opening days of this their second return to New York were a period of great joy to Angela. Unlike that first time when she was returning after seven months of loneliness and unhappiness to a sick husband and a gloomy outlook, she was now looking forward to what, in spite of her previous doubts, was a glorious career of dignity, prosperity and abundance. Eugene was such an important man now. His career was so well marked and in a way almost certified. They had a good bit of money in the bank. Their investments in stocks, on which they obtained a uniform rate of interest of about seven per cent., aggregated $30,000. They had two lots, two hundred by two hundred, in Montclair, which were said to be slowly increasing in value and which Eugene now estimated to be worth about six thousand. He was talking about investing what additional money he might save in stocks bearing better interest or some sound commercial venture. When the proper time came, a little later, he might even abandon the publishing field entirely and renew his interest in art. He was certainly getting near the possibility of this.

The place which they selected for their residence in New York was in a new and very sumptuous studio apartment building on Riverside Drive near Seventy-ninth Street, where Eugene had long fancied he would like to live. This famous thoroughfare and show place with its restricted park atmosphere, its magnificent and commanding view of the lordly Hudson, its wondrous woods of color and magnificent sunsets had long taken his eye. When he had first come to New York it had been his delight to stroll here watching the stream of fashionable equipages pour out towards Grant's Tomb and return. He had sat on a park bench many an afternoon at this very spot or farther up, and watched the gay company of horsemen and horsewomen riding cheerfully by, nodding to their social acquaintances, speaking to the park keepers and road scavengers in a condescending and superior way, taking their leisure in a comfortable fashion and looking idly at the river. It seemed a wonderful world to him at that time. Only millionaires could afford to live there, he thought—so ignorant was he of the financial tricks of the world. These handsomely garbed men in riding coats and breeches; the chic looking girls in stiff black hats, trailing black riding skirts, yellow gloved, and sporting short whips which looked more like dainty canes than anything else, took his fancy greatly. It was his idea at that time that this was almost the apex of social glory—to be permitted to ride here of an afternoon.

Since then he had come a long way and learned a great deal, but he still fancied this street as one of the few perfect expressions of the elegance and luxury of metropolitan life, and he wanted to live on it. Angela was given authority, after discussion, to see what she could find in the way of an apartment of say nine or eleven rooms with two baths or more, which should not cost more than three thousand or three thousand five hundred. As a matter of fact, a very handsome apartment of nine rooms and two baths including a studio room eighteen feet high, forty feet long and twenty-two feet wide was found at the now, to them, comparatively moderate sum of three thousand two hundred. The chambers were beautifully finished in old English oak carved and stained after a very pleasing fifteenth century model, and the walls were left to the discretion of the incoming tenant. Whatever was desired in the way of tapestries, silks or other wall furnishing would be supplied.

Eugene chose green-brown tapestries representing old Rhine Castles for his studio, and blue and brown silks for his wall furnishings elsewhere. He now realized a long cherished dream of having the great wooden cross of brown stained oak, ornamented with a figure of the bleeding Christ, which he set in a dark shaded corner behind two immense wax candles set in tall heavy bronze candlesticks, the size of small bed posts. These when lighted in an otherwise darkened room and flickering ruefully, cast a peculiar spell of beauty over the gay throngs which sometimes assembled here. A grand piano in old English oak occupied one corner, a magnificent music cabinet in French burnt woodwork, stood near by. There were a number of carved and fluted high back chairs, a carved easel with one of his best pictures displayed, a black marble pedestal bearing a yellow stained marble bust of Nero, with his lascivious, degenerate face, scowling grimly at the world, and two gold plated candelabra of eleven branches each hung upon the north wall.

Two wide, tall windows with storm sashes, which reached from the floor to the ceiling, commanded the West view of the Hudson. Outside one was a small stone balcony wide enough to accommodate four chairs, which gave a beautiful, cool view of the drive. It was shielded by an awning in summer and was nine storeys above the ground. Over the water of the more or less peaceful stream were the stacks and outlines of a great factory, and in the roadstead lay boats always, war vessels, tramp freighters, sail boats, and up and down passed the endless traffic of small craft always so pleasant to look upon in fair or foul weather. It was a beautiful apartment, beautifully finished in which most of their furniture, brought from Philadelphia, fitted admirably. It was here that at last they settled down to enjoy the fruit of that long struggle and comparative victory which brought them so near their much desired goal— an indestructible and unchangeable competence which no winds of ill fortune could readily destroy.

Eugene was quite beside himself with joy and satisfaction at thus finding himself and Angela eventually surrounded by those tokens of luxury, comfort and distinction which had so long haunted his brain. Most of us go through life with the furniture of our prospective castle well outlined in mind, but with never the privilege of seeing it realized. We have our pictures, our hangings, our servitors well and ably selected. Eugene's were real at last.

CHAPTER XLII

THE affairs of the United Magazines Corporation, so far as the advertising, commercial and manufacturing ends at least were concerned, were not in such an unfortunate condition by any means as to preclude their being quickly restored by tact, good business judgment and hard work. Since the accession to power of Florence White in the commercial and financial ends, things in that quarter at least had slowly begun to take a turn for the better. Although he had no judgment whatsoever as to what constituted a timely article, an important book or a saleable art feature, he had that peculiar intuition for right methods of manufacture, right buying and right selling of stock, right handling of labor from the cost and efficiency point of view, which made him a power to be reckoned with. He knew a good manufacturing man to employ at sight. He knew where books could be sold and how. He knew how to buy paper in large quantities and at the cheapest rates, and how to print and manufacture at a cost which was as low as could possibly be figured. All waste was eliminated. He used his machines to their utmost capacity, via a series of schedules which saved an immense amount of waste and demanded the least possible help. He was constantly having trouble with the labor unions on this score, for they objected to a policy which cut out duplication of effort and so eliminated their men. He was an iron master, however, coarse, brutal, foul when dealing with them, and they feared and respected him.

In the advertising end of the business things had been going rather badly, for the reason that the magazines for which this department was supposed to get business had not been doing so well editorially. They were out of touch with the times to a certain extent—not in advance of the feelings and emotions of the period, and so the public was beginning to be inclined to look elsewhere for its mental pabulum. They had had great circulation and great prestige. That was when they were younger, and the original publishers and editors in their prime. Since then days of weariness, indifference and confusion had ensued. Only with the accession of Colfax to power had hope begun to return. As has been said, he was looking for strong men in every quarter of this field, but in particular he was looking for one man who would tell him how to govern them after he had them. Who was to dream out the things which would interest the public in each particular magazine proposition? Who was to draw great and successful authors to the book end of the house? Who was to inspire the men who were directing the various departments with the spirit which would bring public interest and success? Eugene might be the man eventually he hoped, but how soon? He was anxious to hurry his progress now that he had him.

It was not long after Eugene was seated in his advertising managerial chair that he saw how things lay. His men, when he gathered them in conference, complained that they were fighting against falling circulations.

"You can talk all you want, Mr. Witla," said one of his men gloomily, "but circulation and circulation only is the answer. They have to keep up the magazines here. All these manufacturers know when they get results. We go out and get new business all the time, but we don't keep it. We can't keep it. The magazines don't bring results. What are you going to do about that?"

"I'll tell you what we are going to do," replied Eugene calmly, "we're going to key up the magazines. I understand that a number of changes are coming in that direction. They are doing better already. The manufacturing department, for one thing, is in splendid shape. I know that. In a short time the editorial departments will be. I want you people to put up, at this time, the best fight you know how under the conditions as they are. I'm not going to make any changes here if I can help it. I'm going to show you how it can be done—each one separately. I want you to believe that we have the greatest organization in the world, and it can be made to sweep everything before it. Take a look at Mr. Colfax. Do you think he is ever going to fail? We may, but he won't."

The men liked Eugene's manner and confidence. They liked his faith in them, and it was not more than ten days before he had won their confidence completely. He took home to the hotel where he and Angela were stopping temporarily all the magazines, and examined them carefully. He took home a number of the latest books issued, and asked Angela to read them. He tried to think just what it was each magazine should represent, and who and where was the man who would give to each its proper life and vigor. At once, for the adventure magazine, he thought of a man whom he had met years before who had since been making a good deal of a success editing a Sunday newspaper magazine supplement, Jack Bezenah. He had started out to be a radical writer, but had tamed down and become a most efficient newspaper man. Eugene had met him several times in the last few years and each time had been impressed by the force and subtlety of his judgment of life. Once he had said to him, "Jack, you ought to be editing a magazine of your own."

"I will be, I will be," returned that worthy. Now as he looked at this particular proposition Bezenah stuck in his mind as the man who should be employed. He had seen the present editor, but he seemed to have no force at all.

The weekly needed a man like Townsend Miller—where would he find him? The present man's ideas were interesting but not sufficiently general in their appeal. Eugene went about among the various editors looking at them, ostensibly making their acquaintance, but he was not satisfied with any one of them.

He waited to see that his own department was not needing any vast effort on his part before he said to Colfax one day:

"Things are not right with your editorial department. I've looked into my particular job to see that there is nothing so radically behindhand there but what it can be remedied, but your magazines are not right. I wish, aside from salary proposition entirely, that you would let me begin to make a few changes. You haven't the right sort of people upstairs. I'll try not to move too fast, but you couldn't be worse off than you are now in some instances."

"I know it!" said Colfax. "I know it! What do you suggest?"

"Simply better men, that's all," replied Eugene. "Better men with newer ideas. It may cost you a little more money at present, but it will bring you more back in the long run."

"You're right! You're right!" insisted Colfax enthusiastically. "I've been waiting for someone whose judgment I thought was worth two whoops to come and tell me that for a long time. So far as I'm concerned you can take charge right now! The salary that I promised you goes with it. I want to tell you something, though! I want to tell you something! You're going in there now with full authority, but don't you fall or stub your toe or get sick or make any mistakes. If you do, God help you! if you do, I'll eat you alive! I'm a good employer, Witla. I'll pay any price for good men, within reason, but if I think I'm being done, or made a fool of, or a man is making a mistake, then there's no mercy in me—not a single bit. I'm a plain, everyday blank, blank, blank" (and he

used a term so foul that it would not bear repetition in print),
"and that's all there is to me. Now we understand each
other."

Eugene looked at the man in astonishment. There was a
hard, cold gleam in his blue eyes which he had seen there before. His presence was electric—his look demoniac.

"I've had a remark somewhat of that nature made to me
before," commented Eugene. He was thinking of Summerfield's "the coal shute for yours." He had hardly expected to
hear so cold and definite a proposition laid down so soon after
his entry upon his new duties, but here it was, and he had to
face it. He was sorry for the moment that he had ever left
Kalvin.

"I'm not at all afraid of responsibility," replied Eugene
grimly. "I'm not going to fall down or stub my toe or make
any mistakes if I can help it. And if I do I won't complain
to you."

"Well, I'm only telling you," said Colfax, smiling and good-
natured again. The cold light was gone. "And I mean it in
the best way in the world. I'll back you up with all power
and authority, but if you fail, God help you; I can't."

He went back to his desk and Eugene went upstairs. He
felt as though the red cap of a cardinal had been put upon
his head, and at the same time an axe suspended over him. He
would have to think carefully of what he was doing from now
on. He would have to go slow, but he would have to go.
All power had been given him—all authority. He could go
upstairs now and discharge everybody in the place. Colfax
would back him up, but he would have to replace them. And
that quickly and effectively. It was a trying hour, notable but
grim.

His first move was to send for Bezenah. He had not seen
him for some time, but his stationery which he now had headed
"The United Magazines Corporation," and in one corner "Office of the Managing Publisher," brought him fast enough. It
was a daring thing to do in a way thus to style himself managing
publisher, when so many able men were concerned in the work,
but this fact did not disturb him. He was bound and determined to begin, and this stationery—the mere engraving of it
—was as good a way as any of serving notice that he was in
the saddle. The news flew like wild fire about the building,
for there were many in his office, even his private stenographer,
to carry the news. All the editors and assistants wondered
what it could mean, but they asked no questions, except among

themselves. No general announcement had been made. On the same stationery he sent for Adolph Morgenbau, who had exhibited marked skill at Summerfield's as his assistant, and who had since become art editor of *The Sphere*, a magazine of rising importance. He thought that Morgenbau might now be fitted to handle the art work under him, and he was not mistaken. Morgenbau had developed into a man of considerable force and intelligence, and was only too glad to be connected with Eugene again. He also talked with various advertising men, artists and writers as to just who were the most live editorial men in the field at that time, and these he wrote to, asking if they would come to see him. One by one they came, for the fact that he had come to New York to take charge not only of the advertising but the editorial ends of the United Magazines Corporation spread rapidly over the city. All those interested in art, writing, editing and advertising heard of it. Those who had known something of him in the past could scarcely believe their ears. Where did he get the skill?

Eugene stated to Colfax that he deemed it advisable that a general announcement be made to the staff that he was in charge. "I have been looking about," he said, "and I think I know what I want to do."

The various editors, art directors, advertising men and book workers were called to the main office and Colfax announced that he wished to make a statement which affected all those present. "Mr. Witla here will be in charge of all the publishing ends of this business from now on. I am withdrawing from any say in the matter, for I am satisfied that I do not know as much about it as he does. I want you all to look to him for advice and counsel just as you have to me in the past. Mr. White will continue in charge of the manufacturing and distributing end of the business. Mr. White and Mr. Witla will work together. That's all I have to say."

The company departed, and once more Eugene returned to his office. He decided at once to find an advertising man who could work under him and run that branch of the business as well as he would. He spent some time looking for this man, and finally found him working for the Hays-Rickert Company, a man whom he had known something of in the past as an exceptional worker. He was a strong, forceful individual of thirty-two, Carter Hayes by name, who was very anxious to succeed in his chosen work, and who saw a great opportunity here. He did not like Eugene so very well—he thought that he was over-estimated—but he decided to work for him. The latter put him in at ten thousand a year and then turned his attention to his new duties completely.

The editorial and publishing world was entirely new to Eugene from the executive side. He did not understand it as well as he did the art and advertising worlds, and because it was in a way comparatively new and strange to him he made a number of initial mistakes. His first was in concluding that all the men about him were more or less weak and inefficient, principally because the magazines were weak, when, as a matter of fact, there were a number of excellent men whom conditions had repressed, and who were only waiting for some slight recognition to be of great value. In the next place, he was not clear as to the exact policies to be followed in the case of each publication, and he was not inclined to listen humbly to those who could tell him. His best plan would have been to have gone exceedingly slow, watching the men who were in charge, getting their theories and supplementing their efforts with genial suggestions. Instead he decided on sweeping changes and not long after he had been in charge he began to make them. Marchwood, the editor of the *Review,* was removed, as was Gailer of the *Weekly.* The editorship of the *Adventure Story Magazine* was given to Bezenah.

In any organization of this kind, however, great improvements cannot be effected in a moment, and weeks and months must elapse before any noticeable change can be shown. Instead of throwing the burden of responsibility on each of his assistants and leaving it there, making occasional criticisms, Eugene undertook to work with each and all of them, endeavoring to direct the policy intimately in each particular case. It was not easy, and to him at times it was confusing. He had a great deal to learn. Still he did have helpful ideas in a score of directions daily and these told. The magazines were improved. The first issues which were affected by his judgment and those of his men were inspected closely by Colfax and White. The latter was particularly anxious to see what improvement had been made, and while he could not judge well himself, he had the means of getting opinions. Nearly all these were favorable, much to his disappointment, for he hoped to find things to criticize.

Colfax, who had been watching Eugene's determined air, the energy with which he went about his work and the manner in which he freely accepted responsibility, came to admire him even more than he had before. He liked him socially—his companionship after business hours—and began to invite him up to the house to dinner. Unlike Kalvin, on most of these occa-

sions he did not take Angela into consideration, for having
met her he was not so very much impressed with her. She
was nice, but not of the same coruscating quality as her husband. Mrs. Colfax expressed a derogatory opinion, and this
also made it difficult. He sincerely wished that Eugene were
single.

Time passed. As Eugene worked more and more with the
various propositions which this situation involved, he became
more and more at his ease. Those who have ever held an
executive position of any importance know how easy it is, given
a certain degree of talent, to attract men and women of ability
and force according to that talent. Like seeks like and those who
are looking for advancement in their world according to their
talents naturally drift to those who are more highly placed and
who are much like themselves. Advertising men, artists, circulation men, editors, book critics, authors and all those who
were sufficiently in his vein to understand or appreciate him
sought him out, and by degrees he was compelled to learn to
refer all applicants to the heads of departments. He was compelled to learn to rely to a certain degree on his men, and having
learned this he was inclined to go to the other extreme and
rely too much. In the case of Carter Hayes, in the advertising
department, he was particularly impressed with the man's efficiency, and rested on him heavily for all the details of that work,
merely inspecting his programs of procedure and advising him in
difficult situations. The latter appreciated this, for he was
egotistic to the roots, but it did not develop a sense of loyalty
in him. He saw in Eugene a man who had risen by some fluke
of fortune, and who was really not an advertising man at heart.
He hoped some day that circumstances would bring it about
that he could be advertising manager in fact, dealing directly
with Colfax and White, whom, because of their greater financial
interest in the business, he considered Eugene's superiors, and
whom he proposed to court. There were others in the other
departments who felt the same way.

The one great difficulty with Eugene was that he had no
great power of commanding the loyalty of his assistants. He
had the power of inspiring them—of giving them ideas which
would be helpful to themselves—but these they used, as a rule,
merely to further their own interests, to cause them to advance
to a point where they deemed themselves beyond him. Because
in his manner he was not hard, distant, bitter, he was considered,
as a rule, rather easy. The men whom he employed, and he
had talent for picking men of very exceptional ability, some-

times much greater than his own in their particular specialties, looked upon him not so much as a superior after a time, as someone who was in their path and to whose shoes they might properly aspire. He seemed so good natured about the whole work—so easy going. Now and then he took the trouble to tell a man that he was getting too officious, but in the main he did not care much. Things were going smoothly, the magazines were improving, the advertising and circulation departments were showing marked gains, and altogether his life seemed to have blossomed out into comparative perfection. There were storms and daily difficulties, but they were not serious. Colfax advised with him genially when he was in doubt, and White pretended a friendship which he did not feel.

CHAPTER XLIII

THE trouble with this situation was that it involved more power, comfort, ease and luxury than Eugene had ever experienced before, and made him a sort of oriental potentate not only among his large company of assistants but in his own home. Angela, who had been watching his career all these years with curiosity, began to conceive of him at last as a genius in every respect—destined to some great pre-eminence, in art or finance or the publishing world or all three. She did not relax her attitude in regard to his conduct, being more convinced than ever that to achieve the dizzy eminence to which he was now so rapidly ascending, he must be more circumspect than ever. People were watching him so closely now. They were so obsequious to him, but still so dangerous. A man in his position must be so careful how he dressed, talked, walked. "Don't make so much fuss," he used to say to her. "For heaven's sake, let me alone!" This merely produced more quarrels, for Angela was determined to regulate him in spite of his wishes and in his best interests.

Grave men and women in various walks of life—art, literature, philanthropy, trade, began to seek him out, because in the first place he had an understanding mind and because in the next place, which was much more important, he had something to give. There are always those in all walks of life who are seeking something through those avenues which a successful person represents, whatever they may be, and these together with those others who are always intensely eager to bask in the reflected glory of a rising luminary, make a retinue for every successful man. Eugene had his retinue, men and women of his own station or beneath it, who would eagerly shake his hand with an "Oh, yes, indeed. Managing Publisher of the United Magazines Corporation! Oh, yes, yes!" Women particularly were prone to smile, showing him even white teeth and regretting that all good looking and successful men were married.

In July following his coming from Philadelphia the United Magazines Corporation moved into its new building, and then he was installed into the most imposing office of his career. A subtle assistant, wishing to ingratiate the staff in Eugene's good graces, suggested that a collection be taken up for flowers.

His room, which was done in white, blue and gold with rose wood furniture, to set it apart from the prevailing decorative scheme and so make it more impressive, was scattered with great bouquets of roses, sweet peas and pinks, in beautiful and ornate vases of different colors, countries and schools. His great rosewood flat-topped desk, covered with a thick, plate glass through which the polished wood shone brightly, was decorated with flowers. On the morning of his entry he held an impromptu reception, on which occasion he was visited by Colfax and White, who after going to look at their new rooms, came to his. A general reception which followed some three weeks later, and in which the successful representatives of various walks of life in the metropolis took part, drew to the building a great crowd, artists, writers, editors, publishers, authors and advertising men who saw him in all his glory. On this occasion, Eugene, with White and Colfax did the receiving. He was admired at a distance by striplings who wondered how he had ever accomplished such great results. His rise had been so meteoric. It seemed so impossible that a man who had started as an artist should change and become a dominant factor in literature and art from a publishing point of view.

In his own home his surroundings were equally showy; he was as much a figure as he was in his office. When he was alone with Angela, which was not so often, for naturally they did a great deal of entertaining, he was a figure even to her. Long ago she had come to think of him as someone who would some day dominate in the art world; but to see him an imposing factor in the city's commercial life, its principal publishers' representative, having a valet and an automobile, riding freely in cabs, lunching at the most exclusive restaurants and clubs, and associating constantly with someone who was of importance, was a different matter.

She was no longer so sure of herself with him, not so certain of her power to control him. They quarreled over little things, but she was not so ready to begin these quarrels. He seemed changed now and deeper still. She was afraid, even yet, that he might make a mistake and lose it all, that the forces of ill will, envy and jealousy which were everywhere apparent in life, and which blow about so easily like gusts of wind, would work him harm. Eugene was apparently at ease, though he was troubled at times for his own safety, when he thought of it, for he had no stock in the company, and was as beholden to Colfax as any hall boy, but he did not see how he could easily be dispensed with. He was *making good*.

Colfax was friendly to him. He was surprised at times to
see how badly the manufacturing arrangements could go awry,
affecting his dates of issue, but White invariably had a good excuse. Colfax took him to his house in the country, his lodge in
the mountains, on short yachting and fishing trips, for he liked
to talk to him, but he rarely if ever invited Angela. He did
not seem to think it was necessary to do this, and Eugene was
afraid to impress the slight upon his attention, much as he
dreaded the thoughts which Angela must be thinking. It was
Eugene here and Eugene there, with constant calls of "where
are you, old man?" from Colfax, who appeared not to want
to be away from him.

"Well, old man," he would say, looking him over much as
one might a blood horse or a pedigree dog, "you're getting on.
This new job agrees with you. You didn't look like that when
you came to me," and he would feel the latest suit Eugene might
be wearing, or comment on some pin or tie he had on, or tell
him that his shoes were not as good as he could really get, if
he wanted to be perfect in dress. Colfax was for grooming his
new prize much as one might groom a blood horse, and he was
always telling Eugene little details of social life, the right things
to do, the right places to be seen, the right places to go, as
though Eugene knew little or nothing.

"Now when we go down to Mrs. Savage's Friday afternoon,
you get a Truxton Portmanteau. Have you seen them? Well,
there's the thing. Got a London coat? Well, you ought to
have one. Those servants down there go through your things
and they size you up accordingly. Nothing less than two dollars
each goes, and five dollars to the butler, remember that."

He assumed and insisted after a fashion which Eugene resented quite as much as he did his persistent ignoring of Angela,
but he did not dare comment on it. He could see that Colfax
was variable, that he could hate as well as love, and that he
rarely took any intermediate ground. Eugene was his favorite
now.

"I'll send my car around for you at two Friday," he would
say, as though Eugene did not keep a car, when he was planning one of his week-end excursions. "You be ready."

At two, on that day, Colfax's big blue touring car would come
speeding up to the entrance of the apartment house and Eugene's
valet would carry down his bags, golf sticks, tennis racket and
the various paraphernalia that go with a week-end's entertainment, and off the car would roll. At times Angela would be
left behind, at times taken, when Eugene could arrange it;

but he found that he had to be tactful and accede to Colfax's indifference mostly. Eugene would always explain to her how it was. He was sorry for her in a way, and yet he felt there was some justice in the distinction. She was not exactly suited to that topmost world in which he was now beginning to move. These people were colder, sharper, shrewder, than Angela. They had more of that intense sophistication of manner and experience than she could achieve. As a matter of fact, Angela had as much grace and more than many of the four hundred, but she did lack that quickness of wit or that shallow self-sufficiency and assurance which are the almost invariable traits of those who shine as members of the smart set. Eugene was able to assume this manner whether he felt it or not.

"Oh, that's all right," she would say, "as long as you're doing it for business reasons."

She resented it nevertheless, bitterly, for it seemed such an uncalled for slur. Colfax had no compunctions in adjusting his companionship to suit his moods. He thought Eugene was well suited to this high life. He thought Angela was not. He made the distinction roughly and went his way.

It was in this manner that Eugene learned a curious fact about the social world, and that was that frequently in these highest circles a man would be received where his wife would not and vice versa, and that nothing very much was thought of it, if it could be managed.

"Oh, is that Birkwood," he heard a young swell once remark, concerning an individual in Philadelphia. "Why do they let him in? His wife is charming, but he won't do," and once in New York he heard a daughter ask her mother, of a certain wife who was announced—her husband being at the same table —"who invited her?"

"I'm sure I don't know," replied her mother; "I didn't. She must have come of her own accord."

"She certainly has her nerve with her," replied the daughter —and when the wife entered Eugene could see why. She was not good looking and not harmoniously and tastefully dressed. It gave Eugene a shock, but in a way he could understand. There were no such grounds of complaint against Angela. She was attractive and shapely. Her one weakness was that she lacked the blasé social air. It was too bad, he thought.

In his own home and circle, however, he thought to make up for this by a series of entertainments which grew more and more elaborate as time went on. At first when he came back from Philadelphia it consisted of a few people in to dinner, old friends, for he was not quite sure of himself and did not know how many would come to share his new honors with him. Eugene had never got over his love for those he had known in his youth. He was not snobbish. It was true that now he was taking naturally to prosperous people, but the little ones, the old-time ones, he liked for old lang syne's sake as well as for themselves. Many came to borrow money, for he had associated with many ne'er do wells in his time, but many more were attracted by his fame.

Eugene knew intimately and pleasantly most of the artistic and intellectual figures of his day. In his home and at his table there appeared artists, publishers, grand opera stars, actors and playwrights. His large salary, for one thing, his beautiful apartment and its location, his magnificent office and his friendly manner all conspired to assist him. It was his self-conscious boast that he had not changed. He liked nice people, simple people, natural people he said, for these were the really great ones, but he could not see how far he had come in class selection. Now he naturally gravitated to the wealthy, the reputed, the beautiful, the strong and able, for no others interested him. He hardly saw them. If he did it was to pity or give alms.

It is difficult to indicate to those who have never come out of poverty into luxury, or out of comparative uncouthness into refinement, the veil or spell which the latter comes eventually to cast over the inexperienced mind, coloring the world anew. Life is apparently striving, constantly, to perfect its illusions and to create spells. There are, as a matter of fact, nothing but these outside that ultimate substance or principle which underlies it all. To those who have come out of inharmony, harmony is a spell, and to those who have come out of poverty, luxury is a dream of delight. Eugene, being primarily a lover of beauty, keenly responsive to all those subtleties of perfection and arrangement which ingenuity can devise, was taken vastly by the nature of this greater world into which, step by step apparently, he was almost insensibly passing. Each new fact which met his eye or soothed his sensibilities was quickly adjusted to all that had gone before. It seemed to him as though all his life he had naturally belonged to this perfect world of which country houses, city mansions, city and country clubs, expensive hotels and inns, cars, resorts, beautiful women, affected manners, subtlety of appreciation and perfection of appointment generally were the inherent concomitants. This was the true heaven— that material and spiritual perfection on earth, of which the world was dreaming and to which, out of toil, disorder, shabby ideas, mixed opinions, non-understanding and all the ill to which the flesh is heir, it was constantly aspiring.

Here was no sickness, no weariness apparently, no ill health or untoward circumstances. All the troubles, disorders and imperfections of existence were here carefully swept aside and one saw only the niceness, the health and strength of being. He was more and more impressed as he came farther and farther along in the scale of comfort, with the force and eagerness with which life seems to minister to the luxury-love of the human mind. He learned of so many, to him, lovely things, large, wellkept, magnificent country places, scenes of exquisite beauty where country clubs, hotels, seaside resorts of all descriptions had been placed. He found sport, amusement, exercise, to be tremendously well organized and that there were thousands of people who were practically devoting their lives to this. Such a state of social ease was not for him yet, but he could sit at the pleasures, so amply spread, between his hours of work and dream of the time to come when possibly he might do nothing at all. Yachting, motoring, golfing, fishing, hunting, riding, playing tennis and polo, there were experts in all these fields he found. Card playing, dancing, dining, lounging, these seemed to occupy many people's days constantly. He could only look in upon it all as upon a passing show, but that was better than nothing. It was more than he had ever done before. He was beginning to see clearly how the world was organized, how far were its reaches of wealth, its depths of poverty. From the lowest beggar to the topmost scene—what a distance!

Angela scarcely kept pace with him in all these mental peregrinations. It was true that now she went to the best dressmakers only, bought charming hats, the most expensive shoes, rode in cabs and her husband's auto, but she did not feel about it as he did. It seemed very much like a dream to her— like something that had come so suddenly and so exuberantly that it could not be permanent. There was running in her mind all the time that Eugene was neither a publisher, nor an editor, nor a financier at heart, but an artist and that an artist he would remain. He might attain great fame and make much money out of his adopted profession, but some day in all likelihood he would leave it and return to art. He seemed to be making sound investments—at least, they seemed sound to her, and their stocks and bank accounts, principally convertible stocks, seemed a safe enough margin for the future to guarantee peace of mind, but they were not saving so much, after all. It was costing them something over eight thousand dollars a year to live, and their expenses were constantly growing larger rather than smaller. Eugene appeared to become more and more extravagant.

"I think we are doing too much entertaining," Angela had once protested, but he waived the complaint aside. "I can't do what I'm doing and not entertain. It's building me up. People in our position have to." He threw open the doors finally to really remarkable crowds and most of the cleverest people in all walks of life—the really exceptionally clever—came to eat his meals, to drink his wines, to envy his comfort and wish they were in his shoes.

During all this time Eugene and Angela instead of growing closer together, were really growing farther and farther apart. She had never either forgotten or utterly forgiven that one terrific lapse, and she had never believed that Eugene was utterly cured of his hedonistic tendencies. Crowds of beautiful women came to Angela's teas, lunches and their joint evening parties and receptions. Under Eugene's direction they got together interesting programmes, for it was no trouble now for him to command musical, theatrical, literary and artistic talent. He knew men and women who could make rapid charcoal or crayon sketches of people, could do feats in legerdemain, and character representation, could sing, dance, play, recite and tell humorous stories in a droll and off-hand way. He insisted that only exceptionally beautiful women be invited, for he did not care to look at the homely ones, and curiously he found dozens, who were not only extremely beautiful, but singers, dancers, composers, authors, actors and playwrights in the bargain. Nearly all of them were brilliant conversationalists and they helped to entertain themselves—made their own entertainment, in fact. His table very frequently was a glittering spectacle. One of his "Stunts" as he called it was to bundle fifteen or twenty people into three or four automobiles after they had lingered in his rooms until three o'clock in the morning and motor out to some out-of-town inn for breakfast and "to see the sun rise." A small matter like a bill for $75.00 for auto hire or thirty-five dollars for a crowd for breakfast did not trouble him. It was a glorious sensation to draw forth his purse and remove four or five or six yellow backed ten dollar bills, knowing that it made little real difference. More money was coming to him from the same source. He could send down to the cashier at any time and draw from five hundred to a thousand dollars. He always had from one hundred and fifty to three hundred dollars in his purse in denominations of five, ten and twenty dollar bills. He carried a small check book and most frequently paid by check. He liked to assume that he was known and frequently imposed this assumption on others.

"Eugene Witla! Eugene Witla! George! he's a nice fellow,"—or "it's remarkable how he has come up, isn't it?" "I was at the Witlas' the other night. Did you ever see such a beautiful apartment? It's perfect! That view!"

People commented on the interesting people he entertained, the clever people you met there, the beautiful women, the beautiful view. "And Mrs. Witla is so charming."

But down at the bottom of all this talk there was also much envy and disparagement and never much enthusiasm for the personality of Mrs. Witla. She was not as brilliant as Eugene —or rather the comment was divided. Those who liked clever people, show, wit, brilliance, ease, liked Eugene and not Angela quite so much. Those who liked sedateness, solidity, sincerity, the commoner virtues of faithfulness and effort, admired Angela. All saw that she was a faithful handmaiden to her husband, that she adored the ground he walked on.

"Such a nice little woman—so homelike. It's curious that he should have married her, though, isn't it? They are so different. And yet they appear to have lots of things in common, too. It's strange—isn't it?"

CHAPTER XLIV

IT was in the course of his final upward progress that Eugene came once more into contact with Kenyon C. Winfield, Ex-State Senator of New York, President of the Long Island Realty Company, land developer, real estate plunger, financier, artist, what not—a man very much of Eugene's own type and temperament, who at this time was doing rather remarkable things in a land speculative way. Winfield was tall and thin, black haired, black eyed, slightly but not offensively hook nosed, dignified, gracious, intellectual, magnetic, optimistic. He was forty-eight years of age. Winfield was a very fair sample of your man of the world who has ideas, dreams, fancies, executive ability, a certain amount of reserve and judgment, sufficient to hold his own in this very complicated mortal struggle. He was not really a great man, but he was so near it that he gave the impression to many of being so. His deep sunken black eyes burned with a peculiar lustre, one might almost have fancied a tint of red in them. His pale, slightly sunken face had some of the characteristics of your polished Mephisto, though not too many. He was not at all devilish looking in the true sense of the word, but keen, subtle, artistic. His method was to ingratiate himself with men who had money in order to get from them the vast sums which he found it necessary to borrow to carry out the schemes or rather dreams he was constantly generating. His fancies were always too big for his purse, but he had such lovely fancies that it was a joy to work with them and him.

Primarily Winfield was a real estate speculator, secondarily he was a dreamer of dreams and seer of visions. His visions consisted of lovely country areas near some city stocked with charming country houses, cut up with well paved, tree shaded roads, provided with sewers, gas, electricity, suitable railway service, street cars and all the comforts of a well organized living district which should be at once retired, exclusive, pleasing, conservative and yet bound up tightly with the great Metropolitan heart of New York which he so greatly admired. Winfield had been born and raised in Brooklyn. He had been a politician, orator, insurance dealer, contractor, and so on. He had succeeded in organizing various suburban estates—Winfield, Sunnyside, Ruritania, The Beeches—little forty, fifty, one hundred and two hundred acre flats which with the help of "O. P. M." as he always called other people's money he had divided off into blocks, laying out charmingly with trees and sometimes a strip of green grass running down the centre, concrete sidewalks, a set of noble restrictions, and so forth. Anyone who ever came to look at a lot in one of Winfield's perfect suburbs always found the choicest piece of property in the centre of this latest burst of improvement set aside for the magnificent house which Mr. Kenyon C. Winfield, the president of the company, was to build and live in. Needless to say they were never built. He had been round the world and seen a great many things and places, but Winfield or Sunnyside or Ruritania or The Beeches, so the lot buyers in these places were told, had been finally selected by him deliberately as the one spot in all the world in which he hoped to spend the remainder of his days.

At the time Eugene met him, he was planning Minetta Water on the shores of Gravesend Bay, which was the most ambitious of all his projects so far. He was being followed financially, by a certain number of Brooklyn politicians and financiers who had seen him succeed in small things, taking a profit of from three to four hundred per cent. out of ten, twenty and thirty acre flats, but for all his brilliance it had been slow work. He was now worth between three and four hundred thousand dollars and, for the first time in his life, was beginning to feel that freedom in financial matters which made him think that he could do almost anything. He had met all sorts of people, lawyers, bankers, doctors, merchants, the "easy classes" he called them, all with a little money to invest, and he had succeeded in luring hundreds of worth-while people into his projects. His great dreams had never really been realized, however, for he saw visions of a great warehouse and shipping system to be established on Jamaica Bay, out of which he was to make millions, if it ever came to pass, and also a magnificent summer resort of some kind, somewhere, which was not yet clearly evolved in his mind. His ads were scattered freely through the newspapers: his signs, or rather the signs of his towns, scattered broadcast over Long Island.

Eugene had met him first when he was working with the Summerfield Company, but he met him this time quite anew at the home of the W. W. Willebrand on the North Shore of Long Island near Hempstead. He had gone down there one Saturday afternoon at the invitation of Mrs. Willebrand, whom he had met at another house party and with whom he had danced. She had been pleased with his gay, vivacious manner and had asked him if he wouldn't come. Winfield was here as a guest with his automobile.

"Oh, yes," said Winfield pleasantly. "I recall you very well. You are now with the United Magazines Corporation,—I understand—someone was telling me—a most prosperous company, I believe. I know Mr. Colfax very well. I once spoke to Summerfield about you. A most astonishing fellow, that, tremendously able. You were doing that series of sugar plantation ads for them or having them done. I think I copied the spirit of those things in advertising Ruritania, as you may have noticed. Well, you certainly have improved your condition since then. I once tried to tell Summerfield that he had an exceptional man in you, but he would have nothing of it. He's too much of an egoist. He doesn't know how to work with a man on equal terms."

Eugene smiled at the thought of Summerfield.

"An able man," he said simply. "He did a great deal for me."

Winfield liked that. He thought Eugene would criticize him. He liked Eugene's genial manner and intelligent, expressive face. It occurred to him that when next he wanted to advertise one of his big development projects, he would go to Eugene or the man who had done the sugar plantation series of pictures and get him to give him the right idea for advertising.

Affinity is such a peculiar thing. It draws people so easily, apart from volition or consciousness. In a few moments Eugene and Winfield, sitting side by side on the veranda, looking at the greenwood before them, the long stretch of open sound, dotted with white sails and the dim, distant shore of Connecticut, were talking of real estate ventures in general, what land was worth, how speculations of this kind turned out, as a rule. Winfield was anxious to take Eugene seriously, for he felt drawn to him and Eugene studied Winfield's pale face, his thin, immaculate hands, his suit of soft, gray cloth. He looked as able as his public reputation made him out to be—in fact, he looked better than anything he had ever done. Eugene had seen Ruritania and The Beeches. They did not impress him vastly as territorial improvements, but they were pretty, nevertheless. For middle-class people, they were quite the thing he thought.

"I should think it would be a pleasure to you to scheme out a new section," he said to him once. "The idea of a virgin piece of land to be converted into streets and houses or a village appeals to me immensely. The idea of laying it out and sketching houses to fit certain positions, suits my temperament exactly. I wish sometimes I had been born an architect."

"It is pleasant and if that were all it would be ideal," returned Winfield. "The thing is more a matter of financing than anything else. You have to raise money for land and improvements. If you make exceptional improvements they are expensive. You really can't expect to get much, if any, of your money back, until all your work is done. Then you have to wait. If you put up houses you can't rent them, for the moment you rent them, you can't sell them as new. When you make your improvements your taxes go up immediately. If you sell a piece of property to a man or woman who isn't exactly in accord with your scheme, he or she may put up a house which destroys the value of a whole neighborhood for you. You can't fix the details of a design in a contract too closely. You can only specify the minimum price the house is to cost and the nature of the materials to be used. Some people's idea of beauty will vary vastly from others. Taste in sections may change. A whole city like New York may suddenly decide that it wants to build west when you are figuring on its building east. So—well, all these things have to be taken into consideration."

"That sounds logical enough," said Eugene, "but wouldn't the right sort of a scheme just naturally draw to itself the right sort of people, if it were presented in the right way? Don't you fix the conditions by your own attitude?"

"You do, you do," replied Winfield, easily. "If you give the matter sufficient care and attention it can be done. The pity is you can be too fine at times. I have seen attempts at perfection come to nothing. People with taste and tradition and money behind them are not moving into new additions and suburbs, as a rule. You are dealing with the new rich and financial beginners. Most people strain their resources to the breaking point to better their living conditions and they don't always know. If they have the money, it doesn't always follow that they have the taste to grasp what you are striving for, and if they have the taste they haven't the money. They would do better if they could, but they can't. A man in my position is like an artist and a teacher and a father confessor and financier and everything all rolled into one. When you start to be a real estate developer on a big scale you must be these things. I have had some successes and some notable failures. Winfield is one of the worst. It's disgusting to me now."

"I have always wished I could lay out a seaside resort or a suburb," said Eugene dreamily. "I've never been to but one or two of the resorts abroad, but it strikes me that none of the resorts here—certainly none near New York—are right. The opportunities are so wonderful. The things that have been done are horrible. There is no plan, no detail anywhere."

"My views exactly," said Winfield. "I've been thinking of it for years. Some such place could be built, and I suppose if it were done right it would be successful. It would be expensive, though, very, and those who come in would have a long wait for their money."

"It would be a great opportunity to do something really worth while, though," said Eugene. "No one seems to realize how beautiful a thing like that could be made."

Winfield said nothing, but the thought stuck in his mind. He was dreaming a seaside improvement which should be the most perfect place of its kind in the world—a monument to himself if he did it. If Eugene had this idea of beauty he might help. At least he might talk to him about it when the time came. Perhaps Eugene might have a little money to invest. It would take millions to put such a scheme through, but every little would help. Besides Eugene might have ideas which should make money both for himself and for Winfield. It was worth thinking about. So they parted, not to meet again for weeks and months, but they did not forget each other.

BOOK III

THE REVOLT

CHAPTER I

IT was when Eugene was at the height of his success that a meeting took place between himself and a certain Mrs. Emily Dale.

Mrs. Dale was a strikingly beautiful and intelligent widow of thirty-eight, the daughter of a well-to-do and somewhat famous New York family of Dutch extraction—the widow of an eminent banker of considerable wealth who had been killed in an automobile accident near Paris some years before. She was the mother of four children, Suzanne, eighteen; Kinroy, fifteen; Adele, twelve, and Ninette, nine, but the size of her family had in no way affected the subtlety of her social personality and the delicacy of her charm and manner. She was tall, graceful, willowy, with a wealth of dark hair, which was used in the most subtle manner to enhance the beauty of her face. She was calm, placid apparently, while really running deep with emotion and fancies, with manners which were the perfection of kindly courtesy and good breeding and with those airs of superiority which come so naturally to those who are raised in a fortunate and exclusive atmosphere.

She did not consider herself passionate in a marked degree, but freely admitted to herself that she was vain and coquettish. She was keen and observing, with a single eye to the main chance socially, but with a genuine love for literature and art and a propensity to write. Eugene met her through Colfax, who introduced him to her. He learned from the latter that she was rather unfortunate in her marriage except from a money point of view, and that her husband's death was no irreparable loss. He also learned from the same source that she was a good mother, trying to bring up her children in the manner most suitable to their station and opportunities. Her husband had been of a much poorer social origin than herself, but her own standing was of the very best. She was a gay social figure, being invited much, entertaining freely, preferring the company of younger men to those of her own age or older and being followed ardently by one fortune hunter and another, who saw in her beauty, wealth and station, an easy door to the heaven of social supremacy.

The Dale home, or homes rather, were in several different places—one at Morristown, New Jersey, another on fashionable

Grimes Hill on Staten Island, a third—a city residence, which at the time Eugene met them, was leased for a term of years— was in Sixty-seventh Street, near Fifth Avenue in New York City, and a fourth, a small lodge, at Lenox, Massachusetts, which was also rented. Shortly after he met her the house at Morristown was closed and the lodge at Lenox re-occupied.

For the most part Mrs. Dale preferred to dwell in her ancestral home on Staten Island, which, because of its commanding position on what was known as Grimes Hill, controlled a magnificent view of the bay and harbor of New York. Manhattan, its lower wall of buildings, lay like a cloud at the north. The rocking floor of the sea, blue and gray and slate black by turn, spread to the east. In the west were visible the Kill von' Kull with its mass of shipping and the Orange Hills. In a boat club at Tompkinsville she had her motor boat, used mostly by her boy; in her garage at Grimes Hill, several automobiles. She owned several riding horses, retained four family servants permanently and in other ways possessed all those niceties of appointment which make up the comfortable life of wealth and ease.

The two youngest of her girls were in a fashionable boarding school at Tarrytown; the boy, Kinroy, was preparing for Harvard; Suzanne, the eldest, was at home, fresh from boarding school experiences, beginning to go out socially. Her début had already been made. Suzanne was a peculiar girl, plump, beautiful, moody, with, at times, a dreamy air of indifference and a smile that ran like a breath of air over water. Her eyes were large, of a vague blue-gray, her lips rosy and arched; her cheeks full and pink. She had a crown of light chestnut hair, a body at once innocent and voluptuous in its outlines. When she laughed it was a rippling gurgle, and her sense of humor was perfect, if not exaggerated. One of those naturally wise but as yet vague and formless artistic types, which suspect without education, nearly all the subtleties of the world, and burst forth full winged and beautiful, but oh, so fragile, like a butterfly from its chrysalis, the radiance of morning upon its body. Eugene did not see her for a long time after he met Mrs. Dale, but when he did, he was greatly impressed with her beauty.

Life sometimes builds an enigma out of common clay, and with a look from a twelve-year-old girl, sets a Dante singing. It can make a god of a bull, a divinity of an ibis, or a beetle, set up a golden calf to be worshipped of the multitude. Paradox! Paradox! In this case an immature and yet nearly perfect body held a seemingly poetic and yet utterly nebulous appreciation of life—a body so youthful, a soul so fumbling that one would ask, How should tragedy lurk in form like this?

A fool?

Not quite, yet so nebulous, so much a dreamer that difficulty might readily follow in the wake of any thoughtless deed.

As a matter of fact, favored as she was by nature and fortune, her very presence was dangerous—provocative, without thought of being so. If a true artist had painted her, synthesizing her spirit with her body, he might have done so showing her standing erect on a mountain top, her limbs outlined amidst fluttering draperies against the wind, her eyes fixed on distant heights, or a falling star. Out of mystery into mystery again, so she came and went. Her mind was not unlike a cloud of mist through which the morning sun is endeavoring to break, irradiating all with its flushes of pink and gold. Again it was like those impearled shells of the South Sea, without design yet suggestive of all perfections and all beauties. Dreams! dreams!— of clouds, sunsets, colors, sounds which a too articulate world would do its best later to corrupt. What Dante saw in Beatrice, what Abélard saw in Héloïse, Romeo in Juliet, so some wondering swain could have seen in her—and suffered a like fate.

Eugene encountered Mrs. Dale at a house party on Long Island one Saturday afternoon, and their friendship began at once. She was introduced to him by Colfax, and because of the latter's brusque, jesting spirit was under no illusions as to his social state.

"You needn't look at him closely," he observed gaily, "he's married."

"That simply makes him all the more interesting," she rippled, and extended her hand.

Eugene took it. "I'm glad a poor married man can find shelter somewhere," he said, smartly.

"You should rejoice," she replied. "It's at once your liberty and your protection. Think how safe you are!"

"I know, I know," he said. "All the slings and arrows of Miss Fortune hurtling by."

"And you in no danger of being hurt."

He offered her his arm, and they strolled through a window onto a veranda.

The day was just the least bit dull for Mrs. Dale. Bridge was in progress in the card room, a company of women and girls gambling feverishly. Eugene was not good at bridge, not quick enough mentally, and Mrs. Dale did not care much for it.

"I have been trying to stir up enough interest to bring to

pass a motor ride, but it doesn't work," she said. "They all have the gambling fever today. Are you as greedy as the others?"

"I'm greedy I assure you, but I can't play. The greediest thing I can do is to stay away from the tables. I save most. That sharp Faraday has cleaned me and two others out of four hundred dollars. It's astonishing the way some people can play. They just look at the cards or make mystic signs and the wretched things range themselves in serried ranks to suit them. It's a crime. It ought to be a penitentiary offense, particularly to beat me. I'm such an inoffensive specimen of the non-bridge playing family."

"A burnt child, you know. Stay away. Let's sit here. They can't come out here and rob you."

They sat down in green willow chairs, and after a time a servant offered them coffee. Mrs. Dale accepted. They drifted conversationally from bridge to characters in society—a certain climber by the name of Bristow, a man who had made a fortune in trunks—and from him to travel and from travel to Mrs. Dale's experiences with fortune hunters. The automobile materialized through the intervention of others, but Eugene found great satisfaction in this woman's company and sat beside her. They talked books, art, magazines, the making of fortunes and reputations. Because he was or seemed to be in a position to assist her in a literary way she was particularly nice to him. When he was leaving she asked, "Where are you in New York?"

"Riverside Drive is our present abode," he said.

"Why don't you bring Mrs. Witla and come down to see us some week-end? I usually have a few people there, and the house is roomy. I'll name you a special day if you wish."

"Do. We'll be delighted. Mrs. Witla will enjoy it, I'm sure."

Mrs. Dale wrote to Angela ten days later as to a particular date, and in this way the social intimacy began.

It was never of a very definite character, though. When Mrs. Dale met Angela she liked her quite well as an individual, whatever she may have thought of her as a social figure. Neither Eugene nor Angela saw Suzanne nor any of the other children on this occasion, all of them being away. Eugene admired the view tremendously and hinted at being invited again. Mrs. Dale was delighted. She liked him as a man entirely apart from his position but particularly because of his publishing station. She was ambitious to write. Others had told her that he was the most conspicuous of the rising figures in the publishing world. Being friendly with him would give her exceptional standing with all his editors. She was only too pleased to be gracious to him. He was invited again and a third time, with Angela, and it seemed as though they were reaching, or might at least reach, something much more definite than a mere social acquaintance.

It was about six months after Eugene had first met Mrs. Dale that Angela gave a tea, and Eugene, in assisting her to prepare the list of invitations, had suggested that those who were to serve the tea and cakes should be two exceptionally pretty girls who were accustomed to come to the Witla apartment, Florence Reel, the daughter of a well-known author of that name and Marjorie Mac Tennan, the daughter of a well-known editor, both beautiful and talented, one with singing and the other with art ambitions. Angela had seen a picture of Suzanne Dale in her mother's room at Daleview on Grimes Hill, and had been particularly taken with her girlish charm and beauty.

"I wonder," she said, "if Mrs. Dale would object to having Suzanne come and help serve that day. She would like it, I'm sure, there are going to be so many clever people here. We haven't seen her, but that doesn't matter. It would be a nice way to introduce herself."

"That's a good idea, I should say," observed Eugene judicially. He had seen the photo of Suzanne and liked it, though he was not over-impressed. Photos to him were usually gross deceivers. He accepted them always with reservations. Angela forthwith wrote to Mrs. Dale, who agreed. She would be glad to come herself. She had seen the Witla apartment, and had been very much pleased with it. The reception day came and Angela begged Eugene to come home early.

"I know you don't like to be alone with a whole roomful of people, but Mr. Goodrich is coming, and Frederick Allen (one of their friends who had taken a fancy to Eugene), Arturo Scalchero is going to sing and Bonavita to play." Scalchero was none other than Arthur Skalger, of Port Jervis, New Jersey, but he assumed this corruption of his name in Italy to help him to succeess. Bonavita was truly a Spanish pianist of some repute who was flattered to be invited to Eugene's home.

"Well, I don't care much about it," replied Eugene. "But I will come."

He frequently felt that afternoon teas and receptions were ridiculous affairs, and that he had far better be in his office at-

tending to his multitudinous duties. Still he did leave early, and
at five-thirty was ushered into a great roomful of chattering,
gesticulating, laughing people. A song by Florence Reel had
just been concluded. Like all girls of ambition, vivacity and
imagination, she took an interest in Eugene, for in his smiling
face she found a responsive gleam.

"Oh, Mr. Witla!" she exclaimed. "Now here you are and
you just missed my song. And I wanted you to hear it, too."

"Don't grieve, Florrie," he said familiarly, holding her hand
and looking momentarily in her eyes. "You're going to sing it
again for me. I heard part of it as I came up on the elevator."
He relinquished her hand. "Why, Mrs. Dale! Delighted, I'm
sure. So nice of you. And Arturo Scalchero—hullo, Skalger,
you old frost! Where'd you get the Italian name? Bonavita!
Fine! Am I going to hear you play? All over? Alas! Marjorie Mac Tennan! Gee, but you look sweet! If Mrs. Witla
weren't watching me, I'd kiss you. Oh, the pretty bonnet!
And Frederick Allen! My word! What are you trying to grab
off, Allen? I'm on to you. No bluffs! Nix! Nix! Why, Mrs.
Schenck—delighted! Angela, why didn't you tell me Mrs.
Schenck was coming? I'd have been home at three."

By this time he had reached the east end of the great studio
room, farthest from the river. Here a tea table was spread
with a silver tea service, and behind it a girl, oval-faced,
radiantly healthy, her full lips parted in a ripe smile, her
blue-gray eyes talking pleasure and satisfaction, her forehead
laid about by a silver filigree band, beneath which her brown
chestnut curls protruded. Her hands, Eugene noted, were
plump and fair. She stood erect, assured, with the least touch
of quizzical light in her eye. A white, pink-bordered dress
draped her girlish figure.

"I don't know," he said easily, "but I wager a guess that this
is—that this is—this is Suzanne Dale—what?"

"Yes, this is," she replied laughingly. "Can I give you a
cup of tea, Mr. Witla? I know you are Mr. Witla from mama''s description and the way in which you talk to everybody."

"And how do I talk to everybody, may I ask, pleasum?"

"Oh, I can't tell you so easily. I mean, I can't find the words,
you know. I know how it is, though. Familiarly, I suppose I
mean. Will you have one lump or two?"

"Three an thou pleasest. Didn't your mother tell me you
sang or played?"

"Oh, you mustn't believe anything ma-ma' says about me!
She's apt to say anything. Tee! Hee! It makes me laugh"—

she pronounced it laaf—"to think of my playing. My teacher says he would like to strike my knuckles. Oh, dear!" (She went into a gale of giggles.) "And sing! Oh, dear, dear! That is too good!"

Eugene watched her pretty face intently. Her mouth and nose and eyes fascinated him. She was so sweet! He noted the configuration of her lips and cheeks and chin. The nose was delicate, beautifully formed, fat, not sensitive. The ears were small, the eyes large and wide set, the forehead naturally high, but so concealed by curls that it seemed low. She had a few freckles and a very small dimple in her chin.

"Now you mustn't laugh like that," he said mock solemnly. "It's very serious business, this laughing. In the first place, it's against the rules of this apartment. No one is ever, ever, ever supposed to laugh here, particularly young ladies who pour tea. Tea, Epictetus well says, involves the most serious conceptions of one's privileges and duties. It is the high-born prerogative of tea servers to grin occasionally, but never, never, never under any circumstances whatsoever——" Suzanne's lips were beginning to part ravishingly in anticipation of a burst of laughter.

"What's all the excitement about, Witla?" asked Skalger, who had drifted to his side. "Why this sudden cessation of progress?"

"Tea, my son, tea!" said Eugene. "Have a cup with me?"

"I will."

"He's trying to tell me, Mr. Skalger, that I should never laaf. I must only grin." Her lips parted and she laughed joyously. Eugene laughed with her. He could not help it. "Ma-ma' says I giggle all the time. I wouldn't do very well here, would I?"

She always pronounced it "ma-ma'."

She turned to Eugene again with big smiling eyes.

"Exceptions, exceptions. I might make exceptions—one exception—but not more."

"Why one?" she asked archly.

"Oh, just to hear a natural laugh," he said a little plaintively. "Just to hear a real joyous laugh. Can you laugh joyously?"

She giggled again at this, and he was about to tell her how joyously she did laugh when Angela called him away to hear Florence Reel, who was going to sing again for his especial benefit. He parted from Miss Dale reluctantly, for she seemed some delicious figure as delicately colorful as Royal Dresden, as perfect in her moods as a spring evening, as soft, soulful, enticing as a strain of music heard through the night at a distance or over the water. He went over to where Florence Reel was standing, listening in a sympathetic melancholy vein to a delightful rendering of "The Summer Winds Are Blowing, Blowing." All the while he could not help thinking of Suzanne—letting his eyes stray in that direction. He talked to Mrs. Dale, to Henrietta Tenmon, to Luke Severas, Mr. and Mrs. Dula, Payalei Stone, now a writer of special articles, and others, but he couldn't help longing to go back to her. How sweet she was! How very delightful! If he could only, once more in his life, have the love of a girl like that!

The guests began to depart. Angela and Eugene bustled about the farewells. Because of the duties of her daughter, which continued to the end, Mrs. Dale stayed, talking to Arthur Skalger. Eugene was in and out between the studio and cloak room off the entry way. Now and then he caught glimpses of Suzanne demurely standing by her tea cups and samovar. For years he had seen nothing so fresh and young as her body. She was like a new grown wet white lily pod in the dawn of the year. She seemed to have the texture of the water chestnut and the lush, fat vegetables of the spring. Her eyes were as clear as water; her skin as radiant new ivory. There was no sign of weariness about her, nor any care, nor any thought of evil, nor anything except health and happiness. "Such a face!" he thought casually in passing. "She is as sweet as any girl could be. As radiant as light itself."

Incidentally the personality of Frieda Roth came back, and— long before her—Stella Appleton.

"Youth! Youth! What in this world could be finer—more acceptable! Where would you find its equal? After all the dust of the streets and the spectacle of age and weariness—the crow's feet about people's eyes, the wrinkles in their necks, the make-believe of rouge and massage, and powder and cosmetics, to see real youth, not of the body but of the soul also—the eyes, the smile, the voice, the movements—all young. Why try to imitate that miracle? Who could? Who ever had?"

He went on shaking hands, bowing, smiling, laughing, jesting, making believe himself, but all the while the miracle of the youth and beauty of Suzanne Dale was running in his mind.

"What are you thinking about, Eugene?" asked Angela, coming to the window where he had drawn a rocking-chair and was sitting gazing out on the silver and lavender and gray of the river surface in the fading light. Some belated gulls were still flying about. Across the river the great manufactory was sending off a spiral of black smoke from one of its tall chimneys. Lamps were beginning to twinkle in its hundred-windowed wall.

A great siren cry broke from its whistle as six o'clock tolled from a neighboring clock tower. It was still late February and cold.

"Oh, I was thinking of the beauty of this scene," he said wearily.

Angela did not believe it. She was conscious of something, but they never quarreled about what he was thinking nowadays. They had come too far along in comfort and solidity. What was it, though, she wondered, that he was thinking about?

Suzanne Dale had no particular thought of him. He was nice—pleasant, good-looking. Mrs. Witla was quite nice and young.

"Ma-ma," she said, "did you look out of the window at Mr. Witla's?"

"Yes, my dear!"

"Wasn't that a beautiful view?"

"Charming."

"I should think you might like to live on the Drive sometime, ma-ma."

"We may sometime."

Mrs. Dale fell to musing. Certainly Eugene was an attractive man—young, brilliant, able. What a mistake all the young men made, marrying so early. Here he was successful, introduced to society, attractive, the world really before him, and he was married to someone who, though a charming little woman, was not up to his possibilities.

"Oh, well," she thought, "so goes the world. Why worry? Everyone must do the best they can."

Then she thought of a story she might write along this line and get Eugene to publish it in one of his magazines.

CHAPTER II

WHILE these various events were occurring the work of the United Magazines Corporation had proceeded apace. By the end of the first year after Eugene's arrival it had cleared up so many of its editorial and advertising troubles that he was no longer greatly worried about them, and by the end of the second year it was well on the way toward real success. Eugene had become so much of a figure about the place that everyone in the great building, in which there were over a thousand employed, knew him at sight. The attendants were most courteous and obsequious, as much so almost as they were to Colfax and White, though the latter with the improvement of the general condition of the company had become more dominating and imposing than ever. White with his large salary of twenty-five thousand a year and his title of vice-president was most anxious that Eugene should not become more powerful than he had already. It irritated him greatly to see the airs Eugene gave himself, for the latter had little real tact, and instead of dissembling his importance before his superiors was inclined to flaunt it. He was forever retailing to Colfax some new achievement in the advertising, circulation, and editorial fields, and that in White's presence, for he did not take the latter very seriously, telling of a new author of importance captured for the book department; a new manuscript feature secured for one or another of the magazines, a new circulation scheme or connection devised, or a new advertising contract of great money value manipulated. His presence in Colfax's office was almost invariably a signal for congratulation or interest, for he was driving things hard and Colfax knew it. White came to hate the sight of him.

"Well, what's the latest great thing you've done?" Colfax said once to Eugene jovially in White's presence, for he knew that Eugene was as fond of praise as a child and so could be bantered with impunity. White concealed a desire to sneer behind a deceptive smile.

"No latest great thing, only Hayes has turned that Hammond Packing Company trick. That means eighteen thousand dollars' worth more of new business for next year. That'll help a little, won't it?"

"Hayes! Hayes! I'll be switched if I don't think he comes pretty near being a better advertising man than you are, Witla.

You picked him, I'll have to admit that, but he certainly knows all about the game. If anything ever happened to you, I think I'd like to keep him right there." White pretended not to hear this, but it pleased him. Hayes should be aided as much as possible by him.

Eugene's face fell, for this sudden twisting of the thread of interest from his to his assistant's achievements damped his enthusiasm. It wasn't pleasant to have his inspirational leadership questioned or made secondary to the work of those whom he was managing. He had brought all these men here and keyed the situation up. Was Colfax going to turn on him? "Oh, very well," he said sweetly.

"Don't look so hurt," returned Colfax easily. "I know what you're thinking. I'm not going to turn on you. You hired this man. I'm simply telling you that if anything should happen to you I'd like to keep him right where he is."

Eugene thought this remark over seriously. It was tantamount to serving notice on him that he could not discharge Hayes. Colfax did not actually so mean it at the moment, though it was the seed of such a thought. He simply left the situation open for consideration, and Eugene went away thinking what an extremely unfavorable twist this gave to everything. If he was to go on finding good men and bringing them in here but could not discharge them, and if then, later, they became offensive to him, where would he be? Why, if they found that out, as they might through White, they could turn on him as lions on a tamer and tear him to pieces! This was a bad and unexpected twist to things, and he did not like it.

On the other hand, while it had never occurred to Colfax before in this particular connection, for he liked Eugene, it fitted in well with certain warnings and suggestions which had been issuing from White who was malevolently opposed to Eugene. His success in reorganizing the place on the intellectual and artistic sides was too much. Eugene's work was giving him a dignity and a security which was entirely disproportionate to what he was actually doing and which was threatening to overshadow and put in the limbo of indifference that of every other person connected with the business. This must be broken. Colfax, for the time being, was so wrapped up in what he considered Eugene's shining intellectual and commercial qualities that he was beginning to ignore White. The latter did not propose that any such condition should continue. It was no doubt a rare thing to find a man who could pick good men and make the place successful, but what of himself? Colfax was naturally

very jealous, he knew, and suspicious. He did not want to be
overshadowed in any way by any of his employees. He did not
feel that he was, so far. But now White thought it would be a
fine thing to stir him up on this score if he could—to arouse his
jealousy. He knew that Colfax did not care so much about the
publishing world, though now that he was in it, and was seeing
that it could be made profitable, he was rather gratified by the
situation. His wife liked it, for people were always talking to
her about the United Magazines Corporation, its periodicals, its
books, its art products and that was flattering. While it might
not be as profitable as soap and woolens and railway stocks with
which her husband was identified, it was somewhat more distinguished. She wanted him to keep it directly under his thumb and
to shine by its reflected light.

In looking about for a club wherewith to strike Eugene, White
discovered this. He sounded Colfax on various occasions by
innuendo, and noted his sniffing nostrils. If he could first reach
Eugene's advertising, circulation and editorial men and persuade
them to look to him instead of to Eugene, he might later reach
and control Eugene through Colfax. He might humble Eugene
by curbing his power, making him see that he, White, was still
the power behind the throne.

"What do you think of this fellow Witla?" Colfax would
ask White from time to time, and when these occasions offered he
was not slow to drive in a wedge.

"He's an able fellow," he said once, apparently most open-
mindedly. "It's plain that he's doing pretty well with those departments, but I think you want to look out for his vanity. He's
just the least bit in danger of getting a swelled head. You want
to remember that he's still pretty young for the job he holds
(White was eight years older). These literary and artistic
people are all alike. The one objection that I have to them is
that they never seem to have any real practical judgment. They
make splendid second men when well governed, and you can do
almost anything with them, if you know how to handle them,
but you have to govern them. This fellow, as I see him, is just
the man you want. He's picking some good people and he's
getting some good results, but unless you watch him he's apt to
throw them all out of here sometime or go away and take them
all with him. I shouldn't let him do that if I were you. I
should let him get just the men you think are right, and then I
should insist that he keep them. Of course, a man has got to
have authority in his own department, but it can be carried too
far. You're treating him pretty liberally, you know."

This sounded very sincere and logical to Colfax, who admired White for it, for in spite of the fact that he liked Eugene greatly and went about with him a great deal, he did not exactly trust him. The man was in a way too brilliant, he thought. He was a little too airy and light on his feet.

Under pretext of helping his work and directing his policy without actually interfering so that it might eventually prove a failure, White was constantly making suggestions. He made suggestions which he told Colfax Eugene ought to try in the circulation department. He made suggestions which he thought he might find advisable to try in the advertising department. He had suggestions, gathered from Heaven knows where, for the magazines and books, and these he invariably sent through Colfax, taking good care, however, that the various department heads knew from what source they had originally emanated. It was his plan to speak to Hayes or Gillmore, who was in charge of circulation, or one of the editors about some thought that was in his mind and then have that same thought come as an order via Eugene. The latter was so anxious to make good, so good-natured in his interpretation of suggestions, that it did not occur to him, for a long time, that he was being played. The men under him, however, realized that something was happening, for White was hand and glove with Colfax, and the two were not always in accord with Eugene. He was not quite as powerful as White, was the first impression, and later the idea got about that Eugene and White did not agree temperamentally and that White was the stronger and would win.

It is not possible to go into the long, slow multitudinous incidents and details which go to make up office politics, but anyone who has ever worked in a large or small organization anywhere will understand. Eugene was not a politician. He knew nothing of the delicate art of misrepresentation as it was practised by White and those who were of his peculiarly subtle mental tendencies. White did not like Eugene, and he proposed to have his power curbed. Some of Eugene's editors, after a time, began to find it difficult to get things as they wanted them from the printing department, and, when they complained, it was explained that they were of a disorderly and quarrelsome disposition. Some of his advertising men made mistakes in statement or presentation, and curiously these errors almost invariably came to light. Eugene found that his strong men were most quickly relieved of their difficulties if they approached White, but if they came to him it was not quite so easy. Instead of ignoring these petty annoyances and going his way about the big things, he stopped occasionally to fight these petty battles and complaints, and these simply put him in the light of one who was not able to maintain profound peace and order in his domain. White was always bland, helpful, ready with a suave explanation.

"It's just possible that he may not know how to handle these fellows, after all," he said to Colfax, and then if anyone was discharged it was a sign of an unstable policy.

Colfax cautioned Eugene occasionally in accordance with White's suggestions, but Eugene was now so well aware of what was going on that he could see where they came from. He thought once of accusing White openly in front of Colfax, but he knew that this would not be of any advantage for he had no real evidence to go on. All White's protestations to Colfax were to the effect that he was trying to help him. So the battle lay.

In the meantime, Eugene, because of this or the thought rather that he might not always remain as powerful as he was, having no stock in the concern and not being able to buy any, had been interesting himself in a proposition which had since been brought to him by Mr. Kenyon C. Winfield, who, since that memorable conversation at the home of the Willebrands on Long Island, had not forgotten him. Winfield had thought of him for a long time in connection with a plan he had of establishing on the South Shore of Long Island, some thirty-five miles from New York, a magnificent seaside resort which should outrival Palm Beach and the better places of Atlantic City, and give to New York, close at hand, such a dream of beauty and luxury as would turn the vast tide of luxury-loving idlers and successful money grubbers from the former resorts to this. Considerable thought had been given by him as to just what its principal characteristics should be, but he had not worked it out to suit himself exactly, and he thought Eugene might be interested from the outlining point of view.

Unfortunately, on the face of it, this was just the sort of scheme which made an appeal to Eugene from all points of view, in spite of the fact that he already had his hands as full as they could be. Nothing interested him quite so much as beauty and luxury in some artistic combination. A summer resort of really imposing proportions, with hotels, casinos, pagodas, resident sections, club houses, a wide board or stone walk along the ocean, and possibly a gambling center which should outrival Monte Carlo, had long since occurred to him as something which might well spring up near New York. He and Angela had visited Palm Beach, Old Point Comfort, Virginia Hot Springs, Newport, Shelter Island, Atlantic City, and Tuxedo, and his impressions of what constituted luxury and beauty had long since widened to magnificent proportions. He liked the interiors of the Chamberlain at Old Point Comfort, and the Royal Ponciana at Palm Beach. He had studied with artistic curiosity the development of the hotel features at Atlantic City and elsewhere. It had occurred to him that a restricted territory might be had out on the Atlantic Ocean near Gravesend Bay possibly, which would include among other things islands, canals or inland waterways, a mighty sea beach, two or three great hotels, a casino for dancing, dining, gambling, a great stone or concrete walk to be laid out on a new plan parallel with the ocean, and at the back of all these things and between the islands and the ocean a magnificent seaside city where the lots should sell at so expensive a rate that only the well-to-do could afford to live there. His thought was of something so fine that it would attract all the prominent pleasure-lovers he had recently met. If they could be made to understand that such a place existed; that it was beautiful, showy, exclusive in a money sense, they would come there by the thousands.

"Nothing is so profitable as a luxury, if the luxury-loving public want it," Colfax had once said to him; and he believed it. He judged this truth by the things he had recently seen. People literally spent millions to make themselves comfortable. He had seen gardens, lawns, walks, pavilions, pergolas, laid out at an expense of thousands and hundreds of thousands of dollars, where few would ever see them. In St. Louis he had seen a mausoleum built upon the lines of the Taj Mahal, the lawn about which was undermined by a steam-heating plant in order that the flowers and shrubs displayed there might bloom all winter long. It had never occurred to him that the day would come when he would have anything to do with such a dream as this or its ultimate fruition, but his was the kind of mind that loved to dwell on things of the sort.

The proposition which Winfield now genially laid before him one day was simple enough. Winfield had heard that Eugene was making a good deal of money, that his salary was twenty-five thousand a year, if not more, that he had houses and lots and some nice stock investments, and it occurred to him, as it would have to anyone, that Eugene might be able to shoulder a comfortable investment in some kind of land speculation, particularly if he could see his way to make much more money in the long run. The idea Winfield had was as follows: He was going to organize a corporation to be known as The Sea Island Development Company, to be capitalized at ten million dollars, some two or three hundred thousand dollars of which was to be laid down or paid into the treasury at the start. Against this latter sum stock to the value of one million dollars, or five shares of one hundred dollars par value each, was to be issued. That is, whoever laid down one hundred dollars in cash was to receive in return three shares of common stock and two of preferred, valued at one hundred dollars each, bearing eight per cent. interest. This ratio was to be continued until $200,000 in cash was in the treasury. Then those who came afterward and were willing to buy were only to receive two shares of common and one of preferred, until one million in cash was in the treasury. After that the stock was to be sold at its face value, or more, as the situation might dictate.

The original sum of two hundred thousands dollars was to go to purchase for the corporation an undeveloped tract of land, half swamp, half island, and facing the Atlantic Ocean beyond Gravesend Bay, now owned by Winfield himself, where a beautiful rolling beach of white sand stretched some three miles in length and without flaw or interruption. This would clear Winfield of a piece of property which was worth, say $60,000, but at present unsaleable, and give him magnificent holdings in the new company besides. He proposed to take a mortgage on this and all improvements the company might make in order to protect himself. At the west end of this tract—inland from the sea— was a beautiful bay, which, though shallow, gave access to a series of inlets and a network of waterways, embracing nine small islands. These waterways, when dredged, would be amply deep enough for yachts and small craft of all descriptions, and the first important thought which occurred to Winfield was that the mud and sand so dredged could be used to fill in the low, marshy levels of soil between them and the sea and so make it all into high, dry, and valuable land. The next thing was to devise a beautiful scheme of improvement, and it was for this that he wished to talk to Eugene.

CHAPTER III

THE matter was not difficult to arrange. Before Winfield had gone ten sentences, Eugene began to take the ideas out of his mind.

"I know something of that property," he said, studying a little outline map which Winfield had prepared. "I've been out there duck shooting with Colfax and some others. It's fine property, there's no doubt of it. How much do they want for it?"

"Well, as a matter of fact, I already own it," said Winfield. "It cost me sixty thousand dollars five years ago when it was a vast, inaccessible swamp. Nothing has been done to it since, but I will turn it over to the company for what it is worth now—two hundred thousand dollars—and take a mortgage for my protection. Then the company can do what it pleases with it; but as president, of course, I should direct the line of development. If you want to make a fortune and have fifty thousand dollars to spare, here is your chance. This land has increased in value from sixty to two hundred thousand dollars in five years. What do you fancy it will be worth in ten years from now the way New York is growing? It has pretty near four million people now. In twenty-five years it is safe to say that there will be fourteen or fifteen millions scattered over this territory which lies within twenty-five miles. Of course, this is thirty-two miles away on a direct line, but what of it? The Long Island Railroad will be glad to put a spur in there which would bring this territory within one hour of the city. Think of it—one of the finest beaches on the Atlantic Ocean within one hour of New York! I expect to interest Mr. Wiltsie, the President of the Long Island, very heavily in this property. I come to you now because I think your advertising and artistic advice are worth something. You can take it or leave it, but before you do anything, I want you to come out and look over the property with me."

All told, in stocks, land, free money in the banks, and what he might save in a year or two, Eugene had about fifty thousand dollars of good hard cash which he could lay his hands on at a pinch. He was well satisfied that Winfield was putting before him one of those golden opportunities which, prudently managed, would make him a rich man. Nevertheless, his fifty thousand was fifty thousand, and he had it. Never again, however, once this other thing was under way, if it were true, would he have to worry about a position, or whether he would be able to maintain his present place in society. One could not possibly say what an investment like this might not lead to. Winfield, so he told Eugene, expected eventually to clear six or eight million dollars himself. He was going to take stock in some of the hotels, casinos, and various other enterprises, which would be organized. He could clearly see how, later, once this land was properly drained and laid out, it would be worth from three to fifteen thousand dollars per lot of one hundred by one hundred feet—the smallest portions to be sold. There were islands which for clubs or estates should bring splendid returns. Think of the leases to yacht and boat clubs alone! The company would own all the land.

"I would develop this myself if I had the capital," said Winfield, "but I want to see it done on a gigantic scale, and I haven't the means. I want something here which will be a monument to me and to all connected with it. I am willing to take my chances pro rata with those who now enter, and to prove my good faith I am going to buy as many shares as I possibly can on the five-for-one basis. You or anyone else can do the same thing. What do you think?"

"It's a great idea," said Eugene. "It seems as though a dream which had been floating about in the back of my head for years had suddenly come to life. I can scarcely believe that it is true, and yet I know that it is, and that you will get away with it just as you are outlining it here. You want to be very careful how you lay out this property, though. You have the chance of a lifetime. For goodness' sake, don't make any mistakes! Let's have one resort that will be truly, beautifully right."

"That's precisely the way I feel about it," answered Winfield, "and that's why I am talking to you. I want you to come in on this, for I think your imagination will be worth something. You can help me lay this thing out right and advertise it right."

They talked on about one detail and another until finally Eugene, in spite of all his caution, saw his dreams maturing in this particular proposition. Fifty thousand dollars invested here would give him two thousand five hundred shares—one thousand preferred, and fifteen hundred common—whose face value, guaranteed by this magnificent piece of property, would be $250,000. Think of it, $250,000—a quarter of a million—and that subject to a natural increase which might readily carry him into the millionaire class! His own brains would be of some value here, for Winfield was anxious to have him lay this out, and this would bring him in touch with not only one of the best real estate men in the city, but would bring him into contact with a whole host of financiers in business, people who would certainly become interested in this venture. Winfield talked easily of architects, contractors, railroad men, presidents of construction companies, all of whom would take stock for the business opportunities it would bring to them later and also of the many strings to be pulled which later would bring great gains to the company and save it from expenditures which would otherwise mean millions in outlay. Thus this proposed extension by the Long Island which would cost that railroad two hundred thousand dollars would cost the Sea Island Company nothing and would bring thousands of lovers of beauty there the moment conveniences were established to receive them. This was true of hotels to be built. Each would bring business for everything else. The company would lease the ground. The great hotel men would do their own building according to restrictions and plans laid down by the Sea Island Company. The only real expenditure would be for streets, sewers, lights, water, walks, trees, and the great one hundred foot wide boardwalk with concrete ornaments which would be the finest sea stroll in the world. But these could be undertaken by degrees.

Eugene saw it all. It was a vision of empire. "I don't know about this," he said cautiously. "It's a great thing, but I may not have the means to dip into it. I want to think it over. Meanwhile, I'll be glad to go out there and look over the ground with you."

Winfield could see that he had Eugene fascinated. It would be an easy matter to land him once he had his plans perfected. Eugene would be the type of man who would build a house and come and live there in the summer. He would interest many people whom he knew. He went away feeling that he had made a good start, and he was not mistaken.

Eugene talked the matter over with Angela—his one recourse in these matters—and as usual she was doubtful, but not entirely opposed. Angela had considerable caution, but no great business vision. She could not really tell him what he ought to do. Thus far his judgment, or rather his moves, had been obviously successful. He had been going up apparently because he was valuable as an assistant, not because he was a born leader.

"You'll have to judge for yourself, Eugene," Angela finally said. "I don't know. It looks fine. You certainly don't want to work for Mr. Colfax all your life, and if, as you say, they are beginning to plot against you, you had better prepare to get

out sometime. We have enough now, really, to live on, if you
want to return to your art."

Eugene smiled. "My art. My poor old art! A lot I've done
to develop my art."

"I don't think it needs developing. You have it. I'm sorry
sometimes I ever let you leave it. We have lived better, but
your work hasn't counted for as much. What good has it done
you outside the money to be a successful publisher? You were
as famous as you are now before you ever started in on this line,
and more so. More people know you even now as Eugene
Witla, the artist, than as Eugene Witla, the magazine man."

Eugene knew this to be so. His art achievements had never
forsaken him. They had grown in fame always. Pictures that
he had sold for two hundred and four hundred had gone up to
as high as three and four thousand in value, and they were still
rising. He was occasionally approached by an art dealer to
know if he never intended to paint any more. In social circles
it was a constant cry among the elect, "Why don't you paint
any longer?" "What a shame you ever left the art world!"
"Those pictures of yours, I can never forget them."

"My dear lady," Eugene once said solemnly, "I can't live by
painting pictures as I am living by directing magazines. Art is
very lovely. I am satisfied to believe that I am a great painter.
Nevertheless, I made little out of it, and since then I have
learned to live. It's sad, but it's true. If I could see my way
to live in half the comfort I am living in now and not run the
risk of plodding the streets with a picture under my arm, I
would gladly return to art. The trouble is the world is always
so delightfully ready to see the other fellow make the sacrifice
for art or literature's sake. Selah! I won't do it. So there!"

"It's a pity! It's a pity!" said this observer, but Eugene was
not vastly distressed. Similarly Mrs. Dale had reproached him,
for she had seen and heard of his work.

"Some time. Some time," he said grandly; "wait."

Now at length this land proposition seemed to clear the way
for everything. If Eugene embarked upon it, he might gradually come to the point at which he could take some official position in connection with it. Anyhow, think of a rising income
from $250,000! Think of the independence, the freedom!
Surely then he could paint or travel, or do as he pleased.

As a matter of fact, after two automobile rides to the nearest
available position on the site of the future resort and a careful
study of the islands and the beach, Eugene devised a scheme
which included four hotels of varying sizes, one dining and

dancing casino, one gambling resort after the pattern of Monte Carlo, a summer theatre, a music pavilion, three lovely piers, motor and yacht club houses, a park with radiating streets, and other streets arranged in concentric rings to cross them. There was a grand plaza about which the four hotels were ranged, a noble promenade, three miles in length, to begin with, a handsome railway station, plots for five thousand summer homes, ranging from five to fifteen thousand in price. There were islands for residences, islands for clubs, islands for parks. One of the hotels sat close to an inlet over which a dining veranda was to be built—stairs were to be laid down to the water so that one could step into gondolas or launches and be carried quickly to one of the music pavilions on one of the islands. Everything that money wanted was to be eventually available here, and all was to be gone about slowly but beautifully, so that each step would only make more sure each additional step.

Eugene did not enter on this grand scheme until ten men, himself included, had pledged themselves to take stock up to $50,000 each. Included in these were Mr. Wiltsie, President of the Long Island; Mr. Kenyon C. Winfield, and Milton Willebrand, the very wealthy society man at whose home he had originally met Winfield. The Sea Island Company was then incorporated, and on a series of dates agreed upon between them and which were dependent upon a certain amount of work being accomplished by each date, the stock was issued to them in ten-thousand-dollar lots and then cash taken and deposited in the treasury. By the end of two years after Eugene had first been approached by Winfield he had a choice collection of gold-colored certificates in the Sea Island Realty and Construction Company, which was building the now widely heralded seaside resort— "Blue Sea"—which, according to those interested, was to be the most perfect resort of its kind in the world. His certificates stated that they were worth $250,000, and potentially they were. Eugene and Angela looking at them, thinking of the initiative and foresight of Mr. Kenyon C. Winfield and the men he was associated with, felt sure that some day, and that not so very far distant, they would yield their face value and much more.

CHAPTER IV

IT had been while he was first perfecting his undertaking with Winfield as to what his relationship to the new Sea Island Construction Company was to be that Eugene had been dwelling more and more fondly upon the impression which Suzanne Dale had originally made upon him. It was six weeks before they met again, and then it was on the occasion of a dance that Mrs. Dale was giving in honor of Suzanne that Eugene and Angela were invited. Mrs. Dale admired Angela's sterling qualities as a wife, and while there might be temperamental and social differences, she did not think they were sufficient to warrant any discrimination between them, at least not on her part. Angela was a good woman—not a social figure at all—but interesting in her way. Mrs. Dale was much more interested in Eugene, because in the first place they were very much alike temperamentally, and in the next place because Eugene was a successful and brilliant person. She liked to see the easy manner in which he took life, the air with which he assumed that talent should naturally open all doors to him. He was not conscious apparently of any inferiority in anything but rather of a splendid superiority. She heard it from so many that he was rapidly rising in his publishing world and that he was interested in many things, the latest this project to create a magnificent summer resort. Winfield was a personal friend of hers. He had never attempted to sell her any property, but he had once said that he might some day take her Staten Island holdings and divide them up into town lots. This was one possibility which tended to make her pleasant to him.

The evening in question Eugene and Angela went down to Daleview in their automobile. Eugene always admired this district, for it gave him a sense of height and scope which was not easily attainable elsewhere about New York. It was still late winter and the night was cold but clear. The great house with its verandas encased in glass was brightly lit. There were a number of people—men and women, whom Eugene had met at various places, and quite a number of young people whom he did not know. Angela had to be introduced to a great many, and Eugene felt that peculiar sensation which he so often experienced of a certain incongruity in his matrimonial state. Angela was nice, but to him she was not like these other women who carried themselves with such an air. There was a statuesqueness and a sufficiency about many of them, to say nothing of their superb beauty and sophistication which made him feel, when the contrast was forced upon him closely, that he had made a terrible mistake. Why had he been so silly as to marry? He could have told Angela frankly that he would not at the time, and all would have been well. He forgot how badly, emotionally, he had entangled himself. But scenes like these made him dreadfully unhappy. Why, his life if he were single would now be but beginning!

As he walked round tonight he was glad to be free socially even for a few minutes. He was glad that first this person and that took the trouble to talk to Angela. It relieved him of the necessity of staying near her, for if he neglected her or she felt neglected by others she was apt to reproach him. If he did not show her attention, she would complain that he was conspicuous in his indifference. If others refused to talk to her, it was his place. He should. Eugene objected to this necessity with all his soul, but he did not see what he was to do about it. As she often said, even if he had made a mistake in marrying her, it was his place to stick by her now that he had. A real man would.

One of the things that interested him was the number of beautiful young women. He was interested to see how full and complete mentally and physically so many girls appeared to be at eighteen. Why, in their taste, shrewdness, completeness, they were fit mates for a man of almost any age up to forty! Some of them looked so wonderful to him—so fresh and ruddy with the fires of ambition and desire burning briskly in their veins. Beautiful girls—real flowers, like roses, light and dark. And to think the love period was all over for him—completely over!

Suzanne came down with others after a while from some room upstairs, and once more Eugene was impressed with her simple, natural, frank, good-natured attitude. Her light chestnut-colored hair was tied with a wide band of light blue ribbon which matched her eyes and contrasted well with her complexion. Again, her dress was some light flimsy thing, the color of peach blossoms, girdled with ribbon and edged with flowers like a wreath. Soft white sandals held her feet.

"Oh, Mr. Witla!" she said gaily, holding out her smooth white arm on a level with her eyes and dropping her hand gracefully. Her red lips were parted, showing even white teeth, arching into a radiant smile. Her eyes were quite wide as he remembered, with an innocent, surprised look in them, which was wholly unconscious with her. If wet roses could outrival a maiden in all her freshness, he thought he would like to see it. Nothing could equal the beauty of a young woman in her eighteenth or nineteenth year.

"Yes, quite, Mr. Witla," he said, beaming. "I thought you had forgotten. My, we look charming this evening! We look like roses and cut flowers and stained-glass windows and boxes of jewels, and, and, and——"

He pretended to be lost for more words and looked quizzically up at the ceiling.

Suzanne began to laugh. Like Eugene, she had a marked sense of the comic and the ridiculous. She was not in the least vain, and the idea of being like roses and boxes of jewels and stained-glass windows tickled her fancy.

"Why, that's quite a collection of things to be, isn't it?" she laughed, her lips parted. "I wouldn't mind being all those things if I could, particularly the jewels. Mama won't give me any. I can't even get a brooch for my throat."

"Mama is real mean, apparently," said Eugene vigorously. "We'll have to talk to mama, but she knows, you know, that you don't need any jewels, see? She knows that you have something which is just as good, or better. But we won't talk about that, will we?"

Suzanne had been afraid that he was going to begin complimenting her, but seeing how easily he avoided this course she liked him for it. She was a little overawed by his dignity and mental capacity, but attracted by his gaiety and lightness of manner.

"Do you know, Mr. Witla," she said, "I believe you like to tease people."

"Oh, no!" said Eugene. "Oh, never, never! Nothing like that. How could I? Tease people! Far be it from me! That's the very last thing I ever think of doing. I always approach people in a very solemn manner and tell them the dark sad truth. It's the only way. They need it. The more truth I tell the better I feel. And then they like me so much better for it."

At the first rush of his quizzical tirade Suzanne's eyes opened quaintly, inquiringly. Then she began to smile, and in a moment after he ceased she exclaimed: "Oh, ha! ha! Oh, dear! Oh, dear, how you talk!" A ripple of laughter spread outward, and Eugene frowned darkly.

"How dare you laugh?" he said. "Don't laugh at me. It's against the rules to laugh, anyhow. Don't you remember growing girls should never laugh? Solemnity is the first rule of beauty. Never smile. Keep perfectly solemn. Look wise. Hence. Therefore. If. And——"

He lifted a finger solemnly, and Suzanne stared. He had fixed her eye with his and was admiring her pretty chin and nose and lips, while she gazed not knowing what to make of him. He was very different; very much like a boy, and yet very much like a solemn, dark master of some kind.

"You almost frighten me," she said.

"Now, now, listen! It's all over. Come to. I'm just a silly-billy. Are you going to dance with me this evening?"

"Why, certainly, if you want me to! Oh, that reminds me! We have cards. Did you get one?"

"No."

"Well, they're over here, I think."

She led the way toward the reception hall, and Eugene took from the footman who was stationed there two of the little books.

"Let's see," he said, writing, "how greedy dare I be?"

Suzanne made no reply.

"If I take the third and the sixth and the tenth—would that be too many?"

"No-o," said Suzanne doubtfully.

He wrote in hers and his and then they went back to the drawing-room where so many were now moving. "Will you be sure and save me these?"

"Why, certainly," she replied. "To be sure, I will!"

"That's nice of you. And now here comes your mother. Remember, you mustn't ever, ever, ever laugh. It's against the rules."

Suzanne went away, thinking. She was pleased at the gaiety of this man who seemed so light-hearted and self-sufficient. He seemed like someone who took her as a little girl, so different from the boys she knew who were solemn in her presence and rather love sick. He was the kind of man one could have lots of fun with without subjecting one's self to undue attention and having to explain to her mother. Her mother liked him. But she soon forgot him in the chatter of other people.

Eugene was thinking again, though, of the indefinable something in the spirit of this girl which was attracting him so vigorously. What was it? He had seen hundreds of girls in the last few years, all charming, but somehow this one—— She seemed so strong, albeit so new and young. There was a poise there—a substantial quality in her soul which could laugh at life

and think no ill of it. That was it or something of it, for of
course her beauty was impressive, but a courageous optimism was
shining out through her eyes. It was in her laugh, her mood.
She would never be afraid.

The dance began after ten, and Eugene danced with first one
and then another—Angela, Mrs. Dale, Mrs. Stevens, Miss
Willy. When the third set came he went looking for Suzanne
and found her talking to another young girl and two society
men.

"Mine, you know," he said smilingly.

She came out to him laughing, stretching her arm in a sinuous
way, quite unconscious of the charming figure she made. She had
a way of throwing back her head which revealed her neck in
beautiful lines. She looked into Eugene's eyes simply and un-
affectedly, returning his smile with one of her own. And when
they began to dance he felt as though he had never really danced
before.

What was it the poet said of the poetry of motion? This was
it. This was it. This girl could dance wonderfully, sweetly, as
a fine voice sings. She seemed to move like the air with the
sound of the two-step coming from an ambush of flowers, and
Eugene yielded himself instinctively to the charm—the hypnotism of it. He danced and in dancing forgot everything except
this vision leaning upon his arm and the sweetness of it all.
Nothing could equal this emotion, he said to himself. It was
finer than anything he had ever experienced. There was joy in
it, pure delight, an exquisite sense of harmony; and even while
he was congratulating himself the music seemed to hurry to a
finish. Suzanne had looked up curiously into his eyes.

"You like dancing, don't you?" she said.

"I do, but I don't dance well."

"Oh, I think so!" she replied. "You dance so easily."

"It is because of you," he said simply. "You have the soul of
the dance in you. Most people dance poorly, like myself."

"I don't think so," she said, hanging on to his arm as they
walked toward a seat. "Oh, there's Kinroy! He has the next
with me."

Eugene looked at her brother almost angrily. Why should
circumstances rob him of her company in this way? Kinroy
looked like her—he was very handsome for a boy.

"Well, then, I have to give you up. I wish there were more."

He left her only to wait impatiently for the sixth and the
tenth. He knew it was silly to be interested in her in this way,
for nothing could come of it. She was a young girl hedged

about by all the conventions and safeguards which go to make for the perfect upbringing of girlhood. He was a man past the period of her interest, watched over by conventions and interests also. There could be absolutely nothing between them, and yet he longed for her just the same, for just this little sip of the nectar of make-believe. For a few minutes in her company, married or not, so many years older or not, he could be happy in her company, teasing her. That sense of dancing—that sense of perfect harmony with beauty—when had he ever experienced that before?

The night went by, and at one he and Angela went home. She had been entertained by some young officer in the army stationed at Fort Wadsworth who had known her brother David. That had made the evening pleasant for her. She commented on Mrs. Dale and Suzanne, what a charming hostess the former was and how pretty and gay Suzanne looked, but Eugene manifested little interest. He did not want it to appear that he had been interested in Suzanne above any of the others.

"Yes, she's very nice," he said. "Rather pretty; but she's like all girls at that age. I like to tease them."

Angela wondered whether Eugene had really changed for good. He seemed saner in all his talk concerning women. Perhaps large affairs had cured him completely, though she could not help feeling that he must be charmed and delighted by the beauty of some of the women whom he saw.

Five weeks more went by and then he saw Suzanne one day with her mother on Fifth Avenue, coming out of an antique shop. Mrs. Dale explained that she was looking after the repair of a rare piece of furniture. Eugene and Suzanne were enabled to exchange but a few gay words. Four weeks later he met them at the Brentwood Hadleys, in Westchester. Suzanne and her mother were enjoying a season of spring riding. Eugene was there for only a Saturday afternoon and Sunday. On this occasion he saw her coming in at half-past four wearing a divided riding skirt and looking flushed and buoyant. Her lovely hair was flowing lightly about her temples.

"Oh, how are you?" she asked, with that same inconsequent air, her hand held out to him at a high angle. "I saw you last in Fifth Avenue, didn't I? Mama was having her chair fixed. Ha, ha! She's such a slow rider! I've left her miles behind. Are you going to be here long?"

"Just today and tomorrow."

He looked at her, pretending gaiety and indifference.

"Is Mrs. Witla here?"

"No, she couldn't come. A relative of hers is in the city."

"I need a bath terribly," said the desire of his eyes, and passed on, calling back: "I'll see you again before dinner, very likely." Eugene sighed.

She came down after an hour, dressed in a flowered organdie, a black silk band about her throat, a low collar showing her pretty neck. She picked up a magazine, passing a wicker table, and came down the veranda where Eugene was sitting alone. Her easy manner interested him, and her friendliness. She liked him well enough to be perfectly natural with him and to seek him out where he was sitting once she saw he was there.

"Oh, here you are!" she said, and sat down, taking a chair which was near him.

"Yes, here I am," he said, and began teasing her as usual, for it was the only way in which he knew how to approach her. Suzanne responded vivaciously, for Eugene's teasing delighted her. It was the one kind of humor she really enjoyed.

"You know, Mr. Witla," she said to him once, "I'm not going to laugh at any of your jokes any more. They're all at my expense."

"That makes it all the nicer," he said. "You wouldn't want me to make jokes at my expense, would you? That would be a terrible joke."

She laughed and he smiled. They looked at a golden sunset filtering through a grove of tender maples. The spring was young and the leaves just budding.

"Isn't it lovely tonight?" he asked.

"Oh, yes!" she exclaimed, in a mellow, meditative voice, the first ring of deep sincerity in it that he ever noticed there.

"Do you like nature?" he asked.

"Do I?" she returned. "I can't get enough of the woods these days. I feel so queer sometimes, Mr. Witla. As though I were not really alive at all, you know. Just a sound, or a color in the woods."

He stopped and looked at her. The simile caught him quite as any notable characteristic in anyone would have caught him. What was the color and complexity of this girl's mind? Was she so wise, so artistic and so emotional that nature appealed to her in a deep way? Was this wonderful charm that he felt the shadow or radiance of something finer still?

"So that's the way it is, is it?" he asked.

"Yes," she said quietly.

He sat and looked at her, and she eyed him as solemnly.

"Why do you look at me so?" she asked.

"Why do you say such curious things?" he answered.

"What did I say?"

"I don't believe you really know. Well, never mind. Let us walk, will you? Do you mind? It's still an hour to dinner. I'd like to go over and see what's beyond those trees."

They went down a little path bordered with grass and under green budding twigs. It came to a stile finally and looked out upon a stony green field where some cows were pasturing.

"Oh, the spring! The spring!" exclaimed Eugene, and Suzanne answered: "You know, Mr. Witla, I think we must be something alike in some ways. That's just the way I feel."

"How do you know how I feel?"

"I can tell by your voice," she said.

"Can you, really?"

"Why, yes. Why shouldn't I?"

"What a strange girl you are!" he said thoughtfully. "I don't think I understand you quite."

"Why, why, am I so different from everyone else?"

"Quite, quite," he said; "at least to me. I have never seen anyone quite like you before."

CHAPTER V

IT was after this meeting that vague consciousness came to Suzanne that Mr. Witla, as she always thought of him to herself, was just a little more than very nice to her. He was so gentle, so meditative, and withal so gay when he was near her! He seemed fairly to bubble whenever he came into her presence, never to have any cause for depression or gloom such as sometimes seized on her when she was alone. He was always immaculately dressed, and had great affairs, so her mother said. They discussed him once at table at Daleview, and Mrs. Dale said she thought he was charming.

"He's one of the nicest fellows that comes here, I think," said Kinroy. "I don't like that stick, Woodward."

He was referring to another man of about Eugene's age who admired his mother.

"Mrs. Witla is such a queer little woman," said Suzanne. "She's so different from Mr. Witla. He's so gay and good-natured, and she's so reserved. Is she as old as he is, mama?"

"I don't think so," said Mrs. Dale, who was deceived by Angela's apparent youth. "What makes you ask?"

"Oh, I just wondered!" said Suzanne, who was vaguely curious concerning things in connection with Eugene.

There were several other meetings, one of which Eugene engineered, once when he persuaded Angela to invite Suzanne and her mother to a spring night revel they were having at the studio, and the other when he and Angela were invited to the Willebrands, where the Dales were also.

Angela was always with him. Mrs. Dale almost always with Suzanne. There were a few conversations, but they were merely gay, inconsequent make-believe talks, in which Suzanne saw Eugene as one who was forever happy. She little discerned the brooding depths of longing that lay beneath his gay exterior.

The climax was brought about, however, when one July day after a short visit to one of the summer resorts, Angela was taken ill. She had always been subject to colds and sore throats, and these peculiar signs, which are associated by medical men with latent rheumatism, finally culminated in this complaint. Angela had also been pronounced to have a weak heart, and this combined with a sudden, severe rheumatic attack completely prostrated her. A trained nurse had to be called, and Angela's sister Marietta was sent for. Eugene's sister Myrtle, who now lived in New York, was asked by him to come over and take charge, and under her supervision, pending Marietta's arrival, his household went forward smoothly enough. The former, being a full-fledged Christian Scientist, having been instantly cured, as she asserted, of a long-standing nervous complaint, was for calling a Christian Science practitioner, but Eugene would have none of it. He could not believe that there was anything in this new religious theory, and thought Angela needed a doctor. He sent for a specialist in her complaint. He pronounced that six weeks at the least, perhaps two months, must elapse before Angela would be able to sit up again.

"Her system is full of rheumatism," said her physician. "She is in a very bad way. Rest and quiet, and constant medication will bring her round."

Eugene was sorry. He did not want to see her suffer, but her sickness did not for one minute alter his mental attitude. In fact, he did not see how it could. It did not change their relative mental outlook in any way. Their peculiar relationship of guardian and restless ward was quite unaffected.

All social functions of every kind were now abandoned and Eugene stayed at home every evening, curious to see what the outcome would be. He wanted to see how the trained nurse did her work and what the doctor thought would be the next step. He had a great deal to do at all times, reading, consulting, and many of those who wished to confer with him came to the apartment of an evening. All those who knew them socially at all intimately called or sent messages of condolence, and among those who came were Mrs. Dale and Suzanne. The former because Eugene had been so nice to her in a publishing way and was shortly going to bring out her first attempt at a novel was most assiduous. She sent flowers and came often, proffering the services of Suzanne for any day that the nurse might wish to be off duty or Myrtle could not be present. She thought Angela might like to have Suzanne read to her. At least the offer sounded courteous and was made in good faith.

Suzanne did not come alone at first, but after a time, when Angela had been ill four weeks and Eugene had stood the heat of the town apartment nightly for the chance of seeing her, she did. Mrs. Dale suggested that he should run down to her place over Saturday and Sunday. It was not far. They were in close telephone communication. It would rest him.

Eugene, though Angela had suggested it a number of times

before, had refused to go to any seaside resort or hotel, even for
Saturday and Sunday, his statement being that he did not care to
go alone at this time. The truth was he was becoming so interested in Suzanne that he did not care to go anywhere save somewhere that he might see her again.

Mrs. Dale's offer was welcome enough, but having dissem-
bled so much he had to dissemble more. Mrs. Dale insisted.
Angela added her plea. Myrtle thought he ought to go. He
finally ordered the car to take him down one Friday afternoon
and leave him. Suzanne was out somewhere, but he sat on the
veranda and basked in the magnificent view it gave of the lower
bay. Kinroy and some young friend, together with two girls,
were playing tennis on one of the courts. Eugene went out to
watch them, and presently Suzanne returned, ruddy from a walk
she had taken to a neighbor's house. At the sight of her every
nerve in Eugene's body tingled—he felt a great exaltation, and
it seemed as though she responded in kind, for she was particularly gay and laughing.

"They have a four," she called to him, her white duck skirt
blowing. "Let's you and I get rackets and play single."

"I'm not very good, you know," he said.

"You couldn't be worse than I am," she replied. "I'm so
bad Kinroy won't let me play in any game with him. Ha, ha!"

"Such being the case——" Eugene said lightly, and followed
her to get the rackets.

They went to the second court, where they played practically
unheeded. Every hit was a signal for congratulation on the part
of one or the other, every miss for a burst of laughter or a jest.
Eugene devoured Suzanne with his eyes, and she looked at him
continually, in wide-eyed sweetness, scarcely knowing what she
was doing. Her own hilarity on this occasion was almost inexplicable to her. It seemed as though she was possessed of some
spirit of joy which she couldn't control. She confessed to him
afterward that she had been wildly glad, exalted, and played
with freedom and abandon, though at the same time she was
frightened and nervous. To Eugene she was of course ravishing
to behold. She could not play, as she truly said, but it made no
difference. Her motions were beautiful.

Mrs. Dale had long admired Eugene's youthful spirit. She
watched him now from one of the windows, and thought of him
much as one might of a boy. He and Suzanne looked charming
playing together. It occurred to her that if he were single he
would not make a bad match for her daughter. Fortunately he

was sane, prudent, charming, more like a guardian to Suzanne than anything else. Her friendship for him was rather a healthy sign.

After dinner it was proposed by Kinroy that he and his friends and Suzanne go to a dance which was being given at a club house, near the government fortifications at The Narrows, where they spread out into the lower bay. Mrs. Dale, not wishing to exclude Eugene, who was depressed at the thought of Suzanne's going and leaving him behind, suggested that they all go. She did not care so much for dancing herself, but Suzanne had no partner and Kinroy and his friend were very much interested in the girls they were taking. A car was called, and they sped to the club to find it dimly lighted with Chinese lanterns, and an orchestra playing softly in the gloom.

"Now you go ahead and dance," said her mother to Suzanne. "I want to sit out here and look at the water a while. I'll watch you through the door."

Eugene held out his hand to Suzanne, who took it, and in a moment they were whirling round. A kind of madness seized them both, for without a word or look they drew close to each other and danced furiously, in a clinging ecstasy of joy.

"Oh, how lovely!" Suzanne exclaimed at one turn of the room, where, passing an open door, they looked out and saw a full lighted ship passing silently by in the distant dark. A sail boat; its one great sail enveloped in a shadowy quiet, floated wraith-like, nearer still.

"Do scenes like that appeal to you so?" asked Eugene.

"Oh, do they!" she pulsated. "They take my breath away. This does, too, it's so lovely!"

Eugene sighed. He understood now. Never, he said to himself, was the soul of an artist so akin to his own and so enveloped in beauty. This same thirst for beauty that was in him was in her, and it was pulling her to him. Only her soul was so exquisitely set in youth and beauty and maidenhood that it overawed and frightened him. It seemed impossible that she should ever love him. These eyes, this face of hers—how they enchanted him! He was drawn as by a strong cord, and so was she—by an immense, terrible magnetism. He had felt it all the afternoon. Keenly. He was feeling it intensely now. He pressed her to his bosom, and she yielded, yearningly, suiting her motions to his subtlest moods. He wanted to exclaim: "Oh, Suzanne! Oh, Suzanne!" but he was afraid. If he said anything to her it would frighten her. She did not really dream as yet what it all meant.

"You know," he said, when the music stopped, "I'm quite beside myself. It's narcotic. I feel like a boy."

"Oh, if they would only go on!" was all she said. And together they went out on the veranda, where there were no lights but only chairs and the countless stars.

"Well?" said Mrs. Dale.

"I'm afraid you don't love to dance as well as I do?" observed Eugene calmly, sitting down beside her.

"I'm afraid I don't, seeing how joyously you do it. I've been watching you. You two dance well together. Kinroy, won't you have them bring us ices?"

Suzanne had slipped away to the side of her brother's friends. She talked to them cheerily the while Eugene watched her, but she was intensely conscious of his presence and charm. She tried to think what she was doing, but somehow she could not—she could only feel. The music struck up again, and for looks' sake he let her dance with her brother's friend. The next was his, and the next, for Kinroy preferred to sit out one, and his friend also. Suzanne and Eugene danced the major portions of the dances together, growing into a wild exaltation, which, however, was wordless except for a certain eagerness which might have been read into what they said. Their hands spoke when they touched and their eyes when they met. Suzanne was intensely shy and fearsome. She was really half terrified by what she was doing—afraid lest some word or thought would escape Eugene, and she wanted to dwell in the joy of this. He went once between two dances, when she was hanging over the rail looking at the dark, gurgling water below, and leaned over beside her.

"How wonderful this night is!" he said.

"Yes, yes!" she exclaimed, and looked away.

"Do you wonder at all at the mystery of life?"

"Oh, yes; oh, yes! All the time."

"And you are so young!" he said passionately, intensely.

"Sometimes, you know, Mr. Witla," she sighed, "I do not like to think."

"Why?"

"Oh, I don't know; I just can't tell you! I can't find words. I don't know."

There was an intense pathos in her phrasing which meant everything to his understanding. He understood how voiceless a great soul really might be, new born without an earth-manufactured vocabulary. It gave him a clearer insight into a thought he had had for a long while and that was that we came, as Wordsworth expressed it, "trailing clouds of glory." But from where? Her soul must be intensely wise—else why his yearning to her? But, oh, the pathos of her voicelessness!

They went home in the car, and late that night, while he was sitting on the veranda smoking to soothe his fevered brain, there was one other scene. The night was intensely warm everywhere except on this hill, where a cool breeze was blowing. The ships on the sea and bay were many—twinkling little lights—and the stars in the sky were as a great army. "See how the floor of heaven is thick inlaid with patines of bright gold," he quoted to himself. A door opened and Suzanne came out of the library, which opened on to the veranda. He had not expected to see her again, nor she him. The beauty of the night had drawn her.

"Suzanne!" he said, when the door opened.

She looked at him, poised in uncertainty, her lovely white face glowing like a pale phosphorescent light in the dark.

"Isn't it beautiful out here? Come, sit down."

"No," she said. "I mustn't stay. It is so beautiful!" She looked about her vaguely, nervously, and then at him. "Oh, that breeze!" She turned up her nose and sniffed eagerly.

"The music is still whirling in my head," he said, coming to her. "I cannot get over tonight." He spoke softly—almost in a whisper—and threw his cigar away. Suzanne's voice was low.

She looked at him and filled her deep broad chest with air. "Oh!" she sighed, throwing back her head, her neck curving divinely.

"One more dance," he said, taking her right hand and putting his left upon her waist.

She did not retreat from him, but looked half distrait, half entranced in his eyes.

"Without music?" she asked. She was almost trembling.

"You are music," he replied, her intense sense of suffocation seizing him.

They moved a few paces to the left where there were no windows and where no one could see. He drew her close to him and looked into her face, but still he did not dare say what he thought. They moved about softly, and then she gurgled that soft laugh that had entranced him from the first. "What would people think?" she asked.

They walked to the railing, he still holding her hand, and then she withdrew it. He was conscious of great danger—of jeopardizing a wonderfully blissful relationship, and finally said: "Perhaps we had better go."

"Yes," she said. "Ma-ma would be greatly disturbed if she knew this."

She walked ahead of him to the door.

"Good night," she whispered.

"Good night," he sighed.

He went back to his chair and meditated on the course he was pursuing. This was a terrible risk. Should he go on? The flower-like face of Suzanne came back to him—her supple body, her wondrous grace and beauty. "Oh, perhaps not, but what a loss, what a lure to have flaunted in front of his eyes! Were there ever thoughts and feelings like these in so young a body? Never, never, never, had he seen her like. Never in all his experiences had he seen anything so exquisite. She was like the budding woods in spring, like little white and blue flowers growing. If life now for once would only be kind and give him her!

"Oh, Suzanne, Suzanne!" he breathed to himself, lingering over the name.

For a fourth or a fifth time Eugene was imagining himself to be terribly, eagerly, fearsomely in love.

CHAPTER VI

THIS burst of emotion with its tentative understanding so subtly reached, changed radically and completely the whole complexion of life for Eugene. Once more now the spirit of youth had returned to him. He had been resenting all this while, in spite of his success, the passage of time, for he was daily and hourly growing older, and what had he really achieved? The more Eugene had looked at life through the medium of his experiences, the more it had dawned on him that somehow all effort was pointless. To where and what did one attain when one attained success? Was it for houses and lands and fine furnishings and friends that one was really striving? Was there any such thing as real friendship in life, and what were its fruits—intense satisfaction? In some few instances, perhaps, but in the main what a sorry jest most so-called friendships veiled! How often they were coupled with self-interest, self-seeking, self-everything! We associated in friendship mostly only with those who were of our own social station. A good friend. Did he possess one? An inefficient friend? Would one such long be his friend? Life moved in schools of those who could run a certain pace, maintain a certain standard of appearances, compel a certain grade of respect and efficiency in others. Colfax was his friend—for the present. So was Winfield. About him were scores and hundreds who were apparently delighted to grasp his hand, but for what? His fame? Certainly. His efficiency? Yes. Only by the measure of his personal power and strength could he measure his friends—no more.

And as for love—what had he ever had of love before? When he went back in his mind, it seemed now that all, each, and every one, had been combined in some way with lust and evil thinking. Could he say that he had ever been in love truly? Certainly not with Margaret Duff or Ruby Kenny or Angela— though that was the nearest he had come to true love—or Christina Channing. He had liked all these women very much, as he had Carlotta Wilson, but had he ever loved one? Never. Angela had won him through his sympathy for her, he told himself now. He had been induced to marry out of remorse. And here he was now having lived all these years and come all this way without having truly loved. Now, behold Suzanne Dale with her perfection of soul and body, and he was wild about her

—not for lust, but for love. He wanted to be with her, to hold her hands, to kiss her lips, to watch her smile; but nothing more. It was true her body had its charm. In extremes it would draw him, but the beauty of her mind and appearance—there lay the fascination. He was heartsick at being compelled to be absent from her, and yet he did not know that he would ever be able to attain her at all.

As he thought of his condition, it rather terrified and nauseated him. To think, after having known this one hour of wonder and superlative bliss, of being compelled to come back into the work-a-day world! Nor were things improving at the office of the United Magazines Corporation. Instead of growing better, they were growing worse. With the diversity of his interests, particularly the interest he held in the Sea Island Realty and Construction Company, he was growing rather lackadaisical in his attitude toward all magazine interests with which he was connected. He had put in strong men wherever he could find them, but these had come to be very secure in their places, working without very much regard to him since he could not give them very much attention. White and Colfax had become intimate with many of them personally. Some of them, such as Hayes, the advertising man, the circulation manager, the editor of the *International Review,* the editor in charge of books, were so very able that, although it was true that Eugene had hired them it was practically settled that they could not be removed. Colfax and White had come to understand by degrees that Eugene was a person who, however brilliant he might be in selecting men, was really not capable of attention to detail. He could not bring his mind down to small practical points. If he had been an owner, like Colfax, or a practical henchman like White, he would have been perfectly safe, but being a natural-born leader, or rather organizer, he was, unless he secured control in the beginning, rather hopeless and helpless when organization was completed. Others could attend to details better than he could. Colfax came to know his men and like them. In absences which had become more frequent, as Eugene became more secure, and as he took up with Winfield, they had first gone to Colfax for advice, and later, in Colfax's absence, to White. The latter received them with open arms. Indeed, among themselves, his lieutenants frequently discussed Eugene and agreed that in organizing, or rather reorganizing the place, he had done his great work. He might have been worth twenty-five thousand a year doing that, but hardly as a man to sit about and cool his heels after the work was done. White had persistently whispered suggestions of Eugene's commercial inefficiency for the task he was essaying to Colfax. "He is really trying to do up there what you ought to be doing," he told him, "and what you can do better. You want to remember that you've learned a lot since you came in here, and so has he, only he has become a little less practical and you have become more so. These men of his look more to you now than they do to him."

Colfax rejoiced in the thought. He liked Eugene, but he liked the idea better that his business interests were perfectly safe. He did not like to think that any one man was becoming so strong that his going would injure him, and this thought for a long time during Eugene's early ascendancy had troubled him. The latter had carried himself with such an air. Eugene had fancied that Colfax needed to be impressed with his importance, and this, in addition to his very thorough work, was one way to do it. His manner had grated on Colfax after a time, for he was the soul of vainglory himself, and he wanted no other gods in the place beside himself. White, on the contrary, was constantly subservient and advisory in his manner. It made a great difference.

By degrees, through one process and another, Eugene had lost ground, but it was only in a nebulous way as yet, and not in anything tangible. If he had never turned his attention to anything else, had never wearied of any detail, and kept close to Colfax and to his own staff, he would have been safe. As it was, he began now to neglect them more than ever, and this could not fail to tell rather disastrously in the long run.

In the first place the prospects in connection with the Sea Island Construction Company were apparently growing brighter and brighter. It was one of those schemes which would take years and years to develop, but it did not look that way at first. Rather it seemed to be showing tangible evidences of accomplishment. The first year, after a good deal of money had been invested, considerable dredging operations were carried out, and dry land appeared in many places—a long stretch of good earth to the rear of the main beach whereon hotels and resorts of all sorts could be constructed. The boardwalk was started after a model prepared by Eugene, and approved—after modification—by the architect engaged, and a portion of the future great dining and dancing casinos was begun and completed, a beautiful building modeled on a combination of the Moorish, Spanish and Old Mission styles. A notable improvement in design had been effected in this scheme, for the color of Blue Sea, according to Eugene's theory, was to be red, white, yellow, blue, and green, done in spirited yet simple outlines. The walls of all buildings were to be white and yellow, latticed with green. The roofs, porticos, lintels, piers, and steps were to be red, yellow, green, and blue. There were to be round, shallow Italian pools of concrete in many of the courts and interiors of the houses. The hotels were to be western modifications of the Giralda in Spain, each one a size smaller, or larger, than the other. Green spear pines and tall cone-shaped poplars were to be the prevailing tree decorations. The railroad, as Mr. Winfield promised, had already completed its spur and Spanish depot, which was beautiful. It looked truly as though Blue Sea would become what Winfield said it would become; the seaside resort of America.

The actuality of this progress fascinated Eugene so much that he gave, until Suzanne appeared, much more time than he really should have to the development of the scheme. As in the days when he first went with Summerfield, he worked of nights on exterior and interior layouts, as he called them—façades, ground arrangements, island improvements, and so on. He went frequently with Winfield and his architect in his auto to see how Blue Sea was getting on and to visit monied men, who might be interested. He drew up plans for ads and booklets, making romantic sketches and originating catch lines.

In the next place, after Suzanne appeared, he began to pay attention almost exclusively in his thoughts to her. He could not get her out of his head night or day. She haunted his thoughts in the office, at home, and in his dreams. He began actually to burn with a strange fever, which gave him no rest. When would he see her again? When would he see her again? When would he see her again? He could see her only as he danced with her at the boat club, as he sat with her in the swing at Daleview. It was a wild, aching desire which gave him no peace any more than any other fever of the brain ever does.

Once, not long after he and she had danced at the boat club together, she came with her mother to see how Angela was, and Eugene had a chance to say a few words to her in the studio, for they came after five in the afternoon when he was at home. Suzanne gazed at him wide-eyed, scarcely knowing what to think, though she was fascinated. He asked her eagerly where she had been, where she was going to be.

"Why," she said gracefully, her pretty lips parted, "we're going to Bentwood Hadley's tomorrow. We'll be there for a week, I fancy. Maybe longer."

"Have you thought of me much, Suzanne?"

"Yes, yes! But you mustn't, Mr. Witla. No, no. I don't know what to think."

"If I came to Bentwood Hadleys, would you be glad?"

"Oh, yes," she said hesitatingly, "but you mustn't come."

Eugene was there that week-end. It wasn't difficult to manage.

"I'm awfully tired," he wrote to Mrs. Hadley. "Why don't you invite me out?"

"Come!" came a telegram, and he went.

On this occasion, he was more fortunate than ever. Suzanne was there, out riding when he came, but, as he learned from Mrs. Hadley, there was a dance on at a neighboring country club. Suzanne with a number of others was going. Mrs. Dale decided to go, and invited Eugene. He seized the offer, for he knew he would get a chance to dance with his ideal. When they were going in to dinner, he met Suzanne in the hall.

"I am going with you," he said eagerly. "Save a few dances for me."

"Yes," she said, inhaling her breath in a gasp.

They went, and he initialled her card in five places.

"We must be careful," she pleaded. "Ma-ma won't like it."

He saw by this that she was beginning to understand, and would plot with him. Why was he luring her on? Why did she let him?

When he slipped his arm about her in the first dance he said, "At last!" And then: "I have waited for this so long."

Suzanne made no reply.

"Look at me, Suzanne," he pleaded.

"I can't," she said.

"Oh, look at me," he urged, "once, please. Look in my eyes."

"No, no," she begged, "I can't."

"Oh, Suzanne," he exclaimed, "I am crazy about you. I am mad. I have lost all reason. Your face is like a flower to me. Your eyes—I can't tell you about your eyes. Look at me!"

"No," she pleaded.

"It seems as though the days will never end in which I do not see you. I wait and wait. Suzanne, do I seem like a silly fool to you?"

"No."

"I am counted sharp and able. They tell me I am brilliant. You are the most perfect thing that I have ever known. I think of you awake and asleep. I could paint a thousand pictures of you. My art seems to come back to me through you. If I live I will paint you in a hundred ways. Have you ever seen the Rossetti woman?"

"No."

"He painted a hundred portraits of her. I shall paint a thousand of you."

She lifted her eyes to look at him shyly, wonderingly, drawn by this terrific passion. His own blazed into hers. "Oh, look at me again," he whispered, when she dropped them under the fire of his glance.

"I can't," she pleaded.

"Oh, yes, once more."

She lifted her eyes and it seemed as though their souls would blend. He felt dizzy, and Suzanne reeled.

"Do you love me, Suzanne?" he asked.

"I don't know," she trembled.

"Do you love me?"

"Don't ask me now."

The music ceased and Suzanne was gone.

He did not see her until much later, for she slipped away to think. Her soul was stirred as with a raging storm. It seemed as though her very soul was being torn up. She was tremulous, tumultuous, unsettled, yearning, eager. She came back after a time and they danced again, but she was calmer apparently. They went out on a balcony, and he contrived to say a few words there.

"You mustn't," she pleaded. "I think we are being watched."

He left her, and on the way home in the auto he whispered: "I shall be on the west veranda tonight. Will you come?"

"I don't know, I'll try."

He walked leisurely to that place later when all was still, and sat down to wait. Gradually the great house quieted. It was one and one-thirty, and then nearly two before the door opened. A figure slipped out, the lovely form of Suzanne, dressed as she had been at the ball, a veil of lace over her hair.

"I'm so afraid," she said, "I scarcely know what I am doing. Are you sure no one will see us?"

"Let us walk down the path to the field." It was the same way they had taken in the early spring when he had met her here before. In the west hung low a waning moon, yellow, sickle shaped, very large because of the hour.

"Do you remember when we were here before?"

"Yes."

"I loved you then. Did you care for me?"

"No."

They walked on under the trees, he holding her hand.

"Oh, this night, this night," he said, the strain of his intense emotion wearying him.

They came out from under the trees at the end of the path. There was a sense of August dryness in the air. It was warm, sensuous. About were the sounds of insects, faint bumblings, cracklings. A tree toad chirped, or a bird cried.

"Come to me, Suzanne," he said at last when they emerged into the full light of the moon at the end of the path and paused. "Come to me." He slipped his arm about her.

"No," she said. "No."

"Look at me, Suzanne," he pleaded; "I want to tell you how much I love you. Oh, I have no words. It seems ridiculous to try to tell you. Tell me that you love me, Suzanne. Tell me now. I am crazy with love of you. Tell me."

"No," she said, "I can't."

"Kiss me!"

"No!"

He drew her to him and turned her face up by her chin in spite of her. "Open your eyes," he pleaded. "Oh, God! That this should come to me! Now I could die. Life can hold no more. Oh, Flower Face! Oh, Silver Feet! Oh, Myrtle Bloom! Divine Fire! How perfect you are. How perfect! And to think you love me!"

He kissed her eagerly.

"Kiss me, Suzanne. Tell me that you love me. Tell me. Oh, how I love that name, Suzanne. Whisper to me you love me."

"No."

"But you do."

"No."

"Look at me, Suzanne. Flower face. Myrtle Bloom. For God's sake, look at me! You love me."

"Oh, yes, yes, yes," she sobbed of a sudden, throwing her arm around his neck. "Oh, yes, yes."

"Don't cry," he pleaded. "Oh, sweet, don't cry. I am mad for love of you, mad. Kiss me now, one kiss. I am staking my soul on your love. Kiss me!"

He pressed his lips to hers, but she burst away, terror-stricken.

"Oh, I am so frightened," she exclaimed all at once. "Oh, what shall I do? I am so afraid. Oh, please, please. Something terrifies me. Something scares me. Oh, what am I going to do? Let me go back."

She was white and trembling. Her hands were nervously clasping and unclasping.

Eugene smoothed her arm soothingly. "Be still, Suzanne," he said. "Be still. I shall say no more. You are all right. I have frightened you. We will go back. Be calm. You are all right."

He recovered his own poise with an effort because of her obvious terror, and led her back under the trees. To reassure her he drew his cigar case from his pocket and pretended to select a cigar. When he saw her calming, he put it back.

"Are you quieter now, sweet?" he asked, tenderly.

"Yes, but let us go back."

"Listen. I will only go as far as the edge. You go alone. I will watch you safely to the door."

"Yes," she said peacefully.

"And you really love me, Suzanne?"

"Oh, yes, but don't speak of it. Not tonight. You will frighten me again. Let us go back."

They strolled on. Then he said: "One kiss, sweet, in parting. One. Life has opened anew for me. You are the solvent of my whole being. You are making me over into something different. I feel as though I had never lived until now. Oh, this experience! It is such a wonderful thing to have done— to have lived through, to have changed as I have changed. You have changed me so completely, made me over into the artist again. From now on I can paint again. I can paint you." He scarcely knew what he was saying. He felt as though he were revealing himself to himself as in an apocalyptic vision.

She let him kiss her, but she was too frightened and wrought to even breathe right. She was intense, emotional, strange. She did not really understand what it was that he was talking about.

"Tomorrow," he said, "at the wood's edge. Tomorrow. Sweet dreams. I shall never know peace any more without your love."

And he watched her eagerly, sadly, bitterly, ecstatically, as she walked lightly from him, disappearing like a shadow through the dark and silent door.

CHAPTER VII

IT would be impossible to describe even in so detailed an account as this the subtleties, vagaries, beauties and terrors of the emotions which seized upon him, and which by degrees began also to possess Suzanne, once he became wholly infatuated with her. Mrs. Dale, was, after a social fashion, one of Eugene's best friends. She had since she had first come to know him spread his fame far and wide as an immensely clever publisher and editor, an artist of the greatest power, and a man of lovely and delightful ideas and personal worth. He knew from various conversations with her that Suzanne was the apple of her eye. He had heard her talk, had, in fact, discussed with her the difficulties of rearing a simple mannered, innocent-minded girl in present day society. She had confided to him that it had been her policy to give Suzanne the widest liberty consistent with good-breeding and current social theories. She did not want to make her bold or unduly self-reliant, and yet she wanted her to be free and natural. Suzanne, she was convinced, from long observation and many frank conversations, was innately honest, truthful and clean-minded. She did not understand her exactly, for what mother can clearly understand any child; but she thought she read her well enough to know that she was in some indeterminate way forceful and able, like her father, and that she would naturally gravitate to what was worth while in life.

Had she any talent? Mrs. Dale really did not know. The girl had vague yearnings toward something which was anything but social in its quality. She did not care anything at all for most of the young men and women she met. She went about a great deal, but it was to ride and drive. Games of chance did not interest her. Drawing-room conversations were amusing to her, but not gripping. She liked interesting characters, able books, striking pictures. She had been particularly impressed with those of Eugene's; she had seen and had told her mother that they were wonderful. She loved poetry of high order, and was possessed of a boundless appetite for the ridiculous and the comic. An unexpected faux pas was apt to throw her into uncontrollable fits of laughter and the funny page selections of the current newspaper artists, when she could obtain them, amused her intensely. She was a student of character, and of her own mother, and was beginning to see clearly what were the motives that were prompting her mother in her attitude toward herself, quite as clearly as that person did herself and better. At bottom she was more talented than her mother, but in a different way. She was not, as yet, as self-controlled, or as understanding of current theories and beliefs as her mother, but she was artistic, emotional, excitable, in an intellectual way, and capable of high flights of fancy and of intense and fine appreciations. Her really sensuous beauty was nothing to her. She did not value it highly. She knew she was beautiful, and that men and boys were apt to go wild about her, but she did not care. They must not be so silly, she thought. She did not attempt to attract them in any way. On the contrary, she avoided every occasion of possible provocation. Her mother had told her plainly how susceptible men were, how little their promises meant, how careful she must be of her looks and actions. In consequence, she went her way as gaily and yet as inoffensively as she could, trying to avoid the sadness of entrancing anyone hopelessly and wondering what her career was to be. Then Eugene appeared.

With his arrival, Suzanne had almost unconsciously entered upon a new phase of her existence. She had seen all sorts of men in society, but those who were exclusively social were exceedingly wearisome to her. She had heard her mother say that it was an important thing to marry money and some man of high social standing, but who this man was to be and what he was to be like she did not know. She did not look upon the typical society men she had encountered as answering suitably to the term high. She had seen some celebrated wealthy men of influential families, but they did not appear to her really human enough to be considered. Most of them were cold, self-opinionated, ultra-artificial to her easy, poetic spirit. In the realms of real distinction were many men whom the papers constantly talked about, financiers, politicians, authors, editors, scientists, some of whom were in society, she understood, but most of whom were not. She had met a few of them as a girl might. Most of those she met, or saw, were old and cold and paid no attention to her whatever. Eugene had appeared trailing an atmosphere of distinction and acknowledged ability and he was young. He was good looking, too—laughing and gay. It seemed almost impossible at first to her that one so young and smiling should be so able, as her mother said. Afterwards, when she came to know him, she began to feel that he was more than able; that he could do anything he pleased. She had visited him once in his office, accompanied by her mother, and she had been vastly impressed by the great building, its artistic finish, Eugene's palatial surroundings. Surely he was the most remarkable young man she had ever known. Then came his incandescent attentions to her, his glowing, radiant presence and then——

Eugene speculated deeply on how he should proceed. All at once, after this night, the whole problem of his life came before him. He was married; he was highly placed socially, better than he had ever been before. He was connected closely with Colfax, so closely that he feared him, for Colfax, in spite of certain emotional vagaries of which Eugene knew, was intensely conventional. Whatever he did was managed in the most offhand way and with no intention of allowing his home life to be affected or disrupted. Winfield, whom also Mrs. Dale knew, was also conventional to outward appearances. He had a mistress, but she was held tightly in check, he understood. Eugene had seen her at the new casino, or a portion of it, the East Wing, recently erected at Blue Sea, and he had been greatly impressed with her beauty. She was smart, daring, dashing. Eugene looked at her then, wondering if the time would ever come when he could dare an intimacy of that character. So many married men did. Would he ever attempt it and succeed?

Now that he had met Suzanne, however, he had a different notion of all this, and it had come over him all at once. Heretofore in his dreams, he had fancied he might strike up an emotional relationship somewhere which would be something like Winfield's towards Miss De Kalb, as she was known, and so satisfy the weary longing that was in him for something new and delightful in the way of a sympathetic relationship with beauty. Since seeing Suzanne, he wanted nothing of this, but only some readjustment or rearrangement of his life whereby he could have Suzanne and Suzanne only. Suzanne! Suzanne! Oh, that dream of beauty. How was he to obtain her, how free his life of all save a beautiful relationship with her? He could live with her forever and ever. He could, he could! Oh, this vision, this dream!

It was the Sunday following the dance that Suzanne and Eugene managed to devise another day together, which, though, it was one of those semi-accidental, semi-voiceless, but nevertheless not wholly thoughtless coincidences which sometimes come about without being wholly agreed upon or understood in the beginning, was nevertheless seized upon by them, accepted silently and semi-consciously, semi-unconsciously worked out together. Had they not been very strongly drawn to each other by now,

this would not have happened at all. But they enjoyed it none
the less. To begin with, Mrs. Dale was suffering from a sick
headache the morning after. In the next place, Kinroy suggested to his friends to go for a lark to South Beach, which was
one of the poorest and scrubbiest of all the beaches on Staten
Island. In the next place, Mrs. Dale suggested that Suzanne
be allowed to go and that perhaps Eugene would be amused.
She rather trusted him as a guide and mentor.

Eugene said calmly that he did not object. He was eager
to be anywhere alone with Suzanne, and he fancied that some
opportunity would present itself whereby once they were there,
they could be together, but he did not want to show it. Once
more the car was called and they departed, being let off at
one end of a silly panorama which stretched its shabby length
for a mile along the shore. The chauffeur took the car back to
the house, it being agreed that they could reach him by phone.
The party started down the plank walk, but almost immediately,
because of different interests, divided. Eugene and Suzanne
stopped to shoot at a shooting gallery. Next they stopped at a
cane rack to ring canes. Anything was delightful to Eugene
which gave him an opportunity to observe his inamorata, to
see her pretty face, her smile, and to hear her heavenly voice.
She rung a cane for him. Every gesture of hers was perfection; every look a thrill of delight. He was walking in some
elysian realm which had nothing to do with the tawdry evidence
of life about him.

They followed the boardwalk southward, after a ride in the
Devil's Whirlpool, for by now Suzanne was caught in the
persuasive subtlety of his emotion and could no more do as her
honest judgment would have dictated than she could have flown.
It needed some shock, some discovery to show her whither she
was drifting and this was absent. They came to a new dance
hall, where a few servant girls and their sweethearts were
dancing, and for a lark Eugene proposed that they should enter.
They danced together again, and though the surroundings were
so poor and the music wretched, Eugene was in heaven.

"Let's run away and go to the Terra-Marine," he suggested, thinking of a hotel farther south along the shore. "It
is so pleasant there. This is all so cheap."

"Where is it?" asked Suzanne.

"Oh, about three miles south of here. We could almost
walk there."

He looked down the long hot beach, but changed his mind.

"I don't mind this," said Suzanne. "It's so very bad that

it's good, you know. I like to see how these people enjoy themselves."

"But it is *so* bad," argued Eugene. "I wish I had your live, healthy attitude toward things. Still we won't go if you don't want to."

Suzanne paused, thinking. Should she run away with him? The others would be looking for them. No doubt they were already wondering where they had gone. Still it didn't make so much difference. Her mother trusted her with Eugene. They could go.

"Well," she said finally, "I don't care. Let's."

"What will the others think?" he said doubtfully.

"Oh, they won't mind," she said. "When they're ready, they'll call the car. They know that I am with you. They know that I can get the car when I want it. Mama won't mind."

Eugene led the way back to a train which ran to Hugenot, their destination. He was beside himself with the idea of a day all alone with Suzanne. He did not stay to consider or give ear to a thought concerning Angela at home or how Mrs. Dale would view it. Nothing would come of it. It was not an outrageous adventure. They took the train south, and in a little while were in another world, on the veranda of a hotel that overlooked the sea. There were numerous autos of idlers like themselves in a court before the hotel. There was a great grassy lawn with swings covered by striped awnings of red and blue and green, and beyond that a pier with many little white launches anchored near. The sea was as smooth as glass and great steamers rode in the distance trailing lovely plumes of smoke. The sun was blazing hot, brilliant, but here on the cool porch waiters were serving pleasure lovers with food and drink. A quartette of negroes were singing. Suzanne and Eugene seated themselves in rockers at first to view the perfect day and later went down and sat in a swing. Unthinkingly, without words, these two were gradually gravitating toward each other under some spell which had no relationship to everyday life. Suzanne looked at him in the double seated swing where they sat facing each other and they smiled or jested aimlessly, voicing nothing of all the upward welling deep that was stirring within.

"Was there ever such a day?" said Eugene finally, and in a voice that was filled with extreme yearning. "See that steamer out there. It looks like a little toy."

"Yes," said Suzanne with a little gasp. She inhaled her

breath as she pronounced this word which gave it an airy breath-lessness which had a touch of demure pathos in it. "Oh, it is perfect."

"Your hair," he said. "You don't know how nice you look. You fit this scene exactly."

"Don't speak of me," she pleaded. "I look so tousled. The wind in the train blew my hair so I ought to go the ladies' dress-ing room and hunt up a maid."

"Stay here," said Eugene. "Don't go. It is all so lovely."

"I won't now. I wish we might always sit here. You, just as you are there, and I here."

"Did you ever read the "Ode on a Grecian Urn'?"

"Yes."

"Do you remember the lines 'Fair youth, beneath the trees, thou canst not leave'?"

"Yes, yes," she answered ecstatically.

> "'Bold lover, never, never canst thou kiss
> Though winning near the goal—yet, do not grieve;
> She cannot fade, though thou hast not thy bliss,
> For ever wilt thou love and she be fair.'"

"Don't, don't," she pleaded.

He understood. The pathos of that great thought was too much for her. It hurt her as it did him. What a mind!

They rocked and swung idly, he pushing with his feet at times in which labor she joined him. They strolled up the beach and sat down on a green clump of grass overlooking the sea. Idlers approached and passed. He laid his arm to her waist and held her hand, but something in her mood stayed him from any ex-pression. Through dinner at the hotel it was the same and on the way to the train, for she wanted to walk through the dark. Under some tall trees, though, in the rich moonlight pre-vailing, he pressed her hand.

"Oh, Suzanne," he said.

"No, no," she breathed, drawing back.

"Oh, Suzanne," he repeated, "may I tell you?"

"No, no," she answered. "Don't speak to me. Please don't. Let's just walk. You and I."

He hushed, for her voice, though sad and fearsome, was imperious. He could not do less than obey this mood.

They went to a little country farmhouse which ranged along the track in lieu of a depot, and sang a quaint air from some old-time comic opera.

"Do you remember the first time when you came to play tennis with me?" he asked.

"Yes."

"Do you know I felt a strange vibration before your coming and all during your playing. Did you?"

"Yes."

"What is that, Suzanne?"

"I don't know."

"Don't you want to know?"

"No, no, Mr. Witla, not now."

"Mr. Witla?"

"It must be so."

"Oh, Suzanne!"

"Let's just think," she pleaded, "it is so beautiful."

They came to a station near Daleview, and walked over. On the way he slipped his arm about her waist, but, oh, so lightly.

"Suzanne," he asked, with a terrible yearning ache in his heart, "do you blame me? Can you?"

"Don't ask me," she pleaded, "not now. No, no."

He tried to press her a little more closely.

"Not now. I don't blame you."

He stopped as they neared the lawn and entered the house with a jesting air. Explanations about mixing in the crowd and getting lost were easy. Mrs. Dale smiled good naturedly. Suzanne went to her room.

HAVING involved himself thus far, seized upon and made his own this perfect flower of life, Eugene had but one thought, and that was to retain it. Now, of a sudden, had fallen from him all the weariness of years. To be in love again. To be involved in such a love, so wonderful, so perfect, so exquisite, it did not seem that life could really be so gracious as to have yielded him so much. What did it all mean, his upward rise during all these years? There had been seemingly but one triumph after another since the bitter days in River-wood and after. The *World*, Summerfield's, The Kalvin Company, The United Magazine Corporation, Winfield, his beautiful apartment on the drive. Surely the gods were good. What did they mean? To give him fame, fortune and Suzanne into the bargain? Could such a thing really be? How could it be worked out? Would fate conspire and assist him so that he could be free of Angela—or——

The thought of Angela to him in these days was a great pain. At bottom Eugene really did not dislike her, he never had. Years of living with her had produced an understanding and a relationship as strong and as keen as it might well be in some respects. Angela had always fancied since the Riverwood days that she really did not love Eugene truly any more—could not, that he was too self-centered and selfish; but this on her part was more of an illusion than a reality. She did care for him in an unselfish way from one point of view, in that she would sacrifice everything to his interests. From another point of view it was wholly selfish, for she wanted him to sacrifice everything for her in return. This he was not willing to do and had never been. He considered that his life was a larger thing than could be encompassed by any single matrimonial relationship. He wanted freedom of action and companionship, but he was afraid of Angela, afraid of society, in a way afraid of himself and what positive liberty might do to him. He felt sorry for Angela—for the intense suffering she would endure if he forced her in some way to release him—and at the same time he felt sorry for himself. The lure of beauty had never for one moment during all these years of upward mounting effort been stilled.

It is curious how things seem to conspire at times to produce a climax. One would think that tragedies like plants and flowers are planted as seeds and grow by various means and aids to a terrible maturity. Roses of hell are some lives, and they shine with all the lustre of infernal fires.

In the first place Eugene now began to neglect his office work thoroughly, for he could not fix his mind upon it any more than he could upon the affairs of the Sea Island Company, or upon his own home and Angela's illness. The morning after his South Beach experience with Suzanne and her curious reticence, he saw her for a little while upon the veranda of Daleview. She was not seemingly depressed, or at least, not noticeably so, and yet there was a gravity about her which indicated that a marked impression of some kind had been made upon her soul. She looked at him with wide frank eyes as she came out to him purposely to tell him that she was going with her mother and some friends to Tarrytown for the day.

"I have to go," she said. "Mamma has arranged it by phone."

"Then I won't see you any more here?"

"No."

"Do you love me, Suzanne?"

"Oh, yes, yes," she declared, and walked wearily to an angle of the wall where they could not be seen.

He followed her quickly, cautiously.

"Kiss me," he said, and she put her lips to his in a distraught frightened way. Then she turned and walked briskly off and he admired the robust swinging of her body. She was not tall, like himself, or small like Angela, but middle sized, full bodied, vigorous. He imagined now that she had a powerful soul in her, capable of great things, full of courage and strength. Once she was a little older, she would be very forceful and full of strong, direct thought.

He did not see her again for nearly ten days, and by that time he was nearly desperate. He was wondering all the time how he was to arrange this. He could not go on in this haphazard way, seeing her occasionally. Why she might leave town for the fall a little later and then what would he do? If her mother heard she would take her off to Europe and then would Suzanne forget? What a tragedy that would be! No, before that should happen, he would run away with her. He would realize all his investments and get away. He could not live without her. He must have her at any cost. What did the United Magazine Corporation amount to, anyway? He was tired of that work. Angela might have the Sea Island Realty Company's stock, if he could not dispose of it advantageously, or if he could, he would make provision for her out of what he should receive. He had some ready money—a few thousand dollars. This and his art—he could still paint—would sustain them. He would go to England with Suzanne, or to France. They would be happy if she really loved him and he thought she did. All this old life could go its way. It was a dreary thing, anyhow, without love. These were his first thoughts.

Later, he came to have different ones, but this was after he had talked to Suzanne again. It was a difficult matter to arrange. In a fit of desperation he called up Daleview one day, and asked if Miss Suzanne Dale was there. A servant answered, and in answer to the "who shall I say" he gave the name of a young man that he knew Suzanne knew. When she answered he said: "Listen, Suzanne! Can you hear very well?"

"Yes."

"Do you recognize my voice?"

"Yes."

"Please don't pronounce my name, will you?"

"No."

"Suzanne, I am crazy to see you. It has been ten days now. Are you going to be in town long?"

"I don't know. I think so."

"If anyone comes near you, Suzanne, simply hang up the receiver, and I will understand."

"Yes."

"If I came anywhere near your house in a car, could you come out and see me?"

"I don't know."

"Oh, Suzanne!"

"I'm not sure. I'll try. What time?"

"Do you know where the old fort road is, at Crystal Lake, just below you?"

"Yes."

"Do you know where the ice house is near the road there?"

"Yes."

"Could you come there?"

"What time?"

"At eleven tomorrow morning or two this afternoon or three."

"I might at two today."

"Oh, thank you for that. I'll wait for you, anyhow."

"All right. Good-bye."

And she hung up the receiver.

Eugene rejoiced at the fortunate outcome of this effort without thinking at first of the capable manner in which she had handled the situation. Truly he said afterwards she must be very courageous to think so directly and act so quickly, for it must have been very trying to her. This love of his was so new. Her position was so very difficult. And yet, on this first call when she had been suddenly put in touch with him, she had shown no signs of trepidation. Her voice had been firm and even, much more so than his, for he was nervously excited. She had taken in the situation at once and fallen into the ruse quite readily. Was she as simple as she seemed? Yes and no. She was simply capable, he thought and her capability had acted through her simplicity instantly.

At two the same day Eugene was there. He gave as an excuse to his secretary that he was going out for a business conference with a well-known author whose book he wished to obtain, and, calling a closed auto, but one not his own, journeyed to the rendezvous. He asked the man to drive down the road, making runs of half a mile to and fro while he sat in the shade of a clump of trees out of view of the road. Presently Suzanne came, bright and fresh as the morning, beautiful in a light purple walking costume of masterly design. She had on a large soft brimmed hat with long feathers of the same shade which became her exquisitely. She walked with an air of grace and freedom, and yet when he looked into her eyes, he saw a touch of trouble there.

"At last?" he said signaling her and smiling. "Come in here. My car is just up the road. Don't you think we had better get in? It's closed. We might be seen. How long can you stay?"

He took her in his arms and kissed her eagerly while she explained that she could not stay long. She had said she was going to the library, which her mother had endowed, for a book. She must be there by half past three or four at the least.

"Oh, we can talk a great deal by then," he said gaily. "Here comes the car. Let's get in."

He looked cautiously about, hailed it, and they stepped in quickly as it drew up.

"Perth Amboy," said Eugene, and they were off at high speed.

Once in the car all was perfect, for they could not be seen. He drew the shades partially and took her in his arms.

"Oh, Suzanne," he said, "how long it has seemed. How very long. Do you love me?"

"Yes, you know I do."

"Suzanne, how shall we arrange this? Are you going away soon? I must see you oftener."

"I don't know," she said. "I don't know what mama is thinking of doing. I know she wants to go up to Lenox in the fall."

"Oh, Pshaw!" commented Eugene wearily.

"Listen, Mr. Witla," said Suzanne thoughtfully. "You know we are running a terrible risk. What if Mrs. Witla should find out, or mama? It would be terrible."

"I know it," said Eugene. "I suppose I ought not to be acting in this way. But, oh, Suzanne, I am wild about you. I am not myself any longer. I don't know what I am. I only know that I love you, love you, love you!"

He gathered her in his arms and kissed her ecstatically. "How sweet you look. How beautiful you are. Oh, flower face! Myrtle Bloom! Angel Eyes! Divine Fire!" He hugged her in a long silent embrace, the while the car sped on.

"But what about us?" she asked, wide-eyed. "You know we are running a terrible risk. I was just thinking this morning when you called me up. It's dangerous, you know."

"Are you becoming sorry, Suzanne?"

"No."

"Do you love me?"

"You know I do."

"Then you will help me figure this out?"

"I want to. But listen, Mr. Witla, now listen to me. I want to tell you something." She was very solemn and quaint and sweet in this mood.

"I will listen to anything, baby mine, but don't call me Mr. Witla. Call me Eugene, will you?"

"Well, now, listen to me, Mr.—Mr.—Eugene."

"Not Mr. Eugene, just Eugene. Now say it. Eugene," he quoted his own name to her.

"Now listen to me, Mr.—now, listen to me, Eugene," she at last forced herself to say, and Eugene stopped her lips with his mouth.

"There," he said.

"Now listen to me," she went on urgently, "you know I am afraid mama will be terribly angry if she finds this out."

"Oh, will she?" interrupted Eugene jocosely.

Suzanne paid no attention to him.

"We have to be very careful. She likes you so much now that if she doesn't come across anything direct, she will never think of anything. She was talking about you only this morning."

"What was she saying?"

"Oh, what a nice man you are, and how able you are."

"Oh, nothing like that," replied Eugene jestingly.

"Yes, she did. And I think Mrs. Witla likes me. I can meet you sometimes when I'm there, but we must be so careful. I mustn't stay out long today. I want to think things out, too. You know I'm having a real hard time thinking about this."

Eugene smiled. Her innocence was so delightful to him, so naïve.

"What do you mean by thinking things out, Suzanne?" asked Eugene curiously. He was interested in the workings of her young mind, which seemed so fresh and wonderful to him. It was so delightful to find this paragon of beauty so responsive, so affectionate and helpful and withal so thoughtful. She was somewhat like a delightful toy to him, and he held her as reverently in awe as though she were a priceless vase.

"You know I want to think what I'm doing. I have to. It seems so terrible to me at times and yet you know, you know——"

"I know what?" he asked, when she paused.

"I don't know why I shouldn't if I want to—if I love you."

Eugene looked at her curiously. This attempt at analysis of life, particularly in relation to so trying and daring a situation as this, astonished him. He had fancied Suzanne more or less thoughtless and harmless as yet, big potentially, but uncertain and vague. Here she was thinking about this most difficult problem almost more directly than he was and apparently with more courage. He was astounded, but more than that, intensely interested. What had become of her terrific fright of ten days before? What was it she was thinking about exactly?

"What a curious girl you are," he said.

"Why am I?" she asked.

"Because you are. I didn't think you could think so keenly yet. I thought you would some day. But, how have you reasoned this out?"

"Did you ever read 'Anna Karénina'?" she asked him meditatively.

"Yes," he said, wondering that she should have read it at her age.

"What did you think of that?"

"Oh, it shows what happens, as a rule, when you fly in the face of convention," he said easily, wondering at the ability of her brain.

"Do you think things must happen that way?"

"No, I don't think they must happen that way. There are lots of cases where people do go against the conventions and succeed. I don't know. It appears to be all a matter of time and chance. Some do and some don't. If you are strong enough or clever enough to 'get away with it,' as they say, you will. If you aren't, you won't. What makes you ask?"

"Well," she said, pausing, her lips parted, her eyes fixed on the floor, "I was thinking that it needn't necessarily be like that, do you think? It could be different?"

"Yes, it could be," he said thoughtfully, wondering if it really could.

"Because if it couldn't," she went on, "the price would be too high. It isn't worth while."

"You mean, you mean," he said, looking at her, "that you would." He was thinking that she was deliberately contemplating making a sacrifice of herself for him. Something in her thoughtful, self-debating, meditative manner made him think so.

Suzanne looked out of the window and slowly nodded her head. "Yes," she said, solemnly, "if it could be arranged. Why not? I don't see why."

Her face was a perfect blossom of beauty, as she spoke. Eugene wondered whether he was waking or sleeping. Suzanne reasoning so! Suzanne reading "Anna Karénina" and philosophizing so! Basing a course of action on theorizing in connection with books and life, and in the face of such terrible evidence as "Anna Karénina" presented to the contrary of this proposition. Would wonders ever cease?

"You know," she said after a time, "I think mama wouldn't mind, Eugene. She likes you. I've heard her say so lots of times. Besides I've heard her talk this way about other people. She thinks people oughtn't to marry unless they love each other very much. I don't think she thinks it's necessary for people to marry at all unless they want to. We might live together if we wished, you know."

Eugene himself had heard Mrs. Dale question the marriage system, but only in a philosophic way. He did not take much stock in her social maunderings. He did not know what she might be privately saying to Suzanne, but he did not believe it could be very radical, or at least seriously so.

"Don't you take any stock in what your mother says, Suzanne," he observed, studying her pretty face. "She doesn't mean it, at least, she doesn't mean it as far as you are concerned. She's merely talking. If she thought anything were going to happen to you, she'd change her mind pretty quick."

"No, I don't think so," replied Suzanne thoughtfully. "You know, I think I know mama better than she knows herself. She always talks of me as a little girl, but I can rule her in lots of things. I've done it."

Eugene stared at Suzanne in amazement. He could scarcely believe his ears. She was beginning so early to think so deeply on the social and executive sides of life. Why should her mind be trying to dominate her mother's?

"Suzanne," he observed, "you must be careful what you do or say. Don't rush into talking of this pellmell. It's dangerous. I love you, but we shall have to go slow. If Mrs. Witla should learn of this, she would be crazy. If your mother should suspect, she would take you away to Europe somewhere, very likely. Then I wouldn't get to see you at all."

"Oh, no, she wouldn't," replied Suzanne determinedly. "You know, I know mama better than you think I do. I can rule her, I tell you. I know I can. I've done it."

She tossed her head in an exquisitely pretty way which upset Eugene's reasoning faculties. He could not think and look at her.

"Suzanne," he said, drawing her to him. "You are exquisite, extreme, the last word in womanhood for me. To think of your reasoning so—you, Suzanne."

"Why, why," she asked, with pretty parted lips and uplifted eyebrows, "why shouldn't I think?"

"Oh, yes, certainly, we all do, but not so deeply, necessarily, Flower Face."

"Well, we must think now," she said simply.

"Yes, we must think now," he replied; "would you really share a studio with me if I were to take one? I don't know of any other way quite at present."

"I would, if I knew how to manage it," she replied. "Mama is queer. She's so watchful. She thinks I'm a child and you know I am not at all. I don't understand mama. She talks one thing and does another. I would rather do and not talk. Don't you think so?" He stared. "Still, I think I can fix it. Leave it to me."

"And if you can you'll come to me?"

"Oh, yes, yes," exclaimed Suzanne ecstatically, turning to

him all at once and catching his face between her hands. "Oh!"
—she looked into his eyes and dreamed.

"But we must be careful," he cautioned. "We musn't do
anything rash."

"I won't," said Suzanne.

"And I won't, of course," he replied.

They paused again while he watched her.

"I might make friends with Mrs. Witla," she observed, after
a time. "She likes me, doesn't she?"

"Yes," said Eugene.

"Mama doesn't object to my going up there, and I could
let you know."

"That's all right. Do that," said Eugene. "Oh, please do,
if you can. Did you notice whose name I used today?"

"Yes," she said. "You know Mr. Witla, Eugene, I thought
you might call me up?"

"Did you?" he asked, smiling.

"Yes."

"You give me courage, Suzanne," he said, drawing close to
her. "You're so confident, so apparently carefree. The world
hasn't touched your spirit."

"When I'm away from you, though, I'm not so courageous,"
she replied. "I've been thinking terrible things. I get frightened sometimes."

"But you mustn't, sweet, I need you so. Oh, how I need
you."

She looked at him, and for the first time smoothed his hair
with her hand.

"You know, Eugene, you're just like a boy to me."

"Do I seem so?" he asked, comforted greatly.

"I couldn't love you as I do if you weren't."

He drew her to him again and kissed her anew.

"Can't we repeat these rides every few days?" he asked.

"Yes, if I'm here, maybe."

"It's all right to call you up if I use another name?"

"Yes, I think so."

"Let's choose new names for each, so that we'll know who's
calling. You shall be Jenny Lind and I Allan Poe." Then
they fell to ardent love-making until the time came when they
had to return. For him, so far as work was concerned, the afternoon was gone.

CHAPTER IX

THERE followed now a series of meetings contrived with difficulty, fraught with danger, destructive of his peace of mind, of his recently acquired sense of moral and commercial responsibility, of the sense of singleness of purpose and interest in his editorial and publishing world, which had helped him so much recently. The meetings nevertheless were full of such intense bliss for him that it seemed as though he were a thousand times repaid for all the subtlety and folly he was practicing. There were times when he came to the ice house in a hired car, others when she notified him by phone or note to his office of times when she was coming in to town to stay. He took her in his car one afternoon to Blue Sea when he was sure no one would encounter him. He persuaded Suzanne to carry a heavy veil, which could be adjusted at odd moments. Another time—several, in fact—she came to the apartment in Riverside Drive, ostensibly to see how Mrs. Witla was getting along, but really, of course, to see Eugene. Suzanne did not really care so much for Angela, although she did not dislike her. She thought she was an interesting woman, though perhaps not a happy mate for Eugene. The latter had told her not so much that he was unhappy as that he was out of love. He loved her now, Suzanne, and only her.

The problem as to where this relationship was to lead to was complicated by another problem, which Eugene knew nothing of, but which was exceedingly important. For Angela, following the career of Eugene with extreme pleasure and satisfaction on the commercial side, and fear and distrust on the social and emotional sides, had finally decided to risk the uncertain outcome of a child in connection with Eugene and herself, and to give him something which would steady his life and make him realize his responsibilities and offer him something gladdening besides social entertainment and the lure of beauty in youth. She had never forgotten the advice which Mrs. Sanifore and her physician had given her in Philadelphia, nor had she ever ceased her cogitations as to what the probable effect of a child would be. Eugene needed something of this sort to balance him. His position in the world was too tenuous, his temperament too variable. A child—a little girl, she hoped, for he always liked little girls and made much of them—would quiet him. If she could only have a little girl now!

Some two months before her illness, while Eugene was becoming, all unsuspected by her, so frenzied about Suzanne, she had relaxed, or rather abandoned, her old-time precautions entirely, and had recently begun to suspect that her fears, or hopes, or both, were about to be realized. Owing to her subsequent illness and its effect on her heart, she was not very happy now. She was naturally very uncertain as to the outcome as well as to how Eugene would take it. He had never expressed a desire for a child, but she had no thought of telling him as yet, for she wanted to be absolutely sure. If she were not correct in her suspicions, and got well, he would attempt to dissuade her for the future. If she were, he could not help himself. Like all women in that condition, she was beginning to long for sympathy and consideration and to note more keenly the drift of Eugene's mind toward a world which did not very much concern her. His interest in Suzanne had puzzled her a little, though she was not greatly troubled about her because Mrs. Dale appeared to be so thoughtful about her daughter. Times were changing. Eugene had been going out much alone. A child would help. It was high time it came.

When Suzanne had started coming with her mother, Angela thought nothing of it; but on the several occasions when Suzanne called during her illness, and Eugene had been present, she felt as though there might easily spring up something between them. Suzanne was so charming. Once as she lay thinking after Suzanne had left the room to go into the studio for a few moments, she heard Eugene jesting with her and laughing keenly. Suzanne's laugh, or gurgling giggle, was most infectious. It was so easy, too, for Eugene to make her laugh, for his type of jesting was to her the essence of fun. It seemed to her that there was something almost overgay in the way they carried on. On each occasion when she was present, Eugene proposed that he take Suzanne home in his car, and this set her thinking.

There came a time when, Angela being well enough from her rheumatic attack, Eugene invited a famous singer, a tenor, who had a charming repertoire of songs, to come to his apartment and sing. He had met him at a social affair in Brooklyn with which Winfield had something to do. A number of people were invited—Mrs. Dale, Suzanne, and Kinroy, among others; but Mrs. Dale could not come, and as Suzanne had an appointment for the next morning, Sunday, in the city, she decided to stay at the Witlas. This pleased Eugene immensely. He had bought a sketching book which he had begun to fill with sketches of Suzanne from memory and these he wanted to show her. Besides, he wanted her to hear this singer's beautiful voice.

The company was interesting. Kinroy brought Suzanne early and left. Eugene and Suzanne, after she had exchanged greetings with Angela, sat out on the little stone balcony overlooking the river and exchanged loving thoughts. He was constantly holding her hand when no one was looking and stealing kisses. After a time the company began to arrive, and finally the singer himself. The trained nurse, with Eugene's assistance, helped Angela forward, who listened enraptured to the songs. Suzanne and Eugene, swept by the charm of some of them, looked at each other with that burning gaze which love alone understands. To Eugene Suzanne's face was a perfect flower of hypnotic influence. He could scarcely keep his eyes off her for a moment at a time. The singer ceased, the company departed. Angela was left crying over the beauty of "The Erlking," the last song rendered. She went back to her room, and Suzanne ostensibly departed for hers. She came out to say a few final words to Mrs. Witla, then came through the studio to go to her own room again. Eugene was there waiting. He caught her in his arms, kissing her silently. They pretended to strike up a conventional conversation, and he invited her to sit out on the stone balcony for a few last moments. The moon was so beautiful over the river.

"Don't!" she said, when he gathered her in his arms, in the shadow of the night outside. "She might come."

"No," he said eagerly.

They listened, but there was no sound. He began an easy pretence to talk, the while stroking her pretty arm, which was bare. Insanity over her beauty, the loveliness of the night, the charm of the music, had put him beside himself. He drew her into his arms in spite of her protest, only to have Angela suddenly appear at the other end of the room where the door was. There was no concealing anything—she saw. She came rapidly forward, even as Suzanne jumped up, a sickening rage in her heart, a sense of her personal condition strong in her mind, a sense of something terrible and climacteric in the very air, but she was still too ill to risk a great demonstration or to declare herself fully. It seemed now once more the whole world had fallen about her ears, for because of her plans and in spite of all her suspicions, she had not been ready to believe that Eugene would really trespass again. She had come to surprise him, if possible, but she had not actually expected to, had hoped not to. Here was this beautiful girl, the victim of his wiles, and here was she involved by her own planning, while Eugene, shame-faced, she supposed, stood by ready to have this ridiculous liaison nipped in the bud. She did not propose to expose herself to Suzanne if she could help it, but sorrow for herself, shame for him, pity for Suzanne in a way, the desire to preserve the shell of appearances, which was now, after this, so utterly empty for her though so important for the child, caused her to swell with her old-time rage, and yet to hold it in check. Six years before she would have raged to his face, but time had softened her in this respect. She did not see the value of brutal words.

"Suzanne," she said, standing erect in the filtered gloom of the room which was still irradiated by the light of the moon in the west, "how could you! I thought so much better of you."

Her face, thinned by her long illness and her brooding over her present condition, was still beautiful in a spiritual way. She wore a pale yellow and white flowered dressing gown of filmy, lacy texture, and her long hair, done in braids by the nurse, was hanging down her back like the Gretchen she was to him years before. Her hands were thin and pale, but artistic, and her face drawn in all the wearisome agony of a mater dolorosa.

"Why, why," exclaimed Suzanne, terribly shaken out of her natural fine poise for the moment but not forgetful of the dominating thought in her mind, "I love him; that's why, Mrs. Witla."

"Oh, no, you don't! you only think you love him, as so many women have before you, Suzanne," said Angela frozenly, the thought of the coming child always with her. If she had only told him before! "Oh, shame, in my house, and you a young, supposedly innocent girl! What do you suppose your mother would think if I should call her up and tell her now? Or your brother? You knew he was a married man. I might excuse you if it weren't for that—if you hadn't known me and hadn't accepted my hospitality. As for him, there is no need of my talking to him. This is an old story with him, Suzanne. He has done this with other women before you, and he will do it with other women after you. It is one of the things I have to bear for having married a man of so-called talent. Don't think, Suzanne, when you tell me you love him, that you tell me anything new. I have heard that story before from other women. You are not the first, and you will not be the last."

Suzanne looked at Eugene inquiringly, vaguely, helplessly, wondering if all this were so.

Eugene hardened under Angela's cutting accusation, but he was not at all sure at first what he ought to do. He wondered for the moment whether he ought not to abandon Suzanne and fall back into his old state, dreary as it might seem to him; but the sight of her pretty face, the sound of Angela's cutting voice, determined him quickly. "Angela," he began, recovering his composure the while Suzanne contemplated him, "why do you talk that way? You know that what you say isn't true. There was one other woman. I will tell Suzanne about her. There were several before I married you. I will tell her about them. But my life is a shell, and you know it. This apartment is a shell. Absolutely it means nothing at all to me. There has been no love between us, certainly not on my part, for years, and you know that. You have practically confessed to me from time to time that you do not care for me. I haven't deceived this girl. I am glad to tell her now how things stand."

"How things stand! How things stand!" exclaimed Angela, blazing and forgetting herself for the moment. "Will you tell her what an excellent, faithful husband you have made me? Will you tell her how honestly you have kept your word pledged to me at the altar? Will you tell her how I have worked and sacrificed for you through all these years? How I have been repaid by just such things as this? I'm sorry for you, Suzanne, more than anything else," went on Angela, wondering whether she should tell Eugene here and now of her condition but fearing he would not believe it. It seemed so much like melodrama. "You are just a silly little girl duped by an expert man, who thinks he loves you for a little while, but who really doesn't. He will get over it. Tell me frankly what do you expect to get out of it all? You can't marry him. I won't give him a divorce. I can't, as he will know later, and he has no grounds for obtaining one. Do you expect to be his mistress? You have no hope of ever being anything else. Isn't that a nice ambition for a girl of your standing? And you are supposed to be virtuous! Oh, I am ashamed of you, if you are not! I am sorry for your mother. I am astonished to think that you would so belittle yourself."

Suzanne had heard the "I can't," but she really did not know how to interpret it. It had never occurred to her that there could ever be a child here to complicate matters. Eugene told her that he was unhappy, that there was nothing between him and Angela and never could be.

"But I love him, Mrs. Witla," said Suzanne simply and rather dramatically. She was tense, erect, pale and decidedly beautiful.

It was a great problem to have so quickly laid upon her shoulders.

"Don't talk nonsense, Suzanne!" said Angela angrily and desperately. "Don't deceive yourself and stick to a silly pose. You are acting now. You're talking as you think you ought to talk, as you have seen people talk in plays. This is my husband. You are in my home. Come, get your things. I will call up your mother and tell her how things stand, and she will send her auto for you."

"Oh, no," said Suzanne, "you can't do that! I can't go back there, if you tell her. I must go out in the world and get something to do until I can straighten out my own affairs. I won't be able to go home any more. Oh, what shall I do?"

"Be calm, Suzanne," said Eugene determinedly, taking her hand and looking at Angela defiantly. "She isn't going to call up your mother, and she isn't going to tell your mother. You are going to stay here, as you intended, and tomorrow you are going where you thought you were going."

"Oh, no, she isn't!" said Angela angrily, starting for the phone. "She is going home. I'm going to call her mother."

Suzanne stirred nervously. Eugene put his hand in hers to reassure her.

"Oh, no, you aren't," he said determinedly. "She isn't going home, and you are not going to touch that phone. If you do, a number of things are going to happen, and they are going to happen quick."

He moved between her and the telephone receiver, which hung in the hall outside the studio and toward which she was edging.

Angela paused at the ominous note in his voice, the determined quality of his attitude. She was surprised and amazed at the almost rough manner in which he put her aside. He had taken Suzanne's hand, he, her husband, and was begging her to be calm.

"Oh, Eugene," said Angela desperately, frightened and horrified, her anger half melted in her fears, "you don't know what you are doing! Suzanne doesn't. She won't want anything to do with you when she does. Young as she is, she will have too much womanhood."

"What are you talking about?" asked Eugene desperately. He had no idea of what Angela was driving at, not the faintest suspicion. "What are you talking about?" he repeated grimly.

"Let me say just one word to you alone, not here before Suzanne, just one, and then perhaps you will be willing to let her go home tonight."

Angela was subtle in this, a little bit wicked. She was not using her advantage in exactly the right spirit.

"What is it?" demanded Eugene sourly, expecting some trick. He had so long gnawed at the chains which bound him that the thought of any additional lengths which might be forged irritated him greatly. "Why can't you tell it here? What difference can it make?"

"It ought to make all the difference in the world. Let me say it to you alone."

Suzanne, who wondered what it could be, walked away. She was wondering what it was that Angela had to tell. The latter's manner was not exactly suggestive of the weighty secret she bore. When Suzanne was gone, Angela whispered to him.

"It's a lie!" said Eugene vigorously, desperately, hopelessly. "It's something you've trumped up for the occasion. It's just like you to say that, to do it! Pah! I don't believe it. It's a lie! It's a lie! You know it's a lie!"

"It's the truth!" said Angela angrily, pathetically, outraged in her every nerve and thought by the reception which this fact had received, and desperate to think that the announcement of a coming child by him should be received in this manner under such circumstances that it should be forced from her as a last resort, only to be received with derision and scorn. "It's the truth, and you ought to be ashamed to say that to me. What can I expect from a man, though, who would introduce another woman into his own home as you have tonight?" To think that she should be reduced to such a situation as this so suddenly! It was impossible to argue it with him here. She was ashamed now that she had introduced it at this time. He would not believe her, anyhow now, she saw that. It only enraged him and her. He was too wild. This seemed to infuriate him—to condemn her in his mind as a trickster and a sharper, someone who was using unfair means to hold him. He almost jumped away from her in disgust, and she realized that she had struck an awful blow which apparently, to him, had some elements of unfairness in it.

"Won't you have the decency after this to send her away?" she pleaded aloud, angrily, eagerly, bitterly.

Eugene was absolutely in a fury of feeling. If ever he thoroughly hated and despised Angela, he did so at that moment. To think that she should have done anything like this! To think that she should have complicated this problem of weariness of her with a thing like this! How cheap it was, how shabby! It showed the measure of the woman, to bring a child into the world, regardless of the interests of the child, in order to hold him against his will. Damn! Hell! God damn such a complicated, rotten world! No, she was lying. She could not hold him that way. It was a horrible, low, vile trick. He would have nothing to do with her. He would show her. He would leave her. He would show her that this sort of thing would not work with him. It was like every other petty thing she had ever done. Never, never, never, would he let this stand in the way. Oh, what a mean, cruel, wretched thing to do!

Suzanne came back while they were arguing. She half suspected what it was all about, but she did not dare to act or think clearly. The events of this night were too numerous, too complicated. Eugene had said so forcibly it was a lie whatever it was, that she half believed him. That was a sign surely of the little affection that existed between him and Angela. Angela was not crying. Her face was hard, white, drawn.

"I can't stay here," said Suzanne dramatically to Eugene. "I will go somewhere. I had better go to a hotel for the night. Will you call a car?"

"Listen to me, Suzanne," said Eugene vigorously and determinedly. "You love me, don't you?"

"You know I do," she replied.

Angela stirred sneeringly.

"Then you will stay here. I want you to pay no attention to anything she may say or declare. She has told me a lie tonight. I know why. Don't let her deceive you. Go to your room and your bed. I want to talk to you tomorrow. There is no need of your leaving tonight. There is plenty of room here. It's silly. You're here now—stay."

"But I don't think I'd better stay," said Suzanne nervously.

Eugene took her hand reassuringly.

"Listen to me," he began.

"But she won't stay," said Angela.

"But she will," said Eugene; "and if she don't stay, she goes with me. I will take her home."

"Oh, no, you won't!" replied Angela.

"Listen," said Eugene angrily. "This isn't six years ago, but now. I'm master of this situation, and she stays here. She stays here, or she goes with me and you look to the future as best you may. I love her. I'm not going to give her up, and if you want to make trouble, begin now. The house comes down on your head, not mine."

"Oh!" said Angela, half terrified, "what do I hear?"

"Just that. Now you go to your room. Suzanne will go to

hers. I will go to mine. We will not have any more fighting here tonight. The jig is up. The die is cast. I'm through. Suzanne comes to me, if she will."

Angela walked to her room through the studio, stricken by the turn things had taken, horrified by the thoughts in her mind, unable to convince Eugene, unable to depose Suzanne, her throat dry and hot, her hands shaking, her heart beating fitfully; she felt as if her brain would burst, her heart break actually, not emotionally. She thought Eugene had gone crazy, and yet now, for the first time in her married life, she realized what a terrible mistake she had made in always trying to drive him. It hadn't worked tonight, her rage, her domineering, critical attitude. It had failed her completely, and also this scheme, this beautiful plan, this trump card on which she had placed so much reliance for a happy life, this child which she had hoped to play so effectively. He didn't believe her. He wouldn't even admit its possibility. He didn't admire her for it. He despised her! He looked on it as a trick. Oh, what an unfortunate thing it had been to mention it! And yet Suzanne must understand, she must know, she would never countenance anything like this. But what would he do? He was positively livid with rage. What fine auspices these were under which to usher a child into the world! She stared feverishly before her, and finally began to cry hopelessly.

Eugene stood in the hall beside Suzanne after she had gone. His face was drawn, his eyes hunted, his hair tousled. He looked grim and determined in his way, stronger than he had ever looked before.

"Suzanne," he said, taking the latter by her two arms and staring into her eyes, "she has told me a lie, a lie, a cold, mean, cruel lie. She'll tell it you shortly. She says she is with child by me. It isn't so. She couldn't have one. If she did, it would kill her. She would have had one long ago if she could have. I know her. She thinks this will frighten me. She thinks it will drive you away. Will it? It's a lie, do you hear me, whatever she says. It's a lie, and she knows it. Ough!" He dropped her left arm and pulled at his neck. "I can't stand this. You won't leave me. You won't believe her, will you?"

Suzanne stared into his distraught face, his handsome, desperate, significant eyes. She saw the woe there, the agony, and was sympathetic. He seemed wonderfully worthy of love, unhappy, unfortunately pursued; and yet she was frightened. Still she had promised to love him.

"No," she said fixedly, her eyes speaking a dramatic confidence. "You won't leave here tonight?"

"No."

She smoothed his cheek with her hand.

"You will come and walk with me in the morning? I have to talk with you."

"Yes."

"Don't be afraid. Just lock your door if you are. She won't bother you. She won't do anything. She is afraid of me. She may want to talk with you, but I am close by. Do you still love me?"

"Yes."

"Will you come to me if I can arrange it?"

"Yes."

"Even in the face of what she says?"

"Yes; I don't believe her. I believe you. What difference could it make, anyhow? You don't love her."

"No," he said; "no, no, no! I never have." He drew her into his arms wearily, relievedly. "Oh, Flower Face," he said, "don't give me up! Don't grieve. Try not to, anyhow. I have been bad, as she says, but I love you. I love you, and I will stake all on that. If all this must fall about our heads, then let it fall. I love you."

Suzanne stroked his cheek with her hands nervously. She was deathly pale, frightened, but somehow courageous through it all. She caught strength from his love.

"I love you," she said.

"Yes," he replied. "You won't give me up?"

"No, I won't," she said, not really understanding the depth of her own mood. "I will be true."

"Things will be better tomorrow," he said, somewhat more quietly. "We will be calmer. We will walk and talk. You won't leave without me?"

"No."

"Please don't; for I love you, and we must talk and plan."

CHAPTER X

THE introduction of this astonishing fact in connection with Angela was so unexpected, so morally diverting and peculiar that though Eugene denied it, half believed she was lying, he was harassed by the thought that she might be telling the truth. It was so unfair, though, was all he could think, so unkind! It never occurred to him that it was accidental, as indeed it was not, but only that it was a trick, sharp, cunning, ill-timed for him, just the thing calculated to blast his career and tie him down to the old régime when he wanted most to be free. A new life was dawning for him now. For the first time in his life he was to have a woman after his own heart, so young, so beautiful, so intellectual, so artistic! With Suzanne by his side, he was about to plumb the depths of all the joys of living. Without her, life was to be dark and dreary, and here was Angela coming forward at the critical moment disrupting this dream as best she could by the introduction of a child that she did not want, and all to hold him against his will. If ever he hated her for trickery and sharp dealing, he did so now. What would the effect on Suzanne be? How would he convince her that it was a trick? She must understand; she would. She would not let this miserable piece of chicanery stand between him and her. He turned in his bed wearily after he had gone to it, but he could not sleep. He had to say something, do something. So he arose, slipped on a dressing gown, and went to Angela's room.

That distraught soul, for all her determination and fighting capacity, was enduring for the second time in her life the fires of hell. To think that in spite of all her work, her dreams, this recent effort to bring about peace and happiness, perhaps at the expense of her own life, she was compelled to witness a scene like this. Eugene was trying to get free. He was obviously determined to do so. This scandalous relationship, when had it begun? Would her effort to hold him fail? It looked that way, and yet surely Suzanne, when she knew, when she understood, would leave him. Any woman would.

Her head ached, her hands were hot, she fancied she might be suffering a terrible nightmare, she was so sick and weak; but, no, this was her room. A little while ago she was sitting in her husband's studio, surrounded by friends, the object of much solicitude, Eugene apparently considerate and thoughtful of her, a beautiful programme being rendered for their special benefit. Now she was lying here in her room, a despised wife, an outcast from affection and happiness, the victim of some horrible sorcery of fate whereby another woman stood in her place in Eugene's affection. To see Suzanne, proud in her young beauty, confronting her with bold eyes, holding her husband's hand, saying in what seemed to her to be brutal, or insane, or silly melodramatic make-believe, "But I love him, Mrs. Witla," was maddening. Oh, God! Oh, God! Would her tortures never cease? Must all her beautiful dreams come to nothing? Would Eugene leave her, as he so violently said a little while ago? She had never seen him like this. It was terrible to see him so determined, so cold and brutal. His voice had actually been harsh and guttural, something she had never known before in him.

She trembled as she thought, and then great flashes of rage swept her only to be replaced by rushes of fear. She was in such a terrific position. The woman was with him, young, defiant, beautiful. She had heard him call to her, had heard them talking. Once she thought that now would be the time to murder him, Suzanne, herself, the coming life and end it all; but at this critical moment, having been sick and having grown so much older, with this problem of the coming life before her, she had no chart to go by. She tried to console herself with the thought that he must abandon his course, that he would when the true force of what she had revealed had had time to sink home; but it had not had time yet. Would it before he did anything rash? Would it before he had completely compromised himself and Suzanne? Judging from her talk and his, he had not as yet, or she thought not. What was he going to do? What was he going to do?

Angela feared as she lay there that in spite of her revelation he might really leave her immediately. There might readily spring a terrible public scandal out of all this. The mockery of their lives laid bare; the fate of the child jeopardized; Eugene, Suzanne, and herself disgraced, though she had little thought for Suzanne. Suzanne might get him, after all. She might accidentally be just hard and cold enough. The world might possibly forgive him. She herself might die! What an end, after all her dreams of something bigger, better, surer! Oh, the pity, the agony of this! The terror and horror of a wrecked life!

And then Eugene came into the room.

He was haggard, stormy-eyed, thoughtful, melancholy, as he entered. He stood in the doorway first, intent, then clicked a little night-lamp button which threw on a very small incandes-

cent light near the head of Angela's bed, and then sat down in a
rocking-chair which the nurse had placed near the medicine table.
Angela had so much improved that no night nurse was needed—
only a twelve-hour one.

"Well," he said solemnly but coldly, when he saw her pale,
distraught, much of her old, youthful beauty still with her, "you
think you have scored a splendid trick, don't you? You think
you have sprung a trap? I simply came in here to tell you that
you haven't—that you have only seen the beginning of the end.
You say you are going to have a child. I don't believe it. It's
a lie, and you know it's a lie. You saw that there was an end
coming to all this state of weariness some time, and this is your
answer. Well, you've played one trick too many, and you've
played it in vain. You lose. I win this time. I'm going to be
free now, I want to say to you, and I am going to be free if I
have to turn everything upside down. I don't care if there were
seventeen prospective children instead of one. It's a lie, in the
first place; but if it isn't, it's a trick, and I'm not going to be
tricked any longer. I've had all I want of domination and trickery and cheap ideas. I'm through now, do you hear me? I'm
through."

He felt his forehead with a nervous hand. His head ached,
he was half sick. This was such a dreary pit to find himself in,
this pit of matrimony, chained by a domineering wife and a
trickily manœuvred child. His child! What a mockery at this
stage of his life! How he hated the thought of that sort of
thing, how cheap it all seemed!

Angela, who was wide-eyed, flushed, exhausted, lying staring
on her pillow, asked in a weary, indifferent voice: "What do
you want me to do, Eugene, leave you?"

"I'll tell you, Angela," he said sepulchrally, "I don't know
what I want you to do just at this moment. The old life is all
over. It's as dead as dead can be. For eleven or twelve years
now I have lived with you, knowing all the while that I was
living a lie. I have never really loved you since we were married. You know that. I may have loved you in the beginning,
yes, I did, and at Blackwood, but that was a long, long while
ago. I never should have married you. It was a mistake, but I
did, and I've paid for it, inch by inch. You have, too. You
have insisted all along that I ought to love you. You have brow-
beaten and abused me for something I could no more do than I
could fly. Now, at this last minute, you introduce a child to
hold me. I know why you have done it. You imagine that in
some way you have been appointed by God to be my mentor and

guardian. Well, I tell you now that you haven't. It's all over.
If there were fifty children, it's all over. Suzanne isn't going to
believe any such cheap story as that, and if she did she wouldn't
leave me. She knows why you do it. All the days of weariness
are over for me, all the days of being afraid. I'm not an ordinary man, and I'm not going to live an ordinary life. You have
always insisted on holding me down to the little, cheap conventions as you have understood them. Out in Wisconsin, out in
Blackwood. Nothing doing. It's all over from now on. Everything's over. This house, my job, my real estate deal—everything. I don't care what your condition is. I love this girl in
there, and I'm going to have her. Do you hear me? I love her,
and I'm going to have her. She's mine. She suits me. I love
her, and no power under God is going to stay me. Now you
think this child proposition you have fixed up is going to stay me,
but you are going to find out that it can't, that it won't. It's a
trick, and I know it, and you know it. It's too late. It might
have last year, or two years ago, or three, but it won't work now.
You have played your last card. That girl in there belongs to
me, and I'm going to have her."

Again he smoothed his face in a weary way, pausing to sway
the least bit in his chair. His teeth were set, his eyes hard.
Consciously he realized that it was a terrible situation that confronted him, hard to wrestle with.

Angela gazed at him with the eyes of one who is not quite
sure that she even sees aright. She knew that Eugene had developed. He had become stronger, more urgent, more defiant,
during all these years in which he had been going upward. He
was no more like the Eugene who had clung to her for companionship in the dark days at Biloxi and elsewhere than a child
is like a grown man. He was harder, easier in his manner, more
indifferent, and yet, until now, there had never been a want of
traces of the old Eugene. What had become of them so suddenly? Why was he so raging, so bitter? This girl, this foolish, silly, selfish girl, with her Circe gift of beauty, by tolerance
of his suit, by yielding, perhaps by throwing herself at Eugene's
head, had done this thing. She had drawn him away from her in
spite of the fact that they had appeared to be happily mated. Suzanne did not know that they were not. In this mood he might
actually leave her, even as she was, with child. It depended on
the girl. Unless she could influence her, unless she could bring
pressure to bear in some way, Eugene might readily be lost to
her, and then what a tragedy! She could not afford to have him
go now. Why, in six months——! She shivered at the thought

of all the misery a separation would entail. His position, their child, society, this apartment. Dear God, it would drive her crazy if he were to desert her now!

"Oh, Eugene," she said quite sadly and without any wrath in her voice at this moment, for she was too torn, terrified and disheveled in spirit to feel anything save a haunting sense of fear, "you don't know what a terrible mistake you are making. I did do this thing on purpose, Eugene. It is true. Long ago in Philadelphia with Mrs. Sanifore I went to a physician to see if it were possible that I might have a child. You know that I always thought that I couldn't. Well, he told me that I could. I went because I thought that you needed something like that, Eugene, to balance you. I knew you didn't want one. I thought you would be angry when I told you. I didn't act on it for a long while. I didn't want one myself. I hoped that it might be a little girl if ever there was one, because I know that you like little girls. It seems silly now in the face of what has happened tonight. I see what a mistake I have made. I see what the mistake is, but I didn't mean it evilly, Eugene. I didn't. I wanted to hold you, to bind you to me in some way, to help you. Do you utterly blame me, Eugene? I'm your wife, you know."

He stirred irritably, and she paused, scarcely knowing how to go on. She could see how terribly irritated he was, how sick at heart, and yet she resented this attitude on his part. It was so hard to endure when all along she had fancied that she had so many just claims on him, moral, social, other claims, which he dare not ignore. Here she was now, sick, weary, pleading with him for something that ought justly be hers—and this coming child's!

"Oh, Eugene," she said quite sadly, and still without any wrath in her voice, "please think before you make a mistake. You don't really love this girl, you only think you do. You think she is beautiful and good and sweet and you are going to tear everything up and leave me, but you don't love her, and you are going to find it out. You don't love anyone, Eugene. You can't. You are too selfish. If you had any real love in you, some of it would have come out to me, for I have tried to be all that a good wife should be, but it has been all in vain. I've known you haven't liked me all these years. I've seen it in your eyes, Eugene. You have never come very close to me as a lover should unless you had to or you couldn't avoid me. You have been cold and indifferent, and now that I look back I see that it has made me so. I have been cold and hard. I've tried to steel myself to match what I thought was your steeliness, and now I see what it has done for me. I'm sorry. But as for her, you don't love her and you won't. She's too young. She hasn't any ideas that agree with yours. You think she's soft and gentle, and yet big and wise, but do you think if she had been that she could have stood up there as she did tonight and looked me in the eyes—me, your wife—and told me that she loved you—you, my husband? Do you think if she had any shame she would be in there now knowing what she does, for I suppose you have told her? What kind of a girl is that, anyway? You call her good? Good! Would a good girl do anything like that?"

"What is the use of arguing by appearances?" asked Eugene, who had interrupted her with exclamations of opposition and bitter comments all through the previous address. "The situation is one which makes anything look bad. She didn't intend to be put in a position where she would have to tell you that she loved me. She didn't come here to let me make love to her in this apartment. I made love to her. She's in love with me, and I made her love me. I didn't know of this other thing. If I had, it wouldn't have made any difference. However, let that be as it will. So it is. I'm in love with her, and that's all there is to it."

Angela stared at the wall. She was half propped up on a pillow, and had no courage now to speak of and no fighting strength.

"I know what it is with you, Eugene," she said, after a time; "it's the yoke that galls. It isn't me only; it's anyone. It's marriage. You don't want to be married. It would be the same with any woman who might ever have loved and married you, or with any number of children. You would want to get rid of her and them. It's the yoke that galls you, Eugene. You want your freedom, and you won't be satisfied until you have it. A child wouldn't make any difference. I can see that now."

"I want my freedom," he exclaimed bitterly and inconsiderately, "and, what's more, I'm going to have it! I don't care. I'm sick of lying and pretending, sick of common little piffling notions of what you consider right and wrong. For eleven or twelve years now I have stood it. I have sat with you every morning at breakfast and every evening at dinner, most of the time when I didn't want to. I have listened to your theories of life when I didn't believe a word of what you said, and didn't care anything about what you thought. I've done it because I thought I ought to do it so as not to hurt your feelings, but I'm through with all that. What have I had? Spying on me, opposition, searching my pockets for letters, complaining if I dared to stay out a single evening and did not give an account of myself.

"Why didn't you leave me after that affair at Riverdale? Why do you hang on to me when I don't love you? One'd think I was prisoner and you my keeper. Good Christ! When I think of it, it makes me sick! Well, there's no use worrying over that any more. It's all over. It's all beautifully over, and I'm done with it. I'm going to live a life of my own hereafter. I'm going to carve out some sort of a career that suits me. I'm going to live with someone that I can really love, and that's the end of it. Now you run and do anything you want to."

He was like a young horse that had broken rein and that thinks that by rearing and plunging he shall become forever free. He was thinking of green fields and delightful pastures. He was free now, in spite of what she had told him. This night had made him so, and he was going to remain free. Suzanne would stand by him, he felt it. He was going to make it perfectly plain to Angela that never again, come what may, would things be as they were.

"Yes, Eugene," she replied sadly, after listening to his protestations on this score, "I think that you do want your freedom, now that I see you. I'm beginning to see what it means to you. But I have made such a terrible mistake. Are you thinking about me at all? What shall I do? It is true that there will be a child unless I die. I may die. I'm afraid of that, or I was. I am not now. The only reason I would care to live would be to take care of it. I didn't think I was going to be ill with rheumatism. I didn't think my heart was going to be affected in this way. I didn't think that you were going to do as you have done, but now that you have, nothing matters. Oh," she said sadly, hot tears welling to her eyes, "it is all such a mistake! If I only hadn't done this!"

Eugene stared at the floor. He wasn't softened one bit. He did not think she was going to die—no such luck! He was thinking that this merely complicated things, or that she might be acting, but that it could not stand in his way. Why had she tried to trick him in this way? It was her fault. Now she was crying, but that was the old hypocrisy of emotion that she had used so often. He did not intend to desert her absolutely. She would have plenty to live on. Merely he did not propose to live with her, if he could help it, or only nominally, anyhow. The major portion of his time should be given to Suzanne.

"I don't care what it costs," he said finally. "I don't propose to live with you. I didn't ask you to have a child. It was none of my doing. You're not going to be deserted financially, but I'm not going to live with you."

He stirred again, and Angela stared hot-cheeked. The hardness of the man enraged her for the moment. She did not believe that she would starve, but their improving surroundings, their home, their social position, would be broken up completely.

"Yes, yes. I understand," she pleaded, with an effort at controlling herself, "but I am not the only one to be considered. Are you thinking of Mrs. Dale, and what she may do and say? She isn't going to let you take Suzanne if she knows it, without doing something about it. She is an able woman. She loves Suzanne, however self-willed she may be. She likes you now, but how long do you think she is going to like you when she learns what you want to do with her daughter? What are you going to do with her? You can't marry her under a year even if I were willing to give you a divorce. You could scarcely get a divorce in that time."

"I'm going to live with her, that's what I'm going to do," declared Eugene. "She loves me, she's willing to take me just as I am. She doesn't need marriage ceremonies and rings and vows and chains. She doesn't believe in them. As long as I love her, all right. When I cease to love her, she doesn't want me any more. Some difference in that, isn't there?" he added bitterly. "It doesn't sound exactly like Blackwood, does it?"

Angela bridled. His taunts were cruel.

"She says that, Eugene," she replied quietly, "but she hasn't had time to think. You've hypnotized her for the moment. She's fascinated. When she stops to think later, if she has any sense, any pride—— But, oh, why should I talk, you won't listen. You won't think." Then she added: "But what do you propose to do about Mrs. Dale? Don't you suppose she will fight you, even if I do not? I wish you would stop and think, Eugene. This is a terrible thing you are doing."

"Think! Think!" he exclaimed savagely and bitterly. "As though I had not been thinking all these years. Think! Hell! I haven't done anything but think. I've thought until the soul within me is sick. I've thought until I wish to God I could stop. I've thought about Mrs. Dale. Don't you worry about her. I'll settle this matter with her later. Just now I want to convince you of what I am going to do. I'm going to have Suzanne, and you're not going to stop me."

"Oh, Eugene," sighed Angela, "if something would only make you see! It is partially my fault. I have been hard and suspicious and jealous, but you have given me some cause to be, don't you think? I see now that I have made a mistake. I have been too hard and too jealous, but I could reform if you would let me try." (She was thinking now of living, not dying.) "I know I could. You have so much to lose. Is this change worth it? You know so well how the world looks at these things. Why, even if you should obtain your freedom from me under the circumstances, what do you suppose the world would think? You couldn't desert your child. Why not wait and see what happens? I might die. There have been such cases. Then you would be free to do as you pleased. That is only a little way off."

It was a specious plea, calculated to hold him; but he saw through it.

"Nothing doing!" he exclaimed, in the slang of the day. "I know all about that. I know what you're thinking. In the first place, I don't believe you are in the condition you say you are. In the next place, you're not going to die. I don't propose to wait to be free. I know you, and I've no faith in you. What I do needn't affect your condition. You're not going to starve. No one need know, unless you start a row about it. Suzanne and I can arrange this between ourselves. I know what you're thinking, but you're not going to interfere. If you do, I'll smash everything in sight—you, this apartment, my job——" He clenched his hands desperately, determinedly.

Angela's hands were tingling with nervous pains while Eugene talked. Her eyes ached and her heart fluttered. She could not understand this dark, determined man, so savage and so resolute in his manner. Was this Eugene who was always moving about quietly when he was near her, getting angry at times, but always feeling sorry and apologizing? She had boasted to some of her friends, and particularly to Marietta, in a friendly, jesting way that she could wind Eugene around her little finger. He was so easy-going in the main, so quiet. Here he was a raging demon almost, possessed of an evil spirit of desire and tearing up his and hers and Suzanne's life for that matter, by the roots. She did not care for Suzanne, though, now, or Mrs. Dale. Her own blighted life, and Eugene's, looming so straight ahead of her terrified her.

"What do you suppose Mr. Colfax will do when he hears of this?" she asked desperately, hoping to frighten him.

"I don't care a damn what Mr. Colfax will or can do!" he replied sententiously. "I don't care a damn what anybody does or says or thinks. I love Suzanne Dale. She loves me. She wants me. There's an end of that. I'm going to her now. You stay me if you can."

Suzanne Dale! Suzanne Dale! How that name enraged and frightened Angela! Never before had she witnessed quite so clearly the power of beauty. Suzanne Dale was young and beautiful. She was looking at her only tonight thinking how fascinating she was—how fair her face—and here was Eugene bewitched by it, completely undone. Oh, the terror of beauty! The terror of social life generally! Why had she entertained? Why become friendly with the Dales? But then there were other personalities, almost as lovely and quite as young—Marjorie McLennan, Florence Reel, Henrietta Tenman, Annette Kean. It might have been any one of these. She couldn't have been expected to shut out all young women from Eugene's life. No; it was Eugene. It was his attitude toward life. His craze about the beautiful, particularly in women. She could see it now. He really was not strong enough. Beauty would always upset him at critical moments. She had seen it in relation to herself— the beauty of her form, which he admired so, or had admired. "God," she prayed silently, "give me wisdom now. Give me strength. I don't deserve it, but help me. Help me to save him. Help me to save myself."

"Oh, Eugene," she said aloud, hopelessly, "I wish you would stop and think. I wish you would let Suzanne go her way in the morning, and you stay sane and calm. I won't care about myself. I can forgive and forget. I'll promise you I'll never mention it. If a child comes, I'll do my best not to let it annoy you. I'll try yet not to have one. It may not be too late. I'll change from this day forth. Oh!" She began to cry.

"No! By God!" he said, getting up. "No! No! No! I'm through now. I'm through! I've had enough of fake hysterics and tears. Tears one minute, and wrath and hate the next. Subtlety! Subtlety! Subtlety! Nothing doing. You've been master and jailer long enough. It's my turn now. I'll do a little jailing and task-setting for a change. I'm in the saddle, and I'm going to stay there. You can cry if you want to, you can do what you please about the child. I'm through. I'm tired, and I'm going to bed, but this thing is going to stand just as it does. I'm through, and that's all there is to it."

He strode out of the room angrily and fiercely, but nevertheless, when he reached it, he sat in his own room, which was on the other side of the studio from Angelas, and did not sleep. His mind was on fire with the thought of Suzanne; he thought of the old order which had been so quickly and so terribly broken. Now, if he could remain master, and he could, he proposed to take Suzanne. She would come to him, secretly no doubt, if necessary. They would open a studio, a second establishment. Angela might not give him a divorce. If what she said was true, she couldn't. He wouldn't want her to, but he fancied from this conversation that she was so afraid of him that she would not stir up any trouble. There was nothing she could really do. He was in the saddle truly, and would stay there. He would take Suzanne, would provide amply for Angela, would visit all those lovely public resorts he had so frequently seen, and he and Suzanne would be happy together.

Suzanne! Suzanne! Oh, how beautiful she was! And to think how nobly and courageously she had stood by him tonight. How she had slipped her hand into his so sweetly and had said, "But I love him, Mrs. Witla." Yes, she loved him. No doubt of that. She was young, exquisite, beautifully rounded in her budding emotion and feeling. She was going to develop into a wonderful woman, a real one. And she was so young. What a pity it was he was not free now! Well, wait, this would right all things, and, meanwhile, he would have her. He must talk to Suzanne. He must tell her how things stood. Poor little Suzanne! There she was in her room wondering what was to become of her, and here was he. Well, he couldn't go to her tonight. It did not look right, and, besides, Angela might fight still. But tomorrow! Tomorrow! Oh, tomorrow he would walk and talk with her, and they would plan. Tomorrow he would show her just what he wanted to do and find out what she could do.

CHAPTER XI

THIS night passed without additional scenes, though as it stood it was the most astonishing and tremendous in all Eugene's experience. He had, not up to the time Angela walked into the róom, really expected anything so dramatic and climacteric to happen, though what he did expect was never really very clear to him. At times as he lay and thought now he fancied that he might eventually have to give Suzanne up, though how, or when, or why, he could not say. He was literally crazed by her, and could not think that such a thing could really be. At other moments he fancied that powers outside of this visible life, the life attested by the five senses, had arranged this beautiful finish to his career for him so that he might be perfectly happy. All his life he had fancied that he was leading a more or less fated life, principally more. He thought that his art was a gift, that he had in a way been sent to revolutionize art in America, or carry it one step farther forward and that nature was thus constantly sending its apostles or special representatives over whom it kept watch and in whom it was well pleased. At other times he fancied he might be the sport or toy of untoward and malicious powers, such as those which surrounded and accomplished Macbeth's tragic end, and which might be intending to make an illustration of him. As he looked at life at times, it seemed to do this with certain people. The fates lied. Lovely, blandishing lures were held out only to lead men to destruction. He had seen other men who seemed to have been undone in this way. Was he to be so treated?

Angela's unexpected and peculiar announcement made it look that way. Still he did not believe it. Life had sent Suzanne across his path for a purpose. The fates or powers had seen he was miserable and unhappy. Being a favorite child of Heaven, he was to be rewarded for his sufferings by having her. She was here now—quickly, forcefully thrust into his arms, so to speak, so that perhaps he might have her all the more quickly. How silly it seemed to him now to have brought her into his own apartment to make love to her and get caught, and yet how fortunate, too, the hand of fate! No doubt it was intended. Anyhow, the shame to him, the shame to Angela and Suzanne, the terrific moments and hours that each was enduring now—these were things which were unfortunately involved in any necessarily great readjustment. It was probable that it had to come about this way. It was better so than to go on living an unhappy life. He was really fitted for something better, he thought—a great career. He would have to adjust this thing with Angela in some way now, either leave her, or make some arrangement whereby he could enjoy the company of Suzanne uninterrupted. There must be no interference. He did not propose to give her up. The child might come. Well and good. He would provide for it, that would be all. He recalled now the conversation he had had with Suzanne in which she had said that she would live with him if she could. The time had come. Their plan for a studio should now be put into effect. It must be secret. Angela would not care. She could not help herself. If only the events of this night did not terrorize Suzanne into retracing her steps! He had not explained to her how he was to get rid of Angela apart from what she had heard this night. She was thinking, he knew, that they could go on loving each other in this tentative fashion, occupying a studio together, perhaps, not caring what the world thought, not caring what her mother thought, ignoring her brother and sister and Angela, and being happy with Eugene only. He had never tried to disillusion her. He was not thinking clearly himself. He was rushing forward in an aimless way, desiring the companionship of her beautiful mind and body. Now he saw he must act or lose her. He must convince her in the face of what Angela had said, or let her go. She would probably be willing to come to him rather than leave him entirely. He must talk, explain, make her understand just what a trick this all was.

Angela had not slept, but lay staring at the ceiling in the dark, her eyes a study in despair. When morning came they were none of them further along in their conclusions than they were the night before, save to know, each separately and distinctly, that a great tragedy or change was at hand. Suzanne had thought and thought, or tried to, but the impulse of blood and passion in her were Eugeneward and she could only see the situation from their own point of view. She loved him, she thought—must love him, since he was so ready to sacrifice so much for her; yet at the same time there was a strange, disconcerting nebulosity about her which, had Eugene fully realized it at this moment, would have terrified him. In her state, which was one of wondering delight at the beauty of life and love—a fatalistic security in the thought that joy was to come to her throughout life—much joy. She could not see the grimness of Eugene's position. She could not understand the agony of a soul that had never really tasted supreme bliss in love, and had wanted, however foolishly, the accessories of wealth, and had never had them. Terrorized lest after the first sip of so wonderful a joy it should be removed forever, Eugene was tingling in the dark of his own room—tingling and yet reaching, almost with outstretched hands, to the splendor of the life that was seemingly before him. Suzanne, however, to whom life had given so much, was resting in a kind of still ease, like that which might fill a drowsy poppyland of joy where all the pleasures had been attained and were being tasted at leisure. Life at its worst to her was not so bad. Witness this storm which had been quelled in part by Eugene and was like to blow over as nothing at all. Things came round of their own accord in time, if one let them. She had always felt so sure that whatever happened no ill would befall her, and here she was courted and protected by Eugene even in his own home!

In this situation, therefore, she was not grieving either for Eugene, for Angela, or for herself. She could not. Some dispositions are so. Eugene was able to take care of himself and her and Angela financially, she thought. She was really looking forward to that better day when this misalliance should be broken up, and Eugene and presumably Angela would be really happier. She wanted Eugene to be much happier, and Angela, for that matter—and through her, if possible, since Eugene's happiness seemed to depend on her. But unlike Eugene, she was already thinking that she could live well enough without him, if it must be. She did not want to. She felt that her greatest happiness would be in repaying him for past ills and pains; but if they must part for a time, for instance, it would not make so much difference. Time would bring them together. But if it didn't—— But it would. Why think otherwise? But how wonderful it was that her beauty, her mere physical beauty, which seemed unimportant to her, made him so wild. She could not know of the actual physical pain gnawing at his vitals, but it was so plain that he was madly stricken with her. His whole face and his burning black eyes riveted on her in intense delight and almost agony proved it. Was she so beautiful? Surely not! Yet he yearned over her so. And it was so delightful.

She arose at dawn and began silently to dress, thinking that she might take a walk, leaving a note for Eugene as to where to come and find her if he could. She had one appointment for the day. Later she would have to go home, but things would come out all right. Since Eugene had compelled Angela to relinquish her determination to inform her mother, all must be well. They would meet, she and Eugene. She would leave her home and be his and they would go anywhere, anywhere Eugene desired, only she would prefer to persuade her mother to see things from her point of view and later countenance some understanding between them here. Because of Angela's and Eugene's position here, she preferred this. Because of her youth and her poetic, erratic conception of life, she assumed that she could overcome her mother and that she and Eugene could live together somewhere in peace. Her friends might either be unaware of the situation, or they could be told, some of them, and they might countenance it because it was so beautiful and natural!

Eugene heard her stirring after a time, and rose and went to her room and knocked. When she opened the door almost fully dressed a thrill of pain passed over his heart, for he thought that she had been intending to slip away without seeing him any more —so little they really knew each other. But as she stood there, a little cool or still or sober from much thought and the peculiar nature of her position, she seemed more beautiful than ever.

"You're not going, are you?" he asked, as she looked up at him with inquiring eyes.

"I thought I'd go for a walk."

"Without me?"

"I intended to see you, if I could, or leave a note for you to come to me. I thought you would."

"Will you wait for me?" he asked, feeling as though he must hold her close forever in order to live. "Just a little bit. I want to change my clothes." He took her in his arms.

"Yes," she said softly.

"You won't go without me?"

"No. Why do you ask?"

"Oh, I love you so!" he replied, and pushed her head back and looked yearningly into her eyes.

She took his tired face between her hands and studied his eyes. She was so enrapt by him now in this first burst of affection that she could see nothing but him. He seemed so beautiful, so hungry! It did not matter to her now that she was in the home of his wife or that his love was complicated with so much that was apparently evil. She loved him. She had thought all night about him, not sleeping. Being so young, it was hard for her to reason clearly as yet, but somehow it seemed to her that he was very unhappily placed, terribly ill-mated, and that he needed her. He was so fine, so clean, so capable! If he did not want Angela, why should she want him? She would not be suffering for anything save his company, and why should she want to hold him? She, Suzanne, would not, if she were in Angela's place. If there were a child, would that make any real difference? He did not love her.

"Don't worry about me," she said reassuringly. "I love you. Don't you know I do? I have to talk to you. We have to talk. How is Mrs. Witla?"

She was thinking about what Mrs. Witla would do, whether she would call up her mother, whether her struggle to have Eugene would begin at once.

"Oh, she's about the same!" he said wearily. "We've had a long argument. I've told her just what I propose to do, but I'll tell you about that later."

He went away to change his clothes, and then stepped into Angela's room.

"I'm going to walk with Suzanne," he said dominantly, when he was ready.

"All right," said Angela, who was so tired she could have fainted. "Will you be back for dinner?"

"I don't know," he replied. "What difference does it make?"

"Only this: that the maid and cook need not stay unless you are coming. I want nothing."

"When will the nurse be here?"

"At seven."

"Well, you can prepare dinner, if you wish," he said. "I will try and be back by four."

He walked toward the studio where Suzanne was, and found her waiting, white-faced, slightly hollow-eyed, but strong and confident. Now, as so often before, he noticed that spirit of self-sufficiency and reliance about her young body which had impressed him so forcibly and delightfully in the past. She was a wonderful girl, this Suzanne, full of grit and ability, although raised under what might have been deemed enervating circumstances. Her statement, made under pressure the night before, that she must go to a hotel and not go home until she could straighten out her affairs, had impressed him greatly. Why had she thought of going out in the world to work for herself unless there were something really fine about her? She was heir to a fortune under her father's will, he had heard her mother say once. This morning her glance was so assured. He did not use the phone to call a car, but strolled out into the drive with her walking along the stone wall which commanded the river northward toward Grant's Tomb. It occurred to him that they might go to Claremont Inn for breakfast, and afterwards take a car somewhere—he did not know quite where. Suzanne might be recognized. So might he.

"What shall we do, sweet?" he asked, as the cool morning air brushed their faces. It was a glorious day.

"I don't care," replied Suzanne. "I promised to be at the Almerdings some time today, but I didn't say when. They won't think anything of it if I don't get there till after dinner. Will Mrs. Witla call up mama?"

"I don't think so. In fact, I'm sure she won't." He was thinking of his last conversation with Angela, when she said she would do nothing. "Is your mother likely to call you up?"

"I think not. Mama doesn't usually bother when she knows where I am going. If she does, they'll simply say I haven't come yet. Will Mrs. Witla tell her, if she calls up there?"

"I think not," he said. "No, I'm sure she won't. Angela wants time to think. She isn't going to do anything. She told me that this morning. She's going to wait until she sees what I am going to do. It all depends now on how we play our cards."

He strolled on, looking at the river and holding Suzanne's hand. It was only a quarter to seven and the drive was comparatively empty.

"If she tells mama, it will make things very bad," said Suzanne thoughtfully. "Do you really think she won't?"

"I'm sure she won't. I'm positive. She doesn't want to do anything yet. It's too dangerous. I think she thinks that maybe I will come round. Oh, what a life I've led! It seems like a dream, now that I have your love. You are so different, so generous! Your attitude is so unselfish! To have been ruled all these years in every little thing. This last trick of hers!"

He shook his head woefully. Suzanne looked at his weary face, her own as fresh as the morning.

"Oh, if I might only have had you to begin with!" he added.

"Listen, Eugene," said Suzanne. "You know I feel sorry for Mrs. Witla. We shouldn't have done what we did last night, but you made me. You know you will never listen to me, until it's too late. You're so headstrong! I don't want you to leave Mrs. Witla unless you want to. You needn't for me. I don't want to marry you; not now, anyhow. I'd rather just give myself to you, if you want me to. I want time though, to think and plan. If mama should hear today, there would be a terrible time. If we have time to think, we may bring her round. I don't care anything about what Mrs. Witla told you last night. I don't want you to leave her. If we could just arrange some way. It's mama, you know."

She swung his hand softly in hers, pressing his fingers. She was deep in thought, for her mother presented a real problem.

"You know," she went on, "mama isn't narrow. She doesn't believe much in marriage unless it's ideal. Mrs. Witla's condition wouldn't make so much difference if only the child were here. I've been thinking about that. Mama might sanction some arrangement if she thought it would make me happy and there was no scandal. But I'll have to have time to talk to her. It can't be done right away."

Eugene listened to this with considerable surprise, as he did to everything Suzanne volunteered. She seemed to have been thinking about these questions a long time. She was not free with her opinions. She hesitated and halted between words and in her cogitations, but when they were out this was what they came to. He wondered how sound they were.

"Suzanne," he said, "you take my breath away! How you think! Do you know what you're talking about? Do you know your mother at all well?"

"Mama? Oh, yes, I think I understand mama. You know she's very peculiar. Mama is literary and romantic. She talks a great deal about liberty, but I don't take in everything she says. I think mama is different from most women—she's exceptional. She likes me, not so much as a daughter as a person. She's anxious about me. You know, I think I'm stronger than mama. I think I could dominate her if I tried. She leans on me now a lot, and she can't make me do anything unless I want to. I can make her come to my way of thinking, I believe. I have, lots of times. That's what makes me think I might now, if I have time. It will take time to get her to do what I want."

"How much time?" asked Eugene thoughtfully.

"Oh, I don't know. Three months. Six months. I can't tell. I would like to try, though."

"And if you can't, then what?"

"Why, then—why, then I'll defy her, that's all. I'm not sure, you know. But I think I can."

"And if you can't?"

"But I can. I'm sure I can." She tossed her head gaily.

"And come to me?"

"And come to you."

They were near One Hundredth Street, under the trees. There was a lone man some distance away, walking from them. Eugene caught Suzanne in his arms and implanted a kiss upon her mouth. "Oh, you divinity!" he exclaimed. "Helen! Circe!"

"No," she replied, with smiling eyes. "No, not here. Wait till we get a car."

"Shall we go to Claremont?"

"I'm not hungry."

"Then we might as well call a car and ride."

They hunted a garage and sped northward, the wonderful wind of the morning cooling and refreshing their fevered senses. Both he and Suzanne were naturally depressed at moments, at other moments preternaturally gay, for he was varying between joy and fear, and she was buoying him up. Her attitude was calmer, surer, braver, than his. She was like a strong mother to him.

"You know," he said, "I don't know what to think at times. I haven't any particular charge against Mrs. Witla except that I don't love her. I have been so unhappy. What do you think of cases of this kind, Suzanne? You heard what she said about me."

"Yes, I heard."

"It all comes from that. I don't love her. I never have really from the beginning. What do you think where there is no love? It is true, part of what she said. I have been in love with other women, but it has always been because I have been longing for some sort of temperament that was congenial to me. I have, Suzanne, too, since I have been married. I can't say that I was really in love with Carlotta Wilson, but I did like her. She was very much like myself. The other was a girl somewhat like you. Not so wise. That was years ago. Oh, I could tell you why! I love youth. I love beauty. I want someone who is my companion mentally. You are that, Suzanne, and yet see what a hell it is creating. Do you think it is so bad where I am so very unhappy? Tell me, what do you think?"

"Why, why," said Suzanne, "I don't think anyone ought to stick by a bad bargain, Eugene."

"Just what do you mean by that, Suzanne?"

"Well, you say you don't love her. You're not happy with her. I shouldn't think it would be good for her or you to have you stay with her. She can live. I wouldn't want you to stay with me if you didn't love me. I wouldn't want you at all if you didn't. I wouldn't want to stay with you if I didn't love you, and I wouldn't. I think marriage ought to be a happy bargain, and if it isn't you oughtn't to try to stay together just because you thought you could stay together once."

"What if there were children?"

"Well, that might be different. Even then, one or the other

could take them, wouldn't you think? The children needn't be made very unhappy in such a case."

Eugene looked at Suzanne's lovely face. It seemed so strange to hear her reasoning so solemnly—this girl!

"But you heard what she said about me, Suzanne, and about her condition?"

"I know," she said. "I've thought about it. I don't see that it makes so very much difference. You can take care of her."

"You love me just as much?"

"Yes."

"Even if all she says is true?"

"Yes."

"Why, Suzanne?"

"Well, all her charges concerned years gone by, and that isn't now. And I know you love me now. I don't care about the past. You know, Eugene, I don't care anything about the future, either. I want you to love me only so long as you want to love me. When you are tired of me, I want you to leave me. I wouldn't want you to live with me if you didn't love me. I wouldn't want to live with you if I didn't love you."

Eugene looked into her face, astonished, pleased, invigorated, and heartened by this philosophy. It was so like Suzanne, he thought. She seemed to have reached definite and effective conclusions so early. Her young mind seemed a solvent for all life's difficulties.

"Oh, you wonderful girl!" he said. "You know you are wiser than I am, stronger. I draw to you, Suzanne, like a cold man to a fire. You are so kindly, so temperate, so understanding!"

They rode on toward Tarrytown and Scarborough, and on the way Eugene told Suzanne some of his plans. He was willing not to leave Angela, if that was agreeable to her. He was willing to maintain this outward show, if that was satisfactory. The only point was, could he stay and have her, too? He did not understand quite how she could want to share him with anybody, but he could not fathom her from any point of view, and he was fascinated. She seemed the dearest, the subtlest, the strangest and most lovable girl. He tried to find out by what process she proposed to overcome the objections of her mother, but Suzanne seemed to have no plans save that of her ability to gradually get the upper hand mentally and dominate her. "You know," she said at one point, "I have money coming to me. Papa set aside two hundred thousand dollars for each of us children when we should come of age, and I am of age now. It is to be held in trust, but I shall have twelve thousand or maybe more from that. We can use that. I am of age now, and I have never said anything about it. Mama has managed all these things."

Here was another thought which heartened Eugene. With Suzanne he would have this additional income, which might be used whatever else might betide. If only Angela could be made to accept his conditions and Suzanne could win in her contest with her mother all would be well. His position need not be jeopardized. Mrs. Dale need hear nothing of it at present. He and Suzanne could go on associating in this way until an understanding had been reached. It was all like a delightful courtship which was to bloom into a still more delightful marriage.

The day passed in assurances of affection. Suzanne told Eugene of a book she had read in French, "The Blue Bird." The allegory touched Eugene to the quick—its quest for happiness, and he named Suzanne then and there "The Blue Bird." She made him stop the car and go back to get her an exquisite lavender-hued blossom growing wild on a tall stalk which she saw in a field as they sped by. Eugene objected genially, because it was beyond a wire fence and set among thorns, but she said, "Yes, now, you must. You know you must obey me now. I am going to begin to train you now. You've been spoiled. You're a bad boy. Mama says that. I am going to reform you."

"A sweet time you'll have, Flower Face! I'm a bad lot. Have you noticed that?"

"A little."

"And you still like me?"

"I don't mind. I think I can change you by loving you."

Eugene went gladly. He plucked the magnificent bloom and handed it to her "as a sceptre," he said. "It looks like you, you know," he added. "It's regal."

Suzanne accepted the compliment without thought of its flattering import. She loved Eugene, and words had scarcely any meaning to her. She was as happy as a child and as wise in many things as a woman twice her years. She was as foolish as Eugene over the beauty of nature, dwelling in an ecstasy upon morning and evening skies, the feel of winds and the sigh of leaves. The beauties of nature at every turn caught her eye, and she spoke to him of things she felt in such a simple way that he was entranced.

Once when they had left the car and were walking about the grounds of an inn, she found that one of her silk stockings had worn through at the heel. She lifted up her foot and looked at it meditatively. "Now, if I had some ink I could fix that up so quickly," she said, laughing.

"What would you do?" he asked.

"I would black it," she replied, referring to her pink heel, "or you could paint it."

He laughed and she giggled. It was these little, idle simplicities which amused and fascinated him.

"Suzanne," he said dramatically at this time, "you are taking me back into fairyland."

"I want to make you happy," she said, "as happy as I am."

"If I could be! If I only could be!"

"Wait," she said; "be cheerful. Don't worry. Everything will come out all right. I know it will. Things always come right for me. I want you and you will come to me. You will have me just as I will have you. Oh, it is all so beautiful!"

She squeezed his hand in an ecstasy of delight and then gave him her lips.

"What if someone should see?" he asked.

"I don't care! I don't care!" she cried. "I love you!"

CHAPTER XII

AFTER dining joyously, these two returned to the city. Suzanne, as she neared New York proper, was nervous as to what Angela might have done, for she wanted, in case Angela told her mother, to be present, in order to defend herself. She had reached a rather logical conclusion for her, and that was, in case her mother objected too vigorously, to elope with Eugene. She wanted to see just how her mother would take the intelligence in order that she might see clearly what to do. Previously she had the feeling that she could persuade her mother not to interfere, even in the face of all that had been revealed. Nevertheless, she was nervous, and her fears were bred to a certain extent by Eugene's attitude.

In spite of all his bravado, he really did not feel at all secure. He was not afraid of what he might lose materially so much as he was of losing Suzanne. The thought of the coming child had not affected them at all as yet. He could see clearly that conditions might come about whereby he could not have her, but they were not in evidence as yet. Besides, Angela might be lying. Still at odd moments his conscience troubled him, for in the midst of his intense satisfaction, his keenest thrills of joy, he could see Angela lying in bed, the thought of her wretched future before her, the thought of the coming life troubling her, or he could hear the echo of some of the pleas she had made. It was useless to attempt to shut them out. This was a terrible ordeal he was undergoing, a ruthless thing he was doing. All the laws of life and public sentiment were against him. If the world knew, it would accuse him bitterly. He could not forget that. He despaired at moments of ever being able to solve the tangle in which he had involved himself, and yet he was determined to go on. He proposed accompanying Suzanne to her friends, the Almerdings, but she changed her mind and decided to go home. "I want to see whether mama has heard anything," she insisted.

Eugene had to escort her to Staten Island and then order the chauffeur to put on speed so as to reach Riverside by four. He was somewhat remorseful, but he argued that his love-life was so long over, in so far as Angela was concerned, that it could not really make so very much difference. Since Suzanne wanted to wait a little time and proceed slowly, it was not going to be as bad for Angela as he had anticipated. He was going to give her a choice of going her way and leaving him entirely, either now, or after the child was born, giving her the half of his property, stocks, ready money, and anything else that might be divisible, and all the furniture, or staying and tacitly ignoring the whole thing. She would know what he was going to do, to maintain a separate ménage, or secret rendezvous for Suzanne. He proposed since Suzanne was so generous not to debate this point, but to insist. He must have her, and Angela must yield, choosing only her conditions.

When he came to the house, a great change had come over Angela. In the morning when he left she was hard and bitter in her mood. This afternoon she was, albeit extremely sad, more soft and melting than he had ever seen her. Her hard spirit was temporarily broken, but in addition she had tried to resign herself to the inevitable and to look upon it as the will of God. Perhaps she had been, as Eugene had often accused her of being, hard and cold. Perhaps she had held him in too tight leading strings. She had meant it for the best. She had tried to pray for light and guidance, and after a while something softly sad, like a benediction, settled upon her. She must not fight any more, she thought. She must yield. God would guide her. Her smile, kindly and wan, when Eugene entered the room, took him unawares.

Her explanation of her mood, her prayers, her willingness to give him up if need be, even in the face of what was coming to her, moved him more than anything that had ever passed between them. He sat opposite her at dinner, looking at her thin hands and face, and her sad eyes, trying to be cheerful and considerate, and then, going back into her room and hearing her say she would do whatever he deemed best, burst into tears. He cried from an excess of involuntary and uncontrolled emotion. He hardly knew why he cried, but the sadness of everything— life, the tangle of human emotions, the proximity of death to all, old age, Suzanne, Angela, all—touched him, and he shook as though he would rend his sides. Angela, in turn, was astonished and grieved for him. She could scarcely believe her eyes. Was he repenting? "Come to me, Eugene!" she pleaded. "Oh, I'm so sorry! *Are you as much in love as that?* Oh, dear, dear, if I could only do something! Don't cry like that, Eugene. If it means so much to you, I will give you up. It tears my heart to hear you. Oh, dear, please don't cry."

He laid his head on his knees and shook, then seeing her getting up, came over to the bed to prevent her.

"No, no," he said, "it will pass. I can't help it. I'm sorry for you. I'm sorry for myself. I'm sorry for life. God will punish me for this. I can't help it, but you are a good woman."

He laid his head down beside her and sobbed, great, aching sobs. After a time he recovered himself, only to find that he had given Angela courage anew. She would think now that his love might be recovered since he had seemed so sympathetic; that Suzanne might be displaced. He knew that could not be, and so he was sorry that he had cried.

They went on from that to discussion, to argument, to ill-feeling, to sympathetic agreement again by degrees, only to fall out anew. Angela could not resign herself to the thought of giving him up. Eugene could not see that he was called upon to do anything, save divide their joint possessions. He was most anxious to have nothing to do with Angela anymore in any way. He might live in the same house, but that would be all. He was going to have Suzanne. He was going to live for her only. He threatened Angela with dire consequences if she tried to interfere in any way. If she communicated with Mrs. Dale, or said anything to Suzanne, or attempted to injure him commercially, he would leave her.

"Here is the situation," he would insist. "You can maintain it as I say, or break it. If you break it, you lose me and everything that I represent. If you maintain it, I will stay here. I think I will. I am perfectly willing to keep up appearances, but I want my freedom."

Angela thought and thought of this. She thought once of sending for Mrs. Dale and communicating with her secretly, urging her to get Suzanne out of the way without forewarning either the girl or Eugene, but she did not do this. It was the one thing she should have done and a thing Mrs. Dale would have agreed to, but fear and confusion deterred her. The next thing was to write or talk to Suzanne, and because she mistrusted her mood in Suzanne's presence she decided to write. She lay in bed on Monday when Eugene was away at the office and composed a long letter in which she practically gave the history of Eugene's life reiterating her own condition and stating what she thought Eugene ought to do.

"How can you think, Suzanne," she asked in one place, "that he will be true to you when he can ignore me, in this condition? He has not been true to anyone else. Are you going to throw your life away? Your station is assured now. What can he add to you that you have not already? If you take him, it is sure to become known. You are the one who will be injured, not he. Men recover from these things, particularly from an infatuation of this character, and the world thinks nothing of it; but the world will not forgive you. You will be 'a bad woman' after this, irretrievably so if a child is born. You think you love him. Do you really love him this much? Read this and stop and think. Think of his character. I am used to him. I made my mistakes in the beginning, and it is too late for me to change. The world can give me nothing. I may have sorrow and disgust, but at least I shall not be an outcast and our friends and the world will not be scandalized. But you—you have everything before you. Some man will come to you whom you will love and who will not ask and willingly make a sacrifice of you. Oh, I beg you to think! You do not need him. After all, sorry as I am to confess it, I do. It is as I tell you. Can you really afford to ignore this appeal?"

Suzanne read this and was greatly shocked. Angela painted him in a wretched light, as fickle, deceitful, dishonest in his relations with women. She debated this matter in her own room, for it could not help but give her pause. After a time, Eugene's face came back to her, however, his beautiful mind, the atmosphere of delight and perfection that seemed to envelop all that surrounded him. It was as though Eugene were a mirage of beauty, so soft, so sweet, so delightful! Oh, to be with him; to hear his beautiful voice; to feel his intense caresses! What could life offer her equal to that? And, besides, he needed her. She decided to talk it out with him, show him the letter, and then decide.

Eugene came in a day or two, having phoned Monday and Tuesday mornings. He made a rendezvous of the ice house, and then appeared as eager and smiling as ever. Since returning to the office and seeing no immediate sign of a destructive attitude on Angela's part, he had recovered his courage. He was hopeful of a perfect dénouement to all this—of a studio and his lovely Suzanne. When they were seated in the auto, she immediately produced Angela's letter and handed it to him without comment. Eugene read it quietly.

He was greatly shocked at what he read, for he thought that Angela was more kindly disposed toward him. Still he knew it to be true, all of it, though he was not sure that Suzanne would suffer from his attentions. The fates might be kind. They might be happy together. Anyhow, he wanted her now.

"Well," he said, giving it back, "what of it? Do you believe all she says?"

"It may be so, but somehow when I am with you I don't seem

to care. When I am away from you, it's different. I'm not so sure."

"You can't tell whether I am as good as you think I am?"

"I don't know what to think. I suppose all she says about you is true. I'm not sure. When you're away, it's different. When you are here, I feel as though everything must come out right. I love you so. Oh, I know it will!" She threw her arms around him.

"Then the letter doesn't really make any difference?"

"No."

She looked at him with big round eyes, and it was the old story, bliss in affection without thought. They rode miles, stopped at an inn for something to eat—Mrs. Dale was away for the day—looked at the sea where the return road skirted it, and kissed and kissed each other. Suzanne grew so ecstatic that she could see exactly how it was all coming out.

"Now you leave it to me," she said. "I will sound mama. If she is at all logical, I think I can convince her. I would so much rather do it that way. I hate deception. I would rather just tell her, and then, if I have to, defy her. I don't think I shall have to, though. She can't do anything."

"I don't know about that," said Eugene cautiously. He had come to have great respect for Suzanne's courage, and he was rather relying on Mrs. Dale's regard for him to stay her from any desperate course, but he did not see how their end was to be achieved.

He was for entering on an illicit relationship after a time without saying anything at all. He was in no hurry, for his feeling for Suzanne was not purely physical, though he wanted her. Because of her strange reading and philosophy, she was defying the world. She insisted that she did not see how it would hurt her.

"But, my dear, you don't know life," said Eugene. "It will hurt you. It will grind you to pieces in all places outside of New York. This is the Metropolis. It is a world city. Things are not quite the same here, but you will have to pretend, anyhow. It is so much easier."

"Can you protect me?" she asked significantly, referring to the condition Angela pleaded. "I wouldn't want—I couldn't, you know, not yet, not yet."

"I understand," he said. "Yes, I can, absolutely."

"Well, I want to think about it," she said again. "I prefer so much to be honest about it. I would so much rather just tell mama, and then go and do it. It would be so much nicer.

My life is my own to do with as I please. It doesn't concern
anybody, not even mama. You know, if I want to waste it,
I. may, only I don't think that I am doing so. I want to live
as I choose. I don't want to get married yet."

Eugene listened to her with the feeling that this was the most
curious experience of his life. He had never heard, never seen,
never experienced anything like it. The case of Christina Channing was different. She had her art to consider. Suzanne had
nothing of the sort. She had a lovely home, a social future,
money, the chance of a happy, stable, normal life. This was
love surely, and yet he was quite at sea. Still so many favorable things had happened, consciously favorable, that he was
ready to believe that all this was intended for his benefit by a
kind, governing providence.

Angela had practically given in already. Why not Suzanne's
mother? Angela would not tell her anything. Mrs. Dale was
not any stronger than Angela apparently. Suzanne might be
able to control her as she said. If she was so determined to try,
could he really stop her? She was headstrong in a way and
wilful, but developing rapidly and reasoning tremendously. Perhaps she could do this thing. Who could tell? They came
flying back along lovely lanes where the trees almost swept their
faces, past green stretches of marsh where the wind stirred in
ripples the tall green cat grass, past pretty farm yards, with
children and ducks in the foreground, beautiful mansions, playing children, sauntering laborers. All the while they were reassuring each other, vowing perfect affection, holding each other
close. Suzanne, as Angela had, loved to take Eugene's face
between her hands and look into his eyes.

"Look at me," she said once when he had dolefully commented
upon the possibility of change. "Look straight into my eyes.
What do you see?"

"Courage and determination," he said.

"What else?"

"Love."

"Do you think I will change?"

"No."

"Surely?"

"No."

"Well, look at me straight, Eugene. I won't. I won't, do
you hear? I'm yours until you don't want me anymore. Now
will you be happy?"

"Yes," he said.

"And when we get our studio," she went on.

"When we get our studio," he said, "we'll furnish it perfectly, and entertain a little after a while, maybe. You'll be my lovely Suzanne, my Flower Face, my Myrtle Blossom. Helen, Circe, Dianeme."

"I'll be your week-end bride," she laughed, "your odd or even girl, whichever way the days fall."

"If it only comes true," he exclaimed when they parted. "If it only does."

"Wait and see," she said. "Now you wait and see."

The days passed and Suzanne began what she called her campaign. Her first move was to begin to talk about the marriage question at the dinner table, or whenever she and her mother were alone, and to sound her on this important question, putting her pronouncements on record. Mrs. Dale was one of those empirical thinkers who love to philosophize generally, but who make no specific application of anything to their own affairs. On this marriage question she held most liberal and philosophic views for all outside her own immediate family. It was her idea, outside her own family, of course, that if a girl having reached maturity, and what she considered a sound intellectual majority, and who was not by then satisfied with the condition which matrimony offered, if she loved no man desperately enough to want to marry him and could arrange some way whereby she could satisfy her craving for love without jeopardizing her reputation, that was her lookout. So far as Mrs. Dale was concerned, she had no particular objection. She knew women in society, who, having made unfortunate marriages, or marriages of convenience. sustained some such relationship to men whom they admired. There was a subtle, under the surface understanding outside the society circles of the most rigid morality in regard to this, and there was the fast set, of which she was at times a welcome member, which laughed at the severe conventions of the older school. One must be careful—very. One must not be caught. But, otherwise, well, every person's life was a law unto him or herself.

Suzanne never figured in any of these theories, for Suzanne was a beautiful girl, capable of an exalted alliance, and her daughter. She did not care to marry her off to any wretched possessor of great wealth or title, solely for wealth's or title's sake, but she was hoping that some eligible young man of excellent social standing or wealth, or real personal ability, such, for instance, as Eugene possessed, would come along and marry Suzanne. There would be a grand wedding at a church of some prominence,—St. Bartholomew's, very likely; a splendid wedding dinner, oceans of presents, a beautiful honeymoon. She used to look at Suzanne and think what a delightful mother she would make. She was so young, robust, vigorous, able, and in a quiet way, passionate. She could tell when she danced how eagerly she took life. The young man would come. It would not be long. These lovely springtimes would do their work one of these days. As it was, there were a score of men already who would have given an eye to attract Suzanne's attention, but Suzanne would none of them. She seemed shy, coy, elusive, but above all, shy. Her mother had no idea of the iron will all this concealed any more than she had of the hard anarchic, unsocial thoughts that were surging in her daughter's brain.

"Do you think a girl ought to marry at all, mama?" Suzanne asked her one evening when they were alone together, "if she doesn't regard marriage as a condition she could endure all her days?"

"No-o," replied her mother. "What makes you ask?"

"Well, you see so much trouble among married people that we know. They're not very happy together. Wouldn't it be better if a person just stayed single, and if they found someone that they could really love, well, they needn't necessarily marry to be happy, need they?"

"What have you been reading lately, Suzanne?" asked her mother, looking up with a touch of surprise in her eyes.

"Nothing lately. What makes you ask?" said Suzanne wisely, noting the change in her mother's voice.

"With whom have you been talking?"

"Why, what difference does that make, mama? I've heard you express precisely the same views?"

"Quite so. I may have. But don't you think you're rather young to be thinking of things like that? I don't say all that I think when I'm arguing things philosophically. There are conditions which govern everything. If it were impossible for a girl to marry well, or if looks or lack of money interfered,— there are plenty of reasons—a thing like that might possibly be excusable, but why should you be thinking of that?"

"Why, it doesn't necessarily follow, mama, that because I am good looking, or have a little money, or am socially eligible, that I should want to get married. I may not want to get married at all. I see just as well as you do how things are with most people. Why shouldn't I? Do I have to keep away from every man, then?"

"Why, Suzanne! I never heard you argue like this before. You must have been talking with someone or reading some outré book of late. I wish you wouldn't. You are too young and too good looking to entertain any such ideas. Why, you can have nearly any young man you wish. Surely you can find someone with whom you can live happily or with whom you would be willing to try. It's time enough to think about the other things when you've tried and failed. At least you can give yourself ample time to learn something about life before you begin to talk such nonsense. You're too young. Why it's ridiculous."

"Mama," said Suzanne, with the least touch of temper, "I wish you wouldn't talk to me like that. I'm not a child any more. I'm a woman. I think like a woman—not like a girl. You forget that I have a mind of my own and some thoughts. I may not want to get married. I don't think I do. Certainly not to any of the silly creatures that are running after me now. Why shouldn't I take some man in an independent way, if I wish? Other women have before me. Even if they hadn't, it would be no reason why I shouldn't. My life is my own."

"Suzanne Dale!" exclaimed her mother, rising, a thrill of terror passing along her heartstrings. "What are you talking about? Are you basing these ideas on anything I have said in the past? Then certainly my chickens are coming home to roost early. You are in no position to consider whether you want to get married or not. You have seen practically nothing of men. Why should you reach any such conclusions now? For goodness' sake, Suzanne, don't begin so early to meditate on these terrible things. Give yourself a few years in which to see the world. I don't ask you to marry, but you may meet some man whom you could love very much, and who would love you. If you were to go and throw yourself away under some such silly theory as you entertain now, without stopping to see, or waiting for life to show you what it has in store, what will you have to offer him. Suzanne, Suzanne"—Suzanne was turning impatiently to a window—"you frighten me! There isn't, there couldn't be. Oh, Suzanne, I beg of you, be careful what you think, what you say, what you do! I can't know all your thoughts, no mother can, but, oh, if you will stop and think, and wait a while!"

She looked at Suzanne who walked to a mirror and began to fix a bow in her hair.

"Mama," she said calmly. "Really, you amuse me. When you are out with people at dinner, you talk one way, and when you are here with me, you talk another. I haven't done anything desperate yet. I don't know what I may want to do.

I'm not a child any more, mama. Please remember that. I'm a woman grown, and I certainly can lay out my life for myself. I'm sure I don't want to do what you are doing—talk one thing and do another."

Mrs. Dale recoiled intensely from this stab. Suzanne had suddenly developed in the line of her argument a note of determination, frank force and serenity of logic which appalled her. Where had the girl got all this? With whom had she been associating? She went over in her mind the girls and men she had met and known. Who were her intimate companions? —Vera Almerding; Lizette Woodworth; Cora TenEyck—a half dozen girls who were smart and clever and socially experienced. Were they talking such things among themselves? Was there some man or men unduly close to them? There was one remedy for all this. It must be acted on quickly if Suzanne were going to fall in with and imbibe any such ideas as these. Travel—two or three years of incessant travel with her, which would cover this dangerous period in which girls were so susceptible to undue influence was the necessary thing. Oh, her own miserable tongue! Her silly ideas! No doubt all she said was true. Generally it was so. But Suzanne! Her Suzanne, never! She would take her away while she had time, to grow older and wiser through experience. Never would she be permitted to stay here where girls and men were talking and advocating any such things. She would scan Suzanne's literature more closely from now on. She would viser her friendships. What a pity that so lovely a girl must be corrupted by such wretched, unsocial, anarchistic notions. Why, what would become of her girl? Where would she be? Dear Heaven!

She looked down in the social abyss yawning at her feet and recoiled with horror.

Never, never, never! Suzanne should be saved from herself, from all such ideas now and at once.

And she began to think how she could introduce the idea of travel easily and nicely. She must lure Suzanne to go without alarming her—without making her think that she was bringing pressure to bear. But from now on there must be a new order established. She must talk differently; she must act differently. Suzanne and all her children must be protected against themselves and others also. That was the lesson which this conversation taught her.

CHAPTER XIII

EUGENE and Angela had been quarreling between themselves most bitterly; at other times Angela was attempting to appeal to his sense of justice and fair play, if not his old-time affection, in the subtlest of ways. She was completely thrown out of her old methods of calculation, and having lost those had really no traditions on which to proceed. Eugene had always heretofore apparently feared her wrath; now he cared nothing for that. He had been subject, in times past, to a certain extent to those alluring blandishments which the married will understand well enough, but these were as ashes. Her charms meant nothing to him. She had hoped that the thought of a coming child would move him, but no, it was apparently without avail. Suzanne seemed a monster to her now since she did not desert him, and Eugene a raving maniac almost, and yet she could see how human and natural it all was. He was hypnotized, possessed. He had one thought, Suzanne, Suzanne, and he would fight her at every turn for that. He told her so. He told her of her letter to Suzanne, and the fact that he had read and destroyed it. It did not help her cause at all. She knew that she had decried him. He stood his ground solidly, awaiting the will of Suzanne, and he saw Suzanne frequently, telling her that he had won completely, and that the fulfilment of their desires now depended upon her.

As has been said, Suzanne was not without passion. The longer she associated with Eugene, the more eager she became for that joyous fulfilment which his words, his looks, his emotions indicated. In her foolish, girlish way, she had built up a fancy which was capable of realization only by the most ruthless and desperate conduct. Her theory of telling her mother and overcoming her by argument or defiance was really vain, for it could not be settled so easily, or so quickly. Because of her mother's appeal to her in this first conversation, she fancied she had won a substantial victory. Her mother was subject to her control and could not defeat her in argument. By the latter token she felt she was certain to win. Besides, she was counting heavily on her mother's regard for Eugene and her deep affection for herself. Hitherto, her mother had really refused her nothing.

The fact that Eugene did not take her outright at this time,—postponing until a more imperative occasion an adjustment of the difficulties which must necessarily flow from their attempted union without marriage—was due to the fact that he was not as desperate or as courageous as he appeared to be. He wanted her, but he was a little afraid of Suzanne herself. She was doubtful, anxious to wait, anxious to plan things her own way. He was not truly ruthless ever, but good natured and easy going. He was no subtle schemer and planner, but rather an easy natured soul, who drifted here and there with all the tides and favorable or unfavorable winds of circumstance. He might have been ruthless if he had been eager enough for any one particular thing on this earth, money, fame, affection, but at bottom, he really did not care as much as he thought he did. Anything was really worth fighting for if you had to have it, but it was not worth fighting for to the bitter end, if you could possibly get along without it. Besides, there was nothing really one could not do without, if one were obliged. He might long intensely, but he could survive. He was more absorbed in this desire than in anything else in his history, but he was not willing to be hard and grasping.

On the other hand, Suzanne was willing to be taken, but needed to be pressed or compelled. She imagined in a vague way that she wanted to wait and adjust things in her own way, but she was merely dreaming, procrastinating because he was procrastinating. If he had but compelled her at once she would have been happy, but he was sadly in need of that desperate energy that acts first and thinks afterward. Like Hamlet, he was too fond of cogitating, too anxious to seek the less desperate way, and in doing this was jeopardizing that ideal bliss for which he was willing to toss away all the material advantages which he had thus far gained.

When Mrs. Dale quite casually within a few days began to suggest that they leave New York for the fall and winter, she, Suzanne and Kinroy, and visit first England, then Southern France and then Egypt, Suzanne immediately detected something intentional about it, or at best a very malicious plan on the part of fate to destroy her happiness. She had been conjecturing how, temporarily, she could avoid distant and long drawn out engagements which her mother not infrequently accepted for herself and Suzanne outside New York, but she had not formulated a plan. Mrs. Dale was very popular and much liked. This easy suggestion, made with considerable assurance by her mother, and as though it would be just the thing, frightened and then irritated Suzanne. Why should her mother think of it just at this time?

"I don't want to go to Europe," she said warily. "We were over there only three years ago. I'd rather stay over here this winter and see what's going on in New York."

"But this trip will be so delightful, Suzanne," her mother insisted. "The Camerons are to be at Callendar in Scotland for the fall. They have taken a cottage there. I had a note from Louise, Tuesday. I thought we might run up there and see them and then go to the Isle of Wight."

"I don't care to go, mama," replied Suzanne determinedly. We're settled here comfortably. Why do you always want to be running off somewhere?"

"Why, I'm not running—how you talk, Suzanne! I never heard you object very much to going anywhere before. I should think Egypt and the Riviera would interest you very much. You haven't been to either of these places."

"I know they're delightful, but I don't care to go this fall. I'd rather stay here. Why should you suddenly decide that you want to go away for a year?"

"I haven't suddenly decided," insisted her mother. "I've been thinking of it for some time, as you know. Haven't I said that we would spend a winter in Europe soon? The last time I mentioned it, you were very keen for it."

"Oh, I know, mama, but that was nearly a year ago. I don't want to go now. I would rather stay here."

"Why would you? More of your friends go away than remain. I think a particularly large number of them are going this winter."

"Ha! Ha! Ho! Ho!" laughed Suzanne. "A particularly large number. How you exaggerate, mama, when you want anything. You always amuse me. It's a particularly large number now, just because you want to go," and she laughed again.

Suzanne's defiance irritated her mother. Why should she suddenly take this notion to stay here? It must be this group of girls she was in with, and yet, Suzanne appeared to have so few intimate girl friends. The Almerdings were not going to stay in town all the winter. They were here now because of a fire at their country place, but it would only be for a little while. Neither were the TenEycks. It couldn't be that Suzanne was interested in some man. The only person she cared much about was Eugene Witla, and he was married and only friendly in a brotherly, guardian-like way.

"Now, Suzanne," she said determinedly, "I'm not going to have you talk nonsense. This trip will be a delightful thing for you once you have started. It's useless for you to let a silly notion like not wanting to go stand in your way. You are just at the time when you ought to travel. Now you had better begin to prepare yourself, for we're going."

"Oh, no, I'm not, mama," said Suzanne. "Why, you talk as though I were a very little girl. I don't want to go this fall and I'm not going. You may go if you want to, but I'm not going."

"Why, Suzanne Dale!" exclaimed her mother. "Whatever has come over you? Of course you'll go. Where would you stay if I went? Do you think I would walk off and leave you? Have I ever before?"

"You did when I was at boarding school," interrupted Suzanne.

"That was a different matter. Then you were under proper supervision. Mrs. Hill was answerable to me for your care. Here you would be alone. What do you think I would be doing?"

"There you go, mama, talking as though I was a little girl again. Will you please remember that I am nearly nineteen? I know how to look after myself. Besides, there are plenty of people with whom I might stay if I chose."

"Suzanne Dale, you talk like one possessed. I'll listen to nothing of the sort. You are my daughter, and as such, subject to my guardianship. Of what are you thinking? What have you been reading? There's some silly thing at the bottom of all this. I'll not go away and leave you and you will come with me. I should think that after all these years of devotion on my part, you would take my feelings into consideration. How can you stand there and argue with me in this way?"

"Arguing, mama?" asked Suzanne loftily. "I'm not arguing. I'm just not going. I have my reasons for not wanting to go, and I'm not going, that's all! Now you may go if you want to."

Mrs. Dale looked into Suzanne's eyes and saw for the first time a gleam of real defiance in them. What had brought this about? Why was her daughter so set—of a sudden, so stubborn and hard? Fear, anger, astonishment, mingled equally in her feelings.

"What do you mean by reasons?" asked her mother. "What reasons have you?"

"A very good one," said Suzanne quietly, twisting it to the singular.

"Well, what is it then, pray?"

Suzanne debated swiftly and yet a little vaguely in her own mind. She had hoped for a longer process of philosophic discussion in which to entrap her mother into some moral and intellectual position from which she could not well recede, and by reason of which she would have to grant her the license she desired. From one remark and another dropped in this and the preceding conversation, she realized that her mother had no logical arrangement in her mind whereby she included her in her philosophical calculations at all. She might favor any and every theory and conclusion under the sun, but it would mean nothing in connection with Suzanne. The only thing that remained, therefore, was to defy her, or run away, and Suzanne did not want to do the latter. She was of age. She could adjust her own affairs. She had money. Her mental point of view was as good and sound as her mother's. As a matter of fact, the latter's attitude, in view of Suzanne's recent experience and feelings, seemed weak and futile. What did her mother know of life any more than she? They were both in the world, and Suzanne felt herself to be the stronger—the sounder of the two. Why not tell her now and defy her. She would win. She must. She could dominate her mother, and this was the time to do it.

"Because I want to stay near the man I love," she finally volunteered quietly.

Mrs. Dale's hand, which had been elevated to a position of gesticulation before her, dropped limp, involuntarily, to her side. Her mouth opened the least bit. She stared in a surprised, anguished, semi-foolish way.

"The man you love, Suzanne?" she asked, swept completely from her moorings, and lost upon a boundless sea. "Who is he?"

"Mr. Witla, mama—Eugene. I love him and he loves me. Don't stare, mama. Mrs. Witla knows. She is willing that we should have each other. We love each other. I am going to stay here where I can be near him. He needs me."

"Eugene Witla!" exclaimed her mother, breathless, a look of horror in her eyes, cold fright in her tense hands. "You love Eugene Witla? a married man! He loves you! Are you talking to me? Eugene Witla!! You love him! Why I can't believe this. I'm not in my right mind. Suzanne Dale, don't stand there! Don't look at me like that! Are you telling me, your mother? Tell me it isn't so! Tell me it isn't so before

you drive me mad! Oh, great Heavens, what am I coming to?
What have I done? Eugene Witla of all men! Oh, God, oh,
God, oh, God!"

"Why do you carry on so, mama?" asked Suzanne calmly.
She had expected some such scene as this—not quite so intense,
so hysterical, but something like it, and was, in a way, prepared
for it. A selfish love was her animating, governing impulse—a
love also that stilled self, and put aside as nothing all the
world and its rules. Suzanne really did not know what she was
doing. She was hypnotized by the sense of perfection in her
lover, the beauty of their love. Not practical facts but the
beauty of the summer, the feel of cool winds, the glory of skies
and sunlight and moonlight, were in her mind. Eugene's arms
about her, his lips to hers, meant more than all the world beside.
"I love him. Of course, I love him. What is there so strange
about that?"

"What is strange? Are you in your right mind? Oh, my
poor, dear little girl! My Suzanne! Oh, that villain! That
scoundrel! To come into my house and make love to you, my
darling child! How should you know? How could I expect
you to understand? Oh, Suzanne! for my sake, for the love of
Heaven, hush! Never breathe it! Never say that terrible thing
to me again! Oh, dear! Oh, dear! Oh, dear!!! That I
should live to see this! My child! My Suzanne! My lovely,
beautiful Suzanne! I shall die unless I can stop this! I shall
die! I shall die!"

Suzanne stared at her mother quite astonished at the violent
emotion into which she had cast her. Her pretty eyes were
open wide, her eyebrows elevated, her lips parted sweetly. She
was a picture of intense classic beauty, chiseled, peaceful, self-
possessed. Her brow was as smooth as marble, her lips as arched
as though they had never known one emotion outside joy. Her
look was of a quizzical, slightly amused, but not supercilious
character which made her more striking than ever if possible.

"Why, mama! You think I am a child, don't you? All
that I say to you is true. I love Eugene. He loves me. I
am going to live with him as soon as it can be quietly arranged.
I wanted to tell you because I don't want to do anything secretly,
but I propose to do it. I wish you wouldn't insist on looking
on me as a baby, mama. I know what I am doing. I have
thought it all out this long time."

"Thought it all out!" pondered Mrs. Dale. "Going to live
with him when it can be arranged! Is she talking of living
with a man without a wedding ceremony being performed?

With a man already married! Is the child stark mad? Something has turned her brain. Surely something has. This is not my Suzanne—my dear, lovely, entrancing Suzanne."

To Suzanne she exclaimed aloud:

"Are you talking of living with this, with this, oh, I don't dare to name him. I'll die if I don't get this matter straightened out; of living without a marriage ceremony and without his being divorced? I can't believe that I am awake. I can't! I can't!"

"Certainly I am," replied Suzanne. "It is all arranged between us. Mrs. Witla knows. She has given her consent. I expect you to give yours, if you desire me to stay here, mama."

"Give my consent! As God is my witness! Am I alive? Is this my daughter talking to me? Am I in this room here with you? I." She stopped, her mouth wide open. "If it weren't so horribly tragic, I should laugh. I will! I will become hysterical! My brain is whirling like a wheel now. Suzanne Dale, you are insane. You are madly, foolishly insane. If you do not hush and cease this terrible palaver, I will have you locked up. I will have an inquiry made into your sanity. This is the wildest, most horrible, most unimaginable thing ever proposed to a mother. To think that I should have lived with you eighteen long years, carried you in my arms, nursed you at my breast and then have you stand here and tell me that you will go and live unsanctioned with a man who has a good true woman now living as his wife. This is the most astounding thing I have ever heard of. It is unbelievable. You will not do it. You will no more do it than you will fly. I will kill him! I will kill you! I would rather see you dead at my feet this minute than to even think that you could have stood there and proposed such a thing to me. It will never be! It will never be! I will give you poison first. I will do anything, everything, but you shall never see this man again. If he dares to cross this threshold, I will kill him at sight. I love you. I think you are a wonderful girl, but this thing shall never be. And don't you dare to attempt to dissuade me. I will kill you, I tell you. I would rather see you dead a thousand times. To think! To think! To think! Oh, that beast! That villain! that unconscionable cur! To think that he should come into my house after all my courtesy to him and do this thing to me. Wait! He has position, he has distinction. I will drive him out of New York. I will ruin him. I will make it impossible for him to show his face among decent people. Wait and see!"

Her face was white, her hands clenched, her teeth set. She had a keen, savage beauty, much like that of a tigress when it shows its teeth. Her eyes were hard and cruel and flashing. Suzanne had never imagined her mother capable of such a burst of rage as this.

"Why, mama," she said calmly and quite unmoved, "you talk as though you ruled my life completely. You would like to make me feel, I suppose, that I do not dare to do what I choose. I do, mama. My life is my own, not yours. You cannot frighten me. I have made up my mind what I am going to do in this matter, and I am going to do it. You cannot stop me. You might as well not try. If I don't do it now, I will later. I love Eugene. I am going to live with him. If you won't let me I will go away, but I propose to live with him, and you might as well stop now trying to frighten me, for you can't."

"Frighten you! Frighten you! Suzanne Dale, you haven't the faintest, weakest conception of what you are talking about, or of what I mean to do. If a breath of this—the faintest intimation of your intention were to get abroad, you would be socially ostracized. Do you realize that you would not have a friend left in the world—that all the people you now know and are friendly with would go across the street to avoid you? If you didn't have independent means, you couldn't even get a position in an ordinary shop. Going to live with him? You are going to die first, right here in my charge and in my arms. I love you too much not to kill you. I would a thousand times rather die with you myself. You are not going to see that man any more, not once, and if he dares to show his face here, I will kill him. I have said it. I mean it. Now you provoke me to action if you dare."

Suzanne merely smiled. "How you talk, mama. You make me laugh."

Mrs. Dale stared.

"Oh, Suzanne! Suzanne!" she suddenly exclaimed. "Before it is too late, before I learn to hate you, before you break my heart, come to my arms and tell me that you are sorry— that it is all over—that it is all a vile, dark, hateful dream. Oh, my Suzanne! My Suzanne!"

"No, mama, no. Don't come near, don't touch me," said Suzanne, drawing back. "You haven't any idea of what you are talking about, of what I am, or what I mean to do. You don't understand me. You never did, mama. You have always looked down on me in some superior way as though you knew a great deal and I very little. It isn't that way at all. It isn't true. I know what I am about. I know what I am doing. I love Mr. Witla, and I am going to live with him. Mrs. Witla understands. She knows how it is. You will. I don't care anything at all about what people think. I don't care what any society friends do. They are not making my life. They are all just as narrow and selfish as they can be, anyhow. Love is something different from that. You don't understand me. I love Eugene, and he is going to have me, and I am going to have him. If you want to try to wreck my life and his, you may, but it won't make any difference. I will have him, anyhow. We might just as well quit talking about it now."

"Quit talking about it? Quit talking about it? Indeed, I haven't even begun talking yet. I am just trying to collect my wits, that's all. You are raging in insanity. This thing will never be. It will nev-er be. You are just a poor, deluded slip of girl, whom I have failed to watch sufficiently. From now on, I will do my duty by you, if God spares me. You need me. Oh, how you need me. Poor little Suzanne!"

"Oh, hush, mama! Stop the hysteria," interrupted Suzanne.

"I will call up Mr. Colfax. I will call up Mr. Winfield. I will have him discharged. I will expose him in the newspapers. The scoundrel, the villain, the thief! Oh, that I should have lived to see this day. That I should have lived to have seen this day!"

"That's right, mama," said Suzanne, wearily. "Go on. You are just talking, you know, and I know that you are. You cannot change me. Talking cannot. It is silly to rave like this, I think. Why won't you be quiet? We may talk, but needn't scream."

Mrs. Dale put her hands to her temples. Her brain seemed to be whirling.

"Never mind, now," she said. "Never mind. I must have time to think. But this thing you are thinking will never be. It never will be. Oh! Oh!"—and she turned sobbing to the window.

Suzanne merely stared. What a peculiar thing emotions were in people—their emotions over morals. Here was her mother, weeping, and she was looking upon the thing her mother was crying about as the most essential and delightful and desirable thing. Certainly life was revealing itself to her rapidly these days. Did she really love Eugene so much? Yes, yes, yes, indeed. A thousand times yes. This was not a tearful emotion for her, but a great, consuming, embracing joy.

CHAPTER XIV

FOR hours that night, until one, two, and three o'clock in the morning; from five, six and seven on until noon and night of the next day, and the next day after that and the fourth day and the fifth day, the storm continued. It was a terrible, siege, heart burning, heart breaking, brain racking; Mrs. Dale lost weight rapidly. The color left her cheeks, a haggard look settled in her eyes. She was terrified, nonplussed, driven to extremities for means wherewith to overcome Suzanne's opposition and suddenly but terribly developed will. No one would have dreamed that this quiet, sweet-mannered, introspective girl could be so positive, convinced and unbending when in action. She was as a fluid body that has become adamant. She was a creature made of iron, a girl with a heart of stone; nothing moved her—her mother's tears, her threats of social ostracism, of final destruction, of physical and moral destruction for Eugene and herself, her threats of public exposure in the newspapers, of incarceration in an asylum. Suzanne had watched her mother a long time and concluded that she loved to talk imposingly in an easy, philosophic, at times pompous, way, but that really there was very little in what she said. She did not believe that her mother had true courage—that she would risk incarcerating her in an asylum, or exposing Eugene to her own disadvantage, let alone poisoning or killing her. Her mother loved her. She would rage terribly for a time this way, then she would give in. It was Suzanne's plan to wear her down, to stand her ground firmly until her mother wearied and broke under the strain. Then she would begin to say a few words for Eugene, and eventually by much arguing and blustering, her mother would come round. Eugene would be admitted to the family councils again. He and Suzanne would argue it all out together in her mother's presence. They would probably agree to disagree in a secret way, but she would get Eugene and he her. Oh, the wonder of that joyous dénouement. It was so near now, and all for a little courageous fighting. She would fight, fight until her mother broke, and then— Oh, Eugene, Eugene!

Mrs. Dale was not to be so easily overcome as Suzanne imagined. Haggard and worn as she was, she was far from yielding. There was an actual physical conflict between them once when Suzanne, in the height of an argument, decided that she would call up Eugene on the phone and ask him to come down and help her settle the discussion. Mrs. Dale was determined that she should not. The servants were in the house listening, unable to catch at first the drift of the situation, but knowing almost by intuition that there was a desperate discussion going on. Suzanne decided to go down to the library where the phone was. Mrs. Dale put her back to the door and attempted to deter her. Suzanne tried to open it by pulling. Her mother unloosed her hands desperately, but it was very difficult, Suzanne was so strong.

"For shame," she said. "For shame! To make your mother contest with you. Oh, the degradation"—the while she was struggling. Finally, angry, hysteric tears coursed involuntarily down her cheeks and Suzanne was moved at last. It was so obvious that this was real bitter heart-burning on her mother's part. Her hair was shaken loose on one side—her sleeve torn.

"Oh, my goodness! my goodness!" Mrs Dale gasped at last, throwing herself in a chair and sobbing bitterly. "I shall never lift my head again. I shall never lift my head again."

Suzanne looked at her somewhat sorrowfully. "I'm sorry, mama," she said, "but you have brought it all on yourself. I needn't call him now. He will call me and I will answer. It all comes from your trying to rule me in your way. You won't realize that I am a personality also, quite as much as you are. I have my life to live. It is mine to do with as I please. You are not going to prevent me in the long run. You might just as well stop fighting with me now. I don't want to quarrel with you. I don't want to argue, but I am a grown woman, mama. Why don't you listen to reason? Why don't you let me show you how I feel about this? Two people loving each other have a right to be with each other. It isn't anyone else's concern."

"Anyone else's concern! Anyone else's concern!" replied her mother viciously. "What nonsense. What silly, love-sick drivel. If you had any idea of life, of how the world is organized, you would laugh at yourself. Ten years from now, one year even, you will begin to see what a terrible mistake you are trying to make. You will scarcely believe that you could have done or said what you are doing and saying now. Anyone else's concern! Oh, Merciful Heaven! Will nothing put even a suggestion of the wild, foolish, reckless character of the thing you are trying to do in your mind?"

"But I love him, mama," said Suzanne.

"Love! Love! You talk about love," said her mother bitterly
and hysterically. "What do you know about it? Do you
think he can be loving you when he wants to come here and
take you out of a good home and a virtuous social condition
and wreck your life, and bring you down into the mire, your
life and mine, and that of your sisters and brother for ever and
ever? What does he know of love? What do you? Think of
Adele and Ninette and Kinroy. Have you no regard for
them? Where is your love for me and for them? Oh, I have
been so afraid that Kinroy might hear something of this. He
would go and kill him. I know he would. I couldn't prevent it.
Oh, the shame, the scandal, the wreck, it would involve us all
in. Have you no conscience, Suzanne; no heart?"

Suzanne stared before her calmly. The thought of Kinroy
moved her a little. He might kill Eugene—she couldn't tell—
he was a courageous boy. Still there was no need for any
killing, or exposure, or excitement of any kind if her mother
would only behave herself. What difference did it make to her,
or Kinroy, or anybody anywhere what she did? Why couldn't
she if she wanted to? The risk was on her head. She was
willing. She couldn't see what harm it would do.

She expressed this thought to her mother once who answered
in an impassioned plea for her to look at the facts. "How many
evil women of the kind and character you would like to make
of yourself, do you know? How many would you like to know?
How many do you suppose there are in good society? Look at
this situation from Mrs. Witla's point of view. How would
you like to be in her place? How would you like to be in
mine? Suppose you were Mrs. Witla and Mrs. Witla were the
other woman. What then?"

"I would let him go," said Suzanne.

"Yes! Yes! Yes! You would let him go. You might, but
how would you feel? How would anyone feel? Can't you see
the shame in all this, the disgrace? Have you no comprehension at all? No feeling?"

"Oh, how you talk, mama. How silly you talk. You don't
know the facts. Mrs. Witla doesn't love him any more. She
told me so. She has written me so. I had the letter and gave
it back to Eugene. He doesn't care for her. She knows it.
She knows he cares for me. What difference does it make if
she doesn't love him. He's entitled to love somebody. Now I
love him. I want him. He wants me. Why shouldn't we
have each other?"

In spite of all her threats, Mrs. Dale was not without subsidiary thoughts of what any public move on her part would certainly, not probably, but immediately involve. Eugene was well known. To kill him, which was really very far from her thoughts, in any save a very secret way, would create a tremendous sensation and involve no end of examination, discussion, excited publicity. To expose him to either Colfax or Winfield meant in reality exposing Suzanne to them, and possibly to members of her own social set, for these men were of it, and might talk. Eugene's resignation would cause comment. If he left, Suzanne might run away with him—then what? There was the thought on her part that the least discussion or whisper of this to anybody might produce the most disastrous results. What capital the so-called "Yellow" newspapers would make out of a story of this character. How they would gloat over the details. It was a most terrible and dangerous situation, and yet it was plain that something had to be done and that immediately. What?

In this crisis it occurred to her that several things might be done and that without great danger of irremediable consequences if she could only have a little time in which Suzanne would promise to remain quiescent and do so. If she could get her to say that she would do nothing for ten days or five days all might be well for them. She could go to see Angela, Eugene, Mr. Colfax, if necessary. To leave Suzanne in order to go on these various errands, she had to obtain Suzanne's word, which she knew she could respect absolutely, that she would make no move of any kind until the time was up. Under pretense that Suzanne herself needed time to think, or should take it, she pleaded and pleaded until finally the girl, on condition that she be allowed to phone to Eugene and state how things stood, consented. Eugene had called her up on the second day after the quarrel began and had been informed by the butler, at Mrs. Dale's request, that she was out of town. He called the second day, and got the same answer. He wrote to her and Mrs. Dale hid the letter, but on the fourth day, Suzanne called him up and explained. The moment she did so, he was sorry that she had been so hasty in telling her mother, terribly so, but there was nothing to be done now save to stand by his guns. He was ready in a grim way to rise or fall so long as, in doing either, he should obtain his heart's desire.

"Shall I come and help you argue?" he asked.

"No, not for five days. I have given my word."

"Shall I see you?"

"No, not for five days, Eugene."

"Mayn't I even call you up?"

"No, not for five days. After that, yes."

"All right, Flower Face—Divine Fire. I'll obey. I'm yours to command. But, oh, sweet, it's a long time."

"I know, but it will pass."

"And you won't change?"

"No."

"They can't make you?"

"No, you know they can't, dearest. Why do you ask?"

"Oh, I can't help feeling a little fearful, sweet. You are so young, so new to love."

"I won't change. I won't change. I don't need to swear. I won't."

"Very well, then, Myrtle Bloom."

She hung up the receiver, and Mrs. Dale knew now that her greatest struggle was before her.

Her several contemplated moves consisted first, in going to see Mrs. Witla, unknown to Suzanne and Eugene, learning what she knew of how things were and what she would advise.

This really did no good, unless the fact that it fomented anew the rage and grief of Angela, and gave Mrs. Dale additional material wherewith to belabor Eugene, could be said to be of advantage. Angela, who had been arguing and pleading with Eugene all this time, endeavoring by one thought and another to awaken him to a sense of the enormity of the offense he was contemplating, was practically in despair. She had reached the point where she had become rather savage again, and he also. In spite of her condition, in spite of all she could say, he was cold and bitter, so insistent that he was through with the old order that he made her angry. Instead of leaving him, as she might have done, trusting to time to alter his attitude, or to teach her the wisdom of releasing him entirely, she preferred to cling to him, for there was still affection left. She was used to him, he was the father of her coming child, unwelcome as it was. He represented her social position to her, her station in the world. Why should she leave him? Then, too, there was this fear of the outcome, which would come over her like a child. She might die. What would become of the child?

"You know, Mrs. Dale," she said at one point significantly, "I don't hold Suzanne absolutely guiltless. She is old enough to know better. She has been out in society long enough to know that a married man is sacred property to another woman."

"I know, I know," replied Mrs. Dale resentfully, but cautiously, "but Suzanne is so young. You really don't know how much of a child she is. And she has this silly, idealistic, emotional disposition. I suspected something of it, but I did not know it was so strong. I'm sure I don't know where she gets it. Her father was most practical. But she was all right until your husband persuaded her."

"That may be all true," went on Angela, "but she is not guiltless. I know Eugene. He is weak, but he will not follow where he is not led, and no girl need be tempted unless she wants to."

"Suzanne is so young," again pleaded Mrs. Dale.

"Well, I'm sure if she knew Mr. Witla's record accurately," went on Angela foolishly, "she wouldn't want him. I have written her. She ought to know. He isn't honest and he isn't moral as this thing shows. If this were the first time he had fallen in love with another woman, I could forgive him, but it isn't. He did something quite as bad six or seven years ago, and only two years before that there was another woman. He wouldn't be faithful to Suzanne if he had her. It would be a case of blazing affection for a little while, and then he would tire and cast her aside. Why, you can tell what sort of a man he is when he would propose to me, as he did here, that I should let him maintain a separate establishment for Suzanne and say nothing of it. The idea!"

Mrs. Dale clicked her lips significantly. She considered Angela foolish for talking in this way, but it could not be helped now. Possibly Eugene had made a mistake in marrying her. This did not excuse him, however, in her eyes for wanting to take Suzanne under the conditions he proposed. If he were free, it would be an entirely different matter. His standing, his mind, his manners, were not objectionable, though he was not to the manner born.

Mrs. Dale went away toward evening, greatly nonplussed by what she had seen and heard, but convinced that no possible good could come of the situation. Angela would never give him a divorce. Eugene was not a fit man morally for her daughter, anyhow. There was great scandal on the verge of exposure here in which her beloved daughter would be irretrievably smirched. In her desperation, she decided, if she could do no better, she would try to dissuade Eugene from seeing Suzanne until he could obtain a divorce, in which case, to avoid something worse, she would agree to a marriage, but this was only to be a lip promise. The one thing she wanted to do was to get Suzanne to give him up entirely. If Suzanne could be spirited away, or dissuaded from throwing herself away on Eugene, that would be the thing. Still, she proposed to see what a conversation with Eugene would do.

The next morning as he was sitting in his office wondering what the delay of five days portended, and what Suzanne was doing, as well as trying to fix his mind on the multitudinous details which required his constant attention, and were now being rather markedly neglected, the card of Mrs. Emily Dale was laid on his table, and a few moments later, after his secretary had been dismissed, and word given that no one else was to be allowed to enter, Mrs. Dale was shown in.

She was pale and weary, but exquisitely dressed in a greenish blue silk and picture hat of black straw and feathers. She looked quite young and handsome herself, not too old for Eugene, and indeed once she had fancied he might well fall in love with her. What her thoughts were at that time, she was not now willing to recall, for they had involved the probable desertion or divorce, or death of Angela, and Eugene's passionate infatuation for her. All that was over now, of course, and in the excitement and distress, almost completely obliterated. Eugene had not forgotten that he had had similar sensations or imaginations at the time, and that Mrs. Dale had always drawn to him in a sympathetic and friendly way. Here she was, though, this morning coming upon a desperate mission no doubt, and he would have to contend with her as best he could.

The conversation opened by his looking into her set face as she approached and smiling blandly, though it was something of an effort. "Well," he said, in quite a business like way, "what can I do for you?"

"You villain," she exclaimed melodramatically, "my daughter has told me all."

"Yes, Suzanne phoned me that she told you," he replied, in a conciliatory tone.

"Yes," she said in a low, tense voice, "and I ought to kill you where you stand. To think that I should have ever harbored such a monster as you in my home and near my dear, innocent daughter. It seems incredible now. I can't believe it. That you should dare. And you with a dear, sweet wife at home, sick and in the condition she is in. I should think if you had any manhood at all—any sense of shame! When I think of that poor, dear little woman, and what you have been doing, or trying to do—if it weren't for the scandal you would never leave this office alive."

"Oh, bother! Don't talk rot, Mrs. Dale," said Eugene quietly, though irritably. He did not care for her melodramatic

THE "GENIUS" 617

attitude. "The dear, darling little woman you speak of is not as
badly off as you think, and I don't think she needs as much of
your sympathy as you are so anxious to give. She is pretty
well able to take care of herself, sick as she is. As for killing
me, or you or anyone else, well that wouldn't be such a bad idea.
I'm not so much in love with life. This is not fifty years ago,
though, but the nineteenth century, and this is New York City.
I love Suzanne. She loves me. We want each other desperately.
Now, an arrangement can be made which will not interfere
with you in any way, and which will adjust things for us. Suzanne is anxious to make that arrangement. It is as much her
proposition as it is mine. Why should you be so vastly disturbed?
You know a great deal about life."

"Why should I be disturbed? Why should I? Can you sit
in this office, you a man in charge of all this vast public work,
and ask me in cold blood why I should be disturbed? And my
daughter's very life at stake. Why should I be disturbed and
my daughter only out of her short dresses a little while ago and
practically innocent of the world. You dare to tell me that she
proposed! Oh, you impervious scoundrel! To think I could be
so mistaken in any human being. You, with your bland manners
and your inconsistent talk of happy family life. I might have
understood, though, when I saw you so often without your wife.
I should have known. I did, God help me! but I didn't act
upon it. I was taken by your bland, gentlemanly attitude. I
don't blame poor, dear little Suzanne. I blame you, you utterly
deceiving villain and myself for being so silly. I am being
justly rewarded, however."

Eugene merely looked at her and drummed with his fingers.

"But I did not come here to bandy words with you," she went
on. "I came to say that you must never see my daughter again,
or speak of her, or appear where she might chance to be, though
she won't be where you may appear, if I have my way, for you
won't have a chance to appear anywhere in decent society very
much longer. I shall go, unless you agree here and now never
to see or communicate with her any more, to Mr. Colfax, whom
I know personally, as you are aware, and lay the whole matter
before him. I'm sure with what I know now of your record,
and what you have attempted to do in connection with my
daughter, and the condition of your wife, that he will not
require your services very much longer. I shall go to Mr.
Winfield, who is also an old friend, and lay the matter before
him. Privately you will be drummed out of society and my
daughter will be none the worse for it. She is so very young

that wnen the facts are known, you are the only one who will
bear the odium of this. Your wife has given me your wretched
record only yesterday. You would like to make my Suzanne your
fourth or fifth. Well, you will not. I will show you something you have not previously known. You are dealing with a
desperate mother. Defy me if you dare. I demand that you
write your farewell to Suzanne here and now, and let me take
it to her."

Eugene smiled sardonically. Mrs. Dale's reference to Angela
made him bitter. She had been there and Angela had talked
of him—his past to her. What a mean thing to do. After all,
Angela was his wife. Only the morning before, she had been
appealing to him on the grounds of love, and she had not told
him of Mrs. Dale's visit. Love! Love! What sort of love
was this? He had done enough for her to make her generous
in a crisis like this, even if she did not want to be.

"Write you a statement of release to Suzanne?" he observed,
his lips curling—"how silly. Of course, I won't. And as for
your threat to run to Mr. Colfax, I have heard that before
from Mrs. Witla. There is the door. His office is twelve flights
down. I'll call a boy, if you wish. You tell it to Mr. Colfax
and see how much farther it goes before you are much older.
Run to Mr. Winfield also. A lot I care about him or Mr.
Colfax. If you want a grand, interesting discussion of this
thing, just begin. It will go far and wide, I assure you. I love
your daughter. I'm desperate about her. I'm literally crazy
about her"—he got up—"she loves me, or I think she does.
Anyhow, I'm banking all on that thought. My life from the
point of view of affection has been a failure. I have never really
been in love before, but I am crazy about Suzanne Dale. I am
wild about her. If you had any sympathy for an unhappy, sympathetic, emotional mortal, who has never yet been satisfied in a
woman, you would give her to me. I love her. I love her. By
God!"—he banged the desk with his fist—"I will do anything
for her. If she will come to me, Colfax can have his position,
Winfield can have his Blue Sea Corporation. You can have her
money, if she wants to give it to you. I can make a living abroad
by my art, and I will. Other Americans have done it before me.
I love her! I love her! Do you hear me? I love her, and
what's more, I'm going to have her! You can't stop me. You
haven't the brains; you haven't the strength; you haven't the resources to match that girl. She's brighter than you are. She's
stronger, she's finer. She's finer than the whole current day
conception of society and life. She loves me and she wants to

give herself to me, willingly, freely, joyously. Match that in your petty society circles if you can. Society! You say you will have me drummed out of it, will you? A lot I care about your society. Hacks, mental light weights, money grubbers, gamblers, thieves, leeches—a fine lot! To see you sitting there and talking to me with your grand air makes me laugh. A lot I care for you. I was thinking of another kind of woman when I met you, not a narrow, conventional fool. I thought I saw one in you. I did, didn't I—not? You are like all the rest, a narrow, petty slavish follower after fashion and convention. Well," he snapped his fingers in her face, "go on and do your worst. I will get Suzanne in the long run. She will come to me. She will dominate you. Run to Colfax! Run to Winfield! I will get her just the same. She's mine. She belongs to me. She is big enough for me. The Gods have given her to me, and I will have her if I have to smash you and your home and myself and everyone else connected with me. I'll have her! I'll have her! She is mine! She is mine!" He lifted a tense hand. "Now you run and do anything you want to. Thank God, I've found one woman who knows how to live and love. She's mine!"

Mrs. Dale stared at him in amazement, scarcely believing her ears. Was he crazy? Was he really so much in love? Had Suzanne turned his brain? What an astonishing thing. She had never seen him anything like this—never imagined him capable of anything like it. He was always so quiet, smiling, bland, witty. Here he was dramatic, impassioned, fiery, hungry. There was a terrible light in his eyes and he was desperate. He must be in love.

"Oh, why will you do this to me?" she whimpered all at once. The terror of his mood conveying itself to her for the moment, and arousing a sympathy which she had not previously felt. "Why will you come into my home and attempt to destroy it? There are lots of women who will love you. There are lots more suited to your years and temperament than Suzanne. She doesn't understand you. She doesn't understand herself. She is just young, and foolish and hypnotized. You have hypnotized her. Oh, why will you do this to me? You are so much older than her, so much more schooled in life. Why not give her up? I don't want to go to Mr. Colfax. I don't want to speak to Mr. Winfield. I will, if I have to, but I don't want to. I have always thought so well of you. I know you are not an ordinary man. Restore my respect for you, my confidence in you. I can forgive, if I can't forget. You

may not be happily married. I am sorry for you. I don't want
to do anything desperate. I only want to save poor, little Suzanne. Oh, please! please! I love her so. I don't think you
understand how I feel. You may be in love, but you ought to
be willing to consider others. True love would. I know that
she is hard and wilful and desperate now, but she will change
if you will help her. Why, if you really love her, if you have
any sympathy for me or regard for her future, or your own, you
will renounce your schemes and release her. Tell her you made
a mistake. Write to her now. Tell her you can't do this and
not socially ruin her and me and yourself, and so you won't do
it. Tell her that you have decided to wait until time has made
you a free man, if that is to be, and then let her have a chance
of seeing if she will not be happy in a normal life. You don't
want to ruin her at this age, do you? She is so young, so
innocent. Oh, if you have any judgment of life at all, any
regard, any consideration, anything, I beg of you; I beg as her
mother, for I love her. Oh!" Tears came into her eyes again
and she cried weakly in her handkerchief.

Eugene stared at her. What was he doing? Where was he
going? Was he really as bad as he appeared to be here? Was
he possessed? Was he really so hard-hearted? Through her
grief and Angela's and the threats concerning Colfax and Winfield, he caught a glimpse of the real heart of the situation. It
was as if there had been a great flash of lightning illuminating
a black landscape. He saw sympathetically, sorrow, folly, a
number of things that were involved, and then the next moment,
it was gone. Suzanne's face came back, smooth, classic, chiseled,
perfectly modeled, her beauty like a tightened bow; her eyes, her
lips, her hair, the gaiety and buoyancy of her motions and her
smile. Give her up! Give up Suzanne and that dream of the
studio, and of joyous, continuous, delicious companionship? Did
Suzanne want him to? What had she said over the phone? No!
No! No! Quit now, and her clinging to him. No! No!
No! Never!! He would fight first. He would go down fighting. Never! Never! Never!

His brain seethed.

"I can't do it," he said, getting up again, for he had sat down
after his previous tirade. "I can't do it. You are asking something that is utterly impossible. It can never be done. God
help me, I'm insane, I'm wild over her. Go and do anything
you want to, but I must have her and I will. She's mine! She's
mine! She's mine!"

His thin, lean hands clenched and he clicked his teeth.

"Mine, mine, mine!" he muttered, and one would have thought him a villain in a cheap melodrama.

Mrs. Dale shook her head.

"God help us both!" she said. "You shall never, never have her. You are not worthy of her. You are not right in your mind. I will fight you with all the means in my power. I am desperate! I am wealthy. I know how to fight. You shall not have her. Now we will see which will win." She rose to go and Eugene followed her.

"Go ahead," he said calmly, "but in the end you lose. Suzanne comes to me. I know it. I feel it. I may lose many other things, but I get her. She's mine."

"Oh," sighed Mrs. Dale wearily, half believing him and moving towards the door. "Is this your last word?"

"It is positively."

"Then I must be going."

"Good-bye," he said solemnly.

"Good-bye," she answered, white faced, her eyes staring.

She went out and Eugene took up the telephone; but he remembered that Suzanne had warned him not to call, but to depend on her. So he put it down again.

CHAPTER XV

THE fire and pathos of Mrs. Dale's appeal should have given Eugene pause. He thought once of going after her and making a further appeal, saying that he would try and get a divorce eventually and marry Suzanne, but he remembered that peculiar insistency of Suzanne on the fact that she did not want to get married. Somehow, somewhere, somewhy, she had formulated this peculiar ideal or attitude, which whatever the world might think of it, was possible of execution, providing he and she were tactful enough. It was not such a wild thing for two people to want to come together in this way, if they chose, he thought. Why was it? Heaven could witness there were enough illicit and peculiar relationships in this world to prevent society from becoming excited about one more, particularly when it was to be conducted in so circumspect and subtle a way. He and Suzanne did not intend to blazon their relationship to the world. As a distinguished artist, not active, but acknowledged and accomplished, he was entitled to a studio life. He and Suzanne could meet there. Nothing would be thought of it. Why had she insisted on telling her mother? It could all have been done without that. There was another peculiar ideal of hers, her determination to tell the truth under all circumstances. And yet she had really not told it. She had deceived her mother a long time about him simply by saying nothing. Was this some untoward trick of fate's, merely devised to harm him? Surely not. And yet Suzanne's headstrong determination seemed almost a fatal mistake now. He sat down brooding over it. Was this a terrific blunder? Would he be sorry? All his life was in the balance. Should he turn back?

No! No! No! Never! It was not to be. He must go on. He must! He must! So he brooded.

The next of Mrs. Dale's resources was not quite so unavailing as the others, though it was almost so. She had sent for Dr. Latson Woolley, her family physician—an old school practitioner of great repute, of rigid honor and rather Christian principles himself, but also of a wide intellectual and moral discernment, so far as others were concerned.

"Well, Mrs. Dale," he observed, when he was ushered into her presence in the library on the ground floor, and extending his hand cordially, though wearily, "what can I do for you this morning?"

"Oh, Dr. Woolley," she began directly, "I am in so much trouble. It isn't a case of sickness. I wish it were. It is something so much worse. I have sent for you because I know I can rely on your judgment and sympathy. It concerns my daughter, Suzanne."

"Yes, yes," he grunted, in a rather crusty voice, for his vocal cords were old, and his eyes looked out from under shaggy, gray eyebrows which somehow bespoke a world of silent observation. "What's the matter with her? What has she done now that she ought not to do?"

"Oh, doctor," exclaimed Mrs. Dale nervously, for the experiences of the last few days had almost completely dispelled her normal composure, "I don't know how to tell you, really. I don't know how to begin. Suzanne, my dear precious Suzanne, in whom I have placed so much faith and reliance has, has——"

"Well, tell me," interrupted Dr. Woolley laconically.

When she had told him the whole story, and answered some of his incisive questions, he said:

"Well, I am thinking you have a good deal to be grateful for. She might have yielded without your knowledge and told you afterwards—or not at all."

"Not at all. Oh, doctor! My Suzanne!"

"Mrs. Dale, I looked after you and your mother before you and Suzanne. I know something about human nature and your family characteristics. Your husband was a very determined man, as you will remember. Suzanne may have some of his traits in her. She is a very young girl, you want to remember, very robust and vigorous. How old is this Witla man?"

"About thirty-eight or nine, doctor."

"Um! I suspected as much. The fatal age. It's a wonder you came through that period as safely as you did. You're nearly forty, aren't you?"

"Yes, doctor, but you're the only one that knows it."

"I know, I know. It's the fatal age. You say he is in charge of the United Magazines Corporation. I have probably heard of him. I know of Mr. Colfax of that company. Is he very emotional in his temperament?"

"I had never thought so before this."

"Well, he probably is. Thirty-eight to thirty-nine and eighteen or nineteen—bad combination. Where is Suzanne?"

"Upstairs in her room, I fancy."

"It might not be a bad thing if I talked to her myself a little, though I don't believe it will do any good."

Mrs. Dale disappeared and was gone for nearly three-quarters

of an hour. Suzanne was stubborn, irritable, and to all preliminary entreaties insisted that she would not. Why should
her mother call in outsiders, particularly Dr. Woolley, whom she
knew and liked. She suspected at once when her mother said
Dr. Woolley wanted to see her that it had something to do
with her case, and demanded to know why. Finally, after much
pleading, she consented to come down, though it was with the
intention of showing her mother how ridiculous all her excitement was.

The old doctor who had been meditating upon the inexplicable tangle, chemical and physical, of life—the blowing
hither and thither of diseases, affections, emotions and hates
of all kinds, looked up quizzically as Suzanne entered.

"Well, Suzanne," he said genially, rising and walking slowly
toward her, "I'm glad to see you again. How are you this
morning?"

"Pretty well, doctor, how are you?"

"Oh, as you see, as you see, a little older and a little fussier,
Suzanne, making other people's troubles my own. Your mother
tells me you have fallen in love. That's an interesting thing
to do, isn't it?"

"You know, doctor," said Suzanne defiantly, "I told mama
that I don't care to discuss this, and I don't think she has
any right to try to make me. I don't want to and I won't. I
think it is all in rather poor taste."

"Poor taste, Suzanne?" asked Mrs. Dale. "Do you call our
discussion of what you want to do poor taste, when the world
will think that what you want to do is terrible when you
do it?"

"I told you, mama, that I was not coming down here to discuss this thing, and I'm not!" said Suzanne, turning to her
mother and ignoring Dr. Woolley. "I'm not going to stay. I
don't want to offend Dr. Woolley, but I'm not going to stay
and have you argue this all over again."

She turned to go.

"There, there, Mrs. Dale, don't interrupt," observed Dr.
Woolley, holding Suzanne by the very tone of his voice. "I
think myself that very little is to be gained by argument.
Suzanne is convinced that what she is planning to do is to her
best interest. It may be. We can't always tell. I think the
best thing that could be discussed, if anything at all in this
matter can be discussed, is the matter of time. It is my opinion
that before doing this thing that Suzanne wants to do, and which
may be all right, for all I know, it would be best if she would

take a little time. I know nothing of Mr. Witla. He may be a most able and worthy man. Suzanne ought to give herself a little time to think, though. I should say three months, or six months. A great many after effects hang on this decision, as you know," he said, turning to Suzanne. "It may involve responsibilities you are not quite ready to shoulder. You are only eighteen or nineteen, you know. You might have to give up dancing and society, and travel, and a great many things, and devote yourself to being a mother and ministering to your husband's needs. You expect to live with him permanently, don't you?"

"I don't want to discuss this, Dr. Woolley."

"But you do expect that, don't you?"

"Only as long as we love each other."

"Um, well, you might love him for some little time yet. You rather expect to do that, don't you?"

"Why, yes, but what is the good of this, anyhow? My mind is made up."

"Just the matter of thinking," said Dr. Woolley, very soothingly and in a voice which disarmed Suzanne and held her. "Just a little time in which to be absolutely sure. Your mother is anxious not to have you do it at all. You, as I understand it, want to do this thing right away. Your mother loves you, and at bottom, in spite of this little difference, I know you love her. It just occurred to me that for the sake of good feeling all around, you might like to strike a balance. You might be willing to take, say six months, or a year and think about it. Mr. Witla would probably not object. You won't be any the less delightful to him at the end of that time, and as for your mother, she would feel a great deal better if she thought that, after all, what you decided to do you had done after mature deliberation."

"Yes," exclaimed Mrs. Dale, impulsively, "do take time to think, Suzanne. A year won't hurt you."

"No," said Suzanne unguardedly. "It is all a matter of whether I want to or not. I don't want to."

"Precisely. Still this is something you might take into consideration. The situation from all outside points of view is serious. I haven't said so, but I feel that you would be making a great mistake. Still, that is only my opinion. You are entitled to yours. I know how you feel about it, but the public is not likely to feel quite the same. The public is a wearisome thing, Suzanne, but we have to take it into consideration."

Suzanne stared stubbornly and wearily at her tormentors.

Their logic did not appeal to her at all. She was thinking of Eugene and her plan. It could be worked. What did she care about the world? During all this talk, she drew nearer and nearer the door and finally opened it.

"Well, that is all," said Dr. Woolley, when he saw she was determined to go. "Good morning, Suzanne. I am glad to have seen you again."

"Good morning, Dr. Woolley," she replied.

She went out and Mrs. Dale wrung her hands. "I wish I knew what was to be done," she exclaimed, gazing at her counselor.

Dr. Woolley brooded over the folly of undesired human counsel.

"There is no need for excitement," he observed after a time. "It is obvious to me that if she is handled rightly, she will wait. She is in a state of high strung opposition and emotion for some reason at present. You have driven her too hard. Relax. Let her think this thing out for herself. Counsel for delay, but don't irritate. You cannot control her by driving. She has too stern a will. Tears won't help. Emotion seems a little silly to her. Ask her to think, or better yet, let her think and plead only for delay. If you could get her away for two or three weeks or months, off by herself undisturbed by your pleadings and uninfluenced by his—if she would ask him of her own accord to let her alone for that time, all will be well. I don't think she will ever go to him. She thinks she will, but I have the feeling that she won't. However, be calm. If you can, get her to go away."

"Would it be possible to lock her up in some sanatorium or asylum, doctor, until she has had time to think?"

"All things are possible, but I should say it would be the most inadvisable thing you could do. Force accomplishes nothing in these cases."

"I know, but suppose she won't listen to reason?"

"You really haven't come to that bridge yet. You haven't talked calmly to her yet. You are quarreling with her. There is very little in that. You will simply grow further and further apart."

"How practical you are, doctor," observed Mrs. Dale, in a mollified and complimentary vein.

"Not practical, but intuitional. If I were practical, I would never have taken up medicine."

He walked to the door, his old body sinking in somewhat

upon itself. His old, gray eyes twinkled slightly as he turned.

"You were in love once, Mrs. Dale," he said.

"Yes," she replied.

"You remember how you felt then?"

"Yes."

"Be reasonable. Remember your own sensations—your own attitude. You probably weren't crossed in your affair. She is. She has made a mistake. Be patient. Be calm. We want to stop it and no doubt can. Do unto others as you would be done by."

He ambled shufflingly across the piazza and down the wide steps to his car.

"Mama," she said, when after Dr. Woolley had gone her mother came to her room to see if she might not be in a mellower mood, and to plead with her further for delay, "it seems to me you are making a ridiculous mess of all this. Why should you go and tell Dr. Woolley about me! I will never forgive you for that. Mama, you have done something I never thought you would do. I thought you had more pride—more individuality."

One should have seen Suzanne, in her spacious boudoir, her back to her oval mirrored dressing table, her face fronting her mother, to understand her fascination for Eugene. It was a lovely, sunny, many windowed chamber, and Suzanne in a white and blue morning dress was in charming accord with the gay atmosphere of the room.

"Well, Suzanne, you know," she said, rather despondently, "I just couldn't help it. I had to go to someone. I am quite alone apart from you and Kinroy and the children"—she referred to Adele and Ninette as the children when talking to either Suzanne or Kinroy—"and I didn't want to say anything to them. You have been my only confidant up to now, and since you have turned against me——"

"I haven't turned against you, mama."

"Oh, yes you have. Let's not talk about it, Suzanne. You have broken my heart. You are killing me. I just had to go to someone. We have known Dr. Woolley so long. He is so good and kind."

"Oh, I know, mama, but what good will it do? How can anything he might say help matters? He isn't going to change me. You're only telling it to somebody who oughtn't to know anything about it."

"But I thought he might influence you," pleaded Mrs. Dale.

"I thought you would listen to him. Oh, dear, oh, dear. I'm so tired of it all. I wish I were dead. I wish I had never lived to see this."

"Now there you go, mama," said Suzanne confidently. "I can't see why you are so distressed about what I am going to do. It is my life that I am planning to arrange, not yours. I have to live my life, mama, not you."

"Oh, yes, but it is just that that distresses me. What will it be after you do this—after you throw it away? Oh, if you could only see what you are contemplating doing—what a wretched thing it will be when it is all over with. You will never live with him—he is too old for you, too fickle, too insincere. He will not care for you after a little while, and then there you will be, unmarried, possibly with a child on your hands, a social outcast! Where will you go?"

"Mama," said Suzanne calmly, her lips parted in a rosy, baby way, "I have thought of all this. I see how it is. But I think you and everybody else make too much ado about these things. You think of everything that could happen, but it doesn't all happen that way. People do these things, I'm sure, and nothing much is thought of it."

"Yes, in books," put in Mrs. Dale. "I know where you get all this from. It's your reading."

"Anyhow, I'm going to. I have made up my mind," added Suzanne. "I have decided that by September fifteenth I will go to Mr. Witla, and you might just as well make up your mind to it now." This was August tenth.

"Suzanne," said her mother, staring at her, "I never imagined you could talk in this way to me. You will do nothing of the kind. How can you be so hard? I did not know that you had such a terrible will in you. Doesn't anything I have said about Adele and Ninette or Kinroy appeal to you? Have you no heart in you? Why don't you wait, as Dr. Woolley suggests, six months or a year? Why do you talk about jumping into this without giving yourself time to think? It is such a wild, rash experiment. You haven't thought anything about it, you haven't had time."

"Oh, yes, I have, mama!" replied Suzanne. "I've thought a great deal about it. I'm fully convinced. I want to do it then because I told Eugene that I would not keep him waiting long; and I won't. I want to go to him. That will make a clear two months since we first talked of this."

Mrs. Dale winced. She had no idea of yielding to her daughter, or letting her do this, but this definite conclusion as to the time brought matters finally to a head. Her daughter was out of her mind, that was all. It gave her not any too much time to turn round in. She must get Suzanne out of the city—out of the country, if possible, or lock her up, and she must do it without antagonizing her too much.

CHAPTER XVI

MRS. DALE'S next step in this struggle was to tell Kinroy, who wanted, of course, in a fit of boyish chivalry, to go immediately and kill Eugene. This was prevented by Mrs. Dale, who had more control over him than she had over Suzanne, pointing out to him what a terrifically destructive scandal would ensue and urging subtlety and patience. Kinroy had a sincere affection for his sisters, particularly Suzanne and Adele, and he wanted to protect all of them. He decided in a pompous, ultra chivalrous spirit that he must help his mother plan, and together they talked of chloroforming her some night, of carrying her thus, as a sick girl, in a private car to Maine or the Adirondacks or somewhere in Canada.

It would be useless to follow all these strategic details in their order. There were, after the five days agreed upon by Suzanne, attempted phone messages by Eugene, which were frustrated by Kinroy, who was now fulfilling the rôle of private detective. Suzanne resolved to have Eugene summoned to the house for a discussion, but to this her mother objected. She felt that additional meetings would simply strengthen their bond of union. Kinroy wrote to Eugene of his own accord that he knew all, and that if he attempted to come near the place he would kill him at sight. Suzanne, finding herself blocked and detained by her mother, wrote Eugene a letter which Elizabeth, her maid, secretly conveyed to the mail for her, telling him how things stood. Her mother had told Dr. Woolley and Kinroy. She had decided that September fifteenth was the time she would leave home, unless their companionship was quietly sanctioned. Kinroy had threatened to kill him to her, but she did not think he had anything to fear. Kinroy was just excited. Her mother wanted her to go to Europe for six months and think it over, but this she would not do. She was not going to leave the city, and he need not fear, if he did not hear anything for a few days at a time, that anything was wrong with her. They must wait until the storm subsided a little. "I shall be here, but perhaps it is best for you not to try to see me just now. When the time comes, I will come to you, and if I get a chance, I will see you before."

Eugene was both pained and surprised at the turn things had taken, but still encouraged to hope for the best by the attitude

Suzanne took toward it all. Her courage strengthened him. She was calm, so purposeful! What a treasure she was!

So began a series of daily love notes for a few days, until Suzanne advised him to cease. There were constant arguments between her, her mother and Kinroy. Because she was being so obviously frustrated, she began to grow bitter and hard, and short contradictory phrases passed between her and her mother, principally originating in Suzanne.

"No, no, no!" was her constantly reiterated statement. "I won't do it! What of it? It's silly! Let me alone! I won't talk!" So it went.

Mrs. Dale was planning hourly how to abduct her. Chloroforming and secret removal after the fashion she had in her mind was not so easy of accomplishment. It was such a desperate thing to do to Suzanne. She was afraid she might die under its influence. It could not be administered without a doctor. The servants would think it strange. She fancied there were whispered suspicions already. Finally she thought of pretending to agree with Suzanne, removing all barriers, and asking her to come to Albany to confer with her guardian, or rather the legal representative of the Marquardt Trust Company, which held her share of her father the late Westfield Dale's estate in trust for her, in regard to some property in western New York, which belonged to her. Mrs. Dale decided to pretend to be obliged to go to Albany in order to have Suzanne sign a waiver of right to any share in her mother's private estate, after which, supposedly, she would give Suzanne her freedom, having also disinherited her in her will. Suzanne, according to this scheme, was then to come back to New York and go her way and her mother was not to see her any more.

To make this more effective, Kinroy was sent to tell her of her mother's plan and beg her for her own and her family's sake not to let the final separation come about. Mrs. Dale changed her manner. Kinroy acted his part so effectively that what with her mother's resigned look and indifferent method of address, Suzanne was partly deceived. She imagined her mother had experienced a complete change of heart and might be going to do what Kinroy said.

"No," she replied to Kinroy's pleadings, "I don't care whether she cuts me off. I'll be very glad to sign the papers. If she wants me to go away, I'll go. I think she has acted very foolishly through all this, and so have you."

"I wish you wouldn't let her do that," observed Kinroy, who

was rather exulting over the satisfactory manner in which this bait was being swallowed. "Mama is broken hearted. She wants you to stay here, to wait six months or a year before you do anything at all, but if you won't, she's going to ask you to do this. I've tried to persuade her not to. I'd hate like anything to see you go. Won't you change your mind?"

"I told you I wouldn't, Kinroy. Don't ask me."

Kinroy went back to his mother and reported that Suzanne was stubborn as ever, but that the trick would in all probability work. She would go aboard the train thinking she was going to Albany. Once aboard, inside a closed car, she would scarcely suspect until the next morning, and then they would be far in the Adirondack Mountains.

The scheme worked in part. Her mother, as had Kinroy, went through this prearranged scene as well as though she were on the stage. Suzanne fancied she saw her freedom near at hand. Only a travelling bag was packed, and Suzanne went willingly enough into the auto and the train, only stipulating one thing—that she be allowed to call up Eugene and explain. Both Kinroy and her mother objected, but, when finally she refused flatly to go without, they acceded. She called him up at the office—it was four o'clock in the afternoon, and they were leaving at five-thirty—and told him. He fancied at once it was a ruse, and told her so, but she thought not. Mrs. Dale had never lied to her before, neither had her brother. Their words were as bonds.

"Eugene says this is a trap, mama," said Suzanne, turning from the phone to her mother, who was near by. "Is it?"

"You know it isn't," replied her mother, lying unblushingly.

"If it is, it will come to nothing," she replied, and Eugene heard her. He was strengthened into acquiescence by the tone of her voice. Surely she was a wonderful girl—a master of men and women in her way.

"Very well, if you think it's all right," said Eugene; "but I'll be very lonely. I've been so already. I shall be more so, Flower Face, unless I see you soon. Oh, if the time were only up!"

"It will be, Eugene," she replied, "in a very few days now. "I'll be back Thursday, and then you can come down and see me."

"Thursday afternoon?"

"Yes. We're to be back Thursday morning."

She finally hung up the receiver and they entered the automobile and an hour later the train.

CHAPTER XVII

IT was a Montreal, Ottawa and Quebec express, and it ran without stopping to Albany. By the time it was nearing the latter place Suzanne was going to bed—and because it was a private car—Mrs. Dale explained that the president of the road had lent it to her—no announcement of its arrival, which would have aroused Suzanne, was made by the porter. When it stopped there shortly after ten o'clock it was the last car at the south end of the train, and you could hear voices calling, but just what it was was not possible to say. Suzanne, who had already gone to bed, fancied it might be Poughkeepsie or some wayside station. Her mother's statement was that since they arrived so late, the car would be switched to a siding, and they would stay aboard until morning. Nevertheless, she and Kinroy were alert to prevent any untoward demonstration or decision on Suzanne's part, and so, as the train went on, she slept soundly until Burlington in the far northern part of Vermont was reached the next morning. When she awoke and saw that the train was still speeding on, she wondered vaguely but not clearly what it could mean. There were mountains about, or rather tall, pine-covered hills, mountain streams were passed on high trestles and sections of burned woodlands were passed where forest fires had left lonely, sad charred stretches of tree trunks towering high in the air. Suddenly it occurred to Suzanne that this was peculiar, and she came out of the bath to ask why.

"Where are we, mama?" she asked. Mrs. Dale was leaning back in a comfortable willow chair reading, or pretending to read a book. Kinroy was out on the observation platform for a moment. He came back though shortly, for he was nervous as to what Suzanne would do when she discovered her whereabouts. A hamper of food had been put aboard the night before, unknown to Suzanne, and Mrs. Dale was going shortly to serve breakfast. She had not risked a maid on this journey.

"I don't know," replied her mother indifferently, looking out at a stretch of burnt woods.

"I thought we were to be in Albany a little after midnight?" said Suzanne.

"So we were," replied Mrs. Dale, preparing to confess. Kinroy came back into the car.

"Well, then," said Suzanne, pausing, looking first out of the

windows and then fixedly at her mother. It came to her as she
saw the unsettled, somewhat nervous expression in her mother's
face and eyes and in Kinroy's that this was a trick and that she
was being taken somewhere—where?—against her will.

"This is a trick, mama," she said to her mother grandly.
"You have lied to me—you and Kinroy. We are not going to
Albany at all. Where are we going?"

"I don't want to tell you now, Suzanne," replied Mrs. Dale
quietly. "Have your bath and we'll talk about it afterwards. It
doesn't matter. We're going up into Canada, if you want to
know. We are nearly there now. You'll know fast enough
when we get there."

"Mama," replied Suzanne, "this is a despicable trick! You
are going to be sorry for this. You have lied to me—you and
Kinroy. I see it now. I might have known, but I didn't believe you would lie to me, mama. I can't do anything just now,
I see that very plainly. But when the time comes, you are going
to be sorry. You can't control me this way. You ought to
know better. You yourself are going to take me back to New
York." And she fixed her mother with a steady look which be-
tokened a mastership which her mother felt nervously and
wearily she might eventually be compelled to acknowledge.

"Now, Suzanne, what's the use of talking that way?" pleaded
Kinroy. "Mama is almost crazy, as it is. She couldn't think
of any other way or thing to do."

"You hush, Kinroy," replied Suzanne. "I don't care to talk
to you. You have lied to me, and that is more than I ever did
to you. Mama, I am astonished at you," she returned to her
mother. "My mother lying to me! Very well, mama. You
have things in your hands today. I will have them in mine later.
You have taken just the wrong course. Now you wait and see."

Mrs. Dale winced and quailed. This girl was the most un-
terrified, determined fighter she had ever known. She wondered
where she got her courage—from her late husband, probably.
She could actually feel the quietness, grit, lack of fear, which had
grown up in her during the last few weeks under the provocation which antagonism had provided. "Please don't talk that
way, Suzanne," she pleaded. "I have done it all for your own
good. You know I have. Why will you torture me? You
know I won't give you up to that man. I won't. I'll move
heaven and earth first. I'll die in this struggle, but I won't give
you up."

"Then you'll die, mama, for I'm going to do what I said.
You can take me to where this car stops, but you can't take me

out of it. I'm going back to New York. Now, a lot you have accomplished, haven't you?"

"Suzanne, I am convinced almost that you are out of your mind. You have almost driven me out of mine, but I am still sane enough to see what is right."

"Mama, I don't propose to talk to you any more, or to Kinroy. You can take me back to New York, or you can leave me, but you will not get me out of this car. I am done with listening to nonsense and pretences. You have lied to me once. You will not get a chance to do it again."

"I don't care, Suzanne," replied her mother, as the train sped swiftly along. "You have forced me to do this. It is your own attitude that is causing all the trouble. If you would be reasonable and take some time to think this all over, you would not be where you are now. I won't let you do this thing that you want to do. You can stay in the car if you wish, but you cannot be taken back to New York without money. I will speak to the station agent about that."

Suzanne thought of this. She had no money, no clothes, other than those she had on. She was in a strange country and not so very used to travelling alone. She had really gone to very few places in times past by herself. It took the edge off her determination to resist, but she was not conquered by any means.

"How are you going to get back?" asked her mother, after a time, when Suzanne paid no attention to her. "You have no money. Surely, Suzanne, you are not going to make a scene? I only want you to come up here for a few weeks so that you will have time to think away from that man. I don't want you to go to him on September the fifteenth. I just won't let you do that. Why won't you be reasonable? You can have a pleasant time up here. You like to ride. You are welcome to do that. I will ride with you. You can invite some of your friends up here, if you choose. I will send for your clothes. Only stay here a while and think over what you are going to do."

Suzanne refused to talk. She was thinking what she could do. Eugene was back in New York. He would expect her Thursday.

"Yes, Suzanne," put in Kinroy. "Why not take ma's advice? She's trying to do the best thing by you. This is a terrible thing you are trying to do. Why not listen to common sense and stay up here three or four months?"

"Don't talk like a parrot, Kinroy! I'm hearing all this from mama."

When her mother reproached her, she said: "Oh, hush,

mama, I don't care to hear anything more. I won't do anything of the sort. You lied to me. You said you were going to Albany. You brought me out here under a pretence. Now you can take me back. I won't go to any lodge. I won't go anywhere, except to New York. You might just as well not argue with me."

The train rolled on. Breakfast was served. The private car was switched to the tracks of the Canadian Pacific at Montreal. Her mother's pleas continued. Suzanne refused to eat. She sat and looked out of the window, meditating over this strange dénouement. Where was Eugene? What was he doing? What would he think when she did not come back? She was not enraged at her mother. She was merely contemptuous of her. This trick irritated and disgusted her. She was not thinking of Eugene in any wild way, but merely that she would get back to him. She conceived of him much as she did of herself—though her conception of her real self was still vague—as strong, patient, resourceful, able to live without her a little while if he had to. She was eager to see him, but really more eager that he should see her if he wanted to. What a creature he must take her mother to be!

By noon they had reached Juinata, by two o'clock they were fifty miles west of Quebec. At first, Suzanne thought she would not eat at all to spite her mother. Later she reasoned that that was silly and ate. She made it exceedingly unpleasant for them by her manner, and they realized that by bringing her away from New York they had merely transferred their troubles. Her spirit was not broken as yet. It filled the car with a disturbing vibration.

"Suzanne," questioned her mother at one point, "won't you talk to me? Won't you see I'm trying to do this for your own good? I want to give you time to think. I really don't want to coerce you, but you must see."

Suzanne merely stared out of the window at the green fields speeding by.

"Suzanne! Don't you see this will never do? Can't you see how terrible it all is?"

"Mama, I want you to let me alone. You have done what you thought was the right thing to do. Now let me alone. You lied to me, mama. I don't want to talk to you. I want you to take me back to New York. You have nothing else to do. Don't try to explain. You haven't any explanation."

Mrs. Dale's spirit fairly raged, but it was impotent in the presence of this her daughter. She could do nothing.

Still more hours, and at one small town Suzanne decided to get off, but both Mrs. Dale and Kinroy offered actual physical opposition. They felt intensely silly and ashamed, though, for they could not break the spirit of the girl. She ignored their minds—their mental attitude in the most contemptuous way. Mrs. Dale cried. Then her face hardened. Then she pleaded. Her daughter merely looked loftily away.

At Three Rivers Suzanne stayed in the car and refused to move. Mrs. Dale pleaded, threatened to call aid, stated that she would charge her with insanity. It was all without avail. The car was uncoupled after the conductor had asked Mrs. Dale if she did not intend to leave it. She was beside herself, frantic with rage, shame, baffled opposition.

"I think you are terrible!" she exclaimed to Suzanne. "You are a little demon. We will live in this car, then. We will see."

She knew that this could not be, for the car was only leased for the outward trip and had to be returned the next day.

The car was pushed on to a siding.

"I beg of you, Suzanne. Please don't make a mockery of us. This is terrible. What will people think?"

"I don't care what they think," said Suzanne.

"But you can't stay here."

"Oh, yes, I can!"

"Come, get off, please do. We won't stay up here indefinitely. I'll take you back. Promise me to stay a month and I'll give you my solemn word I'll take you back at the end of that time. I'm getting sick of this. I can't stand it. Do what you like after that. Only stay a month now."

"No, mama," replied Suzanne. "No, you won't. You lied to me. You're lying to me now, just as you did before."

"I swear to you I'm not. I lied that once, but I was frantic. Oh, Suzanne, please, please. Be reasonable. Have some consideration. I will take you back, but wait for some clothes to arrive. We can't go this way."

She sent Kinroy for the station master, to whom was explained the need of a carriage to take them to Mont Cecile and also for a doctor—this was Mrs. Dale's latest thought—to whom she proposed to accuse Suzanne of insanity. Help to remove her was to be called. She told this to Suzanne, who simply glared at her.

"Get the doctor, mama," she said. "We will see if I have to go that way. But you will rue every step of this. You will be thoroughly sorry for every silly step you have taken."

When the carriage arrived, Suzanne refused to get out. The country driver, a French habitant, reported its presence at the car. Kinroy tried to soothe his sister by saying that he would help straighten matters out if she would only go peacefully.

"I'll tell you, Susie, if it isn't all arranged to suit you within a month, and you still want to go back, I'll send you the money. I have to go back tomorrow, or next day for ma, but I'll give you my word. In fact, I'll persuade mother to bring you back in two weeks. You know I never lied to you before. I never will again. Please come. Let's go over there. We can be comfortable, anyhow."

Mrs. Dale had leased the lodge from the Cathcarts by phone. It was all furnished—ready to live in—even wood fires prepared for lighting in the fireplaces. It had hot and cold water controlled by a hot-water furnace system; acetylene gas, a supply of staples in the kitchen. The service to take care of it was to be called together by the caretaker, who could be reached by phone from the depot. Mrs. Dale had already communicated with him by the time the carriage arrived. The roads were so poor that the use of an automobile was impossible. The station agent, seeing a fat fee in sight, was most obliging.

Suzanne listened to Kinroy, but she did not believe him. She did not believe anyone now, save Eugene, and he was nowhere near to advise her. Still, since she was without money and they were threatening to call a doctor, she thought it might be best perhaps to go peacefully. Her mother was most distracted. Her face was white and thin and nervous, and Kinroy was apparently strained to the breaking point.

"Do you promise me faithfully," she asked her mother, who had begun her pleadings anew, corroborating Kinroy in a way, "that you will take me back to New York in two weeks if I promise to stay that long? This was still within the date in which she had promised to go to Witla, and as long as she got back by that time, she really did not care, provided she could write to her lover. It was a silly arbitrary thing for her mother to have done, but it could be endured. Her mother, seeing no reasonable way to obtain peace, promised. If she could only keep her there two weeks quietly, perhaps that would help. Suzanne could think here under different conditions. New York was so exciting. Out at this lodge all would be still. There was more argument, and, finally, Suzanne agreed to enter the hack, and they drove over toward Mont Cecile and the Cathcarts' Lodge, now vacant and lonely, which was known as "While-a-Way."

CHAPTER XVIII

THE Cathcart Lodge, a long, two-story affair, half-way up a fine covered mountain slope, was one of those summer conveniences of the rich, situated just near enough to the primeval wilds to give one a sense of the unexplored and dangerous in raw nature, and yet near enough to the comforts of civilization, as represented by the cities of Quebec and Montreal, to make one feel secure in the possession of those material joys, otherwise so easily interrupted. It was full of great rooms tastefully furnished with simple summery things—willow chairs, box window-seats, structural book shelves, great open fireplaces, surmounted by handsome mantels, outward swinging leaded casements, settees, pillow-strewn rustic couches, great fur rugs and robes and things of that character. The walls were ornamented with trophies of the chase—antlers, raw fox skins, mounted loons and eagles, skins of bears and other animals. This year the Cathcarts were elsewhere, and the lodge was to be had by a woman of Mrs. Dale's standing for the asking.

When they reached While-a-Way, the caretaker, Pierre, an old habitant of musty log-hut origin, who spoke broken English and was dressed in earth-brown khaki over Heaven knows what combination of clothes beneath, had lighted the fires and was bestirring himself about warming the house generally with the furnaces. His wife, a small, broad-skirted, solid-bodied woman, was in the kitchen preparing something to eat. There was plenty of meat to be had from the larder of the habitant himself, to say nothing of flour, butter, and the like. A girl to serve was called from the family of a neighboring trapper. She had worked in the lodge as maid to the Cathcarts. They settled down to make themselves comfortable, but the old discussion continued. There was no cessation to it, and through it all, actually, Suzanne was having her way.

Meanwhile, Eugene back in New York was expecting word from Suzanne on Thursday, and none came. He called up the house only to learn that Mrs. Dale was out of the city and was not expected back soon. Friday came, and no word; and Saturday. He tried a registered letter "for personal delivery only, return signature demanded," but it came back marked "not there." Then he realized that his suspicions were correct and that Suzanne had fallen into a trap. He grew gloomy, fearful, impatient and nervous by turn, and all at the same time. He drummed on his desk at the office, tried almost in vain to fix his mind on the scores of details which were ever before him, wandered aimlessly about the streets at times, thinking. He was asked for his opinion on art plans, and books, and advertising and circulation propositions, but he could not fix his mind closely on what was being said.

"The chief has certainly got something on his mind which is troubling him these days," said Carter Hayes, the advertising man, to the circulation head. "He's not himself. I don't believe he hears what I'm telling him."

"I've noticed that," replied the latter. They were in the reception room outside Eugene's door, and strolled arm in arm down the richly carpeted hall to the elevator. "There's certainly something wrong. He ought to take a rest. He's trying to do too much."

Hayes did not believe Eugene was trying to do too much. In the last four or five months it had been almost impossible to get near him. He came down at ten or ten-thirty in the morning, left frequently at two and three, had lunch engagements which had nothing to do with office work, and at night went into the social world to dinner or elsewhere, where he could not be found. Colfax had sent for him on a number of occasions when he was not present, and on several other occasions, when he had called on his floor and at his office, Eugene was out. It did not strike him as anything to complain of—Eugene had a right to be about—but as inadvisable, in the managing publisher's own interest. He knew that he had a vast number of things to take care of. It would take an exceptionally efficient man to manage them and not give all his time to them. He would not have thought this if Eugene had been a partner with himself, as were other men in other ventures in which he was interested, but not being so, he could not help viewing him as an employee, one who ought to give all his time to his work.

White never asked anything much save the privilege of working, and was always about the place, alert, earnest at his particular duties, not haughty, but calm and absolutely efficient in every way. He was never weary of consulting with Colfax, whereas Eugene was indifferent, not at all desirous of running to him with every little proposition, but preferring to act on his own initiative, and carrying himself constantly with very much of an air.

In other ways there were other things which were and had been militating against him. By degrees it had come to be rumored about the office that Eugene was interested in the Blue Sea or Sea Island Development and Construction Company, of which there was a good deal of talk about the city, particularly in financial and social circles. Colfax had heard of the corporation. He had been interested in the scheme because it promised so much in the way of luxury. Not much of the panoramic whole so beautifully depicted in the colored insets of a thirty-two-page literary prospectus fathered by Eugene was as yet accomplished, but there was enough to indicate that it was going to be a great thing. Already somewhat over a mile and a quarter of the great sea walk and wall were in place. A dining and dancing pavilion had been built, and one of the smaller hotels—all in accordance with the original architectural scheme. There were a number of houses—something like twenty or thirty—on plots one hundred and fifty by one hundred and fifty feet, built in the most ornate fashion on ground which had formerly been wet marsh grown high with grass. Three or four islands had been filled in and the club house of a minor yacht club had been constructed, but still the Sea Island Development Company had a long way to go before even a third of its total perfection would be in sight.

Eugene did not know the drift of the company's financial affairs, except in a general way. He had tried to keep out of it so far as public notice of him was concerned, though he was constantly lunching with Winfield, Willebrand, and others, and endeavoring to direct as much attention to the wonders and prospects of the new resort as was possible for him to do. It was an easy thing for him to say to one person and another whom he met that Blue Sea was rapidly becoming the most perfect thing in the way of a summer resort that he had ever seen, and this did good; so did the comments of all the other people who were interested in it, but it did not make it anything of a success as yet. As a matter of fact, the true success of Blue Sea depended on the investment of much more than the original ten millions for which it had been capitalized. It depended on a truly solid growth, which could not be rapid.

The news which came to the United Magazines Corporation and eventually to Colfax and White was that Eugene was heavily interested in this venture, that he was secretary or held some other office in connection with it, and that he was giving a great deal of his time to its development, which might better be employed in furthering the interests of the United Magazines Corporation.

"What do you think of that?" asked Colfax of White, on

hearing the news one morning. It had come through the head of the printing department under White, who had mentioned it to Colfax in White's presence by the latter's directions.

"It's just what I've been telling you all along," said the latter blandly. "He isn't interested in this business any more than he is in any other. He's using it as a stepping-stone, and when he's through with it, good-bye. Now that's all right from his point of view. Every man has a right to climb up, but it isn't so good from yours. You'd be better off if you had a man who wanted to stay here. You'd be better off really if you were handling it yourself. You may not want to do that, but with what you know now you can get someone who will work under you quite well. That's the one satisfactory thing about it—you really can get along without him if it comes right down to it now. With a good man in there, it can be handled from your office."

It was about this time that the most ardent phase of Eugene's love affair with Suzanne began. All through the spring and summer Eugene had been busy with thoughts of Suzanne, ways of meeting her, pleasurable rides with her, thinking of things she had done and said. As a rule now, his thoughts were very far from the interests of his position, and in the main it bored him greatly. He began to wish earnestly that his investment in the Sea Island Corporation would show some tangible return in the way of interest, so that he could have means to turn round with. It struck him after Angela's discovery of his intrigue with Suzanne as a most unfortunate thing that he had tied up all his means in this Blue Sea investment. If it had been fated that he was to go on living with Angela, it would have been all right. Then he could have waited in patience and thought nothing of it. Now it simply meant that if he wanted to realize it, it would all be tied up in the courts, or most likely so, for Angela could sue him; and at any rate he would wish to make reasonable provision for her, and that would require legal adjustment. Apart from this investment, he had nothing now save his salary, and that was not accumulating fast enough to do him much good in case Mrs. Dale went to Colfax soon, and the latter broke with him. He wondered if Colfax really would break with him. Would he ask him to give up Suzanne, or simply force him to resign? He had noticed that for some time Colfax had not been as cordial to and as enthusiastic about him as he had formerly been, but this might be due to other things besides opposition. Moreover, it was natural for them to become a little tired of each other. They did not go about so much together, and when they did Colfax was not as high-flown and boyish in his spirits as he had formerly been. Eugene fancied it was White who was caballing against him, but he thought if Colfax was going to change, he was going to change, and there was no help for it. There were no grounds, he fancied, in so far as the affairs of the corporation were concerned. His work was successful.

The storm broke one day out of a clear sky, in so far as the office was concerned, but not until there had been much heartache and misery in various directions—with the Dales, with Angela, and with Eugene himself.

Suzanne's action was the lightning bolt which precipitated the storm. It could only come from that quarter. Eugene was frantic to hear from her, and for the first time in his life began to experience those excruciating and gnawing pangs which are the concomitants of uncertain and distraught love. It manifested itself in an actual pain in his vitals—in the region of the solar plexus, or what is commonly known as the pit of the stomach. He suffered there very much, quite as the Spartan boy may have done who was gnawed by the fox concealed under his belt. He would wonder where Suzanne was, what she was doing, and then, being unable to work, would call his car and ride, or take his hat and walk. It did him no good to ride, for the agony was in sitting still. At night he would go home and sit by one or the other of his studio windows, principally out on the little stone balcony, and watch the changing panorama of the Hudson, yearning and wondering where she was. Would he ever see her again? Would he be able to win this battle if he did? Oh, her beautiful face, her lovely voice, her exquisite lips and eyes, the marvel of her touch and beautiful fancy!

He tried to compose poetry to her, and wrote a series of sonnets to his beloved, which were not at all bad. He worked on his sketch book of pencil portraits of Suzanne seeking a hundred significant and delightful expressions and positions, which could afterwards be elaborated into his gallery of paintings of her, which he proposed to paint at some time. It did not matter to him that Angela was about, though he had the graciousness to conceal these things from her. He was ashamed, in a way, of his treatment of her, and yet the sight of her now was not so much pitiable as objectionable and unsatisfactory. Why had he married her? He kept asking himself that.

They sat in the studio one night. Angela's face was a picture of despair, for the horror of her situation was only by degrees coming to her, and she said, seeing him so moody and despondent:

"Eugene, don't you think you can get over this? You say Suzanne has been spirited away. Why not let her go? Think of your career, Eugene. Think of me. What will become of me? You can get over it, if you try. Surely you won't throw me down after all the years I have been with you. Think how I have tried. I have been a pretty good wife to you, haven't I? I haven't annoyed you so terribly much, have I? Oh, I feel all the time as though we were on the brink of some terrible catastrophe! If only I could do something; if only I could say something! I know I have been hard and irritable at times, but that is all over now. I am a changed woman. I would never be that way any more."

"It can't be done, Angela," he replied calmly. "It can't be done. I don't love you. I've told you that. I don't want to live with you. I can't. I want to get free in some way, either by divorce, or a quiet separation, and go my way. I'm not happy. I never will be as long as I am here. I want my freedom and then I will decide what I want to do."

Angela shook her head and sighed. She could scarcely believe that this was she wandering around in her own apartment wondering what she was going to do in connection with her own husband. Marietta had gone back to Wisconsin before the storm broke. Myrtle was in New York, but she hated to confess to her. She did not dare to write to any member of her own family but Marietta, and she did not want to confess to her. Marietta had fancied while she was here that they were getting along nicely. She had fits of crying, which alternated with fits of anger, but the latter were growing weak. Fear, despondency, and grief were becoming uppermost in her soul again—the fear and despondency that had weighed her down in those lonely days before she married Eugene, the grief that she was now actually and finally to lose the one man whom, in spite of everything, she loved still.

CHAPTER XIX

IT was three days later when he was at his office that a telegram came from Mrs. Dale, which read, "I depend on you,
on the honor of a gentleman, to ignore any message which may
come from my daughter until I see you."

Eugene was puzzled, but fancied that there must be a desperate quarrel on between Suzanne and her mother, wherever
they were, and that it was probable that he would hear from
her now. It was his first inkling as to her whereabouts, for
the telegram was sent off from Three Rivers, in Canada, and he
fancied they must be near there somewhere. The place of des-
patch did him no good from a material point of view, for he
could neither write nor pursue Suzanne on the strength of this.
He would not know where to find her. He could only wait,
conscious that she was having a struggle, perhaps as severe, or
possibly more so, than his own. He wandered about with this
telegram in his pocket wondering when he should hear—what a
day should bring forth, and all those who came in contact with
him noticed that there was something wrong.

Colfax saw him, and asked: "What's the matter, old man?
You're not looking as chipper as you might." He fancied it
might be something in connection with the Blue Sea Corporation.
He had heard, after he had learned that Eugene was in it, that
it would take much more money than had been invested to date
to make it a really successful seaside proposition according to the
original outlines, and that it would be years before it could possibly yield an adequate return. If Eugene had put much money
in it, he had probably lost it or tied it up in a most unsatisfactory way. Well, it served him right for trifling with things he
knew nothing about.

"Oh, nothing," replied Eugene abstractedly. "I'm all right.
I'm just a little run down physically. I'll come round."

"You'd better take a month or so off and brace up, if you're
not in shape."

"Oh, not at all! Not now, anyhow."

It occurred to Eugene that he might use the time to advantage
a little later and that he would claim it.

They proceeded to business, but Colfax noticed that Eugene's
eyes were specially hollow and weary and that he was noticeably

restless. He wondered whether he might be going to break down physically.

Suzanne had drifted along peacefully enough considering the nature of the feeling between her and her mother at this time. After a few days of desultory discussion, however, along the lines now so familiar, she began to see that her mother had no intention of terminating their stay at the time agreed upon, particularly since their return to New York meant, so far as Suzanne was concerned, her immediate departure to Witla. Mrs. Dale began at first to plead for additional delay, and later that Suzanne should agree not to go to New York but to Lenox for a season. It was cold up here already now, though there were still spells of bright warm summery or autumn weather between ten and four in the day, and sometimes in the evening. The nights usually were cold. Mrs. Dale would gladly have welcomed a compromise, for it was terribly lonely, just herself and Suzanne—after the gaieties of New York. Four days before the time of her proposed departure, Mrs. Dale was still obdurate or parleying in a diplomatic way, and Suzanne, disgusted, made the threat which caused Mrs. Dale to wire distractedly to Eugene. Later, she composed the following, which she gave to Gabrielle:

"DEAR EUGENE—

If you love me, come and get me. I have told mama that if she did not keep her word to return with me to New York by the fifteenth, I would write to you and she is still obstinate. I am at the Cathcart Lodge, While-a-Way, eighteen miles north of Three Rivers, here in Canada. Anyone can show you. I will be here when you come. Do not try to write to me as I am afraid I should not get it. But I will be at the Lodge.

"With love,

"SUZANNE."

Eugene had never before received a love appeal, nor indeed any such appeal from any woman in his life.

This letter reached him thirty-six hours after the telegram arrived, and set him to planning at once. The hour had struck. He must act. Perhaps this old world was now behind him forever. Could he really get Suzanne, if he went to Canada to find her? How was she surrounded? He thrilled with delight when he realized that it was Suzanne who was calling him and that he was going to find her. "If you love me, come and get me."

Would he?

Watch!

He called for his car, telephoned his valet to pack his bag and bring it to the Grand Central Station, first ascertaining for himself the time of departure, asked to talk to Angela, who had gone to Myrtle's apartment in upper Seventh Avenue, ready at last to confess her woes to Eugene's sister. Her condition did not appeal to Eugene in this situation. The inevitable result, which he thought of frequently, was still far away. He notified Colfax that he was going to take a few days rest, went to the bank where he had over four thousand dollars on deposit, and drew it all. He then went to a ticket office and purchased a one-way ticket, uncertain where his actions would take him once he saw Suzanne. He tried once more to get Angela, intending boldly to tell her that he was going to seek Suzanne, and to tell her not to worry, that he would communicate with her, but she had not returned. Curiously, through all this, he was intensely sorry for her, and wondered how she would take it, if he did not return. How would the child be arranged for? He felt he must go. Angela was heartsick, he knew that, and frightened. Still he could not resist this call. He could not resist anything in connection with this love affair. He was like a man possessed of a devil or wandering in a dream. He knew that his whole career was at stake, but it did not make any difference. He must get her. The whole world could go hang if he could only obtain her—her, the beautiful, the perfect!

At five-thirty the train departed, and then he sat as it rolled northward speculating on what he was to do when he got there. If Three Rivers were much of a place, he could probably hire an automobile. He could leave it some distance from the lodge and then see if he could not approach unobserved and signal Suzanne. If she were about, she would no doubt be on the lookout. At a sign she would run to him. They would hurry to the automobile. The pursuit might quickly follow, but he would arrange it so that his pursuers would not know which railroad station he was going to. Quebec was the nearest big city, he found by studying the map, though he might return to Montreal and New York or Buffalo, if he chose to go west— he would see how the train ran.

It is curious what vagaries the human mind is subject to, under conditions of this kind. Up to the time of Eugene's arrival in Three Rivers and after, he had no plan of campaign, or of future conduct beyond that of obtaining Suzanne. He did not know that he would return to New York—he did not know that he would not. If Suzanne wished, and it were best, and they could, they would go to England from Montreal, or France.

If necessary, they could go to Portland and sail. Mrs. Dale, on the evidence that he had Suzanne and that of her own free will and volition, might yield and say nothing, in which case he could return to New York and resume his position. This courageous stand on his part if he had only followed it might have solved the whole problem quickly. It might have been the sword that would have cut the Gordian Knot. On the train was a heavy black-bearded man, which was always good luck to him. At Three Rivers, when he dismounted from the train, he found a horseshoe, which was also a lucky sign. He did not stop to think what he would do if he really lost his position and had to live on the sum he had with him. He was really not thinking logically. He was dreaming. He fancied that he would get Suzanne and have his salary, and that somehow things would be much as they were. Of such is the logic of dreams.

When he arrived at Three Rivers, of course the conditions were not what he anticipated. It is true that at times, after a long continued period of dry weather, the roads were passable for automobiles, at least as far as While-a-Way, but the weather had not recently been entirely dry. There had been a short period of cold rain and the roads were practically impassable, save for horses and carryalls. There was a carryall which went as far as St. Jacques, four miles from While-a-Way, where the driver told him he could get a horse, if he wanted one. The owner of this hack line had a stable there.

This was gratifying to him, and he decided to make arrangements for two horses at St. Jacques, which he would take to within a reasonable distance of the lodge and tie in some spot where they would not be seen. Then he could consider the situation and signal Suzanne; if she were there on the lookout. How dramatic the end would be! How happy they would be flying together! Judge then his astonishment on reaching St. Jacques to find Mrs. Dale waiting for him. Word had been telephoned by her faithful representative, the station agent at Three Rivers, that a man of Eugene's description had arrived and departed for While-a-Way. Before this a telegram had come from New York from Kinroy to the effect that Eugene had gone somewhere. His daily habits since Mrs. Dale had gone away had been under observation. Kinroy, on his return, had called at the United Magazines Corporation and asked if Eugene was in the city. Heretofore he had been reported in. When on this day he was reported as having gone, Kinroy called up Angela to inquire. She also stated that he had left the city. He then wired his mother and she, calculating the time of his arrival, and hearing from the station agent of his taking the carryall, had gone down to meet him. She had decided to fight every inch of the way with all the strategy at her command. She did not want to kill him— had not really the courage to do that—but she still hoped to dissuade him. She had not been able to bring herself to resort to guards and detectives as yet. He could not be as hard as he looked and acted. Suzanne was bedeviling him by her support and communications. She had not been able to govern there, she saw. Her only hope was to talk him out of it, or into an additional delay. If necessary, they would all go back to New York together and she would appeal to Colfax and Winfield. She hoped they would persuade him to reason. Anyhow, she would never leave Suzanne for one moment until this thing had been settled in her favor, or brutally against her.

When Eugene appeared she greeted him with her old social smile and called to him affably: "Come, get in."

He looked at her grimly and obeyed, but changed his manner when he saw that she was really kindly in her tone and greeted her sociably.

"How have you been?" he asked.

"Oh, quite well, thank you!"

"And how is Suzanne?"

"All right, I fancy. She isn't here, you know."

"Where is she?" asked Eugene, his face a study in defeat.

"She went with some friends to visit Quebec for ten days. Then she is going from there to New York. I don't expect to see her here any more."

Eugene choked with a sense of repugnance to her airy taradiddles. He did not believe what she was saying—saw at once that she was fencing with him.

"That's a lie," he said roughly, "and it's out of the whole cloth! She's here, and you know it. Anyhow, I am going to see for myself."

"How polite you are!" she laughed diplomatically. "That isn't the way you usually talk. Anyhow, she isn't here. You'll find that out, if you insist. I wouldn't advise you to insist, for I've sent for counsel since I heard you were coming, and you will find detectives as well as guards waiting to receive you. She isn't here, though, even at that, and you might just as well turn round and go back. I will drive you over to Three Rivers, if you wish. Why not be reasonable, now, and avoid a scene? She isn't here. You couldn't have her if she were. The people I have employed will prevent that. If you make trouble, you will simply be arrested and then the newspapers will have it.

Why not be reasonable now, Mr. Witla, and go on back? You
have everything to lose. There is a train through Three Rivers
from Quebec for New York at eleven tonight. We can make
it. Don't you want to do that? I will agree, if you come to
your senses now, and cause me no trouble here, to bring Suzanne
back to New York within a month. I won't let you have her
unless you get a divorce and straighten things out with your
wife, but if you can do that within six months, or a year, and
she still wants you, you can have her. I will promise in writing
to withdraw all objection, and see that her full share of her
property comes to her uncontested. I will help you and her
socially all I can. You know I am not without influence."

"I want to see her first," replied Eugene grimly and disbe-
lievingly.

"I won't say that I will forget everything," went on Mrs.
Dale, ignoring his interpolated remark. "I can't—but I will
pretend to. You can have the use of my country place at
Lenox. I will buy out the lease at Morristown, or the New
York House, and you can live in either place. I will set aside
a sum of money for your wife, if you wish. That may help you
obtain your release. Surely you do not want to take her under
the illegal condition which you propose, when you can have her
outright in this brilliant manner by waiting a little while. She
says she does not want to get married, but that is silly talk,
based on nothing except erratic reading. She does, or she will,
the moment she comes to think about it seriously. Why not
help her? Why not go back now and let me bring her to New
York a little later and then we will talk this all over. I shall
be very glad to have you in my family. You are a brilliant
man. I have always liked you. Why not be reasonable? Come
now and let's drive over to Three Rivers and you take the train
back to New York, will you?"

While Mrs. Dale had been talking, Eugene had been surveying her calmly. What a clever talker she was! How she could
lie! He did not believe her. He did not believe one word that
she said. She was fighting to keep him from Suzanne, why he
could readily understand. Suzanne was somewhere, here, he
fancied, though, as in the case of her recent trip to Albany, she
might have been spirited away.

"Absurd!" said Eugene easily, defiantly, indifferently. "I'll
not do anything of the sort. In the first place, I don't believe you. If you are so anxious to be nice to me, let me see
her, and then you can say all this in front of her. I've come up
here to see her, and I'm going to. She's here. I know she is.

You needn't lie. You needn't talk. I know she's here. Now I'm going to see her, if I have to stay here a month and search."

Mrs. Dale stirred nervously. She knew that Eugene was desperate. She knew that Suzanne had written to him. Talk might be useless. Strategy might not avail, but she could not help using it.

"Listen to me," she said excitedly. "I tell you Suzanne is not here. She's gone. There are guards up there—lots of them. They know who you are. They have your description. They have orders to kill you, if you try to break in. Kinroy is there. He is desperate. I have been having a struggle to prevent his killing you already. The place is watched. We are watched at this moment. Won't you be reasonable? You can't see her. She's gone. Why make all this fuss? Why take your life in your hands?"

"Don't talk," said Eugene. "You're lying. I can see it in your face. Besides, my life is nothing. I am not afraid. Why talk? She's here. I'm going to see her."

He stared before him and Mrs. Dale ruminated as to what she was to do. There were no guards or detectives, as she said. Kinroy was not there. Suzanne was not away. This was all palaver, as Eugene suspected, for she was too anxious to avoid publicity to give any grounds for it, before she was absolutely driven.

It was a rather halcyon evening after some days of exceeding chill. A bright moon was coming up in the east, already discernible in the twilight, but which later would shine brilliantly. It was not cold but really pleasantly warm, and the rough road along which they were driving was richly odorous. Eugene was not unconscious of its beauty, but depressed by the possibility of Suzanne's absence.

"Oh, do be generous," pleaded Mrs. Dale, who feared that once they saw each other, reason would disappear. Suzanne would demand, as she had been continually demanding, to be taken back to New York. Eugene with or without Suzanne's consent or plea, would ignore her overtures of compromise and there would be immediate departure or defiant union here. She thought she would kill them if need be, but in the face of Eugene's defiant persistence on one side, and Suzanne's on the other, her courage was failing. She was frightened by the daring of this man. "I will keep my word," she observed distractedly. "Honestly she isn't here. She's in Quebec, I tell you. Wait a month. I will bring her back then. We will arrange things together. Why can't you be generous?"

"I could be," said Eugene, who was considering all the brilliant prospects which her proposal involved and being moved by them, "but I can't believe you. You're not telling me the truth. You didn't tell the truth to Suzanne when you took her from New York. That was a trick, and this is another. I know she isn't away. She's right up there in the lodge, wherever it is. You take me to her and then we will talk this thing out together. By the way, where are you going?"

Mrs. Dale had turned into a bypath or half-formed road closely lined with small trees and looking as though it might be a woodchoppers' path.

"To the lodge."

"I don't believe it," replied Eugene, who was intensely suspicious. "This isn't a main road to any such place as that."

"I tell you it is."

Mrs. Dale was nearing the precincts of the lodge and wanted more time to talk and plead.

"Well," said Eugene, "you can go this way if you want to. I'm going to get out and walk. You can't throw me off by driving me around in some general way. I'm going to stay here a week, a month, two months, if necessary, but I'm not going back without seeing Suzanne. She's here, and I know it. I'll go up alone and find her. I'm not afraid of your guards."

He jumped out and Mrs. Dale gave up in despair. "Wait," she pleaded. "It's over two miles yet. I'll take you there. She isn't home tonight, anyhow. She's over at the cottage of the caretaker. Oh, why won't you be reasonable? I'll bring her to New York, I tell you. Are you going to throw aside all those fine prospects and wreck your life and hers and mine? Oh, if Mr. Dale were only alive! If I had a man on whom I could rely! Come, get in, and I'll drive you up there, but promise me you won't ask to see her tonight. She isn't there, anyway. She's over at the caretaker's. Oh, dear, if only something would happen to solve this!"

"I thought you said she was in Quebec?"

"I only said that to gain time. I'm so unstrung. It wasn't true, but she isn't at the lodge, truly. She's away tonight. I can't let you stay there. Let me take you back to St. Jacques and you can stay with old Pierre Gaine. You can come up in the morning. The servants will think it so strange. I promise you you shall see Suzanne. I give you my word."

"Your word. Why, Mrs. Dale, you're going around in a ring! I can't believe anything you say," replied Eugene calmly. He was very much collected and elated now since he knew that

Suzanne was here. He was going to see her—he felt it. He had Mrs. Dale badly worsted, and he proposed to drive her until, in the presence of Suzanne, he and his beloved dictated terms.

"I'm going there tonight and you are going to bring her to me. If she isn't there, you know where to find her. She's here, and I'm going to see her tonight. We'll talk of all this you're proposing in front of her. It's silly to twist things around this way. The girl is with me, and you know it. She's mine. You can't control her. Now we two will talk to you together."

He sat back in the light vehicle and began to hum a tune. The moon was getting clearer.

"Promise me just one thing," urged Mrs. Dale despairingly. "Promise me that you will urge Suzanne to accept my proposition. A few months won't hurt. You can see her in New York as usual. Go about getting a divorce. You are the only one who has any influence with her. I admit it. She won't believe me. She won't listen to me. You tell her. Your future is in it. Persuade her to wait. Persuade her to stay up here or at Lenox for a little while and then come down. She will obey you. She will believe anything you say. I have lied. I have lied terribly all through this, but you can't blame me. Put yourself in my place. Think of my position. Please use your influence. I will do all that I say and more."

"Will you bring Suzanne to me tonight?"

"Yes, if you promise."

"Will you bring her to me tonight, promise or no promise? I don't want to say anything to you which I can't say in front of her."

"Won't you promise me that you will accept my proposition and urge her to?"

"I think I will, but I won't say. I want her to hear what you have to say. I think I will."

Mrs. Dale shook her head despondently.

"You might as well acquiesce," went on Eugene. "I'm going to see her anyhow, whether you will or no. She's there, and I'll find her if I have to search the house room by room. She can hear my voice."

He was carrying things with a high hand.

"Well," replied Mrs. Dale, "I suppose I must. Please don't let on to the servants. Pretend you're my guest. Let me take you back to St. Jacques tonight, after you see her. Don't stay with her more than half an hour."

She was absolutely frightened out of her wits at this terrific dénouement.

Eugene sat grimly congratulating himself as they jogged on in the moonlight. He actually squeezed her arm cheerfully and told her not to be so despairing—that all would come out all right. They would talk to Suzanne. He would see what she would have to say.

"You stay here," she said, as they reached a little wooded knoll in a bend of the road—a high spot commanding a vast stretch of territory now lit by a glistening northern moon. "I'll go right inside and get her. I don't know whether she's there, but if she isn't, she's over at the caretaker's, and we'll go over there. I don't want the servants to see you meet her. Please don't be demonstrative. Oh, be careful!"

Eugene smiled. How excited she was! How pointless, after all her threats! So this was victory. What a fight he had made! Here he was outside this beautiful lodge, the lights of which he could see gleaming like yellow gold through the silvery shadows. The air was full of field fragrances. You could smell the dewy earth, soon to be hard and covered deep in snow. There was still a bird's voice here and there and faint stirrings of the wind in the leaves. "On such a night," came back Shakespeare's lines. How fitting that Suzanne should come to him under such conditions! Oh, the wonder of this romance—the beauty of it! From the very beginning it had been set about with perfections of scenery and material environment. Obviously, nature had intended this as the crowning event of his life. Life recognized him as a genius—the fates—it was heaping posies in his lap, laying a crown of victory upon his brow.

He waited while Mrs. Dale went to the lodge, and then after a time, true enough, there appeared in the distance the swinging, buoyant, girlish form of Suzanne. She was plump, healthful, vigorous. He could detect her in the shadows under the trees and behind her a little way Mrs. Dale. Suzanne came eagerly on—youthful, buoyant, dancing, determined, beautiful. Her skirts were swinging about her body in ripples as she strode. She looked all Eugene had ever thought her. Hebe—a young Diana, a Venus at nineteen. Her lips were parted in a welcoming smile as she drew near and her eyes were as placid as those dull opals which still burn with a hidden lustre of gold and flame.

She held out her arms to him as she came, running the last few steps.

"Suzanne!" called her mother. "For shame!"

"Hush, mama!" declared Suzanne defiantly. "I don't care. I don't care. It's your fault. You shouldn't have lied to me.

He wouldn't have come if I hadn't sent for him. I'm going back to New York. I told you I was."

She did not say, "Oh, Eugene!" as she came close, but gathered his face in her hands and looked eagerly into his eyes. His burned into hers. She stepped back and opened wide her arms only to fold them tightly about him.

"At last! At last!" he said, kissing her feverishly. "Oh, Suzanne! Oh, Flower Face!"

"I knew you would come," she said. "I told her you would. I'll go back with you."

"Yes, yes," said Eugene. "Oh, this wonderful night! This wonderful climax! Oh, to have you in my arms again!"

Mrs. Dale stood by, white, intense. To think a daughter of hers should act like this, confound her so, make her a helpless spectator of her iniquity. What an astounding, terrible, impossible thing!

"Suzanne!" she cried. "Oh, that I should have lived to see this day!"

"I told you, mama, that you would regret bringing me up here," declared Suzanne. "I told you I would write to him. I knew you would come," she said to Eugene, and she squeezed his hand affectionately.

Eugene inhaled a deep breath and stared at her. The night, the stars swung around him in a gorgeous orbit. Thus it was to be victorious. It was too beautiful, too wonderful! To think he should have triumphed in this way! Could any other man anywhere ever have enjoyed such a victory?

"Oh, Suzanne," he said eagerly, "this is like a dream; it's like heaven! I can scarcely believe I am alive."

"Yes, yes," she replied, "it is beautiful, perfect!" And together they strolled away from her mother, hand in hand.

CHAPTER XX

THE flaw in this situation was that Eugene, after getting Suzanne in his arms once more, had no particular solution to offer. Instead of at once outlining an open or secret scheme of escape, or taking her by main force and walking off with her, as she more than half expected him to do, here he was repeating to her what her mother had told him, and instead of saying "Come!" he was asking her advice.

"This is what your mother proposed to me just now, Suzanne," he began, and entered upon a full explanation. It was a vision of empire to him.

"I said to her," he said, speaking of her mother, who was near by, "that I would decide nothing. She wanted me to say that I would do this, but I insisted that it must be left to you. If you want to go back to New York, we will go, tonight or tomorrow. If you want to accept this plan of your mother's, it's all right, so far as I am concerned. I would rather have you now, but if I can see you, I am willing to wait."

He was calm now, logical, foolishly speculative. Suzanne wondered at this. She had no advice to offer. She had expected some dramatic climax, but since it had not come about, she had to be content. The truth was that she had been swept along by her desire to be with Eugene. It had seemed to her in the beginning that it was not possible for him to get a divorce. It had seemed also from her reading and youthful philosophizing that it was really not necessary. She did not want to be mean to Angela. She did not want Eugene to mortify her by openly leaving her. She had fancied since Eugene had said that Angela was not satisfactory to him and that there was no real love between them, that Angela really did not care—she had practically admitted as much in her letter—that it would not make so much difference if she shared him with her. What was he explaining now—a new theory as to what they were to do? She thought he was coming for her to take her away like a god, whereas here he was presenting a new theory to her in anything but a god-like way. It was confusing. She did not know how it was that Eugene did not want to leave at once.

"Well, I don't know—whatever you think," she said. "If you want me to stay here another month——"

"No, no!" exclaimed Eugene quickly, conscious of a flaw in

the arrangement, and anxious to make it seem right. "I didn't mean that. Not that. I want you to come back with me now, if possible, tonight, only I wanted to tell you this. Your mother seems sincere. It seems a shame if we can keep friends with her and still have our way, not to do so. I don't want to do any greater harm than I can help unless you are perfectly willing and——" He hesitated over his own thoughts.

At this moment Suzanne could scarcely have told what she felt. The crux of the situation was being put to her for her decision, and it should not be. She was not strong enough, not experienced enough. Eugene should decide, and whatever he decided would be right.

The truth was that after getting her in his arms again, and that in the presence of her mother, Eugene did not feel that he was quite so much the victor as he had imagined, or that the whole problem of his life was solved. He could not very well ignore, he thought, what Mrs. Dale had to offer, if she was offering it seriously. She had said to him just before he came into the presence of Suzanne that unless he accepted these terms she would go on fighting—that she would telegraph to Colfax and ask him to come up here. Although Eugene had drawn his money and was ready to fly if he could, still the thought of Colfax and the desire to keep his present state of social security and gain all Mrs. Dale had to offer besides were deterrents. He hesitated. Wasn't there some way to smooth everything out?

"I don't want you to decide finally," he said, "but what do you think?"

Suzanne was in a simmering, nebulous state, and could not think. Eugene was here. This was Arcady and the moon was high.

It was beautiful to have him with her again. It was wonderful to feel his caresses. But he was not flying with her. They were not defying the world; they were not doing what she fancied they would be doing, rushing to victory, and that was what she had sent for him for. Mrs. Dale was going to help Eugene get a divorce, so she said. She was going to help subsidize Angela, if necessary. Suzanne was going to get married, and actually settle down after a time. What a curious thought. Why that was not what she had wanted to do. She had wanted to flout convention in some way; to do original things as she had planned, as she had dreamed. It might be disastrous, but she did not think so. Her mother would have yielded. Why was Eugene compromising? It was curious. Such thoughts as these formulated in her mind at this time were the most disastrous things that could happen to their romance. Union should have followed his presence. Flight should have been a portion of it. As it was she was in his arms, but she was turning over vague, nebulous thoughts. Something—a pale mist before an otherwise brilliant moon; a bit of spindrift; a speck of cloud, no bigger than a man's hand that might possibly portend something and might not, had come over the situation. Eugene was as desirable as ever, but he was not flying with her. They were talking about going back to New York afterwards, but they were not going together at once. How was that?

"Do you think mama can really damage you with Mr. Colfax?" she asked curiously at one point, after Eugene had mentioned her mother's threat.

"I don't know," he replied solemnly. "Yes, I think she could. I don't know what he'd do, though. It doesn't matter much one way or the other," he added. Suzanne puzzled.

"Well, if you want to wait, it's all right," she said. "I want to do whatever you think best. I don't want you to lose your position. If you think we ought to wait, we will."

"Not if I'm not to be with you regularly," replied Eugene, who was wavering. He was not your true champion of victory —your administrative leader. Foolishly he was spelling over an arrangement whereby he could eat his cake and have it—see Suzanne, drive with her, dance with her, all but live with her in New York until such time as the actual union could be arranged secretly or openly. Mrs. Dale was promising to receive him as a son, but she was merely plotting for time—time to think, act, permit Suzanne, under argument, to come to her senses. Time would solve everything, she thought, and tonight as she hung about, keeping close and overhearing some of Eugene's remarks, she felt relieved. Either he was coming to his senses and beginning to regret his folly or he was being deluded by her lies. If she could keep him and Suzanne apart one more week, and get to New York herself, she would go to Colfax now, and to Winfield, and see if they could not be induced to use their good offices. Eugene must be broken. He was erratic, insane. Her lies were apparently plausible enough to gain her this delay, and that was all she wanted.

"Well, I don't know. Whatever you think," said Suzanne again, after a time between embraces and kisses, "do you want me to come back with you tomorrow, or——"

"Yes, yes," he replied quickly and vigorously, "tomorrow, only we must try and argue your mother into the right frame of mind. She feels that she has lost now since we are together, and we must keep her in that mind. She talks compromise and that's just what we want. If she is willing to have us make some arrangement, why not? I would be willing to let things rest for a week or so, just to give her a chance if she wishes. If she doesn't change then we can act. You could come as far as Lenox for a week, and then come on."

He talked like one who had won a great victory, whereas he had really suffered a great defeat. He was not taking Suzanne.

Suzanne brooded. It was not what she expected—but——

"Yes," she said, after a time.

"Will you return with me tomorrow?"

"Yes."

"As far as Lenox or New York?"

"We'll see what mama says. If you can agree with her—anything you want—I am willing."

After a time Eugene and Suzanne parted for the night. It was agreed that they should see each other in the morning, that they should go back as far as Lenox together. Mrs. Dale was to help Eugene get a divorce. It was a delightfully affectionate and satisfactory situation, but somehow Eugene felt that he was not handling it right. He went to bed in one part of the house —Suzanne in another—Mrs. Dale, fearful and watchful, staying near by, but there was no need. He was not desperate. He went to sleep thinking that the near future was going to adjust everything for him nicely, and that he and Suzanne were eventually going to get married.

CHAPTER XXI

THE next day, after wavering whether they would not spend a few days here in billing and cooing and listening to Mrs. Dale's veiled pleas as to what the servants might think, or what they might know already or suspect from what the station master at Three Rivers might say, they decided to return, Eugene to New York, Suzanne to Lenox. All the way back to Albany, Eugene and Suzanne sat together in one seat in the Pullman like two children rejoicing in each other's company. Mrs. Dale sat one seat away, turning over her promises and pondering whether, after all, she had not yet better go at once and try to end all by an appeal to Colfax, or whether she had better wait a little while and see if the affair might not die down of its own accord.

At Albany the following morning, Suzanne and Mrs. Dale transferred to the Boston and Albany, Eugene going on to New York. He went to the office feeling much relieved, and later in the day to his apartment. Angela, who had been under a terrific strain, stared at him as if he were a ghost, or one come back to life from the dead. She had not known where he had gone. She had not known whether he would ever come back. There was no use in reproaching him—she had realized that long since. The best she could do was to make an appeal. She waited until after dinner, at which they had discussed the mere commonplaces of life, and then came to his room, where he was unpacking.

"Did you go to find Suzanne?" she asked.

"Yes."

"Is she with you?"

"No."

"Oh, Eugene, do you know where I have spent the last three days?" she asked.

He did not answer.

"On my knees. On my knees," she declared, "asking God to save you from yourself."

"Don't talk rot, Angela," he returned coldly. "You know how I feel about this thing. How much worse am I now than I was before? I tried to get you on the phone to tell you. I went to find her and bring her back, and I did as far as Lenox. I am going to win this fight. I am going to get Suzanne, either legally or otherwise. If you want to give me a divorce, you can. I will provide amply for you. If you don't I'm going to take her, anyhow. That's understood between me and her. Now what's the use of hysterics?"

Angela looked at him tearfully. Could this be the Eugene she had known? In each scene with him, after each plea, or through it, she came to this adamantine wall. Was he really so frantic about this girl? Was he going to do what he said? He outlined to her quite calmly his plans as recently revised, and at one point Angela, speaking of Mrs. Dale, interrupted him—"she will never give her up to you—you will see. You think she will. She says she will. She is only fooling you. She is fighting for time. Think what you are doing. You can't win."

"Oh, yes, I can," said Eugene, "I practically have already. She will come to me."

"She may, she may, but at what a cost. Look at me, Eugene. Am I not enough? I am still good looking. You have declared to me time and again that I have a beautiful form. See, see"—she tore open her dressing gown and the robe de nuit, in which she had come in. She had arranged this scene, especially thought it out, and hoped it would move him. "Am I not enough? Am I not still all that you desire?"

Eugene turned his head away in disgust—wearily—sick of their melodramatic appeals. This was the last rôle Angela should have played. It was the most ineffectual, the least appropriate at the moment. It was dramatic, striking, but totally ineffective under the circumstances.

"It's useless acting in that way to me, Angela," he said. "I'm no longer to be moved in that way by you. All marital affection between us is dead—terribly so. Why plead to me with something that has no appeal. I can't help it. It's dead. Now what are we going to do about it?"

Once more Angela turned wearily. Although she was nerve worn and despairing, she was still fascinated by the tragedy which was being played out under her eyes. Would nothing make him see?

They went their separate ways for the night, and the next day he was at his desk again. Word came from Suzanne that she was still in Lenox, and then that her mother had gone to Boston for a day or two on a visit. The fifth day Colfax stepped into his office, and, hailing him pleasantly, sat down.

"Well, how are things with you, old man?" he asked.

"Oh, about the same," said Eugene. "I can't complain."

"Everything going all right with you?"

"Yes, moderately so."

"People don't usually butt in on you here when I'm here, do they?" he asked curiously.

"I've given orders against anything like that, but I'll make it doubly sure in this case," said Eugene, alert at once. Could Colfax be going to talk to him about anything in connection with his case? He paled a little.

Colfax looked out of the window at the distant panorama of the Hudson. He took out a cigar, and cut the end, but did not light it.

"I asked you about not being interrupted," he began thoughtfully, "because I have a little something I want to talk to you about, which I would rather no one else heard. Mrs. Dale came to me the other day," he said quietly. Eugene started at the mention of her name and paled still more, but gave no other outward sign. "And she told me a long story about something that you were trying to do in connection with her daughter—run away with her, or go and live with her without a license or a divorce, or desert your wife, or something to that effect, which I didn't pay much attention to, but which I have to talk to you about just the same. Now, I never like to meddle with a man's personal affairs. I don't think that they concern me. I don't think they concern this business, except in so far as they may affect it unfavorably, but I would like to know if it is true. Is it?"

"Yes," said Eugene.

"Mrs. Dale is an old friend of mine. I've known her for years. I know Mrs. Witla, of course, but not quite in the same way. I haven't seen as much of her as I have of you. I didn't know that you were unhappily married, but that is neither here nor there. The point is, that she seems to be on the verge of making a great scandal out of this—she seems a little distracted to me—and I thought I'd better come up and have a little talk with you before anything serious really happened. You know it would be a rather damaging thing to this business if any scandal were started in connection with you just at present."

He paused, expecting some protest or explanation, but Eugene merely held his peace. He was tense, pale, harried. So she had gone to Colfax, after all. Instead of going to Boston; instead of keeping her word, she had come down here to New York and gone to Colfax. Had she told him the full story? Very likely Colfax, in spite of all his smooth words, would be inclined to sympathize with her. What must he think of him?

He was rather conservative in a social way. Mrs. Dale could be of service to him in her world in one way and another. He had never seen Colfax quite so cool and deliberate as he was now. He seemed to be trying to maintain an exceedingly judicial and impartial tone, which was not characteristic.

"You have always been an interesting study to me, Witla, ever since I first met you," he went on, after a time. "You're a genius, I fancy, if there ever was one, but like all geniuses you are afflicted with tendencies which are erratic. I used to think for a little while that maybe you sat down and planned the things which you have carried through so successfully, but I have since concluded that you don't. You attract some forms of force and order. Also, I think you have various other faculties—it would be hard for me to say just what they are. One is vision. I know you have that. Another is appreciation of ability. I know you have that. I have seen you pick some exceptional people. You plan in a way, but you don't plan logically or deliberately, unless I am greatly mistaken. The matter of this Dale girl now is an interesting case in point, I think."

"Let's not talk of her," said Eugene frigidly and bridling slightly. Suzanne was a sore point with him. A dangerous subject. Colfax saw it. "That's something I can't talk about very well."

"Well, we won't," put in the other calmly, "but the point can be established in other ways. You'll admit, I think, that you haven't been planning very well in connection with this present situation, for if you had been, you would see that in doing what you have been doing you have been riding straight for a fall. If you were going to take the girl, and she was willing, as she appears to be, you should have taken her without her mother's knowledge, old man. She might have been able to adjust things afterward. If not, you would have had her, and I suppose you would have been willing to suffer the consequences, if you had been caught. As it is, you have let Mrs. Dale in on it, and she has powerful friends. You can't ignore her. I can't. She is in a fighting mood, and it looks as though she were going to bring considerable pressure to bear to make you let go."

He paused again, waiting to see if Eugene would say something, but the latter made no comment.

"I want to ask one question, and I don't want you to take any offense at it, for I don't mean anything by it, but it will help to clear this matter up in my own mind, and probably in yours later, if you will. Have you had anything to do in a compromising way with Miss——?"

"No," said Eugene before he could finish.

"How long has this fight been going on?"

"Oh, about four weeks, or a little less."

Colfax bit at the end of his cigar.

"You have powerful enemies here, you know, Witla. Your rule hasn't been very lenient. One of the things I have noticed about you is your utter inability to play politics. You have picked men who would be very glad to have your shoes, if they could. If they could get the details of this predicament, your situation wouldn't be tenable more than fifteen minutes. You know that, of course. In spite of anything I might do you would have to resign. You couldn't maintain yourself here. I couldn't let you. You haven't thought of that in this connection, I suppose. No man in love does. I know just how you feel. From having seen Mrs. Witla, I can tell in a way just what the trouble is. You have been reined in too close. You haven't been master in your own home. It's irritated you. Life has appeared to be a failure. You have lost your chance, or thought you had on this matrimonial game, and it's made you restless. I know this girl. She's beautiful. But just as I say, old man, you haven't counted the cost—you haven't calculated right—you haven't planned. If anything could prove to me what I have always faintly suspected about you, it is this: You don't plan carefully enough ——" and he looked out of the window.

Eugene sat staring at the floor. He couldn't make out just what it was that Colfax intended to do about it. He was calmer in his thinking than he had ever seen him before—less dramatic. As a rule, Colfax yelled things—demonstrated, performed—made excited motions. This morning, he was slow, thoughtful, possibly emotional.

"In spite of the fact that I like you personally, Witla—and every man owes a little something to friendship—it can't be worked out in business, though—I have been slowly coming to the conclusion that perhaps, after all, you aren't just the ideal man for this place. You're too emotional, I fancy—too erratic. White has been trying to tell me that for a long time, but I wouldn't believe it. I'm not taking his judgment now. I don't know that I would ever have acted on that feeling or idea, if this thing hadn't come up. I don't know that I am going to do so finally, but it strikes me that you are in a very ticklish position—one rather dangerous to this house, and you know

that this house could never brook a scandal. Why the newspapers would never get over it. It would do us infinite harm.
I think, viewing it all in all, that you had better take a year
off and see if you can't straighten this out quietly. I don't
think you had better try to take this girl unless you can get a
divorce and marry her, and I don't think you had better try to
get a divorce unless you can do it quietly. I mean so far as
your position here is concerned only. Apart from that, you
can do what you please. But remember! a scandal would affect your usefulness here. If things can be patched up, well
and good. If not, well then they can't. If this thing gets
talked about much, you know that there will be no hope of
your coming back here. I don't suppose you would be willing
to give her up?"

"No," said Eugene.

"I thought as much. I know just how you take a thing of
this kind. It hits your type hard. Can you get a divorce from
Mrs. Witla?"

"I'm not so sure," said Eugene. "I haven't any suitable
grounds. We simply don't agree, that's all—my life has been
a hollow shell."

"Well," said Colfax, "it's a bad mix up all around. I know
how you feel about the girl. She's very beautiful. She's just
the sort to bring about a situation of this kind. I don't want
to tell you what to do. You are your own best judge, but if
you will take my advice, you won't try to live with her without first marrying her. A man in your position can't afford to
do it. You're too much in the public eye. You know you have
become fairly conspicuous in New York during the last few
years, don't you?"

"Yes," said Eugene. "I thought I had arranged that matter with Mrs. Dale."

"It appears not. She tells me that you are trying to persuade her daughter to live with you; that you have no means of
obtaining a divorce within a reasonable time; that your wife is
in a—pardon me, and that you insist on associating with her
daughter, meanwhile, which isn't possible, according to her.
I'm inclined to think she's right. It's hard, but it can't be
helped. She says that you say that if you are not allowed to
do that, you will take her and live with her."

He paused again. "Will you?"

"Yes," said Eugene.

Colfax twisted slowly in his chair and looked out of the
window. What a man! What a curious thing love was!

"When is it," he asked finally, "that you think you might do this?"

"Oh, I don't know. I'm all tangled up now. I'll have to think."

Colfax meditated.

"It's a peculiar business. Few people would understand this as well as I do. Few people would understand you, Witla, as I do. You haven't calculated right, old man, and you'll have to pay the price. We all do. I can't let you stay here. I wish I could, but I can't. You'll have to take a year off and think this thing out. If nothing happens—if no scandal arises—well, I won't say what I'll do. I might make a berth for you here somewhere—not exactly in the same position, perhaps, but somewhere. I'll have to think about that. Meanwhile"—he stopped and thought again.

Eugene was seeing clearly how it was with him. All this talk about coming back meant nothing. The thing that was apparent in Colfax's mind was that he would have to go, and the reason that he would have to go was not Mrs. Dale or Suzanne, or the moral issue involved, but the fact that he had lost Colfax's confidence in him. Somehow, through White, through Mrs. Dale, through his own actions day in and day out, Colfax had come to the conclusion that he was erratic, uncertain, and, for that reason, nothing else, he was being dispensed with now. It was Suzanne—it was fate, his own unfortunate temperament. He brooded pathetically, and then he said: "When do you want this to happen?"

"Oh, any time, the quicker, the better, if a public scandal is to grow out of it. If you want you can take your time, three weeks, a month, six weeks. You had better make it a matter of health and resign for your own good.—I mean the looks of the thing. That won't make any difference in my subsequent conclusions. This place is arranged so well now, that it can run nicely for a year without much trouble. We might fix this up again—it depends——"

Eugene wished he had not added the last hypocritical phrase.

He shook hands and went to the door and Eugene strolled to the window. Here was all the solid foundation knocked from under him at one fell stroke, as if by a cannon. He had lost this truly magnificent position, $25,000 a year. Where would he get another like it? Who else—what other company could pay any such salary? How could he maintain the Riverside Drive apartment now, unless he married Suzanne? How could he have his automobile—his valet? Colfax said nothing about continuing his income—why should he? He really owed him nothing. He had been exceedingly well paid—better paid than he would have been anywhere else.

He regretted his fanciful dreams about Blue Sea—his silly enthusiasm in tying up all his money in that. Would Mrs. Dale go to Winfield? Would her talk do him any real harm there? Winfield had always been a good friend to him, had manifested a high regard. This charge, this talk of abduction. What a pity it all was. It might change Winfield's attitude, and still why should it? He had women; no wife, however. He hadn't, as Colfax said, planned this thing quite right. That was plain now. His shimmering world of dreams was beginning to fade like an evening sky. It might be that he had been chasing a will-o'-the-wisp, after all. Could this really be possible? Could it be?

CHAPTER XXII

ONE would have thought that this terrific blow would have given Eugene pause in a way, and it did. It frightened him. Mrs. Dale had gone to Colfax in order to persuade him to use his influence to make Eugene behave himself, and, having done so much, she was actually prepared to go further. She was considering some scheme whereby she could blacken Eugene, have his true character become known without in any way involving Suzanne. Having been relentlessly pursued and harried by Eugene, she was now as relentless in her own attitude. She wanted him to let go now, entirely, if she could, not to see Suzanne any more and she went, first to Winfield, and then back to Lenox with the hope of preventing any further communication, or at least action on Suzanne's part, or Eugene's possible presence there.

In so far as her visit to Winfield was concerned, it did not amount to so much morally or emotionally in that quarter, for Winfield did not feel that he was called upon to act in the matter. He was not Eugene's guardian, nor yet a public censor of morals. He waived the whole question grandly to one side, though in a way he was glad to know of it, for it gave him an advantage over Eugene. He was sorry for him a little—what man would not be? Nevertheless, in his thoughts of reorganizing the Blue Sea Corporation, he did not feel so bad over what might become of Eugene's interests. When the latter approached him, as he did some time afterward, with the idea that he might be able to dispose of his holdings, he saw no way to do it. The company was really not in good shape. More money would have to be put in. All the treasury stock would have to be quickly disposed of, or a reorganization would have to be effected. The best that could be promised under these circumstances was that Eugene's holdings might be exchanged for a fraction of their value in a new issue by a new group of directors. So Eugene saw the end of his dreams in that direction looming up quite clearly.

When he saw what Mrs. Dale had done, he saw also that it was necessary to communicate the situation clearly to Suzanne. The whole thing pulled him up short, and he began to wonder what was to become of him. With his twenty-five thousand a year in salary cut off, his prospect of an independent fortune in

Blue Sea annihilated, the old life closed to him for want of cash, for who can go about in society without money? he saw that he was in danger of complete social and commercial extinction. If by any chance a discussion of the moral relation between him and Suzanne arose, his unconscionable attitude toward Angela, if White heard of it for instance, what would become of him? The latter would spread the fact far and wide. It would be the talk of the town, in the publishing world at least. It would close every publishing house in the city to him. He did not believe Colfax would talk. He fancied that Mrs. Dale had not, after all, spoken to Winfield, but if she had, how much further would it go? Would White hear of it through Colfax? Would he keep it a secret if he knew? Never! The folly of what he had been doing began to dawn upon him dimly. What was it that he had been doing? He felt like a man who had been cast into a deep sleep by a powerful opiate and was now slowly waking to a dim wondering sense of where he was. He was in New York. He had no position. He had little ready money—perhaps five or six thousand all told. He had the love of Suzanne, but her mother was still fighting him, and he had Angela on his hands, undivorced. How was he to arrange things now? How could he think of going back to her? Never!

He sat down and composed the following letter to Suzanne, which he thought would make clear to her just how things stood and give her an opportunity to retract if she wished, for he thought he owed that much to her now:

"FLOWER FACE:

I had a talk with Mr. Colfax this morning and what I feared might happen has happened. Your mother, instead of going to Boston as you thought, came to New York and saw him and, I fancy, my friend Winfield, too. She cannot do me any harm in that direction, for my relationship with that company does not depend on a salary, or a fixed income of any kind, but she has done me infinite harm here. Frankly, I have lost my position. I do not believe that would have come about except for other pressure with which she had nothing to do, but her charges and complaints, coming on top of opposition here on the part of someone else, has done what she couldn't have done alone. Flower Face, do you know what that means? I told you once that I had tied up all my spare cash in Blue Sea, which I hoped would come to so much. It may, but the cutting off my salary here means great changes for me there, unless I can make some other business engagement immediately. I shall probably have to give up my apartment in Riverside Drive and my automobile, and in other ways trim my sails to meet the bad weather. It means that if you come to me, we should have to live on what I can earn as an artist unless I should decide and be able to find something else. When I came to

Canada for you, I had some such idea in mind, but since this thing has actually happened, you may think differently. If nothing happens to my Blue Sea investment, there may be an independent fortune some day in that. I can't tell, but that is a long way off, and meanwhile, there is only this, and I don't know what else your mother may do to my reputation. She appears to be in a very savage frame of mind. You heard what she said at While-a-Way. She has evidently gone back on that completely.

"Flower Face, I lay this all before you so that you may see how things are. If you come to me it may be in the face of a faded reputation. You must realize that there is a great difference between Eugene Witla, Managing Publisher of the United Magazines Corporation, and Eugene Witla, Artist. I have been very reckless and defiant in my love for you. Because you are so lovely—the most perfect thing that I have ever known, I have laid all on the altar of my affection. I would do it again, gladly—a thousand times. Before you came, my life was a gloomy thing. I thought I was living, but I knew in my heart that it was all a dusty shell—a lie. Then you came, and oh, how I have lived! The nights, the days of beautiful fancy. Shall I ever forget White Wood, or Blue Sea, or Briarcliff, or that wonderful first day at South Beach? Little girl, our ways have been the ways of perfectness and peace. This has been an intensely desperate thing to do, but for my sake, I am not sorry. I have been dreaming a wonderfully sweet and perfect dream. It may be when you know all and see how things stand, and stop and think, as I now ask you to do, you may be sorry and want to change your mind. Don't hesitate to do so if you feel that way. You know I told you to think calmly long ago before you told your mother. This is a bold, original thing we have been planning. It is not to be expected that the world would see it as we have. It is quite to be expected that trouble would follow in the wake of it, but it seemed possible to me, and still seems so. If you want to come to me, say so. If you want me to come to you, speak the word. We will go to England or Italy, and I will try my hand at painting again. I can do that I am sure. Or, we can stay here, and I can see if some engagement cannot be had.

"You want to remember, though, that your mother may not have finished fighting. She may go to much greater lengths than she has gone. You thought you might control her, but it seems not. I thought we had won in Canada, but it appears not. If she attempts to restrain you from using your share of your father's estate, she may be able to cause you trouble there. If she attempts to incarcerate you, she might be successful. I wish I could talk to you. Can't I see you at Lenox? Are you coming home next week? We ought to think and plan and act now if at all. Don't let any consideration for me stand in your way, though, if you are doubtful. Remember that conditions are different now. Your whole future hangs on your decision. I should have talked this way long ago, perhaps, but I did not think your mother could do what she has succeeded in doing. I did not think my financial standing would play any part in it.

"Flower Face, this is the day of real trial for me. I am unhappy, but only at the possible prospect of losing you. Nothing of all these other things really matters. With you, everything would be perfect, whatever my condition might be. Without you, it will be as dark as night. The decision is in your hands and you must act. Whatever you decide, that I will do. Don't, as I say, let consideration for me stand in the way. You are young. You have a social career before you. After all, I am twice your age. I talk thus sanely because if you come to me now, I want you to understand clearly how you come.

"Oh, I wonder sometimes if you really understand. I wonder if I have been dreaming a dream. You are so beautiful. You have been such an inspiration to me. Has this been a lure—a will-o'-the wisp? I wonder. I wonder. And yet I love you, love you, love you. A thousand kisses, Divine Fire, and I wait for your word.

"EUGENE."

Suzanne read this letter at Lenox, and for the first time in her life she began to think and ponder seriously. What had she been doing? What was Eugene doing? This dénouement frightened her. Her mother was more purposeful than she imagined. To think of her going to Colfax—of her lying and turning so in her moods. She had not thought this possible of her mother. Had not thought it possible that Eugene could lose his position. He had always seemed so powerful to her; so much a law unto himself. Once when they were out in an automobile together, he had asked her why she loved him, and she said, "because you are a genius and can do anything you please."

"Oh, no," he answered, "nothing like that. I can't really do very much of anything. You just have an exaggerated notion of me."

"Oh, no, I haven't," she replied. "You can paint, and you can write"—she was judging by some of the booklets about Blue Sea and verses about herself and clippings of articles done in his old Chicago newspaper days, which he showed her once in a scrapbook in his apartment—"and you can run that office, and you were an advertising manager and an art director."

She lifted up her face and looked into his eyes admiringly.

"My, what a list of accomplishments!" he replied. "Well whom the gods would destroy they first make mad." He kissed her.

"And you love so beautifully," she added by way of climax.

Since then, she had thought of this often, but now, somehow, it received a severe setback. He was not quite so powerful. He could not prevent her mother from doing this, and could she really conquer her mother? Whatever Suzanne might think of her deceit, she was moving Heaven and earth to prevent this. Was she wholly wrong? After that climacteric night at St. Jacques, when somehow the expected did not happen, Suzanne had been thinking. Did she really want to leave home, and go with Eugene? Did she want to fight her mother in regard to her estate? She might have to do that. Her original idea had been that she and Eugene would meet in some lovely studio, and that she would keep her own home, and he would have his. It was something very different, this talk of poverty, and not having an automobile, and being far away from home. Still she loved him. Maybe she could force her mother to terms yet.

There were more struggles in the two or three succeeding days, in which the guardian of the estate—Mr. Herbert Pitcairn, of the Marquardt Trust Company, and, once more, Dr. Woolley, were called in to argue with her. Suzanne, unable to make up her mind, listened to her mother's insidious plea, that if she would wait a year, and then say she really wanted him, she could have him; listened to Mr. Pitcairn tell her mother that he believed any court would on application adjudge her incompetent and tie up her estate; heard Dr. Woolley say in her presence to her mother that he did not deem a commission in lunacy advisable, but if her mother insisted, no doubt a judge would adjudge her insane, if no more than to prevent this unhallowed consummation. Suzanne became frightened. Her iron nerve, after Eugene's letter, was weakening. She was terribly incensed against her mother, but she began now for the first time to think what her friends would think. Supposing her mother did lock her up. Where would they think she was? All these days and weeks of strain, which had worn her mother threadbare had told something on her own strength, or rather nerve. It was too intense, and she began to wonder whether they had not better do as Eugene suggested, and wait a little while. He had agreed up at St. Jacques to wait, if she were willing. Only the provision was that they were to see each other. Now her mother had changed front again, pleading danger, undue influence, that she ought to have at least a year of her old kind of life undisturbed to see whether she really cared.

"How can you tell?" she insisted to Suzanne, in spite of the girl's desire not to talk. "You have been swept into this, and you haven't given yourself time to think. A year won't hurt. What harm will it do you or him?"

"But, mama," asked Suzanne over and over at different times, and in different places, "why did you go and tell Mr. Colfax? What a mean, cruel thing that was to do!"

"Because I think he needs something like that to make him pause and think. He isn't going to starve. He is a man of talent. He needs something like that to bring him to his senses. Mr. Colfax hasn't discharged him. He told me he wouldn't. He said he would make him take a year off and think about it, and that's just what he has done. It won't hurt him. I don't care if it does. Look at the way he has made me suffer."

She felt exceedingly bitter toward Eugene, and was rejoicing that at last she was beginning to have her innings.

"Mama," said Suzanne, "I am never going to forgive you for this. You are acting horribly—I will wait, but it will come to the same thing in the end. I am going to have him."

"I don't care what you do after a year," said Mrs. Dale cheerfully and subtly. "If you will just wait that long and give yourself time to think and still want to marry him, you can do so. He can probably get a divorce in that time, anyhow." She did not mean what she was saying, but any argument was good for the situation, if it delayed matters.

"But I don't know that I want to marry him," insisted Suzanne, doggedly, harking back to her original idea. "That isn't my theory of it."

"Oh, well," replied Mrs. Dale complaisantly, "you will know better what to think of that after a year. I don't want to coerce you, but I'm not going to have our home and happiness broken up in this way without turning a hand, and without your stopping to think about it. You owe it to me—to all these years I have cared for you, to show me some consideration. A year won't hurt you. It won't hurt him. You will find out then whether he really loves you or not. This may just be a passing fancy. He has had other women before you. He may have others after you. He may go back to Mrs. Witla. It doesn't make any difference what he tells you. You ought to test him before you break up his home and mine. If he really loves you, he will agree readily enough. Do this for me, Suzanne, and I will never cross your path any more. If you will wait a year you can do anything you choose. I can only hope you won't go to him without going as his wife, but if you insist, I will hush the matter up as best I can. Write to him and tell him that you have decided that you both ought to wait a year. You don't need to see him any more. It will just stir things all up afresh. If you don't see him, but just write, it will be better for him, too. He won't feel so badly as he will if you see him again and go all over the ground once more."

Mrs. Dale was terribly afraid of Eugene's influence, but she could not accomplish this.

"I won't do that," said Suzanne, "I won't do it. I'm going back to New York, that's all there is about it!" Mrs. Dale finally yielded that much. She had to.

There was a letter from Suzanne after three days, saying that she couldn't answer his letter in full, but that she was coming back to New York and would see him, and subsequently a meeting between Suzanne and Eugene at Daleview in her mother's presence—Dr. Woolley and Mr. Pitcairn were in another part of the house at the time—in which the proposals were gone over anew.

Eugene had motored down after Mrs. Dale's demands had been put before him in the gloomiest and yet more feverish frame of mind in which he had ever been,—gloomy because of heavy forebodings of evil and his own dark financial condition—while inspirited at other moments by thoughts of some splendid, eager revolt on the part of Suzanne, of her rushing to him, defying all, declaring herself violently and convincingly, and so coming off a victor with him. His faith in her love was still so great.

The night was one of those cold October ones with a steely sky and a sickle moon, harbinger of frost, newly seen in the west, and pointed stars thickening overhead. As he sat in his car on the Staten Island ferry boat, he could see a long line of southward bound ducks, homing to those reedy marshes which Bryant had in mind when he wrote "To a Waterfowl." They were honking as they went, their faint "quacks" coming back on the thin air and making him feel desperately lonely and bereft. When he reached Daleview, speeding past October trees, and entered the great drawing-room where a fire was blazing and where once in spring he had danced with Suzanne, his heart leaped up, for he was to see her, and the mere sight of her was as a tonic to his fevered body—a cool drink to a thirsting man.

Mrs. Dale stared at Eugene defiantly when he came, but Suzanne welcomed him to her embrace. "Oh!" she exclaimed, holding him close for a few moments and breathing feverishly. There was complete silence for a time.

"Mama insists, Eugene," she said after a time, "that we ought to wait a year, and I think since there is such a fuss about it, that perhaps it might be just as well. We may have been just a little hasty, don't you think? I have told mama what I think about her action in going to Mr. Colfax, but she doesn't seem to care. She is threatening now to have me adjudged insane. A year won't make any real difference since I am coming to you, anyhow, will it? But I thought I ought to tell you this in person, to ask you about it"—she paused, looking into his eyes.

"I thought we settled all this up in St. Jacques?" said Eugene, turning to Mrs. Dale, but experiencing a sinking sensation of fear.

"We did, all except the matter of not seeing her. I think it is highly inadvisable that you two should be together. It isn't possible the way things stand. People will talk. Your wife's condition has to be adjusted. You can't be running around with her and a child coming to you. I want Suzanne to go away for a year where she can be calm and think it all out, and I want you to let her. If she still insists that she wants you after that, and will not listen to the logic of the situation in regard to marriage, then I propose to wash my hands of the whole thing. She may have her inheritance. She may have you if she wants you. If you have come to your senses by that time, as I hope you will have, you will get a divorce, or go back to Mrs. Witla, or do whatever you do in a sensible way."

She did not want to incense Eugene here, but she was very bitter.

Eugene merely frowned.

"Is this your decision, Suzanne, too?" he asked wearily.

"I think mama is terrible, Eugene," replied Suzanne evasively, or perhaps as a reply to her mother. "You and I have planned our lives, and we will work them out. We have been a little selfish, now that I think of it. I think a year won't do any harm, perhaps, if it will stop all this fussing. I can wait, if you can."

An inexpressible sense of despair fell upon Eugene at the sound of this, a sadness so deep that he could scarcely speak. He could not believe that it was really Suzanne who was saying that to him. Willing to wait a year! She who had declared so defiantly that she would not. It would do no harm? To think that life, fate, her mother were triumphing over him in this fashion, after all. What then was the significance of the black-bearded men he had seen so often of late? Why had he been finding horseshoes? Was fate such a liar? Did life in its dark, subtle chambers lay lures and traps for men? His position gone, his Blue Sea venture involved in an indefinite delay out of which might come nothing, Suzanne going for a whole year, perhaps for ever, most likely so, for what could not her mother do with her in a whole year, having her alone? Angela alienated—a child approaching. What a climax!

"Is this really your decision, Suzanne?" he asked, sadly, a mist of woe clouding his whole being.

"I think it ought to be, perhaps, Eugene," she replied, still evasively. "It's very trying. I will be faithful to you, though. I promise you that I will not change. Don't you think we can wait a year? We can, can't we?"

"A whole year without seeing you, Suzanne?"

"Yes, it will pass, Eugene."

"A whole year?"

"Yes, Eugene."

"I have nothing more to say, Mrs. Dale," he said, turning to her mother solemnly, a sombre, gloomy light in his eye, his heart hardening towards Suzanne for the moment. To think she should treat him so—throw him down, as he phrased it. Well, such was life. "You win," he added. "It has been a terrible experience for me. A terrible passion. I love this girl. I love her with my whole heart. Sometimes I have vaguely suspected that she might not know."

He turned to Suzanne, and for the first time he thought that he did not see there that true understanding which he had fancied had been there all the time. Could fate have been lying to him also in this? Was he mistaken in this, and had he been following a phantom lure of beauty? Was Suzanne but another trap to drag him down to his old nothingness? God! The prediction of the Astrologer of a second period of defeat after seven or eight years came back.

"Oh, Suzanne!" he said, simply and unconsciously dramatic. "Do you really love me?"

"Yes, Eugene," she replied.

"Really?"

"Yes."

He held out his arms and she came, but for the life of him he could not dispel this terrible doubt. It took the joy out of his kiss—as if he had been dreaming a dream of something perfect in his arms and had awaked to find it nothing—as if life had sent him a Judas in the shape of a girl to betray him.

"Do let us end this, Mr. Witla," said Mrs. Dale coldly, "there is nothing to be gained by delaying. Let us end it for a year, and then talk."

"Oh, Suzanne," he continued, as mournful as a passing bell, "come to the door with me."

"No, the servants are there," put in Mrs. Dale. "Please make your farewells here."

"Mama," said Suzanne angrily and defiantly, moved by the pity of it, "I won't have you talk this way. Leave the room, or I shall go to the door with him and further. Leave us, please."

Mrs. Dale went out.

"Oh, Flower Face," said Eugene pathetically, "I can't believe it. I can't. I can't! This has been managed wrong. I should have taken you long ago. So it is to end this way. A year, a whole year, and how much longer?"

"Only a year," she insisted. "Only a year, believe me, can't you? I won't change, I won't!"

He shook his head, and Suzanne as before took his face in her hands. She kissed his cheeks, his lips, his hair.

"Believe me, Eugene. I seem cold. You don't know what I have gone through. It is nothing but trouble everywhere. Let us wait a year. I promise you I will come to you. I swear. One year. Can't we wait one year?"

"A year," he said. "A year. I can't believe it. Where will we all be in a year? Oh, Flower Face, Myrtle Bloom, Divine Fire. I can't stand this. I can't. It's too much. I'm the one who is paying now. Yes, I pay."

He took her face and looked at it, all its soft, enticing features, her eyes, her lips, her cheeks, her hair.

"I thought, I thought," he murmured.

Suzanne only stroked the back of his head with her hands.

"Well, if I must, I must," he said.

He turned away, turned back to embrace her, turned again and then, without looking back, walked out into the hall. Mrs. Dale was there waiting.

"Good night, Mrs. Dale," he said gloomily.

"Good night, Mr. Witla," she replied frigidly, but with a sense of something tragic in her victory at that.

He took his hat and walked out.

Outside the bright October stars were in evidence by millions. The Bay and Harbor of New York were as wonderfully lit as on that night when Suzanne came to him after the evening at Fort Wadsworth on her own porch. He recalled the spring odours, the wonderful feel of youth and love—the hope that was springing then. Now, it was five or six months later, and all that romance was gone. Suzanne, sweet voice, accomplished shape, light whisper, delicate touch. Gone. All gone—

> "Faded the flower and all its budded charms,
> Faded the sight of beauty from my eyes,
> Faded the shape of beauty from my arms,
> Faded the voice, warmth, whiteness, paradise."

Gone were those bright days in which they had ridden together, dined together, walked in sylvan places beside their car.

A little way from here he first played tennis with her. A little way from here he had come so often to meet her clandestinely. Now she was gone—gone.

He had come in his car, but he really did not want it. Life was accursed. His own was a failure. To think that all his fine dreams should crumble this way. Shortly he would have no car, no home on Riverside Drive, no position, no anything.

"God, I can't stand this!" he exclaimed, and a little later— "By God, I can't! I can't!"

He dismissed his car at the Battery, telling his chauffeur to take it to the garage, and walking gloomily through all the tall dark streets of lower New York. Here was Broadway where he had often been with Colfax and Winfield. Here was this great world of finance around Wall Street in which he had vaguely hoped to shine. Now these buildings were high and silent—receding from him in a way. Overhead were the clear bright stars, cool and refreshing, but without meaning to him now. How was he to settle it? How adjust it? A year! She would never come back—never! It was all gone. A bright cloud faded. A mirage dissolved into its native nothingness. Position, distinction, love, home—where were they? Yet a little while and all these things would be as though they had never been. Hell! Damn! Curse the brooding fates that could thus plot to destroy him!

Back in her room in Daleview Suzanne had locked herself in. She was not without a growing sense of the tragedy of it. She stared at the floor, recalled his face.

"Oh, oh," she said, and for the first time in her life felt as though she could cry from a great heartache—but she could not.

And in Riverside Drive was another woman brooding, lonely, despondently, desperately, over the nature of the tragedy that was upon her. How were things to be adjusted? How was she to be saved? Oh! oh! her life, her child! If Eugene could be made to understand! If he could only be made to see!

CHAPTER XXIII

DURING the weeks which followed Colfax's talk with him, and Suzanne's decision, which amounted practically to a dismissal, Eugene tried to wind up his affairs at the United Magazines Corporation, as well as straighten out his relationship with Angela. It was no easy task. Colfax helped him considerably by suggesting that he should say he was going abroad for the company, for the time being, and should make it appear imperative that he go at once. Eugene called in his department heads, and told them what Colfax suggested, but added that his own interests elsewhere, of which they knew, or suspected, were now so involved that he might possibly not return, or only for a little while at best. He put forward an air of great sufficiency and self-satisfaction, considering the difficulties he was encountering, and the thing passed off as a great wonder, but with no suspicion of any immediate misfortune attaching to him. As a matter of fact, it was assumed that he was destined to a much higher estate—the control of his private interests.

In his talk with Angela he made it perfectly plain that he was going to leave her. He would not make any pretence about this. She ought to know. He had lost his position; he was not going to Suzanne soon; he wanted her to leave him, or he would leave her. She should go to Wisconsin or Europe or anywhere, for the time being, and leave him to fight this thing out alone. He was not indispensable to her in her condition. There were nurses she could hire—maternity hospitals where she could stay. He would be willing to pay for that. He would never live with her any more, if he could help it—he did not want to. The sight of her in the face of his longing for Suzanne would be a wretched commentary—a reproach and a sore shame. No, he would leave her and perhaps, possibly, sometime when she obtained more real fighting courage, Suzanne might come to him. She ought to. Angela might die. Yes, brutal as it may seem, he thought this. She might die, and then—and then—— No thought of the child that might possibly live, even if she died, held him. He could not understand that, could not grasp it as yet. It was a mere abstraction.

Eugene took a room in an apartment house in Kingsbridge,

where he was not known for the time being, and where he was not likely to be seen. Then there was witnessed that dreary spectacle of a man whose life has apparently come down in a heap, whose notions, emotions, tendencies and feelings are confused and disappointed by some untoward result. If Eugene had been ten or fifteen years older, the result might have been suicide. A shade of difference in temperament might have resulted in death, murder, anything. As it was, he sat blankly at times among the ruins of his dreams speculating on what Suzanne was doing, on what Angela was doing, on what people were saying and thinking, on how he could gather up the broken pieces of his life and make anything out of them at all.

The one saving element in it all was his natural desire to work, which, although it did not manifest itself at first, by degrees later on began to come back. He must do something, if it was not anything more than to try to paint again. He could not be running around looking for a position. There was nothing for him in connection with Blue Sea. He had to work to support Angela, of whom he was now free, if he did not want to be mean; and as he viewed it all in the light of what had happened, he realized that he had been bad enough. She had not been temperamentally suited to him, but she had tried to be. Fundamentally it was not her fault. How was he to work and live and be anything at all from now on?

There were long arguments over this situation between him and Angela—pleas, tears, a crashing downward of everything which was worth while in life to Angela, and then, in spite of her pathetic situation, separation. Because it was November and the landlord had heard of Eugene's financial straits, or rather reverse of fortune, it was possible to relinquish the lease, which had several years to run, and the apartment was given up. Angela, distraught, scarcely knew which way to turn. It was one of those pitiless, scandalous situations in life which sicken us of humanity. She ran helplessly to Eugene's sister, Myrtle, who first tried to conceal the scandal and tragedy from her husband, but afterward confessed and deliberated as to what should be done. Frank Bangs, who was a practical man, as well as firm believer in Christian Science because of his wife's to him miraculous healing from a tumor several years before, endeavored to apply his understanding of the divine science—the omnipresence of good to this situation.

"There is no use worrying about it, Myrtle," he said to his wife, who, in spite of her faith, was temporarily shaken and frightened by the calamities which seemingly had overtaken her brother. "It's another evidence of the workings of mortal mind. It is real enough in its idea of itself, but nothing in God's grace. It will come out all right, if we think right. Angela can go to a maternity hospital for the time being, or whenever she's ready. We may be able to persuade Eugene to do the right thing."

Angela was persuaded to consult a Christian Science practitioner, and Myrtle went to the woman who had cured her and begged her to use her influence, or rather her knowledge of science to effect a rehabilitation for her brother. She was told that this could not be done without his wish, but that she would pray for him. If he could be persuaded to come of his own accord, seeking spiritual guidance or divine aid, it would be a different matter. In spite of his errors, and to her they seemed palpable and terrible enough at present, her faith would not allow her to reproach him, and besides she loved him. He was a strong man, she said, always strange. He and Angela might not have been well mated. But all could be righted in *Science*. There was a dreary period of packing and storing for Angela, in which she stood about amid the ruins of her previous comfort and distinction and cried over the things that had seemed so lovely to her. Here were all Eugene's things, his paintings, his canes, his pipes, his clothes. She cried over a handsome silk dressing gown in which he had been wont to lounge about— it smacked so much, curiously, of older and happier days. There were hard, cold and determined conferences also in which some of Angela's old fighting, ruling spirit would come back, but not for long. She was beaten now, and she knew it—wrecked. The roar of a cold and threatening sea was in her ears.

It should be said here that at one time Suzanne truly imagined she loved Eugene. It must be remembered, however, that she was moved to affection for him by the wonder of a personality that was hypnotic to her. There was something about the personality of Eugene that was subversive of conventionality. He approached, apparently a lamb of conventional feelings and appearances; whereas, inwardly, he was a ravening wolf of indifference to convention. All the organized modes and methods of life were a joke to him. He saw through to something that was not material life at all, but spiritual, or say immaterial, of which all material things were a shadow. What did the great forces of life care whether this system which was maintained here with so much show and fuss was really maintained at all or not? How could they care? He once stood in a morgue and saw human bodies apparently dissolving into a kind of chemical mush,

and he had said to himself then how ridiculous it was to assume
that life meant anything much to the forces which were doing
these things. Great chemical and physical forces were at work,
which permitted, accidentally, perhaps, some little shadow-play,
which would soon pass. But, oh, its presence—how sweet it
was!

Naturally Suzanne was cast down for the time being, for she
was capable of suffering just as Eugene was. But having given
her word to wait, she decided to stick to that, although she had
not stuck to her other. She was between nineteen and twenty
now—Eugene was nearing forty. Life could still soothe her in
spite of herself. In Eugene's case it could only hurt the more. Mrs.
Dale went abroad with Suzanne and the other children, visiting
with people who could not possibly have heard, or ever would
except in a vague, uncertain way for that matter. If it became
evident, as she thought it might, that there was to be a scandal,
Mrs. Dale proposed to say that Eugene had attempted to establish an insidious hold on her child in defiance of reason and
honor, and that she had promptly broken it up, shielding Suzanne, almost without the latter's knowledge. It was plausible
enough.

What was he to do now? how live? was his constant thought.
Go into a wee, small apartment in some back street with Angela,
where he and she, if he decided to stay with her, could find a
pretty outlook for a little money and live? Never. Admit that
he had lost Suzanne for a year at least, if not permanently, in
this suddenly brusque way? Impossible. Go and confess that
he had made a mistake, which he still did not feel to be true?
or that he was sorry and would like to patch things up as before? Never. He was not sorry. He did not propose to live
with Angela in the old way any more. He was sick of her,
or rather of that atmosphere of repression and convention in
which he had spent so many years. He was sick of the idea
of having a child thrust on him against his will. He would
not do it. She had no business to put herself in this position.
He would die first. His insurance was paid up to date. He
had carried during the last five years a policy for something
over eighteen thousand in her favor, and if he died she would
get that. He wished he might. It would be some atonement
for the hard knocks which fate had recently given her, but he
did not wish to live with her any more. Never, never, child or
no child. Go back to the apartment after this night—how
could he? If he did, he must pretend that nothing had happened—at least, nothing untoward between him and Suzanne.

She might come back. Might! Might! Ah, the mockery of it—to leave him in this way when she really could have come to him—should have—oh, the bitterness of this thrust of fate!

There was a day when the furniture was sent away and Angela went to live with Myrtle for the time being. There was another tearful hour when she left New York to visit her sister Marietta at Racine, where they now were, intending to tell her before she came away, as a profound secret, the terrible tragedy which had overtaken her. Eugene went to the train with her, but with no desire to be there. Angela's one thought, in all this, was that somehow time would effect a reconciliation. If she could just wait long enough; if she could keep her peace and live and not die, and not give him a divorce, he might eventually recover his sanity and come to think of her as at least worth living with. The child might do it, its coming would be something that would affect him surely. He was bound to see her through it. She told herself she was willing and delighted to go through this ordeal, if only it brought him back to her. This child—what a reception it was to receive, unwanted, dishonored before its arrival, ignored; if by any chance she should die, what would he do about it? Surely he would not desert it. Already in her nervous, melancholy way, she was yearning toward it.

"Tell me," she said to Eugene one day, when they were alternately quarreling and planning, "if the baby comes, and I—and I—die, you won't absolutely desert it? You'll take it, won't you?"

"I'll take it," he replied. "Don't worry. I'm not an absolute dog. I didn't want it. It's a trick on your part, but I'll take it. I don't want you to die. You know that."

Angela thought if she lived that she would be willing to go through a period of poverty and depression with him again, if only she could live to see him sane and moral and even semi-successful. The baby might do it. He had never had a child. And much as he disliked the idea now, still, when it was here, he might change his mind. If only she could get through that ordeal. She was so old—her muscles so set. Meanwhile she consulted a lawyer, a doctor, a fortune teller, an astrologer and the Christian Science practitioner to whom Myrtle had recommended her. It was an aimless, ridiculous combination, but she was badly torn up, and any port seemed worth while in this storm.

The doctor told her that her muscles were rather set, but with the regimen he prescribed, he was satisfied she would be all right. The astrologer told her that she and Eugene were fated for this storm by the stars—Eugene, particularly, and that he might recover, in which case, he would be successful again in a measure. As for herself, he shook his head. Yes, she would be all right. He was lying. The fortune teller laid the cards to see if Eugene would ever marry Suzanne, and Angela was momentarily gratified to learn that she would never enter his life—this from a semi-cadaverous, but richly dressed and bejeweled lady whose ante-room was filled with women whose troubles were of the heart, the loss of money, the enmity of rivals, or the dangers of childbirth. The Christian Science practitioner declared all to be divine mind—omnipotent, omnipresent, omniscient good, and that evil could not exist in it—only the illusion of it. "It is real enough to those who give it their faith and believe," said the counselor, "but without substance or meaning to those who know themselves to be a perfect, indestructible reflection of an idea in God. God is a principle. When the nature of that principle is realized and yourself as a part of it, evil falls away as the troublesome dream that it is. It has no reality." She assured her that no evil could befall her in the true understanding of Science. God is love.

The lawyer told her, after listening to a heated story of Eugene's misconduct, that under the laws of the State of New York, in which these misdeeds were committed, she was not entitled to anything more than a very small fraction of her husband's estate, if he had any. Two years was the shortest time in which a divorce could be secured. He would advise her to sue if she could establish a suitable condition of affluence on Eugene's part, not otherwise. Then he charged her twenty-five dollars for this advice.

CHAPTER XXIV

TO those who have followed a routine or system of living in this world—who have, by slow degrees and persistent effort, built up a series of habits, tastes, refinements, emotions and methods of conduct, and have, in addition, achieved a certain distinction and position, so that they have said to one "Go!" and he goes, and to another "Come!" and he comes, who have enjoyed without stint or reserve, let or hindrance, those joys of perfect freedom of action, and that ease and deliberation which comes with the presence of comparative wealth, social position, and comforts, the narrowing that comes with the lack of means, the fear of public opinion, or the shame of public disclosure, is one of the most pathetic, discouraging and terrifying things that can be imagined. These are the hours that try men's souls. The man who sits in a seat of the mighty and observes a world that is ruled by a superior power, a superior force of which he by some miraculous generosity of fate has been chosen apparently as a glittering instrument, has no conception of the feelings of the man who, cast out of his dignities and emoluments, sits in the dark places of the world among the ashes of his splendor and meditates upon the glory of his bygone days. There is a pathos here which passes the conception of the average man. The prophets of the Old Testament discerned it clearly enough, for they were forever pronouncing the fate of those whose follies were in opposition to the course of righteousness and who were made examples of by a beneficent and yet awful power. "Thus saith the Lord: Because thou hast lifted thyself up against the God of Heaven, and they have brought the vessels of His house before thee, and thou and thy Lords, thy wives and concubines, have drank wine in them, and thou hast praised the gods of silver and gold, of brass, iron, wood, and stone. . . . God hath numbered thy Kingdom and finished it. Thou art weighed in the balance and found wanting; thy Kingdom is divided and given to the Medes and the Persians."

Eugene was in a minor way an exemplification of this seeming course of righteousness. His Kingdom, small as it was, was truly at an end. Our social life is so organized, so closely knit upon a warp of instinct, that we almost always instinctively flee that which does not accord with custom, usage, preconceived notions and tendencies—those various things which we in our littleness of vision conceive to be dominant. Who does not run from the man who may because of his deeds be condemned of that portion of the public which we chance to respect? Walk he ever so proudly, carry himself with what circumspectness he may, at the first breath of suspicion all are off—friends, relations, business acquaintances, the whole social fabric in toto. "Unclean!" is the cry. "Unclean! Unclean!" And it does not matter how inwardly shabby we may be, what whited sepulchres shining to the sun, we run quickly. It seems a tribute to that providence which shapes our ends, which continues perfect in tendency however vilely we may overlay its brightness with the rust of our mortal corruption, however imitative we may be.

Angela had gone home by now to see her father, who was now quite old and feeble, and also down to Alexandria to see Eugene's mother, who was also badly deteriorated in health.

"I keep hoping against hope that your attitude will change toward me," wrote Angela. "Let me hear from you if you will from time to time. It can't make any difference in your course. A word won't hurt, and I am so lonely. Oh, Eugene, if I could only die—if I only could!" No word as to the true state of things was given at either place. Angela pretended that Eugene had long been sick of his commercial career and was, owing to untoward conditions in the Colfax Company, glad to return to his art for a period. He might come home, but he was very busy. So she lied. But she wrote Myrtle fully of her hopes and, more particularly, her fears.

There were a number of conferences between Eugene and Myrtle, for the latter, because of their early companionship, was very fond of him. His traits, the innocent ones, were as sweet to her as when they were boy and girl together. She sought him out in his lovely room at Kingsbridge.

"Why don't you come and stay with us, Eugene?" she pleaded. "We have a comfortable apartment. You can have that big room next to ours. It has a nice view. Frank likes you. We have listened to Angela, and I think you are wrong, but you are my brother, and I want you to come. Everything is coming out right. God will straighten it out. Frank and I are praying for you. There is no evil, you know, according to the way we think. Now"—and she smiled her old-time girlish smile—"don't stay up here alone. Wouldn't you rather be with me?"

"Oh, I'd like to be there well enough, Myrtle, but I can't do it now. I don't want to. I have to think. I want to be alone.

I haven't settled what I want to do. I think I will try my hand at some pictures. I have a little money and all the time I want now. I see there are some nice houses over there on the hill that might have a room with a north window that would serve as a studio. I want to think this thing out first. I don't know what I'll do."

He had now that new pain in his groin, which had come to him first when her mother first carried Suzanne off to Canada and he was afraid that he should never see her any more. It was a real pain, sharp, physical, like a cut with a knife. He wondered how it was that it could be physical and down there. His eyes hurt him and his finger tips. Wasn't that queer, too?

"Why don't you go and see a Christian Science practitioner?" asked Myrtle. "It won't do you any harm. You don't need to believe. Let me get you the book and you can read it. See if you don't think there is something in it. There you go smiling sarcastically, but, Eugene, I can't tell you what it hasn't done for us. It's done everything—that's just all. I'm a different person from what I was five years ago, and so is Frank. You know how sick I was?"

"Yes, I know."

"Why don't you go and see Mrs. Johns? You needn't tell her anything unless you want to. She has performed some perfectly wonderful cures."

"What can Mrs. Johns do for me?" asked Eugene bitterly, his lip set in an ironic mould. "Cure me of gloom? Make my heart cease to ache? What's the use of talking? I ought to quit the whole thing." He stared at the floor.

"She can't, but God can. Oh, Eugene, I know how you feel! Please go. It can't do you any harm. I'll bring you the book tomorrow. Will you read it if I bring it to you?"

"No."

"Oh, Eugene, please for my sake."

"What good will it do? I don't believe in it. I can't. I'm too intelligent to take any stock in that rot."

"Eugene, how you talk! You'll change your mind some time. I know how you think. But read it anyhow. Will you please? Promise me you will. I shouldn't ask. It isn't the way, but I want you to look into it. Go and see Mrs. Johns."

Eugene refused. Of asinine things this seemed the silliest. Christian Science! Christian rot! He knew what to do. His conscience was dictating that he give up Suzanne and return to Angela in her hour of need—to his coming child, for the time being anyhow, but this awful lure of beauty, of personality, of love—how it tugged at his soul! Oh, those days with Suzanne in the pretty watering and dining places about New York, those hours of bliss when she looked so beautiful! How could he get over that? How give up the memory? She was so sweet. Her beauty so rare. Every thought of her hurt. It hurt so badly that most of the time he dared not think—must, perforce, walk or work or stir restlessly about agonized for fear he should think too much. Oh, life; oh, hell!

The intrusion of Christian Science into his purview just now was due, of course, to the belief in and enthusiasm for that religious idea on the part of Myrtle and her husband. As at Lourdes and St. Anne de Beau Pré and other miracle-working centres, where hope and desire and religious enthusiasm for the efficacious intervention of a superior and non-malicious force intervenes, there had occurred in her case an actual cure from a very difficult and compliated physical ailment. She had been suffering from a tumor, nervous insomnia, indigestion, constipation and a host of allied ills, which had apparently refused to yield to ordinary medical treatment. She was in a very bad way mentally and physically at the time the Christian Science textbook, "Science and Health, with Key to the Scriptures," by Mrs. Eddy, was put into her hands. While attempting to read it in a hopeless, helpless spirit, she was instantly cured—that is, the idea that she was well took possession of her, and not long after she really was so. She threw all her medicines, of which there was quite a store, into the garbage pail, eschewed doctors, began to read the Christian Science literature, and attend the Christian Science church nearest her apartment, and was soon involved in its subtle metaphysical interpretation of mortal life. Into this faith, her husband, who loved her very much, had followed, for what was good enough for her and would cure her was good enough for him. He soon seized on its spiritual significance with great vigor and became, if anything, a better exponent and interpreter of the significant thought than was she herself.

Those who know anything of Christian Science know that its main tenet is that God is a principle, not a personality understandable or conceivable from the mortal or sensory side of life (which latter is an illusion), and that man (spiritually speaking) in His image and likeness. Man is not God or any part of Him. He is an idea in God, and, as such, as perfect and indestructible and undisturbably harmonious as an idea in God or principle must be. To those not metaphysically inclined, this is usually dark and without significance, but to those spiritually or metaphysically minded it comes as a great light. Matter becomes a built-up set or combination of illusions, which may have evolved or not as one chooses, but which unquestionably have been built up from nothing or an invisible, intangible idea, and have no significance beyond the faith or credence, which those who are at base spiritual give them. Deny them—know them to be what they are—and they are gone.

To Eugene, who at this time was in a great state of mental doldrums—blue, dispirited, disheartened, inclined to see only evil and destructive forces—this might well come with peculiar significance, if it came at all. He was one of those men who from their birth are metaphysically inclined. All his life he had been speculating on the subtleties of mortal existence, reading Spencer, Kant, Spinoza, at odd moments, and particularly such men as Darwin, Huxley, Tyndall, Lord Avebury, Alfred Russel Wallace, and latterly Sir Oliver Lodge and Sir William Crookes, trying to find out by the inductive, naturalistic method just what life was. He had secured inklings at times, he thought, by reading such things as Emerson's "Oversoul," "The Meditations of Marcus Aurelius," and Plato. God was a spirit, he thought, as Christ had said to the woman at the well in Samaria, but whether this spirit concerned itself with mortal affairs, where was so much suffering and contention, was another matter. Personally he had never believed so—or been at all sure. He had always been moved by the Sermon on the Mount; the beauty of Christ's attitude toward the troubles of the world, the wonder of the faith of the old prophets in insisting that God is God, that there are no other Gods before him, and that he would repay iniquity with disfavor. Whether he did or not was an open question with him. This question of sin had always puzzled him—original sin. Were there laws which ante-dated human experience, which were in God—The Word—before it was made flesh? If so, what were these laws? Did they concern matrimony—some spiritual union which was older than life itself? Did they concern stealing? What was stealing outside of life? Where was it before man began? Or did it only begin with man? Ridiculous! It must relate to something in chemistry and physics, which had worked out in life. A sociologist—a great professor in one of the colleges—had once told him that he did not believe in success or failure, sin, or a sense of self-righteousness except as they were related to built-up instincts in the race—instincts related solely to the self-preservation and the evolution of the race. Beyond that was nothing. Spiritual morality? Bah! He knew nothing about it.

Such rank agnosticism could not but have had its weight with
Eugene. He was a doubter ever. All life, as I have said before,
went to pieces under his scalpel, and he could not put it together again logically, once he had it cut up. People talked
about the sanctity of marriage, but, heavens, marriage was an
evolution! He knew that. Someone had written a two-volume
treatise on it—"The History of Human Marriage," or something like that—and in it animals were shown to have mated
only for so long as it took to rear the young, to get them to the
point at which they could take care of themselves. And wasn't
this really what was at the basis of modern marriage? He had
read in this history, if he recalled aright, that the only reason
marriage had come to be looked upon as sacred, and for life,
was the length of time it took to rear the human young. It took
so long that the parents were old, safely so, before the children
were launched into the world. Then why separate?

But it was the duty of everybody to raise children.

Ah! there had been the trouble. He had been bothered by
that. The home centered around that. Children! Race reproduction! Pulling this wagon of evolution! Was every man
who did not inevitably damned? Was the race spirit against
him? Look at the men and women who didn't—who couldn't.
Thousands and thousands. And those who did always thought
those who didn't were wrong. The whole American spirit he
had always felt to be intensely set in this direction—the idea of
having children and rearing them, a conservative work-a-day
spirit. Look at his father. And yet other men were so shrewd
that they preyed on this spirit, moving factories to where this
race spirit was the most active, so that they could hire the children cheaply, and nothing happened to them, or did something
happen?

However, Myrtle continued to plead with him to look into
this new interpretation of the Scriptures, claiming that it was
true, that it would bring him into an understanding of spirit
which would drive away all these mortal ills, that it was above
all mortal conception—spiritual over all, and so he thought
about that. She told him that if it was right that he should
cease to live with Angela, it would come to pass, and that if it
was not, it would not; but anyhow and in any event in this
truth there would be peace and happiness to him. He should
do what was right ("seek ye first the Kingdom of God"), and
then all these things would be added unto him.

And it seemed terribly silly at first to Eugene for him to be
listening at all to any such talk, but later it was not so much

so. There were long arguments and appeals, breakfast and dinner, or Sunday dinners at Myrtle's apartment, arguments with Bangs and Myrtle concerning every phase of the Science teaching, some visits to the Wednesday experience and testimony meetings of their church, at which Eugene heard statements concerning marvelous cures which he could scarely believe, and so on. So long as the testimonies confined themselves to complaints which might be due to nervous imagination, he was satisfied that their cures were possibly due to religious enthusiasm, which dispelled their belief in something which they did not have, but when they were cured of cancer, consumption, locomotor-ataxia, goitres, shortened limbs, hernia—he did not wish to say they were liars, they seemed too sincere to do that, but he fancied they were simply mistaken. How could they, or this belief, or whatever it was, cure cancer? Good Lord! He went on disbelieving in this way, and refusing also to read the book until one Wednesday evening when he happened to be at the Fourth Church of Christ Scientist in New York that a man stood up beside him in his own pew and said:

"I wish to testify to the love and mercy of God in my case, for I was hopelessly afflicted not so very long ago and one of the vilest men I think it is possible to be. I was raised in a family where the Bible was read night and morning—my father was a hidebound Presbyterian—and I was so sickened by the manner in which it was forced down my throat and the inconsistencies which I thought I saw existing between Christian principle and practice, even in my own home, that I said to myself I would conform as long as I was in my father's house and eating his bread, but when I got out I would do as I pleased. I was in my father's house after that a number of years, until I was seventeen, and then I went to a large city, Cincinnati, but the moment I was away and free I threw aside all my so-called religious training and set out to do what I thought was the most pleasant and gratifying thing for me to do. I wanted to drink, and I did, though I was really never a very successful drinker." Eugene smiled. "I wanted to gamble, and I did, but I was never a very clever gambler. Still I did gamble a bit. My great weakness was women, and here I hope none will be offended, I know they will not be, for there may be others who need my testimony badly. I pursued women as I would any other lure. They were really all that I desired— their bodies. My lust was terrible. It was such a dominant thought with me that I could not look at any good-looking woman except, as the Bible says, to lust after her. I was vile.

I became diseased. I was carried into the First Church of Christ Scientist in Chicago, after I had spent all my money and five years of my time on physicians and specialists, suffering from locomotor ataxia, dropsy and kidney disease. I had previously been healed of some other things by ordinary medicine.

"If there is anyone within the sound of my voice who is afflicted as I was, I want him to listen to me.

"I want to say to you tonight that I am a well man—not well physically only, but well mentally, and, what is better yet, in so far as I can see the truth, spiritually. I was healed after six months' treatment by a Christian Science practitioner in Chicago, who took my case on my appealing to her, and I stand before you absolutely sound and whole. God is good."

He sat down.

While he had been talking Eugene had been studying him closely, observing every line of his features. He was tall, lean, sandy-haired and sandy-bearded. He was not bad-looking, with long straight nose, clear blue eyes, a light pinkish color to his complexion, and a sense of vigor and health about him. The thing that Eugene noted most was that he was calm, cool, serene, vital. He said exactly what he wanted to say, and he said it vigorously. His voice was clear and with good carrying power. His clothes were shapely, new, well made. He was no beggar or tramp, but a man of some profession—an engineer, very likely. Eugene wished that he might talk to him, and yet he felt ashamed. Somehow this man's case paralleled his own; not exactly, but closely. He personally was never diseased, but how often he had looked after a perfectly charming woman to lust after her! Was the thing that this man was saying really true? Could he be lying? How ridiculous! Could he be mistaken? *This man?* Impossible! He was too strong, too keen, too sincere, too earnest, to be either of these things. Still— But this testimony might have been given for his benefit, some strange helpful power—that kindly fate that had always pursued him might be trying to reach him here. Could it be? He felt a little strange about it, as he had when he saw the black-bearded man entering the train that took him to Three Rivers, the time he went at the call of Suzanne, as he did when horse-shoes were laid before him by supernatural forces to warn him of coming prosperity. He went home thinking, and that night he seriously tried to read "Science and Health" for the first time.

CHAPTER XXV

THOSE who have ever tried to read that very peculiar and, to many, very significant document know what an apparent jumble of contradictions and metaphysical balderdash it appears to be. The statement concerning the rapid multiplication and increased violence of diseases since the flood, which appears in the introduction is enough to shock any believer in definite, material, established natural science, and when Eugene came upon this in the outset, it irritated him, of course, greatly. Why should anybody make such a silly statement as this? Everybody knew that there had never been a flood. Why quote a myth as a fact? It irritated and from a critical point of view amused him. Then he came upon what he deemed to be a jumble of confusion in regard to matter and spirit. The author talked of the evidences of the five physical senses as being worthless, and yet was constantly referring to and using similes based upon those evidences to illustrate her spiritual meanings. He threw the book down a number of times, for the Biblical references irritated him. He did not believe in the Bible. The very word Christianity was a sickening jest, as sickening as it had been to the man in the church. To say that the miracles of Christ could be repeated today could not be serious. Still the man had testified. Wasn't that so? A certain vein of sincerity running through it all—that profound evidence of faith and sympathy which are the characteristics of all sincere reformers—appealed to him. Some little thoughts here and there—a profound acceptance of the spiritual understanding of Jesus, which he himself accepted, stayed with him. One sentence or paragraph somehow stuck in his mind, because he himself was of a metaphysical turn—

"Become conscious for a single moment that life and intelligence are purely spiritual, neither in nor of matter, and the body will then utter no complaints. If suffering from a belief in sickness, you will find yourself suddenly well. Sorrow is turned into joy when the body is controlled by spiritual life and love."

"God is a spirit," he recalled Jesus as saying. "They that worship Him must worship in spirit and in truth."

"You will find yourself suddenly well," thought Eugene. "Sorrow is turned into joy."

693

"Sorrow. What kind of sorrow? Love sorrow? This probably meant the end of earthly love; that that too was mortal."

He read on, discovering that Scientists believed in the immaculate conception of the Virgin Mary, which struck him as silly; also that they believed in the ultimate abolition of marriage as representing a mortal illusion of self-creation and perpetuation, and of course the having of children through the agency of the sexes, also the dematerialization of the body—its chemicalization into its native spirituality, wherein there can be neither sin, sickness, disease, decay nor death, were a part of their belief or understanding. It seemed to him to be a wild claim, and yet at the time, because of his natural metaphysical turn, it accorded with his sense of the mystery of life.

It should be remembered as a factor in this reading that Eugene was particularly fitted by temperament—introspective, imaginative, psychical—and by a momentarily despairing attitude, in which any straw was worth grasping at which promised relief from sorrow, despair and defeat, to make a study of this apparently radical theory of human existence. He had heard a great deal of Christian Science, seeing its churches built, its adherents multiplying, particularly in New York, and enthusiastically claiming freedom from every human ill. Idle, without entertainment or diversion and intensely introspective, it was natural that these curious statements should arrest him.

He was not unaware, also, from past reading and scientific speculation, that Carlyle had once said that "matter itself—the outer world of matter, was either nothing, or else a product due to man's mind" (Carlyle's Journal, from Froude's Life of Carlyle), and that Kant had held the whole universe to be something in the eye or mind—neither more nor less than a thought. Marcus Aurelius, he recalled, had said somewhere in his meditations that the soul of the universe was kind and merciful; that it had no evil in it, and was not harmed by evil. This latter thought stuck in his mind as peculiar because it was so diametrically opposed to his own feelings that the universe, the spirit of it that is, was subtle, cruel, crafty, and malicious. He wondered how a man who could come to be Emperor of Rome could have thought otherwise. Christ's Sermon on the Mount had always appealed to him as the lovely speculations of an idealist who had no real knowledge of life. Yet he had always wondered why "Lay not up for yourselves treasures upon earth, where moth and rust doth corrupt, and where thieves break through and steal" had thrilled him as something so beautiful that it must be true "For where your treasure is there will your heart be also." Keats had said "beauty is truth—truth beauty," and still another "truth is what is."

"And what is?" he had asked himself in answer to that.

"Beauty," was his reply to himself, for life at bottom, in spite of all its teeming terrors, was beautiful.

Only those of a metaphysical or natural religious turn of mind would care to follow the slow process of attempted alteration, which took place during the series of months which followed Angela's departure for Racine, her return to New York at Myrtle's solicitation, the time she spent in the maternity hospital, whither she was escorted on her arrival by Eugene and after. These are the deeps of being which only the more able intellectually essay, but Eugene wandered in them far and wide. There were long talks with Myrtle and Bangs—arguments upon all phases of mortal thought, real and unreal, with which Angela's situation had nothing to do. Eugene frankly confessed that he did not love her—that he did not want to live with her. He insisted that he could scarcely live without Suzanne. There was the taking up and reading or re-reading of odd philosophic and religious volumes, for he had nothing else to do. He did not care at first to go and sit with Angela, sorry as he was for her. He read or re-read Kent's "History of the Hebrews"; Weiniger's "Sex and Character"; Carl Snyder's "The World Machine"; Muzzey's "Spiritual Heroes"; Johnston's translation of "Bhagavad Ghita"; Emerson's essay on the Oversoul, and Huxley's "Science and Hebrew Tradition" and "Science and Christian Tradition." He learned from these things some curious facts which relate to religion, which he had either not known before or forgotten, i.e., that the Jews were almost the only race or nation which developed a consecutive line of religious thinkers or prophets; that their ideal was first and last a single God or Divinity, tribal at first, but later on universal, whose scope and significance were widened until He embraced the whole universe—was, in fact, the Universe—a governing principle—one God, however, belief in whom, His power to heal, to build up and overthrow had never been relinquished.

The Old Testament was full of that. Was that. The old prophets, he learned to his astonishment, were little more than whirling dervishes when they are first encountered historically, working themselves up into wild transports and frenzies, lying on the ground and writhing, cutting themselves as the Persian zealots do to this day in their feast of the tenth month and resorting to the most curious devices for nurturing their fanatic spirit, but always setting forth something that was astonishingly spiritual and great. They usually frequented the holy places and were to be distinguished by their wild looks and queer clothing. Isaiah eschewed clothing for three years (Is. 22, 21); Jeremiah appeared in the streets of the capital (according to Muzzey) with a wooden yoke on his neck, saying, "Thus shalt Juda's neck be bent under bondage to the Babylonian" (Jer. 27; 2 ff); Zedekiah came to King Ahab, wearing horns of iron like a steer, and saying, "Thus shalt thou push the Syrians" (I Kings 22, 11). The prophet was called mad because he acted like a madman. Elisha dashed in on the gruff captain, Jehu, in his camp and broke a vial of oil on his head, saying, "Thus saith the Lord God of Israel, I have made thee king over the people of the Lord"; then he opened the door and fled. Somehow, though these things seemed wild, yet they accorded with Eugene's sense of prophecy. They were not cheap but great—wildly dramatic, like the word of a Lord God might be. Another thing that fascinated him was to find that the evolutionary hypothesis did not after all shut out a conception of a ruling, ordaining Divinity, as he had supposed, for he came across several things in the papers which, now that he was thinking about this so keenly, held him spellbound. One was quoted from a biological work by a man named George M. Gould, and read:

"Life reaches control of physical forces by the cell-mechanism, and, so far as we know, by it solely." From reading Mrs. Eddy and arguing with Bangs, Eugene was not prepared to admit this, but he was fascinated to see how it led ultimately to an acknowledgment of an active Divinity which shapes our ends. "No organic molecule shows any evidence of intellect, design or purpose. It is the product solely of mathematically determinate and invariable physical forces. Life becomes conscious of itself through specialized cellular activity, and human personality, therefore, can only be a unity of greater differentiations of function, a higher and fuller incarnation than the single cell incarnation. Life, or God, is in the cell. . . . (And everywhere outside of it, quite as active and more so, perhaps, Eugene reserved mentally.) The cell's intelligence is His. (From reading Mrs. Eddy, Eugene could not quite agree with this. According to her, it was an illusion.) The human personality is also at last Himself and only Himself. . . . If you wish to say 'Biologos' or God instead of Life, I heartily agree, and we are face to face with the sublime fact of biology. The cell is God's instrument and mediator in materiality; it is the mechanism of incarnation, the word made flesh and dwelling among us."

The other was a quotation in a Sunday newspaper from some man who appeared to be a working physicist of the time—Edgar Lucien Larkin:

"With the discovery and recent perfection of the new ultra-violet light microscope and the companion apparatus, the micro-photographic camera, with rapidly moving, sensitive films, it seems that the extreme limit of vision of the human eye has been reached. Inorganic and organic particles have been seen, and these so minute that (the smallest) objects visible in the most powerful old-style instruments are as huge chunks in comparison. An active microscopic universe as wonderful as the sidereal universe, the stellar structure, has been revealed. This complexity actually exists; but exploration has scarcely commenced. Within a hundred years, devoted to this research, the micro-universe may be partially understood. Laws of micro-movements may be detected and published in textbooks like those of the gigantic universe suns and their concentric planets and moons. I cannot look into these minute moving and living deeps without instantly believing that they are mental—every motion is controlled by mind. The longer I look at the amazing things, the deeper is this conviction. This micro-universe is rooted and grounded in a mental base. Positively and without hope of overthrow, this assertion is made—the flying particles know where to go. Coarse particles, those visible in old-time microscopes, when suspended in liquids, were observed to be in rapid motion, darting to all geometrical directions with high speed. But the ultra-violet microscope reveals moving trillions of far smaller bodies, and these rush on geometric lines and cut-out angles with the most incredible speed, specific for each kind and type."

What were the angles? Eugene asked himself. Who made them? Who or what arranged the geometric lines? The "Divine Mind" of Mrs. Eddy? Had this woman really found the truth? He pondered this, reading on, and then one day in a paper he came upon this reflection in regard to the universe and its government by Alfred Russel Wallace, which interested him as a proof that there might be, as Jesus said and as Mrs. Eddy contended, a Divine Mind or central thought in which there was no evil intent, but only good. The quotation was: "Life is that power which, from air and water and the substances dissolved therein, builds up organized and highly complex structures possessing definite forms and functions; these are presented in a continuous state of decay and repair by internal circulation of fluids and gases; they reproduce their like, go through various phases of youth, maturity and age, die and quickly decompose into their constituent elements. They thus form continuous series of similar individuals and so long as external conditions render their existence possible seem to possess a potential immortality.

"It is very necessary to presuppose some vast intelligence, some pervading spirit, to explain the guidance of the lower forces in accordance with the preordained system of evolution we see prevailing. Nothing less will do. . . .

"If, however, we go as far as this, we must go further. . . . We have a perfect right, on logical and scientific grounds, to see in all the infinitely varied products of the animal and vegetable kingdoms, which we alone can make use of, a preparation for ourselves, to assist in our mental development, and to fit us for a progressively higher state of existence as spiritual beings.

" . . . It seems only logical to assume that the vast, the infinite chasm between ourselves and the Deity, is to some extent occupied by an almost infinite series of grades of beings, each successive grade having higher and higher powers in regard to the origination, the development and the control of the universe.

" . . . There may have been a vast system of co-operation of such grades of beings, from a very high grade of power and intelligence down to those unconscious or almost unconscious cell souls posited by Haeckel. . . .

"I can imagine the . . . Infinite Being, foreseeing and determining the broad outlines of a universe. . . .

"He might, for instance, impress a sufficient number of his highest angels to create by their will power the primal universe of ether, with all those inherent properties and forces necessary for what was to follow. Using this as a vehicle, the next subordinate association of angels would so act upon the ether as to develop from it, in suitable masses and at suitable distances, the various elements of matter, which, under the influence of such laws and forces as gravitation, heat, and electricity, would thenceforth begin to form those vast systems of nebulæ and suns which constitute our stellar universe.

"Then we may imagine these hosts of angels, to whom a thousand years are as one day, watching the development of this vast system of suns and planets until some one or more of them combined in itself all those conditions of size, of elementary constitution, of atmosphere, of mass of water and requisite distance from its source of heat as to insure a stability of constitution and uniformity of temperature for a given minimum of millions of years, or of ages, as would be required for the full development of a life world from amœba to man, with a surplus of a few hundreds of millions for his adequate development.

"We are led, therefore, to postulate a body of what we may term organizing spirits, who would be charged with the duty of so influencing the myriads of cell souls as to carry out their part of the work with accuracy and certainty. . . .

"At successive stages of the development of the life world, more and perhaps higher intelligences might be required to direct the main lines of variation in definite directions, in accordance with the general design to be worked out, and to guard against a break in the particular line, which alone could lead ultimately to the production of the human form.

"This speculative suggestion, I venture to hope, will appeal to some of my readers as the very best approximation we are now able to formulate as to the deeper, the most fundamental causes of matter and force of life and consciousness, and of man himself, at his best, already a little lower than the angels, and, like them, destined to a permanent progressive existence in a world of spirit."

This very peculiar and apparently progressive statement in regard to the conclusion which naturalistic science had revealed in regard to the universe struck Eugene as pretty fair confirmation of Mrs. Eddy's contention that all was mind and its infinite variety and that the only difference between her and the British scientific naturalists was that they contended for an ordered hierarchy which could only rule and manifest itself according to its own ordered or self-imposed laws, which they could perceive or detect, whereas, she contended for a governing spirit which was everywhere and would act through ordered laws and powers of its own arrangement. God was a principle like a rule in mathematics—two times two is four, for instance—and was as manifest daily and hourly and momentarily in a hall bedroom as in the circling motions of suns and systems. God was a principle. He grasped that now. A principle could be and was of course anywhere and everywhere at one and the same time. One could not imagine a place for instance where two times two would not be four, or where that rule would not be. So, likewise with the omnipotent, omniscient, omnipresent mind of God.

CHAPTER XXVI

THE most dangerous thing to possess a man to the extent of dominating him is an idea. It can and does ride him to destruction. Eugene's idea of the perfection of eighteen was one of the most dangerous things in his nature. In a way, combined with the inability of Angela to command his interest and loyalty, it had been his undoing up to this date. A religious idea followed in a narrow sense would have diverted this other, but it also might have destroyed him, if he had been able to follow it. Fortunately the theory he was now interesting himself in was not a narrow dogmatic one in any sense, but religion in its large aspects, a comprehensive resumé and spiritual co-ordination of the metaphysical speculation of the time, which was worthy of anyone's intelligent inquiry. Christian Science as a cult or religion was shunned by current religions and religionists as something outré, impossible, uncanny—as necromancy, imagination, hypnotism, mesmerism, spiritism—everything, in short, that it was not, and little, if anything, that it really was. Mrs. Eddy had formulated or rather restated a fact that was to be found in the sacred writings of India; in the Hebrew testaments, old and new; in Socrates, Marcus Aurelius, St. Augustine, Emerson, and Carlyle. The one variation notable between her and the moderns was that her *ruling unity* was not malicious, as Eugene and many others fancied, but helpful. Her *unity* was a *unity* of love. God was everything but the father of evil, which according to her was an illusion—neither fact nor substance—sound and fury, signifying nothing.

It must be remembered that during all the time Eugene was doing this painful and religious speculation he was living in the extreme northern portion of the city, working desultorily at some paintings which he thought he might sell, visiting Angela occasionally, safely hidden away in the maternity hospital at One Hundred and Tenth Street, thinking hourly and momentarily of Suzanne, and wondering if, by any chance, he should ever see her any more. His mind had been so inflamed by the beauty and the disposition of this girl that he was really not normal any longer. He needed some shock, some catastrophe greater than any he had previously experienced to bring him to his senses. The loss of his position had done something. The loss of Suzanne had only heightened his affection for her. The condition of Angela had given him pause, for it was an interesting question what would become of her. "If she would only die!" he said to himself, for we have the happy faculty of hating most joyously on this earth the thing we have wronged the most. He could scarcely go and see her, so obsessed was he with the idea that she was a handicap to his career. The idea of her introducing a child into his life only made him savage. Now, if she should die, he would have the child to care for and Suzanne, because of it, might never come to him.

His one idea at this time was not to be observed too much, or rather not at all, for he considered himself to be in great disfavor, and only likely to do himself injury by a public appearance—a fact which was more in his own mind than anywhere else. If he had not believed it, it would not have been true. For this reason he had selected this quiet neighborhood where the line of current city traffic was as nothing, for here he could brood in peace. The family that he lived with knew nothing about him. Winter was setting in. Because of the cold and snow and high winds, he was not likely to see many people hereabouts—particularly those celebrities who had known him in the past. There was a great deal of correspondence that followed him from his old address, for his name had been used on many committees, he was in "Who's Who," and he had many friends less distinguished than those whose companionship would have required the expenditure of much money who would have been glad to look him up. He ignored all invitations, however; refused to indicate by return mail where he was for the present; walked largely at night; read, painted, or sat and brooded during the day. He was thinking all the time of Suzanne and how disastrously fate had trapped him apparently through her. He was thinking that she might come back, that she ought. Lovely, hurtful pictures came to him of re-encounters with her in which she would rush into his arms, never to part from him any more. Angela, in her room at the hospital, received little thought from him. She was there. She was receiving expert medical attention. He was paying all the bills. Her serious time had not yet really come. Myrtle was seeing her. He caught glimpses of himself at times as a cruel, hard intellect driving the most serviceable thing his life had known from him with blows, but somehow it seemed justifiable. Angela was not suited to him. Why could she not live away from him? Christian Science set aside marriage entirely as a human illusion, conflicting with the indestructible unity of the individual with God. Why shouldn't she let him go?

He wrote poems to Suzanne, and read much poetry that he found in an old trunkful of books in the house where he was living. He would read again and again the sonnet beginning, "When in disgrace with fortune and men's eyes"—that cry out of a darkness that seemed to be like his own. He bought a book of verse by Yeats, and seemed to hear his own voice saying of Suzanne,

> "Why should I blame her that she filled my days
>   With misery . . .

He was not quite as bad as he was when he had broken down eight years before, but he was very bad. His mind was once more riveted upon the uncertainty of life, its changes, its follies. He was studying those things only which deal with the abstrusities of nature, and this began to breed again a morbid fear of life itself. Myrtle was greatly distressed about him. She worried lest he might lose his mind.

"Why don't you go to see a practitioner, Eugene?" she begged of him one day. "You will get help—really you will. You think you won't, but you will. There is something about them —I don't know what. They are spiritually at rest. You will feel better. Do go."

"Oh, why do you bother me, Myrtle? Please don't. I don't want to go. I think there is something in the idea metaphysically speaking, but why should I go to a practitioner? God is as near me as He is anyone, if there is a God."

Myrtle wrung her hands, and because she felt so badly more than anything else, he finally decided to go. There might be something hypnotic or physically contagious about these people— some old alchemy of the mortal body, which could reach and soothe him. He believed in hypnotism, hypnotic suggestion, etc. He finally called up one practitioner, an old lady highly recommended by Myrtle and others, who lived farther south on Broadway, somewhere in the neighborhood of Myrtle's home. Mrs. Althea Johns was her name—a woman who had performed wonderful cures. Why should he, Eugene Witla, he asked himself as he took up the receiver, why should he, Eugene Witla, ex-managing publisher of the United Magazines Corporation, ex-artist (in a way, he felt that he was no longer an artist in the best sense) be going to a woman in Christian Science to be healed of what? Gloom? Yes. Failure? Yes. Heartache? Yes. His evil tendencies in regard to women, such as the stranger who had sat beside him had testified to? Yes. How strange! And yet he was curious. It interested him a little to speculate as to whether this could really be done. Could he be healed of failure? Could this pain of longing be made to cease? Did he want it to cease? No; certainly not! He wanted Suzanne. Myrtle's idea, he knew, was that somehow this treatment would reunite him and Angela and make him forget Suzanne, but he knew that could not be. He was going, but he was going because he was unhappy and idle and aimless. He was going because he really did not know what else to do.

The apartment of Mrs. Johns—Mrs. Althea Johns—was in an apartment house of conventional design, of which there were in New York hundreds upon hundreds at the time. There was a spacious areaway between two wings of cream-colored pressed brick leading back to an entrance way which was protected by a handsome wrought-iron door on either side of which was placed an electric lamp support of handsome design, holding lovely cream-colored globes, shedding a soft lustre. Inside was the usual lobby, elevator, uniformed negro elevator man, indifferent and impertinent, and the telephone switchboard. The building was seven storeys high. Eugene went one snowy, blustery January night. The great wet flakes were spinning in huge whirls and the streets were covered with a soft, slushy carpet of snow. He was interested, as usual, in spite of his gloom, in the picture of beauty the world presented—the city wrapped in a handsome mantle of white. Here were cars rumbling, people hunched in great coats facing the driving wind. He liked the snow, the flakes, this wonder of material living. It eased his mind of his misery and made him think of painting again. Mrs. Johns was on the seventh floor. Eugene knocked and was admitted by a maid. He was shown to a waiting room, for he was a little ahead of his time, and there were others—healthy-looking men and women, who did not appear to have an ache or pain—ahead of him. Was not this a sign, he thought as he sat down, that this was something which dealt with imaginary ills? Then why had the man he had heard in the church beside him testified so forcibly and sincerely to his healing? Well, he would wait and see. He did not see what it could do for him now. He had to work. He sat there in one corner, his hands folded and braced under his chin, thinking. The room was not artistic but rather nondescript, the furniture cheap or rather tasteless in design. Didn't Divine Mind know any better than to present its representatives in such a guise as this? Could a person called to assist in representing the majesty of God on earth be left so unintelligent artistically as to live in a house like this? Surely this was a poor manifestation of Divinity, but——

Mrs. Johns came—a short, stout, homely woman, gray, wrinkled, dowdy in her clothing, a small wen on one side of her mouth, a nose slightly too big to be pleasing—all mortal deficiencies as to appearance highly emphasized, and looking like an old print of Mrs. Micawber that he had seen somewhere. She had on a black skirt good as to material, but shapeless, commonplace, and a dark blue-gray waist. Her eye was clear and gray though, he noticed, and she had a pleasing smile.

"This is Mr. Witla, I believe," she said, coming across the room to him, for he had got into a corner near the window, and speaking with an accent which sounded a little Scotch. "I'm so glad to see you. Won't you come in?" she said, giving him precedence over some others because of his appointment, and re-crossed the room preceding him down the hall to her practice room. She stood to one side to take his hand as he passed.

He touched it gingerly.

So this was Mrs. Johns, he thought, as he entered, looking about him. Bangs and Myrtle had insisted that she had performed wonderful cures—or rather that Divine Mind had, through her. Her hands were wrinkled, her face old. Why didn't she make herself young if she could perform these wonderful cures? Why was this room so mussy? It was actually stuffy with chromos and etchings of the Christ and Bible scenes on the walls, a cheap red carpet or rug on the floor, inartistic leather-covered chairs, a table or desk too full of books, a pale picture of Mrs. Eddy and silly mottoes of which he was sick and tired hung here and there. People were such hacks when it came to the art of living. How could they pretend to a sense of Divinity who knew nothing of life? He was weary and the room here offended him. Mrs. Johns did. Besides, her voice was slightly falsetto. Could *she* cure cancer? and consumption? and all other horrible human ills, as Myrtle insisted she had? He didn't believe it.

He sat down wearily and yet contentiously in the chair she pointed out to him and stared at her while she quietly seated herself opposite him looking at him with kindly, smiling eyes.

"And now," she said easily, "what does God's child think is the matter with him?"

Eugene stirred irritably.

"God's child," he thought; "what cant!" What right had he to claim to be a child of God? What was the use of beginning that way? It was silly, so asinine. Why not ask plainly what was the matter with him? Still he answered:

"Oh, a number of things. So many that I am pretty sure they can never be remedied."

"As bad as that? Surely not. It is good to know, anyhow, that nothing is impossible to God. We can believe that, anyhow, can't we?" she replied, smiling. "You believe in God, or a ruling power, don't you?"

"I don't know whether I do or not. In the main, I guess I do. I'm sure I ought to. Yes, I guess I do."

"Is He a malicious God to you?"

"I have always thought so," he replied, thinking of Angela.

"Mortal mind! Mortal mind!" she asseverated to herself. "What delusions will it not harbor!"

And then to him:

"One has to be cured almost against one's will to know that God is a God of love. So you believe you are sinful, do you, and that He is malicious? It is not necessary that you should tell me how. We are all alike in the mortal state. I would like to call your attention to Isaiah's words, 'Though your sins be as scarlet, they shall be as white as snow; though they be red like crimson, they shall be as wool.'"

Eugene had not heard this quotation for years. It was only a dim thing in his memory. It flashed out simply now and appealed, as had all these Hebraic bursts of prophetic imagery in the past. Mrs. Johns, for all her wen and her big nose and dowdy clothes, was a little better for having been able to quote this so aptly. It raised her in his estimation. It showed a vigorous mind, at least a tactful mind.

"Can you cure sorrow?" he asked grimly and with a touch of sarcasm in his voice. "Can you cure heartache or fear?"

"I can do nothing of myself," she said, perceiving his mood. "All things are possible to God, however. If you believe in a Supreme Intelligence, He will cure you. St. Paul says 'I can do all things through Christ which strengtheneth me.' Have you read Mrs. Eddy's book?"

"Most of it. I'm still reading it."

"Do you understand it?"

"No, not quite. It seems a bundle of contradictions to me."

"To those who are first coming into Science it nearly always seems so. But don't let that worry you. You would like to be cured of your troubles. St. Paul says, 'For the wisdom of this world is foolishness with God.' 'The Lord knoweth the thoughts of the wise—that they are vain.' Do not think of me as a woman, or as having had anything to do with this. I would rather have you think of me as St. Paul describes anyone who works for truth—'Now then we are ambassadors for Christ, as though God did beseech you by us, we pray you in Christ's stead, be ye reconciled to God.'"

"You know your Bible, don't you?" said Eugene.

"It is the only knowledge I have," she replied.

There followed one of those peculiar religious demonstrations so common in Christian Science—so peculiar to the uninitiated—in which she asked Eugene to fix his mind in meditation on the Lord's prayer. "Never mind if it seems pointless to you now. You have come here seeking aid. You are God's perfect image and likeness. He will not send you away empty-handed. Let me read you first, though, this one psalm, which I think is always so helpful to the beginner." She opened her Bible, which was on the table near her, and began:

"He that dwelleth in the secret place of the most high shall abide under the shadow of the Almighty.

"I will say of the Lord, He is my refuge and my fortress; my God; in him will I trust.

"Surely he shall deliver thee from the snare of the fowler, and from the noisome pestilence.

"He shall cover thee with his feathers, and under his wings shalt thou trust: his truth shall be thy shield and thy buckler.

"Thou shalt not be afraid for the terror by night, nor for the arrow that flieth by day. Nor for the pestilence that walketh in the darkness; nor for destruction that wasteth at noonday.

"A thousand shall fall at thy side, and ten thousand at thy right hand; but it shall not come nigh thee.

"Only with thine eyes shalt thou behold and see the reward of the wicked.

"Because thou hast made the Lord, which is my refuge, even the most High, thy habitation; There shall no evil befall thee, neither shall any plague come nigh thy dwelling.

"For he shall give his angels charge over thee, to keep thee in all thy ways.

"They shall bear thee up in their hands, lest thou dash thy foot against a stone.

"Thou shalt tread upon the lion and the adder, the young lion and the dragon shalt thou trample under foot.

"Because he hath set his love upon me, therefore will I deliver him. I will set him on high, because he hath known my name.

"He shall call upon me, and I will answer him: I will be with him in trouble. I will deliver him and honor him.

"With long life will I satisfy him, and show him my salvation."

During this most exquisite pronunciamento of Divine favor Eugene was sitting with his eyes closed, his thoughts wandering over all his recent ills. For the first time in years, he was trying to fix his mind upon an all-wise, omnipresent, omnipotent generosity. It was hard and he could not reconcile the beauty of this expression of Divine favor with the nature of the world as he knew it. What was the use of saying, "They shall bear thee up in their hands lest thou dash thy foot against a stone," when he had seen Angela and himself suffering so much recently? Wasn't he dwelling in the secret place of the Most High when he was alive? How could one get out of it? Still—— "Because he hath set his love on me—therefore will I deliver him." Was that the answer? Was Angela's love set on him? Was his own? Might not all their woes have sprung from that?

"He shall call upon me and I shall answer. I will deliver him in trouble. I will deliver him and honor him."

Had he ever really called on *Him?* Had Angela? Hadn't they been left in the slough of their own despond? Still Angela was not suited to him. Why did not God straighten that out? He didn't want to live with her.

He wandered through this philosophically, critically, until Mrs. Johns stopped. What, he asked himself, if, in spite of all his doubts, this seeming clamor and reality and pain and care were an illusion? Angela was suffering. So were many other people. How could this thing be true? Did not these facts exclude the possibility of illusion? Could they possibly be a part of it?

"Now we are going to try to realize that we are God's perfect children," she said, stopping and looking at him. "We think we are so big and strong and real. We are real enough, but only as a thought in God—that is all. No harm can happen to us there—no evil can come nigh us. For God is infinite, all power, all life. Truth, Love, over all, and all."

She closed her eyes and began, as she said, to try to realize for him the perfectness of his spirit in God. Eugene sat there trying to think of the Lord's prayer, but in reality thinking of the room, the cheap prints, the homely furniture, her ugliness, the curiousness of his being there. He, Eugene Witla, being prayed for! What would Angela think? Why was this woman old, if spirit could do all these other things? Why didn't she make herself beautiful? What was it she was doing now? Was this hypnotism, mesmerism, she was practicing? He re-

membered where Mrs. Eddy had especially said that these were
not to be practiced—could not be in Science. No, she was no
doubt sincere. She looked it—talked it. She believed in this
beneficent spirit. Would it aid as the psalm said? Would it
heal this ache? Would it make him not want Suzanne ever any
more? Perhaps that was evil? Yes, no doubt it was. Still——
Perhaps he had better fix his mind on the Lord's Prayer. Divinity could aid him if it would. Certainly it could. No doubt of
it. There was nothing impossible to this vast force ruling the
universe. Look at the telephone, wireless telegraphy. How
about the stars and sun? "He shall give his angels charge
over thee."

"Now," said Mrs. Johns, after some fifteen minutes of silent
meditation had passed—and she opened her eyes smilingly—"we
are going to see whether we are not going to be better. We are
going to feel better, because we are going to do better, and because we are going to realize that nothing can hurt an idea in
God. All the rest is illusions. It cannot hold us, for it is not
real. Think good—God—and you are good. Think evil and
you are evil, but it has no reality outside your own thought.
Remember that." She talked to him as though he was a little
child.

He went out into the snowy night where the wind was whirling the snow in picturesque whirls, buttoning his coat about him.
The cars were running up Broadway as usual. Taxicabs were
scuttling by. There were people forging their way through
the snow, that ever-present company of a great city. There were
arc lights burning clearly blue through the flying flakes. He
wondered as he walked whether this would do him any good.
Mrs. Eddy insisted that all these were unreal, he thought—
that mortal mind had evolved something which was not in accord with spirit—mortal mind "a liar and the father of it," he
recalled that quotation. Could it be so? Was evil unreal?
Was misery only a belief? Could he come out of his sense of
fear and shame and once more face the world? He boarded a
car to go north. At Kingsbridge he made his way thoughtfully
to his room. How could life ever be restored to him as it had
been? He was really forty years of age. He sat down in his
chair near his lamp and took up his book, "Science and Health,"
and opened it aimlessly. Then he thought for curiosity's sake
he would see where he had opened it—what the particular page
or paragraph his eye fell on had to say to him. He was still
intensely superstitious. He looked, and here was this paragraph
growing under his eyes:

"When mortal man blends his thoughts of existence with the spiritual, and works only as God works, he will no longer grope in the dark and cling to earth because he has not tasted heaven. Carnal beliefs defraud us. They make man an involuntary hypocrite—producing evil when he would create good, forming deformity when he would outline grace and beauty, injuring those whom he would bless. He becomes a general mis-creator, who believes he is a semi-God. His touch turns hope to dust, the dust we all have trod. He might say in Bible language, 'The good that I would, I do not, but evil, which I would not, I do.'"

He closed the book and meditated. He wished he might realize this thing if this were so. Still he did not want to become a religionist—a religious enthusiast. How silly they were. He picked up his daily paper—the *Evening Post*—and there on an inside page quoted in an obscure corner was a passage from a poem by the late Francis Thompson, entitled "The Hound of Heaven." It began:

> "I fled Him, down the nights and down the days;
> I fled Him, down the arches of the years . . .

The ending moved him strangely:

> Still with unhurrying chase,
> And unperturbèd face
> Deliberate speed, majestic instancy
> Came on the following Feet,
> And a voice above their beat—
> "Naught shelters thee, who wilt not shelter Me."

Did this man really believe this? Was it so?

He turned back to his book and read on, and by degrees he came half to believe that sin and evil and sickness might possibly be illusions—that they could be cured by aligning one's self intellectually and spiritually with this Divine Principle. He wasn't sure. This terrible sense of wrong. Could he give up Suzanne? Did he want to? No!

He got up and went to the window and looked out. The snow was still blowing.

"Give her up! Give her up!" And Angela in such a precarious condition. What a devil of a hole he was in, anyway! Well, he would go and see her in the morning. He would at least be kind. He would see her through this thing. He lay down and tried to sleep, but somehow sleep never came to him right any more. He was too wearied, too distressed, too wrought up. till he slept a little, and that was all he could hope for in these days.

CHAPTER XXVII

IT was while he was in this state, some two months later, that the great event, so far as Angela was concerned, came about, and in it, of necessity, he was compelled to take part. Angela was in her room, cosily and hygienically furnished, overlooking the cathedral grounds at Morningside Heights, and speculating hourly what her fate was to be. She had never wholly recovered from the severe attack of rheumatism which she had endured the preceding summer and, because of her worries since, in her present condition was pale and weak though she was not ill. The head visiting obstetrical surgeon, Dr. Lambert, a lean, gray man of sixty-five years of age, with grizzled cheeks, whose curly gray hair, wide, humped nose and keen gray eyes told of the energy and insight and ability that had placed him where he was, took a slight passing fancy to her, for she seemed to him one of those plain, patient little women whose lives are laid in sacrificial lines. He liked her brisk, practical, cheery disposition in the face of her condition, which was serious, and which was so noticeable to strangers. Angela had naturally a bright, cheery face, when she was not depressed or quarrelsome. It was the outward sign of her ability to say witty and clever things, and she had never lost the desire to have things done efficiently and intelligently about her wherever she was. The nurse, Miss De Sale, a solid, phlegmatic person of thirty-five, admired her spunk and courage and took a great fancy to her also because she was lightsome, buoyant and hopeful in the face of what was really a very serious situation. The general impression of the head operating surgeon, the house surgeon and the nurse was that her heart was weak and that her kidneys might be affected by her condition. Angela had somehow concluded after talks with Myrtle that Christian Science, as demonstrated by its practitioners, might help her through this crisis, though she had no real faith in it. Eugene would come round, she thought, also, for Myrtle was having him treated absently, and he was trying to read the book, she said. There would be a reconciliation between them when the baby came—because—because—— Well, because children were so winning! Eugene was really not hard-hearted—he was just infatuated. He had been ensnared by a siren. He would get over it.

Miss De Sale let her hair down in braids, Gretchen style, and fastened great pink bows of ribbon in them. As her condition became more involved, only the lightest morning gowns were given her—soft, comfortable things in which she sat about speculating practically about the future. She had changed from a lean shapeliness to a swollen, somewhat uncomely object, but she made the best of a bad situation. Eugene saw her and felt sorry. It was the end of winter now, with snow blowing gaily or fiercely about the windows, and the park grounds opposite were snow-white. She could see the leafless line of sentinel poplars that bordered the upper edges of Morningside. She was calm, patient, hopeful, while the old obstetrician shook his head gravely to the house surgeon.

"We shall have to be very careful. I shall take charge of the actual birth myself. See if you can't build up her strength. We can only hope that the head is small."

Angela's littleness and courage appealed to him. For once in a great many cases he really felt sorry.

The house surgeon did as directed. Angela was given specially prepared food and drink. She was fed frequently. She was made to keep perfectly quiet.

"Her heart," the house surgeon reported to his superior, "I don't like that. It's weak and irregular. I think there's a slight lesion."

"We can only hope for the best," said the other solemnly. "We'll try and do without ether."

Eugene in his peculiar mental state was not capable of realizing the pathos of all this. He was alienated temperamentally and emotionally. Thinking that he cared for his wife dearly, the nurse and the house surgeon were for not warning him. They did not want to frighten him. He asked several times whether he could be present during the delivery, but they stated that it would be dangerous and trying. The nurse asked Angela if she had not better advise him to stay away. Angela did, but Eugene felt that in spite of his alienation, she needed him. Besides, he was curious. He thought Angela would stand it better if he were near, and now that the ordeal was drawing nigh, he was beginning to understand how desperate it might be and to think it was only fair that he should assist her. Some of the old pathetic charm of her littleness was coming back to him. She might not live. She would have to suffer much. She had meant no real evil to him—only to hold him. Oh, the bitterness and the pathos of this welter of earthly emotions. Why should they be so tangled?

The time drew very near, and Angela was beginning to suffer severe pains. Those wonderful processes of the all-mother, which bind the coming life in a cradle of muscles and ligaments were practically completed and were now relaxing their tendencies in one direction to enforce them in another. Angela suffered at times severely from straining ligaments. Her hands were clenched desperately, her face would become deathly pale. She would cry. Eugene was with her on a number of these occasions and it drove home to his consciousness the subtlety and terror of this great scheme of reproduction, which took all women to the door of the grave, in order that this mortal scheme of things might be continued. He began to think that there might be something in the assertion of the Christian Science leaders that it was a lie and an illusion, a terrible fitful fever outside the rational consciousness of God. He went to the library one day and got down a book on obstetrics, which covered the principles and practice of surgical delivery. He saw there scores of pictures drawn very carefully of the child in various positions in the womb—all the strange, peculiar, flower-like positions it could take, folded in upon itself like a little half-formed petal. The pictures were attractive, some of them beautiful, practical as they were. They appealed to his fancy. They showed the coming baby perfect, but so small, its head now in one position, now in another, its little arms twisted about in odd places, but always delightfully, suggestively appealing. From reading here and there in the volume, he learned that the great difficulty was the head—the delivery of that. It appeared that no other difficulty really confronted the obstetrician. How was that to be got out? If the head were large, the mother old, the walls of the peritoneal cavity tight or hard, a natural delivery might be impossible. There were whole chapters on Craniotomy, Cephalotripsy, which in plain English means crushing the head with an instrument. . . .

One chapter was devoted to the Cæsarian operation, with a description of its tremendous difficulties and a long disquisition on the ethics of killing the child to save the mother, or the mother to save the child with their relative values to society indicated. Think of it—a surgeon sitting in the seat of judge and executioner at the critical moment! Ah, life with its petty laws did not extend here. Here we came back to the conscience of man which Mrs. Eddy maintained was a reflection of immanent mind. If God were good, He would speak through that— He was speaking through it. This surgeon referred to that inmost consciousness of supreme moral law, which alone could guide the practitioner in this dreadful hour.

Then he told of what implements were necessary, how many assistants (two), how many nurses (four), the kinds of bandages, needles, silk and catgut thread, knives, clamp dilators, rubber gloves. He showed how the cut was to be made—when, where. Eugene closed the book, frightened. He got up and walked out in the air, a desire to hurry up to Angela impelling him. She was weak, he knew that. She had complained of her heart. Her muscles were probably set. Supposing these problems, any one of them, should come in connection with her. He did not wish her to die.

He had said he had—yes, but he did not want to be a murderer. No, no! Angela had been good to him. She had worked for him. Why, God damn it, she had actually suffered for him in times past. He had treated her badly, very badly, and now in her pathetic little way she had put herself in this terrific position. It was her fault, to be sure it was. She had been trying as she always had to hold him against his will, but then could he really blame her? It wasn't a crime for her to want him to love her. They were just mis-mated. He had tried to be kind in marrying her, and he hadn't been kind at all. It had merely produced unrest, dissatisfaction, unhappiness for him and for her, and now this—this danger of death through pain, a weak heart, defective kidneys, a Cæsarian operation. Why, she couldn't stand anything like that. There was no use talking about it. She wasn't strong enough—she was too old.

He thought of Christian Science practitioners, of how they might save her—of some eminent surgeon who would know how without the knife. How? How? If these Christian Scientists could only *think* her through a thing like this—he wouldn't be sorry. He would be glad, for her sake, if not his own. He might give up Suzanne—he might—he might. Oh, why should that thought intrude on him now?

When he reached the hospital it was three o'clock in the afternoon, and he had been there for a little while in the morning when she was comparatively all right. She was much worse. The straining pains in her side which she had complained of were worse and her face was alternately flushed and pale, sometimes convulsed a little. Myrtle was there talking with her, and Eugene stood about nervously, wondering what he should do—what he could do. Angela saw his worry. In

spite of her own condition she was sorry for him. She knew
that this would cause him pain, for he was not hard-hearted,
and it was his first sign of relenting. She smiled at him,
thinking that maybe he would come round and change his attitude entirely. Myrtle kept reassuring her that all would be
well with her. The nurse said to her and to the house doctor
who came in, a young man of twenty-eight, with keen, quizzical eyes, whose sandy hair and ruddy complexion bespoke a
fighting disposition, that she was doing nicely.

"No bearing down pains?" he asked, smiling at Angela, his
even white teeth showing in two gleaming rows.

"I don't know what kind they are, doctor," she replied.
"I've had all kinds."

"You'll know them fast enough," he replied, mock cheerfully.
"They're not like any other kind."

He went away and Eugene followed him.

"How is she doing?" he asked, when they were out in the
hall.

"Well enough, considering. She's not very strong, you know.
I have an idea she is going to be all right. Dr. Lambert will
be here in a little while. You had better talk to him."

The house surgeon did not want to lie. He thought Eugene
ought to be told. Dr. Lambert was of the same opinion, but
he wanted to wait until the last, until he could judge approxi-
mately correctly.

He came at five, when it was already dark outside, and
looked at Angela with his grave, kindly eyes. He felt her
pulse, listened to her heart with his stethoscope.

"Do you think I shall be all right, doctor?" asked Angela
faintly.

"To be sure, to be sure," he replied softly. "Little woman,
big courage." He smoothed her hand.

He walked out and Eugene followed him.

"Well, doctor," he said. For the first time for months Eugene was thinking of something besides his lost fortune and
Suzanne.

"I think it advisable to tell you, Mr. Witla," said the old
surgeon, "that your wife is in a serious condition. I don't want
to alarm you unnecessarily—it may all come out very satisfactorily. I have no positive reason to be sure that it will not.
She is pretty old to have a child. Her muscles are set. The
principal thing we have to fear in her case is some untoward
complication with her kidneys. There is always difficulty in the
delivery of the head in women of her age. It may be neces-

sary to sacrifice the child. I can't be sure. The Cæsarian operation is something I never care to think about. It is rarely used, and it isn't always successful. Every care that can be taken will be taken. I should like to have you understand the conditions. Your consent will be asked before any serious steps are taken. Your decision will have to be quick, however, when the time comes."

"I can tell you now, doctor, what my decision will be," said Eugene realizing fully the gravity of the situation. For the time being, his old force and dignity were restored. "Save her life if you can by any means that you can. I have no other wish."

"Thanks," said the surgeon. "We will do the best we can."

There were hours after that when Eugene, sitting by Angela, saw her endure pain which he never dreamed it was possible for any human being to endure. He saw her draw herself up rigid time and again, the color leaving her face, the perspiration breaking out on her forehead only to relax and flush and groan without really crying out. He saw, strange to relate, that she was no baby like himself, whimpering over every little ill, but a representative of some great creative force which gave her power at once to suffer greatly and to endure greatly. She could not smile any more. That was not possible. She was in a welter of suffering, unbroken, astonishing. Myrtle had gone home to her dinner, but promised to return later. Miss De Sale came, bringing another nurse, and while Eugene was out of the room, Angela was prepared for the final ordeal. She was arrayed in the usual open back hospital slip and white linen leggings. Under Doctor Lambert's orders an operating table was got ready in the operating room on the top floor and a wheel table stationed outside the door, ready to remove her if necessary. He had left word that at the first evidence of the genuine childbearing pain, which the nurse understood so well, he was to be called. The house surgeon was to be in immediate charge of the case.

Eugene wondered in this final hour at the mechanical, practical, business-like manner in which all these tragedies—the hospital was full of women—were taken. Miss De Sale went about her duties calm, smiling, changing the pillows occasionally for Angela, straightening the disordered bedclothes, adjusting the window curtains, fixing her own lace cap or apron before the mirror which was attached to the dresser, or before the one that was set in the closet door, and doing other little things without number. She took no interest in Eugene's tense attitude, or Myrtle's when she was there, but went in and out, talking, jesting with other nurses, doing whatever she had to do quite undisturbed.

"Isn't there anything that can be done to relieve her of this pain?" Eugene asked wearily at one point. His own nerves were torn. "She can't stand anything like that. She hasn't the strength."

She shook her head placidly. "There isn't a thing that any-one can do. We can't give her an opiate. It stops the process. She just has to bear it. All women do."

"All women," thought Eugene. Good God! Did all women go through a siege like this every time a child was born? There were two billion people on the earth now. Had there been two billion such scenes? Had he come this way?—Angela? every child? What a terrible mistake she had made—so un-necessary, so foolish. It was too late now, though, to speculate concerning this. She was suffering. She was agonizing.

The house surgeon came back after a time to look at her condition, but was not at all alarmed apparently. He nodded his head rather reassuringly to Miss De Sale, who stood beside him. "I think she's doing all right," he said.

"I think so, too," she replied.

Eugene wondered how they could say this. She was suf-fering horribly.

"I'm going into Ward A for an hour," said the doctor. "If any change comes you can get me there."

"What change could come," asked Eugene of himself, "any worse than had already appeared? He was thinking of the drawings, though, he had seen in the book—wondering if An-gela would have to be assisted in some of the grim, mechanical ways indicated there. They illustrated to him the deadly possi-bilities of what might follow.

About midnight the expected change, which Eugene in ago-nized sympathy was awaiting, arrived. Myrtle had not re-turned. She had been waiting to hear from Eugene. Although Angela had been groaning before, pulling herself tense at times, twisting in an aimless, unhappy fashion, now she seemed to spring up and fall as though she had fainted. A shriek accom-panied the movement, and then another and another. He rushed to the door, but the nurse was there to meet him.

"It's here," she said quietly. She went to a phone outside and called for Dr. Willets. A second nurse from some other room came in and stood beside her. In spite of the knotted cords on Angela's face, the swollen veins, the purple hue, they were calm. Eugene could scarcely believe it, but he made an intense effort to appear calm himself. So this was childbirth!

In a few moments Dr. Willets came in. He also was calm, business like, energetic. He was dressed in a black suit and white linen jacket, but took that off, leaving the room as he did so, and returned with his sleevs rolled up and his body incased in a long white apron, such as Eugene had seen butchers wear. He went over to Angela and began working with her, saying something to the nurse beside him which Eugene did not hear. He could not look—he dared not at first.

At the fourth or fifth convulsive shriek, a second doctor came in, a young man of Willets' age, and dressed as he was, who also took his place beside him. Eugene had never seen him before. "Is it a case of forceps?" he asked.

"I can't tell," said the other. "Dr. Lambert is handling this personally. He ought to be here by now."

There was a step in the hall and the senior physician or obstetrician had entered. In the lower hall he had removed his great coat and fur gloves. He was dressed in his street clothes, but after looking at Angela, feeling her heart and temples, he went out and changed his coat for an apron, like the others. His sleeves were rolled up, but he did not immediately do anything but watch the house surgeon, whose hands were bloody.

"Can't they give her chloroform?" asked Eugene, to whom no one was paying any attention, of Miss De Sale.

She scarcely heard, but shook her head. She was busy dancing attendance on her very far removed superiors, the physicians.

"I would advise you to leave the room," said Dr. Lambert to Eugene, coming over near him. "You can do nothing here. You will be of no assistance whatsoever. You may be in the way."

Eugene left, but it was only to pace agonizedly up and down the hall. He thought of all the things that had passed between him and Angela—the years—the struggles. All at once he thought of Myrtle, and decided to call her up—she wanted to be there. Then he decided for the moment he would not. She could do nothing. Then he thought of the Christian Science practitioner. Myrtle could get her to give Angela absent treatment. Anything, anything—it was a shame that she should suffer so.

"Myrtle," he said nervously over the phone, when he reached her, "this is Eugene. Angela is suffering terribly. The birth is on. Can't you get Mrs. Johns to help her? It's terrible!"

"Certainly, Eugene. I'll come right down. Don't worry."

He hung up the receiver and walked up and down the hall
again. He could hear mumbled voices—he could hear muffled screams. A nurse, not Miss De Sale, came out and wheeled
in the operating table.

"Are they going to operate?" he asked feverishly. "I'm Mr.
Witla."

"I don't think so. I don't know. Dr. Lambert wants her
to be taken to the operating room in case it is necessary."

They wheeled her out after a few moments and on to the elevator which led to the floor above. Her face was slightly
covered while she was being so transferred, and those who were
around prevented him from seeing just how it was with her, but
because of her stillness, he wondered, and the nurse said that a
very slight temporary opiate had been administered—not enough
to affect the operation, if it were found necessary. Eugene
stood by dumbly, terrified. He stood in the hall, outside the
operating room, half afraid to enter. The head surgeon's warning came back to him, and, anyhow, what good could he do?
He walked far down the dim-lit length of the hall before him,
wondering, and looked out on a space where was nothing but
snow. In the distance a long lighted train was winding about a
high trestle like a golden serpent. There were automobiles
honking and pedestrians laboring along in the snow. What a
tangle life was, he thought. What a pity. Here a little while
ago, he wanted Angela to die, and now,—God Almighty, that
was her voice groaning! He would be punished for his evil
thoughts—yes, he would. His sins, all these terrible deeds
would be coming home to him. They were coming home to
him now. What a tragedy his career was! What a failure!
Hot tears welled up into his eyes, his lower lip trembled, not
for himself, but for Angela. He was so sorry all at once. He
shut it all back. No, by God, he wouldn't cry! What good
were tears? It was for Angela his pain was, and tears would
not help her now.

Thoughts of Suzanne came to him—Mrs. Dale, Colfax, but
he shut them out. If they could see him now! Then another
muffled scream and he walked quickly back. He couldn't
stand this.

He didn't go in, however. Instead he listened intently, hearing something which sounded like gurgling, choking breathing.
Was that Angela?

"The low forceps"—it was Dr. Lambert's voice.

"The high forceps." It was his voice again. Something
clinked like metal in a bowl.

"It can't be done this way, I'm afraid," it was Dr. Lambert's voice again. "We'll have to operate. I hate to do it, too."

A nurse came out to see if Eugene were near. "You had better go down into the waiting room, Mr. Witla," she cautioned. "They'll be bringing her out pretty soon. It won't be long now."

"No," he said all at once, "I want to see for myself." He walked into the room where Angela was now lying on the operating table in the centre of the room. A six-globed electrolier blazed close overhead. At her head was Dr. Willets, administering the anæsthetic. On the right side was Dr. Lambert, his hands encased in rubber gloves, bloody, totally unconscious of Eugene, holding a scalpel. One of the two nurses was near Angela's feet, officiating at a little table of knives, bowls, water, sponges, bandages. On the left of the table was Miss De Sale. Her hands were arranging some cloths at the side of Angela's body. At her side, opposite Dr. Lambert, was another surgeon whom Eugene did not know. Angela was breathing stertorously. She appeared to be unconscious. Her face was covered with cloths and a rubber mouth piece or cone. Eugene cut his palms with his nails.

So they have to operate, after all, he thought. She is as bad as that. The Cæsarian operation. Then they couldn't even get the child from her by killing it. Seventy-five per cent. of the cases recorded were successful, so the book said, but how many cases were not recorded. Was Dr. Lambert a great surgeon? Could Angela stand ether—with her weak heart?

He stood there looking at this wonderful picture while Dr. Lambert quickly washed his hands. He saw him take a small gleaming steel knife—bright as polished silver. The old man's hands were encased in rubber gloves, which looked bluish white under the light. Angela's exposed flesh was the color of a candle. He bent over her.

"Keep her breathing normal if you can," he said to the young doctor. "If she wakes give her ether. Doctor, you'd better look after the arteries."

He cut softly a little cut just below the centre of the abdomen apparently, and Eugene saw little trickling streams of blood spring where his blade touched. It did not seem a great cut. A nurse was sponging away the blood as fast as it flowed. As he cut again, the membrane that underlies the muscles of the abdomen and protects the intestines seemed to spring into view.

"I don't want to cut too much," said the surgeon calmly—

almost as though he were talking to himself. "These intestines are apt to become unmanageable. If you just lift up the ends, doctor. That's right. The sponge, Miss Wood. Now, if we can just cut here enough"—he was cutting again like an honest carpenter or cabinet worker.

He dropped the knife he held into Miss Wood's bowl of water. He reached into the bleeding wound, constantly sponged by the nurse, exposing something. What was that? Eugene's heart jerked. He was reaching down now in there with his middle finger—his fore and middle fingers afterwards, and saying, "I don't find the leg. Let's see. Ah, yes. Here we have it!"

"Can I move the head a little for you, doctor?" It was the young doctor at his left talking.

"Careful! Careful! It's bent under in the region of the coccyx. I have it now, though. Slowly, doctor, look out for the placenta."

Something was coming up out of this horrible cavity, which was trickling with blood from the cut. It was queer—a little foot, a leg, a body, a head.

"As God is my judge," said Eugene to himself, his eyes brimming again.

"The placenta, doctor. Look after the peritoneum, Miss Wood. It's alive, all right. How is her pulse, Miss De Sale?"

"A little weak, doctor."

"Use less ether. There, now we have it! We'll put that back. Sponge. We'll have to sew this afterwards, Willets. I won't trust this to heal alone. Some surgeons think it will, but I mistrust her recuperative power. Three or four stitches, anyhow."

They were working like carpenters, cabinet workers, electricians. Angela might have been a lay figure for all they seemed to care. And yet there was a tenseness here, a great hurry through slow sure motion. "The less haste, the more speed," popped into Eugene's mind—the old saw. He stared as if this were all a dream—a nightmare. It might have been a great picture like Rembrandt's "The Night Watch." One young doctor, the one he did not know, was holding aloft a purple object by the foot. It might have been a skinned rabbit, but Eugene's horrified eyes realized that it was his child—Angela's child—the thing all this horrible struggle and suffering was about. It was discolored, impossible, a myth, a monster. He could scarcely believe his eyes, and yet the doctor was striking it on the back with his hand, looking at it curiously. At the same moment came a faint cry—not a cry, either—only a faint, queer sound.

"She's awfully little, but I guess she'll make out." It was Dr. Willets talking of the baby. Angela's baby. Now the nurse had it. That was Angela's flesh they had been cutting. That was Angela's wound they were sewing. This wasn't life. It was a nightmare. He was insane and being bedeviled by spirits.

"Now, doctor, I guess that will keep. The blankets, Miss De Sale. You can take her away."

They were doing lots of things to Angela, fastening bandages about her, removing the cone from her mouth, changing her position back to one of lying flat, preparing to bathe her, moving her to the rolling table, wheeling her out while she moaned unconscious under ether.

Eugene could scarcely stand the sickening, stertorous breathing. It was such a strange sound to come from her—as if her unconscious soul were crying. And the child was crying, too, healthily.

"Oh, God, what a life, what a life!" he thought. To think that things should have to come this way. Death, incisions! unconsciousness! pain! Could she live? Would she? And now he was a father.

He turned and there was the nurse holding this littlest girl on a white gauze blanket or cushion. She was doing something to it—rubbing oil on it. It was a pink child now, like any other baby.

"That isn't so bad, is it?" she asked consolingly. She wanted to restore Eugene to a sense of the commonplace. He was so distracted looking.

Eugene stared at it. A strange feeling came over him. Something went up and down his body from head to toe, doing something to him. It was a nervous, titillating, pinching feeling. He touched the child. He looked at its hands, its face. It looked like Angela. Yes, it did. It was his child. It was hers. Would she live? Would he do better? Oh, God, to have this thrust at him now, and yet it was his child. How could he? Poor little thing. If Angela died—if Angela died, he would have this and nothing else, this little girl out of all her long, dramatic struggle. If she died, came this. To do what to him? To guide? To strengthen? To change? He could not say. Only, somehow, in spite of himself, it was beginning to appeal to him. It was the child of a storm. And Angela, so

near him now—would she ever live to see it? There she was
unconscious, numb, horribly cut. Dr. Lambert was taking a last
look at her before leaving.

"Do you think she will live, doctor?" he asked the great
surgeon feverishly. The latter looked grave.

"I can't say. I can't say. Her strength isn't all that it
ought to be. Her heart and kidneys make a bad combination.
However, it was a last chance. We had to take it. I'm sorry.
I'm glad we were able to save the child. The nurse will give
her the best of care."

He went out into his practical world as a laborer leaves his
work. So may we all. Eugene went over and stood by Angela. He was tremendously sorry for the long years of mistrust that had brought this about. He was ashamed of himself, of life—of its strange tangles. She was so little, so pale,
so worn. Yes, he had done this. He had brought her here
by his lying, his instability, his uncertain temperament. It was
fairly murder from one point of view, and up to this last hour
he had scarcely relented. But life had done things to him,
too. Now, now—— Oh, hell, Oh, God damn! If she would
only recover, he would try and do better. Yes, he would. It
sounded so silly coming from him, but he would try. Love
wasn't worth the agony it cost. Let it go. Let it go. He
could live. Truly there were hierarchies and powers, as Alfred
Russel Wallace pointed out. There was a God somewhere.
He was on His throne. These large, dark, immutable forces,
they were not for nothing. If she would only not die, he would
try—he would behave. He would! he would!

He gazed at her, but she looked so weak, so pale now he
did not think she could come round.

"Don't you want to come home with me, Eugene?" said
Myrtle, who had come back some time before, at his elbow.
"We can't do anything here now. The nurse says she may not
become conscious for several hours. The baby is all right in
their care."

The baby! the baby! He had forgotten it, forgotten Myrtle.
He was thinking of the long dark tragedy of his life—the
miasma of it.

"Yes," he said wearily. It was nearly morning. He went out
and got into a taxi and went to his sister's home, but in spite
of his weariness, he could scarcely sleep. He rolled feverishly.

In the morning he was up again, early, anxious to go back and
see how Angela was—and the child.

CHAPTER XXVIII

THE trouble with Angela's system, in addition to a weak heart, was that it was complicated at the time of her delivery by that peculiar manifestation of nervous distortion or convulsions known as eclampsia. Once in every five hundred cases (or at least such was the statistical calculation at the time), some such malady occurred to reduce the number of the newborn. In every two such terminations one mother also died, no matter what the anticipatory preparations were on the part of the most skilled surgeons. Though not caused by, it was diagnosed by, certain kidney changes. What Eugene had been spared while he was out in the hall was the sight of Angela staring, her mouth pulled to one side in a horrible grimace, her body bent back, canoe shape, the arms flexed, the fingers and thumbs bending over each other to and fro, in and out, slowly, not unlike a mechanical figure that is running down. Stupor and unconsciousness had immediately followed, and unless the child had been immediately brought into the world and the womb emptied, she and it would have died a horrible death. As it was she had no real strength to fight her way back to life and health. A Christian Science practitioner was trying to "realize her identity with good" for her, but she had no faith before and no consciousness now. She came to long enough to vomit terribly, and then sank into a fever. In it she talked of Eugene. She was in Blackwood, evidently, and wanted him to come back to her. He held her hand and cried, for he knew that there was never any recompense for that pain. What a dog he had been! He bit his lip and stared out of the window.

Once he said: "Oh, I'm no damned good! I should have died!"

That whole day passed without consciousness, and most of the night. At two in the morning Angela woke and asked to see the baby. The nurse brought it. Eugene held her hand. It was put down beside her, and she cried for joy, but it was a weak, soundless cry. Eugene cried also.

"It's a girl, isn't it?" she asked.

"Yes," said Eugene, and then, after a pause, "Angela, I want to tell you something. I'm so sorry. I'm ashamed. I want you to get well. I'll do better. Really I will." At the same time he was wondering, almost subconsciously, whether he would or no. Wouldn't it be all the same if she were really well—or worse?

She caressed his hand. "Don't cry," she said, "I'll be all right. I'm going to get well. We'll both do better. It's as much my fault as yours. I've been too hard." She worked at his fingers, but he only choked. His vocal cords hurt him.

"I'm so sorry. I'm so sorry," he finally managed to say.

The child was taken away after a little while and Angela was feverish again. She grew very weak, so weak that although she was conscious later, she could not speak. She tried to make some signs. Eugene, the nurse, Myrtle, understood. The baby. It was brought and held up before her. She smiled a weak, yearning smile and looked at Eugene. "I'll take care of her," he said, bending over her. He swore a great oath to himself. He would be decent—he would be clean henceforth and for ever. The child was put beside her for a little while, but she could not move. She sank steadily and died.

Eugene sat by the bed holding his head in his hands. So, he had his wish. She was really dead. Now he had been taught what it was to fly in the face of conscience, instinct, immutable law. He sat there an hour while Myrtle begged him to come away.

"Please, Eugene!" she said. "Please!"

"No, no," he replied. "Where shall I go? I am well enough here."

After a time he did go, however, wondering how he would adjust his life from now on. Who would take care of—of——

"Angela" came the name to his mind. Yes, he would call her "Angela." He had heard someone say she was going to have pale yellow hair.

The rest of this story is a record of philosophic doubt and speculation and a gradual return to normality, his kind of normality—the artistic normality of which he was capable. He would—he thought—never again be the maundering sentimentalist and enthusiast, imagining perfection in every beautiful woman that he saw. Yet there was a period when, had Suzanne returned suddenly, all would have been as before between them, and even more so, despite his tremulousness of spirit, his speculative interest in Christian Science as a way out possibly, his sense of brutality, almost murder, in the case of Angela—for, the old attraction still gnawed at his vitals. Although he had Angela, junior, now to look after, and in a way to divert him,—a child whom he came speedily to delight in—his fortune to restore, and a sense of responsibility to that abstract thing, society or public opinion as represented by those he knew or who knew him, still there was this ache and this non-controllable sense of adventure which freedom to contract a new matrimonial alliance or build his life on the plan he schemed with Suzanne gave him. Suzanne! Suzanne!—how her face, her gestures, her voice, haunted him. Not Angela, for all the pathos of her tragic ending, but Suzanne. He thought of Angela often—those last hours in the hospital, her last commanding look which meant "please look after our child," and whenever he did so his vocal cords tightened as under the grip of a hand and his eyes threatened to overflow, but even so, and even then, that undertow, that mystic cord that seemed to pull from his solar plexus outward, was to Suzanne and to her only. Suzanne! Suzanne! Around her hair, the thought of her smile, her indescribable presence, was built all that substance of romance which he had hoped to enjoy and which now, in absence and probably final separation, glowed with a radiance which no doubt the reality could never have had.

"We are such stuff as dreams are made on and our little life is rounded with a sleep." We are such stuff as dreams are made on, and only of dreams are our keen, stinging realities compounded. Nothing else is so moving, so vital, so painful as a dream.

For a time that first spring and summer, while Myrtle looked after little Angela and Eugene went to live with her and her husband, he visited his old Christian Science practitioner, Mrs. Johns. He had not been much impressed with the result in Angela's case, but Myrtle explained the difficulty of the situation in a plausible way. He was in a terrific state of depression, and it was while he was so that Myrtle persuaded him to go again. She insisted that Mrs. Johns would overcome his morbid gloom, anyhow, and make him feel better. "You want to come out of this, Eugene," she pleaded. "You will never do anything until you do. You are a big man. Life isn't over. It's just begun. You're going to get well and strong again. Don't worry. Everything that is is for the best."

He went once, quarreling with himself for doing so, for in spite of his great shocks, or rather because of them, he had no faith in religious conclusions of any kind. Angela had not been saved. Why should he?

Still the metaphysical urge was something—it was so hard to suffer spiritually and not believe there was some way out. At times he hated Suzanne for her indifference. If ever she came back he would show her. There would be no feeble urgings and pleadings the next time. She had led him into this trap, knowing well what she was doing—for she was wise enough—and then had lightly deserted him. Was that the action of a large spirit? he asked himself. Would the wonderful something he thought he saw there be capable of that? Ah, those hours at Daleview—that one stinging encounter in Canada!—the night she danced with him so wonderfully!

During a period of nearly three years all the vagaries and alterations which can possibly afflict a groping and morbid mind were his. He went from what might be described as *almost* a belief in Christian Science to almost a belief that a devil ruled the world, a Gargantuan Brobdingnagian Mountebank, who plotted tragedy for all ideals and rejoiced in swine and dullards and a grunting, sweating, beefy immorality. By degrees his God, if he could have been said to have had one in his consciousness, sank back into a dual personality or a compound of good and evil—the most ideal and ascetic good, as well as the most fantastic and swinish evil. His God, for a time at least, was a God of storms and horrors as well as of serenities and perfections. He then reached a state not of abnegation, but of philosophic open-mindedness or agnosticism. He came to know that he did not know what to believe. All apparently was permitted, nothing fixed. Perhaps life loved only change, equation, drama, laughter. When in moments of private speculation or social argument he was prone to condemn it loudest, he realized that at worst and at best it was beautiful, artistic, gay, that, however, he might age, groan, complain, withdraw, wither, still, in spite of him, this large thing which he at once loved and detested was sparkling on. He might quarrel, but it did not care; he might fail or die, but it could not. He was negligible—but, oh, the sting and delight of its inner shrines and favorable illusions.

And curiously, for a time, even while he was changing in this way, he went back to see Mrs. Johns, principally because he liked her. She seemed to be a motherly soul to him, contributing some of the old atmosphere he had enjoyed in his own home in Alexandria. This woman, from working constantly in the esoteric depths, which Mrs. Eddy's book suggests, demonstrating for herself, as she thought, through her belief in or understanding of, the oneness of the universe (its non-malicious, affectionate control, the non-existence of fear, pain, disease, and death itself), had become so grounded in her faith that evil positively did not exist save in the belief of mortals, that at times she almost convinced Eugene that it was so. He speculated long and deeply along these lines with her. He had come to lean on her in his misery quite as a boy might on his mother.

The universe to her was, as Mrs. Eddy said, spiritual, not material, and no wretched condition, however seemingly powerful, could hold against the truth—could gainsay divine harmony. God was good. All that is, is God. Hence all that is, is good or it is an illusion. It could not be otherwise. She looked at Eugene's case, as she had at many a similar one, being sure, in her earnest way, that she, by realizing his ultimate fundamental spirituality, could bring him out of his illusions, and make him see the real spirituality of things, in which the world of flesh and desire had no part.

"Beloved," she loved to quote to him, "now are we the sons of God, and it doth not yet appear what we shall be, but we know that when he shall appear"—(and she explained that *he* was this universal spirit of perfection of which we are a part)— "we shall be like him; for we shall see him as He is."

"And every man that has this hope in him purifieth himself even as He is pure."

She once explained to him that this did not mean that the man must purify himself by some hopeless moral struggle, or emaciating abstinence, but rather that the fact that he had this hope of something better in him, would fortify him in spite of himself.

"You laugh at me," she said to him one day, "but I tell you you are a child of God. There is a divine spark in you. It must come out. I know it will. All this other thing will fall away as a bad dream. It has no reality."

She even went so far in a sweet motherly way as to sing hymns to him, and now, strange to relate, her thin voice was no longer irritating to him, and her spirit made her seemingly beautiful in his eyes. He did not try to adjust the curiosities and anomalies of material defects in so far as she was concerned. The fact that her rooms were anything but artistically perfect; that her body was shapeless, or comparatively so, when contrasted with that standard of which he had always been so conscious; the fact that whales were accounted by her in some weird way as spiritual, and bugs and torturesome insects of all kinds as emanations of mortal mind, did not trouble him at all. There was something in this thought of a spiritual universe —of a kindly universe, if you sought to make it so, which pleased him. The five senses certainly could not indicate the totality of things; beyond them must lie depths upon depths of wonder and power. Why might not this act? Why might it not be good? That book that he had once read—"The World Machine"— had indicated this planetary life as being infinitesimally small; that from the point of view of infinity it was not even thinkable —and yet here it appeared to be so large. Why might it not be, as Carlyle had said, a state of mind, and as such, so easily dissolvable. These thoughts grew by degrees, in force, in power.

At the same time he was beginning to go out again a little. A chance meeting with M. Charles, who grasped his hand warmly and wanted to know where he was and what he was doing, revived his old art fever. M. Charles suggested, with an air of extreme interest, that he should get up another exhibition along whatever line he chose.

"You!" he said, with a touch of heartening sympathy, and yet with a glow of fine corrective scorn, for he considered Eugene as an artist only, and a very great one at that. "You,— Eugene Witla—an editor—a publisher! Pah! You—who could have all the art lovers of the world at your feet in a few years if you chose—you who could do more for American art in your life time than anyone I know, wasting your time art directing, art editing—publishing! Pouf! Aren't you really ashamed of yourself? But it isn't too late. Come now—a fine exhibition! What do you say to an exhibition of some kind next January or February, in the full swing of the season? Everybody's interested then. I will give you our largest gallery. How is that? What do you say?" he glowed in a peculiarly Frenchy way,—half commanding, half inspiring or exhorting.

"If I can," said Eugene quietly, with a deprecating wave of the hand, and a faint line of self-scorn about the corners of his mouth. "It may be too late."

" 'Too late! Too late!' What nonsense! Do you say that to me? If you can! If you can! Well, I give you up! You with your velvet textures and sure lines. It is too much. It is unbelievable!"

He raised his hands, eyes, and eye-brows in Gallic despair. He shrugged his shoulders, waiting to see a change of expression in Eugene.

"Very good!" said Eugene, when he heard this. "Only I

can't promise anything. We will see." And he wrote out his address.

This started him once more. The Frenchman, who had often heard him spoken of and had sold all his earlier pictures, was convinced that there was money in him—if not here then abroad —money and some repute for himself as his sponsor. Some American artists must be encouraged—some *must* rise. Why not Eugene? Here was one who really deserved it.

So Eugene worked, painting swiftly, feverishly, brilliantly— with a feeling half the time that his old art force had deserted him for ever—everything that came into his mind. Taking a north lighted room near Myrtle he essayed portraits of her and her husband, of her and baby Angela, making arrangements which were classically simple. Then he chose models from the streets,—laborers, washerwomen, drunkards—characters all, destroying canvases frequently, but, on the whole, making steady progress. He had a strange fever for painting life as he saw it, for indicating it with exact portraits of itself, strange, grim presentations of its vagaries, futilities, commonplaces, drolleries, brutalities. The mental, fuzzy-wuzzy maunderings and mean-derings of the mob fascinated him. The paradox of a decaying drunkard placed against the vivid persistence of life gripped his fancy. Somehow it suggested himself hanging on, fighting on, accusing nature, and it gave him great courage to do it. This picture eventually sold for eighteen thousand dollars, a record price.

In the meantime his lost dream in the shape of Suzanne was traveling abroad with her mother—in England, Scotland, France, Egypt, Italy, Greece. Aroused by the astonishing storm which her sudden and uncertain fascination had brought on, she was now so shaken and troubled by the disasters which had seemed to flow to Eugene in her wake, that she really did not know what to do or think. She was still too young, too nebulous. She was strong enough in body and mind, but very uncertain philosophically and morally—a dreamer and opportunist. Her mother, fearful of some headstrong, destructive outburst in which her shrewdest calculations would prove of no avail, was most anxious to be civil, loving, courteous, politic—anything to avoid a disturbing re-encounter with the facts of the past, or a sudden departure on the part of Suzanne, which she hourly feared. What was she to do? Anything Suzanne wanted—her least whim, her moods in dress, pleasure, travel, friendship, were most assiduously catered to. Would she like to go here? would she like to see that? would this amuse her? would that be pleasant?

And Suzanne, seeing always what her mother's motives were, and troubled by the pain and disgrace she had brought on Eugene, was uncertain now as to whether her conduct had been right or not. She puzzled over it continually.

More terrifying, however, was the thought which came to her occasionally as to whether she had really loved Eugene at all or not. Was this not a passing fancy? Had there not been some chemistry of the blood, causing her to make a fool of herself, without having any real basis in intellectual rapprochement. Was Eugene truly the one man with whom she could have been happy? Was he not too adoring, too headstrong, too foolish and mistaken in his calculations? Was he the able person she had really fancied him to be? Would she not have come to dislike him—to hate him even—in a short space of time? Could they have been truly, permanently happy? Would she not be more interested in one who was sharp, defiant, indifferent—one whom she could be compelled to adore and fight for rather than one who was constantly adoring her and needing her sympathy? A strong, solid, courageous man—was not such a one her ideal, after all? And could Eugene be said to be that? These and other questions tormented her constantly.

It is strange, but life is constantly presenting these pathetic paradoxes—these astounding blunders which temperament and blood moods bring about and reason and circumstance and convention condemn. The dreams of man are one thing—his capacity to realize them another. At either pole are the accidents of supreme failure and supreme success—the supreme failure of an Abélard for instance, the supreme success of a Napoleon, enthroned at Paris. But, oh, the endless failures for one success.

But in this instance it cannot be said that Suzanne had definitely concluded that she did not love him. Far from it. Although the cleverest devices were resorted to by Mrs. Dale to bring her into contact with younger and to her—now—more interesting personalities, Suzanne—very much of an introspective dreamer and quiet spectator herself, was not to be swiftly deluded by love again—if she had been deluded. She had half decided to study men from now on, and use them, if need be, waiting for the time when some act, of Eugene's, perhaps, or some other personality, might decide for her. The strange, destructive spell of her beauty began to interest her, for now she knew that she really was beautiful. She looked in her mirror very frequently now—at the artistry of a curl, the curve of her chin, her cheek, her arm. If ever she went back to Eugene how well she would repay him for his agony. But would she? Could she? Would he have not recovered his sanity and be able to snap his fingers in her face and smile superciliously? For, after all, no doubt he was a wonderful man and would shine as something somewhere soon again. And when he did—what would he think of her—her silence, her desertion, her moral cowardice?

"After all, I am not of much account," she said to herself. "But what he thought of me!—that wild fever—that was wonderful! Really he was wonderful!"

CHAPTER XXIX

THE dénouement of all this, as much as ever could be, was still two years off. By that time Suzanne was considerably more sobered, somewhat more intellectually cultivated, a little cooler—not colder exactly—and somewhat more critical. Men, when it came to her type of beauty, were a little too suggestive of their amorousness. After Eugene their proffers of passion, adoration, undying love, were not so significant.

But one day in New York on Fifth Avenue, there was a re-encounter. She was shopping with her mother, but their ways, for a moment, were divided. By now Eugene was once more in complete possession of his faculties. The old ache had subsided to a dim but colorful mirage of beauty that was always in his eye. Often he had thought what he would do if he saw Suzanne again—what say, if anything. Would he smile, bow —and if there were an answering light in her eye, begin his old courtship all over, or would he find her changed, cold, indifferent? Would he be indifferent, sneering? It would be hard on him, perhaps, afterwards, but it would pay her out and serve her right. If she really cared, she ought to be made to suffer for being a waxy fool and tool in the hands of her mother. He did not know that she had heard of his wife's death—the birth of his child—and that she had composed and destroyed five different letters, being afraid of reprisal, indifference, scorn.

She had heard of his rise to fame as an artist once more, for the exhibition had finally come about, and with it great praise, generous acknowledgments of his ability—artists admired him most of all. They thought him strange, eccentric, but great. M. Charles had suggested to a great bank director that his new bank in the financial district be decorated by Eugene alone, which was eventually done—nine great panels in which he expressed deeply some of his feeling for life. At Washington, in two of the great public buildings and in three state capitols were tall, glowing panels also of his energetic dreaming,—a brooding suggestion of beauty that never was on land or sea. Here and there in them you might have been struck by a face—an arm, a cheek, an eye. If you had ever known Suzanne as she was you would have known the basis—the fugitive spirit at the bottom of all these things.

But in spite of that he now hated her—or told himself that

he did. Under the heel of his intellectuality was the face, the beauty that he adored. He despised and yet loved it. Life had played him a vile trick—love—thus to frenzy his reason and then to turn him out as mad. Now, never again, should love affect him, and yet the beauty of woman was still his great lure—only he was the master.

And then one day Suzanne appeared.

He scarcely recognized her, so sudden it was and so quickly ended. She was crossing Fifth Avenue at Forty-second Street. He was coming out of a jeweler's, with a birthday ring for little Angela. Then the eyes of this girl, a pale look—a flash of something wonderful that he remembered and then——

He stared curiously—not quite sure.

"He does not even recognize me," thought Suzanne, "or he hates me now. Oh!—all in five years!"

"It is she, I believe," he said to himself, "though I am not quite sure. Well, if it is she can go to the devil!" His mouth hardened. "I will cut her as she deserves to be cut," he thought. "She shall never know that I care."

And so they passed,—never to meet in this world—each always wishing, each defying, each folding a wraith of beauty to the heart.

L'ENVOI

THERE appears to be in metaphysics a basis, or no basis, according as the temperament and the experience of each shall incline him, for ethical or spiritual ease or peace. Life sinks into the unknowable at every turn and only the temporary or historical scene remains as a guide,—and that passes also. It may seem rather beside the mark that Eugene in his moral and physical depression should have inclined to various religious abstrusities for a time, but life does such things in a storm. They constituted a refuge from himself, from his doubts and despairs as religious thought always does.

If I were personally to define religion I would say that it is a bandage that man has invented to protect a soul made bloody by circumstance; an envelope to pocket him from the unescapable and unstable illimitable. We seek to think of things as permanent and see them so. Religion gives life a habitation and a name apparently—though it is an illusion. So we are brought back to time and space and illimitable mind—as what? And we shall always stand before them attributing to them all those things which we cannot know.

Yet the need for religion is impermanent, like all else in life. As the soul regains its health, it becomes prone to the old illusions. Again women entered his life—never believe otherwise—drawn, perhaps, by a certain wistfulness and loneliness in Eugene, who though quieted by tragedy for a little while was once more moving in the world. He saw their approach with more skepticism, and yet not unmoved—women who came through the drawing rooms to which he was invited, wives and daughters who sought to interest him in themselves and would scarcely take no for an answer; women of the stage—women artists, poetasters, "varietists," critics, dreamers. From the many approaches, letters and meetings, some few relationships resulted, ending as others had ended. Was he not changed, then? Not much—no. Only hardened intellectually and emotionally—tempered for life and work. There were scenes, too, violent ones, tears, separations, renouncements, cold meetings—with little Angela always to one side in Myrtle's care as a stay and consolation.

In Eugene one saw an artist who, pagan to the core, enjoyed reading the Bible for its artistry of expression, and Schopenhauer, Nietzsche, Spinoza and James for the mystery of things which they suggested. In his child he found a charming personality and a study as well—one whom he could brood over with affectionate interest at times, seeing already something of himself and something of Angela, and wondering at the outcome. What would she be like? Would art have any interest for her? She was so daring, gay, self-willed, he thought.

"You've a Tartar on your hands," Myrtle once said to him, and he smiled as he replied:

"Just the same I'll see if I can't keep up with her."

One of his occasional thoughts was that if he and Angela, junior, came to understand each other thoroughly, and she did not marry too soon, he could build a charming home around her. Perhaps her husband might not object to living with them.

The last scene of all may be taken from his studio ·in Montclair, where with Myrtle and her husband as resident housekeepers and Angela as his diversion he was living and working. He was sitting in front of his fireplace one night reading, when a thought in some history recalled to his mind a paragraph somewhere in Spencer's astonishing chapters on "the unknowable" in his "Facts and Comments," and he arose to see if he could find it. Rummaging around in his books he extracted the volume and reread it, with a kind of smack of intellectual agreement, for it suited his mood in regard to life and his own mental state in particular. Because it was so peculiarly related to his own viewpoint I quote it:

"Beyond the reach of our intelligence as are the mysteries of the objects known by our senses, those presented in this universal matrix are, if we may say so, still further beyond the reach of our intelligence, for whereas, those of the one kind may be, and are, thought of by many as explicable on the hypothesis of creation, and by the rest on the hypothesis of evolution, those of the other kind cannot by either be regarded as thus explicable. Theist and Agnostic must agree in recognizing the properties of Space as inherent, eternal, uncreated—as anteceding all creation, if creation has taken place. Hence, could we penetrate the mysteries of existence, there would still remain more transcendent mysteries. That which can be thought of as neither made nor evolved presents us with facts the origin of which is even more remote from conceivability than is the origin of the facts presented by visible and tangible things. . . . The thought of this blank form of existence which, explored in all directions as far as eye can reach, has, beyond that, an unexplored region compared with which the part imagination has traversed is but infinitesimal—the thought of a space, compared with which our immeasurable sidereal system dwindles to a point, is a thought too overwhelming to be dwelt upon. Of late years the consciousness that without origin or cause, infinite space has ever existed and must ever exist produces in me a feeling from which I shrink."

"Well," said Eugene, turning as he thought he heard a slight noise, "that is certainly the sanest interpretation of the limitations of human thought I have ever read"—and then seeing the tiny Angela enter, clad in a baggy little sleeping suit which was not unrelated to a Harlequin costume, he smiled, for he knew her wheedling, shifty moods and tricks.

"Now what are you coming in here for?" he asked, with mock severity. "You know you oughn't to be up so late. If Auntie Myrtle catches you!"

"But I can't sleep, Daddy," she replied trickily, anxious to be with him a little while longer before the fire, and tripping coaxingly across the floor. "Won't you take me?"

"Yes, I know all about your not being able to sleep, you scamp. You're coming in here to be cuddled. You beat it!"

"Oh, no, Daddy!"

"All right, then, come here." And he gathered her up in his arms and reseated himself by the fire. "Now you go to sleep or back you go to bed."

She snuggled down, her yellow head in his crook'd elbow while he looked at her cheek, recalling the storm in which she had arrived.

"Little flower girl," he said. "Sweet little kiddie."

His offspring made no reply. Presently he carried her asleep to her couch, tucked her in, and, coming back, went out on the brown lawn, where a late November wind rustled in the still clinging brown leaves. Overhead were the stars—Orion's majestic belt and those mystic constellations that make Dippers, Bears, and that remote cloudy formation known as the Milky Way.

"Where in all this—in substance," he thought, rubbing his hand through his hair, "is Angela? Where in substance will be that which is me? What a sweet welter life is—how rich, how tender, how grim, how like a colorful symphony."

Great art dreams welled up into his soul as he viewed the sparkling deeps of space.

"The sound of the wind—how fine it is tonight," he thought. Then he went quietly in and closed the door.

THE END